Copyright 2022 Nathan Neuharth

The Lords of Secret Things

Night Horse Publishing House

ISBN 9798815316126

Cover: the Satanic Rites of Dracula, Hammer Films, 1973

The Lords of Secret Things

An Anthology of Horror

By Nathan Neuharth

CONTENTS

Etherion

Grave Flowers

Satan

Blackwood

Grimsinger

Phantasies

Secret People

Cthulhu Domine

The Order of Dog Blood

The Lizard Prince

The Philosophy of Murder

Darker Than You Think

Dampir

Beautifully Damaged

Suicide of Shiloh Darling

Harbinger of the Coming Race

Eyes Afire

In Noctus Sol

Etherion

     Travis Winters sits alone on a black leather bar stool, cracked and worn with age. Having lost track of the number of beers he's drunk he avoids looking in the mirror behind the bar. Looking himself in the eye is the last thing he wants to do tonight. He lost his temper with Meredith again. Things have been going downhill between them for some time now. He senses it and she can too.

     They've been arguing more and more often. If not arguing then ignoring each other. When they have been doing things together like watching a movie on the couch or attending a family function they smile and touch, but the smiles are strained and the touches lack passion.

     When they have sex Travis enjoys it, but Meredith says nothing. It's become an act of just going through the motions. More often than not she simply pulls her panties off in bed at night and let's him have a quickie from behind. He can feel her slipping away.

     Last night they fought because she stayed out late avoiding him. Travis sits alone in their house waiting for her to come home, pacing, growing more and more jealous as the clock ticks and the evening grows long. His mind races. What is she doing? Who is she with? Is she lying? Is she cheating? No, she wouldn't.

     She's recently made a new group of friends, but Travis hasn't met them yet. He hates the way she talks about them, feeling left out. The excitement in her voice, the smile hiding something he can't touch. Why hasn't she introduced him to them yet?

     So last night she came home very late again. He was up waiting, furious. He'd been sitting on the couch in silence, watching the clock, chain smoking, until finally Meredith walked in at midnight. She got off work at 8 PM.

     He's afraid of losing her. Afraid she's going to leave him. Her beauty, her confidence, her talent, all makes him feel so insecure, so unworthy.

     She opened the front door with an ear to ear grin, stinking of liquor, enthusiastic. One look at him sitting on their couch wiped the joy from her face.

     They argued immediately. His fault. She was happy, in a wondrous mood, and he stole it away with his jealousy, his sarcasm, and his scolding. Their voices rose as the debate and interrogation ascended into screams and shouts climaxing with his open hand slapping her face.

     That ended the argument. She told him that was it. She couldn't live like this anymore. If they had one more fight like this it was over, she would leave.

The finality of her tone told him this was no hollow threat.

Travis felt the same pitiful guilt he always does after one of their fights turns physical. That, mixed with the dread fear of losing her and his feeling of worthlessness caused him to sob like a child. And she comforted him, held him in a motherly way like she has so many times before. Travis cradled in her arms as she whispers and soothes, "My lost, lost little boy", tucking a strand of hair behind his ear and gingerly petting.

They made love after that. Not from behind with her telling him to hurry up, but with a passion closer to what it was like when they first started dating. That is the only time there is passion in their love making now, after a fight. He fell asleep feeling relieved and secure, believing she wouldn't leave. For some reason sex makes him feel worthy, meaningful.

Today she went to work and Travis was fine at first, but as his day progressed doing chores, washing the dishes, mowing the lawn, insecurity and suspicion grew. Something wasn't right with this new group of friends. He could feel it. Meredith hasn't cheated on him yet, but she wants to. She likes one of the men in her new group of friends.

Why wouldn't she leave him? He's unemployed and has been for months. They are broke and he can't find work. Travis has been getting more and more depressed every day, gaining weight, being reclusive, avoiding his friends due to the shame of failures.

He made up his mind. He would tell Meredith when she came home from work she would not hang out with this new group of friends any longer, and he will find work soon, start exercising, start seeing a therapist to help cope with depression. They will start doing more things together as a couple and heal their breaking relationship.

Things didn't turn out as planned. Meredith came home from work on time to find that he'd made a romantic dinner, evening lighting candles. But she didn't like the idea of giving up her new friends. She flat out refused. Jealousy exploded into rage. She must like one of these new friends. Why else be so protective? He smashed a wine glass against the wall before flipping the dining room table over. Food, wine, and dishes flung into the air, splattering and shattering everywhere. On the wall, the carpet, and on Meredith.

She took off her wedding ring and chucked it across the dining room screaming for him to leave or she would call the police. Travis begged and cried for two hours before she actually called the police. She was on all fours cleaning the mess of his tantrum up when the authorities arrived.

The police made him leave.

He's been sitting in this bar stool drinking ever since. In the mirror across from him he looks in his eyes, feeling nothing but regret, self-loathing, and loss. Seeing nothing but a failure. A true loser.

In the mirror Travis watches a feline woman dressed in black moving with grace like smoke into the bar stool next to him. Her eyes capture him in the mirror. She has an exotic appearance about her with olive skin, big round dark eyes, and long obsidian silk hair.

He turns with hesitation to greet this enigmatic lass, giving a polite, unsure smile. Having already been shunned by every woman in the bar due to his drunken eagerness he's quite afraid of further rejection. He's made a fool of himself all night with obvious desperation. It's not that he wants a woman other than Meredith, but that he needs a warm body to help him forget Meredith.

"May I buy you a drink?" She asks with a conceited and seductive voice.

Travis is flabbergasted, at a loss for words, before this woman who seems to have stepped out of a dark and erotic dream. Her full lips remind him of a cat, thin just at the top where a person puts their index finger when hushing. This cat woman is dressed in all black with a slit dress showing off firm legs and plump cleavage with long lace sleeves.

"Well?" She prods with a knowing look, having enjoyed Travis's eyes examining her body up and down. He notices her incisors are slightly longer than her other teeth when she smiles making her seem all the more feline, like an Egyptian goddess with modern goth tastes in style. This woman wants to be unique and succeeds with aces.

"Um, okay, yeah," he mumbles. "Thank you."

She orders their drinks and remains at his side stirring the ice in her glass with a short, slender straw.

"So," Travis fishes for something to break the ice, "What are you up to tonight?"

"Stalking you," she gives a devilish grin.

Travis's mouth hangs open, taken back.

"I'm fooling you," she giggles, "I needed a break from my research. A nightcap sounded right."

"What kind of research?"

"I'm an anthropologist. Planning a trip to Iraq for an excavation."

"Wow. I'm impressed. Sounds like you're a big deal."

She responds with a delightful chuckle, "Just another member of the expedition."

Travis imagines dating this anthropologist woman. Being seen by Meredith. He wants to make Meredith jealous in hopes of winning her back. For her to see that he's not worthless, that other women desire him. "Where are you from?"

She gives a shy smile, eyes fluttering, "You don't remember me."

Travis raises an eyebrow, giving a crooked smile, "I'm sorry. Do we know each other?"

She gives a slight nod, smug, takes a sip from her little straw, "We were in high school together."

Travis mouth makes an O with sudden realization, "Farah! Farah Somers! What the hell? I didn't recognize you at all. You look different."

"Doesn't surprise me. You didn't talk to me in school. No one did."

Travis flushes, "I'm sorry. I guess I thought I was pretty cool back then. Young and dumb and full of cum."

Farah cocks her head to the side, "Looks like you still think you're pretty cool," she drapes her hand over his shoulder letting her fingers slide down the sleeve of his red and black western shirt. "Nice ensemble. I remember you were always a stylish boy."

Travis smirks with pride, "You look pretty good yourself." He remembers her in high school more vividly now. A very timid girl. She hung out with some of the goth kids. Back then she suffered from excessive acne and dressed like she thought she was a vampire. Memories of his high school friends making fun of her return to him. They made her cry at lunch time once. So quiet and sad, he's astonished that this is that same girl. "Sounds like you've done very well for yourself since high school."

She shrugs, flirts, "I had a huge crush on you back then and you never noticed me."

Travis blushes, "Are you serious? I didn't know." He wants her now, but knows in high school he foolishly wouldn't have given her a chance.

"Seriously," Farah answers and changes the subject, "What have you been up to since high school, Mr. Travis Winters?"

"It's not much of a story," Travis feels that familiar insecurity returns. Not only is he unemployed, but homeless as well since Meredith kicked him out.

"I'll order a couple of more drinks," she puts her hand on his, "I'm curious to hear what the infamous Travis Winters has done with his life. Honestly, I can't believe I'm sitting here next to you. I'm only back in Applegate for a short time. I just about fell over when I saw you sitting here looking all glum."

"Alright," Travis gives in, "I could use another drink, but I warn you, I haven't been as successful as you it seems."

"I've done alright," she admits with cool confidence and orders the drinks from the bartender, "After high school I went to college in Boston on an academic scholarship. I have a doctorate in anthropology and have been working ever since."

"Married? Kids?"

"No," she answers, tight lipped, "You?"

"Recently separated. One son."

"Who were you married to?"

"You might have known her from high school. Meredith Madland."

"Oh, my god," Farah squeals, "Of course I remember her! She was a stuck up snob!"

Travis laughs, "I can't dispute that."

"Did you go to college?"

"Psychology. I was a mental health therapist for eight years."

"Impressive," she taps her glass against his.

"I'm currently unemployed."

"Oh, that sucks. I'm sure you'll find something."

"No doubt," Travis looks at himself in the mirror behind the bar again.

They talk on, getting reacquainted, socially lubed with alcohol. Farah tells him about the recent passing of her father. That is her reason for returning to Applegate, to put his affairs in order. Travis confesses to mistakes he's made and having nowhere to go. He tells her about his son Sidney. By the time the bartender shouts, "Last call!", they are holding one another, kissing, whispering, and Farah Somers takes her lifelong crush, Travis Winters, home with her.

In the morning Travis wakes alone and naked in Farah's bed with a slight headache, feeling dehydrated from the alcohol. His memory toward the end of last night is fuzzy, but after moments he remembers her bringing him here after the bar closed. Her recently departed father's house.

Travis stretches, yawns, rubs his eyes, and lays in bed for a while letting the sleepiness fade. The bedroom is large and luxurious. The sheets are burgundy silk and the feather comforter warm and cozy. The walls are bare and the rest of the room spartan. An oak dresser with a tall mirror attached to it. A fine nightstand next to the bed. A wood roll top desk and standing lamp. Immaculately neat and clean. Farah's father must have been a fairly wealthy man. In high school Travis had assumed she was poor white trash being a goth, not that he gave her much thought back then. But he remembers her. For some reason she must have stuck out to him.

As he looks around, spotting his clothes crumbled at the foot of the bed, he wonders where she is and as he dresses wonders which of the three closed doors to take.

The first door Travis opens leads into a deep walk in closet with two rows of clothes hanging and a dozen shoes beneath them. Dress shirts and pants. Suit coats. Belts and suspenders hang on the wall. He looks at himself in a mirror hanging at the back of the closet.

He feels a hot flash and sweats as a hangover sets in. The second door opens to a large bathroom with a double sink, shower, toilet, shower, and hottub.

Shaking his head with envy he quietly closes the door after sipping some water in cupped hands at the sink and splashing his face. Farah seems like a genuinely nice woman, even beautiful, but she is not his wife. She has certainly blossomed since high school, but thoughts of Meredith bring on a rush of guilt.

The third door takes him into a wide hallway. He realizes this is an old house as he steps into the living room, still wondering where Farah is as he admires a large television screen on one wall, a leather couch, bear skin rug, shelves full of books, and a brick fireplace. Her father had a lot of money it seems.

Truthfully Travis has no plans for the day, no idea where to go, or what to do. Maybe his friend, Tobias Doherty will let him crash on his couch until he gets on his feet. He likely will.

Tobias and Travis haven't spoken in almost a year, maybe more than a year, but they had been close friends once, even though they talk less and less as the years go by. Travis tells himself it's just what people do as they get older. Get jobs, get married, start families, have less time for friends.

He faintly hears Farah's voice coming from another room in the house and moves in that direction. Down the hall and into a kitchen with stainless steel appliances. Something smells good in there. Through the kitchen window he notice's a swimming pool with a diving board in the back. The yard is enclosed by a red brick wall.

The sound of Farah's voice grows louder as he walks from the kitchen into a dining room. He's getting closer to her. She is engaged in a conversation with someone. He can't hear the other person speaking. She must be on the phone. If not this is going to be awkward.

Following the hall further and coming to a closed door, he can hear her on the other side. It's a heated conversation. A debate more than an argument. He calls out, "Farah?"

She falls silent and the door opens.

"Hi," Farah stands smiling dressed all in black again. This time a long, sleeveless dress that looks like one piece of form fitting fabric. Blue lipstick and silver eyeshadow. Travis is relieved to see he wasn't just wearing beer goggles last night. She is as attractive as the night. A curvy, hourglass body so different from Meredith. Meredith has small breasts with perky nipples, he used to tease her, saying he could hang his hat on her nipples. Farah's breasts are much larger with softer nipples. Meredith has an athletic build, a firm stomach, defined muscles. Farah is just soft all over. He blinks several times fighting off arousal. What is he doing? He doesn't want anyone but his wife. He doesn't want to be here.

"Good morning," he clears his throat, "how are you?"

"I'm good," she beams like the sunrise, "I have some breakfast ready for you in the kitchen. I left it in the stove to keep it warm. I didn't want to wake you. You were sleeping like a babe."

"You made me breakfast?" Travis is touched by the gesture. He feels a mix of emotions. Guilt. Confusion. Flattered. He knows he doesn't want Farah. He wants Meredith.

"I did," she pecks his cheek.

He looks over her shoulder into the room she exited, no one is there. He notices a black and white framed photograph of a man on the wall. The man is thin and handsome with a cleft chin. "Were you on the phone?"

"No."

"I thought I heard you talking to someone."

"No," she shakes her head with an innocent smile and takes his hand, leading him back toward the kitchen. "I was doing some reading in my father's office."

"Oh," Travis doesn't believe her, "What were you reading?"

"Brushing up on my Milton. Maybe I was reading aloud. I do that without realizing it sometimes." She blushes, not seeming as confident as last night at the bar.

It's a tasty breakfast. Steak and eggs with hash browns, orange juice, and coffee. Travis drinks his coffee black. Farah with cream and sugar.

They make small talk as he eats hoping the food will alleviate his hangover some. She brings him aspirin and washes the dishes when he's done as he sits at the table smoking a cigarette.

Travis can sense that she is infatuated with him. She is so happy chatting with him as he sits there struggling to find the words to tell her he should be going. It was nice to see her after all these years, and they should hang out again some time. He has no intention of hanging out with her again, but he has no ill feelings toward her and he doesn't want to hurt her feelings. The words are on the tip of his tongue as he stands to announce his departure.

Farah has just finished the dishes, tossing a dish towel over her shoulder, she smiles at him, "I was thinking we can go for a swim after we get your things. Maybe tonight we can go to that movie you mentioned you want to see and try out that new Japanese place you were talking about last night. I could go for some saki and sushi for dinner."

Travis blinks, "Get my stuff?"

"Oh," Farah looks concerned, "It might be better if you do that yourself. You're right. I don't want to cause any drama for Merdith. It would be scandalous if I showed up with you."

"You want me to stay here?" Travis stutters.

"Were you that drunk last night?" Farah laughs, sliding her arms around his waist, "You said you don't have anywhere to go and I invited you to stay here and you said yes."

"I did?" Travis blushes.

A look of hurt on her face she takes a step back letting one arm drop away from him, the other squeezes his shirt, "You don't want to stay?"

"No," he struggles, "I want to. Are you sure it's okay? I don't want to be a burden. I don't even have a job right now."

Farah gives a cheshire grin and rushes him with a hug, "You're not a burden, silly boy. I know you don't have a job. I don't care. I love you. I've always loved you."

He accepts her hug and whispers, "I love you too," wondering how and why those words are escaping his lips.

"Alright then," she announces with renewed vigor, "Go get your things so we can have our first day and date together."

"Uh," Travis looks at the kitchen floor, feeling shameful and useless, "I don't have a car."

"Oh," she chuckles, shrugs, pats his cheek, "I guess that means I'm driving."

Travis surrenders, "Meredith will be at work. There won't be any drama."

Farah kisses him and they make love on the kitchen table before they leave.

Like Travis expected Meredith isn't home. Farah waits outside in her car. When he steps inside his clothes are already packed and stacked in the living room. The site of the bags and suitcases drives the finality of the pending divorce through his heart like a stake. The house is as quiet as a cemetery. Memories flood through his mind as he walks through what was his home just a short time ago. Hot tears warm his eyes.

Peeking in his son's room makes the pang in his heart all the sharper. He knows Meredith won't keep Sidney away from him, but it won't be the same. He won't see Sidney every day. He'll miss out on the little things. Making him dinner. Making sure he brushes his teeth, does his homework, and goes to bed on time. He will now see his only son grow up from a distance. At arm's length. A weekend father.

With a last look around the house and a long sigh he lugs his belongings out to Farah's waiting car. There is a note from him on Meredith's bed and another on his Sidney's telling them both he loves them. Saying goodbye.

Travis and Farah's first date is surprisingly pleasant. She is a highly intelligent woman and gifted conversationalist with an air of arrogance that does get under his skin at moments.

Farah decides not to sell her father's house as originally intended so she can stay in Applegate with Travis. Things went well for the first three months. Travis even gets a job at a children's clinic after only a month together. He suspects Farah may have pulled some strings.

One evening Travis wakes in bed to find Farah gone. The clock on the nightstand reads 3:33 AM. Her absence concerns him. It's unusual. They had gone to bed together as they have every night over the past three months.

He rises wearing only boxers. The wood floor is cold against his feet so he puts on a pair of black slippers that are next to the bed. Fumbling in the dark he hears Farah speaking with someone like that first morning together.

She's in her father's office again. He stands close to the closed door listening. Goosebumps rise on his arms at the sound of her voice. Farah is speaking in a guttural tongue. A language he can't decipher. It sounds as if she's praying. It's unsettling.

Travis opens, barging in, "Farah, are you alright?"

She is seated on the floor and abruptly stops talking, looking at him with glazed eyes, a scowl of irritation, and suddenly it's washed away with a warm smile, "I'm fine, Travis."

"It's late. I was worried when I woke up and you were gone. I heard you talking. What are you doing?"

Farah's eyes dart around the room, "You caught me." She shrugs and stands, "I was talking to my father. I do that sometimes when I miss him."

"Oh," Travis regrets interrupting her, "What language was that?"

"Sumerian," she answers. Her father was a linguistics professor at Northington University, Applegate's most prestigious school.

"I didn't know you could speak it."

She gives a serious nod, speaking with a professional voice, "Speak. Read. Write. Sumerian. Latin. Greek. Hebrew. My father was interested in dead languages. Only a handful of people in the world can speak Sumerian. My father was fluent in over a dozen languages."

Travis is impressed and intimidated by Farah's talents. Familiar feelings of inadequacy creep into his thoughts. "I'll go back to sleep."

"No," she gently takes his hand, "stay for a while. I'll come back to bed with you."

Travis nods.

"I want to show you something," she walks to a painting on the wall, wearing only a black shirt and panties. Travis admires her long legs and buttock. There is a strong sexual element to their relationship. As she lifts the painting off the wall Travis's curiosity is awakened. "My father wasn't very innovative when it came to hiding this safe."

Travis walks to her side paying close attention as she works the safe's combination lock.

"This is something very secret I'm sharing with you," she gives him a sincere look, "You must promise to never tell anyone what I'm about to show you."

"I promise," he whispers expecting to see jewels or gold or bonds. Instead there are six old books stacked in the safe, their bindings facing out.

"These are some of the rarest books on Earth. My father spend most of his life researching them, tracking them down. There are people who would kill for a copy of just one of them. They are priceless." She steps aside letting Travis have a closer look.

There is no disputing the age of these ragged tomes. He reads the titles. *The Book of Eibon. The Mysteries of the Worm. The Book of Iod. The Necronomicon. Unaussprechlichen Kulten. The Book of Etherion.*

Eyes wide with fascination his finger traces the spine of *the Book of Iod*.

"That one is an ancient Hebrew text," Farah explains, "Mostly dealing with the Qlippothic side of the Kabalah. The evil side. These are dark books. Save *Etherion*."

"Wait a minute," Travis gives an entertained smile, "*The Necronomicon*. I know this book. It's fake. H. P. Lovecraft invented it for his horror stories. It doesn't exist outside of his imagination."

"Imagination is one of the most powerful forces in the universe," Farah rebukes, "Thought alone created the universe."

That wipes the smile from his face, "Maybe that's so, but it's still a fictional book. Lovecraft himself admitted it in so many letters."

"A fan of Lovecraft?"

"I read some in high school."

"Many people would like the world to go on believing these are fanciful books."

"They're not real?"

"Oh, Travis, my baby, these books are very real. Lovecraft was an atheist and believed his tales to be figments of his imagination and fragments of his dreams. The dream lands are very real. The visions that came to Lovecraft were awful truths. He tried to deny them but I think on those dreadful and lonely nights he knew the reality of them. The insanity of them. What the self-denied seer confronted in the planes of his unconscious mind were the machinations of the demiurgos. The great, uncaring manipulators of reality. The adversity of escape. The gatekeepers, the torturers, the wardens, the guardians, and the rebels. The swaying of an unknown war."

Travis is mesmerized by her melodic tone. "You're telling me you think *the Necronomicon* is real? And Lovecraft didn't know it?"

"All of these books and more are as real as you and I. The rare person may scribe them from the akasic. Those with three eyes." She strokes his cheek, "There are more things in heaven and earth, Horatio,than are dreamt of in your philosophy."

Travis looks closer at the books scrutinizing, "Can I look through them?"

"No," Farah hisses like a cat, "The books are cursed. Even touching them can bring misery."

Travis looks at his finger then smirks at her, tilting his head to the side, "Come on, you don't believe that."

Farah licks her lips, "My father found this copy of *the Necronomicon* in Italy hidden within a wall at the Abbey of Thelema. It is a handwritten copy, penned by Aleister Crowley. Crowley copied it from John Dee's edition. Dee had copied it from an earlier edition found in Jerusalem during the Crusades."

"This is nuts," Travis suddenly feels lightheaded. "Unbelievable. Do you think the magic in these books works?"

"I do," Farah answers with defiance.

"Tell me about the other books."

"*Unaussprechlichen Kulten* is German. It means 'of unspeakable cults' or something close to that. My father found it in Germany. He had to join an occult group called Fraternitas Saturni to obtain it. Some of them are still searching for it. *The Book of Eibon* was written by a wizard in ancient Hyerborea. This copy was given to my father in 1974 by a man named Julius Evola. He was on his deathbed when he entrusted it to him. *The Book of Iod* was written by a man named Khut-Nah. This copy was found hidden in Peru. De Vermis Mysteriis, *the Mysteries of the Worm*. Father found this copy in Syria."

"And *the Book of Etherion?*"

Farah lets out a sigh and leans back against the desk as she talks, "That's a fascinating story as well. They all are. This was the last book added to the collection. It was found just before he died. It is said to be written by an ancient Atlantean priest named Galabram. The first copy appeared in ancient Greece, well, ancient Egypt actually. The Egyptian priesthood allowed Solon to make a copy of the text when he was in Egypt. That book found its way to the hands of both Plato and Socrates. It was said that Aristotle refused to read it but did pass it on to Alexander the Great. It ended up in the library of Alexandria and was thought destroyed when the library was burned. It resurfaced many years later in the hands of a former Catholic priest named Eliphas Levi. After that it was given to H. P. Blavatsky by a mysterious man. She brought it to India where she had moved the headquarters of her Theosophical Society. That's where I found it and brought it back here to my father."

"Incredible," Travis whispers, eyeing the pale blue tome, "All of them."

Farah continues her narrative, "Contained in that book are the secrets and keys of the ether. The substance from which all physical creation comes. With it a magician can alter reality. Some say the intelligence of the ether itself, Etherion, and it's servitors can be summoned. With that book reality can be re-written however the user desires. Or so the legend goes. The other books are much darker, but this one is more neutral, more the power of nature alone."

Farah shuts the safe door, locking the cursed books from sight. She gives Travis a teasing smile, "Let's go to bed, honey."

Several days later Travis drops his son off at Meredith's after his weekend visit. He stands in the doorway of his old house cordially talking with his ex-wife but she won't let him inside. He doesn't ask to come in. She doesn't invite him in. He suddenly breaks down and begs her to give him one last chance. She denies him, "Travis, I know this is hard, but you have to accept it. I've started to see other people. It will be easier for you if you just let me go. Let me go and move on with your life. You have Farah now."

"Only because I can't have you," he mumbles, holding back tears.

"I'm sorry. We're done. I know it hurts, but there is no going back."

He nods with a long face and returns to his car, Farah's car. What is he doing? Farah is a sweet woman. A bit of an oddball but she's rich, beautiful, intelligent, and treats him well. So much guilt and love for these two women is tearing him apart. It's a matter of losing his family. That's what hurts the most. The loss of the family that he, Meredith, and Sidney were.

Travis decides to take the long way home. To just drive for a while and clear his thoughts, to pull himself together. He drives aimlessly, chain smoking, he needs a stiff drink. He pulls over at a city park and watches children play on the swings, slide, and merry go round. Parents serene at picnic tables. Families looking blissful and carefree. He would do anything to be with Meredith again. Farah would be alright. She would survive without him. She's strong. Meredith. Anything for Merdith. Whatever it takes.

An epiphany. Travis knows what he has to do. Knows what he will do.

That evening Travis lies in bed waiting for Farah to fall asleep. He pretends to sleep, still, listening to her breathing slow into slumber until he is sure it is the breath of sleep.

To be certain he listens a while longer. She seems to be in a deep sleep. With slow, delicate movements he rolls away from her and out of the bed feeling the familiar cool wood beneath his bare feet. She does not stir. He's naked. They made love before going to sleep. The room is dark but his eyes have adjusted to the dimness.

He tests each step before putting his full weight on the floor boards as he tip toes out of the room. One floorboard creaks and Travis freezes, feeling a rush of excitement and fear of discovery. After a few moments of listening to her steady breathing he continues, exiting the room and making his way through the hall and across the house to her father's study.

Inside the study he gently closes the door, turns on a desk lamp, and moves to the safe, nervously removing the painting.

While setting the painting down he catches a glimpse of an old man in a mirror on the wall. The sight of the elderly man scrutinizing him startles him so that he nearly drops the painting. He looks away just for a moment to catch the painting and when he looks back the phantom in the mirror is gone.

There is no one there. He is alone in the room. With a chill of fear courses thought his body with the realization that the old man in the mirror looked like Farah's father. It has to be his nerves. Guilt. He always feels guilt. There is no one there. No one. Farah is fast asleep.

Carefully setting the painting on a velvet cushioned loveseat he turns back to the safe. His hands are clammy as he works the combination lock. There is nervous sweat dripping down the small of his back.

The safe pops open and he can smell the old books inside the safe. They are beautiful radiating forbidden wisdom. He only looks at them afraid to move. Afraid to touch the cursed books. Travis is suddenly acutely aware of the silence of the night. He is alone but he doesn't feel alone. It feels as if each of the books is a sentience of its own. It feels as if something in the room watches and waits. Her father's spirit? What if Farah catches him? What will she do? She'll never trust him again. Paranoia. A voice inside his shouts with disgust, take up the book you coward!

With an unsteady hand he reaches toward the books imagining he feels a cold, foreboding aura surrounding them. There is only one that he wants. Careful to not touch the others Travis slides *the Book of Etherion* away from the others and out of the safe.

He still feels like somebody's watching him as he quickly closes the safe and places everything back in order. The ancient grimoire goes into a briefcase. He's going to bring it to work with him tomorrow.

The following day Travis neglects work and spends the day reading the stolen book. He skips eating at lunch break behind a locked office door with his nose buried in the book. His lunch is longer than it should be. Co-workers think he's catching up on paperwork.

After work he calls Farah and tells her he's going to visit his old friend, Tobias, for a while before coming home. He hears the disappointment in her voice but she says she understands.

Instead he goes to a coffee shop and continues to devour the contents of the book. When he finally finished reading it the sun was setting. He sits in quiet contemplation drinking cold, black coffee.

Looking the book over again he spills his coffee on the floor realizing for the first time that *the Book of Etherion* is not written in English. How the hell did he read it? How did he not notice this before?

A female coffee shop employee with dreadlocks and a nose piercing comes over and begins to clean up his mess with a dish towel. He wonders if she can tell his mind has suddenly broken. Travis apologizes to her, "I'm sorry."

"It's okay," she smiles up at him. "Can I get you a new coffee?"

"No, thank you," he places a large tip on the table for her, then holds the book open to her, "Can you read this?"

She curls her nose, "No. It's Greek to me."

Travis nods and closes the book, standing to leave.

"What is it?"

"Just an old book," he answers and hurries out of the shop in a confused daze.

Outside the wave of confusion continues to assault him. He is swirling in dreamy surrealism. Has he lost his mind?

The book is written in ancient Greek.

When he arrives home the lights are still on. Farah is likely up and waiting for him. She is always so sweet to him, sometimes he feels like she is too sweet, that she likes him too much. Bordering on suffocation. Or maybe her behavior is ordinary and he's the one obsessed with Meredith.

Travis enters the house with *the Book of Etherion* hidden inside his briefcase. He expects Farah to come running but instead stands alone in the entryway tugging his shoes off. He hears Farah having a conversation with someone. He thinks she must be on the phone as he wanders deeper into the house. Who is she talking to? Her tone sounds hushed and heated. She's in her father's office. My god! Does she know he took the book?

The office door is wide open, the light shining into the dark hallway. He stands at the end of the hall eavesdropping.

"It doesn't matter," Farah argues, "I love him." She pauses, her voice rising and falling in volume making it difficult to make out the entire conversation. "Everything is working out... we adjust... no... let it be..."

Travis hears someone else in the room whispering. Farah abruptly stops talking, "Travis?"

Travis walks into the office. She is dressed in her usual black. A black robe, dark hair pulled back. Her soft, round face reminds him of the moon. "Hi," is his timid response.

"I was getting worried," she says.

"Nothing to worry about."

She embraces him with a kiss, "I missed you!"

"Tell me the truth, Farah. Who were you talking to?"

Her smile holds back laughter and eyes so wide it frightens him. He realizes there is a madness in her eyes he's never noticed before. She answers, "My father. I've told you before."

"He's dead."

"Death is not the end, my pretty man," she tilts her head and bats her eyes, "Let's go to bed. I'm glad you're back. I don't like being away from you."

"Alright," he kisses her forehead, surrendering.

They make love before sleep. The act of their love making is intense and apocalyptic. Travis loses himself in the movements. He feels they are no longer there but two souls merging in the bed and floating through space. As if time has stopped and extended all at once. They exist in all time, everywhere. They have made love a hundred thousand times before, over millions of years, through many lives and masks. Their power flows through them, building, ascending, fucking among the stars and gods. When he cums Meredith's face invades his soul and he bursts into tears, sobbing in Farah's arms. "Sh," she soothes and pets.

Travis drifts to sleep like a babe in her arms, their sweat mingled. So soft and sweet, god, let him lay here forever. Her breasts. Her smell. Her breath. Her touch. And he sleeps safe in her arms against olive skin and thumping hearts.

Later in the night Travis is not sure if he's awake or dreaming or half dreaming. He struggles to be awake in the dreaming. In the dreaming he stands alone in an open field. Somewhere. Somewhere. The sky is blue and endless. Wind blows tall yellow and gold grass in waves of majesty. He feels so alive in the vastness. The sun is a great god looking down with giving rays of life. The hidden moon is its lover. Life is all around him in every breath and particle.

A smooth handsome man with pale ice blue piercing stands before him like a master of reality. They are suddenly standing together in a stone structure with open windows, doorways, and roof. There is a paternal familiarity about the man. His physical beauty is intimidating. A scowl of judgment. He grabs Travis with one hand and pushes him to his knees.

Travis wakes. Farah and his naked bodies still entangled, cool wetness of sweat and love on the sheet beneath them. He lies still in the darkness staring up at the ceiling, listening to her slow, deep breathing.

Swift, delicate, and graceful he removes himself from the bed and her safe embrace and walks naked to the briefcase. Not bothering to dress, he carries it to the old office of her departed father. He sits on the loveseat and opens *the Book of Etherion*, not entirely sure why he's doing this, but entirely sure it must be done.

It's dark but he can read the words of the book and his fingers run over them like a lover's touch. He reads aloud the calling of Etherion, pauses, looks to the invisible man before him and whispers, "Meredith.

Travis utters more passages from the book, pleading the service and boon of the intelligence of the ether.

The room illuminates as bright as day. The man from his dream stands before him. The room swirls violently, silently, the heart of a hurricane rushing, rainbow lights, papers and furniture spin around in a cyclone of overwhelming, deafening sound like the crash of machinery, yet the room is so silent and still. No sound. All sound. Chaos and order. Absolute.

Travis feels his ears popping like mountainous elevation. The blinding light is clear and vivid. The sound is a vacuum of nature's crashing rage. Transparent energy explodes all around him, boiling, living, and dying.

The aura of a white dove radiates off the man before him. The beautiful blank man is the center of the room, the center of the storm. Everything crashes outward in endless overlapping ripples as if the man has just parted reality like Moses parted the sea. As if they are in a sphere of pure thought, pure creation, pure destruction.

Whatever reality is Travis finds himself musing beneath his fear. Thoughts race. Atomic energy. Nuclear energy. Electricity. Cosmic radiation. Dark matter. Dark energy. Electromagnetic. Nebula. Black hole. White hole. Wormhole. Supernova. Big bang. Big rip. Something unfathomably powerful and unknown. He doesn't know. He feels madness like a pressure against his skull. He sees the old man, Farah's father, watching from the mirror.

The man before him, Travis knows it must be Etherion, stands like a god holding out a choice in the palm of each hand.

Etherion speaks to Travis without moving his mouth or making a sound, without words. And without words Travis understands. His blue eyes are too burrowing tearing through Travi's body, mind, and soul to the primordial essence of what Travis is.

Etherion's appearance is so stunning, uncanny, utterly beautiful and terrible at once. Sharp angular features absent emotion and expression. Neither Travis nor Etherion move in this absence of time and space. Travis is naked before the god thing.

Etherion's skin is smooth and molded to a perfection no human can match. He looks so human yet so obviously not human. He doesn't know what he is. Too immaculate. Too terrifying.

Travis feels sick with guilt and remorse flowing like sludge, oil, and rot. This man who knew Atlantis knows all there is to know of Travis. All his sins and secrets.

Atlantis. A high priest named Galabram. The word isn't right. Atlantis is what we call it today but it is not its proper name. It is Olympus. Eden. Elysium. Avalon. Asgard. Arcadia.

Etherion is no longer visible, replaced by the form of the powder blue skinned priest Galabram. Spheres of swirling energy like soapy floating bubbles orbit the Atlantean.

Travis feels ill with sin, ugly, weak, unworthy of anything.

The man-god before him could crush him with a thought, snap his ribs like twigs.

The sound and wind that are not there are overwhelming, driving his sanity away, he would cry, sob, and wail but movement no longer exists, flesh and words are no more. Travis is no more, only a minute strand of something else, a single hair of a beast.

The man-god stands with amazing posture, square shoulders, sculpted muscles, a sheer silk robe of sea green blowing in the paradoxical currents. Priestly arms at his sides held out slightly from it's torso, palms flat, facing Travis. A choice in each hand.

Tears wet Travis's face, a silent scream from his entire being. An infinite shrieking that would hoarse and tear raw his throat for months. He feels as if he is exploding with emotion. Fear. Rage. Guilt. Pain. Shame. Regret. Loneliness. Bliss. Never ending.

A multicolored sphere hovers before each palm. The other bubbles flutter around the man-god without moving. A choice in each hand. Travis knows the ugliness of his hidden self. If only he could reach redemption. Forgiveness. A second chance of some sort.

The warmth of the morning sun shining through the bedroom window wakes Farah from her slumber. She stretches and yawns, opening her eyes, naked, tangled in a sheet, an arm searching for her absent lover.

She studies his indented pillow a moment and the empty side of their bed and then rises sky clad, feet padding the wood floor to the window. She stands with her arms raised in a V gazing out at the glorious sunrise before drawing the curtain.

Farah picks her robe from the floor and covers herself before exiting the bedroom, "Travis?"

Popping her head into first the kitchen, then the living and dining room, she makes her way to her father's study, "Travis?"

She stands in the doorway of the study, tears stream down her round olive cheeks, her hand covering her mouth.

Travis is sitting deathly still on the velvet loveseat. Naked with wide unblinking eyes. *The Book of Etherion* clutched in dead hands.

Across town that same morning Meredith wakes startled, in a cold sweat. She dreamed of Travis. He was crying and reaching out to her. Feeling uneasy, a little frightened, she quickly realizes it was only a dream as she comes more fully back to the wakeful world.

A man next to her in bed rolls over, putting an arm over her, "Hey, babe. What's wrong?"

The man's name is Lamont. They have been dating since before Travis and her separated. He was the unknown factor among her new group of friends Travis was always so jealous of. He is the man that helped her find the courage to leave her husband.

The warmth of their bodies brings Meredith comfort. She squeezes his hand and kisses it, "Nothing. Just a dream."

Ten years later.

Sidney sits in his mother's hospital room watching her sitting in her wheelchair and opening a birthday present. She is a long-term patient at Caldwell Asylum. He visits her only a few times a year. Mostly the holidays. He feels guilt for not visiting more often, but struggles to see her when she's acting crazy. Times like this when she is lucid, taking her medication, are not so bad, if still sad. She was worse when he was younger, when she was first committed. She said such odd things, behaved in such bizarre ways, she was always so nervous and frightened that it frightened him. He was only a boy then. Thirteen years old when she first came to the hospital to stay for good. He was ten when his father passed away.

Sidney misses his father and was heartbroken when his parents divorced. The little boy he was then was even angry with them, confused, lost. He just wanted his parents back together. He hated their replacements. Farah for his father. Lamont for his mother. He didn't even like their names and was secretly thrilled when Lamont left his mother. Lamont couldn't cope with her sudden mental illness.

Now as he watches his mother open her presents he almost wishes Lamont would have stayed, so she would have someone else to visit her.

Meredith's hair is frizzy, clean but plagued with split ends, and knots. She doesn't like to brush her hair. She is a sickly thing, wrinkled, appearing much older than her true age. His eyes are always wide and buggy, paranoid, always darting. She wears a hospital gown most of the time.

Meredith looks up at her son with love and gratitude in her eyes, grinning, holding new water color paint and brushes, "Thank you, Sidney. I'll paint something for you."

"That would be great, mom," Sidney gives a tender smile.

"Something warm and colorful," she wheels to a small table near the window. The glass is laced with what looks like chicken wire. She picks up a plastic knife and cuts a small piece off her birthday cake.

"Mom," Sidney chuckles, joining her, "Take the candles out first."

"Oh," she sounds confused and hurt.

"Hey, it's okay, not a big deal at all," he licks the frosting off a candle bottom.

Meredith has been in a wheelchair ever since she attempted suicide by leaping out a window at the hospital two years ago, breaking both legs, shattering the bone so much it never healed right. She can walk but it's a struggle. She still goes to physical therapy for it.

Meredith hands her son a slice of cake on a paper plate and takes one for herself "How do you like your new job?"

Sidney shrugs, "It's money," he's a full time student at Northington University seeking a degree in psychology like his father. He's been working as a waiter since high school. "It's not that bad. I get along with everyone there. Mostly friendly folks."

He looks around the room as he eats the birthday cake. Meredith's paintings and drawings cover the walls. The drawings are intricate and tediously detailed, strange figures and arcane symbols, monsters and shadows. All dark, terrifying, morbid, violent, chaotic, confused. He studies one drawing that resembles an unborn fetus, eyes too big, skin cracked like a jigsaw puzzle, umbilical cord attached to the belly button of a crucified Christ in the background. The cross is an erect phallus. Jesus holds a bloody spear in one hand and a chalice overflowing with black liquid in the other. The rest of the drawing is covered in a myriad of bats, dragons, and devils screaming.

The painting next to it is a stark contrast to the macabre drawing. Most of the paintings are lovely renditions of his father. Each one is different. So odd, the drawings bleak and horrifying and the paintings rainbows of love. This painting of Travis resembles Jesus the Christ with a sacred heart glowing at his chest, a crown of thorns, and a white dove flying over him.

Meredith claims she dreams of Travis every night. The dreams began the night he died. Sidney realizes that somehow the death of his father broke her.

"Can we talk about dad?" Sidney asks.

Meredith answers with her mouth full of cake, she's working on her second piece, "Are those your words or the words of someone else?"

Sidney groans inside, "My words, mom."

"There are security cameras everywhere," she drops her cake, plate, and plastic fork on to the floor.

"Mom," Sidney gets brown paper towels from the table and begins cleaning up her mess.

"They watch us. Remote viewing. They peek at my thoughts," she is suddenly frightened, eyes darting.

Sidney sighs, sitting back across from her, "I have to leave soon. Visiting hours are almost over."

Meredith stares at him, her eyeballs twitching, then burst into forced, nervous giggling. She speaks in a baby girl voice, "Do you think you were the one wearing the invisible tape?"

"I don't know what you mean."

Meredith grabs his wrist, digging her nails into the skin, hissing, spittle and cake spilling from her mouth, "Do you think she cannot see us? Again who do we speak of this time?"

"Calm down," Sidney hushes.

She screams, "There is indeed love everywhere to be seen, felt, and heard and Meredith knows of these wondrous things!"

"Mom, please, calm yourself. It's okay. We don't have to talk about dad. Lets talk about something else."

"You have told me these things before," she whispers harshly, "as in being the Sidney I believe I may know."

"Okay," Sidney nods, carefully pulling her hand off his wrist, resigned to her loss of coherence.

"And what would be specific as to the memory of you that you think would rattle my brain?"

Meredith is calm again, "Or did I just answer my own question again? She once again thought in mind. Memories stir the pot. The witch's cauldron?"

Sidney looks at his mother with a broken heart. He's seen and heard her insane rambling many times before. He thinks it should get easier as time goes on, but it doesn't."

Meredith cries quietly, "They're coming. Always spying. A black witch. My Travis. My Etherion." She looks at Sidney expecting an answer.

Sidney nods, kisses her on the forehead, "I have to go now, mom. I'll be back to visit again as soon as I can. I love you."

"I love you too, Sidney-poo."

The front door of Sidney's apartment opens up into a small kitchen. He sets his keys on the counter with a short sigh and walks into the living room.

"Hey, baby, how was it?" His fiance sits on a yoga mat barefoot in black spandex pants and a purple sports bra, blonde hair in a bun. Daphne Appleseth. They've been living together for only a few months. The wedding is two months away.

Daphne comes from old money, one of Applegate, South Dakota's founding families. The town was founded in 1875. Her family owned an apple orchard and bee hive among other enterprises. Both ventures were profitable during the summers. The family invested in real estate and electricity, damming up the river that runs through the town. In 1910 her great-grandfather founded a bank and the family's empire has been expanding ever since.

Her mother and father don't approve of the engagement to Sidney. They want her to marry into money, but don't say it outright. The only one in her family that approves of Sidney is her grandmother.

"It was alright," Sidney gives her a sad smile, "She didn't tell me about getting phone calls from Jim Morrison or that she was impregnated by an alien or show me any secret messages from the Vatican this time." He sits on the couch.

Daphne continues to stretch, mimicking the woman on the muted television screen. Tiny beads of sweat sparkle in the window sunlight on her forehead. "Siler stopped by to see you." Siler has been a friend of Sidney since high school.

Sidney admires her body as she works out, the spandex hugging her buttocks. "I'll call him later," he leans forward and playfully slaps her rear, "I'm distracted by this gorgeous ass right now." He leaves his hand there, caressing the curve just above her thigh.

Daphne turns and kisses him. Sidney can smell her sweat, feel it, it turns him on. He loves the way she smells, the firmness of her body. She has an athletic build with small breasts, and a fierce bold nature that stole his heart. His future wife. They make love on the yoga mat.

    Later that night Daphne leaves to visit her girlfriends. More wedding plans. Sidney elected to stay home and lounge.

    He sits in front of his computer wondering why he hasn't been able to stop thinking of his father. The ten year anniversary of his death recently passed and he dreamed of him that night. Sidney hasn't mentioned it to anyone because it frightened him. It wasn't a nightmare by any means, in fact it was a pleasant dream, but his mother went insane from dreaming of him. That's what scares him. Meredith claims she dreams of Travis whenever she sleeps. Every night. The doctor's have diagnosed her as schizophrenic. It is hereditary.

    Sidney knows the story of his father's mysterious death. He's read all the newspaper articles and has them in a scrapbook he made as a boy. Ignoring the computer he flips through the pages of the scrapbook, taking a moment to study each picture that he knows so well. He can close his eyes and picture each photograph in his mind. The photo he is looking at now is his ninth birthday. He's holding up a cake with his parents and they are all smiling.

    After his father passed and his mother was institutionalized Sidney went to live with his grandfather Alfritch Madland. Grandpa Al was a good grandpa. He's healthy for his age and attending the wedding. Whenever Sidney would ask about his father's death Alfirtch would only grumble.

    The last of the Madland family moved to Arizona after Meredith was hospitalized. Grandma Madland, Aunt Angelique, and his cousins. They still send birthday and Christmas cards, but grandma Madland died when Sidney was fifteen. He and his grandfather went to Arizona for the funeral. They usually come to visit once a year. Sidney misses his cousins.

    Sidney is haunted by his father's death. The official story is that he died of a heart attack. Natural causes. But it makes no sense. According to everything Sidney has been able to uncover his father was a healthy man.

    There is one person left that may know something more. He types her name into the search engine on his computer. Farah Somers.

    She was his father's girlfriend after the divorce and he died in her house. She was the one who found him.

    The first website link he clicks on is for Northington University. There is a photo of her with a short bio. She is an attractive older woman with dark hair streaked with lines of gray and dressed in all black. Farah Somers. Professor of Anthropology. He's seen her from a distance on campus a few times, but always stays away from her. Sidney skims the bio. Daughter of Hamilton Somers, former Professor of Linguistics at the same university. There is a contact phone number and email listed.

    Sidney writes her an email.

    Dear Professor Somers,

    My name is Sidney Winters. I don't know if you remember me. My father was Travis Winters. I am wondering if you would be free to have coffee sometime? I have questions about my dad. I would very much appreciate it. Thank you for your time.

    Sincerely,

    Sidney Winters

    He includes his cell phone number. Sidney only remembers meeting her once and that was at his father's funeral. They did not speak to each other. One of his cousins pointed her out and told him that she was his father's girlfriend.

    The next day at work, waiting tables, Sidney receives a phone call from a number he doesn't recognize. At break he listens to the message the caller left. Her voice is melodic and thick as honey.

    "Hello, Sidney. This is Farah Somers. I would be delighted to meet you for coffee. My address is 777 Sunset Drive. I'll be available Saturday afternoon. If you're free come by. Hope to see you or hear from you."

    Sidney is sitting on an upturned five gallon bucket behind the restaurant. He drops his cigarette butt and stamps it out under his shoe, watching traffic buzz by. The address is where his father died.

    Farah paces her father's study. She hasn't changed anything in the room since her father died. There is still a deep red carpet. The loveseat. The desk. An antique lamp. Mirror and painting on the wall. Fireplace. A mellow gold globe of the world in a stylish wood stand. A photograph of her and her father on the desk.

    She is barefoot in a long flowing black dress with shoulder straps and a gold locket hanging down into her cleavage. Long black hair unbound and wild with locks of gray. Pacing, hands balled into fists.

    The door of her father's study is wide open. All the lights throughout the rest of the big house are off. She stands alone in the room ranting and raving.

    "I loved him," she argues, "I love him still and I've lost him. I will talk with Sidney and I will tell him everything! He deserves to know."

Farah stops, frowning at her face half hidden and shadowed by hair in the mirror, "I've always done everything you've asked of me. I've searched for your artifacts. Translated books. Took the job at Northington. I am not foolish enough to dabble with devils. I will do this and you have no choice but to accept it. Accept it out of respect for me."

She begins pacing again, "It's his father. You said they would come and they never have. It's been years. I'm bored of this. I'm going to bed. Do what you will."

Saturday afternoon.

Sidney is in their bedroom having just showered and changed out of his work clothes. He worked the day shift and got off early.

Daphne is in their little bathroom leaning over the sink as she applies makeup. The small bathroom is only accessible from the bedroom of their tiny apartment. It is only the bathroom, bedroom, living room, and narrow kitchen. They are lucky enough to have a corner unit so they have windows on two sides of the apartment.

Sitting on the edge of the bed, pulling on socks, Sidney asks Daphne, "How long will you be gone?" Her grandmother is waiting in the living room to take her shopping for more wedding items and dinner after.

Not taking her eyes off the task at hand she answers, "I don't know. Maybe around eight."

"I'll be home by then," Sidney pulls his shoes on.

"Do I get a kiss good-bye?" Daphne chirps.

Sidney slides into the bathroom and plants a kiss on her cheek. She stops what she's doing and kisses his lips, "I love you."

"I love you too," Sidney says.

"Are you sure this is a good idea? You don't know anything about this woman."

"I'm sure it will be fine."

"Want to watch a movie when I get home tonight?"

"Sure. Sounds like a plan."

"Okay," she returns to the mirror and puts on makeup.

"See you later," Sidney steps into the living room.

Daphne's grandmother sits on their living room couch with her gray cotton ball hair watching a news program on the television. She looks to be in her sixties. Thin. High cheekbones. A proper and respectable lady dressed in bright green and white today. Expensive jewelry sparkling. A gold wedding ring with a huge diamond, a pearl necklace, gold earrings, too much make up in a vain attempt to hide her age.

Sidney likes her though. She doesn't seem spoiled and arrogant like the rest of the family. He often sees her rolling her eyes at her children and grandchildren, yet she loves them like a mother bear.

"Hello Sidney," she greets him as he closes the door.

"Hi," he answers with a bit of a smile.

"You're off to your coffee date?" She teases.

"I am."

"Daphne told me," she picks up a tea cup from the coffee table, "A morbid affair," she sips the hot tea.

Sidney puts his hands in his pockets feeling scolded. He looks at her hand. Thin. Loose, soft skin. Visible veins. Polished nails.

"I understand," she tells him, "You need closure. A sad thing."

Sidney looks around the room. Daphne's Felix the Cat clock hangs on the wall with its black tail wagging. "It's just something I have to do."

She reaches out to him, he lets her take his hand in hers. Delicate skin. She squeezes his hand with surprising strength and firmness, a caring gesture, "Sidney. The Somers are a queer family who have been apart of the woodwork of Applegate as long as the Appleseths and Caldwells. I know of them. Talk with this woman. Do what needs to be done. Then walk away without looking back."

Sidney, captured by the warning in her eyes, unsure how to react, "What's wrong with the Somers?"

She frees his hand to sip her tea, "They are an unlucky family. I don't want their bad luck to rub off on you."

Daphne bounces out of the bedroom, "I'm ready." She grins at Sidney, "You're still here?"

Sidney quickly kissed her cheek, "I'll see you tonight."

Sidney parks his car on the curving street of a neighborhood almost hidden by trees. The house is wide and flat, a single story. The driveway is large enough to park a dozen cars. Trees block a full view of the house from the street. A mostly brick house.

There is a tall potted plant next to the front door. He knocks standing on a welcome mat. Birds chirp somewhere in the yard.

The door opens, he recognizes Farah immediately, her black and gray streaked hair pulled back tight, dusk skin, round, opaque eyes. He can't make out her ethnicity. In the flesh, even being so much older than him, he recognizes the stunning allure his father must have fallen for. She has some obscure aspects about her. Black dress and matching sandals.

Farah gives him an affectionate smile, "Sidney?"

"Yes," he shakes her hand.

She puts her hands on her hips, "You look just like your father. Wow."

Sidney blushes, "Thanks."

"Come inside," she beckons, "I have coffee brewing. I'm pleased you could make it."

Sidney follows her into the old house and decides he likes her taste in decor immediately when he sees the three foot marble statue of some Greek god in the entryway upon the wood floor.

"That's Theseus," she glances back as she leads him into the kitchen.

"Have a seat," she pours two cups of steaming coffee. "Would you like anything? Sugar? Milk? Cream?"

"I like it black."

"Ha. So did Travis."

"Huh."

"Would you like anything to eat? I have fresh scones."

"No thank you," Sidney blows on his coffee.

"Well," she sits at the kitchen table across from him, "I was surprised by your email. I didn't quite know what to think, but I'm pleased to answer any questions you may have."

"I appreciate it. I know it must seem weird or something."

Farah gives a solemn glance, "It's not weird, Sidney. On the contrary, it's normal."

"Okay," he looks down into his coffee, "What was he like?"

"Do you want the truth?"

"Of course."

"He was a tortured man. He tortured himself inside with guilt for everything. There was no logical reason for it. He was intelligent but he didn't know how to cope with his emotions. He was creative and curious, adventurous, alcoholic, generous, polite, brooding. A complex man. And I loved him all the more for it. I truly did."

Sidney nods, "He was a shrink?"

"He had a masters in psychology and was slowly working on a doctorate. He always worked as a therapist. He would have been a great psychologist if he'd lived longer. He was an effective therapist."

"How did you meet him?"

"We went to the same high school." Farah smiles at a memory, "I had such a crush on him back then. He was wild then and people loved him for it. The life of the party. In high school no matter what I did I just could catch his attention. He had a lot of friends. He mellowed with age. Settled down when he married your mother, I suspect. Or matured."

"You were friends in high school?"

"No. Acquaintances. I left Applegate for college. He married Meredith. She went to school with us too."

Sidney sits contemplating, watching the steam rise off his coffee.

"Ask," Farah prods with a softhearted manner.

"How did he die?"

"Do you believe in magic, Sidney?"

"No," Sidney looks offended.

"You said you want the truth. It's nothing people like to accept or take seriously. You will think I'm crazy or eccentric, but I will tell you because it is the truth. Whether you believe it or not, you deserve to know."

"I'm grateful."

"Travis Winters died of natural causes, yes, supernatural causes. He tried to use magic to make your mother love him again. It didn't work the way he expected. He died for his efforts," her eyes filled with tears, "I knew he still loved your mother. I didn't care. I was living a dream being with him, I know he didn't love me like he loved your mother, but he loved me in his way. She would never take him back. I thought maybe after enough time passed he'd love me that way. Once he'd had time to heal from the divorce. He was making plans for you and I to meet. He wanted to wait until he was sure we had a stable relationship before he brought a new woman into your life. He loved you, Sidney. If you don't believe anything I say, believe that. He would light up whenever he spoke of you. He carried your picture in his wallet."

"I didn't know." Sidney isn't sure how to react. He thinks of Daphne's grandma's warning.

"Your mother disliked me. I'm not sure why. Because I was the new woman I suppose. Travis hated Lamont. I was jealous of Meredith."

"I didn't care for Lamont."

"Yes," she nods, "I remember Travis told me that too."

"How did he die? What killed him?"

"*The Book of Etherion.* I found him that morning in my father's study. Dead. On the loveseat with that damned book in his lap. I don't know exactly what he did with it. What unearthly thing he tapped into. Something from the ether killed him. I don't know if it was Etherion or Galabram or some astral zombie. Who knows? He wasn't an occultist. He shouldn't have touched the book. I shouldn't have shown it to him. But the heart moves in mysterious ways."

Sidney isn't sure what to think. This woman may be as crazy as his mom. Maybe his dad was crazy too. All of them are crazy. Yet something about her makes him believe her. Makes him want to believe her. Magic. Astral zombies. Nonsense.

No. Something in her story appeals to him. Maybe he only wants to believe something fantastic about his father. Something magical about him. "My dad died because he played with evil magic?"

"Not evil. No. Etherion is not evil. It is neutral. Etherion is the law of nature. The law of reality. The intelligence of the structure of the universe, or reality. The book can be used for evil, to be sure. Travis was far from being an evil man. Men attempt to master the ether and use it to shape their destinies. To bend the world to their will."

"My mother went crazy after my dad died."

Farah answers with a look of empathy, "I had heard she went to the hospital."

"She says he comes to her in his dreams every night. She can't go to sleep without dreaming about him."

"That is interesting. You know we have something else in common, Sidney. My father died using the same book. Where your father sought eternal love, mine sought eternal life. Both were motivated by fear. Fear of being alone and fear of death."

"Do you still have this book?"

"I do."

"May I see it?"

"I don't know that it's a good idea."

Sidney says nothing, his look of disappointment says everything.

Farah sighs, "The follies of men and women. I will let you have a look at the book. Follow me."

He follows her into the hallway and to an office. When Sidney enters the room he can only focus on one thing. A scarlet loveseat. His father died there. In this room.

"This was my father's office. He used to spend long hours working here when I was a girl," Farah says as she removes a painting from the wall, revealing a safe behind it. "I am trusting you with this. Besides you father, you are the only person I've shown it to." She opens the safe and takes out a light blue book and sets it on the desk. "*The Book of Etherion.* There are few copies in the world. I suspect there may be a dozen out there somewhere. This is the oldest known copy. Hundreds of years old."

Sidney studies the dusty, aged book before picking it up. Did this book kill his father? He sits in the loveseat with the book in his lap.

Farah is disturbed by the sight but suddenly distracted by the mirror on the wall.

Sidney runs his hands over the sea blue cover. He opens it. The pages are fragile and made from unusual paper. The letters on the pages are alien to him. Strange markings, glyphs, and secret symbols. "What language is this?"

Farah looks away from the mirror, "Mostly Ancient Greek with some Egyptian influence. I don't know how Travis deciphered it. An uncanny and amazing feat. Truly. Your father was an special kind of man."

"I wish I could read it."

"What is it you're hoping to find, Sidney?"

"My parents."

"I have a copy of the book. A copy of the original text with a translation. I did it myself. I'm going to regret this. You may borrow the copy to study if you'd like, but I'm telling you now that it's an awful idea."

"Sincerely?"

"It is a dangerous thing," she gives a sad nod, "The book can consume you, destroy you. Few can fathom its secrets. If you take the book you will never be the same again. I don't want to give you the book, but it may be that we are just the playthings of the gods. The choice is yours."

"Thank you. I understand. I won't try any of the magic. I don't even believe in magic."

"You will."

That night Daphne and Sidney cuddle on their couch watching a movie. She didn't ask him much about the meeting with Farah Somers, respecting his privacy, and he didn't mention the book. He shrugged off the few questions about Farah telling her she was just an eccentric and he'd never know what killed his father. Maybe it was only a heart attack. Maybe he and Farah did weird drugs together. She seemed like the type who may have done drugs in her youth. It doesn't matter. It's over.

If it doesn't matter, why did he accept the book?

Life went on as usual. Sidney continued waiting tables and going to school while Daphne took care of most of the wedding plans. Oddly he didn't see Farah at school anymore. He even forgot about *the Book of Etherion* tucked away in the closet.

Until one Monday evening when Daphne went out with her family.

Sidney sits on the couch doing homework on his computer.

Rubbing his tired eyes with the thumb and index finger of one hand, sick of studying, he types Etherion into a search engine on his computer and gets no real results. The book must be nothing. Just the story of an eccentric, lonely woman. Pretty much everything is on the internet. If the book was significant he'd have found something on it.

He walks to the bedroom closest and digs out the book. He'd tossed it in there, almost afraid to read it. When Farah offered it to him he accepted because it seemed like some kind of connection to his dad.

Sidney sits on the bed looking over that pale blue cover. He opens the book to the first page and begins to read.

Daphne enters the bedroom, "Hi, honey."

Sidney blinks, startled, "Hi," he glances at his watch, surprised, he's been reading for four hours yet it felt like mere minutes.

Daphne sets shopping bags next to the dresser and takes off her shoes, "What are you reading?"

"Nothing. Just some weird book that used to be my dad's."

"Oh," Daphne unbuttons her blouse, stepping into the small bathroom, "I'm so exhausted. Have to get up early tomorrow too."

Sidney nods, distracted by the book, "That's cool. I'm going to stay up and read for a while."

"Alright," Daphne sticks out her bottom lip pouting.

Sidney doesn't notice, rises, book in hand, stands in the bathroom doorway and gives her a quick kiss, "I love you. Missed you."

"I love you too, you handsome devil. Don't stay up too late."

"I won't."

Sidney sits on the living room couch engrossed in the book. The moon is visible from the window.

He reads of the rise and fall of Atlantis and other golden ages that have come and gone, of races that walked the Earth long before man, and of races that will walk the Earth when man is gone. He reads of creation and the eternal cycle of life and death which follows. He reads of the ancient priest Galabram who is now a guardian at the gate of paradise and of the god thing Etherion that is the intangible, invisible foundation of the tangible and visible. Of the occult laws of the nature of the universe. The shell encasing the spiritus. Etherion that lets the rare wisdom of man escape the clutches of the usurper god of creation.

"Sidney!" Daphne gasps with worry, "You stayed up all night reading that book?"

Sidney is startled, confused, looking at Daphne and the concern in her eyes and out the window at the dawn. He had not noticed the sunrise and the passage of time.

"I'm sorry," he closes the book with bags under his eyes, "I didn't mean to. I guess I lost track of time."

"This is crazy. You have class today."

"You're right," he stands, putting his arms around her and planting a kiss, "I'm going to sleep for a few hours. Wow. That is nuts."

"Sidney?" Daphne holds his face in her hands staring into his eyes, "Are you wearing contacts?"

"What? No?"

She whispers, shocked, "Your eyes are blue."

Sidney steps away and into the bathroom. In the mirror his familiar face gazes back at him with new eyes. His brown eyes are now bright blue.

Daphne squeezes into the bathroom mirror behind him, her hands on his shoulders.

"That's bizarre," Sidney says while tugging at the skin around his eyes.

"Can you see alright?"

"Yes."

"Does it hurt? Do you feel any different?"

"I feel fine. I feel normal," Sidney lies. It doesn't hurt. He can see better than before. Everything seems crisper, more clear, more detailed, and he feels a serenity like he's never known.

"I'll call a doctor. Make an appointment," she hugs him from behind, "Maybe I should stay home with you today."

"No," Sidney touches her hand and turns to face her, "I'm sure it's nothing. I'm sure it's nothing serious."

"Alright," she kisses his hand, "I'm still worried about you. I'm still going to call a doctor."

He nods, "I'm alright. I'm just going to sleep for a while before class."

Daphne follows him to the bed and slips under the blankets with him. While they make love Sidney feels the sensuality of it more than ever before, like he's making love for the first time. The feel of their skin touching sends waves of shivering ecstasy through his entire body. He quakes with pleasure. Lost in time and their rhythm, so focused and intent. At the end of the coupling they climax together, pressing their hips together in a prolonged orgasm. He feels ripped from time and space with the hot rush flowing into her and he feels the divine spark of creation.

Sidney's eyelids fall shut with exhaustion, his body limp, dead still weight on the mattress. Daphne rises to shower and starts her day.

Sidney is in the bed half asleep and floating in visions of blue ocean waters, sea waves rolling as far as the eye can see, calm and un-thought, he is the surface of the water.

Daphne stands over Sidney watching her fiance sleep. His nostrils flare with oxygen moving in and out, his breath deep and heavy. She kisses his forehead and leaves for the day.

The sound of the door closing wakes Sidney and he rolls out of bed feeling a second wind. He must finish reading *the Book of Etherion*.

He camps out on the bed and finishes his reading. Once again unaware of the passage of time. The room goes silent. He is deaf with new blue eyes looking about the room seeing every fine detail. Every fiber of the carpet and blankets. Every bubble and streak in the painted walls. The dust in the air. The vibrancy and distinction of the colors. Colors so wonderful. Shapes and lines and curves and the geometry of it all. Everything is a perfect miracle. Everything means something, having some importance.

The walls seem alive. Moving in and out with the rhythm of a breathing chest. Everything begins to melt and flow, yet never quite losing its form. A constant flux reverting to its originality. There is a current to everything in the room. All substances like clay, like still, hard liquid. Shadows creep and crawl in the nooks and crannies. Skeletal men writhe and worm about the room, peek around corners, and vanish when he tries to focus on them. He doesn't feel alone. It is as if the room is full of people, not strangers, but unknown familiars.

Sidney feels like he understands everything. The entire functioning of the universe, small and large, as above, so below. Yet there is a confusion caused by the sheer scope of everything. He is confused as to what is happening to him. On the walls lines and cracks in the paint shift and morph into the shapes of Chinese dragons, alive, moving, and vanishing only to be reborn.

He perceives all the particles making up everything in the room, his body, the air. Atoms, molecules, electrons, protons, neutrons and the empty spaces between. Everything alive, a constant shifting, copulation, birth, and death, and rebirth.

His name Sidney seems strange. He is not Sidney Winters. He is essence. He knows what he is without a name. An identity, a self without a name.

The flow of matter like magma. The secrets of the universe and God. He can walk with God. He can walk like God. The body called Sidney rises from the bed and walks toward the breathing, melting, growing, shrinking wall. Reaching out a hand and observing it pass through the wall. The rest of the body, called Sidney Winters, follows and walks into the wall.

In the evening Daphne returns home to find Sidney gone and *the Book of Etherion* open on their bed.

Farah sits at the desk in her deceased father's study, long hair down over her shoulders. Hands folded before her. Alone in the room.

"It was the right thing to do," she says to the empty room, "I still love Travis."

She sits with patience watching the mirror on the wall.

"I'm not a liar," she responds to the silence, "Shame on you. I have coffee on." She briskly makes her way to the kitchen and pours two cups of dark brew.

The old doorbell rings.

She brings a tray with both coffee cups into the study before answering the door.

Daphne stands on the doorstep looking nervous and forlorn, "Professor Somers?"

"Yes."

"My name is Daphne Appleseth. Sidney's fiance."

"I am pleased to meet you, Miss Appleseth. That is an old name around here."

"It is."

"How can I help you, dear?"

"Um. I was wondering if you've seen Sidney?"

"He came to see me once, inquiring about his father. Come in. I've made some fresh coffee if you'd like some."

"Thank you," Daphne follows her into the study. She grows suspicious at the sight of two waiting cups of coffee set on a small table near a scarlet loveseat. "Have you heard from Sidney since that day?"

"I have not," she picks up the coffee and sips, "Help yourself."

"No one has," Daphne chokes, ignoring the coffee. "He disappeared not long after meeting with you."

"I'm very sorry to hear that."

"I've filed a missing persons report but the police haven't been able to find anything. It's like he just fell off the face of the Earth."

"Indeed," Farah nods, setting her coffee cup down, "When we spoke he asked me what his father was like and how he passed."

"After meeting with you he started reading some strange book. He became obsessed with it. He went missing while he was reading that book."

"*The Book of Etherion*," Farah admits, "It changes all who read it. Travis was reading it when he left this world."

Daphne's eyes water, fear in her face, "You think Sidney's dead?"

"I don't know that. I don't know where he is or what happened. In fact the police have already been here asking me if I knew anything. I wish I had something more to tell you."

Daphne sighs, taking up her cup of coffee, "Were you expecting company?"

"Only you."

"What do you mean? How did you know I was coming?"

"I just know things sometimes. Daphne, I empathize with you. I wish I had answers to take away your fears. I don't. I felt you would come today. Like I said, *the Book of Etherion* changes people when they read it. It changed me. My father. Travis. If Sidney read it like you say."

"How?" Daphne's voice is barely more than a whisper.

"I don't know. I can't pretend to understand the mysteries of the universe. The book has a strange power. It reveals things that maybe we're not supposed to know."

"How did the book change you?" Daphne is too distraught with the loss of Sidney to question the validity of their conversation.

"I see things. Things that other people don't see. It's always different. Like Alice, my father went into the looking glass. I believe Travis is wandering the dream lands. I just don't know what happened to Sidney if what you tell me is true."

"It sounds ludicrous."

"To most."

"I believe you. I saw the change in his eyes."

"If I could help you I swear I would."

"Thank you."

They sit in silence.

"I've bothered you long enough," Daphne says, "I should go."

"It was no bother."

"Thank you."

"You're welcome, Daphne."

Farah walks her to the door, "Do you still have the book?"

"No," Daphne lies, "It vanished with Sidney."

Farah nods and watches Daphne walk away for a moment before closing the door.

The night their wedding was to take place, Daphne cries herself to sleep holding a picture of Sidney. Her family and friends called to check on her and offered to spend time with her but she refused, telling them all she just needed to be alone.

Sometime in the early morning hours between dusk and dawn Daphne wakes forgetting that Sidney is gone. She feels his warmth in the bed beside her. She pulls him close, they kiss, embrace, make quiet love in the dark. After, as she lay holding him, the realization of his return dawns on her. With tears of joy she says, "Sidney, I love you. Where have you been?"

She feels his breath tickle her ear as he whispers, "My name is no longer Sidney. I am Enoch. And I love you."

And he is gone.

She knows it was him. She knows his touch, his smell, his voice too well to be deceived.

"No!" She cries out, punching the bed where he was. Again and again. She throws his pillow across the room.

"Come back," she sobs, "Please. Don't leave me."

Daphne cries in the bed for several minutes. When she stops crying she just lies till in the dark, her face wet with tears, staring at nothing.

Daphne rises naked from the bed, feeling the phantom wetness left run cool down her inner thigh. The cool night air gives her goosebumps. She opens the top dresser drawer and takes out an old book with a crystal blue cover.

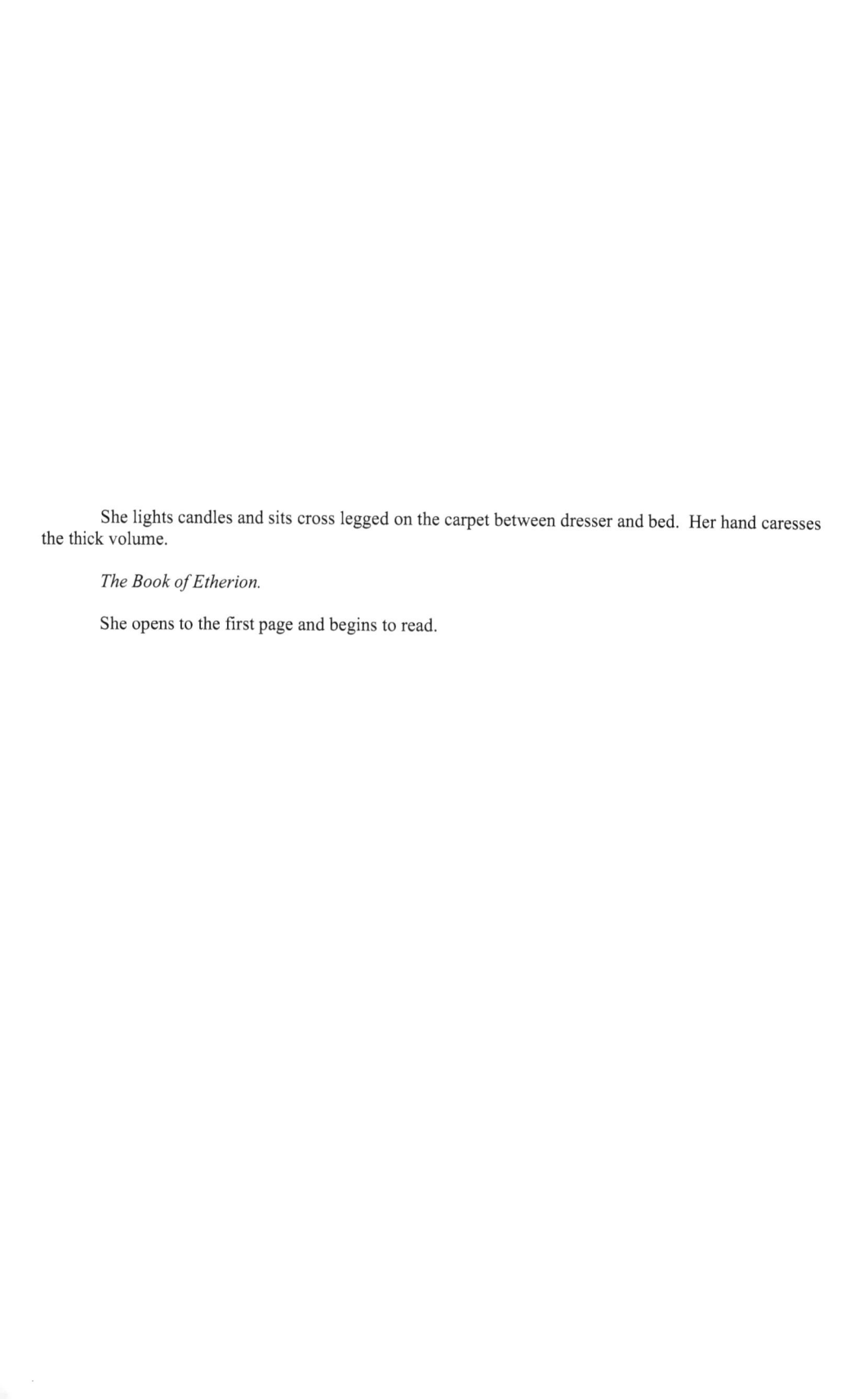

She lights candles and sits cross legged on the carpet between dresser and bed. Her hand caresses the thick volume.

The Book of Etherion.

She opens to the first page and begins to read.

Grave Flowers

Holly Flowers just doesn't care anymore, exhausted, walking home from work in the dark. Her car died so she's been riding the bus to work and walking home at night because the bus system doesn't stay running this late. She hates her job as a waitress at Alphonso Pizza. She wants to do something more with her life, and knows, given the chance she would. If she could just get a break. Another chance at life.

Holly's not as young as she used to be. Thirty-eight and quite a few mistakes. Now her life is weighted down with debt and doubt. Collection agencies harass her daily. Student loans. Medical bills. Old credit cards. She feels hopeless in debt, drowning in debt.

Holly is raising two sons on her own with no child support. Seven year old Omar and fifteen year old Karl. The boys have different fathers. Neither comes around to see them much. Financially they barely squeeze by, collecting food stamps and picking and choosing which bills to pay. Holly struggles to find money for extras like Christmas and birthdays.

It would help if she could find a better paying job, it would make all the difference in the world.

By the time Alphonso's hired her she'd applied for 36 places, turned down by everyone. It's because of her age, her criminal record, and spotty work history. Several years ago she was arrested for DUI, disorderly conduct, and simple assault on three different occasions. That was back when Omar's father left her. She fell apart and drank heavily for about a year. She eventually went to see an income based counselor and started to put the pieces of her life back together.

It's near midnight. The street is quiet. There is a mist and chill in the air. Holly hugs herself to stay warm as she walks. She's wearing her green and red work uniform and apron.

She walks this route home through the same neighborhoods five, sometimes six times a week. It takes about an hour and a half to get home. She enjoys the peace and quiet of the long walk. The exercise is nice, if she wasn't so tired. The walk gives her the chance to clear her head and think about things.

Holly keeps a brisk pace as she walks past familiar houses and street lights. Most of the houses are dark, a few have porch and garage lights on, faint blue television and computer screen light glows out some windows.

The sky is black with dark and gray clouds covering the stars. The clouds move swiftly over a sliver of silver moon. A light sprinkle of rain comes down as she walks in front of a gated cemetery.

"Oh, great," she whispers. Please don't rain on me, she prays. She wants to get home before a hard rain comes down. She stops in front of the cemetery staring across the darkness. Holly always feels uneasy when she walks past it. The other night she frightened herself. She thought she heard the dead whispering to her as she walked past it. She sprinted all the way to the edge of the cemetery before laughing at herself when she realized it was only the wind.

If she were to cut across the cemetery it would cut the rest of her walk in half. It's a long and wide cemetery. The trees and bushes are thick, blacking out the light on the other side of the gates. It's an old cemetery. She'd have to climb the fence.

What is she afraid of? She shakes her head and begins to walk along the sidewalk again, staring at the dark shapes in the cemetery. What must be headstones, mausoleums, statues, bushes, benchs, and trees.

Lightning flashes overhead followed by a low, rumbling thunder.

"Fuck it," Holly climbs the fence. The black iron bars are cold on her hands. She has to be careful, the top of the fence is lined in dull black iron spikes,

As her feet hit the soft soil of the cemetery her pulse instantly races with a mix of fear and excitement. Focus. She just has to walk in a straight line across the cemetery and she just might beat the rain. No reason to look around. Just stare straight ahead.

Taking only a few steps she decides this isn't such a good idea and turns around to climb back out of the cemetery. She lets out a gasp of fright. Staring at her from the other side of the fence is an old man dressed in a black suit and tie.

The old man's gaze is unsettling. A gaunt face with a long, thin nose, beady eyes, and long, white thin and stringy hair. The large nose has a slight bend to one side as if broken in youth. His ears are large with bits of white hair growing from them. His breathing shallow and sickly, "I want you," the old man gives a harsh whisper and points at her with an unsteady finger. The tone of his voice is urgent and perverse.

Holly's hands tremble in fear as she steps backwards, deeper into the cemetery, afraid to take her eyes from the disturbing old man. Her stomach feels queasy. She bumps the back of her heel into a low headstone, almost losing her balance. The old man stands deathly still and staring, unblinking.

With a sudden jerk she spins away from the upsetting old man and jogs away. Her only choice now is to make it to the other side of the cemetery. She wishes she had a weapon or something to protect herself with. In reality the staring man looked too frail to climb the fence. Too old to do much of anything.

As she jogs away a mental image of the old man haunts her with his sagging skin and long fingers. What if he has a weapon? A knife? A gun? Does he want her? What for? To rape her? The thought is beyond repugnant. The withered man must be eighty or ninety years old. Where did he come from all of the sudden?

Holly lets her jog slow to a brisk walk. She has no choice if she is to avoid falling over a headstone or flower pot. It's so dark she can barely see her hand before her face. It would be easy to get lost in the blackness. What was she ever thinking? Then again if she hadn't climbed the fence she would've been on the same side as the old, wrinkled man.

With a sudden whoosh a sheet of rain falls down on her and the cemetery. The rain is so heavy her clothes are immediately soaked through from head to toe. The raging rain pours and slaps down hard joined by a gushing wind whipping her wet hair and apron about. Lightning lights up the cemetery in a blinding flash followed by thunderclaps so loud she can feel them. Holly's whimper goes unheard over the crashing storm and flash flood. She is ankle deep in water and soft earth and grass. It's hard to keep her eyes open against the storm. The rain shifts angles as it comes down. Holly is frightened this may be tornado weather.

She feels like she's walking in a nightmare as water rushes against her feet on the slick grass and she struggles to make progress. Another flash of lightning reveals the statue of a saint and weeping angels before her, its cloaked head down, stone looking blue under the electric light. Holly makes her way to a mausoleum, standing up on the steps to get out of the water.

She stands shivering and holding herself, arms hugging herself, back against the marble tomb wall. She hears a noise over the gushing, whirling storm. The wind whips water against her face. She hears moaning echoing from inside the mausoleum. She tells herself it must be the storm, the howling wind.

In a matter of moments the wind and rain let up, not stopping entirely. Holly hears the groaning within the tomb again. "Oh god," she yowls, stepping away.

A long and stunning bolt of lightning spiders across the sky, lighting everything up for a few seconds. In that flash of light Holly sees the decrepit old man with his white hair drenched like a drowned rat. He is only a dozen feet from her, reaching out his gnarly hands and knobby knuckles, moving slow against the water puddles and muddy path.

Holly shrieks and runs away from him splashing all the way. The water is knee high in places. Her shirt catches on a bush causing her to stumble and fall, her fingers digging into the wet grass. She stands, looking around in the dark. She panics realizing she's lost all sense of direction.

She sloshes forward not sure which direction to go, all the headstones look alike. She sees black silhouettes standing in the distance. They look like people but she knows it's all shadows. She spots a tall headstone and hides behind it, pressing her back against the cold stone. She tries to steady her breath.

She tells herself she must think this through. There is an old man chasing her. There is no doubt about that. Sounds from inside the mausoleum? It had to be the storm. She's frightened is all. Being pursued through a dark storm. She fooled herself just like she did with the whispering wind the other night. This is just a horny old pervert chasing her through a cemetery in the middle of the night. A horny old man and a late autumn thunderstorm.

Holly knows she can do this. She's been through worse and she always survives. She'll get out of this cemetery, make it home, peek at her sleeping children, and curl up warm on the couch to sleep with her familiar pillow and worn just right fluffy feather comforter. The pillow broke in just right. She sleeps on the couch because she can't afford a bigger place. Her kids sleep in the bedroom.

A final breath reinvigorates her courage to run again. She stands, thinking if she just runs hard in a straight line she will come to the end of the cemetery somewhere. As she takes her first step she sees them hovering in front of her and is paralyzed with terror.

A pair of white gloved hands. Hands moving as if attached to a body that's not there. The white hands dance and make odd gestures like a magician casting spells or a maestro before an orchestra. Something in Holly senses the invisible presence of the dancing hands before her. She can't understand the arcane gestures. It's like an alien sign language trying to communicate with her. Trying to teach her. She can almost hear the voice that isn't there and knows in her heart this is no dead man.

Holly Flowers edges her way around the thick headstone and darts away from the hands. Daring a glance back the hands have vanished.

She runs and runs until she is caught in the suction of the mud. Her foot sinks passed the ankle. She tugs hard, yanking free but leaving her shoe in the muck. The old man's voice whispers, "Come to me, Holly. Come to me. I need you. I need you."

Another flash of lightning lets her see clearly the rickety old man waddling toward her with arms reaching blindly.

Holly screams, leaving her shoe behind she sprints through a maze of headstones, trees, and bushes, slipping and sliding. Her tears are lost in the rain as she sobs.

The man crippled with age pursues her at an eager yet feeble pace.

Holly runs and runs until finally smashing her toe against a flat headstone. She rolls in the mud whimpering and holding her foot. Massaging her toe she notices a mausoleum, not sure if it's the one she heard the moaning in earlier. This one's windows are aglow with light. The rain patters against the glass increasing in frequency.

Lightning brightens the sky again and she spots no sign of the old man. The thunder that follows is so loud she jumps.

This is the power of mother nature, she thinks, the power of god. God can do anything. God can kill in the most unsuspecting instant. She's done some bad things in her life. Made some mistakes. But God knows she tries to be a good person. She just gets so lost sometimes. Feels so alone.

She crawls across the soggy cemetery lawn, trying to stay low and hidden. Her toes are throbbing. It may be broken. Her hands and knees sink into the cold water as she makes her way toward the mausoleum. Her apron snags on a flower pot and she leaves it behind in the flooding water.

She crawls up the hard steps of the mausoleum wondering why this one is lit up and not the others. She stands at the door shivering, peering in a window. Electric lamps on the walls inside. The door opens wide when she tries it. She goes inside gently closing the heavy door behind her and begins squeezing water from her clothes. It drips to the stone floor and she enjoys the dry, wondering if she should just wait the storm out. Or maybe even just sleep her until sunrise.   She hopes whatever was moaning before is not in this tomb.

Holly leans against the closed door and slides to the floor resting, listening to the wind and rain twirl outside. The room is bare save the six lanterns lining the walls. A pair of wide, short rectangle doors are embedded in opposite walls. She knows there are coffins inside of them. She imagines the bodies in those coffins and squints to read the aged plaques. It is a family tomb. Obviously a family of wealth.

Eileen. Wife of Dr. Ezekiel Caldwell. Born 1866. Died 1920.

Dr. Ezekiel Caldwell. Born 1860. Died 1932.

Edgar Caldwell. Edith Caldwell. Evelyn Caldwell. Elizabeth Caldwell. Esther Caldwell. Eli Caldwell.

Eli Caldwell was the last to be placed in this tomb. Died 1954.

The Caldwells. Sounds like some old English family maybe. Holly's lips tighten into a forced smirk as she shakes her head, whispering, "We're sharing a room tonight."

The back window of the mausoleum is a stained glass window with the image of an elegant golden cross and a red rose in its center. She notices a trapdoor in the floor beneath the window "I can feel you," the old man's wrinkled face appears in the door's small window above her, water dripping from his chin.

A vital fear rises in Holly again. She presses her back against the door attempting to use her legs as leverage to keep him from coming inside. Maybe he doesn't see her. With a quick glance up that hope dashes away at the sight of his pale face pressed against the glass.

She feels him pushing against the door. He is stronger than he appears. The door is bouncing as he continues to budge it. She can't help crying again. She regrets coming in. She's trapped.

"I can smell you," he hisses, "The scent of flowers between your thighs."

While still holding the door shut Holly fishes her cell phone out to call the police. Her heart sinks as she realizes the rain water has ruined the phone. The old man relentlessly pounds at the door. With each impact it feels like only a matter of time before the door is forced open.

Her mind races, searching for a way out. Maybe she can run past him, back outside. It's her only chance. She squeezes her fists, steeling herself.

The door bursts open sending her skidding across the concrete floor, hitting the wall beneath the stained glass window.

The old man stands in the doorway wheezing, chest rising and falling heavy, grinning yellow teeth, water dripping from his hair and clothes. "I need you," he whispers.

Holly looks back and forth between the trap door and the crazed man. It doesn't appear to have a lock.

The old man advances, unsteady, trembling with a sick lust. She can't rush past without moving within his reach. She has to.

Holly rushes madly toward the exit. Not fast enough.

Bony fingers snag her shirt.

"No!" She screams, jerking away, ripping the front of the shirt in half, exposing a pale green bra beneath.

His other hand grabs her waist, fingers scratching her skin and digging into her waistline, knuckles pressing against her stomach. She jerks away, further tearing her shirt, losing her footing.

Holly falls back hard on the floor and the old man stumbles on top of her, grunting, drooling. His grip was strong on her waist line. Fingers rubbing her pubic hair, attempting to claw his way deeper. His face is so close to her she can smell his rank, sour breath. His other hand releases her torn shirt frantically groping her breast, cold fingers finding their way beneath her bra, rubbing her nipple, kneading.

She grunts, fighting back, grasping at both his hands. She can feel him hard beneath his wet pants grinding against her thigh. With a gleeful grin the old man licks her cheek. A thin line of drool hangs from his mouth to her face. She slaps him across the face and rolls away as he hungrily grabs at her, ripping the bra off. Her elbows scrape across the concrete floor.

The old man crawls after her on hands and knees, panting and huffing with excitement. He gets his hands on her waistline again trying to tug the last of her clothing off.

Holly wriggles away, reaching for the trapdoor. The metal handle is cold and she skins her knuckles as she swings the weighty door open, smashing it into the old man's head.

A line of crimson runs from a cut on the forehead of the momentarily stunned old man. Holly drags herself away from him, wanting to break free and run out the door of the mausoleum back into the rainy night. Instead when she jumps up to flee the perverse man, he catches her arm, yanking hard. The action causes her to lose her balance, falling backward of the old man on the floor. She drops into the open trapdoor banging both her elbow and the back of her head as she falls into the darkness below the mausoleum. The trapdoor slams shut echoing loudly.

It all happened so fast she's not even sure how far she's fallen. The ground beneath her feels like solid earth, a cool dirt floor. Completely naked above her waist, she covers her breasts with her arms and just lays there trying to catch her breath, to calm herself. Her head throbs from the fall and she's suddenly aware of scratches, bruises, aches, and pain. She could just fall asleep exhausted if she weren't so frightened and blinded by complete darkness.

Holly lies there, arms crossed over her chest staring up toward the trapdoor even though it's too dark to see it. It is pitch black, thick as ink or oil. She can't see anything, blinking, hoping her eyes will adjust, afraid the trapdoor will open and the horny rapist will be there drooling.

She doesn't know how much time passes. Why doesn't he open the door? What if he locked it? She'll die down here. What if she's not alone down here? There must be corpses about. She could end up down here forever. No one would know where to look for her. She has to get out somehow, but she's afraid to move. Having her breasts exposed makes her feel even more vulnerable.

More time passes. Fifteen minutes? An hour? She hasn't heard any noise. Not the storm or the old man or anything around her. She sits up feeling sore everywhere.

Holly feels blindly along the ground realizing there is a hard floor beneath the dirt. If she just crawls in one direction long enough she will find a wall. It takes longer than expected. The room must be big. She has paralyzing moments of fear, listening intently, hearing nothing but her own breath. She does find a wall and uses it as a guide to stand, feeling up and down the wall as she walks. It feels like plaster.

Walking slowly and careful, one foot in front of the other. The wall comes to an end, Her heart drops. It's a corner turning to the left. She could be in a maze for all she knows. Lost. Blind. Trapped. Surrounded by ghosts, ghouls, corpses, and perverted old creepers.

A sob escapes her.

Think. Think. She has to think. How to get out of this? How to survive? There has to be a way. Omar and Karl are expecting her home. They need her to take care of them. She's their mother.

Holly checks her pockets. Wet cigarettes and phone. Her lighter! A small plastic lighter! A godsend! Probably too wet to light, but if she dries it...

She shakes it hard for a long time, then holds it to her lips to blow dry it.

Filled with desperation and hope she flicks the lighter and the room blinks with light around her.

Holly screams.

In that blink of light she saw a face before her. Bald, pale, bland features, mouth open, still, elongated, not human. The face wore a rubbery, agony filled expression.

Holly is pressed hard against the wall, breathing heavily, experiencing a panic attack, hands clutched against her breasts, lighter gripped within a clammy palm. Her pants are uncomfortably wet and cold, sticking to her legs. She is covered in goosebumps, shivering violently, hiccuping and sobbing. Once again afraid to move, afraid to flick the lighter again and see that awful haunting face. Afraid it will touch her.

Whatever it is, it's not human. Some kind of monster. Some kind of ghoul Oh, God, help me. Ghouls and ghosts and perverts and this black dungeon. This can't be real. She's having trouble thinking clearly. Focusing. Her head is spinning. What is it going to do? She is going to die down here. This thing is going to kill her.

Several minutes pass as she cries and shakes waiting for its touch. Nothing happens. The underground is black and still as death. She tries to stop shaking, not sure if it's more from fear or cold, even her teeth clatter.

Holly holds the lighter in both hands before her like a holy relic and flicks it again. This time the flash does not reveal the spook. A second flick and the tiny flame stays lit. The small glow doesn't illuminate much. She sees that she is standing in a wide hall. The lower half of the walls are a faded green, the upper a rust color. The two halves are split by a decorative border the length of the wall. The design is an endless twist of ribbon, gold on pale sand with leaves sparsely spread along the way.

Just as in the graveyard above Holly has lost all sense of direction. Two options before her, darkness to the left or right.

Where is the haunting thing? Watching her hidden in the shadows? Is the old man down here somewhere? And the ghostly dancing hands?

Holly walks along the wall to her right. Still trembling, careful not to extinguish the flame. If the right doesn't have the trapdoor in the ceiling, the left must. If it's not right she'll backtrack to the left. Either way she is going to get out.

She feels the heat of the lighter almost burning her thumb, but she will not move her finger. She'd rather burn her thumb than be blind again. She worries about the lighter fluid too, the flame is low.

Holly doesn't have to walk as far as she expected. The hallway opens into a large room with a black and white checkered floor. She can't see beyond her globe of light to determine how large the room actually is. She holds the lighter up high to see the ceiling to no avail. This can't be where the trapdoor was. The ceiling is too high and the floor too clean.

About to turn back and explore the other direction she spots a long red carpet leading to an elevated platform at the head of the room. It looks like an altar reminding her of going to church with her grandmother as a child. She had refused to go to church anymore when she became a teenager. Much to her grandmother's dismay. Now she regrets this, wishing she would have gone just to appease her now deceased grandmother. Yes this altar brings to mind the Catholic church. A green and gold embroidered silk cloth covers and drapes from it. It looks as though the bible or some other book is meant to be placed upon the altar as a priest or minister would preach to a congregation.

There are five chairs along the wall behind the altar and to Holly's delight there are candles on tall brass stands. She lights them and tucks the lighter back into her pant's pocket.

A symbol is carved into the wall above the chairs, a skull and crossbones with an eye in a triangle on its forehead. A balancing scale hangs from the crossbones.

A narrow tapestry hangs behind each of the five chairs. Each tapestry is a different color depicting a different image.

The room is more visible to her with the tall candles burning. It is a circular room with a great circle of wood chairs all along the wall and around the room. The chairs look to be dark oak with tall backs and leaves, thorns, and roses carved in them. A sun with seven rays is carved at the top of each chair.

Off to one side of the room she spots a dusty black grand piano with a candelabra and skull atop it. She walks over and lights the seven candles atop the piano and uses it to light her way.

Further to the side are tall double doors. She gives them a tug but they don't budge. This place doesn't look like it's been in use for a very long time. The dust on the doorknobs was as thick as the dust on the piano and chairs.

Holly makes her way back to the hall from which she came into this strange chamber. She uses her free arm to cover her breasts as she walks. She is still cold but not shivering uncontrollably like before. She hopes the face she saw in the dark was only her imagination.

The floor is much dirtier in the hall. More dirt than dust. The hallway seems longer than she thought. She passes several doors before coming to the turn she believes was the corner she originally found in her blindness.

She holds back a sudden urge to cry again. A wave of despair. Even with the candelabra lighting her way she may be lost. This must be that corner, there hasn't been another.

Holly walks around the corner and into a smaller room. The hall itself keeps going beyond the room. She holds the candles up with a sense of relief spotting the trapdoor in the ceiling. The moment of victory is crushed by the height of the ceiling. There is no way to reach the trapdoor.

Her only option now is to find another way out. There are several doors further down the hall. She begins her search through the eerie quiet, the only sounds are her breathing and footsteps. After trying several doors she finds one unlocked.

The door is thick old wood. Old fashioned door knobs with skeleton keyholes she thinks, not really knowing. She is horrified in the room. It is some kind of gloomy torture chamber. Iron chains and shackles hang from one wall. Chairs with leather straps for binding. A table covered in knives, pokers, and pinchers, metal devices she doesn't recognize or want to imagine their purpose. A black whip hangs from a hook near the door.

Holly takes a rusted knife from the table and the whip from the wall, hoisting it over her shoulder. She steps quickly from the room afraid of the door shutting and locking her in.

The candlelight, whip, and knife give her a sense of security. If she sees the old man or the ghoul she won't hesitate to stick them. The whip is long and she hopes to use it somehow to climb up to the trap door. Like the Indiana Jones movies she saw as a kid. Maybe she can stack chairs from the big room?

Walking further she comes to a fork in the hall. Right or left? Inspecting both directions she almost drops the candelabra at the sound of a voice behind her.

"These halls are long and dark," a melodic and handsome male voice says.

Holly spins violently, an old knife held out before her offensively, breasts swaying, hair a mess, mascara running down her cheeks. Halfway down the hall is a silhouette of a man.

"I won't hurt you," he says in a soft, calm voice, walking leisurely in her direction.

Holly wants to cover her chest but can't with the candles and knife in her hands. She takes a step back, panicked, contemplating fleeing left or right down the unexplored halls.

The man steps within the halo of the candlelight. He is shirtless in black boots, leather pants, and a silver oval belt buckle. The man is younger than her, maybe twenty-seven, thin, she can see his ribs, a firm stomach, and unexpectedly handsome. Holly thinks he looks like a rock star or a movie star with long, curling, waving hair like a lion's mane. The candlelight reflects in his dark blue eyes. His face is like a sculpture of a Greek god. Holly is confused, distracted unreasonably by his beauty.

She blinks, fighting back tears, fight or flight? She doesn't tremble this time. The young man's eyes casually look her up and down, lingering a moment on her breasts. He looks her directly in the eye and smiles showing off full lips and perfect white teeth.

She whispers, "Who are you?"

"My name is Morgan Keith, I won't hurt you," holding his hands up in a gesture of surrender.

"What do you want?" Keeping the knife between them.

"The same as you," he shrugs with a cocksure smile, "Out of the darkness."

"What is this place?" She asks, still not prepared to trust this seductive man, "How did you get here?"

Morgan looks at her with longing in his dark eyes, head tilting to the side, hands on his hips, "This place is so many things. A tomb. Labyrinth. Brothel. Temple. A forgotten lair of a hellfire club." He searches her face for any recognition sparked by his tender words.

"I don't know what that is," Holly admits, still pointing the knife at him.

Morgan gives a lazy shrug, "A sex club. A fiend club. It doesn't matter."

"How did you get here?"

"Through a door," he smirks.

"Please," her voice quivers, "help me get out of here."

"I want to help you. What is your name?"

"Holly," wiping her nose with the back of her hand, "Holly Flowers."

"Of course," batting long eyelashes.

"Just take me out of here!" She raises her voice, shaking the knife at him.

"Will you help me Holly? Will you help me out of this place?" Morgan Keith turns away from her walking back into the darkness, disappearing from the candlelight. She listens to his boot steps fade to silence.

"Morgan?" She asks the darkness. "Please don't leave. Morgan?"

"I want to help you, Holly Flowers," his voice echoes through the hall, sounding as if it could be coming from any direction. "I sincerely do. For me to help you, you must help me. On my honor, by my word, I swear if you help me escape this darkness I will help you."

"I don't understand," Holly timidly walks forward holding the candelabra out before her, covering her breasts with her knife arm. "Why can't you get out? Why do you need my help?" She searches further, "Where are you?"

Holly whips around at the sound of Morgan's voice behind her, "I need you to help me finish something that was started a long time ago."

He's not there. She's sure his voice was behind her.

"How can you help me out if you can't get out?" She asks the shadows.

"You must trust me," his voice was genuine.

"Why can't you get out?"

"We must make love to be freed of this hellfire."

"Make love!" She exasperates, spinning, searching for him, "You're as bad as that sick pervert above! A rapist!"

"No," he whispers in her ear, standing close, restraining both her wrists firmly with his arms around her. She tries to pull away but he's too strong. "I am not like him. Never like him. I will not rape you. If you choose to be with me it will be of your own free will."

His bare chest against her back feels warm and comforting.

"I won't hurt you, Holly," he lets her go gently and backs away.

She turns to face him, the knife loose in her hand. His eyes are stark and compelling. "This is no time to try to get laid," she protests.

"That is not what I am about."

"Oh please," she points at her bare breasts, "What is this?"

"It is elegant."

She just looks at him, drowning in his starry eyes.

"Do you believe in magic?" Morgan asks.

She is at a loss for words. He must be crazy. He believes in himself.

Morgan whispers, "We can make love and be free. I will not force you. Or we can be imprisoned in the darkness forever."

Holly desperately wants out. Morgan seems so genuine and sincere, such an enigmatic gentleman. She's always prided herself on being a good judge of character. He is so enchanting, so handsome. He may be her only hope. She whispers back at him, "Promise me you'll get me out of here."

"I promise you," he says as they step toward each other.

Holly reaches up draping her knife arm over his shoulder and kisses him. Morgan's lips are soft and his kiss is delicate. One of his hands finds the small of her back, the other caresses her cheek. He pulls back from her lips, "Not here." Morgan takes the knife from her and puts her hand in his. He sets the knife on the floor, "You don't need this." And he leads her through the long hallway.

As they walk Holly feels her excitement growing with thoughts of sex with this unknown man. She likes the feel of his fingers intertwined with hers. She watches the shape and sway of his shoulders. She's not afraid. This seems no more mad than the rest of the night.

Morgan leads her back into the circular room with the black and white checkered floor, piano, and altar. They stand before the altar and he places the candelabra upon it. And there he kisses her. In the back of her mind she is surprised by her building passion for him.

They grope and pet and grip each other lost in sweet throes of devotion. Her breasts press against his chest as they kiss and love, awkwardly tearing each other's pants down. They tumble with affection to the floor.

A sigh of pleasure escapes Holly when she feels him inside her for the first time and quickly becomes enamored in their congress. She wants him. More at this moment than anything she's ever wanted before. She never wants him to stop. She doesn't want to be anywhere but right now.

Holly's head tilts back in ancient delight, moaning weakly. Her eyes open. The tall chairs around the room are now filled. Not quite human things still and observing. They all have the same forlorn, haunting face she saw earlier with the first flick of her lighter. Round, black, hollow eyes. Bald, tortured expressions. Expressions of agony and remorse. Elongated, smooth heads. Thin, skeletal bodies. So thin they look to be only skin stretched over bones. Necks, fingers, limbs all out of proportion. Bodies naked. They have no reproductive organs between their legs.

Holly gazes back at Morgan's face too lost in lust and ecstasy to be disturbed by these sickly witnesses. Harder. Faster. They are both grunting and screaming in thrilling revelry now. Morgan's face is pleasure. She sees the night sky in his eyes. The look of god on his face, his melodic moans bring her to orgasm.

Squeezing her thighs tight around him, trying to pull him closer, she sees the dancing white hands floating at the altar. The hands of the conductor. The maestro.

Oh, god, she prays, never to let him go.

Morgan falls against her, panting, whispering, "Thank you."

Holly wakes to the chirp of early morning birds. She is naked, confused, curled next to a generous marble headstone. The grass is moist from the night's storm. The golden sun is just rising bright in the east. She looks around for her clothes, not finding them. It is unusually warm for an autumn morning.

Covered in scrapes, bruises, and smears drying mud, the last thing she remembers is making love with Morgan and wonders if it was all just a dream. But no. Her hand touches her stomach. He was here.

She stands unashamed of her nudity, walking through the cemetery grateful for daylight. Under the sun it is beautiful, peaceful, and serene. And there is the mausoleum of the Caldwells. Giving the door a tug to find it locked. She looks up to the red, white, and blue flag hanging limp at the top of a pole near the mausoleum. Etched on the side of the old tomb she noticed pictures of the dead Caldwells. The one labeled Eli Caldwell oddly resembles the old man who chased her.

Holly wonders who they were. What happened to Morgan?

She takes down the flag and wraps herself in it for the long walk home.

Satan

Atticus growls into the microphone, guttural, hoarse, the last song of the encore, cover of the legendary fathers of black metal *Venom*'s classic *In League with Satan*, "I'm in league with Satan! I was raised in Hell! I walk the streets of Salem! Amongst the living dead! I need no one to tell me! What's wrong or right! I drink the blood of children! Stalk my prey at night!"

Black and white face paint smeared down his face glistening with beads of sweat under the stage lights. Long hair matted like black pointed razor icicles swinging chaotically. Dry ice fog rolls across the stage. Spotlights circle blue and red. Clad in black leather and sharp silver studs, a crucifix dangling wildly from his neck. White contacts giving his eyes a chilling, undead appeal. "Look out! Beware! When the full moon's high and bright! In every way I'm there! In every shadow at night!"

Atticus holds the microphone out over the crowd at the front of the stage. Heshen metalheads mosh in a pit before him. Headbangers line the perimeter. And the crowd chants, "Cause I'm evil! In league with Satan! Evil! In league with Satan!"

The drum's steady beat. Like primal tribal dancing. The crowd is maniacal like unarmed Vikings in black t-shirts and blue jeans. A fight breaks out in the madness of the pit. Atticus bobs his head to the music, heavy guitar, looking down with approval, "I'm in league with Satan! I obey his commands! With the goat of Mendes! Sitting at his left hand! I'm in league with Satan! I love the dead! No one prayed for Sodom! As the people fled!"

A long haired teen rides on a sea of hands atop the crowd, blood and sweat smattered across his forehead and cheeks. A trio of pale skinned goth girls on the shoulders of the crowd flash their breasts. Atticus beats his chest, stomps thick heeled black studded boots, and hoarsely sings on.

"This is Courtney Kennedy with LCFR Radio. With me is Atticus Killroy, lead singer of *Daimon Rapist*, a black metal band that has been sweeping the underground with their third album, *God's Cunt*. Atticus, tell me about the founding of Daimon Rapist." *Slayer*'s *Angel of Death* plays quietly in the background.

"When I put together Daimon Rapist I wanted to bring horrifying darkness into the world. We've tried to return to the roots of black metal and bring its dignity back to life with an artistic assault to the listener. Each song is a fuck you to the world and all people. I want our music to be an initiation of death."

"That's unspeakably interesting," Courtney nods, "Were you in any bands prior to *Daimon Rapist*?"

"I was in a band called *Jesus Wept*. We never signed to a label. A few of *Jesus Wept*'s songs are on *Daimon Rapist*'s first album. Gizzard Slut was in that band with me."

"Gizzard Slut is the name of your female bass player? What about the other members of *Daimon Rapist*? How did they come to be in the band?"

"I met our drummer Ragnarok Rex at a pub in Sweden. He had just quit the band *Christian Holocaust* after beating up their vocalist. We got drunk together and burned a church down. It was fun at the time but it's a cliché now. Reverend Erroneous met us through a friend and tried out for the band. He could play guitar and after talking with him we decided he was the right guy for the job."

"What inspired or influenced you, Mr. Killroy?"

"Mm. I don't know. Horror movies. *The Shining. Lord of Illusions. Prince of Darkness*. I like them all, big Hollywood ones and the cheap B and C ones," he laughs, "*The Church of Satan. Flowers of Evil* by Baudelaire. *The Heart of Darkness* by Joseph Conrad. I like to read. Musically I like the early black metal bands like *Venom. Mercyful Fate. Bathory. Kreator. Mayhem*. Don't get me wrong, I love the more recent stuff. The older one just has a special place in my heart. They were the trailblazers. They had the courage to be the first."

"What's your opinion of the current black metal scene?"

Atticus shrugs, "I don't know. It's annoying. Everyone wants to be famous like *Cradle of Filth*. They just want to use standard riffs and get laid. Mike Patton inspired me to experiment musically. That's how we ended up putting disco and country western elements in our music. There are those out there playing now that I respect and enjoy but I don't feel like anyone's pushing the envelope besides shock value."

"You believe *Daimon Rapist* is pushing the envelope?"

"We're trying. I don't want to be an imitation. I want to be a trailblazer. Making music is like solving puzzles. Like *the Lament Configuration*. I want to make music that takes people somewhere."

Atticus' head rests against the chill window of their car staring out at the wet pavement reflecting street light. Light rain patters against the window. *Gorgoroth* rages from the car's speakers. Thin, long haired Erroneous is passed out in the backseat next to Atticus, his heavy black boots propped up on the unconscious band mate. Atticus makes fists, admiring the pentagram tattoos on the backs of his hands.

Rex is driving, while Gizzard sucks his cock, "Hey, you sure you wanna go home? We're going to the show. Everyone's gonna ask where you are."

"Yes," Atticus looks back out the window at the drizzling night, "I want to go home."

The band squats in an abandoned house near the edge of the city. Atticus knows they are the darkness at the edge of town. A communal living of nihilists. Eat, shit, and sleep together. Make music together.

Atticus stands in his bedroom, naked, by candlelight. Spray painted in dried dripping red on the wall before him is a large inverted pentagram. "I am ready, oh dark lord. I feel your strength within me and wish to honor you in my life. I am one of the Devil's own. Hail Satan." The reflection of the candlelight flickers in his eyes, "So it is done!"

His nude body glowing Halloween orange in the candlelight, he steps back, picking up the glossy black bass guitar of Gizzard. Flicks a switch on the amp and it buzzes to life. He strums a first chord and becomes lost in the music he is creating. It starts slow and deep. Quiet. Rising. Steady rising. Eyes closed. Gentle swaying. More. Building. Building up. Opening a door with sound. He hums with the guitar. A skull cupped microphone at his side. His vocals. "Yeah. Ah. Yeah. Hey. Ah. We make love. Yeah. Hey. Yeah. Scream and meat. The Antichrist. Ah. Yes."

Dancing now. The cradled instrument, his partner, his lover. "Like human bones scraping across the pavement. Real savage!"

A sudden explosion of black music. Bursting forth from the amp. Head and hair flailing about. Side step, flicking a drum machine on. His hand violently beats the bass. Gnashing his teeth. Screaming in the microphone, "Suck! Fuck! Yeah! Alright! The blackness rose! Ripping at the end of the world! Blood fuck on my tongue tonight!" He babbles into the microphone, whatever comes to mind, free flowing. "Hell on my mind! I will fight! I will fight! I don't care! Bleed in my heart! Creeping in graveyards eating the darkest of sluts desolation and fornication gnawing on God's flesh as blood drips from the thighs of Eden!"

Atticus growls and roars, spits and moans. A black pillar of nothing rises from the floor before him like a geyser of oil, a shadow of a man. The dark thing swirls into a blond sky clad man. Smirking with an ice blue soul bearing stare.

Atticus lets his eyelids flutter open, catching sight of the sculpted man and dropping the bass in startled fright. A piercing screech brings the music to an end. There is only the electric buzz of the amplifier. He steps back, ready to fight, ignoring their nudity, "Who the fuck are you!" Atticus stumbles back looking and waving for a weapon of some, picking the bass back up, ready to swing.

"Who do you think," the handsome stranger smirks.

"Fag! I'll kill you!"

The strange one laughs, "Yeah you will," a sleight flick of the wrist and Atticus slams against the dark bedroom wall held immobile by invisible hands, the bass below his feet on the floor. Atticus fruitlessly struggles against the inhuman phantom bonds, hanging on the wall like a crucified Christ.

"Tell me who I am, child," the odd man grins with diamond sparkling blue eyes. Like the eyes of a wolf caught in headlights.

"Satan," Atticus whispers.

"Good chap," Satan nods approval, "Why did you call me and offer your soul, little Faustus?"

"To destroy the world," Atticus answers unsure. "Whatever you want."

Satan shrugs, picking up the bass guitar and sitting on the edge of the bed.

"Why are you naked?" Atticus asks.

"Why are you?" Satan's long fingernails caress the strings of the instrument.

"I don't know," Atticus answers, still pinned to the wall, "It felt right."

Satan sighs, "When we're done playing I'll kill you. Make it look like you committed suicide because you're ashamed of being a homosexual."

"I'm not gay," Atticus shivers.

"That's not the point," Satan smiles, snaps his fingers and he's instantly dressed in an old fashioned tuxedo. "I hate all of you. That's the point. I don't just want to kill you all. I want you to wail and suffer and beg to be erased. Not for death. Beg to be deleted from existence. To utterly cease to be. There is no fiery burning Hell. This world you live in is Hell but you monkeys are all too ignorant to understand that. You know nothing. Would you like to know something? Would you like to know what I am?"

Atticus tries to nod against the supernatural restraints.

"Hmph," Satan snarls. "The thing all you Satan worshippers don't realize is that I hate you all and your suffering brings me joy. I'm programmed that way. It's my sustenance. You give yourselves over to me and destroy in my name, which I dig, but you fall so short. My true stars are the governments and religions. Do you know how many people the Jews, Christians, and Muslims have tortured and killed in the name of the demiurge? In the name of Yahweh, Jesus, and Allah? Oh, they're so good at being evil it just tickles me. Add the politicians, military, lawyers, and bankers to the mix and you have my complete army. Yes, I say it again. My truest ignorant followers are the Jews, Christians, Muslims, governments, and money mongers. Now, Atticus, if you had summoned me asking to be a banker, a president, a rabbi, a priest, a soldier, I would have been inclined to aid your struggle. But instead you've bored me with the shocking stage Satanism. Burning churches and tattooed pentagrams! Don't you know churches are my fuel?

"I didn't exist until the churches created me. What am I? I am the personification of evil. Me and Hitler. You see, it's the lies and the belief in me that gives me life. Before the Abrahamic religions came along enslaving people I was null and void. I've been Satan for a few thousand years now. I was alive before I became Satan but barely. I was an astral zombie. Almost a mindless ether animal floating about the Abyss. The Abrahamic beliefs created a shell for me to inhabit. Pure luck, pure fate drew me to it. Now do you understand what I am?"

"I think so," Atticus answers.

"I am a vampire fed by human indignity. By greed and fear. Lust and envy. The Demiurgos imprisons you in this reality. Hiding the Source from you. Keeping you blind, mute, and deaf. Senseless. Whatever is in man that causes him to shudder, that causes misery, loneliness, rage, regret, that is my glory. Everyone of you black metal lovers, what am I to you? I am everything you're angry at! I am everything that hurts you! I am your ever unhappiness. The Demiurge hopes to keep you locked in this black iron prison, recycling. The Source apart awaiting the divine escapees. I am the eraser. I will erase you when you die." Satan bellows with uncontrolled laughter, "I am against you and your music! I loathe Satanic metal as much as anything else."

Atticus watches handsome Satan, speechless.

"Ah, well," Satan cracks the bass guitar in half with effortless ease, "Let's begin your honest education." He stands as Atticus floats away from the wall and on to the bed, on to his stomach, helpless and paralyzed.

"What are you doing?" Atticus cries out.

"Fucking your ass, buddy," Satan unzips his black pants.

"No!" Atticus protests as he feels the Devil's cock enter him painfully.

Satan whispers seductively in his ear, "You should have called Lucifer or Samael. The archangels who always get a bad rap. Heroes of humanity. They're the ones who fight for you. Not I. I'm born of the only place evil comes from. The human mind."

An hour later Satan withdraws his manhood from the sore mouth of Atticus. Atticus's head pulls to the side, exhausted, defeated, deflated. "Fool," Satan sits on the bed by the metal singer's head leafing through a copy of *the Satanic Bible*. "You think I want an end to child molesting Catholic priests and Christian bigots? I revel in Muslim acts of terror. The horror of bankers, police, and politicians," he trails off then rips *the Satanic Bible* in half, "*The Church of Satan*, my left butt cheek."

Atticus gives a childish groan.

"So true, enough," a razor blade appears in Satan's hand. He slashes both of Atticus's wrists. Red blood spills onto the bed sheet. He stands before the dying Atticus, paper in hand, "Your suicide note, and I quote, I can't live with myself anymore. I'm so sorry. I can't live with my sexual urges any longer. Don't cry for me. I'm free. I love you John. End quote."

Atticus lets out a weak whimper as his life drains from his wrists onto the bed.

"Ta ta, worshiper," Satan flamboyantly snaps his fingers and vanishes from sight.

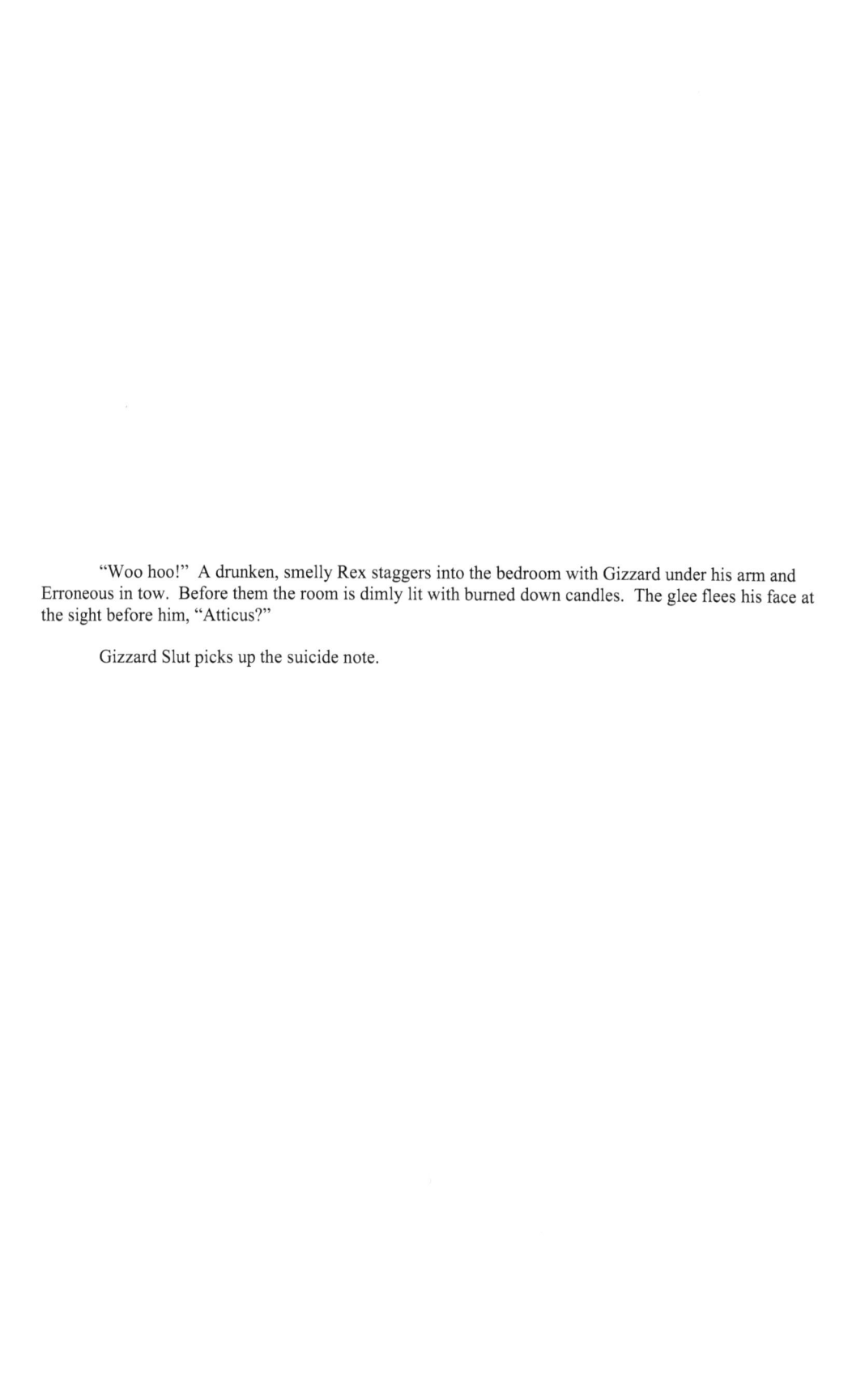

"Woo hoo!" A drunken, smelly Rex staggers into the bedroom with Gizzard under his arm and Erroneous in tow. Before them the room is dimly lit with burned down candles. The glee flees his face at the sight before him, "Atticus?"

Gizzard Slut picks up the suicide note.

Blackwood

      Seven friends from high school travel down a long, winding highway through rolling hills of green and occasional patches of trees. Every so often they spot cattle and farm houses, tractors in fields, barns, cornstalks. They've been driving two hours since they left their hometown of Applegate. Since graduation it has become an unspoken tradition that they get together at least once a summer for a week-long camping trip. They've almost reached their destination. *Hot, Hot, Hot* by *the Cure* plays on the van's stereo.

      Chandler Given is driving the dark blue van. His van. He purchased it for touring with his punk rock band, *Jesus Wept*. Chandler never actually graduated high school having dropped out when he was sixteen years old. He's currently living with his girlfriend, Ginger, in a loft downtown. Chandler's hair is a thick, jet black mohawk and there are several safety pins in his ears. Dark brown eyes, a thin pointed nose, sharp angular eyebrows, and pale moon white skin. He's wearing a black and white *Revolting Cocks* t-shirt with the sleeves cut off, green cutoff army pants, and black military boots decorated with studs and spikes. Both his arms are covered in tattoos and he has a thin black mustache next to a gold lip ring.

      Also in the van is his girlfriend, Ginger Jonadab, who is working as a waitress at a downtown diner four blocks from their loft. She walks to work every day. She's a struggling artist, a painter working mostly in oils. There is a collection of her work hanging in a coffee shop right now. Chandler and Ginger have been dating four years now. She has horned rimmed glasses, blonde hair, blue eyes, a very thin frame, thin boned, short, petite, only 5' 1" and she usually dresses in vintage clothes she hunts thrift stores for. When shopping she often says it's best to mix a little old with a little new. Ginger is sitting in the back of the van next to Hattie and Amber.

      In the seat in front of the girls is Celeste and her boyfriend Dustan. In the passenger seat playing co-pilot is Ira.

      Hattie Archer graduated from college in the spring with a degree in social work. She's working part-time as a tour guide at a museum and as a substitute teacher. She is a recovering alcoholic actively participating in a twelve step program. Amber and Celeste often give her a hard time about not drinking, Amber because she misses drinking with Hattie and Celeste because she's unconsciously threatened due to her own excessive drinking. Hattie has had a crush on Ira since high school but Ira seems unaware of this and Hattie is too reserved to be more forward. They did make out once in high school and even had sex another time, but neither spoke of the incidents afterward and haven't to date. Hattie is short but not as petite as the fiery Ginger.

      Celeste Abington is acknowledged as the bitch of the group by her own proud admission. She comes from wealth and isn't afraid to let that be known. Gold blonde, blazing azure eyes, privileged, entitled, and brilliant. Her IQ is astounding and she's a member of MENSA. Everyone is usually annoyed by her once she starts to get drunk because she becomes the most belligerent and obnoxious of their group of friends, often an embarrassment, pissing and puking, laughing and cussing at all the wrong times. All diamonds and glamor, always tan with lightly freckled nose and cheeks. She flaunts her large breasts, wearing a form fitting violet shirt and black pants today. She's finished a degree in political science and is working on a law degree while she interns for a senator. She is hopelessly in love with Chandler but is dating Dustan. Celeste is viciously protective of all her friends, especially the step-siblings Chandler and Amber. Amber is her best friend.

Amber Ferro's parents divorced when she was three years old. Her father passed away when she was five. Her mother married Chandler's father when she was seven. Chandler and Amber are as close as blood. Chandler is overprotective of her and flew into a violent rage when he found out she was stripping, demanding she quit the job. Of course Amber refused. She's happy with the money she's making, paying her way through college. Promiscuous and flirtatious with heart shaped lips, bleach blonde hair, and big blue doe eyes.

Dustan Fitzgerald is a late comer to this group of friends. There was some resistance when he first joined their tribe back in high school, he was often the butt of jokes and ditched, but the hazing only lasted a few months before he was fully accepted among them. These seven friends are not the tribe in it's entirety but they are the core. Dustan is loud, cocky, and opinionated. Dark brown curly hair like a Brillo pad, fine blue eyes.

Ira Whitfield is emotional, passionate, and sensitive. A halfbreed. Half German and half Sioux Indian. He told Chandler about the ghost town of Blackwood one night and Chandler was intrigued enough to suggest they camp there this summer. Ira didn't think it was a great idea because even though it is essentially a ghost town a few houses still have residents. It was back in the 1970s when everyone got up and left the small town. The story Ira had heard from his cousins on the reservation is that one Sunday morning in the middle of a church service the front door swung open with a bang. The interruption was caused by a tall man in a penguin tuxedo marching up the aisle, the congregation stunned and awed, feet clicking to the head of the church. No one spoke a word, not even the preacher. The man turned to look over all the people. He had a pointed goatee, an arrowhead tipped tail, and black hooves in place of feet. They say he stood at the front of the church grinning before marching back down the aisle and out the door he went. No one saw him again.

Many of the town folk, the preacher included, were sure the man was no other than Old Scratch himself came to Blackwood. The people began to move away with reports of bizarre happenings, UFO sightings, little green men, deer people, and restless ghosts. It didn't take long before the town was deserted. Ira's not sure how many people still live there, maybe four or five households hidden among the trees and hills. All old Native families. Blackwood is deep into the reservation, far from anywhere, founded a century ago near the river bottom. The area has always been surrounded with local legends. In the late 1970s after most of the town folk were gone it became a hotspot for BigFoot hunters. They never found BigFoot but Ira remembers his mom telling him about seeing their giant football field lights searching the night.

Amber is texting with an elfish smile to Hattie and Ginger, "Cas is coming."

"What?" Hattie asks, "On his own?"

"Yeah," Amber beams, "He's only an hour behind us."

"Why didn't he just ride with us?" Ginger laughs.

Hattie answers with gossip delight, "They were fighting before we left."

"Oh," Ginger is smiling, "That's crazy. At least he's coming. You guys are always fighting."

"No we're not," Amber defends.

Both Ginger and Hattie laugh at that.

Castor Gail is Ira's best friend since grade school. He lives with Amber and Chandler. Amber and Cas have been dating on and off since they were freshmen. Cas and Dustan paint houses together for an independent contractor. Cas is American Indian too with less blood than Ira but darker skin, water blue eyes, a round nose, and exceptional good looks. Things between Amber and Cas have become much more volatile since she began stripping. He can't handle it, jealousy, with good reason, Amber has never been terribly faithful to him even with her pronouncements of undying love.

"There it is," Ira announces to Chandler with a hint of adventure.

"Wow," Chandler smiles, slowing the van as they enter Blackwood, "This is a ghost town."

The first thing they see is an old abandoned school off to the right. All the windows are broken out, some are boarded up with plywood, spray paint graffiti covers the brick walls in places, the playground equipment is overgrown with tall weeds and rusted.

There is only one paved road that goes through the town and it's crumbling, riddled with potholes and cracks. The rest of the roads are dirt. It was never a large town and it's been reclaimed by mother nature. The vegetation is mostly greens and wheat yellows, there are many, many gnarly trees about Blackwood. The town rests between high-reaching hills, the main street snug and winding down the middle. The town is not much more than the main street with dirt roads leading to houses. The houses look as bad as the school with broken down doors, hollow windows, paint peeled and faked to nearly nothing, broken boards litter about, holes in walls, more graffiti, leaning porches. The single church has it's windows and doors boarded. Curiously no vandals have touched the church.

The seven friends stare out the van windows with mixed expressions of awe, amusement, and indifference. The van rolls to a stop alongside the main street near the school.

"I have to leave a piss," Dustan climbs out the side door of the van. Everyone follows, standing, stretching, taking in their surroundings.

"Hey," Hattie says to Ira, "Where are we going to camp?"

"I don't know," Ira answers in a soft voice, "This isn't a campground, maybe down by the river."

"We can set up our tents anywhere we want," Chandler explains.

"I want beer," Celeste whines.

"Me too," Amber concurs.

Ginger pulls a blue plastic cooler with a white lid toward the front of the van's interior, opens it, and begins to dole out cans of beer.

"Well," Chandler says after a swig of beer and sigh of refreshment, "Let's find a place to set up camp."

Ira nods, "I'd prefer to camp off the highway, by the river is best I think."

Chandler nods as the pair begin walking together, "You said a few people still live here. It doesn't look like it."

"It's been five years since I was here last," Ira answers, but it didn't look like people lived here then either. Maybe the last of them moved away. We'll be able to tell when it gets dark. They'll have lights on in their houses I'm sure. There were only 3 or 4 with people back then. I'd prefer it if there are still people here if we stay away from them."

"Let's see how close we can get to the river then," Chandler takes the lead.

"Right next to it I'm sure," Ira answers.

Near the van, Celeste, who finished two beers before they even arrived in Blackwood, says, "I have to pee too. Come with me Amber."

Amber nods and they walk toward the abandoned school together.

Staying near the van, Dustan asks Ginger and Hattie, "Where'd Chandler and Ira go?"

Ginger shrugs, "To find a place to camp."

"I'm gonna go after them," Dustan wanders off.

The main street is really just the highway going through the center of the town. It has sharp curves and the houses on the right side of the road (the furthest from the river) are elevated on the hill, the left side houses are level with the road.

Walking in the general direction that Chandler and Ira went, Dustan strolls through the yard of a house. There is an old wood outhouse in the back. Dustan thinks there is no way he's using an outhouse.

Dustan spots someone peeking around the corner of the outhouse at him. Just the side of her face, one eye and a bit of hair. "Hi," he waves, "Do you live here?" He looks at the weathered house as soon as he asks the question thinking no one could possibly be living there. The windows are all broken out. He thinks maybe it's *the Hills Have Eyes* type hillbillies but then remembers they're on a reservation. If anyone is out here it's probably Indians.

The girl doesn't answer and disappears behind the outhouse. He walks around the back of the outhouse but she's not there. He could see both sides of the outhouse. There is no way she could sneak off without him seeing. Dustan feels a chill of fear. He walks in a circle around the outhouse more than once.

From inside the abandoned house he hears what sounds like the giggle of a little girl. He takes a step away from the outhouse and examines the house and all its windows.

To his left he notices Chandler and Ira walking in his direction. He walks to join them, not wanting to be alone anymore.

"We found a good place to camp," Chandler says, walking with a branch in his hand for no apparent reason. He tosses it into tall grass and weeds. "There is even a rope tied to a tree for swinging into the river."

"This is the Tacket Station," Ira says, looking over the big house Dustan heard the giggle from. "People say it's haunted. A lot of weird things happened there." The Tacket Station is slightly east of the main part of Blackwood, not actually part of the town. "A judge lived there in the 1880s. He uses to hang people on that big tree," Ira points.

Dustan and Chandler both look up at the enormous elder tree with its thick branch reaching out like an arm. They both imagine a dead man hanging on a noose from that branch.

Ira continues his tale, "People's cars die in front of the Tacket Station at night for no reason. A guy I used to know told me about a farmer who's tractor died on the road here just as the sun was going down. He looked the tractor over and couldn't figure out what was wrong with it. Of course the farmer knew the stories about the place. He sat there in the dark trying to fix his tractor in the dark when a phone starting ringing inside the Tacket Station. No one had lived there since the 1960s and this was in the 1980s. The house had no electricity, there shouldn't have been a phone ringing. The farmer ran all the way home. The next day the tractor started just fine."

"Bullshit," Dustan says, trying to hide his discomfort.

"What else happened here?" Chandler asks eager for more.

Ever the story teller Ira obliges, "There was a white family living here in the sixties. The last family to live in the house. They adopted a Native American girl. People say they were cruel to her. Abused her. The husband beat her. He beat the girl to death. That was back when white people could still kill Indians and get away with it. That was before the American Indian Movement."

"Damn," Chandler says, "What a dick."

"The family that lived there before them in the fifties went crazy," people say. The husband shot his wife and threw their baby out the upstairs window in the winter. Then he shot himself. Some people say they still hear the baby crying at night."

"Jesus," Chandler eyes the house.

"Why are we camping here?" Dustan mumbles.

By the time Cas arrives the sun is setting and they have their tents set up by the river surrounding a campfire. Cas parks his car next to the van. Amber is waiting by herself near the van for him to arrive. They kiss and make up immediately before making their way to the campsite.

Celeste, Hattie, Ginger, Chandler, Dustan, and Ira are stripped to their undergarments yipping and hollering, taking turns swinging off the rope and splashing into the river. They laugh and play and swim.

Chandler shouts from the water holding up a victorious fist, "Castor!"

Everyone except Hattie and Ira make their way to the shore to meet their late coming companion Cas.

Hattie feels the mud squish against her feet and between her toes as she makes her way in the running water to Ira. "How's school?"

"It's good," Irma answers. He's attending Northington University majoring in accounting with only a year left until he's done. "How's your new job?"

"It's fun," she smiles shyly. She has a big nose, Ira has always thought it makes her very cute, the prominent nose on such a petite and delicate frame. Her wet shoulders glimmering in the sunset, Ira remembers their moment together in high school. He wonders if he made a mistake letting her get away. Hattie continues, "I like giving tours. I get to do activities with the kids."

"I don't think I could be a tour guide."

"I didn't think I could at first," Hattie admits, "I guess I just made myself do it and now I love it. It sucked at first. I was so scared."

"That's pretty cool. You've really changed your life. I'm proud of you. Pretty amazing."

Hattie blushes, "Thanks."

They stand in oafish silence for a time.

Hattie shivers. They both have goosebumps. She adores his broad shoulders, his overall shape, his tender eyes, soft voice, and wet brown hair.

"It's cold," Ira says, hugging himself, "Let's go sit by the fire."

"Okay," Hattie agrees, sounding more disappointed than she meant to.

This tribe of eight friends grew and bonded together gathered around the fire. Drinking beer. Smoking cigarettes and marijuana. Dancing. Laughing. Telling stories of their past adventures and glories. Gossiping about old acquaintances. Dreaming about the future. Debating movies, music, and video games. Telling jokes. Flirting. Smiling. Farting. Getting louder and looser as the summer night drifts on.

Until Hattie is the only sober one, listening to her friends rant and rave over the crackle of burning wood.

"I want to go for a walk," Celeste announces with bluster, "Come on, Amber, Chandler," she slurs, "Let's walk." She puts her arms around both of them.

"I'm coming," Cas jumps up.

"Me too," Ira adds.

Hattie follows the group of drunken adventurers without a word.

Dustan sits across the campfire from Ginger, staring jealously into the flickering flames, feeling its heat on his face as he sips a can of beer and puffs a cigarette. He doesn't trust Celeste with Chandler when she's drunk. Why didn't he go with? He saw the way she was looking at Chandler. He feels his anger grow.

"What's wrong?" Ginger asks bluntly, sitting on a tree stump.

"Nothing," he shakes his head.

Ginger laughs, "What are you so pissed about, bro?"

"What are you talking about," Dustan crosses his arms.

Ginger smirks, "It's obvious you're jealous but it's stupid. Chandler is dedicated to me. He'd never cheat on me and he doesn't like Celeste anymore. He thinks she's bat shit crazy."

"I'm not jealous," Dustan lies.

Chandler, Celeste, Hattie, Ira, Amber, and Cas walk down the main street of the ghost town together, drunk on alcohol and friendship.

Celeste has her arm around Chandler, using him for balance, talking loud, whining, spoiled.

Hattie and Ira lag behind the other four. Hattie smiles at Ira with her heart shaped lips, "Will you wander off with me?"

"Okay," Ira shrugs.

Cas looks at the dark road ahead of them as they walk, paying no attention to the desertion of Hattie and Ira. The grass and weeds on either side of the street are tall and tangled. The abandoned houses sit, watching their trespass, like dull, dried corpses with black windows for eyes. Chandler and Celeste have stumbled more than a dozen feet from Cas and Amber. Celeset whispers in his ear as he plays indifference.

Parked on gravel near the school are Chandler's van and Cas's car. Cas and Amber walk to his car with intention.

"I'm sorry," Amber says in a hush, "I promise I won't hang out with him again. I just won't have any friends"

"Amber," Cas grits his teeth in secret, "You get pissed as hell if I hung out with some bird like that. You know you would. You're always jealous."

Amber sighs, "I know, but I swear to God nothing happened. He's just a friend. I love you and I don't want anyone but you."

Cas counters, "You may not want him but that doesn't mean he doesn't want you."

Amber kisses his cheek, "He can want all he wants, I belong to you."

"That's not the point," Cas debates, "It's disrespectful to me to hang out with him."

"Enough. It's over. It's done. I won't kick it with him again."

"Fine," Cas opens the car door.

"Why are we getting in the car?" Amber asks as she opens the other door.

"Just get in."

Chandler spies Cas and Amber climbing into the car. Celeste is leaning against the van talking, she never seems to stop talking. Chandler slides the side door of the van open, takes Celeste by the hand, and pulls her inside with him.

"What are you doing?" Celeste smiles.

Chandler shuts the van door and pushes her onto the seat with him.

"Oh," she says as they begin to kiss and fondle with a vigorous release of pent up lust and frustration, working frantically to undress each other. Deep swallowing kisses, wet, familiar, hungry bodies, desperate to be together again. In moments they are engaged in heated, urgent sex together on the floor of the van.

Cas is kissing Amber inside his car, trying to push her bra up. Amber giggles and shoves him back, "We're not doing it in the car."

"Fine," Cas pouts, "Let's do it in the grass."

"What is that?" Amber looks concerned out the car window.

Up a tree covered hill, a short distance from the abandoned school, they see lights dancing through the trees.

"I don't know," Cas answers, curious as he gets out of the car for a better look.

"Screw it," Dustan complains, "I'm going to have a piss and pass out in the tent."

Ginger shrugs, "I'm going to find Chandler." She throws her empty beer can in the fire and walks away.

Dustan curses under his breath and walks into the dark foliage to urinate before retiring to his tent.

Ginger walks briskly over grass, weeds, and dirt. She wants to get to the others as quick as she can, being alone in the dark makes her uneasy. She feels like someone is watching her from the trees but she's a rational woman and knows it's likely only an animal. She wonders about this ghost town Blackwood. Maybe it wasn't such a good idea to camp her. Something about the town gives her the creeps. What is she so afraid of all of a sudden? It's just dark.

What she didn't admit to Dustan is that she doesn't trust Celeste. Chandler would never cheat on her, but Ginger wouldn't be surprised if Celeste tried. There is no sense in letting Chandler put up with her uncouth advances.

As Ginger walks past an abandoned house she feels the urge to run but forces herself to be brave and walk. Ginger prides herself on her strength. She is a strong, bold, take no shit kind of woman. She's not afraid of the dark. She's not afraid of an old, empty house.

Ginger reaches the main street and spots someone down the road, "Hey," she waves, realizing the person is saying something. She can't make out who the person is and what they're saying. Ginger smiles, skipping toward the pedestrian, straining to her what they're saying.

"I'm enjoying Jesus every day," an older woman's voice sings.

Ginger slows, not recognizing the voice.

It's an old, plump woman, it's too hard to make out more than that from this distance in the dark. The woman continues her approach, wearing a red sweater, a violet scarf over her hair, and a light, possibly brown knee length skirt. "I'm enjoying Jesus every day," she woman sings on and on, her voice deep and off.

"Ginger!" Ira shouts from behind her.

Ginger looks back to see Ira and Hattie standing in the road together.

"I'm enjoying Jesus every day," the woman sings.

"Who are you?" Ginger asks the woman.

"I'm enjoying Jesus every day!"

Ginger shivers and sprints back to her friends.

"Who is that?" Ira asks, watching the woman turn away, walking into the overgrown yard of another abandoned house, still singing.

"I don't know," Ginger catches her breath.

"Why'd you run from her?" Ira chuckles.

"I don't know," Ginger shakes her head, embarrassed.

All three of them watch the woman disappear inside a dark house and fall silent. The house is as battered and decrepit as the rest of the houses in the town. It doesn't look like a house anyone lives in.

"Okay," Ira whispers, "That is a little weird."

Hattie steps close to Ira, feeling a sudden pinch of jealousy at the arrival of Ginger. She knows it's silly, but the heart is rarely rational. All Hattie can think about is the conversation she and Ira were having. He asked her if she ever wonders what could have been. What could have been between them? If they'd dated? Ira had reached out, taking her hand in his. Hattie was sure they were about to kiss until they were interrupted by the Jesus singing.

As soon as they spotted Ginger standing in the road, Ira let go of Hattie's hand. She wants him to hold her hand. She wants to reach out and take his hand, but she's afraid of potential rejection. What if he doesn't want to hold her hand? What if Ginger sees him brush her off? Oh, Ira, please, I love you, her heart cries inside.

"Must be someone who still lives here," Ira tries to convince himself.

"Where's Chandler?" Ginger asks.

"I don't know," Ira answers, "Last I saw everyone was walking toward the school."

"What the hell's going on over there?" Cas looks at the queer orange light flickering beyond the trees as he stands in front of the van with Amber at his side.

Chandler pops out of the van tugging his shirt on, leaving the door open, "Looks like a fire."

"Chandler," Celeste slurs, "Come back." She tumbles out of the van pulling her pants on, shirtless, wearing only her bra.

"Jesus," Cas says, "Put on some clothes."

"Fuck you," Celeste screeches.

"What the hell is this?" Ginger runs up, confronting Chandler and Celeste, "Are you kidding me!"

Ira and Hattie jog up behind Ginger joining everyone just as they hear a shrill scream from the fire lit woods beyond the school.

The primal drive of the scream silences the friends. They stare in the direction of the illuminated trees.

"What was that?" Amber asks everyone with a nervous cheshire grin.

They hear more sounds, like animal movement in the trees.

"Let's check it out," Chandler says with gusto.

"I don't think so," Ginger grabs his bicep, driving her fingernails into his skin.

"Chandler and I are getting back together," Celeste announces.

"No we're not," Chandler counters.

"You bitch," Ginger glares at Celeste.

There is another cry from the woods.

"Sounds like someone is hurt," Cas says, looking back and forth between the screaming trees and the love triangle.

"Let's check it out," Ira says, leading Hattie toward the dark tree line. Cas and Amber follow.

"Fuck all of you," Celeste begins to cry, "Dustan and I are leaving." She marches away from them.

Ira glances back at the quiet, close argument that is simmering between Ginger and Chandler after Celeste's departure. Ginger hasn't let go of his arm and their faces are almost touching as Ginger growls, sighs, and cries. Ira feels sorry for Ginger. He knows Chandler will never stop messing around with Celeste, they have a twisted relationship. Ira's always had a crush on Ginger. His feelings are mixed because he cherishes his friendship with Chandler and thinks he might have feelings for Hattie. He thinks

Chandler has made a huge mistake. Ginger isn't as glamorous as Celeste but she's a better girlfriend and much more cool and hip.

       Dustan lays in his tent tossing and turning on the sleeping bags. The ground is hard and uncomfortable. He normally loves camping, but tonight he can't stop fuming about Chandler and Celeste. He sees the way Celeste looks at him and talks about him. She acts like Chandler's cooler than Dustan. It irritates him, makes him feel insecure, like he's not man enough for her. Everyone talks about how cool Chandler is. Chandler and Cas and even Ira. It's like Dustan is a second stringer. Screw them, he thinks in the dark, rolling on his belly, trying to force sleep to come.

       Just as Dustan begins to fall asleep, dreaming he his jogging down a sidewalk at night, truly still half awake and half asleep, the sidewalk ends abruptly, jerking Dustan awake the moment he falls. The sleeping bag is damp with sweat, even though he's stripped to his underwear.

       With an unsteady jerking motion the zipper of the tent opens. Dustan lifts his head to see the silhouette of Celeste entering the shadow veiled tent. They don't say anything to each other. Dustan is relieved she's finally come to the tent, relieved to have her away from Chandler. His anger disappears.

       Celeste crawls over his legs, pulling the unzipped sleeping bag off of Dustan. She wordlessly slides a hand beneath his underwear and strokes him. Dustan's smile is hidden by the darkness, whispering, "Oh, baby, I'm glad you're back." When he feels the warm silk soft of her wet mouth engulf his manhood, he lets his head fall back, closing his eyes, enjoying the ride. His arms rest at his sides as she pleasures him and his legs and toes stiffen with joy. After several minutes of tongue and hand, Celeste positions herself over his waist, straddling him.

       "Oh, yes, baby," Dustan groans as she comes down on him. It doesn't take long before they find a steady rhythm.

       "Oh, god, I just want to do this all night," Dustan whispers. This is all that matters, he thinks, Celeste loves me. He whispers to her, "That's my pussy."

       Celeste, hands on Dustan's chest for balance, says, "It's your pussy."

       Dustan immediately recognizes that it's not Celeste's voice. He is shocked, speechless, caught in the passion of sex, unable to stop, part of him even more excited knowing it's not Celeste. The possibilities race through his mind, each exciting him more than the last. Ginger. Hattie. Amber. For a moment in his mind's eye he's having sex with them all.

       "Who are you?" Dustan fumbles for a flashlight while still in the act of copulation.

       The woman ignores him, riding harder.

       Dustan flicks the flashlight on and the dome tent lights up.

He screams, trying to squirm, bat, and kick his way from under the woman. He doesn't know who she is. Naked. Panting. Sweating. Too thin. Anorexic skinny. She looks like skin pulled over a skeleton and not much more. The skin is loose and sagging in places. He can make out every bone of her rib cage above her sunken stomach and her joints are knobby, seeming out of proportion. He can see the shape of her skull in her face, cheek bones, temples, blackened eye sockets.

The woman's hair is brittle and tangled. Teeth yellow. Eyes bloodshot. Spittle oozes from the sides of her mouth. She's not clean. Her skin looks like she hasn't bathed in months. Her teeth seem too large for her gaunt face and drooping eyelids.

"Oh, my God!" Dustan screams, pushing her away.

The haggard woman tries to stay mounted on him. She screams back at him, "I'm skinny for you! Can't you see! I love you so much I'm skinny for you!"

"Oh, God," Dustan tries to crab crawl away as she tries to climb back on top of him.

With a lurch forward she vomits on his naked chest. The vomit is hot and wet with a bitter smell to it. He feels it splash against his skin and run down his sides and stomach.

Dustan swings the flashlight at the gaunt, puking woman, smacking the side of her head, breaking skin, drawing blood. With a gnarled, feral frown her hands wrap around his neck, squeezing.

Dustan tries to pry her fingers away, surprised by her strength, an iron grip, hands clamped around his neck. He can't breathe.

Swinging the flashlight again and again against the side of her head. Half her face and hair is covered in blood, but she doesn't let up. The woman is crushing his windpipe.

His body panics and jerks as Dustan's brain laments for oxygen. His body tingles at first and his vision becomes fuzzy, closing. A moment later he is gone, soul fluttering up like a lost bird above his flesh.

Cas, Amber, Ira, and Hattie make their way up the shallow hill toward the orange glowing trees. Ira is more excited by the mystery than afraid, trying not to smile as they walk toward the noise and firelight.

So distracted that Ira is now holding her hand, Amber can't think of anything else. Her heart is thumping and stomach fluttering as she thinks, Ira, Ira, Ira, I love you.

The four friends wear expressions of awe, confusion, and fear looking down from within the patch of trees. At the bottom of the slightly sloping hill is a thick, high, blazing bonfire. They can feel its heat from where they stand.

A great black bull stands near it with it's smooth coat reflecting the firelight. Dancing, gyrating, and chanting around the bull and blaze are thirteen ecstasy drunk, furious sky clad women. Their ages range from young to old, each moving in her own unique way like women possessed, unshaven, and hair unbound.

One woman's eyes are rolling back showing only white. Some of them are sexually singular, some in pairs. They all howl, scream, and moan in diverse old languages.

An older woman with feline features and long, wild black hair stands beside the big bull with a machete in hand, its silver blade shining in the firelight. She chants, "Paon! Paon! Iao Paon! Paon!"

The four friends are mesmerized by the surreal frenzy. Cas and Ira are both frightened and aroused. Hattie's hand sweats in Ira's grasp. Ira can't stop smiling.

Hattie moves closer to Ira, "Let's get out of here."

Ira and the others ignore her plea caught up in the unfolding spectacle.

The machete rises and Ira's eyes widen with fascination and horror. The blade swings down swift and hard, cutting deep into the thick of the bull's neck. She hacks again and again. Blood spatters her bare chest and pours out onto the ground as she swings the blade deeper and deeper into the animal's flesh until at last the bull's head falls to the ground and the body collapses. The friends are shocked by the brutality of the act.

The other women surge and descend upon the fallen beast like a pack of rabid jackals. They tear flesh away with their hands and mouths. Their bodies swirl in a frenzy of blood, smearing it on themselves, still dancing, cheering, laughing, and chanting.

The women are oblivious to the four friends witnessing their sacred rite from the sparse grove of trees and shadows.

Cas has his hand over his mouth fighting the urge to retch.

"Holy shit," Amber whispers.

"Run," Cas leads their sprint away from the carnage back through the trees the way they have come from.

They do not speak or stop running until they make it back to the vehicles. At the vehicles more terror awaits.

Ginger and Chandler are nowhere to be seen.

Instead, gathered around the van and car, inspecting them as if they've never seen such wonders before are a dozen short hairy men. Maybe three feet tall with glowing eyes. Some are tinkering, poking and playing at the tires, trying to open the doors, touching the windows, sniffing antennae, peering underneath the vehicles.

The four friends stand frozen in fear and confusion looking at these little men, they look like miniature cavemen. Big Foot's children. The little men with fur covered faces see the friends and suddenly transform into stumps of wood. Save one standing between them and the van with staring, glowing eyes, unmoving.

"What do you want?" Hattie cries out. They can still hear the crazed women beyond the trees.

The little furry man-thing points a tiny finger in their direction. Ira feels goosebumps raise all over his body.

Amber lets loose a scream and all four friends run away down the main street of Blackwood. Hattie still holds Ira's hand, afraid to let go. Amber and Cas make better time, getting ahead of Ira and Hattie.

Ira notices a light on in a window of a house partially hidden by trees. He tugs Hattie off the road and up the long, rutted driveway toward that house. He thinks he remembers it as being one of the few residents still living in Blackwood the last time he was here.

"What's going on?" Hattie sniffles, "What about Cas and Amber? Where are we going?"

"I don't know," Ira answers, still leading her toward the house.

It's a small home with a big yard. A pickup truck is parked next to an outhouse. Ira knocks on the front door of the little house.

"What are we doing?" Hattie whispers.

"Calm down," Ira reassures.

From the inside they can hear someone shuffling toward the door and see a shadow pass by the window. An elder Native American man with a large, red nose and a round belly opens the door. He's wearing a flannel shirt with cutoff sleeves, faded blue jeans, and cowboy boots. Long white hair hangs past his shoulders. The man's dark eyes give Hattie and Ira a skeptical look.

"Wyatt," Ira says, "Please let us in."

The dark skinned old man nods with a stoic expression.

The house seems even smaller inside. Only three rooms. A small kitchen, living room, and bedroom. In the kitchen there is an old wood stove next to a table, sink, refrigerator, and freezer. The carpet and furniture in the living room are worn and torn. The doorway to the bedroom is blocked by a ragged hanging sheet. There is a small television sitting on a stand in the living room along with a couch, recliner, coffee table, and an overflowing bookshelf. There is a mess of newspapers, old magazines, and a coffee cup on the coffee table.

Wyatt Painted Bear sits in the recliner. He's known Ira since Ira was a young boy. He'd always felt sorry for Ira being a halfbreed that many of the full blood kids would tease, but the boy Ira always solemnly stood his ground. Wyatt was friends with Ira's grandparents before they died. It's been years since Ira and Wyatt have seen each other.

"What are you doing here, Ira Whitfield?" Wyatt asks.

Ira and Hattie sit close together on the couch, Hattie nearly clinging to Ira. She looks around the room. A buffalo skull and peace pipe hang on one wall. On the other walls are old black and white photographs of Native Americans. The pictures look like they're from the 1950s.

"Chotina," Ira says, feeling remorseful for having come to Blackwood, "Chuhutina. Not just one. A whole bunch of them."

"Chotina?" Hattie asks.

"That is not good," Wyatt shakes his head with evident sorrow. "You shouldn't have come to Blackwood with wasichus. You know better than to bring all these white people here. They don't know how to respect the spirit world. Especially on a night like tonight."

"I didn't think it would be a big deal," Ira laments, "I don't know what makes this night different from any others."

"I don't understand," Hattie says.

"Blackwood is a crossroad between this world and the spirit worlds," Wyatt explains, "Ira knows this. He grew up with the stories."

"I never saw anything before," Ira says, "I just wanted to camp out and have some fun with my friends. I didn't think the stories were real."

"You knew the stories were real when you were younger," Wyatt scolds, "You've been in the white world too long."

"A crossroad?" Hattie probes Wyatt further, "What are chotinas? Who were those crazy women?"

Wyatt remains calm, speaking with his thick Native American accent, "This is a sacred place. Along the river bottom for miles it is so. The walls between the spirit world and this world are thin here. The doors open easier. Spirits walk freely here and other things. Lost things, running or hiding. Someone did a bad thing here in Blackwood once. Opened a door that should not have been opened. Now this place is tainted. The chotinas are harbingers. They are not evil. They are warning of evil. That is why they are often here in Blackwood. They come to warn you away." Wyatt sips his coffee, "If you're thirsty there is coffee or water in the kitchen."

"No thank you," Hattie says, polite as can be.

Continuing to answer their questions, Wyatt continues, "The women you saw, they are white witches. They have been coming to Blackwood since it was deserted. I think they had something to do with the tainting. They come four times a year. It's a full moon. You came on the wrong night. The witches make the spirits and things restless."

"What do the witches want?" Ira aska.

"Nothing good," is Ira's reply.

"This is crazy," Hattie shakes her head, "It can't be real."

"We saw it with our own eyes," Ira reminds her.

"We need to call the police," Hattie exclaims, "Call someone." She takes her cell phone out of her pocket and just stares at it.

"What are we going to tell the police?" Ira asks, "Naked witches killed a bull? Big Foot's babies looked at our cars? There are ghosts in Blackwood?"

"You know what it means to be chosen by them," Wyatt says in a mournful voice to Ira.

Ira nods, "We have to leave Blackwood right away."

"I don't understand what's happening," Hattie says.

"Something bad is coming for us," Ira tells her, "It would be selfish of us to bring it to Wyatt. We have to leave." He looks at Wyatt, "Thank you for letting us in."

Celeste is on her butt in the grass and dirt before the dying flames of the campfire. She has a beer in one hand and a cigarette in the other. She's too upset to go to sleep in the tent with Dustan. She wants to leave but not with Dustan. She wants Chandler. She wants Ginger to die. She's decided she doesn't even like Dustan. She never has. She doesn't hate him either. Celeste gazes into the fire. She only started dating Dustan to make Chandler jealous. It didn't work. Tears smear her mascara. Chandler loves her. Why is he with Ginger?

No. He doesn't love her does he? He was only drunk and horny. Celeste doesn't know what to do. Things shouldn't be this difficult. She and Chandler should be together like they always used to be. It's that simple. Celeste is trapped in a circle of heartache and resentment.

Hearing voices approach, she glances up to see Chandler and Ginger approaching, hand in hand. Smoldering anger begins to burn anew. The infidelity was meant to break them up. Seeing them together makes her feel hopeless.

Chandler and Ginger completely ignore Celeste glaring at them and retire to their tent. Being ignored fuels her anger. She throws her empty beer can in the fire.

With a sigh Celeste gives up and walks to her tent. Climbing inside the tent she smells vomit and thinks Dustan must have gotten too drunk and puked. Blindly finding the flashlight, she feels something wet on it, "Dustan!" She screeches with anger, the flashlight turns on, "you disgusting idiot!"

Dustan lies still, not breathing, eyes open and unblinking, vomit covers his chest. She thinks he must have died choking on his own vomit. Alcohol poisoning. She notices the blood on her fingers and the flashlight. Celeste's heart drops like a brick to her stomach. Dustan is dead. She screams and screams again.

Celeste trips as she rushes out of the tent, "Chandler!" she cries, "He's dead! He's dead!"

"What the hell?" Ginger growls emerging from her tent with Chandler.

"Dustan's dead!" Celeste sobs.

"What are you talking about?" Ginger asks, anger hesitating.

"Dustan!" Celeste wails, still holding the bloody flashlight.

Chandler takes the flashlight from her and inspects the tent. He comes back out to Celeste and Ginger, and says in an odd calm, "She's right. Dustan is dead."

"Oh, my God," Ginger says, "What happened?"

"I don't know," Celeste wipes her eyes, "I just found him like that."

"We have to call the police," Chandler pulls a cell phone from his pocket and dials 911.

Celeste sits by the fire, crying, opening a fresh beer, and lighting a cigarette.

"Jesus," Ginger stands outside Dustan's tent with her hand over her mouth, afraid to look inside, "I can't believe this."

Chandler listens to the ringing on his cell phone, "Hello?" A tinny voice answers.

"My friend is dead," Chandler says, "We need help."

Silence is the only response on the other end of the phone.

"Did you hear me? Our friend is dead. We need help. Is this 911?"

"It's alright, Mr. Given." the voice answers, "It is the way of all flesh. Everything dies."

"What?" Chandler feels an uneasiness in his stomach, "How do you know my name? Caller ID?"

The inhuman voice answers, sounding electronic or insect like, "Chandler Given. You do not believe your father loves you and you are afraid you are an alcoholic like he is. You don't know if you love Ginger or Celeste or if you love either of them. You are not sure you know what love is. You possess a very mechanical consciousness, pretend you don't care about things, your true self hidden deep within. Not unlike many of your race."

"Who is this?" Chandler's voice trembles.

"My name is Cold," the voice replies, "You are standing near the Missouri River with Ginger Jonadab and Celeste Abington and a flashlight in your other hand."

"How do you know?" Chandler looks around for someone spying on them in the darkness.

"Mr. Given," the voice addresses him.

"What?" Chandler is sweating now.

"You will die tonight."

Chandler hears a click and his phone dies. He looks at the cell phone in his hand like some malignant cancer.

"What just happened?" Ginger asks her boyfriend with concern.

"I don't know," he whispers, "Try your phone. Call 911."

Ginger dials the emergency number. It rings three times before being answered. She holds the phone away from her ear at the sound of a high pitched squeaking.

Chandler looks at Ginger and Celeste, "We need to get everyone together and get out of here."

Cas and Amber walk together along the main street making their way back to the campsite. They approach the dark house Ira called the Tacket Station. Amber grabs Cas by the arm, "What is that?" She points at a large tree in the front yard.

The house is shadowed in black, the windows and doorways are midnight voids. Tall grass grows wild about the house, its thin blades reaching up its sides. Cas sees what Amber is pointing at. The silhouette of a man hanging dead by a rope from a long branch of the tree.

"Holy shit," Cas whispers.

At the front door of the house they hear a clacking noise. Amber pulls herself tight against Cas, shivering with fright. Something emerges from the house moving toward them. At first Cas thinks it's a large dog or some other four legged animal. Clacking and clicking as it approaches, stepping out from under the shade of the trees and into the moonlight they see more clearly what it is. Something hard to describe, hard to register as real. Not an animal but a twisted man crawling toward them on both hands and feet. His head is bent too far to one side as if his neck is broken. The man is naked. Skin ruddy, tinted red, bruised, and broken. He looks like all of his bones were broken and healed at unnatural angles. The crawling man couldn't stand upright if he wanted to. The scar tissue is thick covering most of his mangled body. The joints are all bent in the wrong directions. A sliver of drool hangs from his mouth. A few patches of hair remain on his head. Cas thinks the crawling man looks like a burn victim after being thrown off a cliff. He groans and suddenly crawls faster than what seems possible.

Amber and Cas scream together and sprint toward the campsite. They only make it a few dozen feet before spotting Chandler, Ginger, and Celeste walking their way.

"We have to get out of here," Chandler shouts to them, "Back to the van!"

"There's little hairy men all over the van!" Cas exclaims.

Amber screams, feeling the crooked teeth of the crawling man sink into the flesh of her thigh. The bent man jerks his head back, taking a mouthful of meat with it.

Inside the Tacket Station an old fashion phone begins to ring.

Cas takes Amber in his arms, saving her from the bent man, but the man is too quick, digging his teeth and rotten fingernails into Amber's calf.

Chandler strikes the crawling thing in the head with his flashlight again and again. Attacking with furious abandon to protect his stepsister. The bent man hisses, holding up a hand to shield the blows but Chandler doesn't let up.

Cas holds Amber up as she limps and wails, blood gushing from her leg wounds. Celeste backs away from the gory scene before her watching horror stricken as the crawling man's head caves in like a melon beneath Chandler's blows.

Ginger stands a mute witness, hands pressed against her face.

The twisted man lay seemingly dead on the ground as Chandler continues to beat him until Ginger touches his arm to calm him down, "It's over. It's dead. Stop."

Chandler drops the broken, gore smeared flashlight, his hands and arms shaking, whimpering. Ginger hugs him tight.

"We have to bandage her leg," Cas says, taking off his shirt and ripping it into strips.

Seeming to sober, Celeste helps Cas tie the cloth around Amber's leg. "Am I going to die?" Amber cries quietly.

"You're going to be fine," Cas kissed her, trying not to think about how much blood she's losing.

"You're fine, sis," Chandler collects himself, "It looks worse than it is."

"What are we going to do?" Hattie asks as they walk away from Wyatt Painted Bear's home.

"I don't know," Ira sighs as they walk back out to the main street. "Leave. Go home."

"What was all that Wyatt was talking about? Do you know what's going on here?"

"Not really. I told Chandler it wasn't a good idea to camp out here. Everyone says it's a haunted town. I've never seen anything before tonight."

All around the town the night is filled with yipping and howling. Hattie grabs Ira's arm, "What is that?"

"Coyotes. I used to like to listen to them out here when I was a kid."

"You lived here?"

"No. About a half hour east on my grandparent's farm."

Chandler, Ginger, Cas, Amber, and Celeste are coming up the main street to meet Ira and Hattie. Amber is limping, hoisted up between Chandler and Cas.

"Where's Dustan?" Ira asks.

"He's dead," Chandler answers, "We're getting out of here."

"What happened?" Ira asks.

"We don't know," Cas says, "Let's just go."

"But those things are all over the cars," Hattie reminds them.

"Fuck 'em," Chandler growls.

"Look at that," Celeste points, exhausted.

They all look up at the full moon. Gray clouds have surrounded the pale orb to make it look like an eye looking down on them.

"We're in hell," Celeste adds, cracking open another can of beer.

The seven friends approach Chandler's van and Cas's car. Huddled close, protectively, eyes alert and darting all around as to not be taken unaware. Ahead the van and car appear unmolested. The tree trunks still litter the area. Cas wonders if they really saw the little men or if it was just some kind of mirage. Maybe it was these wood chunks all along and they were just so inebriated the shadow play merely tricked them. He thinks of the crawling man, the hanging man, the crazy women. It's too much. The little men were real. He's afraid the wood will come back to life when they get too close to the vehicles.

"Let's get out of here," Chandler digs keys out of his pocket and jangles them.

"Yeah," Ira and Hattie both agree at the same time.

Before they have a chance to make any progress the dozen and one bloody witches charge from the darkness of the trees. Screaming wild and feral, their bodies slick with red blood.

"Run!" Chandler shouts and everyone runs to the van.

As Chandler opens the driver's side door to the van the dark haired witch with the machete attacks him. The blade sinks into the back of his head with a sickening thud just like it had the black bull. Watching from the passenger side door Ira is shocked by the strength of the witch's blow. Chandler slumps over the driver's seat, legs still dangling on the ground as she works the machete back out of his skull.

It is a moment of immaculate chaos. Everyone is screaming and shouting, fighting. The naked bloody witches swarm over them, scratching, biting, pulling hair, kicking, punching. The remaining six friends are fighting for their lives. Ira stumbles and falls after being slapped across the face. He's on his feet again and bumps into the side of the van, swatting a witch away. Another jumps before him bellowing with large crimson breasts and belly jiggling. Her thighs, calves, and ankles are thick, short and stout. Ira finds himself laughing hysterically.

Ira feels like he can hear music in the night as time seems to slow with this danse macabre. He stops fighting back, but does his best to evade assaults. He's astounded by the beauty and dreaminess of the experience. Crazed, blood coated, screaming women murdering his friends around stumps of wood that used to be Chotinas. His friends crying and fighting back. The moon eye looking down on them all. The cool breeze on this hot summer night. The rolling hills and trees, a myriad of shadows. The abandoned houses. The melody of screaming. He sees Hattie take up a block of wood that used to be a little man and hit a witch in the face with it, dropping the witch to the ground. The witch lay there, face smashed, body twitching. She hits another. Again and again. Another witch catches Hattie by the hair, yanking her back, Hattie loses her grip on the wood and it tumbles to the ground. She fights back, clawing at the witch.

Four of the women have overpowered Cas. He's on the ground struggling against them. They seem to be biting him. Tearing. Ripping. Eating. Praying.

Amber is down too. A witch jumps up and down on her corpses triumphantly.

Ginger grabs Ira by the arm, "We have to get out of here! Run! Run!"

Ira nods, seeing Celeste crying inside the van. She pushed Chandler out and locked herself inside. Bloody witches have climbed atop it, pounding, stomping, jumping. Several witches pick up hunks of wood and beat the vehicles. The windshield of Cas's car shatters. Ira knows it's only a matter of time until they break through to Celeste.

Ira, Hattie, and Ginger run away together on the main street. He feels a hot pang slice into the back of his thigh and turns to face the cackling, machete wielding wench raising her arm to slice again.

He gives her a friendly smile. Smiles at the death she swings. He remembers scenes from his childhood. Being a little boy. Singing sad songs alone in the woods. He thinks of Hattie and realizes he should have loved her, should have married her.

Ginger growls and tackles the witch before the blade connects with Ira. The two women wrestle on the crumbled pavement. Ira is about to bend down and help Ginger when he sees the machete impaled in Ginger's abdomen.

"Come on!" Hattie huffs, taking his hand, leading him, running together. A pair of witches join the assault on Ginger.

They run and don't look back. They run down the highway following it out of the ghost town. They run until they are breathing hard and their lungs are burning and their legs ache.

Ira is fascinated by how dark it is out here in the country compared to in the city and how many more stars can be seen in the sky without the pollution of city lights. If he lives through this he will marry Hattie and they will live in the country.

They slow to a fast walk after some time, still breathing hard, panting, sweating. Ira feels the warmth of his blood dripping down the back of his leg. It's beginning to throb. He can feel his heart beat in the gash in his thigh. Funny that it was numb until now. Now it hurts so much he doesn't want to move it, doesn't want to go on.

Hattie takes his hand. Ira is hyper-aware of the sensation. The soft, delicate touch of her fingers. She has tiny fingers compared to his. Her hair is soft, silky, rich. Big eyes, cute nose, small mouth. Little ears. She is alive. Flowing with fear and sweat and blood and oxygen. She's covered in skin. Ira wonders if he's thinking right? Or is he just seeing things right for the first time in his life? The big perfect pale moon above is surrounded by twinkling stars against the black sky. The clouds around the moon have blown away. God, what a beautiful night. Everything is beautiful. The world. Hattie. Everything.

Hattie stands close to him, facing him, his hand on her shoulder. Ira could swim in her eyes forever. Her expression is quizzical. Ira just wants to admire her face for the rest of his life. Each delicate curve, shape, and crease. He gives her a warm, genuine smile full of tenderness and love. They kiss softly, longingly, closing eyes, caressing her chin, drinking in every moment, the firm of her hips, her tongue touching his, her scent.

Behind them on the highway they can hear the approach of witches running after them, they look back, barely making the figures out. They look back into each other's eyes.

"We have to keep running," Hattie urges.

Ira looks serene, "Hattie."

"What, Ira? We need to go!"

"I love you."

She looks at him a moment, tears glistening in her eyes, "I love you, too."

"If I fall behind, you have to keep going."

"You'll be fine," she cried now, "Come on. Let's go."

"Promise me."

"Stop it," she tugs on his arm, wiping away tears.

"Promise me that if I fall behind you'll keep going."

"I promise," she cries.

Ira nods, "If I should fall behind, let me go. I want you to live."

Hattie nods, sniffles, wiping her nose with the back of her hand. "I promise. If you fall behind I'll keep going."

"Then let's run," Ira smiles.

They run. Not fast. It's obvious Ira can't keep up with her now. His limp is growing worse.

Hattie looks back seeing two witches in pursuit. Still naked and crazed.

"Come on," she cries, pulling Ira along.

"Go, Hattie, run on."

"Please, Ira," she sobs.

Don't break your promise to me, Hattie. Please. Run on. Run now." He lets her go and gives her a gentle shove.

She looks at him, crying hard, and runs, leaving Ira and the coming witches behind, blinded by her own tears.

Ira smiles on, watching her disappear into the night ahead of him. The pain in his leg comes and goes between unbearable and only a tingling. He can hear the witches breathing, feet padding, and Ira turns just at the right moment, when both women are within his reach. Catching one by the hair with his left hand, jerking her head back. His right hand grips the other one's throat, slamming her down hard against the pavement. The back of her head thuds against the highway.

The beauty and serenity have vanished like a wisp in the wind. There is a single objective in his life, one drive, one purpose for existing: Hattie must get away. Ira will stop them no matter the cost.

Ira's fingers dig into the witches neck as he strangles the life from her. She claws and kicks to no avail. The other witch wails like a feverish banshee trying to break free of his hold on her hair. His hand is twisted in the hair, she can not get away.

The first witch quits fighting as her life and soul ebb away. The other witch now has Ira's full attention. Ira's arm is scratched and bleeding from her fingernails. Ira's leg gives out and he falls, taking the witch down with him, hugging her close. He begins to strangle her as well using both hands, he begins to smash her head against the highway until her life is gone.

Ira rolls on his back, laying in the center of the highway between the dead witches, gazing up at the stars. So beautiful. Just like heaven. He is content to die, hearing an owl hoot off in the trees somewhere.

Hattie doesn't know how long she's been running. An hour? Two? She feels a euphoric exhaustion. Legs aching with shin splints. Ira is gone. She knows it in her heart. They're all gone. All of her friends. She doesn't know what to do but keeps walking toward home. A two hour drive. How long will it take to walk?

She hears a car and looks back at approaching headlights. Did someone else survive? No. A farmer? Highway Patrol? Someone. Anyone. Please stop. Please help me.

Hattie stands along the side of the highway waving her arms.

The car slows. A big, old car. A sedan. Maybe from the 1970s. She's not sure, she doesn't know much about cars besides pumping gas and changing oil.

She walks to the passenger's side door, the interior dome light flickers on, looking in, feeling her sweat cooling in the summer breeze. The driver is a dark haired man, maybe 35 years old. His hair is cut short, black, curly, well kept. A sharp goatee points down from his chin. Eyebrows angled. Handsome. All his features are sharp. A white button up shirt. He looks at her with heavy lidded eyes.

"Will you take me to town? To the police?" Hattie asks, feeling relieved.

The man nods, reaches across the seat and opens the door for her. She wipes her face and eyes with her hands, her makeup is smeared. Hattie gets in the car and crosses her arms trying to comfort herself as the man starts driving.

Hattie looks out the window at the dark side of the highway wondering what just happened. How could any of this happen? Ira. Ira. Everyone. Everything.

A moment later she realizes the driver hasn't turned the dome light off. She thinks that is odd. Hattie looks at the driver. He's staring at her with a disturbing grin on his face rather than watching the highway ahead of him. Unblinking. Unmoving. She slides closer to the passenger door, noticing the driver's feet. Not feet. Hooves. Goat's feet.

"Please let me go," Hattie whispers.

Grimsinger

A hunched figure stands veiled by darkness and black bushes at the front of a typical house in a middle class residential neighborhood peering into a full basement window. It's a humid summer night. The man is bundled in filthy rags, a dirty dark violet stocking cap, a dark sailor's coat, worn leather boots, and tight leather gloves. His hands rest on the rust colored window sill.

The family room on the other side of the glass glows and flickers with television light. Three young women in pajamas lounge on a full L-shaped couch in the dark engrossed in a movie. A slumber party, the peeping tom thinks.

Drool slides out the corner of the voyeur's mouth. One of the women has her legs propped up on a coffee table wagging fuzzy slippers back and forth while cradling a bowl of popcorn in her lap. Her hair is tied back, glasses hang at the tip of her nose, stretchy black pants, and an oversized red shirt.

The brunette next to her wears a tank top, men's boxers, and eats a bowl of ice cream. The third woman sits cross legged on the section of couch nearest the window, a sleeping bag wrapped over her legs.

The big television screen hanging on the wall presents a bare chested, handsome young man, staring longingly into the eyes of an equally attractive woman. The man's skin is pale white, he has tiny fangs, and a forlorn, angst filled expression.

The man on the screen laments, "Cassandra, you don't understand what I am. I'm cursed. We come from different worlds, night and day. We can never be together."

Cassandra's eyes tear up, "I don't care, Sebastian. All I know is that I love you. When we're together it feels right and when we're apart all I can think of is that night we kissed. I don't care what anyone says. We belong together. We can make it work."

"I'm a monster," the sexy Hollywood vampire whines, "A killer."

"I know what you are and I don't have a choice but to love you. I know you feel it too. We're meant to be." She throws herself into his arms, dramatic, romantic music plays as they kiss and the camera pans away as it begins to rain on them.

"Oh, my gawd," the cross legged woman moans, "Sebastian is so freaking hot."

"I'd fuck him," the woman in the tank top declares.

The other two young women squeal. The girl with the popcorn bowl laughs, "Ruby, you're such a slut!"

"Oh, whatever, Tiff," Ruby smirks, "You'd fuck him too."

"No, I wouldn't," Tiff says with mock shock.

The third says, "Mm. I would."

"Naomi!" Tiff laughs.

"Wow," Ruby giggles at Tiff, "You are so frigid."

"I'm not frigid."

"You are so," Ruby argues, "The only time you'll even make out with a guy is when you're half drunk."

"Like you don't make out with guys when you're drunk," Tiff rolls her eyes.

With a cocky grin Ruby says, "With the right guy I do more than that."

"Would you guys shut up," Naomi complains, tossing her hands up, "I've been waiting to see this movie since forever."

Tiff and Ruby comply.

A small black and white shaggy Shih Tzu patters into the room. The girls ignore the dog, watching the romantic vampire movie. The little dog sniffs around the room before coming to the window where it growls and yips at the hump of shadow beyond the glass.

"Be quiet, Timmy," Tiff scolds lightly.

"What a wimpy name for a dog," Ruby chuckles.

"Uh," Tiff exaggerates her hurt, "He's not wimpy."

The hunched man's eyes glitter and glow pink. Timmy whimpers and runs away as fast as his short legs will carry him.

"Oh, poor puppy," Naomi coos watching Timmy run up carpeted stairs, "You hurt his feelings, Ruby."

"This is the part where Cassandra realizes she's in love with Duncan the zombie," Ruby mumbles.

"You spoiler bitch," Naomi says.

"Oops," Ruby appears genuinely regretful, "Sorry."

Outside the window the spying man feels his hunger being aroused. Pink eyes follow the length of Ruby's smooth, bare, long legs. Her boxers are bunched up, pushing the fabric up high enough to expose where the crease of her thigh ends and becomes the soft curve of her buttocks.

The man outside the window slowly rubs himself, his hand over his crotch, taking his time, while his eyes move up to her firm stomach. Ruby is braless beneath her tank top and he can see the shape of her nipples against the clothes. Her tank top is cut low, the curves of her cleavage unknowingly teasing him. If she moved just right her breasts would be exposed.

The man behind the window, Royce Grimsinger, lusts for all three of these young women with a predatory craving. A greedy yearning that drives him to madness. His hand reaches into his pants to stroke himself properly. Royce glimpses the television screen, irritated, he hates these romantic vampires, the trendy zombies, and other supernatural nightmares made silly in current popular culture.

When Ruby, Tiff, and Naomi see him they will not be starry eyed and fall head over heels in dreamy love for him.

Royce Grimsinger has been a vampire for a long time. He's been wandering North America, terrorizing, raping, and murdering since 1776. How did the cattle come to romanticize his kind? The undead are possessed of a satanic curse, lustful killers of men and women. The starvation and desire are beyond will. Royce has been a savage, rabid, wild animal ever since he was killed and turned all those years ago.

That's what a vampire is, a disease that intensifies instincts and urges to an inhuman degree. A primal blood lust. To be a vampire is to take what you want, feed on the weak, survival of the fittest, masters dominating slaves.

Remembering back to that fateful night when his life was destroyed while a nation was born. The death of Royce Grimsinger. He had been leaving a Masonic Lodge, a patriot and soldier of the revolution, proudly serving under General George Washington. That was a man of providence, he thinks, a man other men hope to be. Royce himself does feel something conflicted between the man he was then and the man he is now, they are nothing alike, that Royce was someone else. That Royce was alive. They have nothing in common except the same memories.

The vampire taps lightly on the window.

Ruby and Tiff both scream. Naomi didn't hear the tapping and looked at them confused and startled, "What?"

Tiff is hanging on Ruby's shoulder. A nervous chuckle escapes Ruby.

"The window," Tiff squeaks.

All three look at the coral eyes glowing in the dark on the other side of the glass. They are caught in the glare of those evil eyes. None of them say a word, transfixed.

Tiff stands and walks rigidly to the window. Inside herself somewhere she is vaguely aware that she doesn't want to do this, but the eyes are like a beacon calling her home.

"Don't," Ruby mutters.

The rapping on the window continues and a hoarse voice says, "Little girl, little girl, won't you let me in?"

"Tiff," Ruby stands stiff, eyes pooling with tears. A strap of her tank top hangs off her shoulder.

Naomi is equally paralyzed with fear under the iron grip of invading and unnatural will power.

Tiff unlocks the window with a quiet click.

"That's a good girl," Royce whispers hidden in shadow.

Tiff opens the window, lost and drowning inside herself. She feels a crushing, claustrophobic dizziness, her mouth waters as if she might vomit.

Royce holds his eyes open wide, unblinking, fighting to keep all his prey's eyes trapped in his. It is no easy task to enthrall three at once, but he's had over two hundred years of practice.

With steady, nimble reflexes and an iron grip, filthy Royce crawls through the window, never blinking or moving his steely gaze from the trinity of young women.

With nonchalant ease he draws a roll of silvery gray duct tape from his coat pocket and hands it to Tiff with a hoarse whispering, like the breath of a rotting corpses, "Bind your friends."

She stands holding the duct tape, unsure.

"Their ankles and wrists," he commands with hushed dominance.

Royce carefully removes his gloves one finger at a time as Tiff wraps the tape around the whimpering Naomi's wrists.

Naomi and Ruby are bound on the couch with duct tape over their mouths, wide and teary eyed.

Grimsinger takes off his coat and hat, settling comfortably on the couch between the captured women. Tiff stands white faced before him, a line of drool sneaking out the corner of her mouth. The television light flickers behind her to the sound of dramatic music.

"I hate these films," Royce growls, "I should hunt the writers and kill them all." He picks up a remote control from the coffee table and hits the mute button.

"Take off your clothes," he orders Tiff in a soft voice. He has no fear. He has not known fear for many years.

Leaning back on the couch, his long, thin fingers absentmindedly pet Ruby's shoulder. The skin is pale, the knuckles knobby, nail's as long as raven's claws. The cold hand slides beneath Ruby's shirt, fondling her breast. With a blinding motion he rips her tank top from her body. The undead beast continues to fondle Ruby, while his other hand finds its way under Naomi's shirt. He wants to rub himself all over these sweet, young women.

Royce Grimsinger studies the naked form of Tiff before him. Small breasts. She isn't as curvy as the other two but still a nubile beauty that drives the animal within. Thin lips. Dark gold shoulder length hair. Hazel eyes. A sharp chin. Thin, long nose.

It has been too long since he's taken concubines.

"Take off your glasses," he says with care.

As Tiff complies, she wonders why she can't see his face. It seems blank, featureless, blurry, except for the demanding pink eyes and white, reaching, sharp, ever grinning teeth.

"Suck my cock," Royce sneers.

Tears run down the duct tape covering Ruby's mouth as she watches her friend since grade school kneel before this violating stranger's parted legs. She squeezes her eyes shut, still hearing the sound of his zipper.

Ruby's mind races. There must be a way to escape. They have to get away from this vile man. She must break free. Her eyes meet Naomi's for some sign of communication. All she sees in her other friend's eyes is sheer terror. Tiff works vigorously, an obedient slave.

The frightening man lets out a shuddering sigh of pleasure and roughly pulls Tiff up onto his lap, kissing her deeply, an arm wrapped around her, fingernails digging into her bottom, drawing blood. The scent of the blood excites him more. With his free hand he flips Ruby onto her stomach as if she weighs nothing and cackles to them all, "The night is long, my loves. So, so long."

The only thing Ruby can think as he feels his chill enter her is that she doesn't want this. She doesn't want to be here. This can't be happening, but it is. He pounds into her with a fury, holding the limp, bare Tiff close all the while. "Suck my nipple," the blank smiling face orders the docile Tiff.

Hours pass as Royce plays and has his way with them. All three young women lay in an exhausted, defeated coil against his stone, cold flesh. The feel of his skin disturbs Ruby. She wonders why she can't break away from this man, even feels a shameful guilt.

"I love you," Tiff whispers earnestly. The first of the women to speak since he invaded their lives this hot, summer night.

Ruby's jaw tightens in anger.

Royce's fingernail slices the duct tape gag from Naomi, leaving a hairline cut, and rips the tape away. "I love you, my lord, my master," she cries, "Please, have me again."

Tiff watches his jagged teeth, thinking they look nothing like Sebastian's. Royce's teeth remind her of a shark.

Ruby tries to squirm away.

"Ah, fiery Ruby," Royce leans close enough for her to smell the rot of death on his breath, "I think I love you the most." With that his teeth painfully sink into her neck. The blood was so hot against his icy dead lips.

Ruby can't believe how much it hurts. It's nothing like it looks in the movies. She can feel her heart throbbing in her throat as he sucks with astounding strength. She feels her blood rushing into his greedy mouth. It hurts so much. She can feel nothing but the burning pain. It feels like she's falling as he slurps and slavers. Rivers of blood run over her body, down his face and chest. She dies in the bony hands of this nightmare.

Mason Orlando pulls his rusted out, beat up, dented, old Ford pickup into the driveway at the back of the house. The garage and driveway are only accessible from the alley behind the house. Before him the red and gold sun is setting over the roof and treeline beyond it. The garage is too full of junk to park inside of it. The truck's radio is set on an oldies station. Only one speaker works and it's blown, sounding tinny. He turns the truck off and the rumbling motor sputters and quits. He gets out listening to the engine tink, tink, tink under the hood as he walks toward the house.

"Eh," a man in his late forties with greasy, wiry black hair grunts at Mason, holding up a can of cheap beer, giving a brown toothed smile. His face is craggy, pockmarked, with a red nose with broken veins, eyelids drooping with drunkenness. "Have a beer with me, Mase."

"Maybe later, Wes," Mason answers, brushing dust and dirt from worn work clothes, blue jeans and a collar stretched t-shirt, "I'm beat. Hungry. Need a shower."

Wesley Jonadab is Mason's uncle. The brother of his mother. Alcoholic. He hasn't had a job in years, since before Mason can remember. Uncle Wes spends most of his time sitting at the picnic table in the backyard or down in the dingy, damp basement, chain smoking and drinking beer or whiskey. Whatever he can get his hands on.

"Ma made dinner," Wes returns his attention to his beer.

Mason lives in this little house with his Uncle Wes, Uncle Leroy, Cousin Eva, Aunt Misty, and Grandma Tasha. The Jonadabs.

Wes, Leroy, and Misty are siblings to Mason's mom, Liz. Wes, Leroy, and Liz all have the same father, Grandma Tasha's deceased husband. Misty has a different dad. Eva is Misty's daughter. She's still in high school. Mason's mom comes around from time to time, always drunk or angry or both. He'd prefer it if she just stopped coming around. It's always been the same. He was raised by his Grandma Tasha.

Misty has a job cleaning motel rooms. She's the head maid now. Whenever Leroy gets a job he usually loses it after getting the first paycheck. Sometimes the second or third. He gets too drunk and misses work. Grandma Tasha likes to drink too. Misty doesn't.

They mostly live off Grandma Tasha's social security checks and food stamps. That was until Mason quit high school four years ago and started working as a carpenter. He's twenty now, helping to support the family. He wants to get his own place but guilt keeps him here. Mason likes to drink too, but he's more of a weekend warrior. On the weekends he gets rip roaring drunk with the rest of the family or goes out and spends too much money at the bar.

The Jonadabs are a big extended family with a soiled reputation about Applegate. There are several aunts, uncles, cousins, and hanger ons who come over. You never know who's going to be sleeping on one of the couches or floor. On weekends there might be half a dozen kin sleeping here.

People around town call them white trash and Mason wears that label with a defiant pride. People can't hurt him with it if he claims it.

Mason has a three year old son named Spencer Lewis Charger. He keeps up on his child support and gets to hang out with his boy every other weekend. Spencer is a half-breed, his mother is full blooded Sioux, Bonita Charger. She was Mason's girlfriend through most of high school. Bonita cheated on Mason and Mason beat the guy up, ending up thrown in jail for his troubles. Bonita broke up with him while he was in jail. She got pregnant by that guy too. His name was Jason. Jason is history and Bonita keeps going through boyfriends like it's a hobby.

Mason goes into the house, the backdoor opens to the kitchen and living room, which are one big room only divided by the carpet ending where the linoleum begins. Family members are scattered about. Leroy is on the couch next to cousin Ryan. Ryan is Aunt Dena's son. Dena is the sister of Grandma Tasha and their dead brother George. Ryan's a couple of years older than Mason.

Grandma and Eva sit on a couch across from them. Grandma is sipping vodka, she doesn't share her bottles. They're all watching HBO on the television. Misty is in the kitchen washing dishes. Her hair is very long, black, and shining, hanging to her waist in a ponytail. She's dressed in blue jeans and a t-shirt with a buffalo head on it. Misty is a half-breed too. Skinny with knobby elbows, a long face and nose. She smiles at Mason, "I saved some dinner for you," she nods at the stove top without taking her hands from the dishwater.

"Thanks," Mason lifts a dish towel off a black cast iron frying pan. Hidden beneath are fried potatoes and a pork chop. He takes a plate out of a cupboard and butters two slices of bread.

"How was work?" Misty asks.

"Another day, another dollar," Mason says while pouring a glass of milk.

"Hey," Leroy bellows, he looks like a chubby version of his brother Wes. Wes is all skin and bones. Leroy has man boobs and a beer belly. His hair is shorter than Wes's. "What do you say? Buy us a twelve pack?"

"If you go get it," Mason says with a mouth full of food, sitting at the kitchen table watching HBO with them.

Leroy chuckles, he's always jolly and joking, "You gonna make me walk to the liquor store?"

"If you want beer," Mason takes a twenty dollar bill from his wallet, "Get me a pack of smokes too."

Grinning, Leroy asks, "I don't 'spose you got enough to get me a pack too? I'm gonna get my last paycheck from that asbestos job on Friday."

Mason takes another bill from his wallet, "Yeah."

"Alright," Leroy cheers, "That's my nephews!"

Royce sits on a red satin couch, arms spread out on the big cushions, legs propped up on a foot stool. A tall, full length mirror before him. Off to one side of the mirror an old television set inside a black entertainment stand. In a black silk gown, Ruby is curled up on a chair near him.

The house is rented in the name of Wade Suede, Royce's human guardian. It's an old tradition among vampires to have a human who wants to become a vamp watch over things while sleeping in a coffin during daylight hours. Royce's coffin is in the basement, along with three new ones for Ruby, Tiff, and Naomi. It's night and Wade is sleeping. Most often the guardians are discarded before earning the curse of bloodletting. He doesn't truly mind Wade, they sleep opposite hours so he doesn't have to suffer his company, and the man is obedient. He's thinking of actually cursing Wade, creating a coven of his own. Why should he continue to follow the traditions of those arrogant elders back in Eastern Europe?

Wade rented this house over a year ago, but they only moved in a month ago. Prior to that they were living in Spokane, Washington mostly feeding off homeless, prostitutes, and junkies. Royce always had bad luck in Applegate but just can't seem to stay away. There is something odd about this little city. Applegate. What a silly name. The history books say it gets the name from the orchards of the Appleseth's, but Royce knows the truth of it. He was here when it was founded as a little settlement, it was still the Dakota Territory then. The name has nothing to do with apple orchards and everything to do with the apple the serpent gave Eve in the Garden of Eden. That was a fiasco. The families of the Caldwells, Appleseths, the Madlands, the Somers, the Flowers, and the Jonadabs all fought with the Sioux Indians. That old medicine man, Painted Bear, cursed their families for seven generations when they killed him. That was the winter of 1875.

Royce didn't return until the spring of 1947. Most of those who'd known him were dead by then. That didn't last long either when that damned Hamilton Somers had tried to prove he was a vampire hunter. Royce's guardian was killed that time and he was invited to Romania by *the Order of the Dragon*. The pompous asses.

Like a fool he returned to Applegate in autumn of 1993 for revenge, but Hamilton was dead by then and his daughter was living with some sad looking man. Somehow she had warded her home in a way that he couldn't get close. He gave up and left.

Now here it is, a fourth return, the summer of 2013, and why? He was born in 1751 making him 262 years old and he's tired of hiding. This strange little city seems the perfect place to make his home for a while. And there is someone living here in particular he wants to kill.

The vampire stares in the mirror where his reflection should be if he were still human. He only sees the empty satin couch and feels as empty himself. He turns his attention to the television, "There is a reason I've come here," he nods at the screen, addressing Ruby.

It is an entertainment gossip show. The anchorwoman is interviewing Irma Imbrumia, author of the mega-popular teen vampire romance novels called *the Blood Moon Chronicles*. The books are now a series of sappy, popular movies. The latest of which Ruby, Tiff, and Naomi had been watching the night he raped and killed them.

"I don't understand," Ruby sounds bored, his fangs showing behind lips as red as a virgin's blood and skin as pale as the moon. It's different for all of them. Every vampire's curse is different.

"You will, lovely," Royce looks back at his absent reflection in the mirror. How is it that people have come to love vampires so much? There was a time when the mere mention of the undead evoked fear and dread. It is the appeal of the immortality and sexuality of the undead. Fools. It is a curse from

Satan himself. It is terror. It is gruesome. The legend of the vampire has been romanticized and perverted into something Royce can't tolerate. It is an insult to the afflicted. He will change this. Royce will make the world tremble and fear the dark again. Thinking of these romantic vampires stirs a rage within him. "I will teach you what we are, daughter. As my father taught me."

"Yes, master," Ruby says.

"My true father is called Taveda Pazos. He killed me in 1776, visiting from his homeland. Spain. That is where he resides now. He is more vicious than I. You do not want to meet him."

"How many of us are there?"

"Not many."

Ruby only looks at him with meek, magnetic eyes.

"I will teach you all I know. If you are loyal and survive, one day I may set you free. We are the children of Satan, Ruby. The first of our kind was Cain. We are sinners and killers. Denounce God, swear yourself His enemy, and our lord Satan may curse you to be one of the hungry undead. To walk the Earth, no longer welcome in Heaven."

"I didn't do that."

"No. You didn't. Humans are our lessers. They are food and slaves, nothing more. You and your friends were human. We do whatever I want to humans."

She only watches him.

He continues, actually fond of Ruby, "There are said to be four kinds of vampires. I learned this from the elders of the Dragon. We, the undead vampires. Astral vampires. Psychic vampires. And Star vampires. Astral vampires have no physical body. Psychic vampires suck the souls of others. I know nothing of the star vampires. The elders revere them."

"We are the undead," Ruby smiles, showing her two fangs.

"We are. Most of us are nomadic rogues hiding in graveyards, caves, and dark places. A few of us have joined together in covens. Each coven has a father or mother, the master. You are now of my coven. Nothing else matters but my will. Do you understand?"

"Master," she nods submissively.

"All coven masters answer to *the Order of the Dragon*. The Order exterminates all rogues who cause problems. They watch for worthy rogues to initiate, like myself."

"Dracula is real?" Ruby is dumbfounded.

"Very real. He is the grandmaster of *the Order of the Dragon*. Him and the others of the Order I know of. Elizabeth Bathory. Marquis de Sade. Nosferatu. Christabel. Rasputin. Below them are the mothers and fathers of the covens. Below us are you. Below you are the rogues. Below the rogues are humans."

Ruby listens intently.

"Vlad is the one who decided to bring order to the undead. In the 15th Century. His father was of *the Order of the Dragon*, supposed defenders of Christianity. When Satan chose Vlad he turned the Order into the bane of the Abrahamic religions." Royce smirks, licking his lips, "The goals of the Order have nothing to do with vampires."

Ruby is afraid of Royce and nothing else, "How do we die, Master?"

"We are already dead. You mean to ask, how are our bodies destroyed. Holy water and holy symbols will hurt us, but only if the wielder has a true faith in a God of light. Roses will always hurt. Garlic will turn your stomach. An iron or wood stake will paralyze us until removed. Fire and decapitation will destroy us, but that is all. Sunlight is unpleasant but it will not destroy us. That is all. We are immortal."

"Everything they say about us true? Except sunlight?"

"Much is true. Sunlight hurts the eyes, irritates the skin after a while, and we are stronger at night."

"Why do we sleep in coffins?"

"A tradition. Grave earth has healing properties, less so than blood. In time you will develop powers. It is different for us all. Some can turn into bats. Wolves. Rats. Creatures of the night. Some read and control minds. Hear thoughts. Some turn to mist. Some fly. There can be many things that come with age, but many of us go mad before that. Only the strong survive."

"What can you do, master?"

Royce laughs, "Never tell others what you can do, lovely."

"Why are you telling me these things, master?"

"You will be my bride."

Ruby crawls into his lap.

"Yes," he swoons, "Enough talk. Let's play and feed."

Ruby kisses him, "May we eat first?"

"Yes, my little devil whore. We will feast first."

They saunter together from into a bedroom.

In the bedroom Tiff looks up at them weak and pale, dried tears on her face, fright in her eyes. She is gagged and handcuffed naked to the bed, arms and legs spread, ankles and wrists bound to the bed posts. Naomi is in a similar state, unconscious, handcuffed to an old water radiator.

"Mm," Ruby gives a wicked smile, eyeing the bite marks and dried blood on Tiff as she climbs onto the bed. Tiff struggles and whimpers. Ruby takes her hard by the hair and sinks her teeth into soft flesh.

Mason loads tools into a worn out tool bag on the wood floor of an unfinished room they are working on. A brown leather tool belt is strapped around his waist. A hammer swings from the belt as he walks and he holds his hands out like a gunfighter so they don't hit the bulging tool belt. He's dressed in work boots, blue jeans, and a white t-shirt with the sleeves cut off the says *Ferguson Construction* on the front of it. There is a pack of cigarettes in the shirt pocket over his left breast. Steel toe boots tap on the sawdust covered floor as he walks about, tool belt jangling.

He balances a four foot level on his shoulder as he walks outside to his truck. This add on to the house is mostly framing and plywood with the beginnings of a roof right now. He sets the level, tool bag, and tool belt in the back of his truck. A company truck is parked next to his. Mason nods and waves at the driver, his foreman, as it pulls away.

Lighting a cigarette inside his truck, Mason looks at the setting sun. They worked late again tonight. The sun is mostly gone. He looks at the big house with envy, trying to imagine what it would be like to live in something like that. This is more than a remodel job. They're adding eight goddamned rooms and a bathroom.

Electricians and plumbers will be here to join the carpenters on Monday. Thank God it's Friday. Man, he just can't imagine what it would be like to have that much money. To live in this house. Part of Mason is annoyed, what do they do to deserve something like this and not him? He works hard, usually 50 hours a week. The owner is supposed to be a big deal, someone famous. That's what his foreman, Dale, said. A chick who wrote some books. Dale said she has a house in Miami and LA too. Wow.

The lights are on in the finished part of the house. They're home. Whoever lives there. It's not a mansion, but an old ranch house they're pretty much turning into one. Not far off is a big red barn in front of a grove of trees. A little forest that covers half the property. A double garage is attached to the house.

A fat black cat sits in the grass in the front yard of the house arrogantly staring at Mason with eyes glowing yellow in the setting sunlight. Mason notices a woman move past an upstairs window. In a ground floor window he sees a television light flickering.

Checking his pockets before starting the truck he can't find his cell phone. The truck itself actually doesn't need a key to start it, but Mason doesn't tell anyone that. Leroy or Wes or someone would steal it and probably either wreck it or get it impounded. "Damn it," he mutters, unable to find his cell phone. He realizes he left his lunchbox inside and his phone inside of it.

When he hops out of the truck the black cat darts from sight around the corner of the house.

Mason goes back inside and stumbles about in the dark, cussing, he knows it's on the west side of the site where they've been taking their breaks. It's getting dark and it's almost black inside. They are a crew of four carpenters and one clean up guy.

Ferguson Construction is a growing company. Glen Ferguson is the owner. He started out on his own when he got out of prison for selling cocaine. It's an American dream type story. Glen joined Narcotics Anonymous and has made himself rich with the company. Now he has about 80 guys working for him and keeps expanding. Mason wishes he had as much money as Glen too, but Glen is a pretty decent guy. He takes care of his employees. Gives out great Christmas bonuses. Gives them a big fat turkey every Thanksgiving. And pays better than most of the companies around town.

A woman's high pitched scream from inside the house cuts into the silence of the night. Mason stands perfectly still in the eerie quiet that follows. Nothing but the sound of a cricket chirping. A jolt of fear rushes through him.

He moves slowly and carefully back outside to his truck and takes a nail gun and hammer out of the back. There is no movement in the white glowing windows of the big house.

Mason isn't sure what to do. That was a terrible scream. Knock on the door? Shout? Go find his phone and call the police? That's it. What was he thinking. Go back into the job site and find his phone. If his goddamned hands and knees would stop shaking.

His instincts tell him something awful is going on. It was a shriek like he's never heard before. Burglars? A domestic dispute turned deadly? Damn it. Where did he put that lunchbox?

Mason fumbles in the dark, tripping over a two by four, grunts and cusses more when he hits the floor, dropping the nail gun and hammer, scraping his palms. Ow. A wood splinter in his palm. So much for stealth.

The front door of the house swings open and a woman sprints across the yard, down the long driveway toward the gravel road. They are in the country on the outskirts of town.

Groping blindly he finds both the nail gun and hammer. He gets back on his feet, thinking that woman must be the writer. A tall, thin man walks out the front door patiently following the woman.

Something about the man's walk, the gaping strides, disturbs Mason. It is as if the man is enjoying watching her try to run away. She looks back screaming, begging, "No! Please! Leave me alone!" She trips and falls, sobbing. The thin man continues at a steady pace.

Mason charges out of the unfinished addition to the house. The man is nearly upon the woman and Mason realizes she is in pain, wounded somehow. "Please don't hurt me!" She begs, holding her hands up to fend her assailant off.

Running at them without time to think, Mason simply reacts, adrenaline rushing, fight or flight. He's not going to let this man hurt that woman. His left hand raises the nail gun.

Thump. Thump. Thump. Thump.

The nails impale the man's back.

The man twists around like a snake attack to face Mason. He seems more angry than hurt. Mason's mind flashes through possibilities. This man must be on drugs. He lets loose more nails.

Thump. Thump. Thump. Thump.

Four nails in the man's chest and stomach.

Mason can't see his face. Only a wide grin and penetrating eyes.

The man roars like a wild beast, not the sound of a man Mason is covered in fear and sweat.

The man opens his mouth wider than a man should just as Mason fires more nails into him. Pink eyes and no face. Teeth like a shark. Eyes that rape Mason's soul. He feels all hope fade as those bright eyes begin to dominate and suffocate him.

Thump, thump, thump, thump, thump, thump, thump, thump.

The first nail lands in one of the man's eyes, a shot of pure luck, the tiny metal missile rips through the soft eyeball like gelatin and settles in the brain.

After unloading the nail gun into the man with the violating eyes, he throws the tool down, charging the still standing, staggering man, letting out a cry of some long forgotten warrior escaping from the recesses of his DNA. He screams in tribal rage bringing the hammer down on the man's skull. Blood splatters with the sound of a melon being crushed. The sound and feel of it makes Mason feel sick in his stomach. He swings again stumbling back and falling on his butt, hand gripping the hammer slippery with his sweat. Spots of blood on his hands and clothes. He vomits between his legs, partially on himself.

The woman stands witness to the killing, shock, hands over her mouth, "We have to go. There are more of them. We have to get away," she cries, hiccups, "They killed my children. My husband."

Mason pulls his shirt off over his head, using it to wipe away vomit and blood, "We have to call the police."

The woman ignores him, wandering down the driveway in a daze. Mason doesn't know what to do. Find his phone? Follow the woman? Instead he fetches his cigarettes from his shirt pocket and tosses the shirt onto the grass. He has to go inside. To check the children. They can't be dead. This can't be happening. He saw the children playing in the yard when he was working earlier today. They were running and laughing in the afternoon.

His mind won't accept dead children, pink eyes, and dragon's teeth.

Mason marches back toward the house, squeezing the blood dripping hammer like it's a holy relic. Shirtless, puffing a cigarette, thinking of his son Spencer and how much he loves him, regretting the way things ended with Bonita. He realizes he still loves her. When this is over he's going to hug Spencer and tell him how much he loves him and that he will always love him no matter what happens.

The front door of the house is wide open. Mason's blind fury takes him inside.

Inside Mason is staggered by beauty and horror. Three young women. He immediately recognizes one of them from high school.

Seen through the kitchen doorway one of the women is perched atop a table, blood stained blonde hair hides her face, as she is hunched over the limp body of a little boy clutched in her grip. Mason will never forget the slurping, gulping noise as she drinks from his neck.

All three women are dressed in ridiculous Halloween Gothic black clothes.

Another woman is on the couch in what seems to be a living room attached to a dining room. A man is spread out on the couch, head resting in her lap as if asleep. The woman hisses at Mason, head tilted in a dangerous, flirtatious hunger. The lower half of her face is a mask of blood dripping from her lips and chin. A clown-like circle of red at the tip of her nose. She's the one her recognizes. Ruby. She was a wild rich girl, one of the cool kids, one of the popular kids, a different social bracket than he and his friends. He had a hopeless crush on her. To Mason, middle class means rich. Does she remember him? She was a cheerleader who hung out with jocks and preps. He was a burn out that ran with metal heads and punk rockers.

Having remembered Ruby he realizes the third woman is Naomi. She stands off to the side holding a dead little boy up by his hair, feet dangling a foot off the carpet. His baby blue pajamas are soaked in red around the shoulders and down his chest. The dead boy's eyes stare hauntingly blank.

The room becomes a haze, he has tunnel vision. Outrage. Horror. He feels like he's not really in the room but watching this nightmare from somewhere else. The animal in Mason's soul takes control, knows it's all too real. The animal in Mason moves while the thinking and emotional parts of his souls rise up out of his body and the room. He looks down at himself, panting, blood dripping hammer. He feels humid and muggy.

Mason dashes into the kitchen, Tiff's head still down too caught up in feeding to care about anything else. At the same time Naomi drops the boy to the floor. Ruby blinks her eyes several times in recognition and whispers, "Mason Orlando." She remembers him. In high school she wanted to date him but couldn't even tell her friends she liked him. She was too embarrassed. He was poor and dirty.

Tiff looks up bearing razor teeth a thin curving line of bloody drool linking her chin to the dead man. The hammer hits her right temple shattering the bone around her eye socket, twisting her head to the side. A trail of blood splatters across the kitchen wallpaper.

Mason cocks the hammer back. Tiff shrieks red with rage. Her right eye was hidden and mashed beneath bloody flesh and broken bone. This time the claw of the hammer catches her other temple, digging deep, ripping flesh, blood, bones, and eyeball away as Mason pulls it back.

Screaming, flailing blindly, Tiff falls off the table and onto the floor.

Naomi grabs Mason from behind, fingernails breaking open his skin. She lifts him off his feet and throws him across the kitchen. His body slams into the refrigerator, putting a big dent in the door. He bounces to the floor, hammer clattering away, the fridge door swinging open.

Screaming and screaming, Tiff runs around the kitchen banging into the walls, table, and counter, lashing out, throwing anything she can grab. An eyeball on the floor next to the hammer. She presses her palms against her missing eyes and pulls them away, never letting up her screams.

In the living room Ruby looks sadly down at the corpse in her lap. In the kitchen Naomi stands over Mason who slips in blood trying to get up. Unheard over Tiff's manic screams she says calmly, "I'm losing you."

Naomi growls down at Mason, "I remember you," and kicks him in the stomach. Mason slides over the floor smacking the wall with a thump.

Looking up, faintly seeing her nipples through the fabric of her blouse, Mason giggles at the absurdity of being turned on by this killer. He crawls away in pain with no place to go, trying to stand, using the wall for support. He leaves bloody hand prints along the wall.

He tries to catch his breath, he's taller than Naomi. Her skin is jaundiced yellow, the whites of her eyes a cream yellow. She looks sick or dead, too thin, skin too tight, aged beyond her youth.

Tiff stops screaming, seeming almost mindless, she sniffs and searches with her hands finding the dead boy on the tabletop and returns to licking and drinking at his throat.

Naomi grins at Mason with sharp teeth.

"He's mine," Ruby is next to Naomi, Mason didn't even see her move from the living room.

Naomi growls, curling her nose in anger, yellow eyes glaring, "No more than mine."

With unnatural speed Naomi's teeth cut into his neck just above the collar bone, a sharp focused pain.

Ruby grabs Naomi by the hair and bites into Naomi's shoulder.

Naomi yells and her jaw lets Mason go. He falls back and catches his balance against the wall again.

"What are you doing, bitch?" Naomi tries to fight Ruby off.

Ruby lets her pit bull grip go and steps away from Naomi with a charming, blood soaked smile, "I will lie with him."

Mason bolts. He runs pass them all and out of the kitchen, out of the house without looking back. He doesn't stop until he reaches his old truck, only then does he pause to look back.

Ruby and Naomi walk joyfully, hand in hand across the dark lawn toward him, in no particular hurry.

Mason can't think. Panic. What to do? Escape. Survive. They are killers. Not human. Vampires aren't real. A stake through the heart. Fire. Sunlight. He's seen the movies.

There is only one thing to do. Run. Flee. Get away. He climbs in the truck and starts it without bothering with the key. It rumbles to life like a grumpy old man. He slams the gear in reverse, pressing the gas pedal to the floorboard. A cloud of dust, grass, and dirt spits up from the tires.

Naomi sprints and leaps into the back of the pickup. Ruby only stands, watching.

The truck skids sideways when it hits the gravel road. Naomi's fist shatters the back window out. Mason puts it in drive and accelerates. Naomi loses her balance and tumbles out of the truck, bouncing across the road and into the grassy ditch.

In the rear-view mirror Mason sees Ruby standing serene in the center of the road. He turns on the headlights just in time to see the nail punctured man walking along the roadside with his head half caved in oozing with blood and gore, dragging the woman by her wrist behind him. She looks dead. Mason sees all of this too late. The truck hits the man, smashing a headlight, sending the man spinning violently away. The truck bumps up and down as it drives over the dead woman.

The speedometer's needle is buried past 110 mph as he escapes back toward the city.

Mason pulls his truck into the driveway behind their house, shuts off the engine, and half falls out of the vehicle. It feels like his ribs are broken or cracked. Hard to breathe. Bruises and scrapes all over. He fights off the pain.

Leroy and Wes are seated on lawn chairs under the back porch light with a cigarette and beer in each hand, and an open twelve pack of beer on the ground beneath them. The lawn is more dirt and weeds than grass. They are laughing at something Leroy said, but both stop and seem to sober at the sight of the shirtless bloody approach of Mason.

Leroy jumps up, "Mason! What the hell happened?"

At the sound of his uncle's voice Mason begins to tremble and cry, falling to his knees, trying to say something coherent but the words are lost between sobs.

Leroy kneels down and squeezes his shoulder, "Hey, bro. It's alright. You're home now. We'll take care of you, man." He looks back at Wes, "Get Misty."

Wes runs inside the house in a drunken panic.

A moment later he returns following his sister Misty out just as Leroy is helping Mason to his feet. "Oh, my God, Mason!" She runs to support his other arm as soon as she sees his condition.

Eva stands in the back doorway with a look of fright on her face.

"Turn on the shower," Misty tells her daughter. Eva turns and steps in the bathroom.

As Leroy and Misty help Mason through the door she asks, "What happened, Mason?" Wes is at their back wanting to help somehow.

Inside Grandma Tasha is passed out in a chair. Eva's homework is set out, interrupted on the kitchen table.

"I don't know," Mason seems dazed, still shaky.

"Let's get him in the shower," Misty takes charge speaking to Leroy, who nods and helps guide Mason into the bathroom.

Eva squeezes out of the way and Misty says to her, "Wipe up any blood you see."

Eva nods and finds a dishrag hanging over the faucet of the kitchen sink.

"Hurry up," Misty ushers Mason to stand in the bathtub, "Just get in the shower," she looks at Leroy, "Find some clean clothes."

"Okay," Leroy steps out of the bathroom as Mason stands under the water with his pants and boots on.

"Just leave the clothes in the tub when you're done," Misty assures him, "Everything will be alright." She steps out of the bathroom and closes the door.

The warm water feels good on his skin as he watches the water pool and swirl pink down the drain. He sits, enjoying the water running over him, beginning to steam while he works his boots off.

Misty takes Leroy and Wes outside to clean any blood from the truck.

In the early afternoon the following day police knocked on the door of the Jonadab's house, not for the first time. Their family is known for having run-ins with the police. Three squad cars are parked in the alley behind the house. Three more are parked on the street in front of the house. Uniformed police and plain clothes detectives are at the front and backdoor.

Feeble, wrinkled, silver hair, Grandma Tasha opens the backdoor. She moves slowly, before she has a chance to say anything a mid-thirties, hook nosed, short black haired detective says, "Hello, ma'am. I'm Detective Dustin Krainock. We have a warrant for the arrest of Mason Orlando."

"Oh," Tasha responds, not trusting them, "He's not here. Didn't come home from work last night."

"We have a warrant to search the premises," Krainock explains with polite authority.

"You can come in and look," Tasha waves a hand, annoyed, "He's not here." She wobbles back to her chair at the edge of the living room.

Misty is at the front door letting more police in.

Leroy and Ryan are in the living room watching HBO. The television volume is low. Eva is at school.

The detectives interrogate everyone, asking many questions about Mason, repetitively, asking for clarification more than once, while the uniformed officers search the house from top to bottom.

In the dimly lit basement Wes stamps out a cigarette in a glass bronze ashtray, seated at the edge of his messy bed with thin worn and stained sheets, watching a small television propped up on a metal folding chair. There is a door size *Daimon Rapist* poster on the wall at the foot of the bed next to an old, dusty record player. A broken basket of dirty laundry is next to that.

One of the black uniformed police officers turns up his nose at the smell of Wes and his bed. The pillowcase and sheets look as if they haven't been washed in years.

The Jonadab's are polite, timid, and cooperative. After over an hour the detectives are satisfied that Mason isn't in the house. As they are leaving, Detective Krainock says to everyone seated in the living room now, "If Mason shows up, call us immediately. He's wanted for questioning in a homicide investigation. I don't need to remind you that harboring a fugitive and tampering with an investigation are crimes."

The family sits in silence watching the television after the police leave. Anxiety is in the air. Misty gets up and looks out the front window, Leroy looks out the back and says, "They're gone."

"Yeah," Misty agrees, "I'll check on him." She walks to the basement door and down the stairs. She enters Wes's bedroom, the door to his room is only a sheet hanging from the ceiling.

Wes nods at her, stands and carefully peels the poster off the wall. Behind the poster the drywall is cut and he removes it with effort. Inside the hole in the wall Mason is seated uncomfortably on a sleeping bag. He looks up at his plain faced aunt. She took the day off of work for him.

"You're all over the news," Misty crossed her arms, "They're saying you robbed some rich lady. Raped her. Killed her family. Burned down their house."

Mason's heart drops from his chest to his feet. He knew it would turn out bad. It always does for Jonadabs. Hearing Misty say it makes him feel like he's being sucked into a back hole, soul and all. He just wants to curl up in this wall and die. "I didn't do it. I heard the woman scream. I tried to help her and her family. I went into the house with my hammer. They were already dead. There were four killers. Three women and a man. I shot him with my nail gun. I couldn't save anyone. I didn't think I would be able to save myself." He shakes his head, wiping fresh tears away with the back of his hand. "I could see them from the highway when I was driving back into the city."

Misty sighs, "I know you didn't do it. Dale called this morning. I told him we don't know where you are. The police are gone." Wes sits on the bed behind her lighting a new cigarette. "Damn it, Mase. I don't know what to do. This is bad."

"I know."

"I know what needs to be done," Grandma Tasha labors to get down the basement stairs. She holds out a one hundred dollar bill to Mason when she reaches them. "Take this. We'll get as much money together as we can. Take whatever you need from the house. You have to leave town today and never come back."

Misty nods in agreement, her eyes misting, "You'll have to take back roads. North. You can sneak over the border into Canada in a day and a half. You'll have to stay in the wall until we have everything ready for you to go. They'll be looking for your truck. We'll find something else."

Mason gives them a reserved nod, "I love you guys," he chokes.

Leroy and Wes are on one old couch in the living room forever sipping cans of beer and nervously chain smoking. On the opposite couch Eva fidgets with her hair and Ryan uses a remote to aimlessly flip through television channels. Misty and Tasha are at the kitchen table sharing a pot of coffee.

"Ryan," Eva snaps at her older cousin, "would you pick something already."

"I don't know what to watch," Ryan complains, "There's nothing good on."

"One hundred-fifty channels and nothing on," Leroy chuckles.

Misty's cell phone rings and everyone is on pins and needles, all eyes on her, she answers it, "Hello," pause, "Hey, that's great. I will stop over soon." Pause. "Thank you." Pause. "Okay." Pause. "Bye."

Everyone is eager for the news.

"It was Cooper," Misty says, the tension in the room lightening, "I'm going over there now. He has a car for Mason."

"Nice," Ryan nods, dumping the remote in Eva's lap.

Zipping up a dark blue jacket Misty addresses everyone, "I'll be back soon and we'll get Mase out of here."

"Bye, mom," Eva says.

Wes just watches and Leroy waves and Misty walks out the front door and gets in her car. An old dark green Pontiac, leaking oil, one window doesn't roll up, another doesn't roll down, side mirror duct taped in place, rear-view mirror missing. Cooper is another cousin, a mechanic.

As Misty drives away she feels guilty because all she can think about is how much she wants this to be over with, how much she just wants Mason to get away. At the same time she's terrified of getting arrested for helping him, but she has no choice, because anyone who turns their back on family ain't no good.

In the basement hidden inside the wall behind the *Daimon Rapist* poster, Mason is sitting in tight quarters on his sleeping bag, pillow at his back propped up against a wood stud, flashlight on, using a gray utility knife to carve sharp wood stakes. Six in all. He's told no one of the vampires, knowing people will just think he's crazy.

Upstairs the other Jonadabs are still watching HBO. Leroy and Wes sipping beers, Wes's eyes are bloodshot. Tasha is sipping from a coffee mug. Eva is usually in bed by this time on school nights but she knows she can't sleep waiting for her mom to come back with a car for Mason. She's close to her cousin Mason, she doesn't want him to leave. She's afraid she'll never see him again but she doesn't want him to get arrested either. Eva wishes it would all go away and things are normal again. Maybe she can run away with him.

Ryan is pacing in the kitchen. He stops and looks in the refrigerator. There isn't much inside. A half gallon of milk. Eggs. Butter. Ketchup. Mustard. Salad dressing. Soy sauce. Leftover goulash in an old plastic butter container. It looks like the refrigerator hasn't been cleaned in a while. Crumbs on the shelves and dried splotches of something dirty yellow. He closes it and begins paces again, "I'm sure the cops are watching this place."

Leroy nods, red nose shining, "Probably parked down the street."

There is a knock at the front door. Eva looks up at the clock on the living room wall, it's midnight. She knows her mom wouldn't knock.

Wes stumbles up off the couch and answers the door.

A tall man in a dark jacket stands there grinning with the biggest smile Wes has ever seen, and strange eyes, "Hello, sir, I'm inspector Royce. May my associates and I come in?"

Ryan steps into the living room and stands next to the seated Eva.

"Inspector?" Eva whispers to him.

Wes nods, "Yeah, yeah, sure." He walks back to his place on the couch waving for the inspector to follow.

Old Royce Grimsinger saunters into the living room, wide grin, featureless face, sparkling eyes, such masterful mesmerism no one can see his face unless he wills it. Naomi, Tiff, and Ruby creep in behind him all dressed in scant black. Ruby is leading Tiff with a leash attached to spiked dog collar around her thin neck. Tiff's eyes are empty black sockets.

Eva's innocent eyes are caught in Royce's aura of dominance, she can't break free of his stare. His wounds from the confrontation with Mason have completely healed.

Ryan, Leroy, and Tasha don't know what to make of the intruders, it's obvious they are not police. Wes is in a daze from the power of Royce's eyes, his drunkenness weakening his will so that it takes little effort to keep him enthralled.

"Hello, ladies," Leroy gives a nervous smile and slaps his thigh, "Come on over here and have a seat."

Naomi lets out a low growl as she approaches Leroy, who's eyes widen at the idea of her actually doing what he asked.

"Who the hell are you?" Ryan puffs his chest like a rooster.

Ignoring the threat, Royce orders the young undead, "Eat them," never taking his eyes off Eva.

Naomi leaps into Leroy's lap, hideous fangs dig into his throat. Ruby yanks Tiff's leash, sending her flailing, clawing, and screaming at Wes. Ruby moves with a blinding swiftness latching her jaw onto Ryan's jugular before he has a chance to react, they hold each other like lovers in an embrace of death.

Grandma Tasha screams, throwing her coffee mug at Ruby. It bounces off the back of her head, splashing and bouncing to the floor.

In the basement Mason hears his grandmother's scream and kicks the sheet rock out, ripping the poster of his hidden cubbyhole. He climbs out of the wall, tucking wood stakes into his pants line across his lower back, keeping one in his hand.

Bolting up the stairs, taking three steps a stride, Mason charges out the basement door and into the kitchen. His pales with horror at the sight of Ryan sprawled on the floor, face down, a pool of blood spreading out around his head.

Ruby is ripping fragile flesh away from Tasha's throat with a wide eyed frenzy, one hand holding her silver hair wrapped in a fist. Mason yips at the sound of Tasha's neck snapping.

In the living room Tiff and Naomi are mounted on the laps of Leroy and Wes feeding from them, Mason can hear the sickening sounds of their licks and slurps. Royce is on the other couch on top of Eva, kissing and groping her, removing her clothing. Eva seems paralyzed with terror.

Lost in shock, feeling as if he is in Hell, dead and locked in nightmares of torture, the death of Mason's family is too much for him to bare. Too much to feel. Emotion collapses him, breaks him into blankness. Everything appears so crisp and clear. Everything is suddenly beautiful. The life of the colors. The bright red of the blood everywhere. The sandy pixels of the television screen. Lint on the carpet. Dust, streaks, and smudges about the kitchen floor. The frizzy strands of Tasha's silvery hair. Scratches on Leroy's thick glasses. The lace of Eva's bra. The cuticles of Royce's nails. The sounds of smacking lips and tongues lapping up blood. The thunderous sound and feel of his own heart beating.

Mason sprints, jamming the wood stake into Royce's back, just where the heart should be. By the grace of God he succeeds. Royce screams so loud it hurts everyone's ears before he falls silent off of Eva and onto the carpet. Unfortunately Mason put all his weight into the thrust and the tip of the stake punctured Eva's stomach. She's covered in Royce's warm blood feeling like fingertips dripping down her sides.

Without thought Mason impales Naomi's heart with another stake as she turns growling to face him, bearing blood and saliva dripping fangs. He presses so hard she is pinned to the couch and dies with a tired sigh seated between the dead bodies of his uncles Leroy and Wes.

Ruby steps away from Tasha, letting the old woman's body fall to the floor with a thud, wiping blood from her lips, she hisses, "I'm losing control again."

Mason gives her a look of hate, glancing back and forth between Ruby and blind Tiff. Tiff stands with her arms reaching out, seeking, sniffing the air, scarlet dripping from her mouth and running in little rivers down into her cleavage.

"Mason," Ruby says, sounding regretful.

Tiff cackles and jumps across the room at Mason. He tries to dodge her but fails and they crash together into the kitchen table smashing it, rolling on to the floor next to dead Ryan.

Climbing onto all fours, Tiff pants like a dog, her hot breath in Mason's face, her fingers digging into his shoulders. After a few hard, short breaths she stops, collapsing against Mason beneath her.

He shoves her body aside and stands looking down at the stake in her heart. Her own momentum drove it in. She looks hideous without eyes but the expression on her face is peaceful, the fangs are gone, she appears to be an ordinary young woman again. A dead young woman.

Ruby is gone.

Mason stands there looking over the carnage, catching his breath. It's too much to bear. Tasha. Leroy. Wes. Ryan. And surprisingly Eva are all dead.

He marches numb out to the garage and returns with a red gas can. He dowses Tiff in gasoline and lights her afire right there on the kitchen floor between Grandma Tasha and his cousin Ryan.

On the couch he pours gas all over Naomi and sets her on fire between Leroy and Wes.

Misty enters the kitchen through the backdoor, her face twisted in horror the sight of her murdered family, the fire, Mason caught red handed with a gas can. She knows he killed that family now. She knows he's killed their family. Her daughter. Her eyes are blinded by tears. She throws car keys at Mason, "What the hell is wrong with you! You fucking monster! You sick monster!"

Her nephew looks at her, a lump in his throat, the insanity of sorrow in his eyes. Behind him Eva moans and sits up.

The kitchen fire separates Misty from Mason and Eva. Misty is still shouting at him, but it's become muffled to his ears, lost in shock. He doesn't care to hear what she's saying, the curses, but in the back of his mind the word 'bastard' registers. He is that. He doesn't know his father.

The front door bursts open, kicked in by police officers charging in violently, guns drawn on Mason. Their black and blue uniforms and shining gold badges become a blur, he doesn't even register their faces as he drowns in their shouts. Faceless men like the grinning man. The grinning death.

There is a loud blast. Eva shrieking and sobbing. It feels like someone just hit him with a sledgehammer. The back of his head bangs hard against the floor and he loses consciousness listening to Eva crying out, Misty yelling and screaming, police barking, the crackle of flames, the static and tinny voices of police radios, the smell of gasoline and burning flesh, black polished shoes rippling in fire light.

The trial of Mason Orlando is long and sensational. It lasts three months and is in the local news and paper almost everyday until it's over with. Applegate hasn't had a mass murder like this since the Eli Caldwell incident in 1954.

Mason is charged with the murders of Tiff Sailor, Naomi Garland, Irma Imbrumia and her family, Leroy Jonadab, Wes Jonadab, Tasha Jonadab, and one John Doe (Royce Grimsinger). He is also suspected of killing Ruby Korte.

No fingerprint or dental records are found for the John Doe. Another mysterious aspect of the trial is the disappearance of the John Doe's body from the morgue. Inconsistencies are brushed under the rug, the public is outraged at the death of the famous author Irma Imbrumia.

Sitting in the courtroom, dressed in black and white stripes, Mason cried when his Aunt Misty Jonadab testified against him. They only made eye contact once while she was on the stand and her eyes were filled with a hate that cracked his heart in two.

There was much discussion of the death penalty, but the trial took a bizarre turn when Mason took the stand and told the full story of the faceless grinning man and vampires. He had to be kept in protective custody in the jail away from the general population. He was found guilty on ten counts of first degree murder but is sentenced to the Caldwell Asylum as criminally insane.

Adding to the unusual circumstances was the behavior of Eva Jonadab. She refused to speak to police the night of Mason's arrest and disappeared the following day. The police suspect that she simply ran away from home. She had been Mason's only hope as a witness.

A psychologist testified that after significant study he diagnosed Mason with extreme schizophrenia and psychotic tendencies. The doctor's recommendation was that he wasn't even fit to stand trial, having no grasp of reality, completely delusional. This was after Mason began telling stories of Eva and Ruby coming to his window at night.

The point came where even Mason began to question his own sanity, wondering if any of it was real, or if he had killed everyone.

Mason Orlando is still in Caldwell Asylum, a dutiful patient, taking his meds, participating in therapy, admitting that vampires aren't real most of the time, and that even though Eva still comes to his window some nights, she is only a hallucination.

Phantasies

"Every home has a house spirit," the lively old woman explains, "Every home whether it's a house or a castle or a cave or a hut. A guardian spirit that watches over the abode. You see there are many, many spirits in the world. The world is teaming with spirits. Different kinds of intelligence. Nature spirits. Imps. Hobs. Pixies. Sprites. Mischievous tricksters. Malevolent ones. Benevolent ones. Some love humans, some hate us, some are indifferent."

Bon Denbraven is caught in the rapture of the old woman's tale. She always says things that fascinate and illuminate. Her long gray hair is crinkled and frizzy matching her gray eyes. There seems an evident madness in her gray eyes but she is a friendly neighbor and bakes a delicious rhubarb pie. Always working in her yard tending her garden, trimming the grass, trees, and bushes, polishing plaster garden gnomes. Bon is fond of the colorful, stubby statues scattered about her backyard.

The woman's name is Renee Parish, a retired school teacher. Bon has been her neighbor since he moved into his duplex two years ago after finishing college. He nods for her to continue as she talks, giving her subtle cues to show that he is attentive.

Renee speaks with animated expressions, excited, hands gesturing for effect, "Often they are mistaken for ghosts haunting houses. This happens sometimes when the house spirit doesn't care for the tenant." She gives a quick sigh, "Sometimes it happens when they are overly fond of the tenant too."

Bon has always felt a bit sorry for the lonely old neighbor, ever since he learned she has children and grandchildren all too busy to visit her.

"Aren't spirits ghosts?" He asks.

"No, no, no," she answers, "Ghosts are spirits but spirits are not necessarily ghosts. Ghosts are things that have lived in the physical world, most spirits never have. Most spirits were never human."

"I think I understand," Bon chuckles, sipping the cold glass of fresh lemonade she's given him. Bon had just finished mowing his lawn when she brought him the refreshment. "I always enjoy your stories Mrs. Parrish. I'm curious as to what this colorful topic is about?"

One of Renee's eyes always squints more than the other, "If you want good fortune it's best to pay respects to your house spirit."

With a charming smile Bon asks, "How do I do that?"

"Acknowledge them. Talk to them. Let them know you respect them and share a common bond, your home."

"Why are you telling me about house spirits?"

Renee shrugs, "I thought I saw one in your window. Maybe not. I thought it best if I tell you about them. Not many people remember things like that. It would be better if they did."

"Thank you," Bon hands her the now empty glass of lemonade, "It was great. The cookies too. I have to get back inside, get cleaned up before Tanielle gets here. We're going to hang out tonight."

"That's good," Renee nods, carrying two empty lemonade glasses back toward her house, "What are your plans?"

"Not sure yet."

That evening Tanielle and Bon elect to stay home, get Chinese food delivered, and cuddle in the living room watching movies with the lights turned low.

They started dating in college when Bon was a junior. He's twenty-four now and she's twenty-two. Tanielle graduated in the spring. Bon has a degree in psychology and works at a group home for adolescents with behavioral issues. Tanielle is doing an internship with the state having a degree in social work. She and Bon will both be starting graduate school in the fall. Bon had no immediate plans for grad school, planning to take a couple of years off, but Tanielle motivates him, pushes him to do his best. They've talked about getting married and have decided to wait until they both finish grad school. Officially they are engaged.

Tanielle is the more outspoken of the two and takes the leadership role in their relationship. Bon is happy to let her. It's not a matter of dominance, but a matter of cooperation. They know each other well and compliment each other's behaviors. Bon the introvert. Tanielle the extrovert.

She is tall, thin, with small breasts, sandy blonde hair, a long nose which doesn't take from her beauty in the slightest. Blue eyes with humble confidence, a small town girl who moved to the city for school and work. Bon was raised in this little city.

The back of the couch they sit on is up against the wall that divides the duplex in half.

Tanielle's head is beginning to bob, fighting sleep. Bon never falls asleep watching movies. He's a movie buff. It irritates him when she falls asleep during good movies but he knows it's nothing to get upset over.

On the other side of the wall, coming from the new neighbor's side of the duplex, they hear a light knocking which begins to ascend into a loud, rhythmic banging.

Bang. Bang. Bang. Bang. Non-stop.

Tanielle's eyes widen and they look at each other with embarrassed grins.

"No," Tanielle whispers and giggles.

"I think so," Bon whispers and laughs back.

Suddenly they hear a woman's voice moaning with pleasure.

"Oh my God," Tanielle curls her nose, putting her hands over her ears.

Bon just looks at her with a big smile on his face.

Tanielle whispers, "Do you think they know we can hear them?"

Bon shrugs, "Probably not."

The banging and moaning grow louder and more rapid. The woman begins to scream, "Oh, yes! Yes, baby! Right there! Right there! Harder! Harder! Oh! Oh! Oh!"

Tanielle is blushing.

"Oh, I love you!" The woman cries out, "I love the way you fuck me! Oh, yes! Oh, yes!"

Bon's face is lit up, grinning, nervous, feeling dirty and aroused.

Still blushing Tanielle crawls closer to Bon, whispering, "Have you met the new neighbor's yet?"

"No," Bond answers, lying on his back, Tanielle on top of him, "We were at the Twins game the weekend they moved in."

She kisses him feeling naughty with excitement and they make quiet love so the neighbor's can't hear.

The next morning Bon makes French toast for breakfast with coffee, orange juice, and turkey bacon, serving Tanielle in bed. She has to work mid-morning but he has the day off.

Tanielle lives with roommates across town. Bon lives by himself. They've talked about living together but have decided to wait until her lease is up with her friends, to give them plenty of time to find a replacement roommate.

Bon doesn't have any big plans for the day. He's going to lounge. Play video games. Probably go for a run. Maybe do the dishes.

He is very curious about the new neighbors now. He wants to meet them and thinks it's odd he hasn't yet, they've been there almost a month. Bon feels a rush of guilt when he wonders if the woman is attractive. He is committed to Tanielle and always has been.

Later in the day when he does go for a run it's a gorgeous summer afternoon. Not too hot, just enough to make the run easy.

An hour later, slick with sweat, jogging up the sidewalk toward his duplex, Bon spots Renee in her yard tending her luscious garden. He smiles at the sight of her, visiting her always puts him in a good mood. Taking headphones out of his ears he waves, "Hi." And walks toward her, catching his breath.

"Oh, hello, Bon," Renee brushes dirt off her hands and gets off her knees to rest a moment. "How are you today?"

"It's a good day," he gives a pleasant smile, taking a seat in one of her lawn chairs, "How are you?"

"Can't complain. I made salsa last night. All from the garden. I'll give you a jar. I have more veggies than I can eat. I'll give you some. Tomatoes, onions, squash, sweet corn, and apples."

"Oh, wow. That's awesome. Thank you."

"They will just go bad if I don't give them to you."

"I appreciate it. I'm trying to eat healthier. Don't want to get fat."

Renee laughs, "That's a good thing. It's harder to stay in shape the older you get. It's best to start good habits when you're young."

Bon nods, "Renee, why did you tell me about the house spirits yesterday?"

Renee seems to study Bon a moment before answering, "Spirits are real and most people are blind to them. They flutter about like cobwebs in the wind."

"Huh," Bon doesn't believe a word of it.

"There are good spirits and there are bad spirits. I learned when I was a young woman to stay away from bars, brothels, and casinos because the bad spirits are thick in those kinds of places. Astral vampires, incubus, succubus, and the like. Go into any of those places and you will find parasitic spirits hungry for people to latch onto and feed from. They are searching for people suffering from weaknesses, sickness and hurting people."

Bon raises an eyebrow, "Bars, brothels, and casinos? Sounds like you were a wild child back in the day." He chuckles, not terribly interested in the topic. Still wondering why she is telling him things like this, wondering if she is getting senile.

Renee looks at her garden with a slight smile as if remembering her youth, then seems to snap back to the present, "Many Native Americans believed that when you get drunk and blackout a bad spirit takes over your body. All the peculiar and bad things done during the blackout are truly done by the bad spirit. Of course it's no excuse, one shouldn't be getting that drunk to begin with."

"I don't know about that," Bon admits his skepticism, "Honestly, Renee, I mean absolutely no offense but I don't believe in spirits."

"That's alright," she gives a smile of patience, "One day you will know they exist."

"Alright. Well, I have some cleaning to do so I better get inside."

"Oh, just wait," she holds up a hand, "Let me get those vegetables for you."

Bon follows her to her backdoor. At the same time the new neighbor pulls into their shared driveway. Bon looks with eager curiosity. A couple gets out of their black sports car without any emotion. They don't speak to each other. A particularly handsome couple in swanky dress, Bon imagines the dark haired man to some kind of banker or businessman in his dark gray suit and sunglasses. The man's hair is greased back, looking to be in his early thirties.

The woman appears much younger with short blonde hair, an elegant white dress, Very formal. Even at a distance Bon is taken in by her allure. She looks his way making brief eye contact before disappearing inside the duplex.

Renee reappears at her back porch carrying a brown cardboard box filled with a variety of vegetables from the garden.

Bon takes the box, "Thank you. Really. They look good."

"You're too skinny," Renee scolds, poking him in the ribs, "Need some meat on them bones."

"Ha! I'll cook a big greasy burger to eat with these veggies."

"I'm making stew this weekend," Renee offers, "There will be plenty for you and Tanielle."

"Sounds great. You are going to fatten me up."

Renee nods in a motherly way.

Changing the tone of his voice, Bon asks, "Have you met my new neighbors?"

Renee frowns, "Stay away from those two."

"They're jerks? You spoke with them?"

"We haven't been formally introduced. I know people. Just trust the wisdom of an old woman."

Bon nods, perplexed, "Understood."

That night Tanielle stays at her own place and Bon sits in his underwear playing a video game on his computer and chatting online with an old friend from college, sipping beer with the lights low.

He's been playing for hours and his eyes are starting to feel dry and buggy from staring at the computer screen for so long. He thinks it's probably time to get some sleep.

As he starts to shut the computer down the neighbor through the wall again. This time the man is yelling in anger.

"Look at you and your cute fucking face!" Bon finds the man's words and volume unsettling.

The man continues to scream and rant, "You're so fucking cute! Fooling everyone! You don't fool me! I know what a whore you are! I know you, you selfish bitch!"

Bon tiptoes closer to the wall to hear better even though the man is so loud he doesn't need to.

"I know the real you! A liar! That sweet, cute face is all a fucking lie! You stupid fucking whore!"

The maniacal tone of the man's voice frightens Bon. The man's voice is so savage, the intensity disturbing. The man sounds unhinged.

"No! You're not going anywhere!" The man shouts.

Smack.

It sounds like the man slapped her.

Silence.

The sound of footsteps walking away.

The quiet weeping of a woman.

Bon considers calling the police. The fight seems to be over. Maybe he should ignore it.

No. He has to do something. He has to call. He's afraid of the neighbor knowing he's the one who called the police so he steps into the bathroom and closes the door, turns on the ceiling fan, and dials the police to anonymously report a domestic disturbance.

After that he tiptoes back out of the bathroom and shuts off all the lights.

Why is he so nervous?

He gets into bed and listens before falling asleep thinking of the rage in the man's voice. That irrational, dangerous, violent, and cruel voice.

After several minutes that seem to drag on forever the police arrive at the neighbor's door.

The woman answers but their voices are too low and muffled for Bon to make out the specifics of her conversation with the police, but it's apparent she sends them away claiming nothing happened.

Bon lies in the dark listening to silence for a long time before falling asleep.

That night he dreams of horses. Dozens of gallant horses running together in the night. Hooves clapping the ground. Manes blowing like the crests of ocean waves in the night wind.

Sunday morning, the sun is shining as Tanielle parks in Bon's driveway wearing a bikini. She has shorts on over the bikini bottoms and big sunglasses. She and Bon are going to the lake today to grill out, swim, and sunbathe with Hattie, a friend from college, and some other friends.

At the same time the neighbor pulls into his driveway. When Tanielle gets out of her jeep she decides to introduce herself to the man, "Hi."

"Hello," the man greets her with dark eyes, naturally tan skin, and a suit and tie. She can't determine his ethnicity. His accent seems Spanish.

"How do you like your new place?" She gives a friendly smile.

"We like it," the man's smile is forced.

"Where are you from?" She asks innocently.

The man seems to warm up to her, his voice melodic, "Originally I'm from Peru but we've recently moved here from Australia. Sidney."

"Oh, wow," she's impressed, "What brings you here of all places?"

"Work," he nods, "We travel a lot. We'll only be here for two more months."

"What do you do for work?"

"You could call me a financial adviser."

"Cool. I'm Tanielle. My boyfriend, Bon, is your neighbor."

"I'm Moriah Hiler. My wife is Pearl. It's a pleasure," he shakes her hand.

His hand is rough and the grip is strong. She feels something like a shock of static electricity. Some odd tingling in her stomach and heart. Moriah is charismatic like a lightning rod. She swoons, feeling almost dizzy.

When he lets her hand go the feeling vanishes. She stands perplexed, unsure what just happened. The man has an uncanny magnetism.

"I must get inside," Moriah smiles.

"Me too," Tanielle nods still off balance.

Once inside Tanielle tells Bon about meeting Moriah and leaves out the strange sensation she felt.

Bon tells her about the violence he heard from the neighbor and advises her to keep her distance from Moriah.

"He seemed like such a gentleman," Tanielle says with disappointment in her voice, "That's messed up. I just can't believe it."

"Believe it," Bon says as they make their way to her jeep for their short trip to the lake.

Late the next night they are returning from their trip to the lake, both tired and sunburned, "I wish you wouldn't make fun of me in front of your friends."

"It's not that big of a deal, Bon," Tanielle defends her behavior, "They know I'm just joking."

"I don't like it when you tell them you make all the decisions."

"Well, I do."

"No, you don't."

Tanielle is a bit drunk, "Uh, yes I do."

"Regardless, it's something I'd prefer to keep between us. It's no one else's business."

Bon slows the jeep as they approach his house, both suddenly somber at the sight of red flashing lights brightening the darkness. Police cars, an ambulance, and a fire truck. A handful of neighbors watched the incident from their front yards.

"Oh, my God," Tanielle gasps as paramedics carry a body covered in a white sheet from Renee's home.

The jeep idles, a police officer with thin wire rim glasses approaches the driver side window, "Move along folks."

"We live next door," Bon points to his driveway.

"Alright," the officer nods.

"What's happened? Renee is a friend of mine."

The officer's lips tighten in sympathy, "I'm sorry. She had a stroke. She passed away. She called 911 but it was too late. I'm sorry. We tried."

"I understand," Bon says with sadness gripping his gut, "Not your fault."

The police officer motions for the others to let Bon through to his driveway.

When they park Tanielle says, "That's awful. So sad."

"It is," Bon agrees, thinking how quickly death can come, unexpected, swift and final.

Tanielle spends the night. Bon's sleep is restless, fitful. He dreams of Renee.

It's a sunny day and Renee is working in her garden wearing thick gray cotton gloves. Bon is helping her pull weeds.

Renee talks to him about the neighbor, "When he was a child the people of his village called him the boy with the blackest soul. Wherever he went he brought death and discord. A cursed boy. An evil soul. Not a human soul. Only a human body. His mother died giving birth to him. His father went mad and tried to kill him when he was still a child. The father sensed the evil that the boy is. He caught little Moriah torturing animals for pleasure. The people of the village didn't know, they protected the boy, killed the father. They thought the father was mad, possessed by a bad spirit. To their chagrin at the age of thirteen Moriah killed almost everyone in the village. He poisoned most of them. Killed the rest with a knife and his bare hands.

"The few survivors fled to neighboring communities to warn the world of the coming of the son of Ahriman born in the west. The boy began his pilgrimage. Forests, plants, and animals withered and died. Moriah left all black and rotten in his wake. His evil power was unleashed radiating plague and suffering about him. It took time before he learned to pull in his fury. Many died by his hand and heart in those early days. Still people die near him, such as I. But not like then when he was walking black death. Beware he will walk as black death again. He's only bored with death now, more entertained by discord.

"He is a harbinger of discord and death. The usher of the end. His pleasure comes from pain in others. A man-god of strife and misery, the hate of mankind. He eats love and sanity."

"What should I do?" Dreaming Bon asks as he continues to pull weeds from the garden.

"Pull weeds," Renee answers, "There are those who fight evil and there are those who fight for evil."

"I have to kill him."

"Bon! Bon!" Tanielle's stands naked at the front door of his house waving and smiling. Bon looks over at her feeling so much love. In the dream it seems normal for her to be naked.

"Bon! Bon!" Tanielle elbows him in the bed, "Wake up! You're talking in your sleep."

The vivid dream of Renee slips from his mind. He is in his bedroom sleeping next to Tanielle in the dark. At least he was sleeping until she woke him up.

"What?" He rolls away from her, annoyed, sleepy.

"You're talking in your sleep. It's freaking me out."

"Mm," Bon focuses on remembering his dream of Renee. The things she said about the neighbor. What a strange dream. "What did I say?"

"You were talking about the neighbor and Renee. I didn't catch it all, but it was loud enough to wake me up." Tanielle spoons him, "It's so sad she died."

"It is," Bon agrees, kissing the back of Tanielle's hand.

On the other side of the wall separating their duplex, Moriah sits in bed next to his wife, Pearl, who is filing her nails.

"What are we going to do?" Pearl asks only half interested.

Moriah looks over his wife, "I have no fear of this man. I will do what I do."

"Oh," Pearl says, "I hoped we would move. This backwater city is so drab. I was thinking of Paris."

"When we travel we travel with purpose. We're here to make a lot of money, love. That's what we do. Legal evil."

In the morning Tanielle gets up and decides to let Bon sleep in. She enters the bathroom in pajamas, with bed head, and sits on the toilet to pee, looking at herself in the mirror above the sink, eyes still puffy with sleep. Thoughts of Moriah stalking in her mind.

She flushes the toilet and brushes her teeth. Why are they so frightened of Moriah? Neither her nor Bon has come out and admitted they are. She finds it hard to believe that Moriah was the one screaming obscenities at his wife, but she knows Bon isn't lying. What was that nonsense Bon was babbling in his sleep last night? Son of Ahriman? Whatever that means. She takes her shirt off and looks over her red and white tan lines.

Turning on the water in the bath, testing its temperature before turning the shower on, she undresses and steps under the lukewarm water. Lukewarm because of her sunburn.

Obviously something about Moriah has caught their attention and she's just realized what it is for her, thinking back to that handshake, she is attracted to the man. More than just a little. She loves Bon. Undying and faithful, but she is so sexually attracted to this dark, exotic man. He's strikingly handsome with a sexy, deep voice and Spanish accent. Healthy thick black hair. He looks strong. She wants to have sex with him. She imagines having sex with him. She never will. Never would. Her hand slips down between her thighs. Her thoughts of Moriah excite her so much it only takes a few moments until she feels a rush of pleasure followed by the weight of guilt.

Tanielle puts her face under the water. Moriah is a married man. She would never cheat on Bon. It's just a phantasy. Bon must sense her attraction to Moriah, at least on an instinctual level. That must be why he was dreaming of Moriah. It makes sense.

After the shower she glances at the clock and realizes she's running behind schedule, she has to hurry. The drive to work from Bon's is further than the drive from her place to work. She looks down at her sleeping mate and decides to let him keep sleeping, then hurries out the door.

Dashing to her car, juggling her purse, coffee cup, and sunglasses, Tanielle drops her car keys on the driveway pavement. She cusses and kneels down to pick them up. When she stands she notices Moriah in the window on his side of the duplex. He is in his kitchen standing before an open refrigerator in the buff, seemingly unaware or unabashed by the fact that he can be seen from the window. She can't help but stare, frozen by the scene.

Moriah retrieves something from the refrigerator, closes it, and turns to walk away, catching Tanielle gazing up from the driveway. She immediately gets into her jeep, trying to pretend she didn't see anything, knowing she was caught by their brief moment of eye contact. She drives away making an effort not to look up at Moriah again.

Moriah stands in the window looking down with his charismatic smiles, watching her drive away.

Bon awakens feeling refreshed until he stretches and feels the sting of his sunburn. Why didn't they wear sunscreen? He sits in bed prepared to enjoy another day off of work. He hears Tanielle shuffling around in the living room. It sounds like she knocks something over.

"Hey, baby," Bon smiles, "What are you doing in there?"

The response is silence, the shuffling has stopped.

Bon stops smiling. Tanielle is supposed to be at work. Maybe it's an animal? A raccoon? A burglar?

He walks into the living room. Tanielle is not there. The floor is a mess with magazines, newspapers, and toilet paper scattered about. A lamp is tipped over.

The mess is the least of Bon's worries. He stands paralyzed with fear looking at the diminutive naked figure standing in the doorway between the living room and kitchen.

It looks like a little, bald albino man or child with red eyes. Completely hairless with yellow, sharp teeth, breathing heavy. Its head is more round than a human's. Skinny and bony with defined muscles standing a foot and a half tall. No ears. An upturned nose. Round eyes. A wide mouth. Four fingers and toes on each limb.

Bon and the creature both scream and Bon dives back into the bedroom, slamming the door behind him. At the same time the little creature darts into the kitchen.

Bon sits with his back against the door, crying softly, realizing his cell phone is charging in the living room. What the hell is that thing? Some kind of deformed kid? A mutated animal? A goblin? A gremlin?

Bon sits with his back against the door for more than an hour. He thinks of Renee and all of her stories. This thing is like something out of one of her stories. What's it doing out there? He can't hear anything.

Maybe he should check. Maybe he should call Tanielle or the police. The phone is in the living room. He hasn't heard anything for a long while. Or maybe he should call an exterminator. Or just kill the thing himself.

Bon looks around the bedroom and spots his samurai sword on the shelf in the closet. He takes it up and hesitantly opens the bedroom door. The living room looks the same, still a mess. There is no sign of the little albino invader.

Bon enters the kitchen. A box of cereal is spilled across the linoleum floor. A window is open and the screen is ripped out. Bon shuts the window.

Nervous and jumpy, he searches the entire house for the red eyed creature, checking every room, cupboard, every where it could possibly be. He decides it must have left through the kitchen window.

Bon showers and dresses. He cleans while he waits for the police to arrive. He's sweeping up the cereal when they knock.

The police look around and take his statement. Bon downplays the bizarre look of the little man and the officers still don't seem to believe him, but when they fingerprint the kitchen window and discover small prints they are convinced it was a mischievous child. Even then they don't seem to take his plight all too seriously, just a vandalizing youth. Relieved once they leave, Bon is annoyed with himself for making them a fresh pot of coffee.

With a sigh, Bon plops onto the living room couch to stretch, rest a bit, and hopefully salvage what's left of the day. Yet just as he finishes stretching there is a knock at the door.

With a second sigh, he grumbles, "Oh, course."

Opening the door he finds his neighbor standing there. Platinum blonde hair, nice complexion, radiating a brilliant smile at his look of surprise.

"Hi," she chirps, "I'm Pearl. Your neighbor."

"Um. Yeah. I've seen you. I'm Bon."

"Good name. Nice to meet you officially, Bon. I don't mean to be a bother. Oh, I noticed the police were here."

"The police. Yeah. Someone broke in my kitchen window. They think it was kids screwing around."

Pearl gives him an honest look of concern, "That's dreadful. Are you alright?"

"I'm fine. They just made a mess and ripped out the screen in the kitchen window."

"Do you think they'll try to break into my place?"

"I hope not. Just keep your windows locked."

"I've seen your girlfriend. She's very pretty."

"Thank you. She's my fiance."

"My husband's always gone. Working. We're still in the process of unpacking. I know we should be done by now," she gives a soft chuckle, "Seems there is not enough time in the day. Or the week for that matter."

"I know what you mean," Bon shuffles his feet, uncomfortable. He's picking up some kind of flirtatious vibe from her. An unwelcome one. He just wants her to go away. They stand there looking at each other momentarily.

Pearl gives him an unarming smile. So sweet and friendly, so damn nice. He thinks of that night he heard Moriah yelling at her.

"I hate to be a burden, Bon, but I have a huge favor to ask of you. I'd be more than grateful if you could help me."

"What's that?"

"I'm moving some furniture, or I was trying to, but I'm not strong enough," she giggles, "Would you be a dear and aid a damsel in distress? It won't take but a moment."

Ugh, Bon thinks, no, I don't want to help you and your weird husband, scratching his head, "Sure. That's not a problem."

"Oh," she puts her hand on his shoulder, "You're an angel."

Bon follows Pearl into her place. There are many potted exotic plants in the house. Many cardboard boxes. Black leather, cushy furniture. Clear glass table tops on gold legs with matching lamps. He noticed she bolted and chained the door when they came in. Maybe she's afraid because of his break in today.

"Have a seat," she motions to the couch, "Would you like a drink?"

"No, thank you," Bon answers politely, thinking let's just get this over with.

"I need to change into something else quickly. I don't want to scuff this outfit," she winks, "I'll be back in a minute."

Bon looks around the room then sits on the big couch. It's very comfortable. There is something weird about Moriah and Pearl. He seems an utter professional and she is a sweetheart. Both are very proper. Still. They might be crazy. Or something.

Looking around at their things he eyes a grandfather clock. A decorative globe of the world. An oil painting leaning against a wall waiting to be hung. A pendulum at the end of a table. A wine rack. He realizes this is a wealthy couple. Much too wealthy to be living in a duplex or even this neighborhood. They stink of money. Pearl is nice on the surface but Bon senses hubris beneath. She believes she is entitled.

He wishes they weren't neighbors, Moriah sounded like a vicious pig that night he was yelling at her. That memory still makes him feel sorrow for Pearl. No one deserves to be treated that way. Not even a spoiled snob.

A loud crack causes Bon to jump and forget his contemplation. His eyes almost pop out of their sockets at the sight of Pearl.

She has changed her outfit. Now she is wearing a red Nazi armband, a black Nazi officer's cap, thigh high black leather boots with tall, sharp heels. Black panties clipped by black suspenders stretching up over her slender shoulders hardly hiding her rosy nipples. She wears nothing else.

Candy apple red lipstick. A beauty mark near the side of her mouth. A long, black leather whip in her hand. She cracks the whip a second time with a devilish grin. Her body is an hourglass. He's frightened and aroused at the same time.

"What the hell?" He whispers, afraid to move off the couch.

Pearl marches at him, heels clicking against the floor. The whip snaps so close to his face he can feel its wind.

"What are you doing?" His voice cracks, sweating beneath his shirt.

Pearl crawls onto his lap, her knees boxing in his thighs as she quickly wraps the whip around his neck. "Speak to me meekly," she snarls in a thick German accent, "Keep your eyes low, Jew, and address me as Fraulein Werewolf!"

"Okay," Bon stares at her waist, feeling himself go erect, "This is insane. You're fucked up." He puts his hands on her shoulders to push her off of him.

Pearl screams in his face, tightening the whip like a python about his neck, "Do not lay your hands on me, maggot! What do you call me!"

"Hey," Bon chokes, trying to talk but the whip is too tight around his throat.

Pearl loosens the whip's grip, grabs his hand, and forces it onto her breast, "How do you address your master, vermin?"

White as a ghost Bon only looks at her and doesn't remove his hand. He knows he should but he can't find the strength to pull away.

"What is my name?" She growls close to his face.

He says nothing, hand on her breast, afraid to move.

Pearl licks his face.

Bon's other hand follows her to her other breast.

"What's my name, slave?"

Her hands open his pants and she mounts him. Bon notices a swastika tattoo just above her shaved vagina.

"What is my name?" She bites his shoulder.

"Fraulein Werewolf."

Pearl is surprisingly nice and polite when they finish having sex. She doesn't change or dress as Bon helps her move some furniture in a bewildered daze. They don't even mention that they just had sex or that she's dressed like a Nazi porn star before he goes back to his side of the duplex.

In the safety of his own home he sits on a recliner in the living room. He doesn't recline. He doesn't know what to think or feel. He loves Tanielle. How could he be so dumb? He's afraid of Pearl and Moriah. God help him. He just sits in the chair not moving. He can think of nothing else to do, feeling so low and ashamed. So dirty. He's a bad person and his life's about to fall apart. Too depressed to move he only sits there for a long time until the sun finally begins to fade from the living room windows.

Bon's cell phone vibrates in his pocket. He looks at the little screen. Tanielle. He answers.

Her voice makes him feel like crying, "Hey, baby. How was your day?"

"It was fine," he answers in a flat voice.

"What's wrong?"

"Nothing. I don't feel good."

"You're sick?"

"Yes. I think I am."

"Oh, poor baby. Need me to come over and take care of you tonight?"

"No. That's okay. I'm too sick. I'm just going to try to sleep it off. I still need to go to work tomorrow."

"Alright," she sounds worried and disappointed, "You get some rest. I'll be at your place when you get off work tomorrow. I'll make dinner. What do you want to eat?"

"I don't know. I can't think about food right now. Surprise me."

"I hope you feel better, Get some sleep. You sound awful."

"I will."

"I love you."

"I love you too."

"Bye."

"Bye."

Bon hangs up the phone and decides to go to bed. He's too depressed to do anything else. If Tanielle finds out he had sex with Pearl she will leave him. She's not the kind of woman to forgive something like that. What's worse is that Bon can't lie to Tanielle. She'll know. He doesn't want to lie to her either. The right thing to do is tell her the truth. He'll tell her the truth after work tomorrow. It is in the hands of fate now.

Just as Bon is settling into bed there is a loud, angry banging at his door. With a resigned sigh he goes to answer it.

It's Moriah.

His dark eyes red with rage. A vein in his temple is visibly throbbing. Jaw grinding. Knuckles white.

Bon feels meek as a mouse wanting to curl up and hide, to withdraw within himself.

"You fucked my wife," Moriah points, poking him in the chest hard with his finger, actually hurting Bon and forcing him to take a step back.

Bon is speechless.

Moriah shakes his head, visibly calming, "You're barely a man. That's the worst part of it. You're so weak. I could break you with my hands."

Bon feels his hands tremble with fear, he can't find the courage to say anything, Moriah is much bigger than him, he radiates violence and power.

Moriah snickers, "Bon, I'm going to fuck your woman. It seems just. Don't you agree? I'll take her from you." He pauses for a response, getting none he continues, "It will be good for her to be fucked by a man."

Moriah walks away.

Bon shuts the door and just stands there, trembling and sweating. Tomorrow at work he's going to read the classified ads in the newspaper and find a new place to live. Screw his lease. He can only hope Tanielle will still be with him when all is said and done.

There is no way Tanielle would sleep with Moriah. The thought of it, the mental image flashing in his mind, angers him. Jealousy rises. Why didn't he say anything to Moriah? He should have told Moriah to get lost. He can think of a hundred things to say now that he's gone. He should have fought him. He should have grabbed his poking finger and broke it. He should have told him he enjoyed fucking his psychotic wife.

Those are some of Bon's thoughts as he drifts to sleep.

The next day Tanielle decides to leave work early so she can make dinner for Bon. He sounded so sick and pitiful on the phone. She's going to clean his place for him and make some homemade chicken noodle soup, her grandmother's recipe.

And she does just that.

Bon decides to leave work early, going home sick. He didn't sleep well last night and hasn't since the Hilers moved in next door.

Tanielle is at Bon's place. The soup is on the stove. She finishes vacuuming. When she shuts the vacuum off she hears the neighbors having sex again through the wall. She hears what sounds like a bed pounding against the wall and a woman's moans of, "Oh, oh, oh."

She sits on Bons bed feeling embarrassed and guilty for listening to the sounds of their love making, yet she's aroused like in the shower the other morning. She imagines Moriah again. Naked. His hard body against herself. Inside of her.

On the other side of the wall she hears Pearl scream, "Oh, yes. Push it! Yes!"

Tanielle finds herself lying back on the bed, slipping her pants off, touching herself beneath her panties. The muscles in her legs tighten. Eyes closed, listening to the sounds of sex beyond the wall, imagining it's her that Moriah is on top of. She is lost in phantasy.

Bon gets home from work, feeling miserable, dreading his confession to come, he saw Tanielle's jeep parked outside so he knows she's there. He pauses to smell the soup, then walks from the kitchen into the living room and hears the sounds of Moriah and Pearl having sex again next door.

He stops in the living room shocked by the sight before him. He can see Tanielle through the open bedroom door masturbating on his bed. Ejecting from her vagina is a cloudy white substance, ectoplasm, floating in the air. The white substance is taking a humanoid form. A haunting face, feminine, exaggerated, morphing, a neck and shoulders, a white milky body made of thick ectoplasm.

Tanielle continues rubbing herself seeming lost in a sexual trance. The ectoplasmic woman, attached by an umbilical cord like smoke coming from Tanielle's vagina, looks at Bon with an expression of recognition. Bon walks cautiously into the bedroom, Tanielle unaware of his presence, the white ectoplasm woman watches him.

Standing on the carpet, knee high to Bon, is the little albino man, skin white as paper, big round red eyes looking up at the ectoplasm woman with a childlike expression of curiosity.

The ectoplasm woman reaches long, thin fingers out toward Bon and he realizes he is looking at a distorted version of Tanielle. It speaks to him over the shallow, exciting breathing of Tanielle and the neighbors grunting, "Ego sum sponsa caeli."

"What?" Bon asks her, knowing in his heart that he's speaking with Tanielle.

"Te amo, Bon."

He reaches out, gently touching her ectoplasm cheek. Her head moves toward his hand in a loving way. The substance of her feels nice against his hand, soft, wet, dry, sticky, cool and warm all at once.

On the bed Tanielle lets out a cry, her body shuddering in a long orgasm, at the same time Bon hears Moriah and Pearl climaxing on the other side of the wall. Her shuddering ripped the smoky umbilical cord free of her vagina. The white woman smiles sadly at Bon as she flutters quickly up through the ceiling and out of his sight. All that follows is silence and stillness.

The skinny little albino creature gives Tanielle on the bed a forlorn look, a single tear dripping down its pale cheek.

Bon moves to the bed next to Tanielle. She's not breathing. "No, Tanielle," he shakes her, "Wake up! Wake up!"

The tiny albino bows its head respectfully.

"Oh, no," Bon laments, "No, no, no. It's alright," he takes her dead body in his arms, hugging her on the bed next to him, crying hysterically, "It's alright. You're alright."

The white skinned creature begins to quietly exit the room.

"Wait," Bon begs, wiping his face with his hand, "Please, tell me what happened."

The ugly thing looks at him sympathetically, considering, then answers, "Es war der Bose. Die schwarze Seele. Moriah." His tiny hand points to the wall Bon shares with the neighbors and then walks away, disappearing in the living room.

Bon lets him go. He now knows what the creature is. A house spirit like Renee told him about. He is ugly and creepy but good. What else could it be?

In his heart Bon knows what has transpired. Moriah made good on his threat. He took Tanielle away from him forever. He knows what he must do. Life is more clear than it has ever seemed before. Bon feels calm and content, destroyed and reborn by the death of Tanielle. Content because he has an important purpose to go on living for the moment. Holding her tight, kissing her many times, a hand cups her breast, and he considers making love to her one last time, but decides against it because he knows that it was Tanielle that floated away.

Rising from the bed a new man made hard by death and loss. Moriah accused him of not being a man. Of being weak and meek. Bon goes to the bedroom closest, digging back into the shelf above his head. He is going to show Moriah what he is.

Bon takes the long, black sheathed samurai sword from the closest. When he'd bought it at a renaissance festival a few years ago Tanielle had teased him, calling him a nerd. It's true. In his youth he was proud to be a nerd. It was all computer games and comic books. He'd always wanted a sword, even if only because they look cool. He'd wanted one since he was a kid. He remembers when Tanielle called him a nerd she immediately apologized seeing the hurt in his eyes. She said she was sorry and loved him no matter what. Bon knows she meant it. She loved him unconditionally like no one has ever loved him before or likely will again. Now Moriah and his crazy wife have taken that from him. He can't get it back but he can stop them from ever hurting anyone else again. He knows Moriah is one of the evil spirits Renee had tried to teach him about.

Ceremoniously, Bon removes his shirt and shoes, kneeling before the body of his dead fiance and the samurai sword. A katana. He draws it from its sheath. The blade is mirror silver and razor sharp, stainless steel.

He says a prayer of thanks to the house spirit, and prays to God and Renee to take care of Tanielle's soul, and he prays for strength, courage, and guidance to do this one thing. Let me do this one thing, God, and I swear to You I will forever be your servant. I will do what you will me to do, Lord.

With that he stands, sword in hand, and walks out the front door of his house, looking about, hoping none of the other neighbors notice him standing there with a weapon.

Pearl answers the door in a sheer black nightgown, a glass of wine in her hand. Even without makeup Bon can't deny her beauty, but her heart is as black as Moriah's.

"Bon," she purrs, "It's good to see you. If you've come for seconds it's not a good time. My husband's home."

A stone, stoic expression, Bon replies, "I'm here for Moriah."

Pearl smiles seductively at the sword in his hand, the bare chest and feet, "Then come in valiant knight." She disappears inside, leaving the door open for Bon to follow. Her nightgown flows like a cape in the breeze.

She strolls right past her husband who is seated in a black leather chair, a smoking pipe between his lips, legs propped up on a stool, dressed in a maroon robe, a book open in his lap, wine glass at his side, barefoot. *Miracles* by *Jefferson Starship* plays on a stereo. The aroma of the pipe smoke is strong and pleasant.

"Ah, Bon, my boy," he closes the book and puts his bare feet down on the floor, "What a curious surprise," a half cocksure smile on his face, eyeing Bon's samurai sword. He holds the thin book up before setting it down next to his wine glass with the pipe, Sun Tzu's *Art of War*. A masterpiece. Have you read it?"

Bon only glares at Moriah, hand squeezing the hilt of his sword, fighting to restrain himself, fighting for the courage to strike. A new song starts playing on the stereo, *Without You* by *Harry Nilsson*.

Pearl sits on the couch amused by the exchange, feet off the floor, sipping her red wine.

"Pearl," Moriah says, "Be a doll and fetch my sword."

Pearl gives Bon her devilish grin and marches into the bedroom returning with a curved scimitar.

Bon doesn't care. Doesn't take his eyes off the dark and handsome Moriah.

Moriah stands, testing the balance of his sword with a practice swing, smiling at Bon with a new found respect and easy confidence, "This may be one of the most beautiful moments of my life."

Pearl stands back by the bedroom door, licking her lips in anticipation.

Bon holds his long samurai sword before him, not at all skilled in swordplay, never really having used it before.

Moriah takes a fighting stance and a few more practice swings showing off intimidating talent and grace, never breaking eye contact with Bon.

They stalk around each other like hunting tigers. A slow dance of foreplay.

"Strike me, Bon," Moriah dares, "I've already cut out your heart."

The tiny albino creature peeks out from behind the black leather couch and scurries to the stereo. The little ugly house spirit reaches up and presses the repeat button with his scrawny finger and giggles.

Bon swings wildly, frantically, several times. Each blow is parried by Moriah's scimitar with effortless ease. The swords clank when they come together.

Anger overtakes Bon, frustration, stabbing at Moriah, striking over and over again with no success, he knocks a lamp off a glass tabletop.

Moriah doesn't bother to attack, playfully dancing about, swatting Bon's sword away with a delightful smile, seeming able to predict all of Bon's attempts.

Bon's arm is growing tired, he's sweating, breathing hard.

With two quick strokes Moriah slashes each of Bon's cheeks, drawing blood, like red lines of tears stretching from his lower eyelids to his jaw. He dances around the room, Bon spinning to keep up, to defend against Moriah's attacks. He fails.

Moriah's sword cuts a bloody gash across Bon's shoulder blades making a large red X on his back.

Bon manages to block one of the four next blows, but Moriah keeps moving, around and around, slashing Bon, teasing, cutting his skin open in dozens of places over his chest, back, legs, and arms. Each drawing blood deep enough to scar. Blood runs in little rivers all down Bon's body. Droplets of blood spatter the floor and furniture.

Pearl is in the bedroom doorway, thoroughly entertained, hands together before her nose and mouth as if cheerfully praying.

Bon has tears running down his cheeks mixing with the blood, understanding that he can't win this fight. Moriah deserves to die, but Bon doesn't have the power to do it. Moriah can kill him whenever he's ready to.

Moriah leaps onto the glass coffee table, swinging down hard, Bon surprises himself by blocking the attack, but the sword vibrates again, hurting his hand so much he drops the katana to the floor.

Moriah laughs, holding the tip of his sword to Bon's adam's apple, pricking just enough to draw more blood. "Turn that damn stereo off repeat please Pearl."

Bon holds his arms out in surrender.

"This is over," Moriah says, "Not a waste. In the last moments of your life you've discovered there is a man buried beneath the mouse. I only had to dig him out. A pity Tanielle didn't have the opportunity to meet the man before she died. You know I fucked her to death with black magic. I always enjoy the orgasm of death."

Bon clenches his jaw, angry at Moriah's words, angry he killed Tanielle, angry he is going to die by Moriah's sword.

Moriah shrugs, "Any last words?"

Bon only stares in defiance.

"Oh, Bon," Moriah laughs, "I am truly impressed. You're not afraid to die. I can see it in your eyes. We have made a man of you. Very well! I give you three options. I can kill you quickly right now. You can pick up your sorry excuse for a sword and nobly kill yourself right now. Or you may take up your sword and fight me! Either way you die with dignity! Like a warrior! I must warn you. If you choose to fight on I will bleed you out ever so slowly. I will make you suffer before you die." He takes the sword away from Bon's throat and winks at him, "Make your choice."

The albino, hiding behind a chair, shakes his head with sympathy at Bon.

Pearl looks like she feels sorry for Bon.

Cautiously squatting to pick up his fallen sword, keeping his eyes on Moriah and his scimitar. As soon as Bon is standing upright again Moriah makes two more slashes low across Bon's stomach.

Bon arches his sword arm back for an overhead strike.

Moriah puts his sword tip to Bon's neck a second time, bellowing, "This is too easy! I should just put you out of your misery like the lame dog you are!"

Just as *Harry Nilsson* sings out from the stereo, *I can't live, if living is without you!* Bon grabs Moriah's sword tip with his free hand. The blade cuts into his palm and fingers. Moriah's eyes go wide as Bon's sword sweeps down at him.

Moriah sidesteps and avoids the samurai blade all together, but the sword smashes the glass tabletop, it shatters into a thousand tiny diamonds. He falls through the tabletop landing like a tripod on one hand and both knees. Many tiny shards of glass imbed his flesh.

Moriah jerks his sword from Bon's grip, severing the pinky finger completely. In that same moment Bon's sword comes back up, catching Moriah beneath the armpit of his sword arm, cutting deep.

Grunting in pain, Moriah struggles to lift his sword arm with the gaping wound bleeding out beneath his arm.

Bon's sword sweeps across slashing Moriah's throat open. Blood rushes out. Moriah looks at Bon, trying to speak, looking like a fish out of water, as if he doesn't understand what just happened.

Pearl squeaks.

Bon drops to his knees exhausted.

Moriah falls to a bed of broken glass on the floor.

Pearl looks angry, but not distressed over Moriah's death, "Get out of my house."

Bon points his bloody samurai sword at her.

"You killed a son of Ahriman. No one will know this happened," she is undaunted by his threat.

The little albino creature walks to Bon and pats his hand, motioning for them to leave. He carries Bon's severed finger in his other hand.

Bon lowers his sword and follows the house spirit back to his side of the duplex.

When the police arrive Pearl and Moriah's body are gone.

It is determined that Tanielle died of unknown natural causes. The entire incident makes the news. Bon isn't charged with anything in the end since there is nobody. It doesn't take long for the story to be forgotten and just becomes another strange urban legend of Applegate.

The landlord moves Pearl and Moriah's things out. The house spirit disappears but Bon still thinks he senses it from time to time. The only thing left to remind him that it happened is a body covered in hideous scars. Every time he looks in the mirror at the two ugly pink scars stretching down his cheeks he is reminded of Tanielle.

Secret People

Ethan looks at his cell phone again, excited for her to text or call. Disappointed, he tucks it back into his pocket, feeling foolish. It's only been ten minutes since he last looked and the phone would ring if someone were to text or call. On the occasions she does text or call he can't help beaming.

Jaden Jasmine is her name. An unbelievable bird. A tall drink of water. Deep ginger hair. Eyes of azure. Hip absolute. Jaden Jasmine. Charismatic and sizzling. Bright and colorful tattoos up and down her arms. A face that defines symmetry. She looks and talks and sways like a golden age jazz singer. So much style, so much swagger. She knows she's hot and flaunts it with the sweep of her hips. A looker and head turner.

And now she's dating Ethan Ellery.

Jaden is so super cool Ethan always feels like an insecure, fumbling high school boy trying to cop a feel for the first time. He's a reputation of being a real ladies man, a lady killer, but Jaden just kills it with presence.

In his thirties now, Ethan thinks it's time for this old player to cash out and settle down. Retire from the night life and the scene. He couldn't pick a better woman than Jaden.

By the end of the work day she still hasn't contacted him and he's wondering why not. His last text to her was the day before yesterday. They've been talking and spending time together, everything seeming more than fine. In that final text he asked her if she wanted to hang out tonight and she responded with a yes. In that last text he asked her what time and there has been nothing but silence since.

Ethan has always been a worrier and tells himself that's what he's doing now. Over analyzing. She's probably just been too busy to get back at him. Hopefully nothing's happened, like a car accident or illness.

Or maybe she's decided she doesn't dig him anymore? Doesn't want to date him? Doesn't want to hang out? Just wants to be friends?

Why wouldn't she just tell him that if it is the case? It seems like a humane thing to do. Not to leave him hanging and wondering. Not knowing is the worst.

Ethan says goodbye to his co-workers and heads for home. It's a twenty-five minute drive. He zones, listening to music, puffing a cigarette, wishing he didn't smoke. *Atlantis* by *Donovan* plays from the car stereo.

Ethan is a daydreamer. Daydreaming about Jaden and a fantasy future together. Just kicking it, falling in love, becoming closer, more intimate, laughing, smiling, confiding, making love, maybe marriage.

When Ethan gets home he waves at his neighbors as he unlocks his door, old Renee, sitting out by her garden visiting with that conceited couple, Tanielle and Bon, who live in the next house over.

Inside the first thing he does after flipping the lights on is turn on music. He's a music lover. The house is filled with the sound of *the Violent Femmes* performing *Good Feeling*. He eats cold pizza for dinner, shaves, and showers. He sings along in the shower. Getting out and dancing while he dries off. Now *Blister in the Sun* by the same band. He sings to himself in the mirror.

Ethan's made a decision. Jaden didn't say what time to come over, but she did say to come over. So he is going to show up. When the sun begins to set. That's night. She agreed to hang out tonight.

He curls weights, dances, sings, smokes cigarettes, keeping an eye on the clock.

The other week Ethan and Jaden were at a bookstore together, browsing, sipping coffee. When Ethan stepped away a young man, unseen, approached Jaden and poked her shoulder with a single finger, startling her. Ethan observed, perplexed.

The man explains with a suave smile, "I wanted to make sure you're real."

Jaden only laughed and walked away. Ethan felt a sting of jealousy but understood the man's inquiry. He feels pressure to always be on his toes, always on guard, and always do his best to deserve the angel Jaden.

The first evening Jaden and Ethan spent together they sip wine straight from the bottle and listened to Nina Simone until the sun came up and they fell in bed together. She whispered love in his ear and begged him to hold her tighter as they drifted into satisfied slumber. That was over a month ago. They've been on fire ever since.

At least until two days ago when she stopped responding to him. Maybe he shouldn't go see her tonight. No. He likes her too much. There must be an explanation. He's going to see her tonight. Ethan sends her a text message, *Hey, pretty girl, I'm on my way*. He sits staring at the phone in his hand for a few minutes. Ten minutes pass. Screw it. Warrior up. He's going. Maybe she lost her phone.

The drive to Jaden's place is relatively short, she doesn't live far from his house. The sun is just down as he pulls up in front of her house. Her black car is parked in the driveway. The lights in her house are dim. For a moment Ethan wonders if he should go to the front or backdoor. In the past he's always gone through the backdoor. He feels nervous fluttering in his stomach walking up the driveway to her backyard. Anticipation. Fear of rejection. Excitement. The faint sound of a radio murmuring from the open garage.

Ethan turns the corner to the backyard and there she sits alone in all her gorgeous splendor. Jaden Jasmine. Her back to him, sitting at her small outdoor table under the porch light, a cigarette in hand, bottle of beer in the other. He stands for a moment wondering what she's thinking.

"Hey," Ethan announces himself.

Jaden looks back at him with a half smile, "I thought I heard a car door."

Relieved by the sight of her, Ethan takes a seat in the chair at the opposite side of the table. "I didn't know if I should come. You didn't answer my text the other day."

"Maybe you shouldn't have," she gives a smug shrug.

"Oh." Ethan is startled, uncomfortable. He can't read her at all, intuition blinded. Jaden is a mystery. Ethan's voice is meek, "Sorry. I can leave."

She looks at him hard, accusing, takes a drag of her smoke and looks away.

"Do you want me to leave?" Ethan starts to stand.

"Do whatever you want."

Ethan lights his own cigarette and says nothing. Sinead O'Connor sings quietly from the garage. Jaden's little black dog sniffs around the backyard.

"Have a beer with me," Jaden pushes a bottle across the table to him. There are four more unopened bottles on the table before her. She likes to drink.

"I don't like to drink and drive," Ethan evades.

"One beer won't hurt. Or two."

Ethan surrenders, "I guess I can have a beer with you. He really doesn't like to drink and drive and the idea of drinking makes him uneasy because he knows how easy it is for him to get caught up in that alcoholic euphoria and if she doesn't let him crash here he'll be stuck having to drive home drunk. He decides if worse comes to worse he will just walk home.

Ethan cracks his beer open and they sit in silence a while longer.

"Maybe I'm afraid of being hurt," Jaden says, not looking at him.

"I won't hurt you."

"What if I fall in love with you?"

"I won't go anywhere."

Ethan drives down the highway with his sunglasses on, smoking a cigarette. Fields of tall corn stalks pass by out the window. The car stereo plays unfamiliar metal music. He looks at his phone again to make sure he hasn't missed a call or text from Jaden. He has no reason to think this. Why does he always check?

Jaden hasn't contacted him in days. More than a week. It's obvious she's no longer interested in dating him.

Why is he driving around aimlessly smoking cigarettes and blaring music? Who cares if she doesn't like him? Oh, it hurts. He's restless and doesn't know what else to do. He can't sit still. He has to keep moving. Has to keep moving away from the pain. His heartaches. People have always told him he's too emotional of a guy.

Maybe he shouldn't have told her about the secret people. She gave him a weird look when he told her about it all. A look somewhere between fear and laughter. But she had agreed to another date! She stood him up for that date. She hasn't returned any of his dozen messages over the past week.

Ethan told her that he is the reincarnation of Jim Morrison, the poet and singer of the Doors, and that he remembers bits and pieces of other lives as well. He was the mother of the man who killed Rasputin. The alchemist Nicholas Flamel. Olympia, mother of Alexander the Great. The Mohammedan philosopher, Avicenna. Sophocles, the ancient Greek dramatist. Voltaire. Sir Borre, the illegitimate son of King Arthur and Lyzianor (A previous incarnation of Adolf Hitler was my half-brother back then). Geoffrey de St. Omer, a founding Knight Templar. The father of the Mayan priest king, Lord Pacal Votan. Amenhotep, son of Hapu. Tiresias, the blind prophet of Thebes. A hermit pilgrim.

He remembers fragments of those lives. Flashes. Puzzles. Memories. Emotions.

He doesn't understand why he keeps being born. He doesn't want to be born anymore. He just wants to stay in Heaven.

These memories had come to him the first time when he put himself into a trance via self-hypnosis. It worked and fascinated him. Was it only his imagination? Or was it real?

Ethan began to research past lives and reincarnation on the internet. Eventually he came into contact with a man in Thailand who is a self-proclaimed expert on reincarnation. The man's name was Stalin. He agreed to work with Ethan in uncovering past lives.

Ethan wondered why people choose to reincarnate. There must be a reason. Or is there no choice in the matter?

He discovered that Adolf Hitler and King Arthur were two great souls who continue to reincarnate, always in conflict with each other. Good and evil souls that keep reincarnating and fighting the same war over and over throughout history.

Ethan's come to believe that he is one of these souls. One of these reincarnating spirit warriors. Every time he is born he brings change. He came to realize he needed to make contact with the other secret people once he remembered who he is. He had to make contact with others to fully understand his purpose in life and figure out what his role was this time in the unknown war.

He needed a teacher. A master. To learn how to unlock his mind.

If he could remember more with ease it would elevate his consciousness to the level of soul and spirit. To let the soul guide him rather than the animal body.

He did this. He found the others. At first he made contact with humans around the globe. New Age people and similar. He joined a few cults. A number of years passed and he realized he'd only found fellow searchers, not masters.

Ethan began to use trances, hypnotism, meditation, yoga, all the techniques he learned in his studies and among the cultists in search for a master. For the masters. The hidden, secret masters.

He began experiments with remote viewing, astral projection, telepathy, channeling. When he finally broke through to the other side he used the Kabbalah as a road map. The Tree of Life.

He's made contact with all sorts of beings. Non-human intelligence. Aliens. Ghosts. Demons. Angels. Gods. Elementals. Faeries. Vampires. He began to feel as if his sanity was slipping, communicating with these entities was difficult. Physically taxing to maintain the ritual work and trances. The entities became easier to make contact with as he became more adept. They wanted to talk. They wanted to communicate. Ethan learned quickly that he couldn't trust what was being said to him. They all talk in riddles. Ridiculous riddles with slippery motives. It got to the point he couldn't tell who was on who's side. Now he realizes many of them had differing, unrelated agendas.

Something in his mind did give way. He'd succeeded in transforming himself. When sleeping dreams became powerful, remembering them all upon awakening. Dreaming of past lives, the future, conversations, explorations. This is where he found the secret masters. In the dreaming.

There were other effects. He'd always had a natural empathy, it seems this was greatly expanded. A sixth sense now. He knows things he shouldn't know for no rational reason. Spirits and astral things often distract. Social life is difficult with the ability to sense so deeply into people's unconscious minds. Deeper than they can see themselves. This causes him to say awkward and inappropriate things. Leaving those around him uncomfortable. Small talk is his bane as he is always drawn like an arrow flung to the heart of the matter.

Now he has found the secret masters in sleep and does as they say. The masters guide his actions in this war. Contact proves his worth as a spirit warrior. An urban shaman. They've taught him to open his mind wide, to become immortal by no longer losing consciousness between lives, that stretch between death and rebirth. Ethan has been working toward this in all of his lives.

The masters are early people of the Earth. The secret people. Many lived on Earth long before man came to be. Their races eventually changed, evolving into the next races. Handfuls of people from each race have ascended. The ascended are the secret masters.

The original secret masters of Earth were called the Brotherhood of the Snake. Eventually the Brotherhood suffered internal squabbles diverging into three dominant philosophies regarding the laws of the universe. Alas, the Brotherhood of the Snake began to plot and fight among themselves.

This unknown war began in ancient Atlantis. It was there the Brotherhood ruled that particular golden age prior to the civil war. The revolution. The rebellions. As is common knowledge today, Atlantis suffered and was destroyed in a cataclysm. The survivors of the three philosophies spread throughout the world founding the first civilizations of the newest race of Earthlings called the humans.

The unknown war continues, directing affairs from secret places, deep corners of the world and mind. Some of these secret places have become legendary. Shamballa. Agartha. Shangri La. Olympus.

Asgard. Arcadia. Eden. Avalon. Oz. Wonderland.

Ethan is one of these old ones. He continually reincarnates as a human to take part in this lingering, unknown war.

The two most aggressive factions of the Brotherhood of the Snake have become known as the Illuminati and the Luminari. The Brotherhood of the Sun and the Brotherhood of the Moon. The three philosophies have been the founders of all the major religions of the human race.

Secret societies all through history have been waging this war on each other. Masons. Knights Templar. Rosicrucians. Cathars. Essenes. The Order of the Dragon. The Nazis. The cults of Mithra, Orpheus, and Dionysus. The ancient mystery schools. The Assassins. The Hospitalers and Teutonic Knights. The Knights of the Garter. The Hellfire Club. The list is so very long.

Cagliostro. Cassanova. Comte Germaine. Mesmer. Thomas Paine. Adam Weishaupt. George Washington. The Enlightenment was a deciding time in the unknown war. The French, American, and Russian revolutions.

Ethan wonders if maybe he shouldn't have told Jaden about all of this. He admits it was early in their relationship to bring it up. The relationship was new and they hadn't connected on an intimate enough level for such a revelation. She obviously couldn't handle it.

Now the secret masters have scolded him for allowing himself to become so easily distracted by a woman. They're right. It's just that he gets so lonely only talking with non-humans. He wants more than universal love, he longs to be loved by a woman. The masters instruct him to let this go and know God. To know God is love, they say. Knowledge of God is love.

He had intended to produce a moon child with a priestess. To make Jaden that priestess. Several in fact. Infants born with the souls of gods. That was to be his contribution to the war this time around.

Baby gods to fight alongside him and the Luminari. This, he realizes, was motivated by his lust for companionship.

Now he's not sure what to do.

The secret masters told him that tonight he would be contacted by a new teacher. His most frequent teachers in the astral and the dreaming have been Rudolph Steiner, H. P. Blavatsky, and Aleister Crowley. They did not give him the name of his new coming master. They've announced that he is ready to be initiated into the next inner circle. In what he hopes is the last inner circle of the Luminari.

There always comes a time in the progression of the searcher when they must choose one of the three philosophies of the broken Brotherhood of the Snake. The right, left, or middle. Ethan chose the left. The right is to reunite with the Source. The left to stand with the Source. The middle is to stand witness.

Ethan feels he is close to achieving his conscious immortality. He thinks he must have been near this level of consciousness in his last few lives. Give or take. Enough to leave a trail of breadcrumbs.

Breaking free from his thoughts, Ethan sees a young woman standing alongside the highway with her thumb out. A car with its hood up is near her on the shoulder of the road.

He pulls over. She jogs to the passenger side of the car wearing a bright smile. Long, curly hair dangles like fire to her waist. Eyes a startling green, rich and clear. A face carved by Aphrodite.

"Hi," she chirps, "Thanks for stopping. My car died. Will you give me a ride to the next town?"

"No cell phone?"

"No."

"Want me to call someone for you?"

"No. Just a ride would be awesome."

"That's fine. Get in."

She gets in the car.

"What's wrong with your car?" He asks.

"Pretty sure it's the alternator. I knew it was going to go out but I was hoping there was enough juice to make it to the next town."

"I don't know much about cars," Ethan admits.

"That's okay. I just need the ride."

"I'm Ethan."

"Betsy," her smile is sunshine.

"Nice to meet you, Betsy."

"Nice to meet you, Ethan."

They drive on for a while. Betsy tells him all about her family. Her dad is a dick that she fights with all the time. She's eighteen. Her parents are getting a divorce. Her younger brother is mentally handicapped. Brain damage. Her older sister is twenty-five and married to a cop and living in California. She wants to move away too. She can't stand being at home now that her parents are getting a divorce. It's about time. They always fight anyway. She's glad they're getting a divorce. Her dad moved up but still comes around all the time and argues with her mom just to be a dick. Now her brother wants to move in with their dad. He doesn't understand that their dad just wants him to live with him so he won't have to pay child support. At least that's what her mom thinks.

Anyways, that's what she's really doing. Running away, but it's not really running away since she is eighteen now. She's an adult. She stole her dad's car, that's the car she just left dead on the side of the highway. When he drops her at the next town she plans to hitchhike to California to stay with her sister and her cop husband. They don't have any kids yet. Her sister is a hairstylist who just shaved her head to donate it to cancer patients who lose their hair during chemotherapy.

She talks in a quiet voice, timid, yet surprisingly open. She's afraid. Not of Ethan, but of life in general.

Ethan feels comfortable with Betsy. He tells her about the secret masters and the unknown war, the whole story, just like he did with Jaden. Betsy takes it all in, genuinely interested, and doesn't give him the freaked out look Jaden had. He feels connected to this girl.

"What are the Illuminati and Luminari fighting over?" She asks.

"Some are fighting for the ascension of mankind. Some are fighting against it. It's complicated because it's so hard to tell the difference between the factions and some fight for both causes in both orders."

"That doesn't make sense."

"Some want to re-united with God, love it that way. Some want to be like God, love it that way. Some want to watch God, love it that way."

"Oh," she looks out the window at the trees and farms they pass by.

"Betsy," Ethan says, "I don't have anything to do. I can drive you to California."

Her face lights up like a carnival, "Oh, my gawd! Are you serious?"

"Yeah. I don't mind. A road trip sounds like fun. I need a vacation."

"Are you sure?"

"Yeah. I really don't mind."

"That would be amazing."

Ethan and Betsy drive along the highway together talking, laughing, confessing, confiding, and listening to music. They have a natural affinity for each other. Fast, easy friends, relaxed comfort.

Ethan lied to Betsy, he has work in the morning, and they've already been traveling for hours, already crossed the state line. The sun retreated from the sky long ago and he's getting tired. When he doesn't show up for work tomorrow his supervisor will be perplexed. It will take them days to get to California and he probably won't have a job when he comes back, if he comes back. He feels released and free. Freedom and Betsy.

In truth he doesn't even know how to get to California. He'll just keep driving west. Tomorrow he'll buy a road map.

He's done with work. He's not going to call anyone or let anyone know where he is. Let them wonder. Just disappear. He loathed his job. There is enough money in his savings account to sustain them for a while if he's frugal.

The secret masters told him he would meet his new teacher tonight and there she sits in the passenger seat of his automobile looking out the window at the dark night. She's so much younger than him. He's thirty-three. Her youth is intoxicating and infectious.

Ethan's attraction to her is super magnetic, animal magnetic, electromagnetic. Looking at her twirling a strand of red curly hair with her fingers he knows that he will do anything she asks of him. Pale skin, a light sprinkle of freckles across her cheeks and nose, oceans of red fiery hair. Her emerald eyes are close together, nose slender and sharp. Flawless. The beauty of youth and more. My God, he thinks, my Goddess, the most beautiful.

He loves her with all his burning, raging heart after only a few hours together. Betsy looks at him staring at her. He keeps glancing back and forth between the deserted highway before them and her green mystical eyes. She cries beauty. He melts and loses himself in the vision of her.

Betsy is a goddess come to heal, save, and teach. She is everything and all he's ever wanted. Marry me, he imagines saying. Please marry me, Betsy. He can sense it when she looks at him, the unseen electricity flowing between them. Ethan and Betsy.

Oh, God, the excitement, the electric love, the fluttering in his stomach, heart, and groin.

Betsy stares at him as he drives. A mysterious look. Wondering what Ethan's thinking about. She studies him. The shape of his face. His gestures. He's not bad looking for an old guy. Is he really taking her to California? Why? What does he want?

Her. He wants her. She knows it. And she trusts him for no good reason. He wants her and she will let him have what he wants.

Betsy looks down at Ethan's free hand resting on the seat between them. His other hand is on the steering wheel. His fingers are long, thin, feminine. She looks up at him again. Short brown hair just beginning to recede. Hairy arms, skinny. A skinny man. He seems smart. Nice. Wise.

Ethan glances at her again. They both smile before his eyes return to the dark road ahead.

Betsy slides toward him in the seat and puts her hand on his.

Ethan feels her hand touch his. So soft and delicate. Smaller than his. Her fingers are thinner, shorter.

Every fiber of his being focuses on that single touch. Their hands together. He wants her. More than anything, feeling a pressure rising against the fabric of his pants. Ethan begins to sweat. Nervous, flushing with heat.

"We can't drive all night," she slides even closer.

"What should we do?" Ethan's voice cracks.

"Sleep," she gives a sly smile.

"Um. I didn't think about that. We could get a motel room?"

"Can you afford it?"

"Tonight I can."

"I have some money too. I'll give you some for the room."

"Just one room?"

"We'll save money that way," she gives his hand a pleasant squeeze.

Ethan and Betsy sit together at the foot of a motel room bed. Both nervous and afraid to move or talk or look at each other. A lamp on the nightstand illuminates the room. They both stare at the blank television screen before them.

Ethan wants to touch her. She smells nice. He's afraid to reach out. What if she rejects him? Thinks he's an old creepy man? What does she want? Is she afraid of him?

Betsy wonders why he doesn't touch her. Maybe she's wrong. Maybe he doesn't like her like that? Maybe she should try to kiss him.

He musters the courage to look at her. Her red, vibrant hair. Her green eyes. The flowing sundress against her thighs and hanging over her knees. Thin straps over her smooth shoulders. A smooth forehead touched with just a bit of oil and pimples. High cheekbones. And he is mesmerized again. Her expression is an unknown mystery, a hint of sadness, bright intelligence, insecurity. Who is this young woman? Where did she come from? She fell from a dream and into his life as sudden as a lightning bolt splits a tree. Others pale in comparison, this is no boast, but a simple fact of nature, and act of nature.

A magical woman, elf like, a nymph goddess bound in perfect flesh.

"I feel like I've known you before," she breaks the silence like a boom of thunder with her soft spoken voice, "Like I've known you all my life."

The movement of her lips, those eyes, that nose, oh Gods, he belongs to this young woman, for good or ill, from this day forth, always hers, "I feel it too."

"Maybe we knew each other in a past life."

"In all of them I think."

Betsy smiles showing off straight, white teeth, "I like you a lot. I like being with you."

"I do too," Ethan is afraid of waking up from this perfect dream. She is love, pure love incarnate. That is how he feels for her.

"I hope one day I'll wake up in bed next to you," she whispers and quickly looks away.

Ethan reaches out gently, turning her back to look into his eyes and leans forward to kiss her. Just one, soft kiss.

"No!" She panics and shakes her head, "You'll never talk to me again if we do this!"

"What are you talking about?" He smiles, taken back. Then leaning close again, their noses almost touching, her breath smells like cool mint, "Are you kidding me, Betsy? You're the girl I've been dreaming of. I'll never leave your side again if you don't want me to. I'm in love with you."

With that he kisses her again. Finally, they kiss and kiss. Their passion suddenly unrestrained with a tender fury and she whispers, "I love you," and his obsession is complete.

They kiss each other in a thousand places, holding and groping and exploring. Ethan kisses her shoulders, eagerly pulling her shirt and bra off. She bashfully tries to cover her large breasts for a moment before letting him pull her hands away revealing firm, small pink nipples. He feels them beneath his palms as he kneads.

He pulls back to admire her. Tan lines around her breast turn him on more. His hands tremble with excitement and she works his pants down his hips, knees, ankles.

This is her. This is it. His goddess. His secret teacher. His master. His everything.

"Marry me," he whispers so quietly beneath the sounds of their lovemaking he doesn't expect Betsy to hear it as they tangle and tango in the motel room bed.

"I will marry you," she whispers back with their naked bodies pressed hard together.

Both are lost in the intensity and ecstasy of this first copulation together, both experiencing a spiritual awakening. Ethan knows he has found the Holy Grail and Betsy knows she has pulled the sacred sword from the stone.

One being floating through the universe, spirits exploding into each other, mingling, winding, caressing, blood and souls mixing like two fountains of water poured together, hearts beating in sync, words don't matter, nothing matters but the other. A heated union, a requiem of moans, groans, sweat, lust, sex, crying, screaming, grunting, fucking, and a climatic orgasm of joyous delight that echoes across the universe.

They cradle each other, exhausted like warm candle wax dripping down the stick.

"I need you. I don't want to be strong anymore. My strength comes from your love. My breath. My death." They both whisper in unison.

"Thank you," Ethan whispers.

"No," Betsy snaps.

Ethan's eyes widened.

She pets his shoulder, tosses him a quick kiss, "I'm sorry. I don't believe in saying thank you. Thank you means the good deed is forgotten. I want something that shows remembrance."

"I said I want to marry you."

With a pixie grin she says, "That will do."

The next day they are back on the highway driving west. The highway ahead of them is all a blur to Ethan, lost in thought, wondering like he often does if he is crazy. Wondering how he could be so lucky as to meet Betsy. She has to be the one the secret masters foretold.

Betsy stares out the passenger window watching the landscape rush by in a monotonous string of trees, fences, tractors, cattle, fields, farms, and power lines. She is quite a quiet girl, shy, bashful and timid. Yet she feels brave with Ethan. She trusts him in her gut, feels safe with him. Betsy looks over at him as he drives. A round nose. Rich blue eyes. In need of a shave. She can tell he's shy too.

Ethan glances at her and smirks, "What are you thinking about?"

Betsy shrugs, "You think I'm your teacher."

Ethan shrugs and focuses on the road, uncomfortable with the question.

She continues her interrogation, "Did you meet anyone else last night?"

"Just you."

She nods as if that settles the matter.

"I don't know," he mumbles.

"You're like fifteen years old than me. What could I possibly teach you? You're a grown man."

"I don't know," Ethan blushes, "I'm sure you know something I need to learn."

Betsy looks back out the window, angry, "Betsy was born eighteen years ago."

Ethan arches an eyebrow and chuckles, "I know."

She crossed her arms and scowls, "Betsy was in a car accident when she was three years old. The same care accident that caused her brother's brain damage and made him simple. Betsy was hurt too. She was in a coma for weeks."

"That's terrible."

"It gets worse," she takes up a bright yellow pack of cigarettes from the dash of the car, lights two, hands one to Ethan, and opens her window a crack. "Betsy wasn't coming back. She was brain dead. Her parents couldn't let her go. They couldn't shut off the life support keeping their little daughter alive."

Ethan is enamored by the story, mouth agape, looking back and forth between the storyteller and the fast approaching highway.

Betsy continues her tale, "Watching Betsy's parents brought elephant sized tears to mine little eyes. I became so misty and blurry with sorrow." She smiles sadly at the memory, "Wow. That hurt."

"I don't understand what you're saying to me," Ethan admits.

"Then just listen to your teacher," Betsy puffs on her smoke, "I thought there was no sense in wasting little Betsy's body. Heck. I got two birds with one stone. I made use of this wonderful body and saved her family from much pain."

"Are you telling me you're not human? Some kind of spirit or demon or something?" Ethan's face reveals shock and horror at the thought. Maybe she's crazy too? Or just pulling his leg?

"I'm human now," she winks, "I was a fey."

"A fairy?"

"A faerie," she whistles. "A bad faerie. I broke the rules riding this body."

"What about the other fairies?"

"We fey are an old people," Betsy explains, "Not quite human. Not quite angel. Something in between. We are the secret people. Long ago when the world was much younger and more fun the humans went to war with us in Britain and the surrounding places. Those were our last strongholds. We were defeated and went into deeper hiding to survive. We slip in and out of the ether with ease."

"You're a fairy?" Ethan bursts out with laughter.

"Don't laugh. You're just as crazy as I am."

"Can you do fairy magic? Sprinkle fairy dust?"

"No," she huffs, "Not while I'm trapped in this body."

"You're trapped?"

Betsy sighs, "It seemed like a good idea at the time, but now I'm trapped in this body until it dies."

"What happened to the real Betsy?"

"She went to Heaven," Betsy answers as if it were a stupid question.

"Be nice."

"I am nice."

"What happens when you die?"

"Same thing that happens to you."

"Oh."

"Am I your teacher?"

"I think so."

"How do your secret people relate to my secret masters?"

"I don't know. They're both really old. I'm sure they're aware of each other. I've never met your secret masters. I think I've heard of them. Maybe."

"Maybe. Maybe they're hidden from each other."

"Ask your masters."

"I could try but they don't talk to me much and they don't always answer. It's all a very subtle and sly relationship."

"Hmpf," Betsy says, "The fey have pretty much blacklisted me since I became human. A lot of them are like racist against humans."

"Oh. I don't know where we're going or what we're doing."

"Does anybody?"

"I hope somebody does."

Betsy shrugs, tossing her cigarette butt out the window, "The secret masters knew enough to tell you I was coming. I don't feel like a teacher."

"I think you are."

"No more than you."

"Well you've taught me about fairies."

"I know where we're going."

"California," Ethan grins.

"Onward! Further! Mush!" She claps and cheers.

"You still want to go to California even though she's not really your sister?"

"She is so. They are my family and I love them. They have been my family since I became Betsy."

"I'm sorry. I thought you were only pretending to be Betsy."

"Pretend something long enough and it becomes true. Haven't you heard the old saying, fake it 'til you make it? Or liars believing their own lies?"

"Mm. Word. That's weird."

"Weird that I grew up in this body with these people as my family and I love them? I had to learn to walk and talk all over again."

"Do they know you're a fairy?"

"They don't know I'm a faerie."

"What are we going to do in California?"

"Hang out with my sister."

"Then what?"

"I don't know."

"I have enough money to get us by for a while, but not forever. We'll need to make money somehow. Eventually."

"I'm not worried about it."

Ethan frowns. She's young. She doesn't know better.

Betsy frowns and slides close to him, taking his hand in hers, giving him a peck on the cheek, and resting her head on his shoulder. "Let's get married before we get there. Let's get married in the next town."

"Really?"

"Now that I've found you, I don't want to lose you again."

"Okay," Ethan kisses her forehead and continues driving.

Things fall into place for their wedding with an uncanny ease. They read a sign as they pull into the first town they come across after their decision to marry. It's a small Midwestern town and the sign says *Welcome to Ogdoad, Population 777 Souls*. They both think it odd but take it as a good omen.

Ethan pays $50 for the marriage license at the town hall. The sheriff had been snoozing in a share with his boots kicked up leaning back in front of the town hall, which it turns out is the same building that houses the sheriff's office, the post office, and the mayor's office.

The sheriff is a bumbling, friendly sort named Andy with a big smile and round sun aged face. He led them into the town hall with a look of glee, helping them obtain the license and introducing them to a man named Wild Bill who goes by the name of Priest. He is the priest of one of Ogdoad's three churches.

Priest is an older gentleman rumored to be a homosexual (according to the sheriff), a junkie, and a writer. No one knows where he's from, he just showed up in town back in 1997.

"We're a small town," jolly Sheriff Andy grins and huffs as he walks Ethan and Betsy to the church. "Good Christian folk. That means we ain't bigots. Priest may be a queer, but that's between his self and the Lord. Ain't nobody else's business."

That statement cemented Betsy and Ethan's already growing respect for the sheriff.

Priest was in his tall, quiet church slumped in the front pew with dilated eyes transfixed on the large crucifix at the front of the chamber. A thin old man, mostly bald, eyes glazed, speech and movement lethargic.

Betsy and Ethan both take note of the needle and rig resting on the bench next to old Priest's thigh.

Ethan and Betsy purchased wedding rings at a pawn shop on Main Street.

The sheriff said he's a good judge of character and always listens to his gut. That's why he decided to let them get the marriage license and that's how he caught Hobbe Sutton last year stealing crops and cattle from many of the surrounding farms in this county. Hobbe is still in the town jail working community service during the days to pay off his fines and restitution, it will likely take him a couple of more years, but they ain't too hard on him, he gets out to work every day but Sunday and old Ms. Reed cooks him a fine supper every night. She's a widow and it's good for her to have something to do.

Betsy and Ethan decided to write their own vows. They did it on the spot, spur of the moment, without much thought but an abundance of heart.

"Our blood mingled blesses me with confidence, comfort, and courage. Our hearts beat as a single drum and our spirits copulate in eternity. I vow to always be yours, from this day on, through thick and thin, wealthy and poverty, illness and health, I am always yours, death does not part."

Priest nods, enthusiastically bored by their vows and entertained by the sheriff's blushing at the newlywed couple's long, wet kiss.

The four cheer and chat before bidding each other farewell. Priest slumping back into the comfort of his pew. The sheriff lazily returns to his chair outside the town hall to sit and snooze in the sun. Ethan and Betsy get in their car and head back out to the highway.

Driving, both beaming, holding hands, Betsy kisses his cheek, leaving lipstick traces. She flicks on the stereo and *Somebody* by *Depeche Mode* plays from the car's speakers.

"Oh, screw this," Betsy scrunches her nose.

"Hey, I dig *Depeche Mode*."

"I wasn't talking about the song. We need to have at least one night to celebrate our first day as husband and wife. Let's get a motel in the next town! Make love all night! Watch TV! Have dinner! Cuddle! And make love some more!"

"Sounds perfect," Ethan inhales, "After California we'll go somewhere. Maybe Mexico, maybe."

"Oh yes, God save the king and queen! After that Central and South America! I know! I know! We'll sneak into the faerie land! There are so many sights to see there. Tir Na Nog. Avaba. Perilous. Elfland. Mag Mell. You know people can always go to the faerie lands instead of Heaven or Hell. Which faerie land would you like to see?"

"I don't know. Avalon. I'd like to visit the Himalayas."

Betsy pouts her lips, "I want to go to a faerie land for our real honeymoon."

Ethan shrugs, "Here's what we'll do. You pick one faerie kingdom and I'll pick a place. It will be an extended honeymoon."

"You want to go someplace where you think your secret masters will be," she teases. "I love you. I'll go anywhere with you."

"I love you too," Ethan says, wondering where they will get the money to go to all these places. A part of him knows everything will work out fine. They can do anything together.

That night they celebrate their wedding in another nameless motel just as Betsy suggested. Toward the end of the night they lay in bed together, both awake, cuddling in the dark beneath the blankets, resting peacefully.

"Do you think it will have a happy ending?" Betsy whispers.

"I hope so," he whispers back.

"If I were your teacher wouldn't I know?"

"I would assume so," Ethan replies, pauses, and continues, "You're not one of the masters? You don't think you're my teacher?"

"I'm just a crazy person like you."

Neither of them speak for several moments.

"Maybe I'm delusional and you're not even here," Ethan whispers.

"I'm real."

"If you were my delusion you would say that."

"If I were real I would say it."

"You're just a ghost. A memory of love lost."

"I'm not a memory. I'm right here next to you." Betsy takes his hand and presses his palm against her chest. "Feel that? My flesh. My heart is beating."

"I feel it. I feel you."

"Maybe I'm the crazy one."

"I want the secret masters to lead me out of this world, but I'm afraid to die."

"I want to return to the fey and I don't want to die either."

"I'm perplexed," Ethan admits.

"Let's forget California," Betsy whispers close.

Ethan nods, tears in his eyes.

Betsy is crying softly, "There is no place for our story to go."

Ethan's tears tickle his face as they trickle down, "I don't want to lose you. To lose this."

Betsy nods, crying, she kisses him hard on the mouth and says, "Everything is only a dream."

"I love you," Ethan whimpers, holding her close.

"Oh," Betsy cries, squeezing him with violence, "I don't want this to end!"

And then she is gone.

Ethan is alone in the bed. His hand feels the warmth of the mattress where she had been. He stands, moving careful in the dark. Her clothes and things are gone.

He walks to the window and pulls back the curtain. It's night outside. On the sidewalk outside the window he sees little people the size of crickets walking in a solemn procession. Between them the little people hold a single rose petal as they walk. On the petal is the tiny body of Betsy.

Ethan gasps, bolting out the motel room door. Outside there is nothing but the empty sidewalk beneath his bare feet. Teary eyes scan.

Nothing. It's true. She's gone. He's crazy.

He steps back into the motel, shutting the door and locking it behind him. The door feels cold against his back as he leans against it for support.

No. She was real. The secret people are real.

Walking in the dimness of the room, carpet feeling pleasant beneath his feet, Ethan comes to stand before a large mirror on the wall.

He stares into the shadowy, crying reflection of himself. Tears glinting in the dark. His hand reaches out to the mirror. When his fingertips touch the glass the surface ripples out like water.

Ethan's car is found abandoned in the motel parking lot. The motel room is empty.

Cthulhu Domine

I want to scream but I can't. I am so afraid. I am paralyzed with fear, unable to make a sound. Am I breathing? I'm holding my breath. Using all of my strength I still can't move. They have strapped my arms and legs down to this cold metal table. I'm surrounded by men and women buzzing in white surgeon's clothing with face masks and caps. The room is dimly lit. This is no hospital.

They are going to hurt me. They are going to cut me. Their silver scalpels are vivid along with other odd, alien, torturous looking instruments in their hands. They have big black inhuman eyes. Oh, my God, what are they doing to me?! They are so close stinking like rotten fish. I'm gagging. They are going to kill me! I remember now! They said it as they wheeled me in this god forsaken room!

Why are there people watching us? Other people in robes, in the shadows, watching. I hear them whispering something insane. Over and over again. "Ph'nglui mglw'nafh Cthulhu R'lyeh wgah'nagl fhtagn."

Finally my voice explodes, "Please! Let me go!" Tears stream down the sides of my face. This is terror like I've never known. Absolutely helpless. There is nothing I can do. They are killing me. They are killing me. It hurts. Oh God, save me, it hurts. Someone please save me!

I wake screaming, soaked in sweat, drool and cum on my bed next to my girlfriend who is shaking me hysterically, "Josh! Josh! Wake up! What's wrong? Josh!"

I'm breathing hard, close to hyperventilating. Her hand feels calming on my chest and I begin to slow my breath. She wraps her arms around me protectively, lovingly.

"I'm okay," a shutter and sigh, relaxing.

She kisses my cheek in the dark, so soft and smelling sweet. "We need to change the sheets." She hops out of bed and flips the momentarily blinding light on before I can respond. I sit at the edge of the bed holding my knees. Why have I been having these horrible nightmares lately? Dreams of fish people and murderous aliens and unspeakable torture. People throwing stones and beating me. Sticking me with needles, scalpels, nails, spears, and knives. So many things, too awful to describe. Too awful to explain. Too awful to remember.

I watch her pulling crisp, clean sheets from the closet. She is so confident, so sure of herself. So caring. Infinite patience. I feel like a burden. I know she loves me. And look at me! I've become a paranoid wreck. A social disaster. She has to know there is something wrong with me. I must be slowly going insane. She has to suspect.

I watch her in awe. Such a lucky man. Her name is Miri Madelaine. I am Joshua Cree. We met years ago in high school. She had the reputation of being a bad girl, from the wrong side of the tracks. I was a nerd. She smoked cigarettes, drank beer, and skipped school. I played Dungeons and Dragons, read comic books, and was a proud member of the chess club. We couldn't have been more different.

Polar opposites.

Her long black hair and brown eyes. My light brown hair and blue eyes. She would cuss and swear and I would blush. She is two years my junior, in the same grade as my brother James. James and I were very close. He died in Iraq serving in the Army not long after high school. I still miss him.

James and Miri ran in the same circle of friends. Back then James was embarrassed that I was his brother. In private things were fine between us, but I wasn't allowed to say hi to him at school. But Miri and James being friends is what caused Miri and I to meet officially. She never noticed me in the halls at school. I always noticed her.

One weekend Miri and her friends came over to smoke pot with my brother and hang out. They stayed the whole weekend as our parents were out of town. Miri ended up intruding into my room discovering my friends and I playing Dungeons and Dragons. I was always the dungeon master. It was awkward at first. None of us had played the fantasy role playing game with a girl before.

Still she was enthusiastic about it and stoned I'm sure. I remember she made an elf cleric named Belle. My friends were just as nervous as I was. They tried to show off, tell stupid jokes, and get her attention. Their attempts at flirtation were embarrassing in their obvious inexperience. I decided to simply do my best at gaming and we played an amazing adventure that weekend. One of the best. By the end of the weekend my friends and I even seemed to forget we were playing with a female.

That first night we gamed until 5 am. She slept in my bed with me to my friends' chagrin. It was the first time I kissed a girl. Or rather she kissed me. We've been together ever since. No one could understand what she saw in me. My brother's group of friends accepted me after that.

We graduated high school. We went to college together. Now we're married and living on the corner of Delaware Street and Third Avenue. She's a teacher and I'm an architect. We recently bought this house and we've been talking about having a baby. To clarify, I have a degree in architecture. I'm working at a call center as a customer service agent. And unhappy doing so. I can't seem to get in with a solid contracting firm.

I dry myself with a fresh towel Miri has brought from the bathroom. I am grateful Miri is a part of my life.

My ears are ringing as I walk out of our house to leave for work and I notice a car parked a block down the street with a man sitting in it. Too far to make him out. As I drive away from our home the man in his car follows me all the way to work, keeping a reasonable distance. The man parks about a block away from my place of employment. I make it obvious I see him by standing at the front door of my work and staring. The man doesn't react or even look in my direction.

Later in the afternoon, I step outside the office building for my lunch break to see my stalker still parked in the car. I approached the vehicle very annoyed. The man in the car is wearing dark glasses, has black hair, a thick mustache, and blue shirt. When the spy realizes I'm marching straight to him he peels away before I reach him. It only serves to piss me off. I know people have been following me, watching me. I don't know why. I haven't told anyone, not even Miri. I'm afraid people will think I'm crazy. Why would people be following me? But it's true. I'm being watched. I feel like a paranoid schizophrenic.

Who are they? What do they want? It was only a few months ago that I began to notice these men in black suits. The first time was when I left the house to go for a jog. The man slowly followed me in his car for my entire run. It alarmed me to say the least.

After my jog I called the police. I've called the police twice. The spies were gone before the police arrived both times. I wrote down the license plate numbers of the different stalkers' vehicles. The police told me those plate numbers don't exist. They are not registered. The police don't believe me. Miri thought it was weird but didn't say anything about it.

I don't know what to do. I can see it in Miri's eyes. She doesn't know whether to believe me or not. I've stopped talking to her about it but I know she sees the paranoia in my watchful eyes.

Miri makes chicken and rice for dinner. It smells wonderful. She is a talented cook. I am grateful for it. I don't doubt for a moment that I am a very lucky man. But the entire time she is busy cooking dinner I can't help but pacing and peeking out the windows wondering why I am being watched and followed. Miri is aware of my distress but doesn't comment on it. I do see the worry in her eyes. But what am I to do? There is a van with a man in it parked down the block who has been watching the house since I got home from work. He followed me to work and home. It's an everyday occurrence.

We sat down to eat dinner together. Miri always shuts the television off while we eat. The food is good as it always is. I can't focus on the conversation we're having. I'm so distracted by my stalkers. I know it's small talk about her day at work. She is disgusted with one of her student's parents. She mentions some people don't deserve to be parents and what a great kid this kid is. This neglected kid. They are not involved or invested in his education or development. They are not interested in their son at all it seems. Miri went so far as to report the parents to the Department of Social Services Child Protection for neglect and suspected abuse. She has no proof and nothing was done other than the report logged. The boy has come to school with bruises and vague explanations as to the cause of them. She's at her wits end. She doesn't know what else to do. The boy is withdrawn and timid. His name is Kent.

I keep nodding as she talks, only half listening. I notice she has a stack of new children's books n the edge of the dining room table. On top is a book titled *'the Berenstein Bears and the Truth'*. Next to the books is a stack of papers for grading with a copy of a news magazine. On the cover of the magazine is reference to an article inside honoring the anniversary the death of Nelson Mandela in prison and another one discussing the miraculous recovery from cancer of the actor Patrick Swayze. I can't take it anymore. I set my fork and napkin delicately on the table next to a jar of Jiffy Peanut Butter and walk over to the window pulling the curtain back just enough to peek out. This is done in the middle of Miri's speech. She is flabbergasted that I simply walked away in mid-sentence. The man in the van is still out there.

"What in God's good name are you doing, Joshua?" Miri sighs.

I look at her, struggling to maintain eye contact. There is no need to answer her question.

"I'm trying to share something important to me and you're ignoring me. That's obvious." Miri is hot. It's been happening more and more often. It hurts me and I'm worried about you."

I remain silent, unsure there is anything to say. I'm ashamed of my paranoia. I honestly don't know if I'm sick or if it's real. I feel sorry for her having to deal with my behavior.

"Are you going to say something?"

I'm still standing at the curtain. I look down at my feet and the carpet. "I'm sorry."

"I'm doubly offended, Josh. I love you. Tell me what's going on with you. Please."

With a deep confessional breath I tell her. "I was followed to work again today. Someone is parked in a van down the street watching our house right now. The same guy who followed me to work and home. He is there right now."

Miri takes a moment of silence while studying Josh. He can't decipher her thoughts. She doesn't believe him. She must think he's sick in the head.

Miri rises from the dinner table and joins Josh at the window, slightly pulling the curtain back so she can see too. "Where?"

"Across the street. About halfway down the block."

"I see it." She says nothing as she examines the van from the window, noting the license plate.

"I can prove it," I announced in sudden realization. "Let's go for a ride right now and the guy will follow us! I know he will."

With an amused smile, an attempt to lighten the mood, Miri says, "Let's go get some ice cream for dessert."

I smile with excitement. This will show her I'm not crazy.

We leave our dinner on the table and walk out the front door. We make it a point not to look back at the man in the van. We don't say a word as we pull out of our driveway and move down the street. I'm driving, watching the van in the rear view mirror. Miri turns on the radio and ironically the song 'Somebody's Watching Me' by Rockwell comes through the car speakers causing us both to laugh.

After traveling only a block the van begins to follow us and it wipes the laughter from my face. "The van is on the move. Don't look back. Use the side mirror."

My wife does use the side mirror to look. Her face pales. "I can't believe it. It is following us."

"I told you."

"Maybe it's only a coincidence."

"Maybe."

When we park in front of the ice cream parlor the van parks a block away, the man watching us. Neither of us make direct eye contact with him. He's a large balding man with glasses. From this distance he seems to be in his mid-thirties. Entering the store we don't say anything but I can see in Miri's demeanor that she believes me now and is frightened.

My strawberry ice cream has graham cracker crumbles sprinkled over it. Miri has vanilla with fruit pieces and nuts over the top. Both bowls of ice cream have chocolate syrup like little rivers swirling down tiny mountains. We sat in our car eating the ice cream without much conversation. The man is watching.

I start the car and we head for home. The van follows.

"Okay," Miri announces, "I shouldn't have doubted you. It's real. This guy is following us and I'm kind of freaked out now. I think we should call the police again."

"I can't understand what they want from me? Are they going to rob us? Is it a serial killer? I agree. Call the police. Have them meet us at our house."

Miri takes her cell phone out of her big brown leather purse and makes the call as I take the scenic route driving us home. She explains everything to the police. They assure her there will be an officer waiting at the house for us.

The van following us is white and long with no side windows. The sight of it is nerve wrecking. As we pull up to our house there are no police cars in sight.

"What do we do?" Miri asks.

"I don't know."

"Keep driving?"

"No. I'm sick of this horse shit." I park in our driveway and exit the car with unstoppable determination, marching to the van.

"Josh, no!" Miri reaches for me but misses.

I'm white knuckled, stomping to the van. To my surprise the man does not speed away like the stalkers have in the past.

Miri follows, but fear of the unknown slows her pace.

The thick man in the driver's seat smiles beneath his dark sunglasses. The shine of his glasses remind me of a snake. There is no fear radiating from the snake eyes. My anger has taken root. "This violation ends today!" I shout.

The driver smirks with amusement.

"What do you want from me!?" I scream. I open the door of the van, grab the big man by the shirt, and yank him out of his seat. He laughs like a hysterical jackal, as if he has never experienced anything so hilarious as me.

Behind me Miri has her hands over her mouth in shock.

The man's laughter fuels my growing anger. I go berserk and punch the man in the jaw. It hurts my fist and the man hardly reacts. I realize there is a very good chance I am about to get my butt kicked. I also notice this man must outweigh me by a hundred pounds and stands six inches taller.

Before I realize what's happening, the side door of the van slides open and four men exit to join the one I just punched. They are all dressed in black suits and ties and wear black demonic face masks with horrific expressions.

The men overpower and subdue me with ease as Miri screams in the background. I feel something club my head inside the van just as the door swings shut. I black out.

Outside the van Miri has dropped to her knees, sobbing, and crying out for help. Some of the neighbors have come out to see what the commotion is. The friendly neighbors big Dan and Roseanne Connor come to Miri's aid as the van speeds from sight and police sirens approach with a whine.

When the police arrive one of them is Roseanne's skinny sister Jackie. The three do their best to calm Miri and get her story. Miri's ears are ringing.

Miri sits on the edge of her bed taking deep, slow breaths, staring out an open window, trying not to cry again. Children are playing in someone's front yard across the street. She has been struggling with the kidnapping of her husband, swinging back and forth between numbness and tears. Her mind fights accepting the fact that Josh is gone. It seems too unreal. Why didn't she believe him sooner?

Days have passed and the police have nothing. The license plates were fake. They can't find the van. None of the witnessing neighbors recognized the kidnappers. Well, the driver was the only one without a black satanic mask hiding his face.

The Connors have been checking on her regularly. Roseanne brought over a casserole yesterday.

Miri has had family staying with her since Josh was taken.

Taken! He was taken! Is he still alive? What do they want? Why did they take him? What are they doing to him?

She has to go back out to the living room and face her family soon. She doesn't want to but there is a detective out there waiting to ask her more questions. The questions never stop. She sighs. Her family. She is grateful, but maybe it would be easier to be alone right now. Her mother, Greta Madeleine, is always there when she needs her. They have always been close.

Her parents divorced years ago. Her father is seldom around. She hasn't seen him often since the divorce. He is a selfish man with a new wife and family. Her stepfather Bret is there though. Bret has been married to her mom for about five years now. Miri can't stand Bret. He's an arrogant know-it all who never stops talking. Josh's uncle Ward Shakespeare showed up this morning. Ward and his deceased wife raised Josh since he was a toddler.

Josh's parents were killed in a plane crash. Something he never liked to talk about. He never actually said that but he would become quiet, uncomfortable, and evasive whenever the issue came up. He claimed to have few memories of them beyond old photographs and forlorn expressions when they are mentioned.

Ward Shakespeare is Josh's father's half-brother. Ward and his wife, Flora, had no children of their own. Josh very much became their son. Josh never complained and was well provided for. He did love his aunt and uncle. Josh's heart broke when Flora passed away. She was a retired secretary for a telecommunications company. Ward is a professor of history here at the University of Haddonfield. They live in Haddonfield, Illinois. Miri is glad Ward is there. He is a leader that oozes confidence. Ward will know what to do.

Miri sits at her vanity looking at the smeared mascara around her eyes. She chuckles and begins to wipe it away. She fixes her makeup enough to present herself to her house guests. With straight shoulders and perfect posture the tall Miri enters the lion's den of her living room.

Entering the living room everyone reacts with pity toward Miri. Their sympathetic looks stir anger in her gut. She is a strong woman. She can survive anything. Seated around her living room in different states of drinking coffee are her mother Greta, stepfather Bret, uncle Ward, and a short, heavyset police detective.

Greta stands and hugs her. "How are you?"

"I'm fine."

Greta nods curtly and sits back down in a chair near the couch.

The stubby detective stands, politely removing his hat and extending a handshake. His fingers are like thick sausages. "Miri Cree? I'm Detective Dwayne Brostek. Assigned to your husband's abduction."

Miri nods and sits gracefully on the couch with Bret and Ward.

"I'm sorry we don't have any leads yet. I promise I will do everything in my power to find Joshua." The detective explains. "I'm here to go over some questions. Maybe jar something in one of us that will spark a lightbulb. I can't imagine how hard this is."

"Thank you," Miri forces a smile.

"Can I get you anything, dear," Greta asks her daughter.

"A glass of ice water," Miri answers, as timid as a mouse.

The rotund Detective Brostek fumbles taking a small note pad out of his coat pocket preparing to begin his line of questioning.

Bret interrupts, "I think we should talk about the history of murder in our little town. We're all thinking about it. I'm only pointing out the elephant in the room. Do the police suspect this is related to that?"

Brostek is flustered. "No, not at all. That was a cult of serial killers, this is a kidnapping. We have no reason to believe that Joshua is not alive. The Cult of the Shape was destroyed. The case closed. It's only a ghost haunting our town's memory now."

Bret grunts disbelief.

The Cult of the Shape was a group of dark occultists who manipulated and brainwashed people into serving as psychotic murderers. Every time the police declared it was over the cult would strike again on and around Halloween. The townsfolk lost faith in their local police department, yet to be fair it has been many years since the cultists have struck and there is no reason to believe any of them are still alive.

Brostek goes into a tirade of questions brushing off Bret's suggestion as nonsense. The Cult of the Shape was before Miri's time, it's more of a local legend than anything. She answers all the detectives' inquiries, many of which she has already answered before. The interrogation becomes a droning dream to her. She answers the questions like a robot, in a monotonous voice, tolerating the necessary annoyance. Miri feels so helpless and hopeless. Part of her feels she will never see her best friend again. Joshua H. Cree. She fights back tears and sips the ice water. The water is wet and refreshing inside her mouth. Greta takes Miri's hand in hers.

Bret is red faced and white knuckled with anger, fidgeting. Greta looks lost for words. Wade seems to possess a limitless reserve of patience, wisdom, and courage. He seems very much in control, thoughtful, and alert to every detail.

After the long hour of questioning is at its end, Detective Brostek rises to leave, replacing his hat on his balding, shining head.

To Miri everything seems so much more clear and crisp, everything seems to have an elusive meaning behind it. She takes everything in. A witness to every particle around her. Every piece of dust in the air. The detective's double chin. The age spots on his hands. The deep, dark blue color and each individual thread of his uniform. The lustrous announcement of his gold badge. The black smooth polish of his shoes. His slight waddle as he exits her home.

Ward wears glasses and has black pepper grey hair combed back. He is in his early sixties but physically healthy and fit. He plays soccer and jogs regularly. Ward is known for a sharp wit, a love of history, and being an outspoken leftist. He's dressed in a faded grey sweatshirt, blue jeans, and worn-out tennis shoes.

Greta is prim and proper, big hair, gaudy jewelry, silver-blue eye shadow always attempting to create the illusion of wealth. Money and social standing have always been a priority to Greta, something Miri did not inherit. Financially things have improved since Greta married the wealthy Bret Hinson.

Bret is always tan or sunburn, his skin having an aged leathery look to it. Often traveling, retired, and often grouchy. He is still the spoiled boy he has been all his life, a fortunate son, born with a silver spoon in hand, he inherited his father's lumber company. Bret doesn't seem to actually work, or at least he hasn't worked since Miri met him. He is an accomplished pianist and a financial whiz. He is abrasive and sometimes obnoxious but Miri doesn't mind him. He loves her mother and that's important.

With a deep inhale through his nose, Ward gingerly slaps his hands against his thighs. "I will find my son by any means necessary." With that confident declaration he rises to leave.

Brett stands, his big eyes bulging, mouth wide. Miri has always thought her stepfather a homely man with eyes and mouth too big, ears too small. "What are you going to do about it?" Brett barks unbelievingly.

"Whatever it takes," Ward answers coolly.

Bret grumbles, not to be out done, "I'm going to the Lodge. My brothers can help find Josh, if anyone can."

It's common knowledge to all present that Bret is referring to a local Masonic Lodge. He storms out of the house to prove he is more resourceful than Ward. The Masons of this community are very tight knit and elitist with a long, strong standing history locally. Family traditions. The Lodge in Haddonfield was dying out in the early 1960s, saved by a man named Jeremiah Moses who moved to town in 1963. He was said to be a wealthy, retired fisherman from somewhere along the east coast, the New England area. At least his accent sounded as if he were from Maine or somewhere about there. It was never clear why he moved to the Midwest.

Children were frightened of Jeremiah Moses due to his physically odd appearance, bordering on deformity. An unfortunately unattractive man. Big eyes spread much too far apart. An abnormally small nose and ears, lips thin. He walked with a cane and a limp. No one knew how old he was exactly. Too the children of the town in the 1960s he was Haddonfield's bogeyman, not the first and not the last.

Jeremiah's reputation was different with the adults than the children. Money tends to do that. He was well respected by the men of the town, the women like the children found him to be repulsive and creepy. Women are not allowed membership into the ranks of the Masons and that may have played a part. He was a very active and proud Mason. (Women and children often called him the toad man behind his back). He was covered in age moles, warts, and odd shaped red birthmarks. He was so old and wrinkled his fingernails fell off, he wore white cloth gloves to hide this.

The town was in financial dire straits when Mr. Moses came along. Unemployment was worse than it had ever been. Businesses were closing. The banks were foreclosing on farms. Alcoholism was becoming an epidemic. Jeremiah Moses was Haddonfield's savior. He came with an abundance of wealth and years of experience as a leader, the captain and owner of a fleet of fishing ships. He still owned and operated his company on the east coast.

The first act of Jeremiah, after purchasing the old Rosenbaum Mansion up on old Carroll Hill just south of town, was to open a manufacturing company building boats, water gear, and fishing equipment exported up through the Great Lakes. He created more than 200 jobs. He revitalized the town and the local Masonic lodge, being a 33rd degree Scottish Rite Mason. He created and strengthened a network of lodges from Haddonfield all of Illinois to the east coast and Ireland. Mr. Moses was immediately elected grandmaster of the lodge. A short while later he was elected town mayor. He succeeded in getting the railroad and an interstate highway to pass through Haddonfield and the town boomed. He bought out several loans to aid farmers and created the JM Credit Union.

Under the leadership of the very strange Jeremiah Moses the Masonic lodge membership became very elitist and paranoid. Jeremiah and the lodge ran the affairs of the town and surrounding counties with an iron grip. The wealthiest and most powerful members of the community joined the lodge, who operated very secretly, but let their membership be known proudly. The Order Eastern Star was reactivated in the area allowing women to operate with the lodge. Membership was by invitation only.

Since Jeremiah Moses passed away not much is said about the local Mason's any longer and Miri doubts they will be of any help. Greta doesn't care for Bret's association with the group, but shortly after they were married she joined the Eastern Star.

Ward gives everyone in the room a stern look and declares, "When I come back I will know what happened to Joshua. I promise you that."

"Thank you." Miri nods with a sniffle as Ward gives her a familial hug and exits the house.

After the men are gone Greta and Miri sit in perplexed silence for a time. Greta can't take the quiet any longer. "I'm sure someone will find him. Brett. Ward. The police. Someone will."

Miri looks at her mother with nothing to say.

Greta then asks, "Are you hungry? I'll make dinner."

Miri nods and covers her legs with a quilt, snuggling with herself on the couch as her mother steps in the kitchen to cook. Just before Greta reaches the kitchen doorway Miri blurts out, "I'm pregnant."

Greta gasps. "Does Josh know?"

Miri shakes her head. Big tears drop from her eyes. "I was going to surprise him this weekend." Her voice cracks.

Greta returns to her daughter and kneels before the couch, taking her hand. "Everything is going to be alright."

Joshua attempts to present courage and defiance yet his body involuntarily shudders with fear. He can feel the motion of the van, an occasional pothole or bump in the road. He guesses they are now on a highway. The blind movement makes him feel dizzy at times. He doesn't understand what's happening. He knows he's inside the white van with the men who manhandled him but he doesn't know who they are or what they want and they have not made a sound. Their silence seems unnatural and unsettling. He is blindfolded and they duct taped his mouth shut. They used duct tape to bind his hands and feet together too. He has tried but he can't break free. Grateful for small favors he's glad they didn't duct tape his eyes.

The van has been traveling for what feels like an hour but he has no real sense of time. Internally he is fighting off panic and shock, focusing on breathing calmly through his nostrils. What worries him the most is not knowing what they want and what they are going to do to him. If they were just going to kill him he would already be dead. That tells him they have other plans in store for him. Nothing that he can't imagine. Torture? Then murder? He has to survive this. No matter what. He will survive. He will escape. He will see Miri again.

Joshua begins to cry softly. He tries to block the memory out but it keeps returning so clearly to his mind and each time he visualizes it Josh fights the urge to scream. He doesn't scream because if he starts he doesn't know if he can stop. What he saw couldn't have been real. The manhandling these brutes gave him must have jarred his perception. The men's hands were deformed. One of them had hands like flippers, the four fingers on each hand were fused together by the skin. One of the men didn't have any fingernails. Their skin was smooth with odd patches of discoloration. One of the men was a hunchback. Another walked with a limp. They didn't quite seem human. They seemed mis-shaped like inbreds.

What the hell is going on?

Making matters more uncomfortable he is bound and lying on the floor of the van. It's not a smooth ride and occasionally one of his captors gives him a kick for good measure. From what Joshua saw briefly of the van's interior was that it is pretty much empty and bare other than his four abductors and the driver. The bumps and turns bounce and jostle him from side to side. He feels he is covered in bruises.

The interior of the van is humid and rank like rotten, dead fish. He's become used to the stink but initially retched. After they gagged him he thought he was going to choke to death on his own vomit but calmed himself enough to force himself to swallow it back down.

Joshua has decided he has to survive this. He will survive. He will escape. Repetitive thought. Focus on survival and escape no matter the cost. Think. Think. Think.

The men who had taken him were all dressed in black. Even black masks. One of the four had strange eyes. Too big and too round. On another he could make out eyebrows so thick and bushy it looked like a single eyebrow. A thick mustache over his eyes. A third had no eyebrows at all.

He sighs through his nostrils at the futility. The van comes to a halt. Its engine shuts off. Joshua's pulse quickens, his heart races, he's sweating again. He hears the van door slide open. Why don't these guys talk to each other? Why don't they say something to him?

Strong, cumbersome hands grab him from all directions. He feels like a worm wiggling to escape. It's useless.

Joshua feels himself being carried out of the van and into fresh air. Cool air and the sound of nearby water. He imagines easy waves caressing a sandy beach. The water is very close. All sense of direction is lost and he has no clue as to how far they carry him. He feels the sensation of ascending stairs. The sound of a door opening and closing behind them. They are inside a house or a building.

The four inbred kidnappers drop him on a concrete floor with a thud. It hurts. Next comes the sound of rattling chains. A cold metal clamp snapping shut around his ankle.

He lays limp on the floor. Resigned. Defeated. Listening to shuffling feet exiting the room and a door shutting behind them.

Now all is darkness and silence. Time is torture.

Ward sits in his idling car outside Saint Thomas's Cathedral. He is looking up at the familiar masterpiece of architecture, studying every intricate curve, corner, and stained glass window. He's attended Mass there every Sunday morning for nearly 25 years, since they moved to Illinois. Flora was a devout Catholic. Their nephew and adopted son, Joshua, attended services there, Sunday school, summer camp, baptism, confirmation, the whole shebang. To Flora's disappointment Josh stopped going to church after graduating high school. She blamed the influence of Miri. Ward has always known that wasn't the case. It was simple biology. Teenage rebellion. The search for self, identity. Testing independence. Leaving the nest.

Ward continues to attend services for his deceased wife. He has many cherished memories of this church and its congregation. Memories of a family growing together.

Ward's father, Earle Shakespeare, was killed in the line of duty serving the true church. He, like Ward, was a holy soldier of Christ. The holy order is a family tradition stretching back for generations. Further back than any cowan or outsider would believe. The famous Shakespeare is an ancestor, of course his name was France's Bacon.

Initiating Joshua was something that should have been done long ago, but Ward always found a reason to postpone the rite. A paternal instinct to protect the boy, who is far from being a boy now. Ward genuinely thinks of Josh as his son and loves him very much.

It doesn't matter now. Someone has him. An enemy of Christ. A servant of the Adversary. It's hard to say which black brethren it may be. The Cult of the Shape? The Order of Dog Blood? The Cult of Ahriman? The Black Templars? It still doesn't matter. Joe was the important one. He was the chosen one, by their order. But the same sacred blood pumps through the hearts of Ward and Joshua. That must be why he was taken. The holy blood. That old blood is all that matters to some. Nothing else.

Ward climbs out of his vehicle listening to the creak of his old knees, missing the dashing youth he once was. Mortality is a drag. Overhead the sky is grey with a blanket of smoky clouds. His knees ache whenever the weather is about to change. He can feel it coming. A storm of some kind.

As he climbs the long concrete steps of Saint Thomas he notices vandalism he didn't see from the car. Written on one of the church's outside walls in green spray paint are the words, "Dagon is rising!"

and "the unholy trinity cometh." Ward's nose curls in disgust. Dead frogs are crucified on tiny crosses and nailed to the church's door. He leaves them in place and enters the church, angry, now knowing who they are dealing with. This is not just the work of teenage satanic hoodlums. It is either the Esoteric Order of Dagon or the Cult of Cthulhu. Or maybe a sect of the Great Old Ones he hasn't learned of. The Outer Gods. Extraterrestrials posing as gods and hiding beneath the seas. Leviathans. Behemoths. Ancient evil from before there was light.

    Ward has spent so much time in the beautiful old church over the years it is like a second home to him. The high arched, vaulted ceilings are painted and decorated with colorful masterpieces of Saints and Angels. His foot falls echo, the acoustics of the church are purposeful and phenomenal. The Priory of Sion have been masters of music, mathematics, and the arts since the days when Pythagoras was their leader.

    A sole figure dressed in black kneels before the altar at the front of the church. An elderly priest. A large crucifix with a life like Jesus the Christ bleeding in agony and dying under a crown of thorns adorns the wall above them. The organ off to one side is enormous. This is a very old church.

    At the sound of Ward's approach the priest ends his silent prayer and struggles to stand using an ornate cane. Ward remembers a day when the priest needed no cane and his stature alone unintentionally demanded respect. The man of the cloth turns to face Ward. They have been fraternal by oath for decades now. The priest wears silver rimmed glasses and is clean shaven with thinning white hair once thick. The skin of his neck hangs like a rooster with old age, his pale blue eyes look tired and sad, his body so frail. Prominent nose and ears seemed to have never stopped growing. He is the man of one thousand wrinkles now.

    "Dario," Ward gives a slight smile and nods.

    Bishop Dario Andolini. Nearly a century old and he refuses to retire even at the urging of the church fathers. This man still has a hidden vitality, a powerful man even with a withering body, respected in the Vatican and tied by blood to the Sicilian Mafia. A man of intelligence, a force of academia. The bond between Ward and Dario is unbreakable.

    "Ward." The elderly priest reaches out and the two men share a secret handshake.

    "We have things to discuss," Ward informs his old friend.

    "We do." Father Andolini nods, his voice aged and quiet. "Let us speak in a quiet place." He struggles to move and motions for Ward to follow him.

    Ward knows where they are going as they walk through a deathly silent maze of hallways, through doors and down stairs of stone, only the sound of their footsteps echo about the halls intruding on the stillness and dust. If Ward had never been down this spiraling maze countless times before he would be lost. The general public has no idea these secret pathways exist beneath the church. It is a temple of the secret church.

    They settle into comfortable ornate leather chairs. These lower levels of the church are styled like gothic dungeons or castles. They feel old. The lighting is soft oil lamps. All the walls, floors, and ceilings are stone. This room is lined with oak shelves of aging books. There is also an elegant desk, a fireplace, and tapestries detailing an esoteric history specific to their order.

    Once they are both comfortably seated they get straight down to the matter at hand. Father

Andolini begins the discussion. "I believe it is the Order of the Sleeping Serpent. Brought to us thanks to Jeremiah Moses. An offshoot of the Esoteric Order of Dagon and the Cult of Cthulhu. Just as dangerous and fanatical." The old man coughs and clears his throat. "I am uncertain. The Sleeping Serpent may have existed before the coming of Jeremiah. It must have."

Ward sighs. "At least it's not the dreadful Druids."

"Blasphemous Druids. A shame to the white and green Druids."

"Is Joshua still alive?"

"That would make sense. Why kidnap him? Why not assassinate him like his parents?"

"It could be a sacrifice."

"It could be. His parents were."

"You believe they killed his parents?"

The bishop nods. "I've divined it. They will kill his or program him eventually."

"I will find him." Ward feels his emotions rising.

"I have contacted the grandmaster. The Poor Soldiers stand with the Priory. Dagon, Cthulhu, all the old ones will fall. Something has changed in the stars. The unknown war stirs. Messiahs arise. Avatars of good and ill. I do not think I will live to see this through. You must take the leadership of the lodge, my old friend."

Ward pales at the words spoken. "This is unthinkable."

"The cycles move around the circle. Time ripples. Ages come to pass. Prophecies are fulfilled. The people of forever. Only you and Joshua are left of the blood. Fools preach the apocalypse."

"What's happened to the others?" Ward asks thoughtfully. He hasn't had contact with others of Sion for many years.

Bishop Andolini observes a moment of silence before he answers. "Many are dead. Those few left, soldiers of the unknown war."

Ward shakes his head in disbelief and regret.

"Ward." The Bishop's voice grave. "The line of James remains hidden and guarded."

"I've always suspected. No matter. I have to find Joshua."

"Make peace with the Lord," Andolini suggests sincerely.

"You as well, old friend." With that statement Ward leaves the church on his mission.

At some point Joshua passed out. He suspects he was drugged because of a groggy feeling and what seems like a chemical hangover. The blindfold and gag are gone. A string of drool hangs off his chin. His eyes take time to focus. It takes time to become aware of his surroundings.

Joshua is flat on his back and chained to a metal table by his wrists, ankles, waist, and neck. There are throbbing aches, pains, and bruises everywhere. He feels like he's been hit by a truck. For a moment he feels like he will vomit again, his mouth waters, the urge passes.

The room is dark and damp, and the humidity is thick. He's naked and it's so hot Joshua is sweating profusely. Above him old lights hang from the grey concrete ceiling. It seems like a warehouse room. Some kind of industrial building. Somewhere is a steady drip of water. The room stinks of dead, rotting fish. He can't see a door but his mobility is limited. The chains around his neck make it difficult to look around. There is nothing in this room but moss, mold, and mildew.

"Good morning."

A familiar voice walks into his line of sight. Bret. His father-in-law. Joshua's eyes widened in horror at the revelation. He screams at the sight of Bret's companions.

They stand upright like men but they are not humans. The creatures shamble more than walk. There is no grace to their movements. They seem like disorientated deformities of nature. Blasphemies of nature. Things that should not exist. One of the beast men is scaly green with bulbous jaundice heavy lidded eyeballs. Thin diamond pupils. Long claws, webbed hands and feet, gills slit on either side of its throat. Completely hairless. The vague shape of a man. Its mouth hangs open with a tongue like a panting dog. Jagged, broken yellow teeth. Its expression is unreadable.

The other man-thing is no less repulsive. It has the round head of a blowfish and is covered in fleshy needles. The skin is amphibious grey, green, and brown, splotchy. The front of its torso is soft off white. A fin like a Mohawk extends from its skull down along its spine and into a long wiggling, restless tail ending in a forked fin. Its hands are craggy lobster claws. There are antennae protruding the sides of its mouth and eyes on the sides of its head. The fish men are so alien Joshua can't tell if there is intelligence behind their round eyes or if they are more like animals.

"Bret?" Joshua's is hyperventilating. Quick short panicked breaths. His heart is racing. Is he having a heart attack? "What are you doing?" His lips and tongue feel thick and numb, his speech slurred.

Bret smiles, his face weather beaten. "I am here to help you become all you are meant to be."

"Son of Mero." Both fish men gurgle and croak and nod respectfully, oddly.

"Stay calm, Josh." Bret instructs, "I'm going to take some of your blood. Struggle and you will only hurt yourself."

"You drugged me?" Josh asks.

"A stinger of Chlagthu." Bret nods in the direction of the fish face with the fleshy needles. "He is a full blood. A Deep One. The poison will wear off. He could have killed you. We all could. Keep that in mind." He sticks the needle in Joshua's arm, drawing blood.

Joshua feels his head swimming, spinning, he feels weak. Bret withdraws the needle and Joshua lets out three hysterical shrieks. One after another. He thinks he must be going insane. This can't be reality.

Ignoring Joshua's behavior Bret points a thumb at the other fish man thing. "This is Moby. A half breed. Son of Jeremiah Moses. Both sons of Dagon."

"Moby Moses," Joshua whispers.

Bret smiles like the Devil. "We are of the Ancient and Accepted Order of the Old Ones. The Lodge of the Sleeping Serpent."

"I don't understand what's happening," Joshua cries and then weeps.

With a glare of frustrated annoyance Bret barks, "Grow some balls. You are a very special boy and I'm going to bring you to life."

Joshua sniffles and coughs attempting to collect himself, calm himself. "Where are we?"

"Riverdale," Bret answers with a red faced grin. "Near Lake Michigan. The Deep Ones have a city beneath the water here." He gives another demented grin. "The time for secrets has passed. I'm going to tell you a very old story."

Joshua gives Bret an unsure look. The heavy breathing of Moby and Chlagthu unsettles Josh. It seems as if they struggle to breathe outside of water. Their eyes unblinking. Josh's face glistens with tears. He struggles to stay calm.

Bret crosses his arms. "The first thing, you little son of a bitch, is that I had to leave the Lodge of the Black Lagoon in Brazil to come up here and not babysit you. I loved it there."

"I'm sorry," Joshua whimpers. "May I have my clothes?"

Bret chuckles. "You are so weak. You will thank me when everything is over." He looks at Moby and Chlagthu. "Why don't we have any chairs in here?"

The Deep Ones only look at Bret as if confused by his words.

Bret sighs. "Forget it." He looks deep into the subdued Joshua's eyes. "I can't fathom that you're a savior and hope of the Priory of Sion."

Joshua can't believe this is his father-in-law. This man is a complete stranger to him. A lunatic. He can't shake the terror. He wishes Miri or Ward would save him. He prays secretly to God and all the angels above for salvation.

"Our gods are older than your gods," Bret boasts. He begins like a teacher lecturing a dunce. "The church of Dagon was founded more than 3000 years before the birth of Jesus the Christ. Dagon was worshiped in Akkad, in Assyria, in Babylon, in Sumer. In many places. Long before the Abrahamic cults rose, following one of the gods of Ur. Dagon leads 200 other gods and the Deep Ones. Together we all serve the mighty dreaming one, the Cthulhu. Curse Dagons treacherous brothers El and Cronus. Curse his enemy Samson. During the ancient times of God wars, the unknown war, the ongoing war, Dagon and Shala's son, the great Hadad, led his armies and allies. They had many allies. Two of their generals were Nergal and Mishaw. Since those battles were lost the Deep Ones have been living on the ocean floors for 80,000 years. Hidden from humanity."

Joshua's eyes widened. "This is some dark fairy tale."

Bret smirks. "The point is Dagon is a god priest, a god soldier, and his followers, like myself, are working toward a common goal. The second coming of Cthulhu. Cthulhu's will be done."

"Okay," Joshua sounds desperate and frightened. "We live in America. Freedom of religion. Let me go. I won't tell anyone about your faith. This doesn't have anything to do with me."

"It's not faith," Bret scolds. "It's knowledge. Use your brain Josh. You wouldn't be here if this all had nothing to do with you." With much sarcasm he adds, "Son of Mero."

Ward returns to Joshua and Miri's home, perturbed. Things are beyond his control, beyond his authority. He has conducted some investigations into the matter and has plans to travel to Riverdale this evening. He has a contact there. A lower ranking member of the secret church named Veronica. She was recruited several years ago by Ward himself. High ranking initiates like Ward have the authority to recruit agents. The Priory works similar to some other mystery schools like the Illuminati, the Great White Brotherhood, and the Silver Star where the initiate only knows his or her recruiter until they reach higher levels of the inner circles where they may be put in contact with others. The trio of orders are allies as are the Poor Soldiers. Initiation becomes more difficult the higher the rank and many recruited agents reach lower levels and remain so.

Veronica is an exception. She has a natural drive toward the light. She has advanced far beyond Ward's expectations and will likely continue to do so. Ward can see her as the head of her own lodge one day. She is talented, reliable, and has come through for him once again, informing him of a lodge called the Sleeping Serpent in Riverdale and she has been spying on their activities. A difficult and dangerous task. Veronica is a wealthy, beautiful, dark haired, resourceful woman. She is an asset to the Priory. Many times over. A golden apple.

The last message Ward received from her was a report that Bret is in town. That likely means Joshua is there if he's still alive. The Priory is well aware that the inner circle of the Haddonfield Masonic Lodge is compromised, infiltrated by the followers of Dagon.

Riverdale isn't a long drive. He wants to check in with Miri before he goes. He knows he shouldn't because getting attached to Miri and her mother can get in the way of his sacred duty but he's grown to love them. He doesn't think Greta is aware of the dark gods Bret worships.

Ward has been keeping tabs on Bret since he first moved to town and began dating Greta. Bret's dedication to the Mason's is what gave him away. It was obvious he wasn't one of the typical wealthy philanthropic alcoholic old socialites that normally join the lodges in these sorry days. It is the modus operandi of the followers of the Old Ones to infiltrate groups like the Mason's.

"How are you holding up?" Ward asks a shaken looking Miri, huddled in a blanket on her couch like she is trying to hide from the world. Her mother Greta is snoozing in a chair across from her, letting out tiny, quiet snores.

"I don't know," Miri mumbles. Her eyes are bloodshot from crying. She stares blankly at the television screen. The volume is too low to understand what the television is saying.

"I'm going to keep searching for him, Miri," Ward assures her. "I just wanted to stop by and make sure you know that. I won't stop until I find him. If there is anything you need, don't hesitate to ask."

Miri looks at Ward. "I need Josh."

Her words and tone break his heart. He can feel her loss and pain.

"What the hell is this?" Greta is suddenly awake and using a remote control to turn up the volume on the television.

The television program has been interrupted by a live news report. All three are stunned by the scene on the TV screen. The local Masonic lodge is in flames. There were reports of gunfire before the fire started. The blaze is out of control. It seems unnaturally so. They watch as the roof collapses. It's obvious the building will not be salvaged. A local historic landmark forever gone. At this time it's not known how many are dead, but six bodies have already been found. The police suspect more dead inside. The identities of the gunmen are unknown.

"Oh, my God," Greta almost shouts. "Bret might be in there!"

Miri bursts into hysterical laughter. "The world goes mad!" Her announcement is immediately followed by tears.

Greta joins Miri on the couch and holds her. Both women cry.

"I need to go," Ward says softly. He knows this was an attack by the Poor Soldiers against the Dagonites. "I will let you know as soon as I know anything about Josh and Bret."

Miri and Greta hardly acknowledge Ward's words. He tightens his lips a moment looking at them, wishing he could do more. "I'll see you both later."

"I need a cigarette," Greta huffs nod follows Ward outside. They stand in the front yard together. Greta has one hand on her hip. "This is crazy. Everything."

"I know," Ward agrees.

"Shit." Greta bites back tears. "I know you will, Ward. You're a good man."

Ward wishes he agreed with that statement.

"I want Josh to meet his child," Greta laments.

Ward fails to hide his surprise. "Miri is pregnant?"

"Yes." Greta rubs her ear. "My ears are ringing."

The call of Cthulhu. Ringing ears. So the legends say. Some legends. "That is bittersweet news. I'm going to find my son, Greta."

After Bret and the Deep Ones left Joshua's damp cell he fell asleep again. This time he dreams of swimming in water. It's not a nightmare. He is free and swimming deep in a salty sea. He can breathe under the water with gill slits on either side of his neck. Several dolphins swim along and play with him. He understands the language of the dolphins. They are good hearted, intelligent, and more sophisticated than humans. They even feel pity for humans. The pleasant dream is interrupted by Bret.

"Wake up," Bret barks like a pit bull. "Wake the hell up, boy." Bret hates Joshua and is happy the charade has ended. He wants to be done with the assignment and return to the Black Lagoon. "The ceremony is about to begin."

Joshua still doesn't understand what's happening. Nothing makes sense. He becomes aware of what's happening. "Oh god! Oh god no! What are you doing? Please Bret! Don't hurt me! Oh god, let me go!"

The dank room is filled with ugly, deformed men and women in long dark cloaks and hoods. Some of them unintentionally fidget, mumble, or wheeze. The floor is ankle deep in water. Water drips like blood down the walls. The cloaked group surrounding him are hideous, each it's own hideous monster. Joshua tastes bile in the back of his throat. The stench of the room is so thick and strong, overwhelming. These things must be what Bret called Deep Ones. Bret is dressed in a cloak like the others. "Your cowardice sickens me, Josh," Bret grumbles.

"W-what ceremony?" Josh stutters.

"Let's call it the chemical wedding of Mero and Dagon," Bret cackles with zeal. He massages one of Joshua's shoulders, "You've slept through most of the ceremony. Stay wide awake for this part. You may like it. Have you ever been raped before?"

"Bret," Joshua sobs.

Bret ignores him and begins a baritone chant the others quickly join. "Ph'nglui mglw'nafh Cthulhu R'lyeh wgah'nagl fhtagn!" It is repeated several times with enthusiasm.

"What are you saying?" Joshua's voice trembles and cracks with fear.

"He comes in dreams," Bret preaches. "He slumbering and dreaming until he dreams time and death away. Even death may die."

A pair of cloaked, deformed Deep Ones limp and waddle into the room. Their faces hidden in the shadows of their hoods. One has tentacles instead of hands. The other has flesh fins. Between them they carry an ornate golden chest etched and carved with images of sea monsters and long forgotten glyphs. It is encrusted with precious jewels. As they approach, Joshua realizes he is still nude and chained down. Only now his legs are chained open, spread eagle. He tries to struggle out of his shackles but he is helpless.

The room erupts in emotional repetitive chanting. The mesmerizing chanting grows louder and louder as if it will never stop. Over and over again. Until Joshua can't stand it anymore and shouts,"Shut up! Shut up! shut up!"

His plea is drowned out by, "Ph'nglui mglw'nafh Cthulhu R'lyeh wgah'nagl fhtagn! Ph'nglui mglw'nafh Cthulhu R'lyeh wgah'nagl fhtagn! Ph'nglui mglw'nafh Cthulhu R'lyeh wgah'nagl fhtagn!"

Some amphibious, some scaly fish, some water mammalian, these things that should not be chanted with all their heart, as if their words will make the world fall apart.

The large gold chest is placed on the wet floor before Joshua's open legs. The box is what he imagines the Ark of Covenant would look like. Joshua urinates on the floor as the box slowly opens. Something is alive inside the box. He can't think straight with all the lunatic chanting.

Tears pour down the sides of his face. Snot runs down, he can taste it on his lips. His body begins to tremble with terror. There is no escape. He screams like he has never screamed before in all his life as the first of the black tentacles wiggle out of the golden chest. Joshua sobs and screams, he bites his tongue in fear. Blood mixes with snot, slobbers, and tears.

He can't stop screaming, his throat becoming raw from shrieking. The dark octopus thing crawls from the box. It is like nothing he's ever imagined before, not in his worst nightmare. Black and grey milky eye balls glare at him with an arrogant intelligence. The tentacles are like slippery rubber eels which sucks on the underside. It's mouth opens like a mutant vagina, a fleshy pink interior.

Tentacles wrap tightly around his legs as it slides and climbs up toward his waist. Its strength is unexpected. He wails and hiccups, sobbing uncontrollably as the creature envelopes his soft phallus inside of its soft, slick maw. He feels suction, a tightening, a physically pleasant sensation. He feels the octopus-things toxins enter his blood stream causing a delirious and ecstatic euphoria. The hideous thing gyrates and pumps at his waist.

The toxins calm him. His screaming subsides. The chanting continues quieter. He experiences visions of making love to Miri. He loses consciousness.

Ward gets out of his car at an old Masonic lodge in Riverdale, Illinois. It's night. A full moon. A low fog in the air. This is the building where Veronica told him he will find Bret and other Dagonites. This is an abandoned building. No longer used by the local Masons but mysteriously left alone and rumored to be haunted. Many of the windows are broken out of the two story building. There are no lights on inside the building. There are no street lights functioning around the building. Ward sees the street lights are all broken out.

He opens the trunk of the car and takes out a large flashlight, sledgehammer, and a black handgun then approaches the front door of the brick building, tries the door, and to his surprise it is unlocked. He sets the sledgehammer next to the side of the door; its intended use was to break the door open.

Following the beam of the flashlight into the ominous quietude he finds the first room empty. Ward is jumpy, sensing something watching from the shadows. With a deep breath he precedes, gun in one hand, flashlight in the other.

After an hour of exploring the old Masonic lodge he deduces that it was recently vacated and in a hurry. People had been living here. Veronica's intelligence is always spot on. Why did they flee this place? Ward is perplexed.

Joshua feels the nausea of sea sickness. The ship sways up and down over the ocean waves ceaselessly. He has private, locked quarters aboard the ship. A small bed. A sink. A toilet. A desk. A chair. Some religious books. Paper and pens. The furniture is bolted to the ground.

Bret has revealed he is a high ranking priest of Dagon. He made many offers for Joshua to join their cult. Joshua refuses. Bret does not give up easily.

How long it's been since he was kidnapped is unknown to him. Weeks? Months? There are no windows in his room. He gets two meals a day. Sea food. Mush. Nothing appetizing. Bret refuses to reveal their location or destination.

When the Deep Ones bring in his food they ignore Joshua's questions. Even when they do speak, many of them are difficult to understand. The door opens and Moby enters with a plate of food. This time Bret follows Moby in with an ear to ear grin.

Joshua sits on the edge of his bed looking at Bret with a dazed and confused expression. A long defeated expression. Everything is futile. Bret is the one with all the cards. Now even if Joshua escaped, what would he do? Jump off the ship and drown in the ocean?

"Josh," Bret begins. "I'm making you a final offer. Turn your will and your life over to Cthulhu. Join the church. Be my apprentice. It will be a chance to learn magic. To learn how the universe works. A chance to see your child grow up. Shala is the mother. You are the father. I'm sure Shala would even marry you like in the days of old, when the Angels would fall." He smirks and chuckles.

Joshua's face twists into a look of outrage. "That monster is pregnant?"

Bret nods proudly. "You are going to be a father of a prophesied son. He will bring the second coming. He will awaken our great lord Cthulhu." His eyes glisten with tears of joy at the thought.

The thought of his violation causes Joshua to shudder. Somehow he finds the strength of defiance within. A spark of strength he never knew existed. "If I had my way I would kill you all. You. Shala. Moby. Chlagthu. The Deep Ones. Dagon. Cthulhu. And the bastard child."

Bret backhands Joshua. His knuckles sting. "You would murder your own child!" He glances at the hunched Moby. "It's time he meets another of our gods." Deep Ones shamble into the room overpowering Joshua.

"Unlike your gods, our gods appear to us, boy." Bret snarls.

Joshua silently prays for salvation as they carry him out of the room and onto the deck of the ship. He doesn't resist. The wind is chilly. It is sunset. He prays for courage. Strength. Serenity. They have already taken everything. They will not have his soul.

His ears are ringing. A familiar ringing. The air is crisp and cold. The taste of salt is on his lips. The stars above are magnificent.

They've bound his hands behind him and drag him to the edge of the ship. The water far below crashes against the side of the vessel. The cultists have taken up their mad chanting once again.

Joshua feels surreal. Serenity. God's granted strength. The peace of finality. They are going to toss him in the sea. With his hands bound he will drown. If he were unbound he would still likely drown. Maybe freeze to death. Become food for the fish. He is a blood sacrifice.

Bret is shouting his religious mumbo jumbo. Prayers and proclamations.

By the look of the stars, Joshua realizes they are far north. He wishes there was a plank to walk. Instead of being fed to sharks he is to be fed to alien gods. He knows Bret is a mad man and wishes he could somehow let Miri and Greta know. A psychopath. Evil.

A knife frees his hands. That same knife stabs into his side. He flinches at the sudden pain. Blood washes down his side. Joshua smiles. Someone pushes him from behind. It happens so fast, an eternal fall to the black water below. When he hits the water he sinks like a dead weight. His life is over. Or soon to be.

Through the water he can see more clearly than expected. His lungs ache with a panicked desire to breathe. The water, so heavy. Blood drifts from his wound like a cloud mixing with the salt water. He sees something large and dark rising from below. A fish God. A leviathan. It makes the ship above seem tiny. Its skin is green. Enormous eyes of gold. A face of tentacles each the size of a whale. Beneath that beard of tentacles is a mouth with teeth like a shark. Each tooth is the size of a car. When the mouth opens the water sucks Joshua in like a whirlpool.

His last thoughts are of his love for Miri. He hopes the loss of their relationship isn't too much. He hopes she grieves and moves on. He loves her more than he loves himself.

Eaten by a god. He feels laughter in his brain as he dies.

Miri steps into her living room wearing a white bathrobe drying her hair with a matching towel. Fresh out of the shower. She is startled to find Ward Shakespeare sitting on her couch, waiting for her.

She is offended and a little creeped out by his intrusion; she makes sure her robe is closed. "What are you doing here, Ward? How did you get in?" The door was locked.

"We need to talk," Ward's voice is grave.

Miri's heart drops like a stone. "Josh?"

"Get dressed. I'll wait."

Miri doesn't understand but she trusts Ward. A few minutes later she returns to her living room, clothed, her hair still damp.

"When we're done talking," Ward informs her, "You will want to pack a few things. We will be leaving."

"You're scaring me," she says. "What are you talking about?"

"We should be scared. I have a story to tell you. A story you won't believe. A story about Joshua."

Miri nods, taking a seat across from Ward.

Ward continues, "There is a secret history to the world. Most people are ignorant and believe what they are told. The ways of the world, the great events, the pivotal events of history, cultures, civilizations, religions, wars, are all guided by the manipulations and opinions, the belief systems of opposing secret societies and at the very top the most skilled magicians, maestros of magic. It is the competing wills of the magicians that determine where we go and what we do as a race. As a people."

Miri looks at Ward with disbelief, as if he's lost all his marbles.

Ward goes on, "The saddest part of it all is that most of us have no choice in the matter. Most of us have no choice in what we believe and what we know. Most people believe what they learn in school. What the governments tell them. What science and the churches say. Miri I am a member of one of these elite groups called the Priory of Sion. The purpose of my particular order is guardianship of a holy bloodline. In hope another messiah or avatar will spring forth."

Miri wonders if the loss of his adopted son has driven him insane.

Ward sighs. "I failed in my sacred duty. More than once. I failed Joseph and I failed Joshua. You would think after 2000 years the bloodline would be a vast spider web of families. But no. They are targets. So many the victims of assassination. They were almost wiped out completely when they were known as the Merovingians. The line is close to extinction again. Josh is dead and your child is the last of his line."

"Josh!" Tears stream down her cheeks. "No! You're crazy! How do you know?"

"We have moles. A group of Dagonites sacrificed him to their gods. I'm so sorry. Now it is my holy duty to protect your child. They don't know you are pregnant. If you want your child to survive you will come with me. Learn our ways. I know this is hard, but they will find out. They will come for you like they came for Josh. They will kill you both. I can't let that happen."

Miri wipes her eyes and smiles. "All children are sacred, Ward."

Ward gives a slight nod. "The Poor Soldiers are waiting to take us to a safe house. They are not of the Priory but we've had a partnership with them for a thousand years. We are ready to have your mother, Greta. She will be joining us."

"Do I have a choice?"

"I'm sorry you don't."

The Order of Dog Blood

Logan Two Hawks smashes a spider crawling across the bathroom floor with the heel of his bare foot. It crept out from beneath the garbage can. He's seated on the toilet with an upset stomach from eating too many jalapeños earlier in the evening. His grandmother made Indian Tacos. It's four o'clock in the morning now and the gurgle of his belly and heartburn woke him from slumber. It was a good sleep too. He was dreaming of a blonde woman at his work. In the dream every time she walked by she would flirtatiously run her fingertips across his back and shoulders. He knows if the Indian Tacos hadn't woken him up he would have gotten laid in the dream tonight by that white girl.

Now bleary eyes and sleepy Logan looks down at the dead spider smashed against the tile floor. Its legs are a broken fragile mess. Regret fills his heart. It is bad luck to kill a spider. The spider is the trickster spirit that comes to visit and should be left alone or caught and released outdoors. His grandmother would scold him for what he's just done. One should always treat the spider with respect.

He wipes the dead arachnid up with toilet paper and flushes it down the toilet whispering, "I'm sorry." With that he returns to bed but his wet dream is lost.

Bob Franklin sees a guy named Quincy Dorne he used to attend high school with from the pizzeria's kitchen window. Bob works at Alphonso's Pizza. The restaurant is new to their small town of 5000 people in Middletown, South Dakota. Alphonso's Pizza is a Midwestern company that has just begun to open franchises in the area. The chain was founded by a one eyed, one legged retired biker from Applegate, South Dakota named Alphonso Broken Arrow. Alphonso is a half breed Sioux Indian that used to ride with a motorcycle club called the Dead Silence.

Bob is full white, born and raised in Middletown. He motions to get his Native American friend and roommate's attention. Bob nods in Quincy's direction, who is standing at the counter awaiting his order. Quincy was an enemy of both Bob and Logan in high school. Now Bob is the guy who makes the pizzas, official title: Pizza Table Cook. Logan is a prep cook with tasks like making salads and pastas along with preparing dough in the morning. He makes the breadsticks, garlic bread, and pizza pies.

Logan shakes his head with a smirk at the sight of Quincy. Quincy was and is a handsome, athletic man. The star quarterback in high school which is a very big deal in small towns. All the cheerleaders wanted to date him which is a big deal among high school boys. Quincy came from an upper middle class family. Those things alone were enough to annoy Bob and Logan but Quincy made it worse by bullying Bob and Logan and their other friends. They were known as the nerd pack. High school was more of a traumatic experience than a learning experience for the nerd pack.

Logan watches and giggles as Bob picks his nose and puts the bugger on Quincy's pizza followed by hacking a goober on to it. Logan almost gags at the sight and thought of eating it. He doesn't like Quincy either, but he's over high school and doesn't think what Bob has done is kosher, but he doesn't voice his opinion. Bob has always been the leader of the nerd pack. The most vocal and most disgruntled. Logan sighs and chalks it up to karma.

Middletown is on the edge of the Yankton Sioux Indian Reservation about two hours from Applegate and half an hour from Blackwood and several other smaller towns like Dante, Marty, Ravina, Avon, and Lake Andes. There are numerous small towns in the area and all across America, one not much different than the next. Being a reservation border town, Middletown's population is about half white and half Native American and the racism is thick coming from both cultures. Tensions rise and ebb often.

The store manager, Olana Robey, comes back into the kitchen with a new hire. Logan feels Deja Vu and begins to sweat as he mixes pizza dough looking at the beautiful blonde woman from his dream last night. How can this be? He dreamed of this girl!

Olana begins teaching the new waitress the ins and outs of maintaining the salad bar. Both are wearing Alphonso aprons. Logan knows this new lady is not from Middletown. Everyone in Middletown knows everyone else. It's a typical small town. The only things to do are get drunk, fuck, and gossip about it.

Bob gives Logan an excited smile and whispers, "Wow!"

Logan smiles, nods agreement and goes back to focusing on his work in an attempt to ignore the new hire. They do make eye contact once and it's more intense than words can explain. Her eyes hold him enchanted. Walking near each other he becomes frozen in his tracks and she notices every time. They look into each other's souls, they've never spoken, don't know the other's name, yet they are already lovers. He holds his breath every time she is near. The butterflies scream *America* in his stomach. She sees him! She knows his soul! She smirks and walks right past him like a delicate devil. He feels the rise of a roller coaster each time she approaches and when she is gone from sight he is deflated.

Being a prep cook, Logan gets off work hours before Bob's shift is over. Logan is making his exit to go home and read for a while before Bob gets there so they can game out together. As he is about to step out the door he notices the new goddess of a waitress sitting at a chair in the break room

"Hey." He smiles. "I'm Freedom."

"Weird name." He regrets saying it as soon as the words fall from his lips. "I am sorry I just said that."

"It's cool. I'm used to it." She smiles back at him showing off immaculate white teeth. "My parents were hippies. My sister's name is Enterprise."

"Cool," Logan responds, not sure what to say next. He stands awkwardly nodding for a moment smiling at her. "Waiting for a ride?"

"No. Just resting before I walk home."

"Oh. That's a drag. Want a ride home?"

Freedom looks into him with her winter blue eyes, measuring, deciding if she trusts him. "It's not really a drag. I like walking. Being outdoors." She shrugs, "But sure. I wouldn't mind a ride home."

"I don't mind at all. It's pretty hot out to be walking."

It has been an abnormally hot and humid summer. Freedom and Logan walk outside to his black van. "You're not a serial killer are you?" She chuckles with a nervousness beneath.

Logan chuckles along with her. "Nah. You're safe with me, my lady."

"Alright. I hate serial killers. Weak, twisted, lost and broken souls. Walking diseases. Besides, I am pretty sure I can take you if you turn out to be a serial killer."

Logan arches a black eyebrow. "Alright then. Let's get out of here."

As they drive Logan leaves the radio off so they can talk. Freedom is his dream girl and he feels if the vibes he's picking up are accurate the feeling is mutual.

"You're new to Middletown?" He asks, keeping his eyes on the road.

She flips the radio on in time to hear the deep melodic voice of singer Jim Morrison chant, "Texas Radio and the Big Beat." She answers him while admiring the summer day outside the passenger window. "I'm from Texas. Lived there most of my life. I was born in LA. My sister left home to go to college in Massachusetts. I decided to start fresh too and wander the world. Enterprise and I were very close. I miss her a lot." She puts her hand on his knee as she talks.

"What made you choose Middletown, South Dakota of all places?"

"My boyfriend lives here."

Logan's heart sinks like a stone to the bottom of the ocean.

Freedom continues, "We met online. Have you heard of the Vampire Junkies?"

"No."

"You should join. It's a goth industrial steampunk social network. Like Facebook for cool people."

"Sounds interesting," he answers. Her hand is still on his knee and Logan realizes this young woman is trouble with a capital T. With a touch of bitterness in his tone he says, "I didn't know we have vampires living here in Middletown."

She gives him a smug glare, clearly offended. "There is no such thing as vampires, only dampir. But dampir probably aren't on vampire junkies. Besides my boyfriend, research brought me here. I want to explore the world. I've been researching cult activities. Satanic cults. It's a hobby. A brief run down is this. The western mystery schools and occult tradition culminate from the Knights Templar into the Rosicrucians and the Masons. From there splinters, there have always been splinters and amalgams, ideologies mixing like different colors of water, one splinter is called the Hermetic Order of the Golden Dawn. A black magician leaves that group to found his own splinters. The Ordo Templi Orientis and the Argentium Astrum. Crowley's ideas were part Golden Dawn and part his own. Then comes Jack Parsons the Californian rocket scientist and follower of Crowley who was hoodwinked and hustled by one L. Ron Hubbard. Mr. Hubbard stole money, a woman, and occult secrets from Jack. He used it all to found his own cult called Scientology using his stolen Crowley knowledge mixed with his own science fiction tastes. This was of course a lucrative cult. Scientology had a splinter group with its own ideas which is most popularly known as the Process Church, but it has had many names. The Process Church worshiped Jehovah, Lucifer, and Satan. Each of its members is encouraged to follow their chosen deity and path. Well the Process splintered with the Satanists becoming a very dangerous, murderous sect. Many sects loosely affiliated and eventually connected with all varieties of organized crime. Some of the groups are known as the Four Pi Movement, the Hand of Satan, the Circe Order of Dog Blood, the Black Cross, the Children of Light, the Family, the Finders, the Servants and the Master, among others. These are Satanists that work in drug trafficking, illegal pornography, snuff films, contract killing, human sacrifices, rape, theft, you name it. They are truly evil, or people succumbed to evil. I work to oppose them. One of these satanic cells is based in North Dakota. I've uncovered reasons to believe there is one of these affiliated satanic cults operating in South Dakota now too. Somewhere between here and Applegate."

Logan looks at Freedom aghast. He thinks she is bat shit crazy. Even knowing that he still wants her with every fiber of his being. So he asks, "Who is your boyfriend?" Some local computer nerd? Everyone knows everyone in Middletown. Satanic cults? Vampires? What the hell?

"Herbert Fearing." She removes her hand from his knee.

"Oh. I don't really know him. We were in high school together. He was kind of a loner. I think he had some friends."

"I know." Freedom smiles. She nods out the window. "This is home."

Logan knows the house. He knows Herbert vaguely. Herbert is into black metal music and dresses like he is in a metal band. A weirdo, nihilist, very quiet, with no friends. He was lower on the social ladder than Logan, Bob, and their circle of friends. Herbert always wears black vinyl looking pants covered in chains and very baggy. Logan thinks he looks like a clown in his black metal clothes, more like costumes.

"Do you want to hang out tonight?" Freedom asks as she is getting out of the van. There is a naughty danger in her eyes.

"Yes. What about Herbert?"

"He lets me have friends. He sleeps all day and works a graveyard shift at the medical supply warehouse. He'll be at work tonight. Don't be scared."

"I'm not scared. I want to hang out."

"Rad. Come over at 10 pm."

As Logan drives away in the direction of his own neighborhood he thinks about Herbert Fearing. Actually he is Herbert Fearing III. Kids in school used to giggle about that too. A very odd duck. Everyone made fun of him but not to his face usually. Everyone was afraid of him because of his size, about six foot four inches tall and his rumored gun, sword, and knife collection. Some people said he liked to kill animals out in the country. And that he was a devil worshiper. Is that why Freedom is with him?

Herbert Fearing has long blond hair and a matching beard. Intense, scary blue eyes. He is socially obtuse and behaves in a way that suggests emotional dysfunction. His family is hard core white trash, the poorest family in Middletown. All backwoods types. Gummo's. Herbert is known to have a violent temper. His claim to fame is that he goes to Renaissance festivals participating in jousting and sword fighting.

Herbert the Hermit is what they called him. It's no surprise he is living out his life vicariously online. Logan shouldn't come back to see Freedom tonight because if Herbert were to find out he would beat the bejesus out of Logan. And it's wrong to see another man's woman. His brain, common sense, and conscience tell him to forget Freedom.

He will be there tonight, on time and sharp as a tack.

Logan Two Hawks, Bob Franklin, and Booker DeFalco sit in their living room together playing video games. The three have been friends since kindergarten. They haven't been out of high school all that long. This is their first adventure together living outside their parent's houses as adults.

The living room is a mess. Logan would prefer it clean but Bob and Booker are lazy about cleaning. Dirty dishes, dirty clothes, empty pizza boxes, and wrappers litter the room. Logan is distracted with Freedom on his mind. Enough so he keeps screwing up and getting killed in the game which is starting to piss Bob off. The trio are serious gamers. Logan wonders if he should go to college someday.

"Hey." Bob pauses the game, annoying Booker. "I want to show you guys something."

Bob Franklin thinks he is the leader of their thunderous trio and he is by default. Logan doesn't care and Booker wishes he was Bob. Bob is always claiming to be a descendant of Benjamin Franklin. Logan doesn't buy it. But who knows. Stranger things have happened. Logan's grandmother insists they are descended from Sitting Bull.

Bob is full white, not a farm boy or redneck or a jock. He never fit in with the other white kids for some reason, except for some of the poor white trash. The main reason Bob is a misfit is because he is socially obnoxious at times. He doesn't know the definition of tact.

Booker is a halfbreed who doesn't know who his father is, even though he has his father's last name. His mom is full blood Indian. Natives around town sometimes call Booker and Logan apples for hanging out with Bob and acting like they are white. The name callers are rival families more than anything so even though it's an annoyance Logan doesn't take it to heart.

"What is it?" Logan asks, not really that curious.

Bob grins ear to ear and pulls a black covered paperback book from his backpack on the hardwood floor. He is seated in his captain's chair, a faded and worn emerald recliner that must be twenty years old. Booker and Logan are on the couch, a brown and orange flowered beast from the 1970s. The couch is very low to the floor due to the peg legs being broken off. All of their furniture is secondhand.

Both Logan and Booker's faces light up at the sight of the black book. The cover is a red arcane symbol with bold white lettering above it. It is the Necronomicon. A book all three young men are familiar with the infamous tome. A fictional book found only in the writings of the horror author H. P. Lovecraft. There have been rumors the old spell book was real. A book for opening portals to other worlds and summoning eldritch beings. Rituals of power. A text written by a mad Arab.

"Where did you find it?" Logan whispers.

"Is it real?" Booker whispers.

"I stole it from a book store in Applegate last weekend when I was visiting my cousins." Bob grins.

Logan turns the book over in his hands inspecting it, flipping through pages. It's a new book, freshly printed. "Lovecraft himself proclaimed the book is fake in his letters. He was an atheist. A strict materialist."

"That is what horrified Lovecraft," Booker tells them.

"God bless the Internet," Bob hoots. "I've been reading up on things online. Even though Lovecraft didn't believe any of it he admits getting material and inspirations from his dreams. In other words from the unconscious of his mind."

Booker and Logan are attentive.

Bob continues, beaming with excitement, "Even though he didn't believe it was real, it is real. He was tapping into something like the astral plane. The ether. A netherworld. There are other dimensions that can be accessed only through alternative states of consciousness because they exist on other levels of reality."

"Weird," Booker thinks out loud. He tucks his long hair behind his ears to keep it out of his face. "It kind of makes sense. If you believe in the supernatural."

"You already said it, Booker," Logan points out. "Lovecraft's own belief system was the source of his greatest fear. Something inside him was screaming out from his unconscious and he remained in denial, the scientific gentleman. The rational man is unable to cope with the irrational."

"I want to do one of the rituals from the book," Bob announces to his friends. "Let's see what happens. How will we ever know if we don't try it?"

"That's kind of freaky," Logan says. "And this looks like someone just wrote the book trying to cash out on the Necronomicon name."

"They did a good job with it," Bob counters. "Maybe that's all that matters. We believe in what we're doing, stirring things up from the unconscious worlds."

Logan knows Bob has already made up his mind. "You think it will work?" Logan asks.

"Maybe," Bob answers. "Only one way to find out."

"I'm in," Booker says, seeming nervous about his decision but unable to resist the temptation.

"Awesome." Bob rubs his hands together diabolically. "We can do it tonight."

"I can't do it tonight," Logan announces. "I have someplace to be."

"What?" Bob barks.

"I'm going to hang out with Freedom."

"You dirty dog!" Bob laughs. "Crazy Herbert is her boyfriend, you fool."

Logan shrugs. "It's probably a good idea to prepare for the Necronomicon ritual first. Give Booker and I a chance to read things over. Make sure everything happens by the book."

"Wise words," Bob nods while thinking about going ahead and doing the ritual without Logan.

Freedom told Logan that Herbert goes to work at 10 pm or rather he has to be there by ten so he leaves the house about twenty minutes prior to that. Logan circles the block a few time scoping out the house and building up his nerve before parking in the front. The lights are on within the little white house. He takes a deep breath and steadies himself before walking up to the front door and knocking. His heart racing and his stomach galloping.

Freedom answers the door giving him her intense stare. "Hey." She holds the door open for him to come inside.

The first thing Logan notices is that she is not wearing a bra beneath her white tank top. It's a man's shirt, slightly baggy on her but the shape of her nipples clear and the movement of her breasts beneath the fabric alluring and maddening. Every time she moves he wants her. He is mad with desire. She is barefoot and wearing black baggy pants with a studded leather belt. There are a couple of little chains hanging from the pants. She says she listens to folk and doom metal, but other stuff too. By other stuff she means other sub-genres of metal music. From the tone of her voice Logan senses she is as nervous as he is.

Freedom gives him a brief tour of the house. It's small and cozy, with low lights. All the windows in the house are open. They don't have air conditioning. It is a breezeless night and still hot and humid enough that they are both sweating.

They talk for hours, small talk that quickly turns into deep conversation that takes odd and bizarre turns. Anyone listening in would question the mental stability of the two. They talk about everything from music to Norse mythology to reincarnation to the Vampire Junkies community to astrology and Nazis and gas masks, swords, knives, guns, sex, death, and the meaning of life. After more than an hour of baring their souls to each other with an uncanny trust for one another they stand close together in the center of the living room as if they are in the center of the universe. And they are in the center of their own universe.

     Logan whispers, "I am a comet lighting up the sky and drawn to you like gravity pulling me down to the world's surface. You are an anchor that prevents me from floating away. You are my gravity. I can't escape."

     Freedom is much shorter than Logan looking up into his eyes; she whispers back, "I've loved you in every life we've lived. I loved you when I was a Viking huntress and you a swan knight crossing the sea with me. Every life we find each other. My spirit is the wolf. You are the lion, your secret self beneath Logan. You know who I am speaking of. Deep, deep. The creator of Logan. I am chained to you. I will never escape you and will always love you. You are the comet caught in my gravity, caught in love, and when we collide the world will die."

     She kisses him on the lips. The sweetest most tender and innocent kiss he's ever felt. Her lips are so pale pink and soft. His heart cries with joy. She has to stand on her tip toes to reach Logan's lips. He places his hands on her hips. He wasn't expecting a kiss.

     "I don't know why I did that," she says with a touch of innocence.

     "It's okay." Logan puts his arms around her. "I liked it. I want to do it again."

     "We're chained," she whispers before the second kiss.

     "I want to feel closer to you."

     In a delirium of passing time they are stripped and making love on the floor. She quietly, softly calls out his name several times. It is an unforgettable moment for the both of them.

     When they are finished, lying on the floor holding each other skin against skin in the night's humidity and sweat, Freedom says, "I feel closer to you."

     She takes out her cell phone and takes several pictures of them naked together.

     "You are gravity pulling me. I can't escape the event horizon." Logan mumbles.

     She rises and walks into another room returning with a long blue, violet, black, and green peacock feather. "I want you to have this."

     Logan takes the feather. "I don't ever want to leave your side." She cuddles back up to him.

     "Someday," she whispers with her head resting on his chest. She kisses him. "Herbert will be home soon. You have to leave. I don't want you to."

     "Leave him. Just come with me now." There is desperation in his voice. "I love you. Marry me."

     "I will. We need each other. I will. Not tonight but soon, my love."

He doesn't want to leave. It feels like one of the hardest things he's ever had to do. What kind of spell does she have over him? On the drive home in the dark early morning hours he tries to sort through mixed emotions. Guilt and shame for infidelity. Fear of Herbert's wrath. Sorrow in the absence of Freedom. The right thing to do must be to stay away and he knows he never will. He has to be with Freedom and will do anything for her.

When he gets home it is past four in the morning. Bob is still up playing a video game and smoking a marijuana cigarette in his green recliner, his feet up. Booker is half snoring on the couch.

"How was it?" Bob asks with a devilish grin, only taking his eyes from the television screen momentarily.

"It was fine." Logan is tired and heart twisted, making his way directly to his bedroom.

Bob snorts and laughs. "You got laid, champ!"

Logan only looks at Bob.

"Don't lie." Bob keeps focusing on the video game he's playing. "Better hope Herbert the hermit doesn't catch wind of it."

Logan changes the subject. "What did you guys do tonight?"

"We messed around with the Necronomicon a little but nothing happened."

"I thought we were going to prepare first."

Bob shrugs. "A trial excursion. We will try again."

Logan nods. "I'm tired. I'm going to bed."

"Sweet dreams are made of these, champion," Bob smiles.

"Good night."

Logan and Freedom begin spending every night together while Herbert Fearing is on the graveyard shift at the medical supply warehouse. When they are not together they are constantly texting each other all day long. Logan is desperately in love with Freedom. Freedom says she loves Logan but they have to wait. She promises she will eventually leave Herbert and they will be together forever.

Herbert knows there is a close friendship between Freedom and Logan. He knows they spend time together. In the beginning he tries to play it cool, that he trusts Freedom enough to allow her to hang out with other guys. The time Freedom and Logan spend together is excessive and obsessive. It becomes obvious Herbert's jealousy and suspicion is growing daily. It is fair to say that Herbert is developing a hate for Logan.

The guilt eats away at Logan but he doesn't have the willpower to stop. He gets very little sleep and starts feeling constant paranoia regarding Herbert Fearing. He is always looking over his shoulder. He knows he is doing wrong and Herbert is a violent man.

How can love be wrong? Logan is frustrated and perplexed as to why Freedom is waiting to break up with Herbert. What is the hold up? And Logan is insanely jealous when Freedom is with Herbert. Logan has become an emotional mess. Always tired from lack of sleep being up all night with Freedom and always emotionally exhausted. At the same time there is an intense, overwhelming excitement created by Freedom's presence. This devastating roller coaster has been going on for several weeks now.

While this dysfunctional love triangle has been spiraling further and further into a volatile situation, Bob has been experimenting with the Necronomicon with little success. Most nights he performs black magic rituals alone, some nights Booker participates, but the failures are beginning to bore Booker.

A frustrated Bob decides he needs more psychic and spiritual energy to succeed with the demonic rituals. He asks the now ever preoccupied Logan to help with the rituals, begs him. Logan can't bear to be away from Freedom so he agrees to help only if she can come too. Bob readily agrees, the more the merrier, the more the psychic energy.

Things happen fast. Bob is too eager to speak with the demons and the dead. That night Logan and Freedom meet Bob and Booker at Bone Field Cemetery on the edge of town just before midnight. Freedom and Logan are holding hands as they approach the meeting place, a statue of Saint Augustine. "It's so dark. I can't see a thing," Freedom tells Logan.

It is pitch black. Clouds blot out the moon and stars above. The cemetery is further shadowed in the night by trees and tombstones. All Logan can make out are shapes of darkness. "It will be fine. We're almost there."

"What's the point of this?" Freedom fearfully squeezes his hand.

"I don't know," Logan admits. "To appease Bob. An act of friendship." He knows his grandmother would be angry and scolding if she knew he was even thinking about dabbling in black magic or magic of any kind. He was raised by his grandmother and she is very traditional, a strong adherent to their tribal beliefs. His entire family would be angry with him. Grandma is the matron of the family, the glue that holds them all together and keeps them proud of their name and culture. Logan himself knows playing with spirits is a dangerous endeavor. "It doesn't matter. The Necronomicon isn't a real book. It's a fake spell book someone named Simon made to turn a quick buck, to cash in on Lovecraft."

"This whole situation is creepy," Freedom complains. "Being here in this graveyard to do some kind of satanic ritual seems like the dumbest thing I've ever done."

"It's not satanic."

"Demons mean the Devil. It's satanic."

"I'm sorry. I'll tell Bob we aren't going to do it and we'll split." Logan assures her.

They share a kiss.

"Thank you," she whispers in his ear.

They hear voices not far off and notice a glow of flickering light causing dancing shadows among the trees and tombstones. The glow is deep within the cemetery, in the back, away from any potential passerby's. When Logan and Freedom reach the low fire light they quickly let go of each other's hands and take a few steps apart to put a false distance between them. Herbert is with Bob and Booker. Both Freedom and Logan are in. Speechless panic. Logan wonders how Bob could set him up like this? He feels so betrayed.

As they approach Bob, Booker, Herbert, and a young woman are just finishing making a large circle and pentagram in the grass with thick piled lines of white flour. There are arcane symbols etched in bronze, copper, and other small, thin sheets of metal. There is a lantern burning along with candles and incense. Logan recognizes the woman immediately, a Middletown native, Jacqueline Fokken.

Herbert glares at Logan, not even attempting to disguise his rage. If eyes could kill Logan would be dead and mutilated. Logan pretends not to notice, smiles, and in a smooth, calming tone says, "Hi, everyone. How's it coming along?"

"Good." Bob grins. "Glad you're here, bud."

Freedom stands next to Herbert and takes his hand. This act seems to calm him and he stops looking at Logan.

Logan does his best to pretend jealousy is not eating him up inside. He is very angry with Bob. He's not happy to see Jackie Fokken there either. She is another social misfit. Long black hair, fairly unattractive, vampire pale skin, all dressed in black. Logan never liked Jackie, she went to high school with them and was very arrogant and stuck up, coming from a well to do family. She thinks very highly of herself and acts as if she is the most intelligent person on the planet. She thinks she's an artist and claims to be a witch. Logan is always polite to her.

Logan stands there looking at everyone including Freedom now standing in the circle and dressed in black robes. Freedom has slipped on a black robe provided by Herbert. Logan knows Freedom doesn't want to do this and neither does he but he can't figure a way out.

"Get in the circle," Bob barks with excitement. "The ceremony is about to begin."

Freedom whispers to no one, "Is everybody in?"

Bob continues, "Tonight we summon the dogs of Hell!"

Reluctantly Logan crosses over into the ceremonial circle with the others. He does his best to avoid eye contact with Freedom or Herbert. His mind races with excuses to get himself and Freedom out of there, but nothing comes to mind. Herbert's presence creates the difficulty. He tells himself the nonsense will be over soon enough. Persevere and he and Freedom will find their life together someday soon.

Everyone stands within the circle, all eyes on Bob and Jackie who have taken charge of performing the rite. The pair prays aloud in some barbarous tongue unknown to Logan. He's not even convinced it's an actual language, for all he knows they are just grunting and spouting gibberish. Bob wields a knife and moves it around creating the shape of an invisible star with his gestures. Logan sees the blade and handle of the knife are decorated in red arcane glyphs of some kind. Jagged geometry of fallen angels.

Before Jackie, who is on her knees, is a deep stone bowl also painted in the blood red eldritch signs of some alien gods. The bowl is filled with what looks like grass, sage, incense, herbs, it smells vaguely of cannabis when she burn the leaves.

Everyone is still and silent once the ceremony is complete. The ceremony was maybe fifteen minutes in its entirety. Everyone looks about the darkness outside their magical circle in fearful anticipation. The black summer night is quiet. Seconds become minutes. Nothing happens. No demon dogs. No unspeakable horrors. No gateways to Hell. The thickest aura in the air is the once again growing tension between Herbert, Freedom, and Logan. Herbert caught a tender look between the secret lovers and is clenching his jaw. Logan is growing more angry at Bob the more he thinks about the situation. Bob knows how complicated it is. Bob is supposed to be Logan's friend. He should have Logan's back. Logan would never do something like this to Bob.

"I guess it didn't work," Booker sighs with a shrug. It never works. He wasn't expecting it to work this time either. Even so he always participates because of that slim unlikely chance something spectacular may happen.

All around them, what sounds to be just outside the perimeter of the circle and filling the entire cemetery is the unsettling barking of dogs. What sounds like dozens of unseen dogs, barking and growling ferociously. Dogs that sound as if they are prepared to rip and tear everyone's flesh apart. Snarling and rabid. The canine madness is nonstop, growing louder and louder. Everyone in the circle looks about, they huddle preparing to be attacked by a pack of wild dogs. It seems like the barking is getting closer and they are about to be ravaged by these unseen dogs of Hell. Booker, Logan, Bob, and Herbert all begin to scream with fear.

"Stay in the circle!" Freedom shouts.

Herbert grabs Freedom in what first appears to be an act to protect her, but quickly becomes an act of using her as a human shield against the coming onslaught of demonic dogs. Freedom's eyes are wide with fright and looking into Logan's equally frightened eyes. There is unspoken love passing between them. Booker is terrified hanging on Bob's shoulder, almost hugging him. Logan sees nothing but excitement in Jackie's eyes. Absolutely no fear.

"I can hear them!" Bob shouts out with a sudden fervor, his eyes almost glazed over. "I can hear it all!" He doesn't seem to be speaking of the dogs.

"No one does anything," the snotty witch Jackie demands loud enough to be heard over the discord of the dogs. "We must banish the Hell hounds before we leave the circle. If you step outside the circle before our rite of banishment you will be cursed, maybe even killed."

Everyone present feels the same growing madness within. They all stand in stiff silence underneath the snarls, growls, and barking as Bob and Jackie go through the gestures of the banishment ritual. Logan notes that it is the reverse of the summoning ritual. The banishment ritual ends with Bob and Jackie chanting together and ending it with a wild howl like the dogs. The cemetery falls silent immediately and Bob and Jackie begin to laugh.

No one leaves the circle. Bob looks ecstatic and melted with pleasure. Jackie is smug and arrogant, above all present. Logan, Freedom, and Booker don't hide their fear.

Jackie is the first to step out of the protective magical circle. "It is over now."

The others hesitantly step out of the circle.

"Or has it only just begun." Jackie says softly to no one in particular. It is not a question.

They all go home without further discussion.

It's midnight. Freedom and Logan are in a small public park together in the heart of the town. It's dark but street lights illuminate the park somewhat. The park is only three blocks from Freedom and Herbert's house. Freedom is sitting on the top of the slide in her usual attire, the braless tank top, baggy, black shorts with chains hanging from the belt loops, and combat boots with chrome spikes. She sits at the top of the slide looking down at Logan who is on a swing letting his feet drag in the wood chips beneath the playground equipment. He doesn't want to look up at her but he does periodically. She stares intensely on purpose. Ever the drama queen, this reincarnating Viking warrioress.

It's a hot summer night. It is the hottest summer in years, record breaking temperatures. Freedom whispers, "When I get to the bottom I go back to the top of the slide."

"I love you Freedom. Leave Fearing. Get it over with. Let's get our own place together. I can't stand to be apart from you."

Freedom's expression is forlorn and distant. "I can't. I have to wait for him to leave me. He will leave me. I can feel it. We only have to wait until the time is right. Then we can be together forever."

"I don't understand. Why wait for him?"

"He is crazy. An emotional time bomb. So pent up and tight. Trust me. I know him. I know what I'm doing. He knows about us even though I deny it. He hates you as a matter of principle not because he wants or loves me. It's a matter of pride. I think he wants Jackie. Have faith. Everything will work out."

"I think Bob wants Jackie too. Where the hell did she come from? Why did she come back to Middletown?"

"I don't know. I don't trust her."

Logan kicks some wood chips. "It's hard waiting."

Freedom slides down and kisses him. Her lips are so soft. He can smell her summer sweat. "I love you."

"Where did you come from?" Bob is smoking a cigarette, sitting on the front steps of their apartment building.

Jackie smiles as if teasing. "You could say I'm a wandering bishop of sorts. I come from all over. My church is invisible. I've come here because you called me."

Bob fails to hide the suspicion on his face. "How did I call you?"

"Playing with the Necronomicon and the black arts." She slides closer to him on the steps. Their shoulders are touching. Her long midnight black hair matched her black clothing. Bob struggles to ignore her allure.

"You say magic is real?" Bob is excited by her touch.

"Something is real." She smiles touching his thigh.

"Tell me," Bob urges. "I want to know everything."

Jackie leans in to whisper in his ear, preceded with a lick, "In bed." Her hand runs up his inner thigh. Bob is hers.

Without a word Bob and Jackie rush into his bedroom and into an eager, aggressive, and lengthy episode of sex. Afterwards they lie naked together, uncovered, cooling sweat beaded on their bodies, sharing a cigarette. She begins speaking to Bob. She has a deep voice for a woman. "My church. My Order. My Coven. We are called the Order of Dog Blood."

"The Order of Dog Blood," Bob whispers in wonderment. "Tell me more."

"I am a satanic witch. Black magic. My Order is loosely affiliated with many small groups nationally and internationally. Intergalactically," she giggles at that.

"What do you mean?"

"Tell me, tell me, tell me," Jackie jokes. "We have been around a very long time. As old as the universe. A long history. A long unknown war. You could say we began to formally organize or reorganize around 1947 when the black magician and prophet died. Of course this prophet, the Great Wild Beast began organizing us before that through thelema and Wicca groups and holy books. A science fiction writer seduced or hoodwinked a rocket scientist around the said time. This writer of fiction, this spinner of tales stole knowledge of the art from the scientist. The scientist had received the knowledge from the prophet. The fiction spinner created a religion of his own with this stolen knowledge with him own twists and beliefs added in. Many people call this cult Scientology. All religions are cults of various sizes. Many cults spawn factions that go their own way. Theological disputes. Often egos run rampant. My path comes from a faction called by many the Process Church, but then more acutely from a faction breaking off of the Process. There are many groups. Many cultists and affiliates and hangers on.

Most ignorant to the origins of everything and the big picture. Most puppets and sheep."

Bob looks at her with a mixed expression of fear and curiosity.

Jackie continues to educate her new student. "The network is made of many cells much like Islamic terrorists and Nazis in hiding. We serve the wisdom of darkness and death. We are what people should fear in the deep of the night. We are shapers of reality. The Angels of Hell. Our reach is far and wide. At the highest levels are the leaders, the rich, the elite, the intelligence agents and so much more. We are winning the war." She grins, kisses Bob's nipple. "In 1947 they tore a hole in reality in the Mojave Desert, continuing the tears in reality created by others such as John Dee and the Enochian reality ripping whirlwind he created. Now more and more the lords and the old creatures bleed through the sky, influencing the world."

"You lost me in there somewhere," Bob admits.

"I've found you," Jackie counters. "I have so much to teach you. We will murder the world."

Bob finds himself internally conflicted. Drawn in by her beauty and words, but horrified by some of it. "You are a devil worshiper?"

She laughs out loud. "You've been trying to summon demons older than the Bible and you're worried about the Devil?"

He feels foolish, but the forbidden is tempting him. "I want to know everything." He can use the power for good.

"I am a witch. My Coven is thirteen. More if you count our students. We chose the name of the Order of Dog Blood in honor of Circe and Hecate. Our high priestess lives in Applegate. Our most sacred rites take place in Blackwood. If you join us you can have me. What would you do to join us?"

"Anything."

"Say you love Satan."

"I love Satan."

Logan arrives home in the early morning hours. Feeling exhausted and somewhat delirious from his constant lack of sleep, sneaking around, and growing paranoia. Booker is still up on the low couch transfixed by a video game. He can see in Booker's eyes that he is stoned immaculate. His eyelids are drooping and his eyes are bloodshot. Upon realizing Logan is in the room, Booker gives his friend a lazy, genuine smile. There is a German Shepherd sitting on the couch next to Booker.

"Where did the dog come from?"

"Mm," Booker answers. "His name is Grimston. Jackie gave him to Bob."

Logan lets the dog sniff his hand before petting the animal and scratching behind its ear affectionately. He notices it has a spiked leather collar with a tiny metal swastika hanging from it. This observation greatly disturbs Logan. A swastika? What the hell is going on with Bob? Ever since he has started messing with black magic and dating this evil witch bitch Jackie. Bob is falling to the dark side.

Logan sits on the couch with Booker and the German Shepherd. The coffee table is a disaster of candy wrappers, overflowing ashtrays, and empty soda bottles. "What do you think of Jackie?"

Booker shrugs. "I don't know. She's Bob's old lady now. They're in his room right now snoozing."

"Where did she come from?" Logan asks. He doesn't trust her. Everything is changing. Bob could easily argue that Logan has changed since he's started having an affair with Freedom.

"I don't know. She's from Middletown. You know that."

"She left," Logan reminds Booker. "Or she disappeared."

"She left to go to college," Booker nods. "A lot of people do that."

"But she disappeared. She was a missing person. Everyone in town knows that. Her mother hung herself overcome with grief. Where was she? Why did she come back now?" Her father had died while she was in high school. He was underneath a car working on it and the jack slipped out. The car crushed him. She was a freshman then. Logan, Bob, and Booker were freshmen when she was a senior.

Booker pauses the game to give Logan his full attention. "I don't know but she has a lot of dogs." He whispers, not wanting to be overheard by Jackie or Bob. Booker seems frightened.

"What's wrong?"

Booker's eyes betray him as he glances at Bob's closed bedroom door. He whispers, "I could use some fresh air. Wanna take a walk?"

Logan nods and the two old friends step outside into the dark night. It is still hot. Even with the odd behavior of Bob and Jackie, Logan finds himself distracted by thoughts of Freedom. They were together earlier this evening. They are together every night and now even during the day while Herbert sleeps.

Booker and Logan walk in silence for a while. It's a quiet night. Both young men light up cigarettes. Freedom hates it that Logan smokes. It's an unspoken agreement that they wait until they are a block away and across the street before they start talking.

Logan gives Booker a nervous side glance. "What's going on?"

"It's fucked up." Booker is obviously shaken by the sound of his voice. He was obviously holding back in the apartment. "They killed a dog right in front of me. I just stood there and watched." There are tears welling up in Booker's eyes.

"Who killed a dog?"

"All of them. Bob. Jackie. Herbert. Bob made me join the stupid cult. Jackie is the leader, but she says there are more of them. Bob and Herbert are really into it."

"Why did they kill the dog?"

"Another ritual. A blood ceremony is what Jackie called it. For power. I don't know. I'm in over my head. Bob isn't Bob anymore. We all signed contracts selling our souls to the Devil. In blood."

"That's crazy, Booker." Logan shakes his head. "That poor dog that's sick. How could you be part of it?"

"I'm afraid of all of them." Booker admits. "Herbert ate the dog's heart. They think they are some kind of black wizards or something."

"Don't go out with them again."

"Jackie has a lot of dogs. All German Shepherds. Haven't you been reading the paper? Talking to people? The cops have been finding dead dogs all over Middletown and the surrounding areas. Cattle mutilations too. I think it's Jackie, Bob, Herbert, and the other cultists she talks about but I've never seen."

Logan realizes his whole world has been Freedom and nothing else. He is obsessed with her. He's paid attention to nothing else. Literally. "We should move out. Let Bob have the place to himself."

"What about the lease?"

"We'll figure something out." Logan feels like Judas. He's been best friends with Bob forever. But what's happening is evil. He can feel it. Jackie has brainwashed Bob. Maybe Herbert has always been evil. "Maybe we can stay with my grandma until we find a place to live. I'll talk with the landlord about the lease. Don't say anything to Bob about it. Things sound dangerous.

"Okay, I trust you." Booker nods.

Logan thinks this may turn out for the best. Freedom can move in with Booker and Logan. They will get away from the stupid devil worshiping garbage and start new lives.

Logan feels like he is living two lives. He is alone in the dark at the same park they always meet waiting for the arrival of Freedom. He watches the sidewalk with impatience and his heart always lights afire with the slow strolling of her emergence from the shadows. Logan is no longer comfortable going to her house since Herbert's suspicion is so blatant and everyone knows about the affair. It would be foolish to even deny it if Herbert approached him, but he would deny it.

Not long ago Logan dropped Freedom off in her driveway after a day of swimming together. Herbert had been trying to call her while Freedom and Logan made love in the shower. Herbert was enraged. He marched out the front door with a red face and an accusing finger pointing right at Logan. Freedom said, "Uh oh, he looks pissed." And he did. He looked like he was going to attack Logan. She quickly exited the car to calm him and Logan sped away feigning ignorance before Herbert reached him. Herbert has since forbidden Freedom to have contact with Logan. They text and meet in secret now but Herbert's new law has not slowed their relationship in the slightest. It's fair to say Logan and Freedom are obsessed with each other.

She appears under a nearby street light all attitude and swagger and Logan's stomach flutters with joy. There she is in her white tank top, baggy black shorts, and combat boots. Logan knows her games. He knows she goes braless in the white tank top to drive him crazy. She loves the attention. She enjoys playing cat and mouse before they make love.

They maintain intense eye contact until she reaches him, both refusing to blink or look away. Before any words are exchanged she throws her arms around him and they kiss with a hungry desperation. "I'm afraid," she whispers, holding Logan tight.

This is Logan's secret life. He has one diminishing life during the day and this secret real life at night with Freedom. He feels he only exists with Freedom. There is power in secrets.

"What are you afraid of?"

They are walking, holding hands now. She is much shorter than he is. Her hand is smaller. Her dark hair reached her waist. She is quite proud of her hair and it is beautiful.

Freedom's eyes tear up. "Herbert took me to another of Jackie's rituals in the graveyard. They gave us LSD without telling us. That was last night. That's why I couldn't see you last night."

"What happened?"

"Bob and Booker were there and another girl named Roxy. Jackie said she met Roxy in London. Jackie says she's traveled all over the place. California, Mexico, New York. Did you know that?"

"No. She is a spoiled rich girl. Her family was always bragging about their vacations and stuff like that. They were the richest family in Middletown I think. She spent the summers away. Every summer. I don't know where. She went to college in Arkham, Massachusetts."

Freedom nods and says, "Roxy and Jackie are both members of the Order of Dog Blood. They say the group has existed for a long time and that Bob is becoming a talented black magician. I thought I was bad ass metal. But sacrificing dogs is fucked up no wrong. We drank the blood! And demons are real! I can feel them! I can hear them! I could see them in the shadows outside the circle!"

"Calm down, baby," Logan hugs her again. "Every little thing will be alright. I talked to my grandmother and she said we can both stay with her until we get our own place. We don't need to see any of them ever again. I can't believe you had to experience all of that. It sounds like a nightmare." Logan feels his initial shock of the story quickly become outrage. "The dogs and the LSD are both fucked up and wrong. Never again. I will protect you."

Freedom cries. "We painted our faces in blood. I was so fucked up from the drugs and so scared I felt like I was under their control. The sacrifice was to the devil. Bob let a demon named Samiel enter his body. He said so many bizarre things. It felt like he would never stop talking. It wasn't Bob's voice.
I couldn't leave the circle. The demon dictated an unholy book through Bob. Roxy was the

scribe. She kept calling us the black circle boys and girls." Freedom is trembling. "It is Satan."

Logan is horrified by her revelations and hugs her close. He thinks of the Necronomicon. That book has nothing to do with what the Order of Dog Blood are doing. It has nothing to do with Satan? Does it? It's about the old gods from Lovecraft's imagination that existed before Satan. Alien gods. If what Booker said is true this is one of many cells, many satanic cults that are loosely connected, more ideology and spirit than structure. This satanic network goes by many names. It seems to be too unreal and insane to be real connecting the Manson Family, the Son of Sam, the Zodiac Killer, and many, many more.

Freedom begins to sob. "Jackie made us celebrate Samiel with an orgy. All of us. An orgy covered in blood.

"Old man Painted Bear lives in Blackwood. He is a medicine man. That's what my grandma and the elders say. We'll go to him. He'll know what to do. I don't want you to ever go back to Herbert's house. Never again."

Freedom nods, wiping her nose and tears. "I want to leave Middletown. I don't want to live here anymore.

Logan agrees. "We're going to get our things and go to my grandma's. We'll tell her everything. She'll know what to do and take us to Painted Bear. She'll help us leave town. That's probably the safest thing to do."

"That's what I want," Freedom says, wiping her face. "I want to get away from here and forget any of this ever happened. I love you, Logan. I never want to be without you. I can't live without you."

"I love you too," Logan replies with warmth in his voice. "After tonight you will never have to be apart from me again."

"Promise?"

"I promise. Let's go pack our things."

"Wait." Freedom looks nervous, thoughtful. "It's too dangerous for you to come to our house. I'm afraid Herbert will shoot you if he sees you there. I know he is at work. I just don't want to take any chances. I'll go pack a bag. It won't take long. I'll meet you at your grandma's in less than an hour."

"I'm not afraid of him."

"I am. Please do this for me. I'd die if anything happened to you."

"Nothing is going to happen to me. I can kick Herbert's ass if I have too."

"You're not bulletproof."

"Maybe I am." Logan grins and kisses her forehead. "Okay, babe. I'll do it your way. Meet me in less than an hour. Promise?"

"Promise."

Logan enters his apartment quickly to pack a few things. He's disappointed to see Bob, Booker, Jackie, and the girl who must be Roxy gathered in the living room. They are not playing video games. Roxy is close to Booker, her hand on his leg. It's obvious Booker is taken by her. Logan acknowledges that she is an oddly attractive girl. Odd because she is so awkward and unique in appearance it makes her attractive. Very pale skin and covered in freckles. Bright green eyes. Long straight strawberry hair.

The four are talking softly, conspiratorially as Logan comes in causing a hush. They stare at him in a way that creeps him out. Logan forces a chuckle. "What the hell are you all being so secretive about?"

There isn't much of a reaction from any of them other than Booker, who can't hide the guilt smeared across his face. Logan notices Booker's eyes dart at something behind him. Before he has the chance to turn around, strong hands grip him like iron. One hand pressing a white cloth over his mouth and nose. The other arm is like a vise around his neck. The muscle is hard as a brick. The last thing Logan sees is as his vision blurs before unconsciousness is the living room quartet up in a babbling panic. Roxy restraining Booker.

Logan wakes in the same cemetery all the so-called Order of Dog Blood has been conducting its either Lovecraftian or Satanic rituals. He is gagged and bound with rope on his knees within a magical circle and pentagram. Thick flour lines in the grass. Bob, Booker, Jackie, Roxy, and Herbert are in the circle with him. He immediately realizes it had to be big Herbert who snuck up behind him. Alarms are going off inside Logan. A tingling danger sense. This is not good.

As he becomes more awake and more aware he realizes he is tied to a thin headstone. The ropes are tight enough to cause pain. He can't wiggle free. A long ceremonial knife and bowl painted in alien symbols rests in the grass before him.

Bob holds his coveted copy of the Necronomicon religiously to his chest. His expression is an unfriendly and hollow one. Jackie grips the Book of Shadows. Herbert has the Satanic Bible.

Logan tries to talk through his gag.

Everyone looks at Roxy. She smiles and nods. "Let the lamb speak."

Jackie removes the gag. Booker refuses to look at Logan.

"What is this?" Logan exasperates. He tries to look brave.

The five members of the Order of Dog Blood ignore him and begin to pray, on their knees with their heads down, attired in long black robes. Logan feels the blackness of mental illness all around him, even before he sees the dogs. Movement in the shadows outside the circle. Low and quiet growling. German Shepherds circling and stalking at a distance like the Minotaur hunting the labyrinth. Logan can feel the heat of anger all around. The dog's black eyes seem to show an unnatural intelligence.

He unintentionally gasps realizing there is a bloody dead dog on the dark grass before him. Its head is severed. Glassy dead eyes give him a vacant stare. Logan's horror continues to build as he realizes he is fully nude and covered from head to toe in what he assumes must be dog blood. His senses are clearing. He sees there are two bowls, not one. The knife is bloody and one bowl is filled with blood. He also realizes each of the five present has a long knife in their hand as they circle him.

"Oh, God," Logan pleads. "Don't do this. Bob. Booker. You can't be serious."

The five continue to circle him closer. Booker's hands are visibly shaking.

Logan struggles violently against his bindings only causing further rope burns on his already raw skin. "Please don't do this!" He sees the hate in Herbert's eyes. "Booker!" His own eyes are crying tears of fear.

"For the dark lord," Jackie says, slashing Logan's arm with her long knife.

"For Satan," Herbert says, stabbing Logan's stomach.

All five begin stabbing Logan all over his body in a frenzied orgy of blood and screams. The dogs all howl. They stab frantically with no mercy as if possessed of some primal rage. As if they can't stop what they've started. It doesn't last long. Logan doesn't live long. His final thoughts are of Freedom and his grandmother.

The five are covered in his blood. Herbert's blade tip actually broke from hitting one of Logan's bones. Roxy tastes Logan's blood on her long knife. Bob's eyes are glazed over with a demonic look. Booker appears to be ill. Jackie is smiling.

Freedom approaches Logan's grandmother's house with her purse slung over her shoulder and a backpack on. The night sky is lit by a full moon. The house is a rust red color. The lawn is more bare earth than grass. A clothes line with white sheets hanging like ghosts swaying in the breeze is at the side of the house. Children's toys are scattered about the yard. Toys of grandchildren. Elder grandmother Kathleen Two Hawks is the matriarch of her large and extended family. Native American family dynamics are culturally different than the European morphed American family unit. They are closer knit and more responsibility for your family members is expected and natural. Any relative that needs a place to stay is welcome in her home. None are turned away.

Kathleen Two Hawks husband died in a car wreck years ago crossing a bridge while inebriated.

Logan has told Freedom many things about his family, even introducing her to some briefly. The whole family is aware and does not approve of Logan's infatuation with the white girl.

There are three cars parked outside the Two Hawks residence and the lights are on inside. Freedom can see grandma doing something in the kitchen. She softly, nervously knocks on the door.

Ross Two Hawks swings the door wide open. The fit, untamed warrior spirit of a man is Logan's older cousin. He has a reputation of being a drunk, a wild man, and an undefeated street brawler. He is always hyper, never seeming comfortable to sit still. His dark brown eyes study her with arrogance and suspicion. She reminds him a a rubber band stretched to its limit. He doesn't like or trust white people. Ross is loud and proud. His hair is short because he recently got out of jail and the local sheriff made him cut it.

"What do you want, wasichu girl?" Ross smirks.

Freedom is intimidated. She musters up the courage to answer. "Logan told me to meet him here." She can hear the television in the living room. It sounds like a generic action movie. The aroma of fresh bread comes from the kitchen.

"He ain't here."

"Who is it?" Grandma asks.

"Logan's white girl," Ross answers.

Grandma appears at the door next to Ross. Her skin is wrinkled and her once black hair streaked with numerous lines of silver. She glares at Freedom and grunts, "What do you want?"

"Logan told me to meet him here." Freedom answers. "I'll wait outside."

Grandma gives her a queer look. Ross chuckles. "Come sit in the kitchen," grandma says.

Ross returns to the living room. His grandmother's word is law as far as he is concerned.

Freedom nervously sits at the kitchen table and watches grandma ignore her and continue baking loaves of bread.

Hours pass.

The light and television in the living room have been turned off and the sound of Ross's snoring echoes from that room. He sleeps on the couch. The other bedrooms are filled with other cousins and such family members.

Grandma Two Hawks has finished making bread and has just finished cleaning up her mess.

Freedom is very worried about Logan. He's never stood her up before and he's not responding to her text messages and phone calls. She stares out the window waiting for her love to appear.

Grandma sees the dedication to her grandson in Freedom's eyes. She's touched by the apparent love even knowing it's a dysfunctional love. She sighs, knowing Logan's want of this girl. She looks at the girl again and sits at the table across from her rather than going to bed. Grandma knows if Logan said he would be here, he would be here.

"Something is wrong," Grandma states this as a fact.

Freedom nods.

"What happened tonight?" Grandma asks with unexpected gentleness.

"I left Herbert tonight." Freedom confesses. Letting those words out uncork a bottle of pent up emotion. Freedom cries as she tells Grandma Two Hawks everything. We were going to escape tonight. Bob and Booker went crazy trying to talk to the Devil. Herbert too. They are Devil worshippers. A girl named Jackie Fokken is their leader. I'm really scared."

Grandma feels something dreadful like the day her husband died. "That Fokken family is no good. Did Herbert know you were leaving tonight?"

"I don't think so, but Logan isn't answering his phone."

"Ross!" Grandma stands pushing herself up from the table and enters the living room doorway. "Ross! Wake up."

Freedom hears him moan. "Let me sleep."

"Logan is in trouble. Now get up." Grandma commands.

The living room light clicks on.

Grandma returns to the kitchen with Ross. Freedom looks at them without knowing what to expect.

"Take Ross and find my grandson, Logan," grandma orders Freedom. She looks to Ross, "I'll call your Uncle Marvin and cousins Rene and Justin."

"I'll find him." Ross says with utter confidence. He looks to Freedom. " Let's go."

They are out the door immediately into the warm summer night. Freedom leaves her purse and backpack in the kitchen. Grandma sits down at the kitchen table and starts making phone calls.

Outside Ross and Freedom walk side by side. "Where do you think Logan is?" Ross asks, seeming angry and clearly protective of his younger cousin.

"He said he was going home to pack a bag and meet me at your grandma's place. We should probably look there." She finds herself fighting off tears. Her guts screams that something is wrong. She tries to ignore it. "Herbert might have tried to fight him."

"Herbert Fearing?" Ross isn't a bad looking man. He's in his early twenties and physically fit from working out in prison on top of being a natural athlete. Before being kicked out of high school he was a state wrestling champ. There are acne scars on his cheeks adding to his rugged good looks.

"Yeah," Freedom explains. "We were going to hide out at your grandma's until we could find our own place to live and get away. Logan wanted to talk with someone named Painted Bear. A medicine man, he said." She pauses. "Ross, I love Logan."

"I love my cousin too," Ross grits his teeth. "Herbert is a weirdo. What the hell did Logan want to go see old man Painted Bear for?"

"Herbert, Bob, and the rest of them started worshiping the Devil."

"Idiots. We better pick up the pace." Ross says. " I'm gonna squash anyone who's laid a finger on Logan."

After some time walking they approach the residences of Logan, Bob, and Booker. Middletown is a small enough town anyone can walk from one end to the other in an hour or so easily. The hour is late and there is a light on in the apartment windows. Without exchanging words they approach the front door and Ross vigorously knocks. When there is no answer he shouts out Logan's name a few times before opening the door and breaking the lock with one swift and powerful kick. The violence of the door slamming open and his earlier shout makes Freedom nervous. She wonders if the neighbors will call the police. Everyone in Middletown knows everyone. Everyone knows Ross and many fear him. So maybe the neighbors will mind their own business.

They are greeted by the loud barking and snarling of a big albino German Shepard with a glint of unusual intelligence in its eyes. Ross and Freedom step back at the sight of the formidable canine, only a few genes away from being a wolf.

"Why didn't it bark when you knocked?" Freedom asks, standing close to Ross for protection.

Ross looks around the apartment, not moving forward, the dog holds its stance, daring Ross to advance. Ross squints taking everything in. "There ain't anybody here." They slowly back away together. The dog does not follow.

Back outside Freedom says, "There is something wrong with that dog."

Ross nods agreement. "Bad spirits. Better tell me more of what's going on. Logan and Bob have been friends since they were kids. Something big and bad must have happened."

Freedom feels something dreadful in her heart, like everything in the world is wrong. Thin tears trickle her cheeks as she talks. "Not much more than what I said. Bob started playing with black magic. Bob, Booker, Herbert, Jackie, and Roxy all became devil worshippers. They summon hounds of Hell and try to talk to the Devil. They tried to get Logan and I to join. We won't. They sacrifice dogs in their evil rituals. I love Logan. We were going to get away from them tonight. Jackie and Roxy are scary, weird satanic witches. I don't know where they came from but they are dating Bob and Booker now. I think Roxy is the leader."

"We don't know where you came from either," Ross points out.

"Texas."

"Damn it." Ross clenches his fists. "That rich white girl Jackie is from Middletown. She ain't no good. Spoiled brat."

Freedom says nothing. Her long hair hides half her face in the dark of the night.

"Where else could they be?" Ross asks.

Freedom shrugs like a mouse. "Maybe Herbert's house or the Bonefield Cemetery."

"Herbert's a freak too." Ross seems furious. "Let's check his place then the cemetery. This is some sick shit."

As they walk, Freedom tells Ross that she doesn't know where Roxy and Jackie live.

Ross responds. "I'm sure Jackie stays at her folks place. I don't know who this Roxy chick is."

Bonefield Cemetery is the oldest cemetery in the county. The allotted land is full, no one else can be buried there. And no one has been buried there since the early 1960s. The oldest graves are from the 1870s. There are many local ghost stories about this graveyard told by whites and Native Americans alike. It's not uncommon for high school kids looking for a thrill to drink there at night. Some of the elders of the tribe say it's a cursed place, like Blackwood and many places along the river bottom. Ross respects his elders in most cases, but sometimes his internal fires lead him astray. He does stay away from cursed places like Bonefield. He is not thrilled with the idea of entering the cemetery at night but he has to for Logan's sake. Family and blood come first. He is a Sioux warrior bound by that proudly. He wonders if the rest of his family will be showing up soon.

Herbert's house was empty. They now walk into the cemetery so dark. Ross got a text. His uncle and cousin are on their way.

Upon making their way through the black cemetery Ross and Freedom see the shadows of men and women dancing by firelight and running about the myriad of old headstones. The flickering fire makes the trees, headstones, and statues of the cemetery dance along. A danse macabre. They keep moving in closer. The fire is outside circle and pentagram drawn on the grass with flour. They see ceremonial bowls, burning incense and candles, a decapitated dog, and a naked, blood soaked Logan tied to a withered tombstone, his head drooped down low. There is no doubt to either of them that he is dead.

Freedom screams and runs to Logan's side, hugging him, holding his lolling head up, sobbing, hysterical. "No! No! I love you!"

Ross's fists are like tight white knuckled hammers as he looks around with hawk eyes for someone to unleash his rage on. Someone to pay for the murder of Logan.

Seeming to dash in from nowhere naked and slick all over with blood, his eyes crazed, possessed. Booker disappears into the shadows as quickly as he appeared.

Before the weeping Freedom can react to the sudden murderous skipping dance of Booker, Ross dives into the magical circle snatching up a long knife that Freedom hadn't even notice was there. He respectfully squeezes Logan's wet shoulder as he moves after Booker into the shadows. She can't let go of Logan. He can't be dead. Maybe if she just holds him and loves him enough he will come back to life. She wails and sobs, covered in Logan's blood.

She then witnesses the approach of Herbert equally nude and blood covered with madness in his eyes. She has never been so afraid of him as she is now. He is so tall and frightening. The look on his face tells her he means to harm her. His expression and the way he carries himself seems inhuman, alien. He is intent on killing her in a vicious manner, a long knife in his hand.

Dogs begin to howl from somewhere in the blackness of the cemetery along with the sounds of humans imitating the howls. Howling and barking. Freedom wishes Ross hadn't run off after Booker. Herbert reaches her before she can get away and his fist collides with the side of Freedom's head. She tumbles away from Logan onto the grass within the magical circle. Her hand finds one of the ceremonial bowls, she grips it, spilling the blood, just as Herbert kicks her in the gut. Gasping for air she swings the ceremonial bowl and with dumb luck blocks his slash with the knife.

Ross finds himself surrounded by the naked and bloody cultists: Booker, Bob, Roxy, and Jackie. All four behave more like animals than humans. Each armed with a long knife. He hears dogs all around but sees none. They circle him like a pack of wolves closing in on prey. Ross feels evil in the wind and prays out loud in his native Dakota tongue to the Great Spirit for courage and strength.

"Hoka hey!" Ross shouts and charges, "It's a good day to die!"

The confrontation is quick and fierce. Ross feels the Great Spirit has answered him and feels the spirits of ancestors rise up inside of him. He has visions of being a warrior long ago fighting white soldiers. Booker gives Ross a look of disbelief when the long knife cuts Booker's throat open. Ross knees Jackie between the legs hard enough to knock her down. Bob screams as he tries backing away as Ross's knife plunges into his stomach and chest over and over again.

Ross hardly feels Roxy's long knife slide deep into his side more than once puncturing his kidney and other vital organs. He backhands her, the knife in his hand slashing up the side of her face. Not a killing stroke but a deep, permanent scar if she lives through the night.

Roxy screams in rage more than pain. Jackie limps to her side. They stand holding hands as they watch Ross bleed to death on the grass. Bob and Booker are both dead on either side of the Sioux warrior. Roxy holds a hand over her bleeding face knowing she will never forget the man. Ross gives them a faint smile as he draws his final breath.

Herbert stomps down on Freedom's hand, breaking several of her fingers. She swings the bowl upward and it hits him squarely in the temple, breaking skin, drawing blood. He stabs at her, the knife nicks her side, cutting her shirt more than anything. Dumb luck strikes again. Herbert slips in the slick and blood soaked grass, falling and cracking his skull on the same headstone Logan is bound too. He twitches a moment and lies still.

Freedom stands very still watching him. She sees he is still breathing. His chest rising and falling. With a deep breath she takes up his long knife and stabs it into his back. Moments later he stops breathing.

She sits next to the slumped bloody body of Logan, holding and kissing his hand. She cries softly. "Remember when I was a Viking and you a knight? The rebellious lovers in every life. Souls chained through time."

Roxy and Jackie stumble up from out of the darkness and observe the eternal lovers. One dead. One forlorn. Jackie raises her knife to kill Freedom. Roxy shakes her head, still bleeding from the gash on her face. "Leave her. The outer ones are coming."

Jackie smiles at that, still disappointed at the prospect of letting Freedom live.

"The witch queen is in Blackwood," Roxy explains. "This girl is lost to madness." With that both satanic witches walk away, leaving the cemetery.

Freedom takes out her cell phone.

"Hello?"

"Enterprise." Freedom begins to sob. "I need help."

Freedom disappears before the Two Hawk family arrives to find Logan, Ross, and the rest of the dead.

The next day the skies turn blood red. Scientists present a myriad of theories to explain the Crimson skies but of course science has always been insufficient to explain the most important questions.

The Lizard Prince

"Hey!" A bearded man with a greying lion's mane of hair wearing dirty black leather pants, worn out boots, a dull silver belt buckle, and Native American style beaded necklace slurs to the dive bar room, standing on a tabletop attempting to keep his balance as he sways with drunkenness. He proudly unzips his pants and proceeds to piss all over the table, surrounding bar stools, the beer stained carpet, and his own leather boots. "I am the Lizard Prince! I can do just about anything!"

"God damn it, Blake!" A rough looking biker in an old patched leather jacket, grubby t-shirt, torn blue jeans, and tangled balding hair shouts up at the pissing man. The bouncer looks more like a biker than a bouncer, and being a regular at the Gold Whiskey Saloon, Blake knows the man is a biker and member of a small local club.

"None of that shit in here!" A red faced bartender with a low cut blouse showing off the cleavage of long breasts hanging nearly to her bellybutton. Her name is Gail and she the lesbian owner of the bar. "I'm tired of your horse shit! You are 86'd! Get that bum the hell out of my bar!"

Without waiting for Blake to finish urinating the biker-bouncer yanks Blake's feet out from beneath him. Blake falls without grace. He first landed flat on his back on the tabletop behind him, bounces off that table and hits his head on the edge of the same tabletop he'd been standing on before landing on the carpet in his own piss. His forehead is bleeding now and the fall has knocked the wind out of him.

The biker-bouncer's name is Mr. Slear. He roughly and rudely lifts Blake off the floor, one hand hanging on his belt from behind, the other hand holding Blake's mane of greying hair. He tosses Blake out the front door. Blake scrapes his palms on the cement sidewalk. "Ouch."

"Stay the hell out of our bar, Blake. You friggin' loser." Mr. Slear turns away and waddles back into the bar. He is a heavy set, round man.

Bleary eyed Blake looks up at the patch on the back of the bouncer's jacket. It says in spooky lettering, 'Devil's Rebels'. The Devils Rebels are a small bike club with a local chapter.

Blake Morrison lays on the sidewalk, pants still unzipped with a peeking shaft, blinking away blood dripping near his eye from the tabletop cut. His head spins when he closes his eyes. He doesn't want to puke so he forces himself to leave his eyes open. Blake only lays there staring up at the stars in the night sky far above the city street lights.

"I'm not an alcoholic," he mumbles, "not to touch the earth," reaching a hand up, "not to reach the stars, nothing left to do but die, die, die."

He passes out on the sidewalk and wakes up under the heat of the summer sun in the same place come morning. Hung over. Sore everywhere. Dehydrated. Thirsty. Shaky. With a severe grunt he pushes himself off the ground and wobbles a moment, covered in dried blood and puke. He feels greasy as he searches pockets for cigarettes and a lighter. Eureka! Blake pulls a crushed pack of cigarettes from his pocket. Three cigarettes. All bent and broken. He rips the butt off one and lights it. Tastes like crap and he zips his pants up. With a hoarse cough he begins the long walk home.

His mouth is so dry. His tongue feels pasty. His headaches. He needs water. These are his predominant thoughts at the beginning of his walk. His mind wanders to other territories as time passes.

Blake Morrison has always told everyone he is a bastard son of the legendary God of rock, Jim Morrison, singer of the Doors and misunderstood poet. No one usually believes him. Blake was born the same year Jim died. 1971.

Blake's mother, a groupie named Penny, was a huge fan of the Doors. She hated being referred to as a groupie, she always said she was a band mate. Penny became a semi-regular girlfriend of Jim whenever he was in California. A secret girlfriend. Blake has conducted some investigations and believes his mother was not the only secret girlfriend of Jim. Blake is also convinced his mother became pregnant intentionally in hopes of getting Jim to stay with her permanently.

Jim never stayed with Penny and never learned he had a son with her. Blake feels a twist of pain in his heart when he thinks of his mother. He knows she never stopped loving Jim and she never dated another man after Jim. She died of a stroke a few years ago, leaving Blake with no surviving family. Going through his mother's things after she passed away he found an old pink shoebox in a closet. The box was filled with love letters from Jim Morrison and a single worn photograph of Penny and Jim together outdoors somewhere. In the picture they are smiling and she has her arms around him. His mother was pretty back then.

Penny stayed a hippie forever. Trapped in time. The world moved forward and she stood in place like a stubborn tree rooted in history. Penny was reclusive and over protective of her son. She named him after William Blake and Arthur Rimbaud. His full name is Blake Rimbaud Morrison.

Blake grew up very proud to be the son of Jim Morrison but it was the rock which shattered him. As a young child the other children didn't know the difference between Jim Morrison and Bugs Bunny, so it made little difference in his early years. When Blake entered his teenage years is when all his social troubles started. Besides having an eccentric mother, which didn't bother him in the slightest. He always felt very loved and cared for by his mother.

It was as a teenager that people started to make fun of him for claiming to be the son of James Douglas Morrison. He was ridiculed and bullied. He was laughed at. Once Blake's story was out in junior high and high school there was nothing to undo the social damage it caused. He was tainted for years and wounded deeply. Even having never met his father, Blake loved him greatly and defended his lineage wholeheartedly in the face of social slaps and strikes at his dignity.

He always wished his father was there to love him. He always wondered if his father would have loved him.

Growing up he researched and studied everything he could find about his father. His father was an icon he could never live up to. A source of feeling inferior. Blake listened to all Jim's music, read his poetry, every book and article he could find, every documentary and movie. He memorized all the song lyrics and poetry and would listen to his father's voice for hours at a time trying to understand the man.

Who was Jim Morrison, the Lizard King, Mr. Mojo Risen, the Exterminating Angel, some leather clad demon? Whatever that means.

He needs his father's love and will never have it. He often imagines Jim's spirit is watching over him.

Blake read the complete works of any author mentioned in reference to Jim Morrison. Any author someone said Jim read. Nietzsche. William Blake. Arthur Rimbaud. Aldous Huxley and many others.

In high school Blake was an outcast, ridiculed, spit on, pushed around, beat up, and always laughed at. The jokes, laughter, and bullying never let up until he finally dropped out of high school.

Another challenge is that aside from his hair he looks like his mother. If one looks close enough there are features of Jim there. A hint of Jim in the eyes.

Blake decided to follow in his father's footsteps becoming a failed poet and rock star. He started a rock band. If people wouldn't believe he is the son of Jim Morrison, Blake would prove it to them. To everyone.

The only problem turned out to be he couldn't write poetry or have any musical talent. He gave up trying to learn to play the guitar after a month. Without the melodic, haunting, blues voice of his father, he screamed more than sang. Blake found his place as the leader of a punk rock band called the End.

Blake had minor success singing for the End. The band even signed with a small label putting out three albums. There were three other members of the End. Pancho Camacho, a Mexican American drummer. Rashid Hamad, a Muslim bass player. Kong Nygun, Vietnamese American guitar player. Blake even had a girlfriend during this short chapter of his life. She was a Native American Oglala Sioux named Wambli Kills In Water.

The End almost broke up because Blake became addicted to heroin. None of the other band members could tolerate his addictive behavior. He stopped showing up for practice, stopped writing songs, and couldn't perform live shows anymore.

They kicked him out of the group and the End went on without him, to be even more successful with Wambli taking his place as the lead singer. She broke up with him when they threw him out of the band. Once Blake was gone the End matured as a band experimenting musically, their albums without him became a mix of gutter punk, goth, and industrial.

Blake is pretty sure the band is still together, but he doesn't follow the music scene anymore so he's not entirely sure. He hasn't talked to any of them in years. He still loves Wambli.

After that Blake worked odd jobs, never able to hold steady employment for an extended period of time because his drug addiction was so severe. He was beyond heroin, consuming any chemical he could get his hands on. His life was out of control. He told himself that is the legacy he inherited from his father. A legacy of addiction. He began to resent his father, blaming him for everything.

Realizing he could not hold a real job Blake became a drug dealer. It worked out well for him for about one year until he broke the cardinal rule of selling drugs and started getting high on his own supply. This caused him to owe the wrong people more money than he could pay. These people could have killed him but the leader of the crew that supplied him had a soft spot for him because he was a fan of the Doors. So instead of killing him they beat him close to death, cut off a pinky finger, and tossed him in an alley dumpster. That was the end of his career as a dope dealer.

Blake's next occupation was thievery and burglary. He stole anything he could sell for drug money. He couldn't afford to support his habit no matter how much he stole. He wasn't good at being a thief or he was just plain unlucky and arrested several times, spending several months in jail. After so many arrests he was given the choice between prison or drug rehab. He chose rehab.

Blake's been off drugs several years. He only drinks now and he drinks daily. In rehab they called it cross addiction. He did try to stay in recovery from addiction but it only lasted a couple months. He knows he's an alcoholic. When he doesn't drink he gets irritable, sick, shaky hands, and sweats.

Making it home to the sleeping room he rents with his monthly disability check he goes straight to the sink, drinking water directly from the faucet. It's a poor neighborhood. The sleeping room is one room with a kitchenette and a tiny bathroom to itself. A dirty sleeping bag and an army green duffle bag sit in the middle of the room on the matted down carpet. He has few possessions. The disability checks are for his severe addiction. It's not much, he survives.

Stripping, aching, he runs a hot bath. It's soothing and he drifts to sleep napping until the water cools. As the water drains from the tub and he dries himself with the only towel he owns, he catches his reflection in the mirror. Blake is disgusted and ashamed of the reflection looking back at him. A withered man he hardly recognizes. He hasn't aged gracefully. Blake is forty-three years old but looks like he's in his late fifties.

Wandering into the main room wearing only his tight, white underwear, sagging a little in the ass with a few holes he gazes blankly out the window at nothing in particular. It's hot. He's tired. Hung over. Tired of everything. Tired of living. Wishes there was an air conditioner in the apartment. Curling up in the sleeping bag he feels safe. His own little sanctuary from the world, warm and snug as a cocoon or womb. It's hot but he wants to feel protected.

Out of money. Down to two broken cigarettes. Out of food. There is only a bottle of ketchup, sour milk, and mustard in the refrigerator. Tomorrow he's going to have to sell some blood and jones. Right now he's too depressed and sore to do anything but lie on the floor.

Late in the night Blake is awakened by a rapping on the door. He doesn't want to get up and answer it, the moon light shines in the open window. He rolls over, ignoring the door, falling back asleep. The person knocking at the door is persistant. Blake sighs with frustration when he realizes the annoyance is not giving up. Rising from the floor, stretching, scratching his butt and hairy chest, one hand absentmindedly rubs his beer belly. A single finger flips the light switch on and he squints as his eyes adjust.

"Who is it?" Blake clears a frog from his throat.

"My name is Indrid," an odd, tinny voice answers from beyond the door. A male voice. "It is important that I speak with you, Blake Morrison. I mean you no harm."

A strange declaration is Blake's first thought, scratching his scruffy beard now and wondering about the odd voice. It could be a mentally ill person. This neighborhood is filled with the forgotten and lost social outcasts and deviants. The people brushed under the rug. Out of sight, out of mind. This neighborhood is the scum of society by middle class plus standards.

There have been no visitors to Blake's sleeping room in a long time. He doesn't have any friends. Only drinking mates. They only come around when there's alcohol around. Blake opens the door out of lonely desperation.

Standing with what looks to be an uncomfortable posture is a man with olive tone skin, electric eyes, hair greased back, a black suit and tie, a white button up shirt, immaculately polished shoes, sunglasses, and a disturbing smile. Blake wonders why Indrid is wearing his sunglasses at night.

"Hello," the man who has identified himself as Indrid greets Blake, never breaking his wide grin or moving his lips. He offers a handshake to Blake.

Blake obliges. Indrid's grip is strong, clammy, and cold. He wipes his palm dry on his underwear after the handshake. "What's going on?" Blake asks. The creepy smile remains as his face is paralyzed with a permanent grin.

"May I come in?" Indrid asks.

Something is so very awkward and odd about this strange visitor. Blake wonders if the man is a ventriloquist. Running fingers through his tangled lion mane of hair, Blake looks down at his dirty underwear and near nudity then shrugs. "Sure."

Indrid doesn't acknowledge that Blake is hardly dressed as he steps into the stale sleeping room. Both men stand in the filthy, bare room in uncanny silence. Blake dazed from just waking. Indrid grinning dumbly. Indrid looks around the room and paces. Blake notices how clumsy Indrid seems to be. As if he only recently learned to walk. Indrid never lets up his grin for a moment.

"Well," Blake urges, growing impatient and distrustful, "I'm not gay if that's what this is about."

"I have no sexual desire for you, Mr. Morrison," Indrid replies, grinning.

This time Blake realizes Indrid's lips aren't moving because he's speaking directly into Blake's mind. He must be hallucinating. Having delirium tremen. Even a hallucination is better than his recent thick and stifling loneliness. "What's up, Indrid?" Blake begins to dig through his duffle bag looking for his cleanest pair of dirty blue jeans.

"I study Earthlings," Indrid answers.

Blake stops what he's doing. It's a mentally ill guy. "Who are you?"

"I am Indrid Cold. I have watched you all your life." Indrid says this as if it's a normal statement. "I was fond of your father. I thought I could ease your misery by informing you of a few things."

Blake feels the chill of fear run up his spine as he realizes the ever grinning man is communicating telepathically and not actually speaking out loud. The visitor stands deathly still with false posture. Blake isn't even sure if Indrid is breathing but he's still grinning. The grin is beginning to freak Blake out. He's thankful Indrid is wearing sunglasses because Blake is certain he doesn't want to see the stranger's eyes. He forgets about putting dirty blue jeans on and begins to pace in his saggy white underwear. He's nervous now. Doesn't want to get too close to Indrid and regrets letting him inside.

"Please stay calm," Indrid's tinny voice says echoes inside Blake's skull. The voice sounds almost electronic. "I will present you with data. Nothing more. Words. I mean you know harm. I come to you in peace."

Blake rests his hands on his hips. No longer pacing and nods, reaches up and feels the fresh scab on his forehead from the night before. "Alright, man. Say your thing."

"The CIA initiated a cloning project," Indrid explains. "Several clones of your father exist about the Earth in multiple locations and professions. This cloning project worked closely with MKUltra. They wanted to be sure the clones were controlled. I know everything about you and your father. Right now you think I am an insane person. I am not a person. Not like you. I come from the planet Lanulu."

Blake steps back away from Indrid Cold. There is nowhere to run. Indrid is between Blake and the door. The window is open but they are on the second floor.

Indrid continues to grin. "One purpose of the cloning project was to make sex slaves for the elite in the world. Conspiracy theorists call them the Illuminati. This is because the Bavarian Illuminati was blacklisted and nearly wiped out in the Eighteenth Century. The elite do not forgive or forget. The stand in the shadow of God. Tonight we shall call it a nameless organization. Those who shall not be named attempted to brainwash your dear father to be used as a sex slave. Jim's will proved to be stronger than expected, which was even more surprising due to his struggles with addiction. I suspect the American Indian shaman who entered your father was his guardian spirit. This would have made him harder to control as well, besides his belief in will to power."

Blake only stares at the strange man in black.

"Your father was an eclectic shaman who struggled when facing his shadow self. He died and became the Exterminating Angel. There is a medium communicating with your father regularly. Her name is Erin Carter." Indrid Cold keeps grinning.

Blake Morrison shakes his head in disbelief.

Indrid's tale is not over. "The Lizard King has a message for you. Go to Erin Carter."

"If you know so much why don't you give me the message?" Blake asks.

"I am something." Indrid turns and exits the sleeping room. His walk is odd.

Blake stands in the center of his room staring at the door Indrid closed behind him wondering what the hell just happened.

Blake sits in the plasma center with a needle stuck in his arm slowly drawing blood. He glances at his blood in the clear tube. It's boring because it takes several hours to sell blood but he needs the money to eat. Maybe get a drink. Browsing through magazines on a small table next to his chair he sees they are all outdated and well read. Nothing interesting. A local daily newspaper that's been dissected. About to give up looking for something to read he finds a gem hidden at the bottom of the pile of old magazines. An old black and white punk rock 'zine. It seems out of place here. Someone else selling blood must have left it behind. Some punk rock junkie or boozer.

He flips through the punk 'zine. It's printed on cheap, thin paper. Most of the bands are unknown to him. Not much of interest. Makes him feel old. The final couple of pages are classified ads. Blake feels his heart rise to his throat when he reads one of the ads. *Psychic Readings by Madame Erin.* The same woman Indrid Cold was talking about last night? How could it be only a coincidence?

He tears the ad out and stuffs it into his jeans pocket. It's a local address.

With the money from selling plasma Blake buys some lunch and a cheap bottle of vodka. He doesn't want to get drunk. Just enough to sip and keep his nerves calm. The food was good. A microwaved burger from a gas station, an apple juice, and a candy bar.

It takes the remainder of the day to walk across town to the address on the Madame Erin's classified ad. When he arrives he's exhausted and thankful he has a little money left to eat again later. He is feeling weak from loss of blood and his mouth is dry. He sighs, realizing he is so out of shape he probably won't live to be an old man. And he'll likely go straight to Hell when he dies.

Looking up at the old house that is partially hidden by arrogant, owly old trees Blake is reminded of Halloween. A dark brown house with window shutters, two stories, a long driveway shadowed by a line of tall bushes. Windows glow with a warm soft yellow-orange. It looks like a comfortable home with character. The home of a friendly witch. Whatever that means.

A black cat hisses at Blake through a screen window when he knocks at the front door. He can hear a radio station quietly playing 1960s music from somewhere within the house. Through the screen door he sees wood floors, a dining room, an entry way, and a living room. All with nice rustic furniture.

A strawberry blonde woman with curious green eyes answers the door. Blake guesses they are close to the same age. Maybe she's a few years younger than him and much healthier looking. Her hair is short. She has a thin nose and a beauty mark. Very pale skin with glasses on and dresses in comfortable looking pajamas pants, slippers, and a tank top covering small breasts. She frowns without saying a word. He feels like an intruder.

"Uh." Blake suddenly feels silly coming to this unknown psychic woman late in the evening. "Someone told me you have a message for me."

She rolls her eyes but doesn't seem surprised by his statement. "I don't know who you are or what you're talking about." Blake can smell beer on her breath through the screen door.

"Are you Erin Carter?"

"Who are you?" She asks defensively.

"Blake Morrison."

Her face softens. "Come in." She opens the screen door. We can talk."

When Blake steps through the doorway into her home the atmosphere is like another world. It's like a time warp into the past. She must be a witch. A new age witch. What do they call that? Wicca. There are candles and incense burning. Erin has a sophisticated decorating sense. Blake spots the dining room table with a table cloth draped over it. Upon the table is a laptop computer. A deck of Tarot cards. A Ouija board. A book on numerology. An ashtray. Two empty beer bottles. A crystal ball.

Behind the dining room table is a wood shelf with glass door cabinets containing expensive, delicate China, a few black and white photographs of people, and various knickknacks. The odor of cat litter is faint in the air. He counts six cats wandering about or perched and arrogantly spying. He suspects she has more felines about the house than the ones he's spotted.

Erin sits at the table before the laptop and lights a cigarette. Blake sits across the table from her. "Could I bum a smoke from you?" He asks insecurely.

She slides an open pack of cigarettes with a lighter on top across the table to him.

"Thank you," Blake lights a cigarette.

"Want a beer?" She stands.

"Yes, please." He smiles, feeling more comfortable than when he first came to her front door. She is attractive.

Erin returns with two cold beers. They both enjoy drinking.

"Do you have any money?" Erin asks, shuffling her Tarot cards.

"Not really," Blake answers.

"I didn't think so." She shrugs. "I normally charge for my services but this is an exceptional circumstance. Your father is persistent. I didn't ask to be psychic. I was just born this way. Ghosts have been confronting me for favors since I was a kid. I'm helping you to get him to leave me alone. And because it's Jim Morrison. I mean, that's pretty neat, pretty cool."

Blake nods.

She gives Blake a tight lipped smile. "Your dad interrupts my life at the most crucial moments."

"I'm sorry."

"Don't be," Erin says. "It's him, not you."

Erin takes a sack of marijuana and cigarette papers out from a drawer in the cabinet behind her. "Let's smoke and get started. Grass makes it easier to connect with the spirit world when I'm feeling lazy about it."

"Okay," Blake says.

"How did you know to find me?" Erin asks as she lights the joint.

"A man came to my house last night. He was kind of creepy."

Erin nods, holding smoke in her lungs as she talks and hands him the joint. "Jim said he knew a man in black."

"He was dressed in a black suit," Blake says just prior to taking a hit.

After smoking the marijuana Blake is paranoid high but still feeling good. Thinking deeply and embarrassed of his dirty clothes. What is going on? Yesterday he was dying a hopeless alcoholic nobody wanted around. Now the odd stranger, his father's ghost, and a wonderfully witchy woman. Life is interesting for the first time in a long time.

The song *Crimson and Clover* comes on the radio after opening another beer.

"Take off your clothes," Erin says out of the blue.

"What?" Blake is embarrassed and excited.

"I could use the Ouija board or tea leaves or tarot cards or my crystal ball," Erin explains as she begins casually undressing. "Ecstasy and orgasm are the most powerful and effective ways to open me up to the spirit world. It's mind blowing." She smiles standing naked before him. She shrugs. "How many women can say they slept with the son of Jim Morrison."

"Not many," Blake admits. He is seated, fully clothed, fully aroused.

Erin walks to Blake and begins taking his clothes off. Her skin is soft. She smells like watermelon, cigarettes, and beer. He cups one of her small breasts in his hand while letting her take his clothes away.

The sex is intense, hot, and long lasting. Blake hasn't been with a woman in years. They do it on the wood floor. He feels the Earth shake beneath him. He shakes beneath her as she rides. When he thinks he can't take it anymore, the momentous mountain of pleasure, when the end of the world climax comes he shouts to the gods above and below in thanks to Erin Carter!

Erin growls, "Coming for you! They want you! They want you! Run! Hide!" She collapses forward onto him. Their naked chests are both slick with mixing sweat. He can feel her breathing hard against him. He thinks he's in love. He came inside of her.

After lying together for an eternity of night Erin sits up and climbs off the exhausted Blake. Their sweat is now cold.

He watches her dress, afraid he will never see her nude again. If she asked him to, he would stay right here with her forever. He would quit drinking. He would get a job. He would do anything she asked of him. He watches her closely hoping to remember every iota of her slender body.

"He seems to think someone wants to kill you because you are his son," she says, almost fully dressed again. "Your father was an eclectic shaman. An urban shaman. He drifted into darkness sometimes as ronin shamans often do. He wiser now that he's dead, he said. As we all will be. Your dad said to quit drinking. Lay off the drugs. He would have if he lived longer but everything happens for a reason."

Blake is dressing, listening intently to his new goddess. She could tell him the world is flat and the center of the universe and he would believe her.

Erin continues, "He says he died in a bar and was carried out to protect the dealers who gave him the bad dope. The most important thing is he wants you to prepare yourself for the mystical enemies that are coming. His enemies. And when they come they will come fast like thunder and lightning striking you down."

"Why?" Blake asks with fear in his voice. "I'm nobody."

"You are the son of Jim Morrison. Blood means more than you think."

"Did he say who is coming for me and why?"

Erin shakes her head, "He did say you have more bastard siblings out there in the world and that after his death certain intelligence agencies instructed his clones to make public appearances to manipulate the public for reasons unknown. Much the same as they did with the king Elvis. He was very clear that the enemy is not the Illuminati. The Illuminati were heroes blacklisted; their history twisted by their enemies. An act of disinformation. What you can call them is the secret elite. The secret elite that stands hidden in the shadow of God. That is where their evil thrives. God's shadow."

"I've had a strange couple of days," Blake shakes his head.

"Strange days indeed," Erin says. "The ghost is gone now. I don't have anything else for you. I did what needed to be done."

"Thank you for the message," Blake says with sincerity.

She nods and scowls. "I would let you stay but there is a dark cloud following you and I have enough troubles. I like you Blake but I can't handle what's coming your way. I'm sorry."

Blake's heart sinks to the pit of his stomach. Good sex. Nothing else. The supposed words of his father. "I dig. I guess I'm gonna split then."

Erin looks away, refusing to make eye contact. "It was nice meeting you, Blake Morrison."

"Later." He steps out into the night. It's much darker now. If he could have anything in the world it would be to stay with Erin Carter.

On the long walk across the city home he wonders and wanders through his mind. The journey takes hours. Is Erin crazy? A con artist? In league with Indrid Cold? If so, what is their con? Blake has nothing. Not a pot to piss in.

So what then? What do they want? Maybe they are Doors fanatics. Blake settles in on what he considers the two most likely conclusions as he reaches the front steps of his home. It's a rundown building with a sign out front leaning against the front wall. Black letters painted on a white piece of plywood. *Sleeping Rooms For Rent Cheap!* Blakes conclusions are that Indrid and Erin are nuts or they are telling the truth. Both ideas are frightening in their own right. If they are crazy, who knows what's next. If they are not crazy, who is coming for him?

The front outdoor light is on as Blake enters the small apartment building. The hallway light is not on. The hallway is black. This is not so unusual. The landlord neglects the property. The light bulb is likely burned out. Using memory to guide himself Blake finds his door. It's not a difficult task. It's a straight hallway. He tries to unlock the door but the key won't fit into the lock. For a moment Blake thinks maybe he's trying the wrong door. But no. He's sure this is the right door. He can't afford a cell phone to use for light, but he has his lighter.

A flip of his wrist and the click of the lighter illuminates the hall enough for Blake to see that he is at the correct door and an eviction notice is taped to the door. Blake sighs feeling hopeless.

"You're a pathetic creature." The voice is a gurgling, buzzing, nightmarish sound from behind him. A voice as if being spoken through a sheet of glass. A voice that doesn't quite seem to come from this world.

Blake whips around in the darkness, startled, having not sensed anyone else present in the hallway. His face twists into horror at the sight of the thing illuminated by his lighter in the deep of the hallway standing so near him.

It is either the most deformed man he's ever set eyes on, a monster straight from space or Hell. An inverted version of the Elephant Man comes to his mind.

Blake only sees the being for the blink of an eye because he bolts from the sleeping rooms screaming as fast as his legs will take him. He does not look back until he is more than a full block away. Gazing at the apartments he's just been evicted from under the haze of the street lights Blake realizes the thing did not follow him on. Maybe it doesn't want to be seen by Joe Public. Who is he kidding? Blake has no idea what it was or if it was real. Was that a demon? He's sweating, panting, and his lungs ache from the short sprint. He curses himself under his breath for being so out of shape.

Whatever the thing in the hallway was, it was a freak of nature. An abomination. Even having only glimpsed it a moment the image is scarred forever into his memory like a photograph. The thing is burned into his brain.

It had a vaguely human shape about it. A human face but with soft, wrinkly, orange leather looking skin. Bald. No facial hair. No eyebrows. The eyeballs were striped vertically like rainbows. Oh, those eyes were unsettling. Blake shivers, walking further from his old home. He needs to put more distance between himself and the nightmare.

On the tip of the creature's chin was a single thick horn, like talon goatee. It was skinny and nude. Its arms and legs reminded Blake of chicken's legs. The skin was covered in pimples of puss and bleeding boils. It had three fingers and three toes on each hand and foot. It was the ugliest creature

Blake's ever seen. He felt evil in its eyes. Evil eyes like razors cutting into his soul.

"Jesus," Blake huffs, walking further and further away. Constantly looking back to make sure the monster is not following him.

Blake wanders and wanders not sure where to go. The night is long and becoming a bit chill. It's too late to get into a homeless shelter even if it had room they wouldn't take him in since he'd been drinking some. There is a knot of despair in his stomach. He has no one to turn to. No friends. No family.

Eventually Blake sneaks into a public park and within a grove of bushes. He curls up on the grass hugging himself to stay warm as he drifts to sleep. He has trouble falling asleep at first due to the discomfort of the ground and the image of the horn chin man that keeps popping into his mind. He's afraid he's losing his mind. Blake stares at the stars. He doesn't remember falling asleep.

"Hey, bum! Wake up!"

Blake hears an authoritative voice stirring him from dreams that slip away as he opens his tired eyes. A swift kick to his stomach knocks the wind out of him and he doubles over on the ground. After a long moment he gasps in pain at the loss of breath.

Two police officers dressed in blue with hats and shiny badges, guns in their black holsters, stand over Blake with looks of disgust.

"Sorry." Blake rubs the sand of sleep from his eyes with one hand and holds his stomach with the other. He's still sore from getting scuffed up at the bar the other night. He's dehydrated. He stinks of sweat and dirty clothes.

"Sorry, my arse, bub." One of the cops spits in his direction. "You're under arrest for being a scumbag."

"For what?" Blake asks in an attempt to de-escalate the situation. It's then that he realizes the young cops are twins. They have to be identical twin brothers. Blake's mouth hangs open in utter shock when he recognizes the twin cops. They look like young Jim Morrison if he had been a clean cut square.

Blake thinks of what the grinning man said. What he warned. What was it all about? Government clones? Sex slaves? God's shadow? He's going completely bat shit crazy or he's slipped into a twilight zone.

"You're under arrest for being a fucking loser," the other Morrison clone guffaws. He takes a pair of twinkling silver handcuffs from a holster on his belt.

The other Jim cop gives a deep belly laugh. "I don't like to speak in absolutes, but you are an absolute fucking fat ass loser!"

Blake bolts. He sprints away through the bushes and trees. Branches scratch and slap him as he runs, like sharp whip fingers trying to hold him back. Without looking back he hears the Jim clones cussing and giving chase. At the same time he's struck by the realization that the pair are young and fit and he's out of shape and sluggish. There is no way he's about to out run them.

There is a bridge stretching over a river at the edge of the park. Blake makes his way there without a thought. Animal instincts of flight have taken over.

"Where do you think you're going?" One of the Jim clones shouts behind him.

"You can't get away." The other one laughs.

Blake makes it to the bridge. An old rusty metal bridge over rushing waters below. It rained a lot recently and the river is overflowing with near roaring rapids. By the time he reaches the center of the bridge it's too late to turn back when he sees two more police officers at the other end blocking his escape. He wants to scream. Blake blinks a few times seeing the new cops are clones of Jimi Hendrix. A hysterical hiccup of a laugh escapes Blake's throat at the absurdity.

Behind him the Jim clones approach with handsome, cocky smiles. One is swinging the handcuffs in a taunting way. The other Jim is patting a billy club into the palm of his open hand.

Blake looks back and forth between the Jim's and Jimi's closing in. No escape. He climbs up the railing of the bridge and plunges down toward the rushing river below. It's not a graceful dive. The four clones watch as Blake twirls head over foot only to belly flop with a stinging slap against the water.

"Looks like it hurt," one of the Jimi's observes.

"Damn," Jim comments. "I wasn't expecting that."

"He's likely drowned," the other Jimi says. The four clones are in the center of the bridge looking down at Blake floating fast away, struggling to keep his head above the surface of the water.

The other Jim clone cop says, "He does have our DNA. Maybe we are underestimating the dude."

One Jimi rolls his eyes.

The other Jimi sarcastically says, "Shit."

The same Jim suggests, "We better follow him. If he gets away I don't want God's Shadow coming down on us."

Blake does his best to keep his head above the water but chokes, coughs, and swallows the river as he flows along with the current. He's not a talented swimmer. He can doggie paddle. Nothing more.

Over the sound of the water rushing and deafening when his ears dip under he hears the rock star clones shouting and taunting from the river's edge. He is making time on them. The distance between them is growing. He spits out water and tries to swim with the river's current.

He rides the water for what feels like a long time until he remembers there are waterfalls along this river just at the edge of the city limits. Blake begins to make his way toward the river's edge. This is harder than expected due to the strength of the current. He can hear the waterfalls crashing not far ahead of him. He can even see where the river drops off. Panic sets in as he races to make it out of the river before he reaches the treacherous falls. It is a race against the current and a life or death struggle. He doggie paddles with a fury trying to go straight to the shore but the current makes his path diagonal.

Blake does make it to the shore and digs his fingers deep into the black mud as he pulls himself out of the water with the last of his strength. His clothes and hair are drenched. The clones are nowhere in sight. He can see the falls very close. Too close for comfort.

Looking back again to be doubly sure the rock star clones are not around. They aren't but he knows they haven't given up their pursuit. What could they possibly want from him? They must be the people his dad's ghost warned him about through Erin Carter. If that's the case they want to kill him for some reason. They can't be real cops?

He struggles to stand for the long walk home. No. He has no home. The wet clothes are uncomfortably sticking to his flesh and heavy. So it is a long walk back to the heart of the city. To a damn homeless shelter. He could use a drink. He considers checking himself back into rehab. Maybe it's time to try the straight and narrow life again.

Blake sits cross legged in an overcrowded homeless shelter in the center of a bunk. The grey blanket feels as rough as a horse blanket. The pillow and mattress are some kind of institutional green plastic with white sheets worn too thin. His clothes aren't as wet as they were but they aren't dry either. The room smells like strong body odor and rotten stinky feet. The air is stale. Somebody opens a window. His boots sit at the foot of the bed and his socks hang off the bed drying.

The large room is filled with dozens of bunk beds. Blake is on the bottom bunk of his. Someone is snoring above him. Outside the sun has almost set. Every bed is filled with vagrants both young and old, man, woman, and child. It's a multicultural situation. He thinks there is something wrong with a social system with this many homeless people. But there are homeless all over the world, aren't there? Maybe his homelessness is his fault. Maybe the world is a fucked up place. Or a place damned to Hell.

"Hey, man. How's it going?"

Blake Morrison recognizes the voice immediately. Anyone would. Blake's blue eyes lift up to witness a clone of the king Elvis Aaron Presley. He looks exactly like a young Elvis if the young Elvis had the sideburns of the old Elvis. An unmistakably handsome man dressed in conservative attire as if he wasn't Elvis. He's smiling, upper lip slightly curled.

"I'm so tired of running," Blake whispers. Tired of this insanity. Tired of his depressing life. His pathetic life. The clones are right. He is a loser. Either reality isn't what he thought it was or he's a mad man. Blake doesn't care which anymore. "I give up. Do what you want. Kill me. Get it over with."

The young Elvis clone gives a friendly chuckle. "I'm not here for that, Blake. I'm a renegade here to help you. I'm running from God's shadow too. We have to get to the light and stay there."

Looking at the iconic man Blake feels a sense of hope that was impossible a moment ago. Blake knows he must look like the walking dead. Hair and beard are a mess. Clothes stink. He fits the role of a bum well. He's measuring this Elvis man. Does he trust this one?

"I get it." The Elvis clone sits on the other end of the bed near Blake. The Elvis sniffs, obviously trying not to react to the smell of Blake. Trying to be polite. "This is what's happening. The men and women in God's shadow are evil. They hide from God there. Calling them devil worshipers wouldn't be accurate but it wouldn't be wrong. It's as good a description as any. God's shadow. The absence of God."

"What's God's shadow?" Blake is feeling ashamed of himself. This Elvis man is neat and trim. He seems like someone who has his life organized. He gives off a charisma of success, prestige, and confidence.

The Elvis clone answers. "It's said that God's shadow is where all the evil hides. There are entire religions and cults hidden in God's shadow. You could call some of the religions secret governments. Selfish, elitist cabals. Some are the wealthiest of the wealthy. A bunch of idiots too."

"Why do they want to kill me?" Blake and the Elvis man are oblivious to the homeless people surrounding them. Many are sleeping. Some quietly converse. Some stare off into space. No one pays attention to Blake and his visitor. "And why are they cloning rock stars?"

"Not only rock stars," the Elvis clone answers. "I've seen clones of James Dean, Marilyn Monroe, Jayne Mansfield, Bridget Bardot, Sharon Tate, Jean Shrimpton, Marlon Brando, and Clark Gable. Just to give you an idea. All the clones are raised and trained to be slaves. Sex slaves and intelligence operatives. Playthings for the rich. Assassins and spies for the merciless. Tools of the shadow psychologists and neuromancers. They study how to control the mob, the common people. What slows people down, keeps them docile and compliant. Unquestioning. The people have no idea what reality is. Only what is spoon fed to them by the powers that be. The haves versus the have nots. Celebrity culture has become a powerful tool in distracting people from what matters most in life. Politics and economics have become so esoteric the common people can't keep up. Most of the world has been brainwashed since birth. Addicted to ignorance and masturbation. Education levels are kept low for a reason. Your father spoke the truth when he told his audience they're all a bunch of fucking slaves."

"What do these people want?" Blake is astounded.

"Base things." The Elvis man shrugs. "What do all the tyrants want? It's greed, lust, envy, power, the seven deadly sins. Control. There is nothing enlightening about it. They've become a disorganized collection of organizations practicing black arts and barely understanding what they are doing. Lost children. All of the world is filled with lost children. Groping blindly through illusions. Misunderstood ideas. Natural selection. Survival of the fittest. Will to power. All of that jive. To have whatever they want and to have it now. Spiritually they are sick and dying. It's hard for the brain to accept what's going down. We're not wired for it. Our consciousness is only one state, one point on the evolutionary chain. If any of that makes sense."

Blake is baffled. "Okay. So why do they want to kill me?"

The Elvis clone chuckles. There is a pair of gold rim sunglasses in his shirt pocket. "Sorry. I went off a bit. It's a good question. You are a biological son of the original Jim Morrison. The Lizard King. Not one of his many clones. This clandestine group pursuing you wants to sacrifice you to the evil thing. In the shadow of God. A thousand angers have kept it alive."

"Why? What evil thing?"

"Do not incline my heart to any evil thing," the young Elvis clone answers. "I don't know which one this particular faction serves. A demon or an alien god. They all want different things. A lot of infighting. Some say the creator of the universe is in the shadow of the true source of all. That the creator is ignorant of this or defiant, I don't have a clue. Everything about reality is so confusing and paradoxical. Okay. Enough of that. You need a straight forward answer. Why do they want to kill you? There is a group of zealots calling themselves the Cult of the Lizard King. Fanatics for your father. There are some disputes over doctrine within the cult. The division is one side believes your father was a shaman prophet and the other side believes he was a messiah of liberation."

"What the hell?" Blake shakes his head in disbelief. "This has to be a conspiracy or some prank to drive me crazy." His eyes wiggle in panic.

The young Elvis clone with the big sideburns nods and smiles. "Reality adjustments are always a trip. The Cult of the Lizard King isn't a bad thing. They smoke a lot of pot and the congregation are a little dark and sullen."

"Fine," Blake exasperates. "You still haven't answered my question."

"Right." The Elvis clone continues to smile. "The network of God's shadow cabals are at war with groups like the Cult of the Lizard King. The Lizard King Cult is opposed to the cloning of Jim Morrison. Who knows what the reasoning for all the public appearances of the Jim clones is. Same with the Elvis sightings. They are up to something. Manipulating the public consciousness somehow. Always to nefarious ends whatever the reason may be. One of the cabal's of God's shadow wants to make a blood sacrifice of you to the evil thing. Straight black magic. A super curse to take out the Cult of the Lizard King."

"This is beyond belief," Blake shakes his head.

"Listen, man," the young Elvis clone says. "My name is Elvis 13. The thirteenth successful clone of the King of Rock and Roll. I'm the leader of a group of renegade clones. We're enemies of God's shadow and all its players. I'm here because I don't want God's shadow to get what it wants. It wants you so I can't let them have you. So what do you say we make like a banana and split from this joint. My place is a more comfortable and safe abode. I found you here which means they can likely find you here too. You'll be safe with me and mine."

Blake nods. "Alright." He doesn't have anywhere else to go. He's lost everything. There is nothing left to lose. Except his life. This Elvis 13 seems like a genuinely nice yet kooky fellow.

Elvis 13 takes Blake to a nice home in the middle of a middle class neighborhood where every house looks the same all up and down the streets. All the same architectural design and painted the same. Shades of grey. Perfect lawns. Double garages. Blake's never understood why someone would want to live in a neighborhood like this. Clone houses. So dull. No individuality. Oh, well. Blake's never made enough money to own his own house so who is he to judge. Maybe his severe poverty is causing him to miss some hidden aesthetic appeal.

Elvis 13 leads Blake Morrison into the grey, generic house. Two stories. A basement it seems. Very nice home. Neat and clean. Retro postmodernism. Big, cushy black leather couches and chairs in the living room. Shag carpet. The inside isn't generic like the neighborhood outside. It's plastic, contemporary, and fashionable plastic 1960s with a mix of outrageous and flamboyant 1970s. James Bond would be comfortable living here in retirement.

To Blake's bewilderment there is a magnificent, voluptuous blonde woman lounging on one of the couches. She is sparsely clothed and cuddled up with a pillow and blanket watching a 52 inch screen television on the wall. *Ray Bradbury Theater* is on the screen. Blake recognizes her too. Another clone. Jayne Mansfield. He can't take his eyes off her beauty.

"Hey, baby." She smiles at the sight of Elvis 13.

"Hey, love." Elvis 13 smiles at her like they share an intimate secret only they know. He walks over and kisses her forehead then introduces Blake. "This is Blake Morrison. Son of Jim Morrison."

"No kidding." She eyes Blake in a flirtatious manner. "Nice to meet you slim."

Blake feels like a mouse suddenly self-conscious of his beer belly. "Hi."

Elvis 13 grins, curling his lip like Elvis does, with pride looking at this beautiful blonde woman. "Blake, this is my wife. Jayne 22."

"This is all new to me." Blake doesn't know what else to say. His life is now surreal.

"It's cool," Elvis 13 says. "Come on. I'll show you to the guest room. Looks like you need a shower and a good night's rest. I think we have some clean clothes you can change into as well. Jayne is going to make you some dinner. We'll get a good night's sleep. You deserve it, sport. Tomorrow you'll meet Brother Blue."

"Who's Brother Blue?" Blake is alarmed again. He can't handle any more surprises.

"Hm." Elvis 13 looks at Jayne 22. "How would you describe Brother Blue, love?"

"A very cool cat," she purrs. "A guru of sorts. The man to talk to about escaping God's shadow."

"Our part's done," Elvis 13 agrees. "For the most part. Tomorrow we'll leave you in the hands of Brother Blue and he'll save your soul. I promise you that. Nothing to worry about. You trust us?"

Blake looks back and forth between the clones and nods. "Blue must be the leader of the renegades?"

"He's got it going on, Blake," Jayne 22 assures him. "No worries. You're safe with us. No one is going to hurt you ever again."

Blake nods again. His life and circumstances are beyond his control. Is anyone's life ever really in their control? Or is that something people just tell themselves for comfort. Maybe everything is in the hand of fate or chaos or God or the universe. Butterflies and hurricanes. He regrets so many things. If he could do it all over again he would and he'd do it differently. He'd make better choices. Stay clean with the End. Marry Wambli.

External circumstances can't be controlled. Or the control is limited. But internal circumstances, people have more control over that. Depending on whether or not you believe the human is an organic robot and computer or the human is a quantum act of consciousness. Whatever that means.

Blake can control his actions. He can take responsibility for his actions from now on. Starting tonight. Tonight is the first night of the rest of his life. A new life. He will be a good person from now on. Do the right thing. Quit drinking. Get a job. Quit being selfish. He almost starts to cry.

"Thank you for helping me, Elvis," Blake says. "Thank you for everything. Both of you. It means a lot that you're helping me."

Jayne 22 gives him an alluring smile as she strolls into the kitchen.

Blake showers and eats the food Elvis 13 and Jayne 22 provide him with. It's very good. A salad with colorful vegetables and tofu. Fruit. Water. They watch television together while they eat. It's so strange to Blake. Elvis 13 and Jayne 22 seem so happy together. It seems so natural. They're living a normal life.

After dinner he sleeps in the guest room. It smells fresh. The sheets are clean. The bed is soft. He hears Elvis 13 and Jayne 22 talking and a while later the sounds of love making. Blake falls asleep grateful yet lonely. He dreams that Wambli still loves him.

The next day Jayne 22 wakes Blake late in the morning. They let him sleep in. She is dressed in a silk bathrobe and puts forth little effort to hide her cleavage from Blake and even seems to be amused by his wandering eyes. Elvis 13 has a hearty breakfast ready for them. Wheat grain French toast, turkey bacon, egg whites, orange juice, and coffee.

Blake doesn't say much as he eats. He is feeling better. Physically and emotionally. He longs for the stability of Elvis 13 and Jayne 22's life together.

The clones make small talk about the weather and the dull neighbors. Jayne gives Elvis a honey do list including several pieces of yard work. They talk about being excited to watch an episode of *Game of Thrones* later tonight. They behave as if nothing is out of the ordinary and are very polite to their house guest. Maybe nothing is out of the ordinary for them. Blake wishes he had a love like they do. He thinks more of Wambli and even of Erin Carter. Maybe later he can visit her again. Ask her on a proper date once he gets on his feet.

After breakfast Jayne 22 hums a tune unfamiliar to Blake as she rinses the dishes and loads the dishwasher. Blake has been distracted by his sexual attraction to her all morning. He feels guilty because he just made a vow last night to be a good man and Elvis 13 seems like a good guy. He doesn't seem to have the strength to stop lusting after Jayne 22 and Blake has the uncanny feeling that Jayne 22 knows it. Looking at her body and her beauty he has no problem understanding why some scientist would choose to clone her. Elvis 13 doesn't seem to mind Blake's longing stares at his wife. It's because Elvis 13 is confident that Blake is absolutely no threat to their relationship.

"How did you sleep?" Elvis 13 asks.

"It was a good night's sleep," Blake answers.

"Good." Elvis 13 sips from a mug of coffee. "Brother Blue is in the basement waiting for you."

Blake is afraid again. Paranoid. This doesn't feel right. Elvis 13 reads the fear in Blake's expression.

"Don't worry," Elvis 13 reassures him. "Brother Blue is super cool. You'll dig him. Once you meet him you'll feel silly for being apprehensive."

"You want me to go into the basement?" Blake asks soberly.

"Yes." Elvis 13 nods at a closed door between the kitchen and living room. "He's expecting you. Don't be scared. He's a teacher. A very wise dude."

"Alright." Blake stands from the breakfast table and makes his way to the basement door. He looks back and the clones who are both watching him with expressions of amusement.

Blake opens the basement door to find a staircase leading down into darkness. He attempts to turn a light switch on the wall at the top of the stairs but when he does so nothing happens. He looks back at the clones again. "The light's burnt out?"

"Don't be afraid of the dark, little Morrison," Jayne 22 smiles. "Close the door behind you. It will be okay. I promise you that."

Jayne playfully sits on her husband's lap as they watch Blake build his courage. Elvis folds the newspaper he was browsing and sets it on the table next to his coffee.

"Go on," Jayne urges.

Something irrational in Blake wants to please her. He takes the first couple of steps down and closes the door behind him standing in fear at the top of the stairs trying to see anything in the black below.

Blake steels himself. That irrational part of him wants to impress Jayne 22. To show her he is no coward. He takes slow blind steps feeling his way down with his feet. One step at a time. Careful not to fall. After several steps down he finally feels the floor. He still can't see anything but darkness.

"Hello?" Blake calls out.

"This darkness is how most people perceive the world without knowing it." A voice from somewhere in the basement responds. The voice sounds muffled, slow, almost like gurgling water. Blake can't determine if it's a masculine or feminine voice.

"Brother Blue?" Blake asks the darkness.

"Yes. Blake Rimbaud Morrison?"

"Yes," Blake answers.

Then there is only silence. The silence grows. Blake is not able to handle it. He feels he will shriek at any moment. Shriek or explode with fright. Maybe he'll piss himself. Finally Blake says, "Brother Blue. I can't see you."

"I can see you," the alien voice responds.

And then Blake Morrison sees Brother Blue. Glowing in a pale blue before him like a floating transparent jellyfish in clear and murky water. It is in the center of the black cellar, whatever it is. Brother Blue's legs are crossed with arms resting on his thighs, palms up as if in some yogic position of meditation hovering in the air it's not unusual in the slightest. Brother Blue is vaguely shaped like a human but is far from being human. He has blue skin, organs, nervous system, and appears to lack a skeletal structure beneath its thin, transparent flesh. The blue flesh looks very soft and delicate. Its head is shaped like a manta ray with shining yellow diamond shaped eyes. Its fingernails are like black pearls. Its limbs are very thin. As thin as bones without flesh.

Blake doesn't know if Brother Blue is a he or an it. Blake worries about his mental health. Is he schizophrenic? Did someone slip him a hallucinogen? Is Brother Blue an alien? A cloning genetic experiment? A spirit? An angel? A demon? Something that should not be?

"I can see you," Blake says.

"I can see you," Brother Blue responds with a voice like a muffled dream.

Blake realizes he is dripping in sweat. Fear sweat. His heart is racing. He is in shock. Every detail is very clear and acute.

"I smell your fear," Brother Blue points out to Blake. "Stay calm. I mean you no harm."

Blake does stand there numb with fear. Paralyzed with fear.

"Elvis 13 spoke to you of the Cult of the Lizard King," Brother Blue addresses Blake. "The cult is soon to break into two factions, much like when the Catholics and the Orthodox broke. It is a sad and unnecessary occurrence. The same theological paradigm with slight differences in philosophy. Too slight to split I think. If they splinter they weaken. The prophet or the messiah? What does this mean to you? It means you will be saved from God's shadow. You will be saved from a torturous and bloody death. To the cult you are either the son of the prophet or the son of the god. Either way you will keep the cult united in love. Without action on your part you are just an ordinary man. Knowledge we know is useless without action. The way you have lived your life proves you are just a man. God's shadow wants to crush all cults like the Cult of the Lizard King. We cannot allow that. I am an advocate of many realities. I know you are the son of the god of rock. You are a demigod."

"I am?" Blake whispers. The sight of Brother Blue still makes him feel he may urinate. Something weird and unseen seems to be radiating from Brother Blue, a pulsating nothing. Almost if reality itself is rippling about the bizarre cobalt thing. "Why me?"

"The creator chose us," Brother Blue explains. "Not the creator I spoke of earlier. The creator created by that creator. Demiurgos after Demiurgos. He created you and me. God Jim, Our world. Our worlds. Everything within our universe is within this creator. A creator gives birth to many creators. Our creator chose you to be the son of Lord Jim. He chose you to be the savior of the Cult of the Lizard King. The creator is the author of us all. The creator moves in mysterious ways as Bono says she does."

"I don't know what you're asking me to do," Blake admits.

"Move with the flow of creation. The current of the universe. Align your will with the will of the universe and you cannot be stopped."

"You mean God?"

Brother Blue shrugs his skinny, boneless shoulders. "A god. There is a hierarchy of consciousness. I often contemplate creation. What is the motive of the creator? Bored and seeking entertainment? Lonely and trying to understand itself? That is profound. Don't you agree?"

"I guess," Blake says. He is dumbfounded. He feels himself begin to relax. His muscles lose tension. Some blue haze has appeared in the heat of their conversation. Blake never noticed it until now. He's no longer nervous. He's feeling euphoric and even finds himself smiling at Brother Blue.

"This is your fate," Brother Blue announces as if it is something Blake should be content with. Still levitating, he spreads his very thin legs wide. A semen like substance sprays out from between his open legs. There is no visible sexual organ. The substance sprays and spews all over Blake like a spider's webbing. The sticky gelatin substance gets in Blake's mouth and he breathes it in. It coats his entire body and hardens like glue. Blake falls backward into a bathtub that he hadn't noticed in the darkness of the basement before this moment. Unknown to Blake the tub was brought all the way from Paris just for him. Fight as he does Blake is quickly cocooned within the bathtub and Brother Blue's spray.

Blake is dreaming. Thank God. He realizes he is asleep and dreaming. It's all just a dream. Such a strange dream to have. Oh, thank God. He's read about this sort of thing before. It's called lucid dreaming. Lucid dreaming is when you become aware of the fact that you are dreaming and can even begin to take action within the dreaming. To make choices in the dreams and control the course of the dreams. To communicate with others in the dreams. This has been a very long dream and it's time to let his mind rest and sleep without dreaming a while before he wakes to a new day.

Blake Morrison wakes up not sure where he is. He must have gotten drunk and blacked out again. Where is he? What kind of hangover is this? Why can't he move? He's tangled in the bed sheets so tightly he feels like he's going to suffocate or have a claustrophobic freak out.

Blake wrestles his way out of the sheets and blankets. He can hear the fabric tear. It's a strange texture and tears away with a surprising ease. It's not quite fabric. More like soft paper mache.

And then he sees the light as he crawls out of the cocoon-crusted bathtub like a man waking from a coma and breaking through an egg shell.

The first thing he notices is his hands. His hands are longer human hands. They are the shape of a man's hands but the skin is that of a snake. He's naked and his entire body is covered in snakeskin. He is a reptilian man. A scaly monster.

The next thing he sees is everything around him. It's like a dizzying carnival of hippies dancing and gyrating around the basement. Dozens of people are celebrating, singing, drum beating, chanting, and love making. Long haired, barefoot hippies like they stepped out of the summer of love. He sees Elvis 13 and Jayne 22 partaking in the celebration of the lizard. There are several celebrity clones mixed in the cult. Brother Blue is nowhere to be seen but he knows this is the Cult of the Lizard King.

The basement is lit up with lanterns, candles, and incense. Tambourines and maracas jingle and jangle. The room is overcrowded. It's a Dionysian orgy.

Blake climbs the rest of the way out of the bathtub and cocoon. His clothes crumble and flake off his lizard body. He's no longer fat and out of shape but sleek and strong. A tall mirror on the east wall gives Blake a look at his new snake stealth form. His new body with diamond yellow eyes, a forked tongue, and fangs. All his hair is gone. The man in the mirror is no longer human. Blake is a two legged serpent.

The time forgotten hippies and star clones circle around Blake and drop to their knees shouting and praying, cheering and elated. "The Lizard King is dead! The Lizard King is dead! Long live the Lizard King!"

Blake Rimbaud Morrison tries to scream out as loud as he can in horror but his voice only lets out frantic hiss after hiss which seems to further excite the cultists.

The Philosophy of Murder

Trena is happily preparing a pasta salad for a potluck she and her husband are attending later this evening. The musician Billy Joel plays softly on a small radio atop a kitchen counter. Something about a lunatic. Trena hums along with the tune as she stirs the pasta with a wood spoon. The potluck dinner is for her mother's birthday. The entire family is getting together for the occasion. As soon as her husband Miah gets home from work she'll put her makeup on and they'll be out the door. She's excited because it's her sister Suzie's eight year old daughter April's birthday too. What are the chances of that? Her mother and her niece are having the same birthday. The chances are 365 to 1. Trena smiles at the thought.

She licks her fingers tasting the Italian seasoning and cool vinegar before covering the glass bowl with plastic wrap and carefully placing it inside the refrigerator. Looking at her thin gold watch Trena decides there is time to wash the dishes before getting ready for the double birthday party. She also realizes that Miah is running a little late which is out of character. He struggles with Obsessive Compulsive Disorder, even taking medication to help cope with his perfectionism. Miah will probably call soon to let her know he's running late. Early in their marriage Miah's perfectionism and tendency to be an overachiever caused some problems. Enough so that they went to marriage counseling for about a year before he was diagnosed. She loves him very much and after that one hump they haven't had many problems. Her biggest problem now is convincing Miah it's time they have children. She thinks about all of this as she rinses dishes and loads the dishwasher. If she has a daughter she'll name her Julia.

The more she thinks about her husband the warmer her heart gets. She feels she is the luckiest woman in the world. Miah is very good to her. Very fair, rational, and logical. He always has the answer, always solves the problems, and she always feels safe when he's around. They have a magnificent life together. Her husband is a successful attorney at a prestigious local firm. She's a pharmacist. They are more than financially stable. Their relationship is healthy. They take turns picking movies and restaurants on date night.

Trena met Miah McDowell while he was still in college. She had just graduated. They've been a couple for eight years, married five years. She grins thinking about kids again. What will they look like? Like Miah or her? A combination of both their best traits? The more she sees Suzie's kids the more she wants children of her own. Miah knows it.

Miah seems to have a knack for kids too. He'll make a wonderful dad. Why is he hesitant? Trena thinks he's afraid. His parents weren't very loving parents. In fact Trena suspects they were abusive. Miah never talks about them. As she starts the dishwasher the backdoor opens. The backdoor leads directly into the kitchen. They usually use the backdoor instead of the front because it's closer to the garage.

Trena turns and smiles at her husband. "Hey, honey." She plants a kiss on his cheek leaving a trace of lipstick she wipes away. "Glad to see you are home. How was work?"

"It was a fine day, Mrs. McDowell," Miah answers. He's wearing a grey suit and scarlet tie. Clean shaven. Hair an immaculate flat top. He sets a brown leather briefcase on the kitchen table.

She takes a deep breath, exhales with a soft smile. "I'll be ready to go to Suzie's in about thirty minutes, Mr. McDowell."

"That sounds fine," Miah answers in monotone. He opens the briefcase with two small clicks.

Trena turns her back to Miah as she wipes the kitchen counter off with a dish towel. "I love you, honey."

"I love you too."

Trena hears her husband's words at the same time she feels a sharp pain in her side. Something overwhelmingly painful. She screams.

Grabbing the counter for balance she feels a second sharp, pointed jab. Her eyes are wide with pain, confusion, and fear. Her hand touches one of the wounds and she raises her hand up before her face, perplexed at the sight of her blood covered fingers.

Trena turns to her husband, "Miah?" Her eyes are filled with tears of pain and horror, sorrow and betrayal. The tears stream down her cheeks causing her mascara to run. She is a beautiful woman, she thinks, not knowing why this is her current thought. Such a strange thought to have at a time like this. What is happening?

Miah holds her arm firmly with one hand, leaving fingermark bruising and keeping her in place. He is squeezing so hard it hurts and cuts off circulation. In his other hand is a large knife coated and dripping to the linoleum floor with her red blood. Trena looks into Miah's eyes or at least that was her intent. Instead she is further disturbed to see the god awful homemade mask her husband is wearing. Her husband of many years. Her husband who is suddenly an insane stranger, an unknown demon she has shared her home and life with.

Miah's mask is a goat's head. An actual hide skinned off of a goat. She can see his evil eyes through two holes cut into the hide of the goat mask. The horns are intact and a goat's beard. She can see stitches on the mask. It is a bit of a patchwork. The hair of the mask looks coarse. Her husband is a dead goat. Or possessed by a dead goat. Her husband is not her husband. It can't be. He is killing her. Her goat husband is killing her with no emotion.

She sobs. "Miah? What are you doing?"

"Shhh," Miah hushes her from beneath the goat mask. "It's okay, honey. Baby. I love you. Everything will be alright." He impales her in the stomach several more times as he speaks to her in such a tender way. He impales her with the razor sharp blade as if it is an act of love.

Trena thinks she's never seen a knife so large before. Where did he get that knife? He seems to enjoy stabbing her, doing it slow but firmly and deep. They do not break eye contact. She's never seen such dementia in his eyes before. She wishes she could see his entire face. The goat mask causes her to feel like she's being killed by the devil himself. How could they be married this long and she never sensed the depth of his depravity, his insanity, his evil sickness, for she knows in this moment he is very much both evil and sick.

"Miah?" She whimpers, feeling weak as she tries to block the knife, but only succeeds in losing some of her fingers as the long razor knife enters her stomach again and again. Now she wails loud like a siren and through the torn holes in the goat mask Miah's eyes seem to light up with joy. She tries to pull away. In her heart she knows this is the ugliest thing she's ever seen or experienced.

Miah holds her in place. He is much stronger than her. He has a routine. He goes to the gym three days a week and jogs before work three mornings a week. He is physically fit. She always admired his body. Miah always observes the Sabbath on Saturdays. He's always been peculiar about his beliefs and routines. Obsessive and a perfectionist. She thought that is what makes him such a financial shark, such a success. His professional career. He says Saturday is the proper day of the Sabbath, but he says he is no Jew. She never thought to question his beliefs. She had even thought some of Miah's eccentricities were cute.

"Sh," Miah continues to attempt to calm her as he kills her. "Trena, I love you. I love you, Trena. I love you so much." He stabs her again and again. She can no longer stand from loss of blood. There is so much blood. The floor is flowing with a growing puddle of blood. She tries to hang on to him, to stay standing but she is sinking to the floor, dying. She knows she is dying. Miah continues to stab her and speaks calmly and tenderly, "It's okay." He sounds so sincere, as if he may cry himself, "Know peace, my love. Eternal sleep."

He comforts her and rips her apart with the knife. Pieces of her clothing and flesh litter the pool of blood on the linoleum floor. He is sitting in the pool of blood with her, holding her lovingly, hushing her, carving her.

Miah McDowell looks at the slumped dead body of his wife cradled in his lap through the eye holes in his goat head mask. The mask makes him feel powerful, like a god, it even gives him a hard on. His hand is soaked in his wife's red blood. He watches with fascination as droplets of blood roll off his fingertips. His clothes are splattered and soaked. So are hers. So much blood. A sea of blood.

The line has been crossed. Miah, the bringer of death, the killer is no longer a fantasy. The dream is real. He will kill and rape and rip and the world will know him and shake. He is exhausted with euphoria and feels an unholy divinity surging through his soul. He feels the warm semen cooling against his thigh as his phallus softens. Miah is the grand sinner. Murder was an intellectual decision. It makes more sense than anything else. He could think of no reason not to kill. The world is meaningless. His life's work will no longer be secret, it will be all there is.

Humans, consciousness, existing, it is all an accident. Only a chance mistake. The biggest mistake to ever occur. The grand fluke. There is no reason for existence. Life brings suffering and pain. Birth brings two things to look forward to with absolute certainty: pain and death. Pleasure is only a vain attempt to dope and dupe one's self of reality. Everything is made of matter and energy, fluxing back and forth between the two states. Nothing can truly be destroyed, only transformed, transferred. All matter is made of atoms. Shit is matter. Nothing is any or worse better than shit. The tragedy of it all is the stumbling birth of consciousness.

There is no soul. There is no God. Fairies aren't real. Thoughts and emotions are chemical reactions within the brain. There is no meaning to life. There is no reason not to murder. No reason not to do whatever you want to do. No reason for anyone to live other than to suffer. There is no reason for hope.

Now Miah McDowell is a killer. He is higher on the food chain. He has elevated his natural status. Man is animal.

Miah has taken life in his hands. He stares at the blood shiny and slick coating all fingers and palm. He is becoming something more than an ordinary man now. He must complete his transformation and the only way to do that is to kill everyone.

"Did you see the new girl in apartment 23?" Chad asks his neighbor and friend Jericho. Chad is a heavy set construction worker, just beginning to bald, a very tall and thick man with a neatly trimmed goatee. Physically Chad is naturally a very strong man, he's a hard worker with a heart of gold that doesn't complain. He is wearing glasses, worn out blue jeans, a black short sleeve shirt, and brown leather steel toe work boots. He's been drinking beer more than usual because he won't admit it but he is very much heartbroken over his longtime girlfriend recently leaving him for another man. Chad is not someone a person would necessarily call a lady's man. He has been blue and been telling himself he will never find another girlfriend for the rest of his life. She was seventeen years old and Chad is twenty-three, so Jericho thinks it's probably not a bad thing that she broke up with Chad. Her name is Diane and she never treated Chad as well as he deserved to be treated. He is such a good natured guy and she would walk all over him. She was spoiled and entitled and was always telling Chad he was fat, always spending his money, and cheating on him, at least Jericho is pretty sure she was cheating and Chad was blinded by love to her actions.

Jericho has been doing his best to cheer Chad up and help keep his mind off of Diane. Diane is now dating Chad's friend Jack. Well, Jack and Chad are no longer friends. Jericho is proud of Chad for breaking Jack's nose.

Jericho has gone so far as to search for a new girlfriend for Chad. Unsuccessfully.

Jack and Jericho are fellow students of the Miskatonic University. Many or most of the residents of the Oldtowne apartment complex on Ravenswood Avenue are students at the university. Chad attended the school when he was nineteen years old but dropped out while he was still a freshman but has continued to live in the apartment ever since and work construction the entire time.

Chad is a year older than Jericho. Jericho only has one year left until he graduates with a BS in Psychology. Chad was taking generals without a major when he was attending. Now the new academic year is just starting. The first classes are on Monday and today is Friday.

"I haven't seen her." Jericho smiles. The two friends are sitting on the patio of Jericho's apartment, grilling brats and drinking from bottles of beer. All the apartment units are single bedrooms and there are 24 units in all.

"Oh, my god," Chad exasperates, "She is smoking hot! A freshman I think. She was moving in the other day with some old dude. Looked like her dad maybe."

"I'll keep an eye out for her." Jericho chuckles. "Maybe you should ask her out." Jericho spent his summer working construction with Chad. Chad took Jericho under his wing and has been teaching him the construction work, which doesn't come naturally to Jericho like it seems to for Chad. Jericho was so ignorant of construction work that Chad even had to teach him how to swing a hammer right when he first started. Chad is very skilled in his craft and happy with the work he does. He is a professional and Jericho can see Chad becoming a foreman and even running his own construction company someday if he wants to.

Chad yawns and stretches while Jericho unfolds today's newspaper and browses the articles. He comes across an article about a murder yesterday and the curiosity of the cat draws him into reading the entire article. What he gleams is this:

A woman named Trena McDowell was found stabbed to death on her kitchen floor. She was stabbed 37 times. There are currently no official suspects but her husband Miah McDowell is missing and wanted for questioning. It is unknown if he is alive or if he is a victim himself. The address where the murder took place is an upper middle class neighborhood not far from Oldtowne Apartments and Miskatonic University.

"What should we do this weekend?" Chad asks. "Celebrate your last weekend of freedom?"

"I think so." Jericho nods.

"We might as well get started now!" Chad proudly holds up his beer bottle like a trophy to the sky.

Jericho grins. "I have a few things to do first. They won't take long."

"Ah," Chad moans. "Like what?"

"Okay." Jericho shrugs. "I need to at least get my clothes out of the dryer. I'll be back in a minute and we will commence."

Chad nods mocking a serious expression. "I will hold down the fort." He takes a bite from a hot brat and ketchup, mustard, and relish squirt out the opposite end.

Jericho walks out of his apartment. He lives on the second floor in unit 13 and Chad lives on the third floor in unit 19. There are three floors to the apartment building not including the basement level, which is where the laundry room and maintenance rooms are located. The landlord also has a locked storage room down there.

It is a very old apartment building with a style and character all its own. It has a haughty, elitist personality, not matching the disposition of most it's residents. If the apartment could speak it would likely declare itself an English gentlemen above the station of the tenants. The building was constructed in 1947 and has been mostly housing for Miskatonic University students ever since. Jericho likes the old Victorian style and structure of the building. He often wonders about the apartment building's history and who has lived here over the years.

Taking the stairs down into the concrete floor laundry room, the light is shut off. That isn't the norm and it irritates him. Who is the moron who shut the light off? It's black dark down there and dangerous finding one's footing on the narrow steps. As he descends a primal instinct of fear of the dark creeps up inside of him. He imagines someone standing hidden in the shadows watching and preparing to jump out and attack him. His hand blindly, quickly finds the light switch on the wall and flicks it on, banishing the darkness.

There is not a soul in the laundry room, only a row of old washing machines and dryers to one side of the room. Jericho pulls his laundry basket off the top of one of the dryers and fills it with clean, warm clothes. He glances at the locked doors of the maintenance and storage room. There are peepholes in both doors and that always creeps Jericho out. The doors are identical to all the apartment unit doors. That must be the reason they have the same peepholes. He wonders if the two rooms were ever apartment units or if they have always been storage and maintenance rooms.

The sound of someone walking down the basement stairs causes Jericho to look up in that direction. A shadow precedes the newcomer. His breath is taken away at the sight of the angel descending. Fireworks explode, lighting up the heavens in Jericho's mind and the archangels blow trumpets announcing the state of love and trust. This vision of a woman must be the new tenant Chad was raving about. He was not exaggerating. She is a blonde golden goddess of sunshine and the spring. The vision of this woman is the rebirth of Jericho. Dumbfounded love at first sight. Pure foolishness. He can't tug his eyes away.

The young woman is carrying a basket of dirty laundry that she sets on the concrete floor while inserting coins into a washing machine. At first she acts oblivious to the presence of Jericho, but he is staring so starry eyed it's impossible for her to ignore him.

"Hi." She smiles and Jericho knows an angel has just earned its wings somewhere in Heaven.

He feels like crying tears of joy at the melodic sound of her voice. His heart is filled with white Christmas and everything nice. The scent of her flowery perfume arouses tickling butterflies in his stomach. "Um." Jericho realizes he must appear a complete fool. "Hi. Sorry. I was caught in a daydream."

"I like daydreams." She continues smiling with perfectly white teeth as his heart melts pleasantly. She finishes loading the washing machine and pours in liquid detergent.

Jericho nods like a panting puppy attempting to mask the awe in his eyes. "I'm Jericho."

"I'm called Enterprise," she introduces herself with a look like a bolt of pale blue lightning that matches her eyes.

"Enterprise?"

She chuckles and rolls her eyes in a playful way. "And my sister is called Freedom. Our parents were uber hippies." Her cheeks slightly blush like rose petals.

"That is an incredible name. Very cool."

Enterprise closes the washing machine and starts it. "Thanks. You have a swell name too. Are you a student at Miskatonic?"

Jericho nods. "You?"

"I am," she answers. "Monday is my first day."

"I'm a senior. If you want to meet some people we're going to see a band called Dead Christians Saturday night. You're welcome to join us. I'm in unit 13 if you wanna go."

"Thank you. I'm not sure what my plans are. I have a friend coming to visit, but I will keep it in mind."

"Cool." Jericho nods.

"See you around." She waves as she exits back up the stairs.

"Later," Jericho mumbles as his heart sinks. He feels like an idiot realizing he's been standing there staring at her the entire time holding his basket of clean clothes. He probably gave her the creeps.

Jack lives in unit 17 right next to Chad, in fact their units share a wall in common. It drives Chad mad with heartache and jealousy. Not only can he hear his ex-girlfriend talking and laughing with Jack every day, he can hear when they have intercourse. He can't make himself stop listening. It's happening right now. Listening to Diane's moans and Jack's groans, Chad is hitting himself in the forehead repeatedly with his fist, clenching his jaw, wishing he could murder Jack. Chad feels trapped inside of a nightmare. The situation seems the jest of a cold hearted God.

Chad decides to go for a walk and take the trash out to the dumpster. It's night as he walks through the old apartment's hallway and alongside the parking lot carrying a black plastic garbage bag. The streetlight which normally illuminates the exterior of the apartment is dark. The bulb must be burned out.

Not meaning to see this, Chad passes by one of the apartment windows on the first floor. The shade is only pulled down halfway hiding the face of the bare breasted woman sitting in front of the window. She is naked doing something, maybe brushing her hair or applying makeup to her face, he's not sure, but he is sure she doesn't realize she is exposed. He feels a rush of guilt moving closer to the window for a better view, growing more aroused with the movement of her breasts.

He knows who everyone is who lives in the apartment building, everyone does. This is Taran LeBlanc in unit 8. She is a junior at Miskatonic this year. Chad feels dirty and wrong but hasn't the willpower to look away. He creeps up until he is standing just outside her window, paranoid of being spotted, he doesn't see anyone else around. It's hard to keep an eye out for witnesses not wanting to take his eyes away from Taran's chest. Chad takes a cell phone out of his pocket and quickly takes several pictures of her boobs in motion. He looks around again seeing no one in the dark. He feels dizzy, hot, sweating at the sight of her beautiful nudity and unzips his pants feeling so wrong.

Chad's excited lust gives over control to the primal reptilian brain, a more primitive part of the mechanics of the mind. So hard to overcome, with a quickness he wets the grass beneath his feet with semen and a crushing guilt makes him feel as if he may vomit. As he rushes to zip his pants up he imagines Jesus the Christ and his dead grandmother looking down at his lustful sin from heaven. He feels damned for eternity in that moment, stumbling away from the window while wiping his hand on his blue jeans. He glances back again at Taran's golden globes. Shame overwhelms. Then he turns to continue on to the dumpster but is stopped dead in his tracks by the sight of a frightening man whose image is forever burned in the memory of his brain like a laser on a shiny disc. A permanent mental image to torture and torment Chad's conscience for the rest of his life.

The man was likely watching Chad from the shadows the entire time, witness to the act of perversion. A man still and with posture sturdy as a tree dressed in a black suit as if dressed for business or a funeral. Chad sees the dark man's eyes peering through the ragged holes of a goat shaped mask with horns and a beard. A mask that looks very real, very much like an actual goat has been murdered and skinned. The eyes are piercing, soul eating, accusing.

Chad drops his garbage sack and dashes for the safety of the apartment. Not looking back, he makes it through the front door and stands pressing his back against it as if to hold the man out, to prevent anyone from entering. That man! Was it a man? It could have been a demon for all Chad knows. Whoever the man is, there is something horrible about him.

Chad is sweating, trembling, and begins to quietly cry, afraid to look out at the goat masked man. A sickness lurches in his stomach and he vomits on the wood floor by the front door. Did anyone else see him masturbating? Is the goat masked man going to tell on him? Is he the devil? Is Chad going to end up in jail for a sex crime?

Chad can't stop crying now. He's afraid to look out and see the man again. Without looking back he runs to his apartment unit and quickly enters, locking the door behind him and shutting off all the lights. Wiping his face and catching his breath, Chad creeps to the window on all fours and peeks out toward the dumpster on the west side of the building. Chad's window faces east.

He sees nothing out of the ordinary. The man is gone. Chad spies the parking lot and dumpster for a long time before retiring to his bed. It's a struggle to sleep and his dreams are filled with images of Taran and the Devil.

Jericho sits in the lecture hall of his philosophy class. The class is called 'Beyond Good and Evil', named for Nietzsche's work of the same name. The class is being taught by a professor of philosophy named Macie Nightengale. It should be an intriguing course. The syllabus outlines topics like the Nazis and the Holocaust, slavery in the United States, the treatment of Native American Indians and Aboriginals in Australia, and other cultural tragedies. Also outlined discrimination, hate crimes, and cults. Jericho is excited for this class.

Three other Oldtown Apartment tenants are present in the large class. Blonde, French-Italian Taran LeBlanc, long Tucker DePriest, and gorgeous Enterprise Sona. Tucker lives in unit 18. He is a young man of average build and looks except for big ears and spectacles. He dresses in thrift store clothes like an old man or a hipster, Jericho isn't sure which. Tucker is an odd duck, a reclusive fellow psychology major. Jericho and Tucker have had several classes together but have never exchanged words. Jericho sometimes thinks what at first seems arrogant from Tucker is actually bashfulness.

Taran is vivacious, sometimes abrasive, short of height and she and Jericho had a brief relationship, which was more like Taran calling Jericho over when she was lonely and drinking, but when Jericho made a move to have a more serious romantic relationship with her she freaked out and ended their relationship. They seldom speak to each other now other than a slight nod and hello in passing. He remembers her final words when the relationship came to an abrupt halt. She said she has a heart as cold as ice.

Enterprise never did take Jericho up on his offer to hang out the last weekend before classes started. He talked to her once in the hall of Oldtown and she told him her sister Freedom had stayed with her that weekend. He did see Freedom too and although she is still in high school she has beauty matching her older sister's.

Still every time Jericho sees Enterprise he becomes a fumbling fool, stumbling over words and shoes. Even now in this class as Professor Nightengale begins her lecture he's driven to distraction, barely picking up on the current discussion of capital punishment as he sinks deeper into the throes of puppy love.

"I don't believe in capital punishment. What gives anyone the right to decide who lives and who doesn't?"

"The murderer decides who dies."

"So we emulate the murderer?"

"It's justice."

"Execution is no different than abortion."

"Only God can judge."

"There is no God."

"That's another discussion entirely."

"We're here to look at all aspects of morality and ethics."

"Atheism is arrogance. It's a declaration that the atheist knows the universe was not created by intelligent design. The atheist is stating they have it figured out. An agnostic is more rational, more reasonable. At least the agnostic is declaring they don't know but have an open mind."

"Gnostics are the wisest."

"What if someone killed your mother or father? A loved one? An innocent child?"

"I would forgive them."

"I don't know what I would do. If someone killed or raped my child and you handed me a gun and put me alone in the room with the killer, I wish I could say I wouldn't kill them, but I can't say for sure. In the passion of the confrontation, the pain of the loss, it is possible I would kill the guilty."

"Nope. I would forgive them, like Jesus would."

"Then what? They accept your forgiveness and go on killing?"

"What happens when a lion kills a wildebeest?"

"Natural born killers?"

"What is the difference between abortion and execution? How can you support one form of killing over another?"

"Where does one draw the line?"

"I don't want to die and I don't want my loved ones to die, therefore killing no is wrong."

"That is an ugly way to look at it."

"Why is it legal for a soldier to kill? Or a police officer?"

"For the greater good."

"Who decides the greater good?"

"The people in charge."

"Who decides who's in charge?"

"Might is right. Today instead of muscle it's money. The people with the most money are in charge and that's a fact, Jack."

"Do violent movies, books, video games, and other forms of media have a relationship with violence?"

"Is art a reflection of life or life a reflection of art?"

"A bit of both?"

"There needs to be some kind of code of conduct. A code of honor. Chivalry. Bushido."

"How do we decide on a common code?"

"A goodness in all of us, deep in all of us."

"The god inside all of us?"

"A right or wrong in all of us that is not cultural but archetypal."

"And justice is?"

"A cultural standard."

"An opinion."

"Justice is the code of conduct but it's based in culture rather than the archetype."

"What do you think, Jericho?" Professor Nightingale asks him out of the blue as she paces the aisles between students.

"Huh?" He is startled, awakened from being mesmerized by Enterprise.

There are a few snickers and soft giggles, a few sneers from classmates who see it's obvious he wasn't fully attentive. Jericho blushes with all eyes on him as he and Enterprise make visual contact.

"Justice? A code of conduct?" The professor reminds him.

"Um. I don't know. The law?"

Later that evening Jericho sits in his little living room reading a local Arkham newspaper. Another homeless man has been found dead. Someone is randomly killing the homeless for sport. A serial killer. All the murders have been stabbing and vicious, averaging 3 dozen per victim. The body count is up to six. The police have no leads, no witnesses.

The preying on the weak disgusts Jericho. How can someone be so demented?

Finishing that article he reads on. The next article isn't any more pleasant. Miah McDowell is still missing. If he is alive or not is unknown. His bank accounts were emptied the day prior to his wife's murder which raises suspicion.

Jericho thinks it is obvious he killed his wife and fled. The cops likely believe the same, but the community is struggling to accept this because McDowell comes from an old wealthy family that has a long Arkham history. His father was the President of Cowan & Carr Bank and Trust. Now Jericho wonders if Miah is the one killing the homeless people? The vagrants are being slain in the same method as Mrs. McDowell. The authorities have to be wondering the same. What would drive a pillar of the community like Miah McDowell to go insane? He was known for philanthropy, volunteering at homeless shelters, attending church every Sunday.

Volunteering at homeless shelters. Lightbulb.

He killed his wife in such a cold blooded way. A man who simply exploded, started killing and can't stop. That is what Jericho thinks. The family name is what's keeping this line of thinking from being printed in the newspapers.

There is a knock at the door. He puts the paper down and answers the door. Outside the window the sun is setting majestically above the inconsequential whims of man. To Jericho's surprise, Enterprise is standing at his door with a soft smile. "Hi," she says.

"Hey," Jericho utters, confused and worried. He's given up all hope of ever courting her, she's two levels above him.

"I don't mean to be a bother, but I'm wondering if you feel like company?" There is an ever slight hint of insecurity in her tone.

"Um, yes. Of course. Come in." Jericho once again feels stupid after every word leaves his mouth.

They sit together in his small living room. All the units of the Oldtowne Apartments are small, single bedrooms with a simple kitchenette and tiny bathroom. All the rooms are laid out exactly the same.

Enterprise looks around Jericho's apartment. The walls are plastered with black and white posters. Jim Morrison. Johnny Cash. David Bowie. Jack Kerouac. Bauhaus. Joy Division. Janis Joplin. Depeche Mode. The Killers. The Bravery.

"You are a music lover." She observes.

"I am," Jericho confesses. "You?"

"I like music." She smiles quietly. It seems she has something to say but isn't saying it. Or at least she has something on her mind. "My musical tastes aren't as dark as yours but I do love the Doors in a special way."

"You think my tastes are dark?"

"In a lovely, cool guy kind of way dark."

He doesn't know what to say to that. "What kind of music do you like? Besides the Doors."

"Happy music. Dance music. Disco. Pop music. Anything upbeat that makes me want to dance."

"Are you thirsty?" Jericho is doing his best to pretend he's not nervous.

Enterprise shrugs. "A glass of water would be fine. Thank you."

A moment later Jericho returns with two glasses of ice water.

Enterprise gazes out the window at the night. "It's beautiful out."

"It is."

"What's your family like?" She asks.

"I don't know," he answers. "They are like a bunch of strangers. We're not that close. Are you close with your family?"

"Mostly my sister," she replies, "our father died a long time ago. Our mother is a kind or crazy hippie, witchy type. Eccentric."

"I'm sorry about your father."

"It's been a long time."

"Do you have a boyfriend?"

Her face turns cherry red with embarrassment. "No. I've never had a boyfriend."

Jericho grins. "Are you kidding me? You're so beautiful. How old are you?"

"Nineteen."

"How come you've never dated before?" Jericho asks this delicately, sensing her defensiveness underneath it all. "You mom didn't allow it?"

"No, not that. I didn't want to. I'd rather focus on school and other things."

"I see," Jericho says crestfallen.

"How old are you?" She asks.

"Twenty-two."

"Do you have a girlfriend?" She asks so softly he almost doesn't hear her words.

"No."

"Why not?"

"Haven't found the right person yet."

"You like me?"

Jericho nods.

"I like you too," she whispers.

Jericho slides close to her and attempts to kiss her.

Enterprise backs away quickly and jumps off the sofa, spilling her glass of ice water onto the floor. "I'm sorry!"

"It's okay." He tries to calm her.

"I have to go." She briskly moves to the door.

"Stay," Jericho says while following her.

"No," her voice cracks, almost in tears, "I have to go."

The door closes and Jericho stands with arms and shoulders slumped, bewildered and defeated.

Walter Noyes is the owner of Oldtowne Apartments. He is in the basement collecting coins from the washing machines and dryers. The door to the maintenance room is ajar. Walter inherited the apartment building from his uncle years ago. His uncle had no children of his own and Walter was next of kin and listed in the will.

Walter enjoys managing rental properties and has accumulated quite a few properties over the years. Enough that it is his sole income beyond investments, it is his full time job. Walter and his wife do not get along, they've been married twenty-five years and will never divorce. Their children are grown and fled the nest long ago. Walter prefers spending his time at the rental properties rather than with his bitter wife. They won't divorce because it would hurt their children and it's against their beliefs. They have both accepted their fate and duty. The love of family and God. There is a third reason they don't divorce, they are sour and stubborn and the hate each other but they love each other even more. Life is strange.

Mr. Noyes enters the dimly lit maintenance room reaching blindly for the string he knows is hanging from a light fixture in the center of the ceiling. After several misses he catches the old string and clicks the light on. A single uncovered bulb hanging.

He starts filling a yellow plastic mop bucket with water from a short black hose attached to the wall. All around him in the maintenance room are a variety of tools, cleaning supplies, wood shelves, a work table, spare air conditioners, and other odds and ends.

Walter Noyes never gets a chance to look into the hollow eyes of the goat mask as Miah takes him firmly by the hair and slits his throat open before he can react or scream once the vocal cord is severed. Blood spills out onto the concrete floor mixing with the running hose water and swirling into a floor drain. Walter dies quickly.

Goat Head, what Miah has started to call himself internally, calmly closes the door of the maintenance room and begins to methodically clean up the mess. The hose and drain are quite convenient. He hasn't spoken a word to anyone since slaying his wife. His world and dialogue are all internal now. Goat Head takes a large ring full of keys from Walter's belt. Keys for every one of Walter's rental properties, including every unit of Oldtowne Apartments.

Jericho nervously knocks on Enterprise's door. She answers wearing pajamas, surprised he is at her door. "Hi," she says, unexpectedly caught in his eyes. She struggles to pretend she doesn't want him there.

"May I come in?"

"Uh." She looks away, avoiding eye contact, the attraction is too much. Enterprise looks over her shoulder, back into her tiny living room, a blanket and a pillow on the sofa. A textbook, notebook, pens, and glass of ice water on the coffee table. She was deep within her studies before he came knocking. "My place is a mess," she offers up as an excuse.

Jericho looks past her and into her apartment unit then chuckles. "If that is messy you must have thought my place was a pig pen."

"No." She shakes her head. "Of course not."

"So I can come in?"

"Okay."

As soon as she shuts the door Jericho kisses her. She doesn't fight it, she wants to kiss him, and they stand in the center of the room as if lost in the stars kissing and fondling. Both on fire and alive.

Enterprise gently pushes Jericho away. "We have to stop."

Jericho is frustrated. "I know you like me. Why are you pushing me away?"

"It has nothing to do with you," she answers with such a sadness it shames Jericho.

"I feel like I've known you all of my life," Jericho confesses. "I am in love with you."

Enterprise's eyes widen in fear and she takes back steps.

"I am sorry." He can't stand the look on her face, he looks instead to the carpet. "I will leave. I won't bother you again."

"If you knew me you wouldn't want me," she explains with eyes now glistening with tears.

Jericho can feel the pain he sees in her eyes. "There is nothing you can do or say that would make me stop loving you."

She looks up at him like a wounded animal. "Do you promise?"

"Yes!" He takes her into his arms and kisses her again. They stumble together in heat through the living room and fall on the sofa together leaving a trail of clothing behind them.

This did not happen overnight. It has been happening since the weekend before school started. Since they first laid eyes on each other. This unexplainable animal magnetism between them, the chemicals between them every time they see each other. Every time they look at each other or share a few words it is like magic. They can talk for hours without ever running out of things to say and when they are silent it is a silent love. They were born for each other. They have an empathic trust and an irrational understanding of each other.

"No," Enterprise says again. "We can't."

Jericho stops attempting to remove her pajama bottoms. He is fully naked, she is from the waist up. Skin against skin.

He pulls back respectfully yet frustrated. "What's wrong?"

"I can't tell you." She trembles with fear and cries softly. "You will hate me. You will call me a freak and tell everyone I'm a monster."

Jericho is perplexed by her words. He isn't sure how to respond to her apparent insecurity. "What are you talking about? You are beautiful." He says this tenderly.

She calms, stands, and walks to the bedroom door. She stands in the doorway partially shadowed, holding the door frame as she needs to.

Jericho rises from the sofa and only watches her.

"I am a hermaphrodite," she whispers almost inaudibly as she takes her pajamas off to stand bare before him, half a silhouette in the open doorway.

Jericho stares with an expression of horror. This beautiful woman he loves is not a woman. She is both a man and woman. The male organ has been surgically removed and there is clearly a scar. He looks into her eyes and feels ashamed of himself when he sees her fragile expectations. "I don't care." He rushes to her standing like a goddess in the shadows and the doorway. He kisses her lips, her neck, her everywhere.

"I have to have surgery every few years," she explains with a hush between his kisses.

"My love is absolute."

Chad sits in his living room exhausted, filthy and stinking from a hard day's labor. He's just finished eating dinner and is now bored staring at the television, sipping a bottle of beer, contemplating a shower. His best friend, Jericho, has been spending most of his free time with Enterprise. Chad understands. He wishes he had a girlfriend himself.

He hears Diane's laughter through the wall interrupting his thoughts. He knows she's not, but it feels like she's laughing at him. For what Chad hears he guesses Jack and Diane are just arriving home from somewhere and Chad is the furthest thing from their minds.

"You are a weak man. Pathetic. Calling you a man is an overestimation." The unknown voice startles Chad. He looks to the source of the voice to see the goat head man exiting his bedroom.

Chad leaps to his feet ready to use the beer bottle as a weapon. "Get the hell out of my apartment! I will call the police!" Chad's voice is more shrill than intended. He reaches for his cell phone which is on the coffee table before him.

Before Chad's hand reaches the phone the goat head man slams a long knife into the phone, splitting it and pinning it to the wood tabletop.

Chad steps back only to bump into the sofa.

"Make another noise and I will gut you like the hog you are from gullet to groin," Goat Head growls, showing off a second long, sturdy day knife in his other hand.

"I'm sorry," Chad nods, thinking this may be the Devil standing before him.

"For what?"

"Looking in Taran's window," Chad whimpers about his confession to the Devil.

"The only thing you should ever feel sorry for is not doing what you truly want to do." Walter's keys hang from the killer's belt. "You should have gone in the window and taken what you wanted."

Chad is frozen with fear even seeing the human eyes beneath the torn holes in the goat mask. The idea that this is a human frightens him as much as the idea that it is the Devil.

The man beneath the goat mask offers, "I will let you live if you kill Jack and Diane and then go fuck Taran well and proper."

Chad eyes the long blade in the man's hand and then at the one stabbed through his phone into the table. He can feel the man's delighted grin beneath the mask.

"Pick up the knife," the masked man urges. "I have the keys."

They can both hear the murmur of Jack and Diane talking in the next room.

"Kill them," the killer whispers. "Taran is my gift to you."

Chad steadies himself and makes eye contact with the masked man. He feels overcome by a sudden calmness and acceptance of his fate. "Never." Chad lunges for the knife stuck in the table. Just as his hand withdraws the blade from the table he feels the other long knife impale his throat, pushing down deep into him. It is only the first of many stabs. He lives long enough to hear the killer say, "There is no God."

Miah contemplates murder as he studies the dead body of Chad bleeding out having just witnessed the life flutter from his eyes. It is an addictive, empowering feeling, taking life. He whispers, "People kill for two reasons. Passion and rationale."

"I can't believe he is dead," Jericho's voice is filled with shock again. He is in bed next to Enterprise. They have just retired for the night. It was Chad's funeral this morning.

Chad stopped showing up for work which was uncharacteristic. He stopped answering his phone and the door. A suspicious Jericho called the police. The police ended up calling a locksmith as they were unable to locate the landlord of Oldtowne or his wife, which was also unusual.

Inside Chad's apartment unit they found him nailed to a wall on the south side of the living room. The killing took place on the blood stained sofa, but someone hung him on the wall and cut him open from throat to belly. His entrails had been found on the floor beneath him.

Everyone in Oldtowne Apartments are now living fear and paranoia. The landlord was eventually found. Dead in the basement. His wife was found dead in their home. Both stabbed to death in the same vicious manner as Chad and the homeless and the wife of McDowell. The police have stationed officers at the apartment building until the killer is caught. One officer parked outside and another walking the halls and exterior of the building. The Arkham public is in an uproar. The local newspapers have sensationalized the killings and the perpetrator has been labeled a serial killer. The serial killer is being called the Arkham Ripper. Most believe it is Miah McDowell.

"I'm scared." Enterprise cuddles Jericho.

"Me too, baby," he whispers. "But everything will be alright."

As they both begin to fall asleep, Enterprise's cell phone rings. She looks at the glowing phone in the dark and tells Jericho, "It's my sister." She answers and walks into the other room to talk in private.

"I know what I'm doing." Jericho hears Enterprise say into the phone in the other room. He tries not to eavesdrop but it's impossible. He doesn't pick up all the conversation but bits and pieces. "I love him. Things will be different." Enterprise is silent for a long time. And then she says, "I understand. I will be there to help you as soon as I can. I love you too."

Enterprise comes back into the bedroom and looks down at Jericho. "I have to go," she says, clearly upset.

"Go where?"

"My sister needs me. I just have to leave. It's an emergency. A private family matter." She is dressing as she speaks.

Jericho is hurt by the fact that being her boyfriend doesn't include him in her family matters.

"What's happening?" He is following her out of the bedroom. She is fully dressed, he is only in his underwear.

"I just have to go now. Trust me."

"Will I see you again?" Something in his gut tells him this is a dire situation. "Wait." She is at the door about to exit his apartment unit and his life. "I love you."

"You can't," she responds stoically.

He follows her into the hallway outside of his apartment unit.

"Oh." Enterprise places her hand over her mouth looking about the hallway.

Jericho is dazed by the bloody, gory massacre. The police officer who was patrolling the halls is dead on the floor. There is so much blood everywhere, painted on the floor, walls, and ceilings. He can't tell whose blood is whose. Jack and Diane are lying dead by the stairs. He recognizes some of the other tenants, dead as well.

"We need to get out of this place," Jericho whispers.

Enterprise nods, not taking her eyes off the dead.

The sound of a young woman crying echoes into the hall.

A man wearing a goat face skin mask with horns, beard, and all enters the far end of the hallway at the top of the stairs. He steps over the dead as if they are nothing but clutter. Dressed in a dark suit, white red soaked shirt and tie, eye holes torn in the mask, and pulling blonde Taran by the hair. Her night clothes are tattered and torn and she sobs. In his other hand a very long knife slick and dripping with blood.

Jericho wishes he had a weapon. They are cornered. He eyes the dead police officer's holstered gun while at the same time considering retreating back into his apartment unit. He realizes that Enterprise doesn't appear to be afraid in the slightest.

Taran looks up at Jericho and Enterprise, her eyes red from crying. "Help me."

"Do you know why people get upset with atheism?" The killer asks them in a matter of fact tone.

No one says anything.

The killer arrogantly chuckles. "It's because people are afraid to die. They know the truth of atheism means there is no afterlife, no spirit, and when they die, they die. End of story. End of their story. They cease to exist as if they were never here to begin with. Their consciousness, their self, everything is gone. Truth horrifies. People are nothing. Consciousness is all chemical reactions within the brain. There is no soul. No God. No meaning to life. Enjoy it while you have it. Accept what we truly are, no better than any organic feces. I am the closest thing to a god, exercising my ability to end life."

"Nonsense." Enterprise laughs as if the killer is a clown.

Jericho's eyes widened at her bold statement.

Taran whimpers, still held painfully by her hair.

The killer's eyes squint in anger beneath the mask. He moves the bloody knife blade to Taran's throat.

"Don't!" Jericho shouts.

"The woman means nothing to me." Enterprise laughs again and shakes her head. "Kill her if you want. That's on you, not us. I will tell you this, Mr. Arkham Ripper, you have no way proving divinity does not exist. Equally no way of objectively proving it does. The absence of proof is not proof. No evidence does not mean the case is solved. Conclusions like that are based on speculation. Opinion."

The killer growls. His anger rises at her lack of fear. "There is no reason to believe the universe exists for a reason! There is no reason to believe in a divine plan or creation or God."

Enterprise shrugs. "Belief is a tool that should be used to accomplish goals. The experience of reality is subjective and that's all it can be. You can only experience your own consciousness. We are all locked in our own independent universes, flesh containing sparks. Subjectivity. Perception. That is all there is. The only tool we have for measurement of existence is our own thoughts. All we have is thought and thought should be used to advantage. Development of consciousness, development of effective and essential thought systems. There are things in this universe we can't measure. Thought is one of those things. How do you measure love? Space? Infinity? Number has no limit. Dreams? What are dreams? What is Deja Vu? Synchronicity? Is it all chemicals? All coincidence and accident? A very mathematically improbable accident, this universe and everything in it. What is precognition? Premonitions? These things can be documented, recorded in a journal, but not proven objectively. The only witness is self."

The killer snarls. "I will kill you all and you will see the void."

"How can you say that when you haven't seen the void yourself?" Enterprise challenges him. "Seems an act of faith, this belief in the void you speak of."

"I will kill her." He presses the razor sharp long knife to Taran's neck firm enough to draw a thin line of blood.

"I have experienced the void." Enterprise informs the killer with undeniable confidence in her voice. It is called the death posture. A meditation technique of silence and stillness, to experience existing without thought or movement, no sensations. A state of death. The heart even slows with the breathing technique if you are dedicated. It is the same experience of existing in the womb."

"Enterprise," Jericho whispers, frightened of the serial killer and his girlfriend's reaction to him now.

Enterprise ignores Jericho and continues. "Atheism is arrogance. It is the assumption that you have figured it out. That you know for certain. The stance of atheism is absolute with no evidence to support it. The truth of the matter from what I've learned is that human consciousness is a quantum experience, the brain and physical body a part of the quantum mechanism. And we are not developed enough to comprehend much of anything other than this animal experience. If you want to prove your convictions, friend, kill yourself and face this void you are so eager to bring others to but fear to enter yourself."

The killer points the knife dripping with crimson at Enterprise. His arm so tense it trembles. Enterprise approaches the point of the blade. Jericho is frozen with shock, it all feels like a dark dream to him. Taran's hair is released and she crumbles to the floor, sobbing softly.

"I am the Devil," the killer whispers in a sinister way.

"Now you are contradicting yourself. There is no Devil without a god. The idea of the

Devil is an Abrahamic duality at the least, I'm sure that is your reference. You just threw atheism and your entire argument out the window." Enterprise taunts. She stands so close the tip of the long knife is just under her chin. "The Devil as in Satan? Or some other devil? I do love a paradox though, I'll give you that much, Mr. Evil. Paradox can lead to ancient wisdom. Serpentine. Be more original. Or more esoteric. How about I am Shaitan? Or I am Samiel? Or some other naughty demon. Leviathan? Legion? Belial? Nergal? Abraxis? Pazuzu? Bezelbub? There are so many to choose from. The Devil you speak of is the bastardized version of so many pagan deities. The Celtic Green Man or the Greek Pan. Maybe Baphomet? No. This is all beyond you. You are no more a unique snowflake than the rest of us. You're a run of the mill, generic serial killer. Killing because you are afraid. Because you are lost and terrified and have given up. Because you are weak. I am n or fond of slashers. I say fuck Jack the Ripper and all the lot of serial killers. They are broken robots, usually smashed by their mothers before anything else comes about. Pure weakness externalized and over compensated. Unsuccessful in society. Culturally retarded. Socially inept. Deep issues of repression, serial killers are their own prisoners. Something shattered against a stone and never put back together correctly. You would do well to seek long term psychoanalysis or analytical psychology. None of that fast food therapy the insurance companies love. That type of therapy is lacking among the general population and is admittedly a major commitment and hard work. Something I doubt you have the strength or stomach for."

Jericho is backed up against his door in horror. Speechless.

"I am not sick!" The killer screams at Enterprise.

Taran crawls away from the entire insane scene.

"McDowell!" Jericho yells.

"You are ruining everything!" The killer screams at Enterprise, the tip of his long knife nicks her chin, drawing blood.

"What you are doing with your killings is an unconscious ritual. Sacrifices of some sort. Attempting to transform into someone or something you like because you hate yourself." Enterprise does not back down.

"Shut up!" The killer screams hysterically. "Shut up! Shut up!"

"Calm down, baby," Enterprise scolds him. I want you to look into my eyes. Deeply. Concentrate."

The killer stares into his eyes through the holes in his rotting goat mask.

Taran has crawled all the way to Jericho and he helps her stand. She is very shaken, no longer crying, but filled with fear.

"If you are caught you won't survive in prison," Enterprise explains. "Everyone is pretty certain of your identity. It is only a matter of time until you are arrested. You killed a police officer. It won't take long at all for the police to come for him. In prison you may be raped.

You may be killed like Dahlmer was. A mop stick up the ass. A painful, slow way to go. Even if you get away today you will eventually be caught. Why? Because your thoughts are irrational. Your philosophy is flawed. There is a good chance you could be executed I suppose. I know you are afraid to die. Prove your convictions. Let your last act be an undeniable act of courage. Enter the void yourself. Marching fearlessly into the void will be the mark you leave behind. Cowboy up. Kill yourself."

The goat mask angles to one side as if thinking childlike.

"It will be your unwritten manifesto," Enterprise urges. "I will tell your story. I promise you that, even if it's undeserved. It will be a bonus reward to the void."

The killer nods.

"Like a samurai," she says.

Taran and Jericho are fascinated and horrified.

"Promise I will be buried with my mask," the killer whispers to Enterprise.

She nods. "It will be."

"Who are you?" The killer asks her.

Taran and Jericho look about the hall of blood and dead, utterly lost as to what is transpired between these two enigmas before them. Both are alien to what is their human condition.

"I am Enterprise."

"Of course you are." The goat masked killer gives a respectful nod before impaling himself in the chest with the long knife. The blade makes a dull quick thud and all are surprised by the strength of the blow. It impales his heart and he drops to his knees as if by intention and falls forward dead within less than a minute.

Taran stands using Jericho for support. Jericho's mouth is hanging open.

Enterprise looks at them. She seems like a different woman. Like an ancient goddess of the hunt and moon. "My tragedy is that I love you, Jericho." She looks to Taran and says, "But she needs you more than I do even if she doesn't realize it. The two of you have been lovers in past lives. You always find each other. My sister needs me."

With those final words she pulls the long knife from the heart of Miah with a grunt and walks out of the Oldtowne Apartment and their lives.

Jericho stands blinking back to reality. What just happened? He had moved to follow Enterprise but Taran grabbed his hand afraid to be alone. He realizes she does need him at this moment. Jericho puts his arms around her.

By the time Taran and Jericho have calmed and collected themselves the police and ambulances are arriving along with fire trucks (the first on the scene), and the media. It turns out the police officer outside in his car was killed as well. Besides Taran and Jericho, Tucker DePriest is the only other survivor of the Arkham Ripper at Oldtowne Apartments.

The police determine the body count since the murder of his wife is thirty-three victims. There may be more unaccounted for. Everyone hopes that is not the case.

Tucker, Taran, and Jericho move into the dorms at Miskatonic University. Jericho has lost all contact with Enterprise. Her phone service has been shut off. Looking into her school records it is discovered her last name was an alias. She is untraceable, as if she has fallen off the face of the world.

As the school year nears its end, people begin to move past the Arkham Ripper and memories of a girl named Enterprise fade from memory. The Arkham Ripper becomes just one more of the dark mysteries of the area. There are many strange things about Arkham that people whisper about. Many rumors and legends spanning back to the founding of the city and prior.

Taran, Tucker, and Jericho end up spending a lot of time together having the shared tragedy in common. As time passes Jericho and Taran rekindle their long extinguished flame and Tucker and Jericho become the best of friends and colleagues. They never discuss the killer or Enterprise, instead the trio become graduate students and work together investigating and theorizing quantum consciousness, local history, and esoteric lore.

Darker Than You Think

Dedicated in honor of Jack Williamson

A pimple and freckled face teenage boy is talking into a cell phone while another snickers in the background.

The boy on the phone says, "I'd like a delivery, please."

There is a pause as the boy listens to the employee on the other end of the phone, grinning big at his cohort.

"What kind of specials do you have?" The angst filled boy asks with an abundance of charm.

Another pause as the boy listens with mock interest.

"That sounds great. Just fine. I'll take the deal with one specialty pizza and one pepperoni pizza. I'll take the bread sticks instead of the dessert pie."

Another listening pause and grin.

"No, thank you. That's everything. I'll be paying in cash. How long until it gets here?"

Chris hangs up the cell phone. He and Josh have been making prank phone calls in one of two ways. Either stealing phones or buying temporary ones at the store.

Both the culprit Chris and his partner in crime giggle hysterically.

"Ha, ha, ha,." Chris laughs. "Mr. Leeds is going to be pissed when the delivery arrives again,"

"You think he suspects?" Josh asks.

"I doubt it. He's just a dumb old jock."

Josh and Chris, a pair of social outcasts at school, have recently taken up the hobby of making prank calls to various staff members and students from their high school.

"I'm proud to be an American!" Josh chants out in mock imitation of their gym/physical health education teacher Mr. Leeds. "You know what makes me feel proud to be American?" Josh jumps up pretending to be Mr. Leeds, "You see those wrestlers back there? Don't be shy boys, stand up! Stand up and be proud to be Americans! Each one of these boys won their matches last night! Makes me darn proud to be American."

"Mr. Leeds is such a dick," Chris laughs. "He doesn't care about anyone but the jocks. I can't believe he's the health teacher. He doesn't know a damn thing about health."

"I doubt he even knows our names," Josh adds.

"Have you seen him jogging in the mornings before school?" Chris asks.

"Yeah, I'm sure everyone has," Josh looks amused.

"Have you noticed he shaves his legs?"

"What?" Josh can't stop laughing at this. "No!"

"I'm serious," Chris chuckles, "He must think it makes him more aerodynamic or something."

Both high school buddies laugh for a couple of minutes.

"God he's a dweeb," Chris says, "Have you noticed he always watches us shower in the locker rooms?"

Josh laughs along with this too," I think everyone has. "Real fucking creepy."

"I heard he spikes his coffee with liquor too," Chris goes on.

"He does," Josh smirks, "I drank some of it once. It's like half coffee and half *Baileys*."

"For real?"

Josh nods, "So basically we have an alcoholic, in the closet gay gym teacher, who favors the jocks over everyone. He deserves every prank we pull on him, not just because of that stuff, because he's a dick to guys like us. He's a bigot toward anyone who's not a jock and he should pay for it."

"He may be the most enormous jerk on the planet," Chris throws in two cents, "but I'd love to bone his daughters!"

"Hell yeah," Josh agrees, "They are smoking hot!"

Gym teacher Mr. Leeds has twin daughters who pretty much every guy at the school has a crush on, but they are socially way out of Chris and Josh's league.

"What do you say we go hide in the bushes and watch the pizza man try to deliver the pizza again?" Chris asks.

"Most definitely," Josh agrees. The pair of friends always hide somewhere nearby to witness the fruits of their pranks.

Elliot Braddock, pizza delivery man extraordinaire, pulls up to Mr. Leeds house. His car is leaking only, the rear view mirror is busted off, and the muffler is dragging. He double checks the address on the delivery ticket before going to the front door and ringing the doorbell.

Hidden around a corner a house away, Chris and Josh try hard to hold back their snickering.

As soon as Elliot sees the tall, red faced man answer the door he senses trouble. He's an old man, maybe late forties, early fifties, but Elliott can tell the man used to have an athletic build. The man has black hair that would be curly if it wasn't cut so short and a thick porn star mustache.

"What's this?" Mr. Leeds grunts with a can of beer in one hand and slurred speech.

Elliott can smell the booze on the man's belligerent breath. "Um, did you order some pizza and breadsticks?"

"Hell, no! Is this some kind of joke? This is the third time this week. Yesterday some slant eye showed up trying to deliver me Chinese food. The day before that three taxi cabs all showed up at the same time from three different cab companies!" Mr. Leeds blusters.

"I apologize, sir, it seems as if someone has been wasting both of our time."

"Don't apologize, boy, you didn't do it. And stand with your shoulders straight like a man."

An attractive teen girl peers out from over Mr. Leeds shoulder, "Did you order us pizza, dad?" She sounds thrilled.

Mr. Leeds takes a deep breath and lets out a pissed off sigh, "How much do I owe you?" No matter what shortcomings Mr. Leeds has, he does have a gracious love for his twin daughters.

"Nothing, sir, it's on the house for the inconvenience. If I take it back to the store it's just gonna sit on the counter and the other employees will eat it. They're all fat and eat enough pizza as it is, so take it for free, please."

"They're all fat," Mr. Leeds laughs more loudly than the joke was funny. He pulls out his wallet and takes out a five dollar bill, "You seem like a good American kid, take this for the pricks wasting your time too."

Handing the food to Mr. Leeds, Elliott smiles sheepishly, "Thank you, very much, sir."

"Now get the hell off my property before I shoot you for trespassing," Mr. Leeds slurs and grumbles. Elliott isn't sure if he is serious about shooting him or not, so he takes no time dawdling back to his old, beat down car. "And keep your shoulders straight when you walk. Walk like a man, damn it."

Elliott straightens his shoulders before getting in the car and driving away.

Both Chris and Josh are disappointed that Mr. Leeds ended up getting free pizza. They decide to go home and finish the night playing video games. It's a school night.

Wesley Woodard sits naked on the floor in a dark and dingy room. The only light in the room comes from the illumination of a city of flickering candles. The naked, pot belly man sits sweating and breathing heavily. Wesley is balding and wearing thick glasses that make his eyes look too big.

He is seated cross legged in the center of a seven point star drawn on the floor about him. There is one circle touching the tip of each of the star's seven points. Around this is a second circle. There is precisely 84 inches of space between the two circles, 7 feet. Seven is one of the sacred numbers he is using in this great work.

There are seven black candles burning at each of the seven points of the star. Scattered about the room there is a myriad rainbow of lit candles. Different incense burns around the room giving it an atmosphere of thin fog.

An arcane symbol is drawn between each of the seven points of the star within the interior circle. Wesley is masturbating vigorously inside the magical circle. On a computer with the monitor shut off so only the volume can be heard, there is a loop playing of a woman screaming in sexual, ecstatic, primal delight, "Oh God, I'm cumming! Oh, God, I'm cumming! Oh, God, I'm cumming! Oh, God, I'm cumming!" Over and over again. This ritual has been going on for an exhausting seven hours. Nearing the seventh hour means the climax of the rite has grown near.

The climax is not the end of a ritual, only a most tremendous point. The point where the maestro's intent is accomplished, as long as everything has gone according to plan and the maestro has the appropriate will to power and talent to succeed. Wesley howls delirious delight as he climaxes, blaring out barbarically, as his entire body and mind tremble uncontrollably experiencing prolonged ejaculation and orgasm, "IAO! IAO! IAO! ABRAXAS! IAO! IAO! IAO! KRONOS! KRONOS! KRONOS! IAO! IAO! IAO! DEMIURGOS! KRONOS! IAO!"

Wesley nearly collapses from the internal power he has unleashed with his manipulation of the akasic. He has not only attained an immaculate state of consciousness with the long built up orgasm, he has sacrificed millions of unborn half children in the form of semen to the ancient god Kronos.

Within the protective circle of the seven pointed star on the floor near Wesley are his magical tools. A dust scented book appears to be more than a hundred years old. A long, sharp, silver dagger. A cup filled with holy water. A cup filled with red wine. An old coin with an odd sigil scratched into both sides. A black wand. A rainbow colored wand. A single dead rose. A personal diary in which he keeps meticulous records of all of his magical work. A quill pen. A jar of India ink. A remote control. A small vial of blood. A well used deck of Tarot cards.

Wesley's shoulders are slumped, sweating profusely, fighting the urge to sleep, but too excited to sleep. This has been a very long process. Eight months of daily rites thus far and there is only one ritual remaining before this great work is completed. He uses the remote control to turn off the loop of the woman's screaming orgasm and all is silent save Wesley's breathing and the faint burning of candle wax and incense.

Seeming to step out from the shadows appear seven black robed figures. Their faces are hidden by the shadows of their hoods. These seven stand as mute witnesses to the callings of Wesley Woodard. They are unseen by all but those who can see into the akasic winds. Wesley has not mastered akasic vision but is improving, a clear and measurable sign of his success. He can see these seven obscure, hidden masters.

Taking in a deep breath, taking all precaution to remain within his protective circle, Wesley laments with deranged joy, on his knees before all of the unseen entities, "I perish and reawaken in the cosmic womb of Saturnius Mons, eradicator and author of entirety. Greatest of all Gods, All Father, High Father, the Almighty. Mightiest of all Gods. Old god of time, sex, and death. Amen."

Wesley continues the final stages of this sixth of the colossal rites of Saturn. "I consume these holy sacraments in the name of the Old Father." Wesley quickly licks up his palm full of warm semen, briefly fighting off a gag reflex, but he swallows it whole. Immediately following that act he opens the small vial of menstrual blood and swallows it like a shot of whiskey.

Around Wesley and his protective circle the seven black robed figures nod their consent as they step back vanishing once again into the darkness as if they were never there.

Wesley smiles weakly with a sweat covered face and hoarse voice, "The sixth rite of Saturnia is complete, my lords."

He collapses to the floor in utter exhaustion and falls asleep right there inside the protective circle.

Joel comes out of the men's restroom at Alphonso's Pizza where he and Elliot both work. Joel is a cook, makes all the pizzas and the pizza dough in the mornings. He is a straight up kitchen employee. Joel wears a grin of amusement as he hands Elliott's cell phone to the assistant manager, overweight Marsha.

"Elliott left his cell phone in the bathroom again, sitting on top of the toilet dispenser like always," Joel snorts.

"What the hell?" Marsha remarks, taking the cell phone from Joel so she could lock it up in the management office until he gets back from delivery. This bothers her because Elliott does it all the time, loses his phone, and it's important to have his phone with him on deliveries. "How does a person lose their phone so much?"

Joel snickers, "He must be rubbing one off to internet porn on his phone."

"Nice, Joel," Marsha shakes her head at his humorless joke. "I'll give it back to him when he gets back."

"Right on," Joel disappears into the kitchen to make more pizza.

Wesley is seated inside the first heptagram just as the night before, within the two protective magical circles. Once again the room is lit only by candle light. One black candle at each point of the star and several others of various colors intentionally placed about the room. The same magical tools as before are within the star with him.

This time Wesley is dressed in a black robe, naked beneath the robe and wearing only a pair of scarlet socks. The strong scents of incense still haze the room. Wesley is not a smoker and doesn't care for all the incense smoke but understands the necessity. He is excited. No one has attempted anything like this before and have come as close to success as he has. Well, that's not entirely true. John Dee. Nicholas Flamel. L. Ron Hubbard. He's sure others whose names have been forgotten from history like the statues of kings which eventually crumble to dust as centuries wear on. He is a chaos maestro. Each maestro has his own methods and philosophies. Wesley chose the path of the chaos maestro for many reasons. Mostly because he doesn't have to listen to the rules of the other maestro's and he can believe whatever it is he chooses to believe. He doesn't have to follow maestro protocol or rules of initiation. No grade work for him. He dropped out of high school for a reason.

On this night, Wesley has the Tarot cards laid out in front of him in a simplified formation he prefers. He's used the Celtic Cross layout for years when he first started practicing magic, but has found the Graal layout works for him best. It only uses five cards. One card for each of the Hallows of the Holy Grail.

The divination before him:

The Five of Wands; strife

The Ten of Wands; oppression

The Eight of Cups; indolence

The Three of Swords; sorrow

The Seven of Disks; failure

Even with the negative outcome of the Tarot divination, Wesley takes it as a good sign for what he is to do. He is preparing for the final and seventh rite of what he has come to call the Apocalypse Working. The liberation of Kronos from Tartarus. Each of these five cards represent the planetary aspect of Saturn.

Mumbling, he diligently records the Tarot divination in his magical diary with his India ink quill pen.

By chance, as he's putting the cards away and back into their black silk covering, a sixth card falls out. Every maestro with even a novice knows this always has meaning and the card is not to be ignored.

He studies the card for a few moments before putting it away with the others. It is a trump card. The card of Death. This only encourages Wesley to move forward. He interprets it to mean symbolic death. The death of his old life and the rebirth of his new life with Kronos.

Nearly against the wall to the west of the room stands a full length antique mirror Wesley purchased at a thrift store a few years ago. The owner of the thrift store didn't realize how much the mirror is actually worth. The owner just thought it was junk and sold it to Wesley for twenty-five dollars. Wesley estimates the mirror to have been crafted some time in the late 1880s. Maybe 1875. Wesley isn't entirely sure of the exact date but he knows he's close.

The mirror is always in that same place on the west end of the room. In the west because that is where the sun sets and Wesley Woodard wants the sun to set for good, to rise again when Kronos has returned.

Wesley could have chosen the older god Ouranos as his master, but he understands Kronos is the right son to choose. Ouranos had to be dealt with for the universe to team freely with life. So Kronos overthrew his father. When Kronos reigned over the universe it was a golden age. The golden age. It could be called the time when mankind lived in Eden. This is known by those who know. Most people in the world are ignorant to the point of being unwitting, contented slaves. The Romans were some of the first to insure the keeping of the slaves and plebians in their place. Of course, it happened through different stages and methods around the world, but this Roman tyranny was one of the most successful. Later when the Roman Empire became the Holy Roman Empire what happened is that the Abrahamic religions took over the role of slave masters. The Jews, Christians, Muslims, and all of their confused offspring. Dyeus fored Kronos to give him the Omphalos, giving men the misguided belief that geo-political power and currency are the most important things about the world and life. Dyeus became an enemy of Gaia when he overthrew Ouranos and has remained so since that time. Gaia went so far as to create Typhon to oppose Dyeus. Dyeus castrated his father as his father had before him. It is said a new god will emerge to usurp Dyeus. Dyeus is mad with paranoia to know which god this is prophesied to be so he may slay the child first. Kronos usurped his father Ouranos to bring a golden age to humanity. Dyeus usurped his father Kronos to enslave humanity and end the golden age. Some of the ancients called Kronos by the name of El. This spiritual war has been waging since long before humanity was even a thought in a god's mind.

Wesley thinks about all of this as he stares into his own eyes in the tall mirror before him. The slaves today call Dyeus by the name of Zeus and are ignorant of their enslavement. Content to be slaves. Most of them. Some among the mortals sense something is wrong. Wesley is one of those sensing mortals.

Kronos was defeated but never killed by Dyeus. Instead he was cut into one thousand pieces and scattered throughout Tartarus, what most people today think of as Hell. Wesley is not the first to work to free Kronos from Tartarus. Many have come before him. It has taken thousands of years to bring all the pieces of Kronos back together. So many have come before Wesley, it brings tears of humility to his eyes knowing he was chosen to be the last of the gods and souls working to restore Kronos to his throne and bring a return to a golden age. Dyeus must die when Kronos returns.

Wesley continues to stare, unblinking into his own eyes in the mirror until his face begins to blur and morph. This is a common practice for a maestro to induce trance and alternative states of consciousness. Those who walk the world calling themselves magicians, pagans, witches, wiccans, whatever their silly labels, they are wrong or simply haven't achieved much progress in the great work. The only other acceptable name of the maestro's is the magi. If you are dealing with a human or human type creature that refers to itself humbly as magi or maestro you know you are likely dealing with the real deal. The great work is different for everyone but it all has the same goal in the end. The goal is the same depending on which school or philosophy of magic you walk. There are three paths Wesley knows of: The right hand path, the left hand path, or the even handed path. It is possible, but unlikely that there are more than these three schools of philosophy all originating several millennia ago as a single theology, a single tribe called *the Brotherhood of the Snake*. There was a rift within *the Brotherhood of the Snake* which started out spreading very slowly like a vaguely, tricky contagious disease. This rift caused the first break and the first outbreak of war. Up until this point the world had not known war, only the golden age of Kronos and the state of nature. When war broke out there were forlorn maestro's that wanted to prevent the war in any way they could. The only problem was they could not stop what had been set in motion. *The Brotherhood of the Snake* had already broken into two factions: *The Brotherhood of the Sun* and *the Brotherhood of the Moon*, *the Illuminati* and *the Luminari* respectively.

Those priests who opposed the separation of the brotherhood chose a leader amongst themselves and created a third order or faction of the great tribe, calling themselves *the Brotherhood of Silence*. Often called *the Quiet Ones*. As war and time went on things became more bewildering and perplexing. The original three orders of the broken tribe all considered themselves still members of the same *Brotherhood of the Snake*, but as time, disagreement, and war slipped forward out of control, the golden age seemed to be lost forever. The three began to break apart over the centuries until eventually some of the factions began to have nothing to do with the original goals and philosophies of the original priesthood. The secret war has gone completely out of control and every century or so another order, faction, or tribe seems to take dominance. The scales are always leaning one way or the other. *The Quiet Ones* do their best to stay out of it all and do their best to stay true to the original philosophies and goals of *the Brotherhood of the Snake* in the beginning.

The maestro Wesley speaks aloud to himself in front of the distant mirror outside his protective circle. In reality he is addressing the invisible entities in the room. Some lingering aimlessly, some looking for weaknesses in the protective circle, some present to witness and record, some actually interested in what is transpiring. Indeed some are hoping for Wesley Woodard's success. Most are bored and apathetic, simply drawn to the high level of activity in the akasic in the area.

"To the old and ancient first father of man, usurped by the lustful bastard Dyeus, I pledge myself to you. I am now your son if you accept me, almighty, absolute Kronos, god of time, sex, and death without which no thing would exist. I humbly kneel before you in a black robe to signify my ignorance to the mysteries. Truthful, noble, and natural father of man, unjustly defeated and imprisoned in Tartarus. Saturn has never ceased orbiting the sun. I humble, bare myself before you," Wesley lies flat on his chest within his protective circle, "My word is my honor, my oath. All that I am is yours. Pure father you will be freed from Tartarus. I pray and worship in the ancient way in preparation of the final rite."

For several minutes, maybe even an hour, Wesley simply stares in the mirror so long his vision blurs and his face morphs into many forms. Like werewolves of moving clay, like the many faces of Christ. Until finally when an unknown and excruciating amount of time has passed something not quite human appears and keeps its form, no longer morphing. Not quite clear but by no means blurry. It is not the face of Wesley looking back at him, he knows and feels this. It is the face of his first father, Kronos. A face too terrible to truly look upon with mortal eyes.

A barbarous voice chants with terminal authority, " In sacrificium, et in vase."

"Yes, my sovereign daimon," Wesley answers with his head bowed low, in absolute submission to the old god.

The old god speaks again, a voice that seems to move through Wesley's body linking a euphoric illness, " Ultima. Sanguis. Antiqua. Imperium. Vindictus."

"I am your servant, my father," Wesley says half in tears half in elation. "I belong to you, Dominus Kronos. Your word is my action. My oath is my blood. I am your hand and your fist."

Kronos vanishes from the magical old mirror without warning.

Wesley lay on his side crying tears of fanatic joy.

Elliot sits in a living room playing video games with fat Joel for the evening. They game out and smoke pot together often. They are both stoned, eating Cheetos, and drinking soda. Both completely content, zoned out, and comfortable.

"Marsha's kinda hot," Joel confesses dully.

Elliot just looks at him, not terribly interested, "Hit that shit."

"What's with you, dude?" Joel bitches, "Did Miranda take your balls when she split?"

Elliott slaps Joel's groin. Joel moans in pain, clutching his crotch, Elliott says, "Just what I thought, a vagina."

"Fuck you, dude," Joel rubs his nuts in an attempt to massage the pain away. "At least I still try to get laid, dick. It's time you quit whining around about her and get used to the idea some other dude is in her balls deep now. You're not as fun to kick it with anymore. It's been like forever. Forget her. You're a cool cat. Chicks dig you. Move on. You'll find a new girlfriend and forget all about Miranda."

"It's only been two months," Elliott retorts.

"Long enough," Joel says, growing bored with the subject. "What do you say we go out and get whiskey drunk tomorrow night?"

"I can't," Elliott answers, "I told Marsha I'd work overtime that next morning."

"Be hungover at work," Joel shrugs. "I do it all the time."

"I hate being hungover at work."

"Come on, sister, no excuses. After work that night then."

"Fine," Elliott answers, "You're right. I need to forget about her. A night of drunken debauchery could do me some good. I'm down."

"Hell yeah!" Joel cheers, starting to focus more on his video game than the conversation.

Wesley stands nervously alongside the bike trails near a grove of trees watching pedestrians, bicyclists, and joggers travel by huffing and sweating. The bike trail is a pavement trail that loops in a great figure eight all across the city of Applegate. He does his best to appear relaxed and incognito, pretending to stretch his legs and back, resting, sipping from a water bottle.

His vehicle is parked very close by. It will only take him a minute, maybe two at the most to get from here to the car. Woodard only has to wait for the perfect moment. He has faith it will come. It is providence. Everything is falling in place like a divine line of domino's collapsing to a magnificent center star.

The perfect moment. Alone. The perfect victim. A moment absent of witnesses. A lone jogger. It doesn't matter who. The prophecies continue to align. A lone woman in headphones and sunglasses, jogging hard, hardly noticing Wesley as she approaches. She wears exercise clothing. Tennis shoes. An athletic build. Very tan and toned.

As an act of divinity she appears, not only alone and unaware, but sweating, exhausted, with no one around, jogging closer to Wesley. His stomach churns. He is so afraid he feels he may defecate in his pants.

Wesley has to move fast. He can tell he is not in as good physical condition as the running lass. It must be staged fast and flawlessly. Perfect timing. The time is right. The time is now.

Crouched with a white cloth in one hand, pretending to tighten his shoe laces, watching from the corner of his eye. She comes closer. He can hear her feet beat the pavement as she runs. He can hear water trickling nearby. Closer now. Wesley's heart is beating faster. All at once he's not sure he can do this. Attempting to hold his hands steady, they tremor. Shudder with primitive fear. Wesley shivers for the old god.

Just as the young jogger passes the crouching Wesley, he bolts upward like a fat panther. She startles at his unexpected movement, but too late. Wesley is holding the white cloth over her mouth, muffling her cries of surprise and protest as she breathes in deeply the chloroform and other herbal agents he's concocted for immediate successful slumber. An alchemical dust worthy of a sandman or faerie.

Moving as quickly as he can, struggling to carry the listless, young woman in his arms, Wesley does manage to get her in the back seat of his car, shutting the door just as a trio of bicyclists zoom past, paying no mind to Wesley. Taking a moment to collect himself, he makes the symbol of the seven pointed star before himself much like a Catholic makes the sign of the cross. Wesley whispers a prayer to Kronos and the collectors of his immortal corpse. Taking a moment to drink more water from his bottle, fighting off a wave of fear, he scans for anyone coming from either end of the bike trail. Spotting no one, he crawls into the backseat of the car, closing the door behind him.

Laboring hastily Wesley uses dark silvery grey duct tape to bind the unknown woman's hands, wrists, and ankles. He uses the white cloth and duct tape to gag her, making sure she can still breath through her nose.

Peering out from the back seat of his car there is no one present. No witnesses.

Shaking with nerves, Wesley gets out of the backseat and takes the driver's seat. Tilting his head back, inhaling deeply. Then he presses his forehead against the steering wheel, wondering how he has come to this place. He did not choose to be chosen. Wesley has been a maestro for years now, but it wasn't until he was worthy that Atlas contacted him in the akasic and the dream lands to aid in the second coming of Kronos.

Wesley lifts his head from the steering wheel and starts the car's engine. "I am the hand of the ancient all-father Kronos."

Josh and Chris relax in Josh's bedroom listening to music. Josh is on the floor browsing through vinyl records. Chris is on the bed tapping his fingers against his chest along to the beat of the music. Both are drinking beer and smoking cigarettes. They have been close friends since middle school.

"Oh, dude, I forgot to tell you, I stole Mr. Leeds cell phone today," Chris sits up bellowing, "Should we order him some more pizza? Chinese food? Taxi cabs? All three?"

"Are you an idiot?" Josh scolds, "They can trace the phone to us."

Chris rolls his eyes, "Really? You think I'm an amateur? How long have we been doing this?" Chris sounds genuinely offended, "I'm a god damned professional criminal."

"Okay," Josh snickers.

"Of course I shut the phone off as soon as I took it and I'll smash it as soon as we place the orders," Chris says like he means business.

"Nah," Josh puts records away and sits on the other end of the bed, "I'm bored with Mr. Leeds. Let's do someone else."

"Like who?"

"I don't know," Josh's shrugs.

"How about Mr. Roth?" Chris suggests.

Josh doesn't appear thrilled with the idea, "Jack Off Roth is a goon, a total weirdo with those googly eyes, but he's actually kind of a nice guy."

Chris cracks up, "You like Jack Off Roth? Do you guys stroke it together in the restroom at school? Does he keep you after school for detention and extracurricular activities?"

"He's never been a prick to me," Josh defends. "Doug was probably lying about catching him jerking off in the restroom anyhow. Doug is always making shit up. It was probably Roth who caught Doug doing it."

Chris shrugs and takes a drink of his beer, "I guess you might be right. Doug is kind of a dud. I mean who in their right mind names their kid Doug? With a name like that the kid is doomed to be a poozer for life no matter what he does. It's almost as bad as being named Tim."

"Some parents don't think enough about naming their kids," Josh thinks aloud, "The name is so important. Regardless of all other factors in life it does play a role in determining the child's outcome in life."

"James Douglas Morrison," Chris says.

"Doesn't count," Josh explains, "First off it's his middle name, which is way different than the first name. Second there are always exceptions to any rule. And if he had been Doug Morrison I doubt the rock god and poet of *the Doors* would have ever existed."

"Well stated," Chris smiles, "and point taken. So who should we order pizza for?"

"The janitor. Mr. Woodard. He's a creepy sucker," Josh offers.

"Absolutely fucking perfect," Chris pulls Mr. Leeds cell phone from his pocket, "That cat is a total creeper."

Chris makes the phone call and then he and Josh go outside to smash the cell phone and watch from a distance the pizza man going to the janitor's door.

Wesley is in his home this evening wearing a black robe. He is in his temple room. The room with the seven pointed star and double circle of protection. All of his usual magical tools are in the star and first circle with him. A black bird is caged inside the circle with them. The servant of the old god chants in barbarous tongue, mostly broken Latin and Greek.

The woman he kidnapped is bound to the floor within the star. Wesley learned her name is Malina Curry going through her things. Her arms and legs are tied apart, making her body vaguely take the shape of a five point star within the seven point star. Malina is on her stomach, naked except for her jogging shorts. Her breasts are hidden from view since she is lying on her chest. Wesley has no sexual interest in her. There is a dried out and dead rose by each of her hands, feet, and her head.

Malina's mouth is gagged. The gag is wet with her saliva. She is wide awake, eyes alert with terror. The occasional whimper escapes her.

In the akasic winds Wesley can see the unseen members of his order. The ancient and secret order of the old gods. These are the same black robed individuals Wesley has seen before. They come to witness his Apocalypse Working. In the beginning none came to watch. The further and more dedicated he became to his occult work, the more they began to appear as watchers. One at first. Eventually more and more with progress he made. Their faces are still hidden beneath the shadows of their hoods. Wesley does not know who they are. He suspects servants of the old gods, Kronos, Atlas, and the other old ones. Not the old gods themselves, but their followers, like Wesley Woodard himself.

There is a clear difference in the atmosphere and attitude of all the robed ones this time. They are more attentive. Even those who seemed bored and half-hearted before seem to be giving Wesley's work their full attention now. Wesley feels pride in this. He is nearing the accomplishment of his great work. His life's work. What he was born to do.

There is another significant difference in the ritual work tonight. A white figure paces trapped between the two protective circles. The first circle aligned with the points of the seven ends of the star. The second outer circle seven feet out from that parallel to the inner circle. This figure is only seen with akasic vision. The development of Wesley's akasic vision is a clear sign he is becoming more than human. A true maestro. The pale figure stalks the circle it is trapped inside like a tiger hungry for it's prey, never taking it's eyes off Wesley or Malina. It pays silent, close attention to the ritual work.

The pacing white figure is the old god Kronos, also known as Saturn, he goes by many names, as do all the old gods. Lengthy hair and savage eyes. He is nude with pearly flesh and no visible sexual organ. He was castrated by his son Dyeus millennia ago. His expression is one of fuming, longing fury. Kronos eyes are black and red like the embers of burning coal. The flesh surrounding his eye sockets wrinkled with age and dark with worry.

Wesley's heart throbs at the vision of his god. He has to focus on the ritual task before him to fight off tremors of pure joy and salvation.

Wesley kneels at the side of the bound woman, Malina, chanting in both Greek and Latin, too softly to make out the words to any but Malina and the extraordinary hearing of Kronos and the black robed witnesses.

With an abysmal breath and the ritual dagger gripped in both Wesley's sweating hands, he begins to carve a seven point star into the flesh of Malina's back. The heptagram. In the center of the star Wesley cuts the sigil of Saturn. Malina's screams of pain are stifled by her gag, which is now soaked through with sweat and saliva. Wesley delicately carves smaller sigils between each of the seven points of the star, one for each of the seven old gods most loyal to high father Kronos during the Titanomachy.

Wesley speaks in a fever of splendor, "Here abide the terminal offering toward the incarnation of the old god. Majus Sanctus Saetern regula aeternalis."

Wesley takes the blackbird, a crow, from its cage with both hands. The crow squawks in protest. With a quickness Wesley cuts the bird's head off, holding it over Malina's back, letting the bird's blood drip down onto her back and mix with her fresh red blood.

Malina is in such pain and shock she is beyond shrieking and struggling.

The black robed figures of the akasic mutley kneel about the magical circles of Wesley.

Kronos stares on at the near completion of the seventh rite with a grin and eyes of everlasting hunger.

Elliott walks away from a house he's just delivered a pizza at. When he gets in the car and drives away he complains aloud to himself, "Never fails. The rich stiff tips and the poor are the generous ones." He lightly punches the ceiling of his car as he drives away annoyed he didn't get a tip. He needs the gas money.

Elliott drives to his next delivery as quickly as he can. Listening to music. Watching the clock. He's cutting it close.

The next house is nondescript. There is nothing unique or outstanding about it, other than it's a big, old, run down house in a seemingly declining middle class neighborhood. Wesley thinks he's more likely to get a tip here than at the last fancy house he was at.

Carrying the pizza's in their red insulated bags up the long flight of stairs to the front door, he notices the lights in the windows are dim and most of the shades are drawn. Doesn't necessarily mean anything, but it does kind of look like no one is home.

The delivery man rings the doorbell, but it seems to be broken, so he begins knocking at the door and waits.

No. He is not getting stiffed again. He is almost out of gas and just needs one lousy tip tonight. He knocks again and waits.

Nothing,

No answer.

He knocks again. And again.

"Not again," Elliott shakes his head and walks the pizzas down the long flight of stairs back to his car which is now running on fumes.

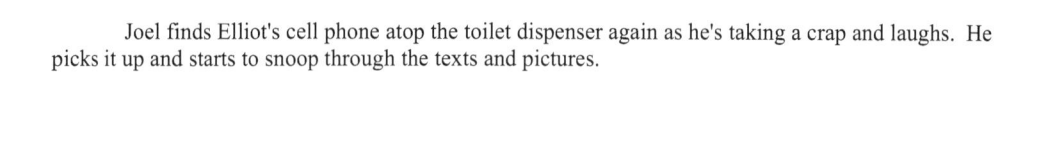

Joel finds Elliot's cell phone atop the toilet dispenser again as he's taking a crap and laughs. He picks it up and starts to snoop through the texts and pictures.

Josh and Chris are hiding in bushes nearby, just around the corner of a neighboring house, snickering, watching Elliott sitting in his car outside the creepy janitor's home.

"Holy shit," Chris whispers, "he's going back up to the door."

Elliot is angry. Even more so because he knows he's trying to deliver pizza to someone who didn't even order it. There has been a rash of prank pizza delivery calls lately.

"Damn it," he slaps his hands on the steering wheel and walks back up the flight of stairs to the front door, leaving the pizzas in the car this time.

At the front door Elliot knocks louder this time and hollers, "I know somebody is in there!"

He stalks around the house, around the yard, attempting to peek in windows, lost in a pointless tantrum of frustration. Most of the windows have blinds and curtains drawn, as if whoever lives in this house is a very private person. Maybe an agoraphobic.

About to give up, Elliott spots something he will never forget through a sliver of a slit in the drapes. Something so bizarre he doesn't know how to react.

In the slight crack between the curtains on the other side of the smudged window Elliott sees a man wearing a hooded black robe pouring blood from a black bird on a woman's back. The woman is tied to the ground and her back is torn up in razor blade cuts deep enough to scar for life. Her back is a slick coat of blood. Blood drips down her sides and pools on the floor around her torso. She is bound to the floor and gagged. There are strange devil markings drawn on the ground all around with lots of candles burning.

Elliott can not see the beings in the akasic, not the black robed witnesses nor the ancient god Kronos. He can only see Wesley and his prisoner, the young beaten, bloody woman. The woman's eyes are squeezed shut in pain and terror. For a moment Elliott is not even sure she is alive.

Then she opens her eyes. Elliott and Malina make eye contact. Her eyes widen in pleading hope and she gives out a muffled scream for mercy.

Elliot darts away from the window, clasping his hands over his mouth to stop himself from making any noises.

Elliott dashes back to his car to get the hell out of there. In his car he searches for his cell phone realizing he's left it at work again. "Damn it," he mutters, wishing he could call the police.

He should just drive away and call the police from Alphonso's Pizza. That's the safest thing to do. The safest thing for him to do. Not the safest thing for that poor woman.

He should just drive away and get help. Maybe find a neighbor and call the police that way.

The mental image of a young woman's red, tearful, begging eyes haunt his memory. Eyes screaming, pleading, please, save me.

There is no time to call the police. She could be dead or worse by the time they arrive. That man is likely still torturing her right now.

"Shit," Elliott mutters, climbing back out of his car. He knows in his gut if he does nothing the woman will be dead soon. It's up to him. He has to do something. He has to stop the torturer. If he takes the time to hunt a phone down it will be too late.

Elliott grits his teeth and marches back up the stairs, saying, "It's a good day to die."

When he reaches the front door, to his utter surprise it's not locked and he walks right into the dingy house. Fear and hesitation slow his pace.

Elliott cautiously makes his way to the freakish ritual room he'd seen from the window. Wesley is standing above the bloodied woman with both hands on a long, red wet dagger's hilt. "Malina," Wesley preaches, about to impale the blade into her back for the final kill, "you will always be remembered for your sacrifice. A saint of a new golden age. And I'm a prophet."

Wesley's back is turned to Elliott. The mad janitor doesn't notice the entrance of the pizza delivery man, so caught up in the act of murder.

In the akasic, Kronos snarls at Elliott, unheard, unseen. Potentially thwarted after so many centuries of preparation.

The black robed figures step back, some disappearing back into the shadows, others linger, curious.

Elliot picks up a tall, brass candlestick.

Old Kronos grins grimly.

Just as Wesley swings down with the dagger in both hands and all his strength behind the plunge to end the mortal life of Malina, Elliott hits Wesley in the side of the head with the candlestick. Elliott doesn't notice his feet scuffle both the protective circles around the seven pointed star drawn on the floor. Both circles are broken. The outer circle holding Kronos in place and the inner circle protecting Wesley. The circles were made of consecrated flour anew each day.

Hidden in the akasic, Kronos raises his arms in victory and triumph and vanishes like dust blown away in the akasic winds.

Elliot clubs Wesley a second time. Wesley drops his knife and it bounces across the floor. All the black robed figures of the akasic have vanished in the shadows now. Wesley falls on his side, holding the side of his now bloody head, whining like a wounded child.

Wesley moans, rolling away from Elliot, still holding his profusely bleeding head as Elliot works quickly to unbind Malina. He uses the same crimson coated dagger Wesley had used. Elliott cuts away her duct tape bindings and gag.

Elliott helps the wounded Malina up, "Let's get you out of here. My name is Elliott."

"I was Malina," she stands without his help. Appearing somewhat dizzy and dazed, blood dripping down her back into scarlet puddles on the floor. Blood is splattered all about the inner circle and the seven point star.

Wesley stands, careful not to get too close to Elliott or Malina, half his face and hair matted in blood. Elliot still has the brass candlestick in one hand and the sacrificial dagger in the other. Elliott is stunned at how ordinary Wesley appears. Beneath the black hood he was expecting to see some demonic maniac.

Malina reaches out and takes the wet dagger from Elliot's hand. He offers no resistance in giving it to her.

"You fool," Wesley scolds Elliot, "Idiot. You have no idea what you've done!"

Elliott scowls at Wesley, "You can tell it to the police when they get here, psycho."

Wesley cackles, "You don't understand, you dimwit! You have set the old god free without restriction. The old god with no human will to balance the scales of justice! It is free! Oh, Christ on a crutch, you've set it free! I wanted to bring back a golden age! Now I don't know what will happen!" Wesley begins to weep, tears mixing with blood on one side of his face.

"I know exactly what I did, you sick son of a bitch," Elliott yells and argues , "I saved an innocent woman from your torment and murder!"

Wesley lifts his arms, raising the black sleeves to reveal arcane tattoos etched all up and down his arms, "You see these, imbecile! My body is covered in the sigils of Saturn! I was giving my flesh to the ancient one! To balance its primordial power with the will of humanity! You've unleashed one of the oldest gods upon the world! I was to be the vessel!" Wesley rages on, nearing hysteria.

Malina, without much more than half a smile, steps forward and in rapid succession sinks the long dagger's blade in Wesley's stomach seven times.

Wesley gasps, stumbling back, he falls against a wall, and slides to a seated position on the floor before them. With resigned eyes he looks back and forth between Elliott and Malina. As he speaks his final words, blood drools from the side of his mouth and down his chin, "And so it is done."

"I thank you for the immolation, Wesley Woodard. It was necessary." Malina smiles devilishly.

Elliott is suddenly confused and not sure of what is transpiring at all.

"Elliott," Malina looks at the pizza delivery man with magnificent, inescapable eyes, blood still draining from her back, mixed with crow's blood. "You shall be my witness. Witness of the new golden age."

Elliott is confused and stands before her dumbfounded. He notices darkening rings around her eyes.

Malina approaches Elliott and he finds himself unable to step away. The old god Malina places her hand on his forehead and Elliott screams like he has never screamed before, not even in night terrors.

When she removes her hand Elliott crumbles to the floor and assumes the fetal position, going so far as to suck his thumb, and wet himself. He lay on the ritual room floor sobbing and blubbering as Malina marched out of Wesley's house with shirtless shoulders straight and blood dagger in hand. She is barefoot, wearing nothing but her tattered, blood stained jogging shorts.

Wesley rests dead across the room from the weeping Elliott.

Josh and Chris step out from hiding among the bushes around a nearby house, both shocked by the outlandish appearance of Malina. They both stand perplexed as the mostly nude woman approaches them.

"Are you okay?" Josh asks with a stutter.

With a quick double flip of her wrist she slashes both Josh and Chris's throats and walks on as if it were nothing as they drop to their knees, gasping and gurgling blood and their last breaths of life.

The sky above takes on a red tint as Malina, the goddess of time, sex, and death parades forward to claim her world once again.

Dampir

Old friends Hodges and Denise pick up Nick from her house.

Nick is blue because his long time girlfriend, Erin, recently broke up with him. Erin left Nick for another man. It was a painful thing for him.

Hodges and Denise have been dating for a long time. They've decided to take Nick on a nature hike to a place called Devil's Creek in an attempt to cheer him up. Hodges and Nick have been friends since grade school.

During the car ride to pick up Nick, Hodges and Denise discuss the situation.

"I'm just wondering about him," Hodges says to Denise. He hasn't been himself since Erin left him. He's been drinking too much. Isolating himself. Spending too much time alone."

"Erin is wicked leaving the way she did," Denise scowls, then smiles at her boyfriend, "but you're a good friend. I understand. This trip is about helping Nick forget about Erin. I support you. I'm worried about him too."

"You're the best," Hodges smiles at Denise.

They pull up to Nick's place where Hodges goes to the door and knocks.

Nick answers appearing glum, bored. "Hey." He stands at the door not inviting him in.

"Hey, Nicky," Hodges greets his friend. "Are you ready to enjoy a beautiful day under the sun?"

"Oh, shit," Nick remarks with no enthusiasm. "I'm sorry. I forgot we were hiking today."

"That's cool," Hodges shrugs, "You don't need anything, it's just a day-long hike. Denise and I brought plenty of food and water."

"I don't know," Nick looks at Hodges feet. "I forgot. Was kind of getting into some reading. Feeling lazy. Maybe another time."

"Don't be ridiculous, man," Hodges says. "Denise is in the car. It's morning and the day is full of potential. Anything could happen."

"I don't know, man," Nick glances back into his small apartment. It's smoky. Nick started smoking again after Erin left. The place is a mess. "I was gonna do some cleaning."

"No," Hodges shakes his head, "You agreed to go with us. You're coming with us."

"Alright," Nick surrenders.

They get in the car and drive off together.

They travel a long road of gated communities as soon as they leave Applegate city limits. It's a nice long drive. Beautiful. A long and winding road. Trees the whole rest of the way until they finally reach the gravel road that leads out to Devil's Creek.

At first the ride is stiff without much talking at all between Hodges and Denise. The first few times they tried to talk to Nick he only gave them one word answers and stared out the window at the scenery.

As they approach a bridge just before Devil's Creek, Nick suddenly asks them, "Have you guys seen Erin around lately?"

Hodges keeps his eyes on the road. Denise gives a nervous look into a rear view mirror into Nick's eyes.

"I haven't seen her," Denise lies.

Hodges makes quick eye contact with his friend in the back seat and goes back to eyes on the road. "I'm not going to lie to you. She's still with that knob Paul and hanging out with all his hipster friends. Screw her. They are a shallow pack of privileged clones. Fuck 'em. Erin showed her true colors. She's a fake. You don't need her. When it came down to it all she cared about was money. She would stay with someone with money even if she's unhappy with him. She's not one of those girls that believes in love. You deserve better."

"We were talking about getting married once," Nick stares out the window at a wide creek as they drive over a bridge. He doesn't want to look back at Hodges or Denise. He has tears in his eyes.

"You're a good looking guy," Denise encourages Nick, "You're going to find a new girlfriend. A better one that deserves you. I know it doesn't feel like it right now. I know it hurts. It hurts like a mother fucker. It won't last forever. It will hurt less in time and one day you will forget you ever knew her."

"It happens to all of us," Hodges adds, "Just don't think about her. Think about the hike and how fun it is out here. All the good times." He smiles, "You know you're a lady killer."

Nick keeps staring out the window at the trees and curves along the gravel road to Devil's Creek. It's called Devil's Creek by the locals because it's around 50 miles from a place called Devil's Gulch where in September 1876 the outlaw Jesse James escaped lawmen by jumping his horse across a 20 foot ravine. Local legend has it that Jesse James wandered Devil's Creek for a time hiding from lawmen.

Before that it was called Homesteaders Creek.

Nick keeps gazing out the window with Erin on his mind, he realizes he's with good friends.

"Maybe I should go back to school. Get a degree in business or something."

"That's a great idea," Hodges enthuses.

"I think my credits from my generals are still good. It wouldn't take that long to do it." Nick looks down at his hands.

"Dude, that's a kick ass idea," Hodges nods, impressed. "I've started back at the gym," Hodges continues. "You should come. It's more fun with a partner, It'll make you feel good."

"Maybe," Nicks nods.

As they park the car, Hodges says, "Remember in high school when we got arrested out here?"

"I didn't get arrested," Nick laughs.

"That's right," Hodges recalls, "You and Mac got away! How the hell did you do that?"

"Jumped the creek just like Jesse James," Nicks laughs.

"Really," Denise laughs.

"But we ended up walking most of the way back to Applegate," Nick admits, "Some farmer picked us up at sunrise and took us back to town, but he thought it was odd so he dropped us off at the police station. No warning. Just took us straight there. I don't know what they thought, but the cops let us go because we were both sober by that time."

"I tried to run," Hodges says, "That park ranger was fast. He was rough too. We tumbled through the dirt together when he tackled me and ripped my shirt."

"And Celeste pissed herself in the cop car!" Nick chuckles.

"You were bad boys," Denise shakes her head.

"Reformed bad boys," Nick smiles.

"I wonder what ever happened to Celeste and Mac?" Hodges asks.

"They're dead," Nick answers.

"What?" Both Hodges and Denise ask together. Denise met them in college.

"Yeah," Nicks shakes his head, "Pretty fucked up. Mac joined the Marines and got killed over in Iraq."

"That's sad," Denise says.

"Yeah," Nick explains, "The vehicle he was driving got hit by an explosive device. You know he moved here from Nevada with his twin brother Jesse back in middle school."

"I remember," Hodges nods, "He was a real good guy. That sucks. What happened to Celeste?"

"Nobody knows," Nick says, "She just disappeared one summer. Nobody knows what happened to her."

"That's weird," Hodges comments, "That happened to a group of people that summer. I remember that. Like 7 or 8 people just vanished from Applegate one summer. I didn't know she was one of them."

"You know what's weird," Nick says, "I was talking to this old Native American guy one time and he told me Jesse James fought some monster out here at Devil's Creek. Some devil."

"He was probably drunk," Hodges says.

"Well I was drunk with him," Nick laughs.

"There's more than that," Hodges says. "There was some lady's head found chopped off out here a few years ago."

"That old Indian guy, Painted Bear was his name I think," Nick goes on, "He says that the devil Jesse James fought out here still lives by the creek and comes out when it's hungry. That's why it's really called Devil's Creek, the guy told me."

"You guys are trying to scare me," Denise says.

"No," Nick says.

"Why are we going there?" Denise huffs.

"Ah, it's all just stories," Hodges answers.

Having parked the car they get out together, stretching. Denise and Hodges each have backpacks. There are picnic tables at the beginning of the Devil's Creek trails. They enjoy the scenery and open air walking across the bridge and creek entering the forest, admiring the running water of the creek as they stroll.

Once on the trail Denise cheers, "Let's go!" And jumps onto Hodges' back who gives her a piggyback ride for a short while up the trail.

Nick lets them get ahead of him, watching with a smile on his face. Internally wondering if he will ever find love again? He wishes he had a love like theirs. Is love so much to ask for? Maybe it is. Maybe some people aren't meant to love or be loved.

His smile fades as he contemplates. Erin broke me. She broke me inside. That is all I know about life right now.

Nick quickened his pace to catch up with Hodges and Denise. He does so just as Hodges is setting Denise down from riding his back.

From up in the hills and the trees above, a woman with long hair mostly hiding her face looks down at the trio of hikers. She is in an old fashioned white dress. The silhouette of her body is clearly visible beneath the fabric of the dress from the sun shining so brightly behind her. She is barefoot. Unseen. Standing more like a feral animal than a human woman.

She continues to follow them as they walk, standing and moving in awkward positions, constantly alert, ready to pounce or run, fight or flight. Always nervous and wide eyed. As she stalks the friends she travels oddly, appearing in places that don't seem possible. As if there is more than one of her or she is somehow teleporting from place to place.

She watches the trio like they are prey.

Her thoughts, in a sweet voice, "I am murder. The last experience. The moment mysteries are revealed. I feel it all. All life."

From this point forward the dark haired, ghostly woman remains an unseen witness for the entirety of their hike.

Nick, Hodges, and Denise walk the trail lazily, happily, the perfect day. The river's edge. Trees all around. Leaves and branches. Weeds and bushes and grass. Insects. Beavers and squirrels and birds. Life springing all about. So peaceful.

Nick sighs, "Life can be so beautiful at times. I mean no matter how much bad there is in the world, there is always still beauty if you take a moment to look. To pause and smell the roses. To take a breath and take it all in. It's a miracle really. A miracle that anything exists at all."

"Those are sweet thoughts," Denise agrees as they walk.

"Yeah," Hodges nods, "It's always a matter of if the cup is half full or empty."

"Words of wisdom," Nick nods, "Words of wisdom."

"What did you mean it's a miracle anything exists at all?" Denise asks, holding out her hands, letting her palm brush over leaves.

"Ah," Hodges answers first, "Nicky is a romantic dreamer! Head always in the clouds wondering what's what!"

Nick laughs, "I guess so. What I was talking about is the fact that anything exists at all. The universe, everything, and there's really no reason for it. The fact that life exists. Humans exist. Planets and stars. A whole universe. It awes me at certain moments. The grandiosity of it all. I think mathematically speaking it's more likely that absolutely nothing exists than for something to exist. I mean if there ever was a time when nothing existed, why would something suddenly exist? The explanation of something suddenly existing spontaneously is just a cop out because people can't figure it. The theory is like poof, it was magic!"

Hodges shrugs as they walk on, still unknowingly observed, "You'll never convince me . I'm an atheist until the end."

Nick shakes his head in total disagreement, "I can understand choosing to be an agnostic, which is saying I won't know until I experience it, but atheism is human arrogance. It's like saying, hey, I figured it out. There is so much that is unknown about existence. We don't understand creation or time or consciousness or if we live in a universe or multiverse. Being an atheist is the equivalent of when men used to say the Earth was flat and the center of the universe. Classic materialism. The pendulum has swung too far in the scientific direction. Paradigms are myriad. There are ways of thinking people have not even discovered yet."

"You think too much," Hodges chuckles.

"He's right though," Denise agrees, "Some nights when I look up at the stars I'm overcome by the magnitude of it all. It makes me feel small and insignificant compared to all the universe. But still a wonder."

Hodges smiles at Denise, "You're a wonder, baby. Never insignificant. None of us." He gives her a hug.

Nick feels the urge to give them some time alone together, "Hey, love birds. I'm gonna go back on the trail and find a tree to piss on. Don't wait for me. I'll catch up in a bit. I just feel like walking alone for a while if that's cool. I feel good. Better than I have in a while. It was a great idea to come out here."

"You sure, Nicky?" Hodges gives him a look of concern.

Vigorously nodding, "For sure. Every little thing's gonna be alright."

"Alright," Hodges nods feeling reassured, "Don't be antisocial for too long."

Nick smirks, "I was born that way."

Hodges and Denise move forward along the trail, hand in hand.

Nick wanders back to find a tree to piss on.

Walking back a ways, Nick's cell phone rings. He looks with shock at the name of the incoming call. Erin.

He just stares at her name, letting the phone ring two more times before answering, hesitant, "Hello?"

The other end of the phone is quiet for a moment. Nick thinks he hears something. Breathing? Sniffling?

"Erin?" He asks into the phone.

"Nicky," her familiar voice sounds weak, as if she's been crying. He knows her well enough to know she is upset about something.

Nick's not sure how to respond. It's been a month since they've spoken. Part of him wants to yell at her. Part of him wants to cry and beg her back. "What's wrong?"

"I'm sorry," she sobs suddenly uncontrollably. "I'm so sorry! I love you Nick! I love you more than anything in the world! I need you! I was wrong. I was so fucking wrong. Please forgive me. Please. I love you so much."

Nick wants to dive in head first and scream yes, I love you. "What happened? What made you change your mind all of the sudden?"

"I was an idiot. I don't know. I got scared. I got confused. Forever is a long time."

"What's changed?"

"He's not you. No one is you. You're the only one. I was born to love you," she cries. "I'll never leave you again. Oh, god!" She screams into the phone, "Please, Nick, I can't live without you. Please give us a second chance. Please."

Nick stands there on the trail listening to her cry on the phone for a few moments. Conflicted. Afraid of losing her again. Not sure if he can survive losing her again. "I love you, Erin."

"I love you," she cries and laughs with joy at the same time, "I love you! Where are you? I need to be with you right now! Please! I never want to be without you again."

"I'm out hiking with Hodges and Denise," Nick answers, "I'm kind of stuck here until they're ready to come home."

"I need you now," she whines.

"Okay," Nick says, "Give me a little time. I have to convince them to bring me home. You can wait at my place for me."

"Okay," she sounds calmer, "Thank you, Nick."

"I love you. I'll see you very soon." Nick grins.

"I love you too, baby," she hangs up the phone.

Nick is beaming. He can't believe Erin actually wants to get back together. He can't stop smiling. It's a surreal moment. Too good to be true. A dream come true.

He still has to take a piss and finds a nice thick tree to water. As he's peeing, he thinks maybe life isn't over. Maybe he will survive after all. He can't stop grinning or thinking about Erin. Life is alright. Three little birds singing on his doorstep.

That's when Nick sees her. The most striking and alluring woman he has ever seen in his life. The abnormal appearance of this woman does nothing to diminish his love of Erin. But something about this moon skinned, long black haired woman captures his attention almost against his will. She is up higher on the hill and in the trees than he is, standing still and odd, staring unblinking, deeply. Her demeanor is so odd in her outdated white dress. She doesn't look like she is dressed to be hiking. Unusual posture, heavy breathing that makes her all the more attractive. Still he loves Erin without a doubt, it's more that he is enthralled with this white woman's unnatural way. She has a unique beauty about her.

Nick only stares at her, unable to move as if a victim of Medusa's gaze. A look of bemusement and wonder on his face.

The woman, her age hard to determine, stares back at Nick with unashamed eye contact, and the intense expression of an animal lust. She appears to be something of a harmless creature.

Nick stands still, thinking he must return to Erin somewhere in the back of his mind, like some overshadowed instinct. He doesn't know how or why to react to the odd girl. Half a smile appears on his face as he lifts a hesitant hand to wave hello. Not really a wave, more just holding his hand up palm out in her direction. An attempt at a friendly gesture. Something is not right about this woman.

The pale moon woman doesn't react at all other than the slightest expression of curiosity. She remains still as a statue, like a timid animal afraid to move.

Nick lowers his hand, still not sure what to do, beginning to wonder if the woman is alright. Another moment passes and Nick says, "Hello?" Sounding unsure of himself.

The odd woman's head turns to one side as if studying him, as if she has never seen a man before. Then she raises her hand in a motion for him to climb up to where she is. He's not sure that's what he wants to do but something draws him. She waves him forward once more, obviously wanting him to follow, yet saying nothing.

Nick feels like he shouldn't, feeling the tug of Erin pulling at his heart strings, but his legs don't listen to the rest of his body and he begins to make his way up to her, feeling more euphoric and mesmerized the closer he comes to her. The only thing he knows in the world at this moment is he must reach the top of the hill to adore this woman. Not as a lover but as a force of nature. Some kind of elemental.

The Dampir (the woman) thinks sweetly, "I can hear your heartbeat. Smell the salt of your sweat. Come to me."

Nick poses before her, dumbfounded as if venerating a golden calf.

The Dampir delicately puts her arms around him as if to embrace Nick in a deep kiss. Inside Nick does not want this, he only wants Erin. Instead of the expected profound kiss she sinks her teeth severely into the flesh of Nick's throat, biting in deep enough to tear a hunk of flesh from his neck, swallowing it before commencing to drink his blood. She has ordinary teeth, not sharp fangs or the teeth of a shark, which in some way makes the attack seem more gruesome.

Nick gasps for air but does not fight back. He holds her shoulders tight as if holding a lover. They gradually slide to the ground together as she stays suctioned to his throat like a giant leech or parasite. She wraps her arms and legs around him like the death grip of a boa constrictor, sucking and slurping his crimson blood. The Dampir licks at the blood like a starved and feverish animal.

Nick does not fight back as he pales, his heart rate slows, and his life begins to slip away. He lays on his back against the grass staring up at the sky and the sun as his breaths become shorter and sharper. Bits of blood drip from either side of his open mouth. Nick appears to be more in a state of ecstasy than death.

In Nick's mind's eye, in the blindness staring at the sun brings him, he whispers almost inaudibly, "Erin."

Hearing the man's last dying word, the Dampir pauses from her blood feast to study Nick's slack dead face for a moment. Her beautiful face is covered in blood from nose to cheeks and chin. She gives a slow shake of her head and whispers in a voice as sweet as an angel, "No."

Then she returns to drinking his blood.

Hodges and Denise walk the trail together, exploring and observing in silence, enjoying nature.

"Nick seems better," Denise reassures her boyfriend.

Hodges agrees, "Yeah. We needed to get him out of the house."

"You think he's alright by himself?"

"He's fine," Hodges answers, "We know these woods. Been coming out here since we were kids, He'll catch up when he's ready. I think he just needs some time to sort things out."

They walk in peace for a few more minutes, very much in love and calm together.

"What do you think everyone will say when we tell them we're getting married? Denise asks. Nick is the first person they have told. They've only been dating a short time, less than a year. Hodges plans to ask Nick to be his best man before they finish their nature hike. "Who cares," Hodges answers, "It's no one's business but our own."

"My mom will be cool about it," Denise says, "but my dad might freak at first."

"My family won't care. I mean they'll be fine with it. They're a pretty accepting bunch."

Denise spots a comfy place to rest, "Let's sit for a while and wait for Nick."

"Yeah," Hodges uses his hand as a sun visor to block its rays and look back on the trail in the direction he expects to see Nick coming from. "He shouldn't be much longer."

The white skinned woman, the Dampir, drags the bleeding corpse of Nick through the forest by one arm. Her strength is surprising. Uncaring. Seemingly unaware of anything around her. She hardly pays attention to where she is going.

In her mind, in an ever sweet voice, "Your blood. Your blood. Your blood on my lips."

She pulls Nick along with an ivory colored arm, as if she's never been in the sun before, eventually bringing his body to hide behind a broken down tree. A log that appears to have been there sometime if the weeds and grass growing around it are any indicator.

After hiding Nick's body behind the timber, the Dampir tears his shirt off and seats herself on the length of wood next to him. The woman uses the tattered shirt to wipe her face clean of blood. She does an unusually good job of cleaning up any signs of the crimson glory.

In the Dampir's mind, in a honeyed voice, preparative, internal, "Forever. Forever. Qayin. Batya of Cathan. Amen."

The unseen, undead woman monitors Denise and Hodges from a distance, hidden by trees, rocks, and shadows.

Striking a graceless pose with her arms out at odd angles, neck crooked in what looks to be an uncomfortable position, legs too far apart.

The Dampir's internal dialogue continues, it's been years since she's had an actual conversation with someone. A handsome, rugged outlaw over a century ago. An American Indian around the same time. She can't remember which she spoke with first and which she spoke with second. Furthermore, the old Dampir's internal dialogue in a whispered sugary voice, "She whispers. She whispers. Always whispers. Heart of cobwebs. Whispers in scarlet. Whispers in red. Whispers in rainbows. Always whispers. Whispers in the dark."

Hodges stands looking back down the trail in the direction Nick should be coming from. He is beginning to look concerned. "It's been too long," he announces to his girlfriend.

Denise agrees, looking cross, "It has been a pretty long time."

Hodges looks at her even more worried now that she's confirmed his concern.

"Maybe he's not doing as well as we thought?" Denise questions delicately.

"I know him," Hodges says, "He was fine. Better than he's been in weeks. I know he was. Nick should have been back by now. Something's wrong."

"Call him," Denise suggests.

Hodges nods and tries to call Nick on his cell phone. No answer. It goes voicemail.

Denise anxiously asks, "Do you think he's suicidal?"

"No," Hodges snaps, more harsh than intended, although he's not convinced himself, "I'm sorry. I don't want to think that."

"Maybe he's hurt," Denise wonders aloud. "He could have fallen in a ravine or something."

"We're probably just getting worried for no reason," Hodges says.

"Yeah," Denise agrees.

"We better look for him," Hodges admits.

The couple begin walking the trail together, back tracking.

The Dampir watches unseen from the foliage, following along, her face clean of blood, always appearing in places that don't make sense geographically.

The internal thoughts of the moon pale Dampir in her childish, mousy voice, "We'll never let you go. Never. We will always be together. Never alone. Never go."

"It's going to get dark soon," Hodges looks to the west, "The sun will be going down."

"I don't want to be out here at night," Denise responds, "I'm getting afraid. I don't know my way around these trails. Maybe it's time to call the police or a park ranger or something."

"Hodges nods, taking charge, "I'm going to walk with you a ways and get you headed in the direction of the car, then I'm going to look for Nick. You just wait at the car for me, Denise. Wait for maybe a half hour and if you haven't heard from me call the police and just wait there at the car for them to come. You'll need to show them which way Nick and I went."

Denise hugs him, "Okay. I love you."

"I love you, little bird."

They follow the trail toward where the car is parked.

The hidden, stalking Dampir continues her internal infantile dialogue, "The Lord created blood and then there was murder."

Frustration grows, after letting Denise go off on her own to wait by the car, Hodges tries calling Nick's cell phone again after wandering the trail a while longer. This time he hears it ring faintly off in the trees.

Hodges dashes up through the trees in the direction of the ringing cell phone, shouting, "Nick! Nick! Where are you?"

At the top of the vegetation covered hill, Hodges finds Nick's cell phone on the ground, in the grass, by itself. When he picks it up he notices spots of blood on it. He holds it close to his lips, thinking hard, upset, distressed.

Hodges looks at the phone. There are thirteen missed text messages. He reads them all. Every message is from Erin. She wants to get back together and it seems Nick agreed to give her a second chance. This bothers Hodges even more because he knows if Erin and Nick are getting back together nothing would stop Nick from going directly to Erin now, this very instant, including canceling the hike. There are several missed calls from Erin as well.

Hodges takes out his own cell phone and calls Denise.

"Baby?" Denise answers.

"Denise," Hodges expresses and she immediately picks up on the edge in his voice, "I want you to stay calm no matter what I say. Promise that before we continue."

"What's going on?" Her voice was shrill.

"I found Nick's phone. There is blood on it. I need you to call the police and stay with the car and wait for them. I'm going to keep looking for Nick. Don't ask questions. I don't know anything more. He's probably hurt somewhere and I need to find him. The most important thing you can do is wait at the car for the police. Promise me you'll do this."

Denise takes a deep breath, calming herself. She trusts Hodges. Enough to do what he's asked in this situation. "Okay, baby. I will do it. I promise."

"Thank you," Hodges says, "I love you. I'll see you very soon."

"I love you too," she hangs up with the unpleasant feeling that she will never hear Hodges say that again. She shakes it off. Nonsense. It's just that Nick is hurt out there somewhere. She does what Hodges asks and calls the police, explaining the situation. The authorities report they will be there soon. Just hang tight and stay with the car. Denise got the feeling the authorities are not urgent to get there.

Hodges continues to scout the area around where he found Nick's cell phone, making wider and wider circles as he goes, until he finds himself standing face to face with the Dampir. Nick's bloody cell phone is still in his hand. It receives another unanswered text message from Erin as Hodges and the Dampir stand frozen in each other's gazes. Hodges does notice a light sprinkling of blood on her white dress. A peculiarly out of fashion dress. Some type of old dress that Hodges isn't sure women wear anymore unless they are in a movie or something like that.

Hodges can't help but admit to himself that her unusual physical appearance does make her seem somewhat appealing. She has long hair that hides her striking eyes. He doesn't know what to make of her but the blood has him on guard.

The dazzling Dampir now stands unsteady, rocking back and forth on her bare feet, never blinking or taking her eyes from Hodges. She reminds him of a snake charmed to dance out of a weave basket. Hodges is too in love with Denise to be swayed by her charms.

"Where is my friend?" Hodges asks in a severe tone.

The Dampir stops moving at the sound of Hodges voice, looking down, very still, as if thinking, deciding on an answer.

A moment later she looks at Hodges with startling, undead eyes and motions for him to follow her.

Reluctantly he follows through the green grass, trees, and brush.

The weird woman doesn't bother to look back to watch whether or not Hodges is following her.

They come to a spot where Nick's body lies face down on the ground near a fallen tree. The bloody ripped wound on his neck was undeniable.

"Oh, Jesus," Hodges drops to his knees at his friend's side and turns him over. The listlessness of Nick's body and the slack expression on his face make it evident he is dead.

"What happened?" Hodges turns to face the queer white woman with animosity.

She only looks at him as if confused, as if she doesn't understand what he's saying, or doesn't understand why he's upset.

"Did you do this?" Hodges ire grows.

The haunted woman looks at him as if about to weep and whispers in desperation, "Mother, may I return into you?"

"What?" Hodges asks, agitated, bewildered.

The ashen Dampir approaches him as slow as a lover and Hodges finds himself a prisoner of her gaze, unable to move or react in any way. The only reaction he is able to evoke are tears for his friend and himself.

"Come back inside," she whispers in her sweet honey voice with so much sincerity and caring in her murmur Hodges believes she truly loves him for a moment as her dull, ordinary teeth tear viciously into the flesh of his throat, ripping out the adam's apple with ease. It is a bloody fountain as she tears into his neck, drinking his blood, nibbling small pieces of skin and tissue.

She holds him as if Hodges is her beloved and she feeds while his body twitches and spurts lines of blood.

The odd Dampir woman gently lies the dead body of Hodges next to his friend Nick, as if it matters in some way.

Denise tries to call Hodges' phone and sends him several texts getting no response. She tries Nick's phone a few times with the same results.

In a moment of panic or survival or love for Hodges she leaves a note for the police under one of her windshield wipers and makes her way back up the trail. She can't stand by and do nothing.

Denise jogs part of the way, taking more than one fork in the road as she travels until realizing she is lost.

"Shit," she cusses, "Shit, shit, shit."

She stands for a moment with her arms crossed unsure what to do.

"Fuck," she grunts, searching for a nice sized branch to defend herself with. After finding the appropriate branch she scans the trees for any signs of Hodges or Nick. Or anything at all.

Denise tries hopelessly to call Hodges on her phone again. No answer.

She calls again this time leaving a message, "I don't know where you are. I don't know what's going on. I called the police like you said and they're on their way. I'm looking for you. I'm lost. I don't know what to do Hodges. I love you." She hangs up the phone, tearful.

Denise sets off walking aimlessly. She despondently dials Hodges phone number several more times as she explores the unfamiliar wilderness. Breaking down she begins to shout his name out to the trees around her, "Hodges! Hodges! Hodges!" Several times until she feels her voice is going hoarse.

The alabaster Dampir is watching and hunting Denise from the trees the entire time. Always unseen. Unnaturally silent. Not even breaking a twig beneath her bare feet.

This time the blood lusting woman has not taken the time to wipe the crimson from her face. From nose to chin the surface of her skin is coated in red blood.

The Dampir's internal thoughts and dialogue continue, as she has not spoken to anyone in many years, in a girlish voice, "Love. She loves. Sweet love. Sweet angel of Cain. This one. She loves once too. He defiled her like no other. Now all there is, is blood. Seas and lives of blood spilling life and drying like salt at the bottom of forgotten ocean floors."

Denise walks randomly along the wooded trails. Downhearted. Feeling hopeless and helpless. "Hodges!" She cries out again.

It is the last time she cries out his name.

Denise halts dead in her tracks at the sight before her.

The Dampir. Breathing heavy and fast. Face half slick with blood. The Dampir stands so calm and still blocking the trail. Her legs spread about shoulder length apart. Arms out like an Old West gunfighter preparing to draw six shooters. Eyes piercing. Drilling into the eyes of Denise like a knife attempting to tear into her soul. Haunting, hypnotizing eyes.

Denise raises her branch to defend herself feeling her adrenaline rising. Fear transforming to anger. "What did you do!? Who are you!?" Denise accuses with venom in her voice.

Dampir bats her eyes like a flirtatious child.

"Answer me, witch!" Denise shouts, hoping the police will show up at any moment.

Dampir gives Denise a slightly amused smirk while remaining still and silent.

"What did you do to them? Hodges and Nick?" She chokes the words out, stepping forward in a threatening manner with the branch held high.

In the blink of an eye the Dampir darts off into the trees, vanishing from sight.

"I called the police," Denise warns, trying to spot the odd woman in the trees. "They're on their way here right now!"

For a while Denise walks cautiously along the trail, ever alert, still holding the branch as she tries to call Hodges one more time.

This time she hears the ringtone of his phone not far off, "Hodges!" She blurts, running blindly in the direction of the noise.

The Dampir studies the movements of Denise from the foliage. Her internal dialogue of thoughts continues, "Freedom like the first breath of a babe from the womb."

Denise sobs when she finds the dead bodies of Nick and Hodges laid out side by side like lovers next to a fallen tree. They are still with death and fresh with blood. Both of their necks are torn apart as if a ferocious animal attacked them. There are not many animals like that in the area. The occasional mountain lion. Wild dogs. Coyotes. Silent pale white women.

Denise sets the branch down, kneels near him, cradling him in her arms, pulling Hodges up close, still sobbing, wailing, hysterical, "No! No! No! No! Hodges! Oh, God, Hodges! No! No! It's alright! It's okay! You're alright! You're alright!" She holds him tight crying uncontrollably, her words lost somewhere in her sobs.

The Dampir appears before the weeping Denise and the fresh corpses, watching with no evident emotion as if trying to understand. Or trying to remember something.

Denise looks up at the Dampir, "No! Get away!" She lets Hodges body down carefully and picks her branch back up, standing. Denise swings the branch in the direction of the Dampir. missing.

The Dampir gives an innocent smile. The undead woman shakes her head so very slowly at Denise and holds her thin arms out as if to embrace the other woman, beckoning Denise forward.

Denise shakes her head with a vengeful grin, "You're absolutely insane."

Dampir's expression looks hurt.

Denise lunges forward using the branch to attack with abandon.

The Dampir reaches out and catches the branch in her grip with astonishing ease, effectively disarming Denise and tossing the branch far off into the trees.

Denise lets out a feral growl, feeling now just as much an animal as the Dampir. She lets out her full animal rage. Fight or flight instincts have taken over leaving little room for thought. Denise begins flailing at the Dampir, slapping her, pulling her hair, kicking at her. The two women fall to the ground together wrestling.

In the face of Denise's assault, the look on the Dampir's face is one of tickled amusement. Instincts drive the Dampir too. Instincts to survive. To eat. The Dampir is much stronger than Denise. She has inhuman strength.

The Dampir grabs a hold of Denise's arm with both hands as Denise has no hope of resisting while the Dampir sinks her teeth into Denise's flesh, ripping a mouthful of meat away. As the Dampir savors the chunk of flesh, Denise manages to get away and runs with all her might back toward the trail. She realizes her only hope of survival is escape. She must escape this inhuman, cannibal woman no matter the cost.

Catching Denise by complete surprise the Dampir leaps low, biting another chunk of fresh meat from Denise's calf.

Denise doesn't give up. She limps and stumbles away, bleeding profusely. She grunts in agony, trying to run away, but the wound in her leg is too great, her run is more of an off balance walk.

The Dampir sits on the ground a moment watching Denise attempt to stagger away, seeming in no hurry to put down her prey. Like a wild cat enjoying the kill.

Looking back, Denise has lost sight of the Dampir. It is gone again. She continues to stumble along the trail, trying to collect herself.

"Where the hell are the police?" She mutters.

She walks on, struggling for moments thinking of Hodges and Nick. Then she thinks of her family. Mom. Dad. Her sisters, Gretchin and Samara. She may never see them again. She may actually die. She doesn't want to die. She doesn't know what to do but keep walking. Try to make it back to the car.

Denise once again stops dead in her tracks letting out an involuntary sob of shock. Before her as if appearing from out of nowhere, standing in her usual awkward posture is the Dampir. It makes no sense how the Dampir got in front of her on the trail. She left her sitting far behind in the opposite direction. There is no way she could have made that distance even if she had been sprinting. But the Dampir does not appear to be out of breath or fatigued at all.

The Dampir only stands in the path, head tilted slightly down, thick, sticky lines of blood hanging like syrup from her chin.

"Leave me alone," Denise whimpers, turning to head the opposite direction on the trail. Limping. Feeling weaker from the loss of blood.

Far ahead at the other end of the trail, the trail she just turned down to leave the Dampir behind, the Dampir appears standing, waiting again. Denise thinks she can't be human whatever she is. She is impossible. She shouldn't exist.

Denise takes her cell phone out of her pocket one last time. Browsing through the list of contacts until she finds the one labeled 'Mom'.

The Dampir walks at a very slow pace toward Denise, in absolutely no hurry.

The cell phone rings and rings as Denise hopes her mother will answer.

The Dampir is much closer now.

The voice mail picks up. The recording of her mother's voice is like the voice of an angel.

"Mom," Denise cries, "Oh, mommy. Mom. I love you. I love you so much. I'm sorry for anything and everything I've ever done wrong. Anything I've ever done to hurt you or dad or Gretchin or Sam. I just want you to know that no matter what, I love you mom. I love dad. I love you my beautiful sisters."

Denise drops the phone to the ground, not hanging it up, as the Dampir's teeth tear into her neck from the side. The voice mail continues to record the final sobs and gurgling protests of Denise as the takes her life away until the only sounds are the Dampir drinking blood and a few animals chirping in the background.

It is the final voice mail Denise's family ever receives from her.

Beautifully Damaged

"Oh, you are damaged so beautifully. Gorgeously broken."

And she is. One eye. Old scars from lashes all zig zagged across her back. Scars up and down the right side of her face, the same side missing the eye. Half the right ear was cut off. Healed bullet holes on her right shoulder. Toes missing from her left foot.

"I'm ugly to look at," she says in a scratchy voice, "But I'm hard to kill."

"No, no," the artist shakes his head, "You are a living work of art. An embodiment of struggling and overcoming. A slave that clawed and crawled her way to freedom. We should all hope to achieve the things you have in life."

"You're as crazy as me," she smirks.

"Maybe. Maybe we're the sane ones and the rest of the world is mad."

"No. There are no sane people."

She stands naked in his studio, the bright, warm lights adjusted just right to create magnificent shadows about her. The artist stands before his blank canvas, a brush in one hand, a cigarette in the other.

"Don't move," he instructs as the brush begins to stroke the white canvas.

Her eyes wander about the studio, studying his works of art. "You are talented," she whispers.

"My work is only as good as my subjects," he says, painting with a sudden fury.

Some time passes. Kasandra thinks about her yoga training. Self taught. Yogic meditations. The pose for the artist Falk is simply a yoga posture. She treats it as such. Remaining perfectly still and silent, removing thought from her mind.

"You're good at this," Falk comments without losing his focus on the painting. "Modeling."

He discovered her at a health food store, in front of the organic vegetables, and propositioned her to model for him. Her first reaction was that he was just some creep. He offered to pay her and she decided she could kill him if he turned out to be a fake. Annoyed by his dreamy talk at first she has to admit that she was caught off guard by his words tonight. How did he know she was a slave?

She had been. A runaway at the age of fourteen because her stepfather couldn't keep his hands to himself, taken in by what she thought were good people who turned out to be using young girls for internet porn. Live video chats. The money was good and it lasted until she was sixteen. Then her boss, who was a good man, was arrested for selling drugs. His whole operation was shut down. She escaped back to the street before she could get thrown into the system, which she feared more than the danger of the streets, and still fears it. The loss of freedom, the suffocation of government, the loss of free will. Foster homes and facilities are as bad as anything the street has to offer. She knows the government is evil.

After the porn game was shut down for her she went into prostitution for a local gang. She hated them all but made money, until the night they decided to run a train on her. She refused to work for them anymore. They beat her and sold her into human trafficking. She found herself living as a sex slave in the North Dakota oil boom passed around among camps of oil and construction workers. That's where she was whipped. The scars on her back. She killed the man. Bit off his cock and escaped.

She stayed and went from prostitution to selling drugs. Rose fast, working with organized crime to run drugs to the oil boom territory. Meth from the bike clubs. Marijuana from Mexican gangs. She soon stepped into crack cocaine and other drugs. LSD. Ecstasy. Heroin. Pills and more pills. Soon Kasandra ran her own gang, her own operation.

That was a nice time in life. She was a high roller. On top of it all. More money than she knew what to do with. Then came the war and bust. A shipment of meth was stolen. She went to war with the gang who stole it. Undercover narcs were involved. Most of her gang and the rival gang were killed or went to prison. That's when she got the scars on her face and lost her eye. Killed a few cops in the process.

Now she's seen the light. She doesn't sell or use drugs anymore. She's become a vigilante known as Silencer. Some say serial killer. She didn't choose the name, the media did. Because she always uses a silencer to kill her prey and wears a full black bodysuit. The media thinks Silencer is a man. Her prey are all those that deserve to die in her eyes. Mostly cops and politicians. Anyone she discovers abusing people. Her favorite is killing the cops though. Any cops she discovers mistreating people. They go down in a ditch at night at the end of her barrel.

Police harassment is a pet peeve.

Falk finishes up the painting, quite pleased with himself, admiring the portrait. "Have a look," he smiles as Kasandra.

Kasandra is impressed. His work almost looks like a photograph. It is her body. Her face. She looks angry and tired. "It's very good."

"Thank you," he steps in the other room and shouts back to her, "Would you like a drink? Scotch on the rocks?"

"Yes, please."

He returns with the drink and hands it to her with a cool smile, "I'd love to paint you again some time."

Kasandra shrugs, "I don't know about that."

"Ah," he nods, dropping the subject. "It's not for everyone."

She glances at his stereo, "Mind if I put on some music."

"Mi casa es su casa."

Soft, quiet classical music comes from the speakers of the stereo.

"Tell me about yourself, Falk," Kasandra says as she begins to dress.

"Not much to tell," he shrugs, "I'm a starving artist. Grew up in the Midwest. Dropped out of art school. Do what I can to get by. Odd jobs sometimes."

"How often do you ask women to model for you?"

"Whenever I discover someone with a unique appearance or presence. It's not always women," he chuckles.

"Are you a bad man, Falk?"

"What? Ha ha," he answers, "I don't know. I like to think I'm a good man but so does everyone. If I'm a bad man it's due to ignorance or maybe emotional immaturity. I try to do the right thing."

"Seems an honest answer," she sips her drink. "Do you like the world?"

"Uh, I don't know. It's okay I guess. There are things that can improve."

"Do you begin all your answers with I don't know?"

"You are the most interesting person I've ever met," he smiles.

She arches an indifferent eyebrow and examines more of his paintings scattered about the studio and plastered on the walls.

"What are your plans tonight? I was thinking of heading downtown for a drink. You're welcome to accompany me."

Kasandra stands in the center of the room, arms outstretched, and whispers, "Life is a mystery, everyone must stand alone, I hear you call my name, and it feels like home."

She drops to her knees and snaps both fingers, rising slowly looking into Falk's eyes with her sole eye. He is dumbfounded. She sings much louder, "When you call my name, it's like a little prayer, down on my knees I want to take you there, in the midnight hour, I can feel your power, down on my knees, I want to take you!"

"*Madonna*," he breathes.

"I hear your voice, it's like an angel sighing, I have no choice, I hear your voice, it feels like flying, I close my eyes, oh, god I think I'm falling, out of the sky, I close my eyes, heaven help me."

"I have that song," he walks to the stereo and plays the *Madonna* song as Kasandra continues to dance about the room.

Falk turns to face her and joins her dance, not close together, both about the room, making it up as they go.

"I've come here to die tonight," she says to Falk as they embrace in a slow dance.

"I know," he answers. "In my arms. It's been a long life. A long night."

"Sex and death are the biggest events in life," she says, resigned.

"Two sides of the same token."

"Maybe."

"I'm surprised you're willing to die."

"I'm tired. I've done more than most. I feel like an old warrior sick of war."

"You are. You deserve rest."

Her eye wet with happy tears, "I need tonight. Hold me tight."

"I'll hold you forever."

"The world died long ago," she weeps, "The people are only living in a dream now."

"Every now and then someone like you wakes up."

"We are always on film. God is always filming."

"Your name is on high in heaven."

"Death for me, a man."

"And every man, a woman."

"Do I have to come back?"

"No."

"The past and future are gone."

"They never were."

"I never found love."

"Neither did I."

"I never stopped looking."

"Neither did I."

"Will you stay with me all through the night?"

"I will."

The Suicide of Shiloh Darling

The horror begins with grieving heartache. The kind of heartache that swallows you whole and feels like there is no coming back from it. The kind of heartache that makes every thought and movement bleed with melancholy. Horror can begin in so many ways. It's something that usually comes unexpected. The horror. Once it arrives it can be brief or prolonged. It is always haunting and scarring. Unforgettable. Always something horrible.

So Shiloh Darling's horror begins with heartache. Not so appalling as murder or monsters, but he can't imagine anything hurting worse or more feeling more petrifying than the loss of Vanessa Balasky. Vanessa was Shiloh's girlfriend for more than a year.

It was a whirlwind romance. They met and fell in love right away. Love at first sight. Neither of them could stand to be away from each other. A Romeo and Juliet kind of love. They couldn't stop holding each other or looking into the other's eyes, telling each other they would die if they ever lost each other. For a moment they had found Heaven together. All their friends were happy for them. Some were envious of the apparent strength of their love. Everyone dreams of a love like they had in the beginning. The kind of love people write stories about, the love of legends.

Shiloh keeps thinking of that Elvis song. *Are You Lonesome Tonight*, "You seemed to change and acted strange, and why I'll never know." He knows that Elvis was so heart broken that it's what killed him. Elvis died of a broken heart.

Shiloh experienced that same second act Elvis was singing about with Vanessa, that strange change. The love of his life suddenly stopped loving him. Not just a little bit. She stopped loving him all together. It was in her behavior before it was verbalized or acted upon, before Shiloh had picked up on it. She started to seem annoyed by him, often giving him the silent treatment for reasons unknown, seeming angry underneath it all, resentful.

In truth Shiloh sensed the change, knew something was wrong, but his heart kept him in denial. He told himself it was just stress or she was just crabby, had a bad day, or she was cranky because she was tired. Whatever excuse his heart could blind him with.

Through it all Shiloh's love for Vanessa remained undiminished. He belonged to her, heart and soul, like they had promised in the beginning, an undying, unconditional love. A daydreamed future together, cuddling in the darkness of their bed together at night whispering secrets and tenderness.

The day came when Vanessa told Shiloh she didn't love him anymore, in fact, had never loved him. This critical and cold strike came from nowhere Shiloh could fathom. It was a mistake, she told him, she'd been lying to him for a long time, pretending she still loved him because she felt sorry for him. But she'd reached a point she just couldn't do it anymore. He was a rebound gone too far. Everything about him annoys her. She hates him, he makes her skin crawl. He whines too much and acts more like a woman than a man. He's too needy and emotional. She doesn't want to be with him anymore. It's over.

This is the end.

Shiloh couldn't understand. He was baffled. Was it all a lie? She did an astounding job of tricking him. With humility Shiloh begged Vanessa to stay together, please give them another chance, he loved her, he could do better, he could be the man she wants him to be. How could she love him so strongly and abruptly stop, seeming to have no emotion about it at all. She was simply turned off to him now. She'd become a stranger he couldn't communicate with.

Vanessa told Shiloh that she just didn't like him anymore, it wasn't a choice, she just wasn't attracted to him anymore.

Vanessa had become Shiloh's best friend. His whole world. He didn't know what to do. She was gone, slipped away without explanation from his fingertips.

This is the horror. The ache and lament of his heart. Some days when he sat home alone he didn't think he'd ever stop crying. He didn't want to live without her. His heart shattered. More than he can bare. He feels let down by life, betrayed, all his love is gone. He's nothing without Vanessa. And she will never return to him. He knows that. It hurts so much it makes him sick to his stomach. He misses her more than he can handle. His life is gone. He doesn't know how to smile.

Shiloh Darling is in a bathtub, naked, steam rising off the surface of the water. The bathroom lights are off and if it weren't for the scented candles he lit he'd be in total darkness. His world is darkness without her.

It hurts more than he imagined it would. It took a long time to build the courage to do it. To convince himself to let go. He's left letters behind for the ones he loves. Family and friends, explaining not to cry, but be happy for him, that his pain is finally over. And one letter for Vanessa, telling her how much he loves her and he's sorry for everything and anything he's done to wrong her. Whatever it may be. He tells her that he won't hurt anymore and wishes her nothing but the best, she deserves a bright future, he'll always love her. It's not her fault. He's a fucked up, emotional person. Always has been. Natural born whatever.

The dark blood runs out of his wrist quicker than Shiloh fancied it would. Dark crimson drops on the edge of the tub and the floor. Blood mixing with bath water, first billowing out like a gloomy storm cloud until the entire bath water is tinted red.

He relaxes, leaning back comfortably in the tub, tears and sweat wet his face. He will be dead before the water cools. Maybe he can fall asleep and dream as he bleeds to death. He just can't hurt anymore. He's been too beat up by life. There has been too much pain in this life. Too many mistakes. That is one thing Vanessa said. She couldn't forgive some of the mistakes he'd made years ago, before they ever met. Shiloh Darling understands. He's not good enough for Vanessa Blasky. She's outstanding. Exceptional. Beautiful, intelligent, and talented. He's just ordinary Shiloh. Nothing special about him. Just a normal, average, nice nobody.

Vanessa and Shiloh come from different worlds. She comes from a good working class Lutheran family with strong values. He comes from the wrong side of the tracks, grew up dirt poor. He always thought he was white trash, for a while he tried to escape that, tried to change his life and follow the rules and do good things, prove he was a good person, but it didn't stick. He can't deny where he came from. Tried to escape and failed. He would do one last thing right. End his pain. Leave Vanessa alone. Runaway. Sleep forever death. A slumber, a dream that never ends.

He'd rather live in a dream with Vanessa than live in the real world without her. But he doesn't know death. Not for sure. No one has seemed to figure that out. Life after death or not. Either way the pain is gone. He either drifts in a forever dream or enters a nothingness of non-existence.

Shiloh doesn't know how much time is passing. He slips in and out of consciousness. Sliding down, head slipping into the water, waking him with panicked gasps for oxygen. He is almost dead. So close. He wishes Vanessa would come running through the door to save his life, remembering that she loved him once. Such a selfish thought.

A meager part of Shiloh doesn't want to die. He left the front door unlocked. He never does that. Anyone who might happen by could walk right in and find him, call an ambulance before it's too late. So much blood loss. He knows it's too late. It's in the hands of the fates now.

Mister Shiloh Darling, no longer Vanessa Balasky's darling. He thinks he sees something in the bathroom candlelight, between the flickering shadows of the gold and orange.

Movement. Silence. Stealth. Moving shadows. Men made of shadow seeping through from another world. A world closer to death. Dark shadows creeping about the small, steam and candle scented room. The candles are burning low now.

Whatever they are, they are dark through and through. Men or women, he can't tell, only the shadows form people. No. They aren't men or women, they are shadow people. Watching him. Waiting. Waiting for him to cross over into death.

Now Shiloh remembers, they've always been there. Since he was a child, an infant even. Always watching from the dark. Witnesses. Silent as shadows, hidden in darkness and shade. Watchers. Like dark angels with unknown intent or purpose.

Yes, that's what they are like, these lurking shadow people, hidden, fallen angels spying on all of us. Witnesses. Watching. Waiting. Creepy and crawling in the gloom. Living shadows. Living in shadows.

There have been times when Shiloh has sensed or glimpsed them before, from the corner of an eye, a flicker gone in a blink, something you thought you saw when you first woke up but realized it must have been the dreaming.

The memories flood back to him as he lays dying in the now lukewarm water. Hushed, mute things in the pitch black. There is some sensation now in Shiloh of what they are about, felt without words or gestures, no symbols, only a black empathy that he vaguely picks up like a radio receiver.

They are sly, devilish things that hold themselves superior to humanity, because they may well be in many ways, something else, some higher form of life than humans, if these are the right words to describe what Shiloh is picking up.   It's like the way a human being looks down on a rat or some kind of rodent.

The shadow things inch and slither all about the darkness of the bathroom, growing more eager the closer Shiloh close to death. They drag themselves across the ceiling, wriggle about the walls, and worm about the floor. Always in shadow, always made of shadow, moving, shifting shadow. Some are like crawling skeleton shadows, others like fat blobs of darkness hungry to swallow all light and life. The shadow people are shape shifters of the single shade of black.

They come close to Shiloh, as if their courage and curiosity builds the closer he comes to their realm, reaching out, so very close, yet never actually touching him. The shadows swarm about the near dark room, it's hard to tell one from another or guess how many are present. One of the shadows works up the daring to dip its elongated, thin, black finger into the blood stained water. The narrow finger tip sends a circle of ripples outward and the shadow thing hastily pulls away. It reminds Shiloh of someone testing the temperature of water with their big toe before plunging into a lake. The thought brings a fading smile to his face with a memory of Vanessa doing just that one weekend they went on a camping trip in the Black Hills.

Shiloh feels himself slipping away, losing consciousness, losing himself, falling asleep, drifting into death.

Vanessa stands outside Shiloh's front door, irritated, unsure of what to do. She leans in close to the door, listening for any movement or signs of life, not wanting to get caught. She has been sending Shiloh text messages for hours and he hasn't responded. She's been trying to reach him most of the day. She broke down and actually tried calling him. More than once. He's a responsible guy. It's unusual for him to be unresponsive.

Not that she cares what he does with his life. They both have their own lives now. The issue is they have a child together and Shiloh said he wants to be a part of that child's life. Now here he is avoiding her and she needs him to watch their daughter.

Vanessa doesn't care what Shiloh is doing. Maybe he's in there with a woman. Maybe he's out drunk somewhere. The house is dark. The lights are off, but that doesn't mean he's not there. He could be in there watching television or goofing off on his computer. The lights are off, yet his car is parked out front. That is unusual. Maybe he's not there. She doesn't know what kind of social life he has now that they've broken up.

She leans close to the door a second time, listening, holding her cell phone in one hand, calling Shiloh's phone. She can hear his phone vibrating inside the house, beyond the door. Maybe on the kitchen table or counter? Vanessa looks through the crack between the edge of the door and the door frame. She can see the deadbolt isn't locked. His door is unlocked, unless the chain is on.

Apprehensive, not sure if she should do it or not, Vanessa turns the door knob slowly, in hopes of not making a sound. She knows she shouldn't do it. She's crossing a boundary, but she's pissed at Shiloh, and underneath that she's also a little worried. The door opens with ease and she cautiously enters his home. Light from the entryway illuminates half the kitchen she enters. There is a distorted rectangle of light framing her silhouette across the kitchen floor. The rest of the house is dark, not a single light on. Maybe Shiloh is asleep. Maybe she should turn around and head back out, she'd be furious if he came into her home without permission.

Vanessa sees the glow from Shiloh's cell phone on the kitchen countertop like she anticipated. Crossing another boundary, she picks up the phone and looks at it. Thirteen missed text messages from her. Three missed calls from her. No one else.

The rest of the house is unlit. Not a single light that she can see anywhere. "Shiloh?" She calls out in a low voice.

To her right she is startled by movement. Someone moving in the shadows of the living room. Vanessa almost screams but flips on the kitchen light switch first. The welcome electric light reveals an empty living room aside from his furniture and such. There was no one there. It must have been the shadows playing tricks with her eyes. Maybe from a passing car's headlights outside.

Vanessa investigates his home, turning on a light in every room as she goes. Every door is open, every light is on, there is no sign of Shiloh except for one place she hasn't looked yet. The bathroom door is shut.

She stands before the closed bathroom door with a feeling of trepidation. Maybe he's in there having sex with some woman. No. Her intuition tells her it's something else. Something not good. She knows she shouldn't have entered his place without his permission, but she knows he's still stuck on her and won't get too mad about it, even if he pretends to be, he'll be happy she's there. He'll probably whine about how much he loves her and misses her. She knows he took the break up hard, but what else could she do? She just doesn't like him anymore.

Why is she so afraid to open the bathroom door? Something is awful. Something is wrong. There is something on the other side of that door she doesn't want to see.

Vanessa knocks faintly on the door, "Shiloh?" Her voice is hesitant, "It's me. Vanessa."

There is no response.

She bites her lip, not sure if she is making the right decision as she opens the bathroom door, immediately noticing the low burning candles. The small room smells pleasant. Shiloh is naked in the bathtub.

Around her the shadows seem to be moving, circling about her like a black slow motion cyclone.

Shiloh wakes in utter darkness, blind from the blackness. He feels his body is still in the cooling bath water. The candles must have burned out. Why isn't he dead?

He stands, a rush of water splashing down his body. Reaching blindly for a towel, he shivers. He finds what he's looking for. The dry towel hanging on the wall. Shiloh is feeling weak and faint, the long cross shaped slashes in his wrists still hurting.

Drying off in the dark he stumbles about reaching for a light switch, hand running along the wall about where he imagines it should be. If he's still alive maybe there is a reason for that.

Maybe he should call someone? Or even call the hospital? Maybe he's made a mistake? Maybe he can live without Vanessa? Or maybe Vanessa will remember the love they had some day and come back to him? Maybe he can just learn to live again, remember who Shiloh Darling is without Vanessa.

Oddly, Shiloh walks around feeling about, hands seeking the light switch. He can't find it. He knows it should be there. His fingers must be just missing it by a hair's breadth. The bathroom isn't that big.

Dropping the towel to the floor, panic rises in his chest, this room is too big. It's not the bathroom. No matter how far he walks or which way he turns he can't find the sink and counter or the toilet, or the door. In fact after moving away from the wall for a moment he can't find the wall again either. Or the bloody water filled bathtub.

"What the hell?" Shiloh whispers, wondering if he is dead. He's cold, goosebumps tighten the skin all over his body, and the cuts on his wrists feel the coldest, like ice.

He must be dead. Dead or dreaming.

It's the only explanation for the sudden vastness of the bathroom. Attempting to back track he has no luck. He's lost in the dark. Involuntary shivering, he wishes he hadn't dropped the towel and feels that much more vulnerable being nude.

What's going on? Is he in Hell? Shiloh doesn't know what to do in this cold blindness. He keeps wandering in the ever dark, hugging himself and rubbing hands and shoulders in an attempt to stay warm. There seems to be no end to the pitch black. He cannot see his fingers in front of his face.

Time seems distorted. Slow. Time seems so very slow. He has no notion of how long he's been walking about. The ground beneath his feet still feels like the linoleum floor of the bathroom.

"Hello?" Shiloh calls out. "Is there anybody here?"

Silence. There is no echo to his voice. Shiloh begins to feel as if he's been walking for miles and fear grows as he suspects there may be no end.

"Am I dead?" Shiloh calls out.

No answer.

He must be dead.

What seems like hours pass.

Weary of walking, possibly delirious, Shiloh suddenly senses something. A single presence veiled by the darkness.

Shiloh feels a familiar fear. It's one of the shadow people standing very near him in the darkness. This is the one that has been watching him all of his life. A leader? Always there hidden in the shadows, like a dark father watching over him. His secret father. Shiloh feels this shadow lord is something like the Devil, if not the Devil himself.

In a sudden moment of illumination Shiloh's eyes adjust to the absolute darkness. It's not that he can see, it's still thick darkness, but he can make out shades of black. He can see the outline of himself, a black on black silhouette. The same as the dark watcher before him, a darker than black silhouette, black on black.

Shiloh feels meek before the watcher. A watcher. He knows in his heart what this means. A fallen angel. The watchers are angels and these shadow ones are the fallen. It seems a distant memory hidden away in the back of Shiloh's brain.

What do the watchers want? Why are they the fallen? What do they do? Shiloh wonders if he is even right about any of this. It feels like lost memories returning. Are all of these shadow people evil? Fallen angels are demons, aren't they?

This dark man is familiar. His presence is foreboding, authoritative, undeniable. This one has been present all of Shiloh's life, hidden in the shadows, a silent witness. Maybe everyone has a guardian angel and a dark angel that also watches over their every move.

Silent.

"Are you Lucifer?" Shiloh dares to whisper, almost stuttering, the sound of his voice so loud in this expansive silence. He feels weak and empty of blood. Cold with the absence of life.

The shadow figure does not respond. Nothing. It only watches. Observes.

Lucifer, Shiloh thinks, the Latin root is Lux Ferro, which means the bringer of light or the bearer of light. Then why the darkness? Why are the watchers shadow people? A punishment from God for Lucifer bringing light to mankind, to be forever bound to the darkness?

There have always been two beings watching Shiloh's life. This watching king of shadow and the old, white bearded man smiling with promises of love, peace, and harmony. Shiloh remembers a dream in which this old man hugged him in a small white church on a lonely hilltop, telling Shiloh he'd always loved him, always will, and forgives him for everything. The old man wore a white robe with hair as long and white as his beard and skin as soft as tissue paper. The old man's love brought tears to Shiloh's eyes. In the very back, last pew of the little white church sat the shadow man, doing what he always does, watching.

His feet still cold on the never ending linoleum floor, still naked, Shiloh begins to weep. He is dead. He is still lost. He is still without Vanessa and their child. He still hurts inside.

It seems more likely he's in Hell than Heaven or Nirvana or Valhalla or any place of peace and paradise.

Shiloh thinks about what he's heard about suicide in the past. Catholics believe people who commit suicide go to Hell. Samurai believe in an honorable suicide. Shiloh's bathtub suicide was not the honorable suicide of a Samurai.

This is utter cold, getting colder, emotionless darkness, it's like the entrance to Hell and the silent, familiar watcher before him is his guide. His unholy guardian angel. Shiloh doesn't care what the dark man thinks of him as he sobs.

Shadow people must not have emotions. At least not the same kind of emotions humans have. It seems that this dark lord does not care that Shiloh is torn apart inside, heart broken, lost, missing Vanessa and their child, realizing his mistake. He weeps and sobs harder, until he feels he may die a second time from crying so much.

After an inestimable amount of uncontrolled, unrestrained lamentation, Shiloh catches his breath and calms. His heart still aches, but he's pulling himself together enough to assess the situation again. He's committed suicide like a coward. Now he is damned to Hell. He did not kill himself like a noble Samurai, but maybe he can accept his damnation with the honor of a Samurai. Accept his punishment and responsibility for his errors. He stands a little taller in the face of Hell.

The dark one is still standing before him, waiting, watching, mute, unmoved. It doesn't care.

"Are you death?" Shiloh whispers.

No response.

"Are you going to talk to me after all these years?"

The dark lord remains silent.

Shiloh feels the darkness around him now, growing thicker like humidity, stifling, quickly suffocating, pulling him down, his soul, that's all that's left, his soul, and the darkness tearing him asunder, crushing him, absorbing him all at once. A black death, an unimagined Hell. A dark lord, a shadow king, an unholy guardian angel, witness of a lifetime claiming it's sinner.

"Death! Death! Death!" Shiloh shrieks out into a new muteness, a drowning, overwhelming silence and darkness, smashing shadow, utter, unheard blackness, choking on shade, like swallowing mouthfuls of blindness, swallowing solid chunks of lies going down like black oil, old death.

All his life the dark lord has been watching and waiting for this. It's all been a lie. Everything. This is Hell now. It's happening. Shiloh struggles to find that Samurai bravery but it's no easy task. He finds himself thinking, 'Was it John Wayne who said courage is being scared shit-less and doing it anyway' ?

Hell is non-existence. A Hell of only shadow, only silence, only nothing.

Infinite hands, limbs, mouths, tentacles, strange things without reason, things that should not exist, even in nightmares, reach for him, grab and grasp and violate, tugging him down further into Hell.

This is not Heaven, Shiloh laughs out loud like a man who's lost his sanity. Did he actually believe God would feel sorry for him and forgive him?

This is something too utterly alien to the human mind.

It is the collapsing of a black hole.

It is the collapsing of a soul.

The grinding and shredding of all that was Shiloh Darling into a mindless ink blot. It is a never ending scream, a never ending gasp for breath. A shutter that shakes forever.

It is the nothing. The becoming of no thing.

The evil. The hater of life.

This shadow is something that holds itself superior to humanity, to all physical existence. To the darkness humanity is only dust.

The eaters of souls.

The inescapable blackness that overcomes and outweighs all.

It is a return to the nothing before the universe was created. The most forlorn, loneliest of all Hells. The immovable darkness against the unstoppable shadow. It is silence cackling. The never ending cracking and shattering of sanity.

Shiloh gasps for air that is not there, grasps for life that does not exist, looks for light which is forever absent, a Faustian fool locked in the ever collapsing tower of evil, unseen obsidian and opal.

Shiloh searches for his voice to cry out, but his voice is gone with everything else. All is gone. There is only black. In the recesses of what's left of his crumbling mind he can hear the faint words of Mick Jagger singing *Paint It Black*.

This eternal, infinite shadow land is overcrowded with endless multitudes of the damned, more frightening because they remain unseen. There is no more room in Hell, but there is nowhere else to go.

Together, Shiloh and all the damned, are crushed, ripped, and raped continuously. This is pain the human mind could never have comprehended, never imagined. A trampling weight too much for the shoulders of even Atlas to bare. An asphyxiating pile of mock flesh, blood, souls, beasts, demons, and the damned of ever kind. A mass like nothing fathomed in physics.

All black. All dark. All shadow. All suffering. All misery. All endless.

Limitless mute agony.

The Devil's greatest trick.

The Devil that existed before the Bible.

The pure black lie.

Now there is only what is to be endured. Sickness. Agony. Breaking.

Sobbing in eternal silence, eternal darkness. There is no time. There is no escape. There is nothing that wants to be here save the lord of shadow, the proud and gleeful king, once the most beautiful of all, throned, unchallenged, upon a black colossal mountain of a vacuum of black nothingness and the most effective, venomous persecution.

From what Shiloh can remember of himself now, he knows he's made a deep, grave error, a regret that rots the marrow of bone, that sears the heart, and aches the lungs with no air. A feeling of remorse and loss that never goes away. The internal torture of all he has done in life haunts him. He tosses, turns, and twists, ever uncomfortable, mangled, crushed, and drowning. He knows he deserves this Hell. The living do not expect this. True damnation.

Shiloh's face is always wet with tears and drool. The good he has done in his life was not enough to make up for the wrong. He was selfish. He did care. He did love.

Hell is a black hole of souls, sins, and infernal beasts forced together into one solid mass and mush of pain, hate, sorrow, and all that is negative. It is helplessness. The vacuum out of time and space.

There have been reports of humans seeing shadow people as far back as the memory of humanity stretches. A dark shifting out of the corner of your eye. The tricks the shadows play. The figure you're sure you saw standing over you just as you woke in the heart of the night.

If you're lucky the shadow figure wasn't trying to steal your breath, pressure your chest, lift your bed, or violate you in some peculiar way.

The shadow people watch like the fallen angels they are. Not all fallen angels fall in the same manner and not all become the same thing when they rise from their divine crater. But there are the shadow people, the fallen watchers, dark angels hidden in shadow, ever present. Dark witnesses of mankind.

God's greatest mistake, some of the fallen say, was not only the creation of man, but creation itself. The almighty war that tore a third of Heaven asunder did not occur until after the creation of man, led by the jealousy of Samael and Lucifer? The records are unclear. Only those present at the turn of events know for sure.

Not all fallen, and not even all the shadow people have the same opinions, like all species they possess traits in common and overlapping beliefs, but they are their own will and action. Some shadows lust with perversion, some stare with wrath and hate, some with envy and jealousy, some with indifference, maybe curious or bored. There are even myths of a few who champion creation, repenting. Other than those mythical fallen, all know their preeminence over humanity. Men are a lesser race. There are a myriad of motives that lurk in the shadows.

Those who have caught glimpses of the shadows over the years have thought many different things, but most felt fear. Even today, among those interesting quirks, some say demon, some say angel, some say ghost. In earlier centuries many said Fey and some said Gobs. In more modern times some say aliens, or ultra-terrestrials, or time travelers, or extra-dimensional beings, or psychological constructs. Dream beings. Hallucinations.

Some say benevolent, others say malevolent.

No one seems to know what they really are, save the wisest of the sages and mages.

Whatever the shadow people are, believe, or choose not to believe, they are there watching you with open eyes from all the shadows and darkness. Reigning in children's closets, under beds, in dusky attics, and all through the night with motives unknown, misunderstood, or incomprehensible.

Faeries. Imps. The dark men in hats. The tall slender man. Men in black. Whatever they are, they have been present since the first wars in Heaven. Since that tremendous, divine rebellion, the cracking of reality, the breaking of the vessel.

"Shiloh?" Vanessa calls out softly, lightly tapping on the now partially open door as she enters the small, candle scented room. It smells so fresh, so clean.

At first glance, Vanessa thinks Shiloh has fallen asleep in the bath, his face so relaxed with peace. She realizes maybe he is fine without her. Maybe he has gotten over their break up. His handsome face is so serene with half a smile seeming to hint at sweet dreams.

The room is so dim as the last of the candles burn down. Not dim enough as she notices the dark shade of the bath water. The numb look and limpness of Shiloh's bare body and posture. His face tilted nearly a third of the way beneath the surface of the water.

"Shiloh!" Her voice rises in sudden realization and panic, "Oh, God, no!" She cries out, rushing to his side, kneeling in a light puddle of blood diluted by water, "What have you done, you bastard!" She is shouting, a flood of tears blinding her.

Vanessa reaches out to her familiar, former lover, fingers coming into contact with his face, flesh too cool. Her hand jerks away in denial of death. He is dead. He is dead. He is dead. The only words she can think of.

"Shiloh!" Vanessa reaches back with both hands, shaking his body, trying to wake him back to life, blood tainted water splashing on her skin and clothes. "Oh, Darling," she collapses in a curled, kneeling position a moment, holding herself, "Don't go," she whispers.

Irrationally she thinks, maybe it's not too late and jumps up, dashing to the light switch to illuminate the situation. It can't be too late. Call someone. An ambulance. Doctors. 911. There has to be something she can do.

He can't be dead. "No! No! No! No!" She moves with a quickness, drawing out her cell phone and reaching for the light switch simultaneously. At the same time her fingers turn on the light, the bulb overhead explodes, burnt out, blowing the breaker for the entire house, and she slips on the water slick floor, falling uncontrollably backward, her head first hitting the corner of the bathroom counter top and then cracking against the hard floor.

A dark fury of shadow people surrounds her, grasping at her in the darkness with the hunger and desperation of madness, gasping, tugging at her life from the eternal night. Elongated, misshapen, shadows stretch, bind, and tangle about her, eager for death.

Her eyes flicker before losing consciousness, seeing these black nightmares horde about her, tearing at her with the gravity of Hell.

On the floor a growing puddle of fresh blood comes from the gashes in her head, mixing with the blood and water of Shiloh. A final glance at Shiloh, trying so hard to keep her eyes open, she sees his head slowly sink beneath the murky water as a legion of shadow people claim her, dragging her down into the dark blight of a true Hell.

This fall and hitting her head was enough to bring her to the same death as Shiloh Darling.

After many years of suffering in the iron grip of darkness, an aeon of anguish, the ever collapsing gravity of the black hole of Hell, entropy. It has always been. Always will be. Always was. The alpha and omega of torment, mourning, and all possible affliction. An overcrowded, private Hell. Alone and claustrophobic, wailing, weeping, screaming in deafening silence.

The endless. The black. The pain that words cannot convey. There is no time in this darkness.

This has always existed for Shiloh, and always will, and it is all there is. Shiloh struggles to remember Shiloh. He is the same as all the prisoners and denizens of Hell. Coherent moments of what's left of Shiloh's mind wonders if there are other Hells, other kinds of torturous, timeless, sleepless nightmares. Never peace. Always pain.

There is something beyond the always horror that was once Shiloh. A puny, vague something that was once Shiloh Darling. Amnesia. Pieces falling apart like a jigsaw puzzle fallen from a table top and scattered in the wind. Self barely exists. Only enough to always suffer.

The vague memory of what self was and what self did and that self will never be self again and was never truly self to begin with.

All phobia. No sense of what is or was self and what is other.

There is only billions of tortured, damned souls, worse than any evil night because night brings the hope of dawn.

It was an eternity ago, a moment ago, a universe ago, that Shiloh gave up being Shiloh and became a part of the conglomerate of a black Hell. It is over but will never be over. All souls pulled to the heart of the black hole.

Shiloh no longer wants to exist. Only to forget. No words.

All at once something changes. What's left of Shiloh senses something. Something secret. Something that does not belong in Hell. Or something Shiloh doesn't want in Hell. Redemption is a selfless act.

Shiloh Darling remembers the scent of flowers and the playfulness of kittens. He remembers something that was once called Shiloh. There was something called Shiloh Darling? It existed? Once upon a time there was a pain he thought would never extinguish. A pain that overwhelmed everything that Shiloh was. Until the stalking shadow people came out of hiding, tearing the soul asunder. All obedient servants of the shadows lord, the king of Black Hell.

Now Shiloh knows the pain he felt in his heart was insignificant compared to damnation.

But for love.

Darling recalls love.

A love he could not live without. A love so near he can sense it within the mass of sludge and tormented souls. She is here. In the endless. In the nothing. In this void of only evil absent time and space.

Shiloh begins to crawl and squirm and slither his way through the murk and muck of black, damned, damaged souls fighting against his every small stride and hint of progress. The pressure, the mass, the weight, the gravity of the greatest collapsed sun.

Shiloh Darling moves against the immovable. He moves mountains and planets of death and Hell, invisibly clawing through rotten flesh and putrid spirit. Hands that are not hands. Arms that are not arms. Limbs that are not limbs. Only memories of what Shiloh was crawling forward and impossibly back together. Reaching even through black burning, charring flames. The black inferno. Hellfire sizzling and cooking Shiloh as the memories struggle to become what was once a man.

Nothing can stop him.

No black hell. No black hole. No unholy or even sacred prison can hold him back now. The scent of flowers led him forth like an archangel to God. He grows stronger with each imagined breath, each imagined heartbeat.

The reconstruction of the soul.

The remembrance of flowers.

There was once something called beauty, something called love, which existed aeons ago.

Quickly, abruptly everything comes back to Shiloh like the swift rush of creation. Like the thing the ignorant scientists called the Big Bang. Like that enigmatic question the mystics and philosophers always sought to answer.

Was there ever nothing? Or was there always something?

Was there ever meaning? Or was it all as meaningless as a cosmic spiral of dung?

No.

It is an epiphany. A word of grace. An epiphany not like touching the demiurge, but like touching the source of all. An euphoric explosion of all his lives, led by Shiloh, returning to him like the second coming of a christ.

The zenith of all his love, the scent of a flower, Vanessa, and his only strength, close to her. After an eternity of struggle, he's found the fragments of what was once Vanessa in this cold, black hell, what was her soul, her mind. He gathers her all together and chooses to believe she does not belong in this dark, damned place.

He is so close to her he can almost touch her, almost feel and hold her. She has forgotten who she is in this dire black hell.

Shiloh reaches out across the span of universes, across the length of ever long shadows, and slightly touches Vanessa. That single moment of contact sparks the memory of Vanessa within Vanessa. She remembers her life, Shiloh, his death, his slit wrists. She remembers slipping in his bloody water. She remembers her own death. Dying with the cracking of her skull. She has been in this black hell alone and crowded ever since, a moment of eternity until Shiloh's fingertips caress her, awakening her like an angel of morning.

Like in the beginning, the very beginning, the alpha, the first point, the first sphere. A perfect circle, an atmosphere protectively surrounds Shiloh and Vanessa. All darkness is expelled from this circle. All the blackness trapped outside their newborn pearl of existence.

They are only two souls floating in and out and around each other with a slow leisure grace. They are the memories of what Shiloh and Vanessa were. Bare before each other. They kiss once. An always kiss that never fades or is forgotten. Never to be anything but Shiloh and Vanessa.

For this moment, in this immaculate sphere, this blooming flower of creation, they are one.

The dark lord steps into their globe of light, silent, deafening, watching as always, leader of archangels and lessers, this immortal, rebellious liar. Hider in the shadows.

"She doesn't belong here," Shiloh demands with defiance he can't restrain.

The shadow man shakes his head with a wisp and chuckle, "Only saints go to Heaven, Shiloh, my darling. Saints and no others."

"No," Shiloh stands, chest puffed out, "keep me. Not her. I will do whatever you ask if you let her free of this black hell. This void and chaos."

"You are already mine," the dark lord whispers, "as is she."

Shiloh stands as if ready to fight, Vanessa behind him.

With an emotionless nod, the dark lord speaks, "For a moment say goodbye."

With those final words the watcher fades back into the blackness outside their illuminated sphere created only by love and will.

Vanessa looks into Shiloh's eyes, the memory of those eyes, holding both his hands, facing each other.

"I feel like I've been in this black prison forever," tears shine in her eyes.

"I know," Shiloh responds, almost too soft to hear.

"You're saving me?"

"Once I promised you I would always protect you."

She vaguely remembers the early whispers of forever love in the beginning of their romance, nodding with a tight lipped smile, holding back emotion like she always does. It's rare for others to know what she feels. Her walls are built thick with history that had nothing to do with Shiloh. The great walls were in place years before they'd met.

He steals one last kiss, "I love you, Vanessa," holding eye contact, hoping she will say the same.

Instead a look of discomfort, "I don't hate you, Shiloh."

"You don't love me," Shioh smiles with tears shining in his eyes now. "I don't understand what happened. I never will. I'll never forget you. I'll always love you."

Vanessa gives him a bright smile and suddenly, vigorously, holds him close against her body, her whisper tickling his ear, "Shiloh Darling..."

She fades as if only the figment of a dream. Shiloh stands there, holding the emptiness where she stood only moments ago. He can still smell the scent of flowers.

Shiloh feels empty, like there is once again nothing left of him. His arms limp at his sides, head drooping, feeling useless. What's left now? She's gone.

Shiloh Darling is still the center of a perfect sphere of illumination surrounding him like a force field shielding out the darkness. Aimless black shadow, crowded distorted suffering, lamenting, raging, tormented, malignant, damned and broken souls swirl, crawl, and claw about the exterior of the white sphere.

He doesn't know what to do or why this perfect sphere of illumination protects him from the black of Hell.

The dark lord who has witnessed Shiloh all his life re-enters the sphere, the darkness and light mingling and mixing like oil and water as he passes through the curved surface of the sphere. The swirling dark lord's passage leaves behind a transitory rainbow of violets.

There is something poignant and beautiful about the dark lord's emergence from the black and into the light of Shiloh's sphere. The man is all shadow, made of mystery. He radiates an aura of the ancient. The dark lord. Its senses, perception, and consciousness far beyond that of anything that Shiloh is. Anything that is human. A very old god. Born before the Earth. Before the galaxy. Before the light. An elder god.

The dark lord, the shadow king speaks with a deep whispering, "In the beginning, when what you children of the Abrahamic religions think of as god, the creator, created existence, it did so with a single point. That was the first act of creation. A single point. A singularity. That single point became a single sphere." The dark lord holds out his shadow arms and hands for dramatic effect gesturing at the sphere they occupy, "Like this sphere of Shiloh." Its voice is a dark, rasping whisper of dominance, of commandment. It makes Shiloh think of a dark christ.

The dark lord's shadow form is as thick as black blood. It continues its hellfire sermon to Shiloh, "This god, this creator, was all before that. Infinite. It existed everywhere. It was all there was and ever had been. There was only the original source."

Shiloh listens like a trapped disciple at a black mass, still aching from the loss of Vanessa, distrusting and resenting this dark lord. This unknown shadow man who has watched him all his life.

Less the enigma it was before it spoke.

The dark one continues like an old philosopher sharing his stone, "To create something other than itself, because it was all, this god thing, this godhead, had to remove itself from itself. It had to retract, withdraw itself, creating a space for something else to exist. This self withdrawal created a space of non-existence. A perfect sphere of non-existence. This perfect sphere was the absence of God. It was within this sphere that creation unfolded. God had to remove itself from creation in order for creation to exist. For something to exist outside itself."

The dark lord chuckles gruffly, "Maybe it was lonely, the godhead. Now you know, Shiloh Darling, that God does not exist in existence. Existence requires God's absence. In God's place became the hierarchy that leads us to and fro. Celestial and earthbound alike. Ascensions and descensions."

Shiloh only looks into the dark lord, into nothingness, blackness, not understanding, speechless. The only thing he knows for certain is Vanessa is gone and he is dead and damned to Hell.

"Contemplate that until it drives you to madness with an eternity of meaninglessness. I will leave you alone here forever. In your own perfect sphere of light like God. Your own private microverse in the heart of the blackest hell. I have always watched you from the shadows and always will. I was there for your birth and death." The black, empty face, the dark lord's entire shadow body fades backward into the black, out of the sphere, exiting completely.

"Who are you, watcher?" Shiloh calls out.

"I have many names. I have no name. I am only a shadow." The dark lord's voice seems to whisper from all around at once. "Think of God. Think of Vanessa. Think of loss." With those final words the dark lord watcher is gone and the immortal soul Shiloh remains alone in a timeless sphere of light with nothing to do but think.

After seconds or aeons of contemplation, Shiloh does realize there is only thought. All else is only dense lies.

Vanessa Balasky wakes in her hospital bed under white sheets, her eyes adjusting to the mid-morning sunlight shining in from a large, clean window. She gazes around, dazed, at the sterile hospital room. It stinks like a dentist's office or cleaning fluids or something like that, she thinks.

Her head is sore. She reaches up and feels the stitches and staples on the back and side of her head. The doctors shaved some of her hair away. She feels vulnerable in her hospital gown.

Vanessa remembers everything. Her eyes are open and the world seems a different place, yet the same. Shiloh was wrong and selfish.

She sits perfectly still looking out the window at the sunlight, no emotion on her face. A single tear sneaks down her cheek. She doesn't move to wipe it away. He can have that. He can have at least one tear.

Shiloh Darling is dead and she is alive.

And only saints go to Heaven.

The Harbinger of the Coming Race

There are three things that put men in jail. Women, drugs, and money. This is in reference to ordinary, civilized men of civilized nations. As civilized as the human ape can get. And excluding political dissidents and anarchists. And the insane. Women, drugs, and money are what put ordinary men in jail and prison. Weak men. Most are. He is not an ordinary man. At least not anymore. Once he was. Yet he is in jail for the same reasons as ordinary men.

Isaac Myrick tries not to be so harsh and judgmental of his fellow inmates because there was a time he was something like them. Never as dumb as them, but incarcerated for the same types of issues. Keep in mind drugs include alcohol under it's umbrella.

Still Isaac looks around at his fellow prisoners and feels nothing but disgust for them. Weak. Mediocre. Con men, car salesmen, and charlatans. All pretending to be tougher and more badass than everyone else in the jail. It's all tattoos and bad attitudes.

The other inmates cackle and tell obnoxious, raunchy jokes as they play cards and tell exaggerated stories of their adventures on the street. How beautiful that last woman was. How much they get laid. Their mighty sexual prowess. What high rollers they were. How big their dicks are. How many fights they won. How many times they outfoxed the pigs. How sly, slick, and cool they all are. This is the average. The standard inside. Their stories combined horse shit blends into one endless concoction of nonsense. They all think they're superman, wronged by the justice system or just in the wrong place at the wrong time. Every yarn and jibe may as well be coming from the same person. That's what it's like. Like they are a bunch of clones. Defective clones.

Isaac hates them all. They are worthless in his eyes. Because they choose to be worthless. They don't deserve to live. Wastes of flesh. He feels only rage and contempt for this human trash. He wants to kill them all. The jailers are in the same category as the inmates in the eyes of Isaac.

He lies alone on his bunk reading a trashy romance novel because there aren't many books to choose from in this jail. There are 50 bunks in this unit so it can hold 100 inmates and it's filled to capacity. All these idiots trapped living together. He doesn't care for the novel he's reading, he's just trying to keep his mind occupied. Make the time go by and not think.

When he was first locked up other inmates tried to befriend him but learned quickly that he had nothing to say and preferred to be left alone. There are those acceptable, invisibles among the inmates. Most of the inmates ignore the existence of Isaac now and he does his best to ignore them. It's hard. They're so annoying. Voices like fingernails scraping chalkboards or concrete.

He sighs quietly, turning the page of the sappy romance novel, listening to one of the other inmates giggle about some mischief. The giggling Inmate A is bragging to Inmate B because Inmate A wiped his ass after taking a shit on Inmate C's pillow case. Inmate A and Inmate C have a beef because they got in an argument over something irrelevant. It's just clashing personalities. No rational reason.

Inmate B laughs and a short while later several inmates snicker when Inmate C goes to sleep, wondering why his pillow smells like shit.

The next day Isaac takes a shower in the afternoon. He prefers showering in the afternoons because the shower room is usually empty then. He hates being in a steamed filled room full of naked hoodlums. A room full of men he can hardly tolerate.

Isaac is annoyed by the entrance of another inmate into the spacious shower room. An elder Native American man. Isaac sees the naked, old Indian, but pays him no mind. A sagging pot belly, skinny legs and arms, long grey hair. The Native is a trustee at the jail so that means instead of leaving for work, he works at the jail, cleaning duties. This jail is for work release, trustees, and general nonviolent overflow.

The two men share no words, but there is an unspoken mutual respect.

Isaac Myrick is not in a prison, it's only jail, better than that he gets work release, meaning as long as the inmates have jobs they get released for the day to work. A major downside to it is that about half the inmates paycheck goes to the county while they are in the work release program.

When the old Indian man leaves the shower room, Isaac rubs one off quickly, just to relax himself a little more than the steaming water already is. The combination of the steam and orgasm loosen Isaac's muscles enough to make him euphoric enough to dream. His imagined fantasy is having sex with the waitress Chastity, a halfbreed with big breasts, a pretty face, and curves like a woman should have. She's a terrible flirt with eyes as big and wide as the actress Karen Black.

Isaac is a construction worker. When he found out he was going to jail and qualified for work release he quickly took a second job at Alphonso's Pizza as a dishwasher and busboy, just to have more hours away from the jail and the monkey men he's locked up with. Fucking knuckleheads and cockroaches. Males but not true men.

When Isaac first walked into his new temporary home, the jail, he was recognized by a few of the other inmates. Guys who knew him on the street or by reputation. This worked to his immediate advantage.

Isaac used to sell drugs and was good at it. In fact it's only been about three months since he gave up the profession. He was in charge of his own crew which he'd put together himself. About two dozen cats. They were well organized street soldiers loyal to him and he was generous to them. He had soldiers that would never snitch and kill any bitch if he asked. He was a natural leader on the street, organizing more than drug distribution, he orchestrated robberies, burglaries, embezzlement from local businesses, and forcefully took out drug dealing competition.

He kept his soldiers happy with a little money, free drugs, parties, and pussy. He had plenty of money. Plenty of everything that most would think a man would want. For a moment he was the king of the street, feared by some, respected by others, envied by a few, and used by many.

It was a good crew. Fun times. The crew fell apart right away without his leadership. They were different types of people who worked for him that wouldn't have normally associated with each other, but came together as a cohesive, effective unit for Isaac. He feels some guilt for leaving them so suddenly.

Isaac was top dog, a high roller for real among those around him, but there is always someone higher on the food chain. The criminal underworld exists as an idea, a word, a notion, but it's actually something more elusive and fluid in the world, it's an ocean of varied fish and sea monsters of all shapes and sizes. Big fish eating little fish every day. Sharks and killer whales. Guppies and minnows. Electric eels and great kraken and unknown depths of crushing water pressure, too much for the ordinary to thrive or survive.

To be the shark Isaac was for a moment he had to do things others wouldn't do. Kick in doors without fear. Meditate on *the Tell Tale Heart* of Poe. He had to conquer not only with a sword but more efficiently with his mind.

One thing he was forced to do was deal with the sea monsters. The bigger fish. The eaters. The fish without hearts. A kraken. Men that shouldn't even be called men because they forgot they had hearts, or maybe they killed or lost their hearts. These are the men only a very few of the crew knew about. These men began to blacken Isaac's heart, a contagiousness that crept it's way into the cracks of his broken heart. Cracks left by things unsaid, by hurts left better off not felt, by things best forgotten.

Isaac rose fast when he started selling drugs, shooting upward like a bolt of ground lightning, electricity spider-crackling skyward like shattered glass and stars lighting up the black night above. He was on the fast track to becoming a local legend, a myth. Everyone downtown knew him for a minute. He was known in every dope house, crack house, and whore house in the little city. All the junkies, drunks, fiends, and wanna-be's sniffed him out like rats following the Piped Piper.

He had it all for a moment. The world in his hands. Underneath it all he had nothing he wanted. One night he killed three men in the early hours of the morning after being awake for three days straight. Washing the blood away, he knew it was the end for him. He could go on and live and die a warrior king of the street, some day forgotten and left gutted in a gutter or maybe wither away in a prison cell. Maybe he could make the big break, the big heist, the big score all the hustlers strive for and run away to South America. But every hustler and dealer is addicted to the next big deal, the next hustle, that next nab and grab, that next handful of diamonds or dust.

Isaac washed a trinity of blood from his body in a hot shower, watching the pink, red swirl of water circle down the drain and knew he'd reached his limit. None of this underworld brought him any true joy. Sex, drugs, money, pointless, unfulfilled, he'd rather be dead. Standing in that shower that morning, or maybe it was noon by that time, he realized he deserved to be dead too. Not just for the three men he'd killed, for a history of crime over the last few years. Not even *Scarface* got away in the end,

Isaac realized. The original gangsters were always washed up half men, surrendered to servitude of a woman, dope, or bills. Ah, he knows there is always an exception to the rule, but he was too tired to take that chance anymore.

He would do none of it. He would find a new route to take, a new way. He would rebuild his life on this foundation of blood and water. A new life born of an unholy trinity of murder.

What does that mean? Sure, murder is wrong, but these men didn't have to die. They chose death when they crossed him. It is nature. Natural. Like when a lion takes down a wildebeest or a cat swallows a bird. He could cry self-defense, the three men tried to rob Isaac. Three men who now lie in weeds and grass being eaten by insects and vermin, recycled by nature. Evil and good are defined by circumstance, not unbreakable dogma. He could have let them kill him, but the instinct of self-preservation kicked in. It confounded Isaac due to his suicidal tendencies he'd been experiencing in secret.

Still a guilt crept out of his cracked and blackened heart. Remorse. A need for something more. Redemption. Atonement. Something sacred.

Ironically Isaac is not in jail for the murders or any other heavy cases. He's in jail on petty marijuana charges and misdemeanors. He was arrested with a small amount of weed, a personal sack. The judge sentenced him because he does have a long list of misdemeanors. The entire situation was twisted and ridiculous compared to the things he's gotten off scot free with. This jail time is so much less than what he deserves.

Why would God let him get away with the things he's done? Maybe he hasn't or isn't going to Heaven. Maybe God has some punishment planned, something grand like burning in Hell. Lakes of fire. Isaac smirks.

"Wipe that grin off your face," a jail guard orders as Isaac stands stark naked in front of the guard in a locker room with metal benches attached to the concrete floor. He goes through this every day, being strip searched before being let back inside the jail. "Are you queer?" The guard barks.

A few of the other buck naked inmates snicker, some remain somber, some ignore it all.

"No," Isaac answers as he lifts his balls for the guard to inspect, "Just thought of something funny," he turns and leans over, spreading his ass cheeks for the guards inspection.

"There's nothing funny about being in jail," the guard grumbles and orders, "Jump up and down on the balls of your heels. Arms up."

Isaac does as he's told, taking note of the guard's name tag, Lee Hosch, a prick like so many of the other guards that treat the inmates no better than dogs. He will remember that name. Many of the guards speak to the inmates like they are less than human. Not all of the guards do, but enough to make the misery of jail life that much worse. A slight majority.

The mistreatment of the inmates is enough to offend Isaac. A few of the guards don't treat them like human beings. Isaac will remember them all. The pricks and the guards who were respectful, yet firm and polite.

"What was so funny?" Hosch interrogates Isaac as he begins dressing in his black and white striped jail clothes. Isaac can't help but glance around the room at the other naked inmates. He's not embarrassed like the first few times he had to go through this routine humiliation, strip searched in a room full of naked, strange men. Isaac could tell the others were embarrassed or as resigned as he now is. Not a lot of eye contact is made, yet Isaac finds himself fascinated by the human body, the human machine. He's not a homosexual by any means. He has no issue with homosexuals. He is absolutely attracted to the female form, almost to the point of weakness. He loves women, sex like a drug, wishful for love, love like a potion to his heart. Women. The most beautiful thing God created. God did create some beautiful things alongside the ugly. But woman, the most mysterious thing a man will ever face. Men are made stupid by women, Isaac is not exempt. They are all fools for women.

   He's looked over the naked men about him daily, surprised at the size and shapes of their cocks. He'd always wondered if his own cock was big or small compared to other men and seeing the other cocks about both young and old, strong and frail, fat and thin, all races, he was disgusted by most of them. He's not a racist. He just doesn't care for the company of most people anymore. But it makes him feel good to look around with validation that Isaac has a good sized cock. Not the biggest, by far not the smallest, based on the collection of some five dozen cocks Isaac has been forced to witness.

   Isaac also takes some pride in his body, not the most fit, but not out of shape either, and half his body is decorated in black tattoos. The guards and the jailhouse record the tattoos as gang related. The authorities keep records of all the inmates tattoos as part of inmate descriptions like mugshots, DNA samples, and fingerprints.

   Isaac's black tattoos are not gang related. Each tattoo is significant with purpose. They are arcane tattoos. Each means something and has power behind it. Holy or unholy bullshit depending on your beliefs.

   He knows the tattoos do intimidate some of the other inmates who don't have tattoos and think Isaac's are gang tats. Actual gang members give Isaac nods of respect pretending they know Isaac is in a set.

   When Isaac first came to jail there were a handful of inmates who already knew him and approached him with enthusiasm, thinking Isaac was still the drug dealer and thief he was months ago. They offer smiles and gifts from the commissary like coffee, soda, sweets, paper, stamps, pencils, envelopes, things like that. Minor items' value inflates in jail. Isaac humbly thanks them all and declines. He doesn't want to owe anyone anything.

   The gifts he does accept are from young street soldiers that still owe him small favors or small money. Two of Isaac's crew are in here. They're the only ones he really talks with and not often. The hoods he knows talk to him quietly in corners or at bunk sides offering to involve him in the jail's contraband operations. Tobacco, gambling, drugs, alcohol, bartering, things like that. Isaac politely declines it all. Keeping things friendly is a delicate balance, he doesn't want them to know he's out of the game until after he's permanently released from jail. It's just safer that way.

   The young thugs spread his old reputation about the jail in whispers, the soldiers remain loyal, and the stories keep the other inmates at a respectful distance, leaving him alone to read trash novels on his bunk. He lets them tell their tales. Some true, some not, some exaggerated. Enough stories to keep everyone away except the few who know him and feel like a privileged elite. A few of them are excited to see Isaac pick up his street crown when he gets out of jail.

   Back to the black tattoos. The arcane symbols look cool and scare wussies, but they are in reality symbols of power and protection of forgotten gods. There are times when Isaac feels a sense of wonder like he is a god walking the Earth, a lion among men. The three murdered men have come to symbolize for Isaac the killers of Hiram Abiff brought to swift, vengeful justice by the hand of Isaac. If he is a lion is he a murderer or a part of nature?

"What was so damn funny?" The guard Hosch asks again, angry at being ignored.

Isaac looks the guard dead in the eyes and answers, "I was wondering if I am evil or not."

The guard's eyes light up as if he's about to burst into laughter, but something demented in Isaac's eyes unnerves him. The inmates who've overheard this brief conversation don't say a word.

"Just get in line for chow," the guard orders, his voice cracks involuntarily.

"You're a fucking weirdo," Ox chuckles in the chow line behind Isaac. Chow is always cheap and sparse. The city spends 26 cents a day to feed each inmate. That includes all three meals for the day. Isaac researched it. Public record. What Isaac doesn't like about this is that the county takes fifty percent of the inmates paychecks beyond court costs, fines, restitution, UA fees, and a 200% increase in the cost of items inmates buy from commissary like soap, snacks, deodorant, slippers, things like that. Today's dinner is a small slab of grey meatloaf. It's black on the outside, grey under the crust shell, watered down ketchup drizzled over the top. A dozen cold french fries, a dozen cold green beans, a cup of coffee, milk, or juice. A small brownie for dessert, actually not a bad meal compared to some nights he gets back to the jail.

Ox sits at a table across from Isaac. They both get back from work later than most of the other inmates sometimes. Isaac likes that, making the cafeteria near empty and private, quiet.

Isaac and Ox have known each other for about a decade. Ox is one of Isaac's soldiers. Ox is a dangerous, unpredictable man, but fiercely loyal to Isaac. Ox would commit any crime Isaac asked him to. Isaac knows it's true. Such an odd friend, Ox is a very large man with blond hair and mustache trimmed exactly like Adolf Hitler. Isaac isn't really sure why Ox wears his hairstyle like that, the big guy has never hinted at anything about Nazis or racism that Isaac can remember.

"So what do you say, my man," Ox says, "I got plans for when we get out. A kick ass new hook up for meth. We're talking a fifty thousand dollar take on our first run," Ox talks with his mouth full of food, "We can flip that shit like *Scarface*. Are you ready to be street king again?" Ox grins, a mad man. He is a man that belongs in lock up, not because he's a bad guy, he's a misunderstood guy that doesn't know how to live by society's rules outside of institutions.

Isaac has always had a soft spot in his heart for Ox. A lot of folks don't care for him but they're afraid of him. Sadly Isaac knows even if Ox gets out of jail the blond man will eventually end up doing life in prison. Isaac can tell Ox doesn't mind being in lock, it seems like Ox likes being in jail.

They didn't sell methamphetamine before. Almost everything else though.

"I don't know what my plans are," Isaac admits to Ox.

"Come on, think about it," Ox can't hide the disappointment in his voice.

"I will," Isaac gives half a smile, half a nod, and a full lie.

"Yeah, King Isaac, the God of Fuck, and Big Ox, back on the streets!"

"Maybe," Isaac mumbles, looking at the food on his tray instead of Ox.

"Maybe?" Ox balks. "It'll be a breeze. What more could you want?"

Isaac answers, "I don't want to be a slave anymore."

Isaac is not in a great mood today. To begin with his foreman forgot to let the jail know his work schedule for this week and they almost didn't let him leave for work in the morning. It was a simple oversight on the part of Isaac's foreman but the jailers were not nice about it. Making the situation even more unpleasant the female guard on duty at the time was very snotty and a basic bitch about everything. Isaac was nothing but polite to her, seething inside.

The same thing happened to another inmate but since it was the third time his boss forgot to call in his schedule they didn't let the old, black bearded inmate go to work. The old man was so angry he kicked a metal door on his way back to the cell block. An intense mistake.

The old man hadn't kicked the door hard. It was more like a child pouting than a violent outburst. The pigs took him down in less than a minute on the female guard's order. The guards tackled and restrained him. He was discharged from the work release program and shipped to regular county jail, effectively losing his job of 25 years. The old man was in jail serving a DUI sentence. An old alcoholic.

Having returned from work this evening Isaac can't help sneering at the female guard who is so rude and venomous to inmates. He hates her. What gives one man the right to have authority over another? Is it just nature? Survival of the fittest? The fittest being the fat, rich, selfish, and power hungry.

As Isaac sits on a bench waiting for his turn to be strip searched and led back to chow and then the cell block, Ox comes marching out of the locker room wearing a beefy, goofy grin, "I got busted, Isaac." Two guards follow him, "They caught me bringing in tobacco. Back downtown to regular county."

"That sucks," Isaac shakes his head.

The guards escort Ox off down a long hall.

Isaac goes through the routine, strip search, and back to the cafeteria to eat. A peanut butter and jelly sandwich tonight. He picks it up off his tray and the sandwich is sludge. Hot for some reason, the bread drips off his fingers with the peanut butter and jelly. He drops it back on the tray, disgusted, wiping his hand clean with a napkin. He drinks his cup of coffee and eats mashed potatoes.

The guards lead him back to the cell block. He's tired. Sore from work.

A handful of inmates sit around a metal table bolted to the concrete floor playing the board game Monopoly, laughing, joking, bragging about their cocks, and all the women and good times they've had partying and how much more fun, sex, and partying they were going to have once they are released from jail.

A trio of inmates get into a shouting match over the television. It is a very important argument. Which station should the television be on, which television show should they be watching. This ruckus brings the guards in to settle them down. Television privileges are revoked for the rest of the night.

Isaac tries to focus on another trashy romance novel. "Lights out." A guard announced through speakers in the walls through the cell block. Lights out really means dim the lights. They don't get to sleep in total darkness, the cameras and guards need to be able to see the inmates all through the night. Make sure there is no contraband, fighting, or butt fucking.

Isaac rips the worn out romance novel in half, down the middle of the spine. Other inmates lie in their bunks whispering, some snoring. Some of the whispering stops when the two halves of the romance novel hit the concrete floor on either side of Isaac's bunk. He drops out of bed as well. The floor is cold on his bare feet. The inmate in the bunk below him gives him a confused look.

Isaac understands the old man kicking the door. He understands the old man being an alcoholic. He understands people wanting to escape this fucked up world. He understands the world of humanity is broken. Designed for the rich to stay rich and keep the lower classes as slaves to various degrees depending upon a person's level of poverty. No matter how you spin it, the truth is the truth. He understands Ox. He understands why there are so many people locked up in jails and prisons. He understands why so many people are lost and trying to find ways to escape through myriad addictions and vises, sex, drugs, alcohol, sports, religion, shopping, money, porn, video games, television, internet, whatever their drug of choice. Whatever makes them numb and forget. Whatever makes them deny the situation they live in. Whatever helps them escape this man made hell we're all trapped in. Call it government and corporation, two great evil slavers.

The pain of humanity is tearing the world apart. The world spirit. It's screaming in pain so loud it hurts Isaac's brain, his mind, his soul. He can see only one way. To start from scratch. Mother Earth will outlive humanity by a very, very long time. The scraps of what was humanity will give birth to the new race, the replacement of the human race. That is the way of nature, the eternal recycling, nothing destroyed, only transformed. It's happened before. Innumerable times. Humans were not the first dominant race on the planet or the first of Earth's long history of civilizations.

It's a spiritual evolution spread out over aeons. It is time to wipe the slate clean. We are born of cosmic dust. That is where all life comes from, all matter, all energy, from the original spiraling cosmic serpent of dust. The seeds of everything, all life. It's time for the rise of the next race.

Always a painful transition, the labor pains of birth, the pangs of death. Death. Birth. Death. Birth. Death. Birth. Never ending.

There are remnants and artifacts of all the races that existed on the Earth before humans.

Ancient, forgotten fingerprints of risen and fallen civilizations. The Earth is not the only planetary intelligence in the universe, she has many godly siblings, always creating more gods with the sperm and eggs of cosmic dust. Making gods is an art and a craft.

Isaac Myrick knows what he will do now. It started with existential loss and pain, the transformation began with the sting of black sigils written all over his body as he fell further into defiance and struggles with meaningless laws and rules. It's all led up to this moment. This epiphany. He has found his calling and in this moment knows who and what he is. He will be one of the remnants of the human race, a witness and advocate of the new and coming race. Isaac will watch humanity die, forlorn, wishing there was another way, but he must be strong. He must endure. Every moment of his life, of his lives, has been building to this moment in time.

A few of the inmates give Isaac curious looks from their beds as he walks toward the shower room, taking off his shirt. He leaves the black and white striped jail clothes on the floor at the door-less doorway of the shower room. It's against the rules to shower after lights out.

"What the hell are you doing?" Wide eyed, bodybuilding, poker playing Sandy asks Isaac with a whisper of concern from his bunk near the shower room. Blue eyed Sandy is Isaac's other soldier. Sandy feels something odd in his friend's behavior.

Half the supposedly sleeping inmates have their heads off their pillows excited for the building drama that will unfold when the guards come in to get Isaac out of the showers.

In a loud proclamation, for all the inmates and guards to hear through their cameras Isaac answers with the confidence of Moses having just been instructed by Yahweh, "Tell the angels to beware! I am no longer afraid!"

With finality and nudity Isaac disappears into the darkness of the shower room.

Behind him the cell block is filled with hushed, excited whispers and giggles.

They hear the showers turned on. Not just one but all of the showers. Soon a cloud of steady steam comes from the shower rooms. Inside the shower room the inmates can hear Isaac chanting in what sounds partially English, partially gibberish, or maybe some language none of them recognize. Sandy swears he hears Isaac say something about baptism.

The elder Native American trustee gets out of his lower bunk bed. "This is not a good thing," his voice filled with trepidation. The younger Native Americans come to his side, they stand near the shut off television, afraid, nervous, and supportive of their elder. Something from their traditional ways speaks to them all in their hearts.

Sandy sits up in his bed, wishing Ox were there, he doesn't know what's going on. Isaac has always been weird, lady killer weird, not this bizarre kind of weird.

More inmates rise as the steam from the shower room thickens like a fog growing out of the shower room entrances. The inmates generally stick to race as they get up. Whites with whites. Mexicans with Mexicans. African Americans with African Americans. They all feel something rising within themselves. Something primal. Safety in numbers. The cell block gets warmer with humidity.

"What's going on?" An inmate in glasses and a beak of a nose shouts, breaking everyone's mesmerized, fearful silence as they stare at the shower room entrances. At that moment, before anyone can answer him, the lights of the whole cell block click on. Guards rush through a door entering the cell block as inmates' eyes adjust to the sudden burst of light.

"Damn," Sandy mutters, staying in his bunk, knowing things are about to get bad for Isaac.

"Everyone back to your bunks!" One of the half dozen guards orders the inmates. Most of them comply, all keeping their eyes on the action. Six guards enter the shower room with billy clubs in their hands.

All the inmates hear the sounds of fighting and cursing from the shower rooms. No one can see what's happening but it sounds brutal.

Sandy hops out of his bunk to go aid Isaac, walking hesitant to the shower room. Another bunked inmate with long hair and a goatee warns Sandy, "Don't do it, dude."

Sandy nods and stands outside the shower room, unsure what to do.

Isaac's chanting had stopped with the entrance of the guards. Now all is silent in the shower room except for the sound of the running water. The inmates are as silent, still as staring stones.

Why haven't the guards brought Isaac out? That's what they're all wondering. That many guards should have taken Isaac down without much effort.

Not a peep from a single inmate as they watch the nude, black tattoo covered Isaac Myrick walk out of the showers dripping from head to toe in blood and water. It's a sight none that survives the night will forget. Not the inmates nor the guards on the other side of the security cameras. Isaac holds a billy club dripping with blood in each hand, his arms dangling at his sides.

"Isaac?" Sandy whispers in shock, standing closer to Isaac than anyone else in the cell block.

"No!" Isaac announces to all present. Outside the cell block more jail guards are gathering and awaiting reinforcements. "I am no longer Isaac. I am the dragon Pariah. I am the harbinger of the coming race."

Sandy drops to his knees, head bowed. Sandy has known Isaac for many years and seen him do many things in life. A professional. Husband of a nuclear family. To lose it all and rise from the ashes a drug lord. He's seen him paint and draw, an artist and poet. So many things that made Isaac seem such a unique and talented man. Now he knows he sees a blood covered messiah before him. Sandy has no doubts. He is a convert. A disciple of Pariah.

Pariah steps forth and begins killing inmates, one after another, bashing in their skulls with the billy clubs. Sandy stays on his knees, trembling with fervor and fear. Most of the inmates fight back but Pariah seems unstoppable. None are able to lay a hand on him.

Pariah looks and points with a blood-covered club to the elder Native American man and his circle of younger inmates, "Keep your people right there in the corner and you will all live through the night."

The old man nods and the younger one huddles around him by the television, avoiding the bloody, whirling clubs and the killing machine calling itself Pariah. The elder Native American notices Pariah only seems to be killing the racist and bigot inmates or the ones who have done cruel things to each other in the cell block, but he does it with an inhuman zeal in his eyes, like a man possessed.

More guards charge into the cell block, this time in full riot gear, guns, tasers, helmets, and plastic shields. Pariah disarms and massacres them all. It's a quick slaughter all caught on the security cameras.

When the violence is finally over about half the inmates are dead, and all the guards.

Pariah stands huffing in the center of the bloodbath, arming himself with guns and riot gear, dressing in a dead guard's uniform. "This is an act of war," Pariah addresses the survivors and the cameras, "Nothing less. The age of man is at its end."

The surviving inmates remain silent, staring in horror at the blood splattered across the floor and bunks, the dozens of dead, the still steaming showers. They stay as far back away from Pariah as they can. All except Sandy.

Pariah looks to the old Native American man, "Gather your people. Prepare them. Unite the tribes. Go now," he points a club to the open cell block door, "before police arrive. The Grandfather guides you. Time is short and war has begun."

The old man nods again and does as Pariah bids with the other Native Americans following him out.

Pariah looks to his old friend, Sandy, "I will find you when it is time." He looks to all the other inmates, the white, black, Mexican, and Asian, "I suggest you all leave. They will likely have the National Guard with them. Those of you afraid of freedom, stay here, I'm sure they will be happy to lock you back up. Those who leave, go find your tribes."

"What about me?" Sandy is still on his knees.

Pariah smiles, "Do what you will."

With that final statement Pariah exits the cell block and jail.

Sandy stays at the jail. Not because he's afraid of freedom, but because he only has two weeks left to serve and he will be released legally.

After two weeks Sandy is released. In the news the incident at the jail is reported as a riot, not the work of one man. The news says nothing about Pariah, but Isaac Myrick is a most wanted man, along with all the others that escaped that night. After the "riot" all the inmates were either released or transferred to other jails. There is a nationwide manhunt for Isaac. Sandy doesn't think they'll find him because he knows Isaac Myrick died that day and gave birth to Pariah.

Pariah. The Dragon. The harbinger of the coming race. He is out there somewhere working in secrecy toward the birth of a new race. The people who will one day take the place of humans. Pariah knows the humans had their chance, not unlike the other races that came before them. It is a natural progression. A biological and spiritual experience. He is not alone. There are others working toward the same goal as him. He is their Messiah, their harbinger.

Pariah communes with the old ones, the remnants of the forgotten races.

Eyes Afire

"There is a conspiracy theory. The grand theory. More than theory. There is a secret government ruling the world. This arrogant entity sits upon the world laughing at us all as it manipulates us with a practiced ease. Ever watching we slaves. It laughs because people don't believe and can't fathom its existence. A great and powerful mind moving us at its whim. It has a plan. It has no respect for us, human beings. Or at least average humans. It has incomprehensible patience and longevity. Judging itself superior to ordinary humans. Working to keep us ordinary and average by far.

"This secret government is one side of a duality. Truly a trinity with the third subtle faction balancing between the two warring factions, but that is not what I'm here to talk about. I'm talking about the evil, satanic secret government.

"It's something like an alien parasite feeding off of humanity. Maybe reptilians like the old soccer player preaches irrationally. It's a little bit like dog-sized, invisible cockroach-shrimp hybrid aliens latched to the back of human necks, sucking out spinal fluid day and night. It's a lot like a gigantic, metallic brain running things incognito, using money as an energy source to tame and control plebeians. Unseen, unbelieved. Sensitive psychics pick up on its existence, confused by the brush with this monster that has existed since before humankind. Magi and maestros sometimes discover the phantom menace. One knows a grand magician if they have truly uncovered this forbidden knowledge. Some actually join the ranks and hierarchy of the hidden government. They call it ascension, their opponents call it descending. Any magician that is a non-believer is either not far advanced in the art or a charlatan. If they are atheists you know they are ignorant. If they are the paradox of atheist and theist, know they are very advanced. If they have gone full circle to atheism and back to spirituality, they may be man-gods. Illuminated. Immortal. Illuminati. The Illuminatus are real! And they are heroic champions of light! They are not the secret government, as so often alleged. That is disinformation. Propaganda. They are men and women either like or on their way to becoming the mighty magi and maestros!

"There was a brilliant surge in the Eighteenth Century, the Enlightenment. A successful striving of humanity. A bright leap in the evolution of human consciousness. Bringing the fire of the sun to the masses. There was so much potential, so many Illuminati leaving their marks upon the world and in the history books. Cagliostro. St. Germain. Cassanova. Adam Weishaupt. Thomas Paine. Franz Mesmer. Benjamin Franklin. To name but a few. The pendulum swung fully to one side. The secret history is so very long and awakening. It is common knowledge among the clandestine but known exoterically as myths, legends, fairy tales, and the lay side of religions.

"The secret government is a genius mathematician. It knows the universe is made of thought and structured with numbers. The secret government is in control. The people do and think what they are told to do and think. The people don't want to hear, believe, or admit they have been hoodwinked, that they are not free thinkers, that their wills are stifled." The elderly man finished his introduction with an enthusiastic twinkle in his eye.

"And who the hell are you?" Gizzard Slut exasperates, an expression of disgust, like the strange old man is a contagious leper. Her cleavage bragging leather is tight, arms covered in colorful tattoos, and thick black eyeliner like an ancient Egyptian goddess making her pale skin seem milk white. She is a punk rock and black metal goddess. Worshiped by fans internationally, even more so since the death of Atticus Killroy. Black hair long, gel and spikes, dyed and streaked with crimson, violet, and jade. Black knee high boots with stiletto heels sharp enough to kill a man.

Gizzard Slut stands on a small stage, posing like an anarchist diva in front of a microphone stand. A bass guitar is cradled in one arm, hanging from a shoulder strap. She is the lead vocalist in a new punk metal band called *Dead Christians*. Standing like sentinels behind her on the stage are the guitar player, Reverend Erroneous, and the drummer, Rex Ragnarok (her ex-lover). Together the trio make up *Dead Christians*. They're currently looking for another guitar player and maybe another bass.

The three used to be in a black metal band on the rise called *Daimon Rapist* until their lead singer and front man, Atticus Killroy, committed suicide. The band decided to go on without Atticus, but out of respect for him they changed their name and style. *Daimon Rapist's* albums have been selling outrageously since his death. Atticus Killroy has become a legend, dying at the age of 27.

Standing shirtless at his drum kit Rev. Erroneus gives Rex a look from behind his long, silk black hair that says he doesn't trust the old man. Rex gives a slight nod of agreement.

The strange old man who interrupted the band's rehearsal is neatly dressed in an expensive black suit and tie with a white shirt. He gives a perk smile with the delivery of his answer to Gizzard Slut's inquiry, "I apologize, my dear, for what must seem random ranting. My name is Atla. You can think of me as your holy guardian angel if you'd like. A lowly, bleeding soldier in this sorrowful and unknown war. These things I tell you are important to know. You are a spearhead of anarchy, but that edge must be sharpened and polished. A potential zeitgeist to be reckoned with, if things play out the way we've planned all these years."

"You want an autograph or something, old dude?" Rex takes a step in the old man's direction giving a show of protection toward Gizzard.

Looking up at her with wonder in his eyes from the edge of the waist high stage, Atla responds, "Will you sign it, Cora Temple?"

Gizzard Slut's blue eyes grow wide with surprise and suspicion. Her real name is not public knowledge, "Who the hell are you?"

The musical trinity are on their first U. S. tour together, promoting *Dead Christians* their self titled first album. Atticus killed himself just before *Daimon Rapist* was scheduled to tour the U. S. Rex Ragnarok and Reverend Erroneous are both from Norway, Atticus Killroy and Gizzard Slut are both Americans. The band is rehearsing for the first show of this tour. *The Kill Everyone Tour*. It's a special show because it's not only the first date of the tour but it's also the home town of both Atticus and Gizzard. Applegate, South Dakota. They left for Norway together at the end of summer after graduating high school, leaving the punk rock band *Jesus Wept*. Gizzard Slut suddenly thinks this old man must be someone from her past but she can't place him.

"This is a private rehearsal," Gizzard Slut growls into the microphone to sound more intimidating, a buffer between her and the old man. "Someone get the geezer out of here. Please."

The smug club manager sporting a pencil thin mustache and sharp, pointy nose comes over with a bulky skinhead bouncer in combat boots and suspenders to escort the old man out of the building. The bouncer takes the old man roughly by the arm without a hint of emotion. Atla doesn't cooperate. "Come on," the bouncer says as he ushers the elder toward the exit.

With youthfulness in his bright eyes and an entertained grin, Atla does not lift his eyes from Gizzard Slut until he is shoved rudely out the door and into the sunlight. His last words are, "Have you come home for war, dear Cora?" Outside Atla squints as his eyes adjust after having been in the dim lighting of the night club.

Inside Gizzard Slut purrs into the microphone, "Alright, come on. Let's do it. Right now."

And the band breaks into a cover of the song *Hook in Mouth* by *Megadeth*.

"What?"

"What?"

"What did you say?"

"We're inside of the skull of the secret government," Atla explains with a chummy smile, "It's kind of like an evil spirit that passes through people, ignorant that they have been influenced."

She's not in the night club anymore. She's in a dark, white domed room with the mysterious old Atla. Gizzard Slut reaches upward with her slender fingers, caressing the white, smooth, curve of the wall, intrigued, confused. How did she get here? Wasn't she just rehearsing? No. They finished rehearsing. She was just on stage, opening with their first song. The show sold out. Why is she here? Did she black out? Is she dreaming? Hallucinating?

"Shhh," Gizzard Slut holds her index finger centered just below her nose. Her face is slack with pleasure. The crowd and the music fall silent and the lights go out. They've just finished their second song. She can feel the energy and excitement of the crowd. Everything is dark except a single spotlight hot on her.

Waiting.

Anticipating.

The band and crowd are in sync and euphoric, intense. There is a fourth band member on stage with them. A second guitar player. A local Applegate musician. She knew him from high school and brought him in just today as a surprise. He's an unknown guitar god.

Waiting.

Dim lights grow slowly.

Waiting for what?

Atla. Who are you?

Rex and Erroneous exchange a look of concern. Gizzard Slut is not saying anything or introducing the next song. She is silent. Looks like she's praying at the microphone. They both wonder if she's on dope. She's not.

The crowd grows restless.

"Give me something," Gizzard Slut suddenly cuts the silence open. Her deft fingers begin playing her bass guitar. A hypnotic rhythm something like *Queen's Another One Bites the Dust*. It's a song the rest of the band doesn't recognize, they realize she is suddenly just jamming, free styling. Both guitars and the drums find their place, following the lead of her bass guitar. She looks mesmerized, eyes mostly closed, head tilted to one side with a flirtatious, far out smile. Fingers strumming her new hot pink instrument. The band gets caught up in this random musical exploration. Like a bunch of hippies jamming, Rex thinks for a moment, before drowning in the music. All together now.

Gizzard Slut sways back and forth with the music. The audience mimics her movement. Stage lights flicker and spin through smoke and fog. The rhythm and music goes on hypnotic forever. On and on and on. So alien, so arcane, so long it seems to lull the band and audience into a trance. The audience sway as a single entity. Their consciousness elevates. It reaches the point they all feel like they are about to scream and explode. They drone on for twenty minutes in all. Some call it temporary madness. Some call it an altered state of consciousness. They all feel the buzz and scream.

"A thousand years," Gizzard Slut sings melodically into the microphone, relieving everyone, "My name is Cora Temple," she whispers. She begins to sing another cover song. *Werewolf* by *CocoRosie*. The first album of *Dead Christians* is all cover songs but one song.

"My soul was filled with crystal light," Gizzard Slut sings. Looking out through the crowd before her, she focuses on the old man in the front row. The strange old man. Atla is back. He is skinny and shirtless, swaying and mesmerized with the rest of the mob. Her eyes flutter and she sings, tilting her head back, remembering being born.

She sees Atla's lips move, forming silent words, "My voice speaks volumes."

"He's a black magic wielder, some say a witch," she sings angelically, returning to her birth. Conception.

This is her birth:

A six winged angel, mighty, majestic, immortal, radiating. Pulsating divine light.

"We are all slivers of divine light," she explains into the microphone as the song ends. The new song begins.

She is light. Surrounded by light. Soul. Myriad souls gathered in a paradise. Surrounded by friends, family, love. Home. She belongs. Knows who she is. What she is.

The angel's voice booms with almighty confidence and respect, "I seek one with these qualities." The list of qualities passes among the aware like a thought.

"Achtariel," Gizzard Slut pleads to the many winged angel who has called her forth, "I do not wish to go. This is my home."

Neither the archangel Achtariel (who does not ordinarily summon souls for incarnation but in rare circumstances) or what is to be Cora Temple are male or female. They are neither and both.

Achtariel answers, lamenting, "You must experience."

As quick as that the light that is the six winged archangel reaches out to her single snowflake soul and she finds herself in the darkness of her new mother's womb.

In the beginning of her warm gestation she still remembers everything but as the fetus develops memories fade. The brain grows, cutting off akasic access like a safety valve turning tighter to filter and close off the knowledge. It becomes hidden knowledge. Full knowledge is magical.

Moments before birth she is only in amnesiac darkness, everything remaining is washed away with a burst of birthing light and eyes opening into the world of flesh and earth.

Cora Temple lets out a hysterical, primal scream at the end of another cover song. *Texas Radio and the Big Beat* by *the Doors*. The audience goes mad with delight. The band is now frantic with the intoxication of the music, no longer mere musicians, but maestros.

Atla leads the crowd like the piped piper, like a fanatic prophet, in a snake dance procession. The snake's tongue darting in and out between reptilian lips. Atla has become the forked tongue leading the mob, its long, slithering body.

"Will you bleed for me, darling?" Cora sings. She begins to speak in tongues as her eyes roll back. Holy fire burns inside her body, wet with fever sweat.

Atla bows and kneels and cheers before her, the crowd follows.

Rex and the other band members begin to sing, "We love our audience! We love our audience! We love our audience!"

"We must go to the desert," Cora snaps, ending her delirious tongues. "Prepare for the night. A long eclipse. Black and vile."

Now Cora recognizes, remembers Atla. Not the old shell of the man, but the ancient soul within, the aura glowing about, the merkabah chariot. She first met him in Atlantis. He went by another name then. He was her son. She remembers him and why he is here now. To oppose the devils. The secret government. And the greatest adversary. The same evil which destroyed Atlantis. She longs for the home and serenity of death, but duty keeps her always alive.

Looking back over her shoulder at the rest of the band she recognizes them from nearly a millennium ago. Knights Templar who fought at her side in Jerusalem.

Cora Temple wakes in her hotel room naked, in bed, sheets cold and wet with sweat. The lights are out. Her eyes see well in the night. She rises and makes her way to the black hole of the bathroom. With the flick of a switch the white light drives out darkness.

Cora stands weary and bare before the mirror, looking into the reflection of her eyes afire, whispering, "I don't know what's real any more."

There is fear in her alluring eyes. Dreams and reality. It's all a dream. The illusion. Brahma. A purposeful mirage.

In existence, above the world, there is a gargantuan, all seeing eye observing her, big brother in the sky. A masculine god stirred by her nudity. This god's will be done.

She lay back down on the hotel room bed with her legs spread like an altar, wishing Atla were real to break this god's sudden possession of her. The deity, Cora's mind, and the dreams are one, mingled as she touches herself sensually. This is how they have sex. Cora Temple and this unseen god.

The nameless god in the akasic thrusting into her like a mighty bull overcome with lust. Both are overcome in a long span of orgasm, an event horizon. When it is over the unnameable god curls into a fetal position on the floor at her feet dangling off the bed, weeping as it slowly fades away.

Cora, no longer Gizzard Slut, regretful of the churches she burned down, sits around a table with several other people in the latter half of the Nineteenth Century. They are spiritualists and theosophists. Cora, who was not Cora in this other linear life, leads the gathering, channeling spirits. A spirit speaks through her with a deep, masculine voice, a thick English accent. A dead man. Little people with rainbow butterfly wings playfully flutter about her.

There is a pop and a flash. One of the people present is photographing the fairies. She was Harriet Kelly and she thought she was a charlatan until the Englishman came into her and the fairies appeared.

Tilting her head back, both Harriet and her wood chair fall back into vertigo.

Cora falls off the hotel room bed, landing roughly on the carpet. Still naked and lazy from the sex. Surprisingly relaxed. Her mind melting.

A knock at the door.

It's the middle of the night, between first and second sleep. Who could it be?

She opens the door, presenting herself tall and proud as a goddess. Followed by insecure hesitation.

Old man Atla stands smiling in the doorway with friendly, soft, wrinkled eyes.

Cora wanders back to the bed, unashamed of her body and the cool liquid running down her inner thigh. As she climbs on the bed, she remembers that Atla was the photographer. Just a friend then. In Jerusalem he was an Assassin. And during the second world war he was her sister.

"How are you, Cora?" Atla asks in a familiar voice as he sits in a chair near the blank television.

"Ugly on the inside," she answers. "Afraid of the darkness inside of me. I know what I'm capable of. Afraid I will fuck everything up again. I know I'm broken. Everything is so delicate. So difficult to balance." Tears stream from her pretty eyes. "I don't want to lose the good things in life. I'm in love. I don't want to screw it up. I feel sick because I know who I am! I wish I was better! A better person! God, save me!"

Atla looks at her sadly.

"Who are you this time?" She demands, lashing out, "Why have you waited until the end to come to me this time?" She angrily wipes tears away. Mascara running down to her cheeks.

"I'm no one of significance," Atla shrugs, "I came when it was time."

Cora nods and sniffles.

Atla speaks, "You are feeling the weakness of flesh. The tug of devils."

Cora takes a deep breath and sighs, "I'm so tired, Atla. I don't think I can do this anymore. Not alone. I want death. Don't make me stay in this world. I miss bliss."

"It is our duty to suffer, my love."

"To what end?" Cora snaps with a razor fire in her voice.

"The dream is over," Atla whispers, "Full circle and death is at the door."

Another knock at the hotel room door making Atla's point startles Cora. The door has her full attention for a moment as she wonders who is there. When she looks back at the chair Atla is gone.

Cora wraps herself in a blanket, feeling cold now, staring at the door. Everything seems so silent.

She remembers being with Atla in the Dark Ages in a place that is called France now. Atla was her wife then, and she was his husband. Betrayed by the Carolingians. Full circle? Cora and Atla? These are their secret names. The names of their immortal souls.

Another knock at the door. This time a knock of impatience followed by the voice of Rex, "I'll do everything I can to help you get in tonight, Gizzard."

She thinks he's probably hoping to get laid. He never gives up. She thought he was done. Getting romantic with Rex was a mistake. She shouldn't have ever started sleeping with him. He gets too attached. It was just sex. Just a good time. She was lonely and Atticus didn't want her. Turns out he was a homosexual. She hadn't had sex with anyone since her best friend Atticus died until the god tonight.

Rex doesn't get it. She likes him as a friend and nothing more. She's just not attracted to him. With an annoyed huff she journeys from the bed to the door. When the door is opened her eyes widen in horror at the figure before her. It is not Rex Ragnarok.

And if we sit perfectly still, what is the meaning of life? If we are still and silent, what is the purpose? Why do we live? It is not to work, slave, and make money. Procreation and pleasure? To not suffer alone? There is something elusive to the entire experience of existence. One grand theme. A theory of everything. What is the purpose of creation? Why is it a mystery? What is the creator's motivation? What is the reason for the source of it all? The original essence which all springs from. Answer these questions and you've answered all questions. Maybe someday when humans learn to think more. To reason more. God as omnipotence and perfection. If this is so, then creation is perfect. Existence is perfect. Everything is as it should be, as it was meant to be. We don't understand suffering and death, but if God is perfect, it must have meaning. If God is good, then it is not for nothing. Is it to give birth to others? Other gods? Companions? Love?

Standing like a frightening scarecrow at the hotel room door before Cora Temple is the angel of death Samael. The vision of Samael is like a stunning, piercing shriek that feels as if it rips eardrums and wounds the heart of the universe, paralyzing all in sight with a spiritual deafness.

The fallen archangel's physical appearance is hidden beneath a ritualistic costume in shades light brown, tan, and black. All rough cloth with a mask marked with a blank expression, slanted eyes, black ivory. Upon his head like the crown of a king are great antlers, almost like tree branches. The tan, thick threaded cloth is draped about him like a cloak. His arms are thin, fingers seem fragile, legs wrapped in strips of black cloth.

Cora stumbles back from the angel of death, retreating back to the bed.

Samael's wings spread after he enters the room and the door shuts softly behind him of it's own accord.

Cora wonders who she really is, sitting before the angel of death. She lets the blanket fall, giving up. The might of Samael is like a shadow blocking out the sun. Reality ripples around the archangel like a stone thrown in oily, swirling rainbow water.

Is she Cora Temple? Gizzard Slut? Harriet? Any one of her queer memories of linear lives? People would say past lives, but she knows time is a part of the grand illusion. All exists always, consciousness splinters into a trillion eyes. She remembers her and Atla living in a world called Valar. They were both elves instead of humans. She has another memory of being an eagle.

Cowering before the radiation of Samael as the angel reaches for her with the touch of death, she knows she is about to end.

"No!" Atla defies the ancient archangel, suddenly appearing as quickly as he vanishes.

Both Samael and Cora look over to the reappearing old man. The old man steps between the angel of death and Cora. Samael's icy fingertips touch Atla's chest, bringing a wave of death.

Atla gasps, clutching at his heart, the agony apparent on his face. "You will not... take her."

Samael hisses in frustration and fades from sight, his cloak spinning in a disintegrating whirlwind.

"Atla!" Cora cries out, reaching to the dying man, wanting to save him with every fiber of her being, but retracts with a sudden pain in her belly. She feels something growing inside of her. Holding her stomach with both hands, she sits back on the bed, looking down at Atla on the floor, "What's happening?"

The old man gazes up at her, gasping like a fish out of water, drowning in air. His eyes roll back and his body stiffens with death.

Cora rolls back onto the bed. She knows what it is. A programming. A pregnancy. The baby inside of her is growing at an extraordinary rate, the sudden expansion of her abdomen, stretching the skin is painful.

Cora looks at her stomach, hands cupped around it. She is already at a full term pregnancy. "I am the temple," she whispers, sweating, panting, grunting in pain, through rapid contractions. The baby is coming.

She is moaning on the bed. Above her instead of the hotel room's speckled popcorn ceiling she sees a canopy of stars. Twinkling diamonds wandering the vast cold, black of space. Ghosts in the night sky. The light of stars long ago extinguished. Her blood drips off the edge of the bed. Beneath the bed a hand reaches out holding a gold chalice, catching the scarlet drops.

Cora groans. The birth is quick. The infant cries. She holds it wet and fresh from God in her arms.

"We've cheated death, little one," Cora says to her child in a loving, motherly voice.

The newborn coos.

She recognizes Atla in the infant's eyes just as her divine amnesia recurs.

In Noctus Sol

    Young Karl Barnes daydreams out the window as his family drives home on a highway returning from his great-grandmother's house. It's an hour long drive. Looking out the window at the ditches and telephone poles zooming by along the edge of the highway Karl imagines himself on a sleek black motorcycle driving alongside his family's car. His imaginary self is dressed in all black leather with a glossy ebony helmet and visor. Black leather gloves and matching boots. He rides in and out of the ditches, ramping and jumping the cycle over the approaches. Skilled and fearless like the motorcyclists he's seen at the circus this last spring.

    His younger brother Kurtis is snoring in the seat next to Karl with a pile full of colorful superhero action figures in his lap. The emerald Green Lantern still clutched in one small hand and the red and blue Superman in the other. The brothers are three years apart in age, riding in the backseat of the family car.

    Their stepfather Terry Langley is driving and their mother Katrina is silent next to him, enjoying the country scenery.

    Grandma Candace and Uncle Floyd didn't come along for the trip on this visit. They often do, but Grandma Candace had some volunteer work she had committed to at the church and Uncle Floyd wanted to stay home alone. Great-grandmother's name is Ellen Rothenberg. Karl likes her alot. She speaks with a thick German accent and often tells him stories about his family and life in Germany many years ago. Karl likes old things. Sometimes he wishes he was born in the olden days.

    Grandma Candace and Uncle Floyd not taking trips to Minnesota to visit Grandman Ellen is one of the many changes that has come along with their stepfather Terry. At first Karl was excited to have a stepfather, but that changed fast. Everything seems to be changing since his mom married Terry. Karl doesn't like Terry and both he and Kurtis are afraid of him. Terry is never nice, even though Karl does try to do whatever he can to make Terry happy and earn his approval, but never seems to succeed. No matter what Karl does, it doesn't seem to make Terry happy. It's almost like Terry gets jealous when Katrina gives either of her sons attention.

    When he was cleaning his room the other day Karl got down on his hands and knees to pick all the lint from the carpet just like Terry had told him to, but Terry still yelled at him, saying it wasn't good enough. Karl was too afraid to ask why he couldn't use the vacuum.

    Karl wishes his mom and dad would get back together. He misses his dad alot. Karl likes to watch the television show *Magnum PI* because Tom Selleck reminds him of his dad. Karl and Kurtis get to visit their dad one weekend a month, but it's not the same. Their dad is remarried and seems more concerned with his new family. Their stepmother isn't very nice to them when they're there and they end up spending most of the time in the basement watching movies alone without their dad.

    Terry doesn't like their dad and gets mad whenever Karl or Kurtis talk about him. Terry yells alot. He's loud, even when he's just talking. And he's tall. Lanky, with wire rim glasses, black curly hair and beard with big, buggy eyes. He's a carpet layer by trade. Terry and their mom argue alot.

Even though Karl is afraid of Terry he feels worse for his little brother. Terry seems to pick on Kurtis more than Karl. Maybe because he's younger, quieter, still chubby with baby fat. Whatever the reason, Kurtis gets grounded more and way more spankings. Bare handed or with the belt. Karl wishes Terry would just go away forever as a song about 'you and me and a dog named Boo' plays on the car's radio.

That catches Karl's attention. A dog named Boo. What a good name for a dog. Karl thinks about the dog they used to have. His name was Spot. Last winter Spot froze to death in a blizzard. Terry left him outside in his doghouse. He said he didn't mean to but Karl has never believed that. It makes Karl sad to think about Spot.

Karl looks back out the window imagining himself on the motorcycle again, but as he turns his head away, as everyone in the vehicle moves out of his line of sight, Karl thinks about that. What if nobody else is real? What if when he turns his head away everyone else shuts down. They stop working and moving. Just turn off like robots. Like a grand conspiracy and everyone else in the world is just a robot that powers down when Karl isn't looking and they start back up when he looks at them. Everyone else in the world are just robots acting for Karl. They only come alive with movement when he can see them. Why would they do that? Why the pretending?

That night they get home to Grandma Candace's house at the top of the hill on North Main Street. It's late. Dark outside. Terry tells Katrina that Karl and Kurtis need to go straight to bed. And they do. Katrina carries Kurtis upstairs and puts him to bed. He doesn't wake up, so sound asleep.

Karl is a little nervous with Kurtis already asleep. The bedroom they are staying in at the front of the house upstairs is scary even when it's not night time. There is a ceiling attic in the closet and a second attic door on the side of the closet wall. A very short, wide hallway connects the boys room with Uncle Floyd's room. There is an attic door in that hallway wall too. Karl wonders why the house needs three attics. He remembers his grandma calling them crawl spaces once, but they're attics to Karl and his younger brother.

One attic is frightening enough.

Grandmother Candace's house is big and old. They all moved in with her and Uncle Floyd only a month ago when Terry lost his job. Karl and Kurtis are both happy to be living with Grandma Candace and Uncle Floyd. It would be better if Terry wasn't there. Karl and Kurtis always have fun playing with Uncle Floyd.

Uncle Floyd has an entire imaginary town spread out across his bedroom floor. Toy cars and farm equipment. Houses made of Lincoln Logs. Grown ups say Uncle Floyd is slow. He cried once when one of the neighborhood kids called him retarded. That upset Karl last summer. Karl understands that Uncle Floyd doesn't act like other grown ups. He acts like one of the kids.

Uncle Floyd is not sleeping in his room right now. He's downstairs with the other grownups. Karl wouldn't be as afraid of the dark if Floyd was in his room or if Kurtis was awake.

Karl lies very still in the dark listening to the quiet. Why can't he hear the grownups talking downstairs? Most nights he can. At least here an occasional laugh or something. It's so very dark up here. Some of the shadows seem thicker, more black than the others. Shadows seem to overlap in places making them seem darker than dark.

Karl closes his eyes to pretend he's asleep to trick whatever unknown thing is watching him from those triple dark shadows. What is watching him? There is something there. Karl can feel it in his heart and soul and bones. Something is there hidden in the darkness. A ghost. Something like a ghost. It's always there. Always watching. No matter if it's day or night. No matter what room of the house Karl is in. This room and the basement are the worst. It's something only felt inside. The feeling of being watched.

Karl hears the door at the bottom of the stairs open and close. Uncle Floyd must be coming up to go to bed. Karl sits up in bed and opens his eyes with a smile of relief, looking across the short hallway into Uncle Floyd's bedroom. There are no doors in the hallway separating the rooms, only a velvet maroon curtain hanging in the doorway between Floyd's room and the hall that is pulled open to one side.

Karl grins with anticipation as he listens to Floyd's footsteps as he climbs the old creaky stairs. The sound of the footsteps reach the top of the stairs and all is silent again. It only takes a moment for the smile to melt from Karl's face as he realizes there is no one standing at the top of the stairs. Uncle Floyd did not come up. A rush of terror comes up from Karl's gut and into his heart, bringing tears to his young eyes. He quickly hides beneath a blanket and slides closer to his slumbering little brother Kurtis.

Karl lies perfectly still, trying to breathe quietly while listening for any movement, praying for the real Uncle Floyd to open the door and come up the stairs. He knows it's there. Watching. Maybe them, instead of it. A house full of ghosts. Why do they watch?

Karl doesn't remember falling asleep.

Karl is playing alone in Grandma Candace's backyard. It's a huge backyard. Long, stretching back into three sections. Stretching back to a length of more than a city block. A very private backyard. The way the trees are arranged is what divides it into three sections. The first section surrounded by trees is closest to the house, containing the white garage with a line of trees behind it, a swing set and small slide, and an old fireplace and chimney made of pink quartz.

The second section of the backyard is enclosed by a square line of trees surrounding a garden. The last and further section of the backyard is an open field of tall grass with a forest of trees at the far end leading down a steep hill forest that eventually ends at railroad tracks below.

Karl is in the first area of the backyard, playing quietly among the brown and grey trees lined behind the garage. Out here, outside the house, Karl feels something too. Something different than in the house. He feels safe out here. What he feels is still like the watchers in the house yet out here these invisible watchers aren't scary. It's more like the spirits of the trees or some kind of spying elves or faeries. Something nice and playful, if a bit mischievous. The tree spirits don't seem to express an aura of responsibility to protect Karl or anyone, they just seem friendly and curious, maybe empathetic. Not necessarily enemies of humans.

Sometimes, like this summer morning, Karl finds himself singing quietly and talking to the tree spirits with a childish innocence and naivety.

"I miss the good old days," Karl whispers to the trees, "The golden days. The way things used to be. When dad was still around and grandpa was alive. Before mom married Terry."

The boy is on his knees before a robust tree with his palms flat against the rough, jagged lines of bark.

Wind blows lightly. Leaves rustle. Sun shines down through the leaves and branches above like a shower of pale gold laser beams. Karl thinks the bark on the tree is so beautiful. All greys and browns and jagged designs like hard, long rivers frozen in wood.

"I know you're here," Karl says in his childish voice, "Why are you hiding from me? Let me see you."

He waits a moment and nothing happens. Then Karl feels a sudden chill and quiver as if something has passed through his soul.

Karl, Kurtis, and Uncle Floyd are playing in the backyard this summer afternoon after eating lunch Grandma Candace made for them. Tomato soup and grilled cheese sandwiches.

"We're going to play black hole!" Karl yells while running circles around Kurtis and Uncle Floyd.

Kurtis pretends he's holding a laser gun, shooting all around him, "The killer robots are everywhere! We're surrounded!"

"I don't want to play black hole," Uncle Floyd complains. He usually only likes to play with cars and farm toys. "I don't like outer space. I want to play the Cheryl Gang!"

"I'm sick of playing the Cheryl Gang," Karl pouts, "I'm sick of bank robbers. He continues imagining he has a laser pistol in his hand, "We're surrounded by killer robots with laser eyes and spinning razor fingers! We have to shoot our way out to get to our starship and we have to hurry because we're floating too close to the black hole! If we're caught in it's gravity we're doomed!"

"We have to get into an escape pod!" Kurtis hollers in his squeaky voice, still blasting away at robots, while running to the swing set and sitting on one of the two swings.

"Let's go!" Karl tugs on Uncle Floyd's hand. Floyd's fingernails are in need of trimming.

"I said I don't wanna play black hole or outer space," Uncle Floyd gets mad and refuses to budge.

"I tried to save him," Karl shouts to his brother, jumping on the swing next to him, "He sacrificed himself so we could live!"

"Let's make it count for something," Kurtis says, "Launch the escape pod."

"Yahoo!" Karl shouts as he and his brother begin swinging high still pretending to shoot killer robots.

"Hey, guys," a familiar young female voice sounds from the trees behind the garage. They all recognize her immediately as she crosses the line of trees into their backyard. Casey Ebner is the neighbor girl. She comes over to play almost every other day.

"Hey, Casey," Kurtis launches off the swing landing awkwardly on his feet, slipping on the grass in an attempt to show off his prowess. "We're playing black hole."

"I wanna show you guys something neat," Casey announces with delight twinkling in her eyes. Casey and Karl are the same age. Kurtis is three years younger than them, but both boys have a competitive crush on her.

"What is it," Karl asks, his curiosity tickled.

"My little brother had a worm in his stomach and it came out of his butt while he was in the bathtub today," she gives a cheerful grin.

Karl gives her a look of disgust, curling his nose.

"I wanna see," Kurtis jumps off his swing, "I wanna see! I wanna see!"

Uncle Floyd grins and giggles, rocking his head as he often does absentmindedly, like a nervous tic, "He pooped out a worm?"

"How did a worm get inside of him?" Kurtis looked confused.

"Did he eat it?" Karl asks, feeling sick to his stomach at the thought of it.

"I don't know," Casey admits, "All I know is that it's still in the bathtub right now if you want to see it."

Karl shakes his head, "I don't want to see that."

"Scaredy cat?" Casey smiles.

"Chicken," Kurtis taunts, "Bock, bock, bock!"

"No," Karl defends, "it sounds weird."

"Fine," Casey raises her nose, "Come on, Kurtis, I'll show you."

"No," Karl sighs, "I'm coming too."

    Uncle Floyd isn't allowed in Casey's house because he's slow. Karl has noticed a lot of people aren't nice to Floyd because they say he's slow. Some people say worse things than that. So Uncle Floyd sits on the back porch of Grandma Candace's house to enjoy the sun. He does that a lot. He says he likes the way the sun feels on him. Sitting in the sun. Karl always thinks that sounds dull.

    The brothers follow Casey back through the trees into her backyard and into her house through the back door. The back door leads into the kitchen. The house isn't as big as Grandma Candace's house. Casey's house is only one floor, not upstairs. The first thing Karl notices is the sour stench of the kitchen. It stinks like rotten food in the garbage hasn't been taken out in days. The air in the house is stale. None of the windows are open and it's humid inside. The shades are all drawn preventing the sunlight from coming in. It's dim and yellowish inside. The linoleum kitchen floor is dirty and stained. It doesn't look like it's been mopped before.

    Casey's home gives Karl an uncomfortable feeling. He feels sad for Casey living in such a mess.

    Grandma Candace doesn't like Casey's parents at all. She always says mean things about them. It's not unusual to hear Casey's parents screaming at each other in the night. They argue and sometimes even throw things around inside their house. At least that's what it sounds like from the outside. One night Grandma Candace drank too much wine and when she heard them fighting, Grandma Candace went next door and started pounding on their walls and windows yelling at them to shut up or she would give them something to holler about. They did get quiet that night, but the whole scene scared Karl and Kurtis.

    Casey's mom is overweight with puffy, big orange hair and round, thick rimmed glasses. She always wears a scowl on her round, flush face. Casey's dad is super skinny and bony, always wearing a stained white V-neck t-shirt every day with his hair slicked back with grease. A strand or two of hair always hangs over his forehead reminding Karl of Adolf Hitler. He wears black horn-rimmed glasses too. Karl thinks it looks like Casey's mom could probably beat up her scrawny dad.

    Casey excitedly leads the boys into the bathroom and the first thing Karl notices in here is the layered brownish, rust colored rings around the inside of the toilet, sink, and tub. There are dirty clothes and mildew scented towels scattered around the floor.

"Is it alive?" Kurtis asks with a sense of awe peering down in the tub.

"I don't know," Casey whispers, "I don't think so."

    Karl doesn't want to look but forces himself to. The worm is a long, stringy, odd, dull yellow color, floating motionless in the water. Goosebumps raise on his arms and he feels a knot tighten in his gut.

"We have to go home," Karl says.

"Are you sure?" Casey looks hurt, "I thought we could have a funeral for it."

"Sorry, we were 'spose to go inside a little bit ago. We can play tomorrow."

"Ah," Kurtis moans disappointed, "I wanna have the funeral."

"Fine," Karl says. "I'm going home before Terry gets home."

Not long later Uncle Floyd, Casey, and Kurtis stand in her back yard by the trees furthest from the house. There is a small mound of fresh dirt before the trio as they stand with solemn expressions. Kurtis made a small cross from twigs tied together with grass. The cross is planted at the top of the small black mound of earth.

"Ashes to ashes, dust to dust," Uncle Floyd says in a somber voice as the sun sets.

That evening Kurtis and Karl go to bed without complaint. Candace, Katrina, and Terry sit around the dining room table drinking coffee and visiting. Of course, Grandma Candace actually has wine in her coffee cup. In truth, Terry is drinking from a 2 liter bottle of cola like he always does.

Uncle Floyd sits in his usual corner on a green stool in the dining room sipping his coffee and mumbling to himself, occasionally giggling quietly at what no one else knows.

"I got hired at Anderson Carpet today," Terry smiles with pride, "start work on Monday."

"That's great news," Katrina reaches across the dark oak dining room table and squeezes his hand in reassurance.

"Bob Anderson seems like a good fellow," Terry nods, "An old fashioned stand up man."

"Mom," Katrina addresses Candace, "Terry and I have our Thursday night meeting to go to. Will you watch the boys for us again?"

Candace shakes her head, "There's a potluck at the church that night. I volunteered for kitchen duty. Sorry."

"It's an important meeting," Katrina laments, "Birthday night."

"Who's birthday?" Candace frowns, "Not yours or Terry's."

"No, it means it's anniversaries for people's sobriety. Our friend Perry has been sober for four years."

"I don't know who Perry is," Candace shakes her head, "If you would have asked me sooner, like on Saturday I could have done it."

"How do we feel about leaving the boys alone with Floyd?" Terry asks.

Floyd is oblivious to their conversation, lost in his own imaginary world of cars, tractors, and the Cheryl Gang. He chuckles quietly and studies his fingernails and knobby knuckles.

"I don't know about that," Katrina looks at her brother Floyd, "I mean leaving them alone with him for a few minutes while we run to the gas station or the grocery store is one thing, but leaving them alone with him for hours seems a little risky. I mean I think Karl is more responsible than Floyd. It's just not a great idea. Maybe it's best if I stay home on Thursday and you go without me."

"We can leave a phone number for Karl to call if there are any emergencies," Terry justifies.

Candace chuckles after taking a shot of wine from her coffee cup, "Last time we let Floyd use the phone home alone the police showed up. He made phone calls to restaurants all over town calling waitresses, asking them for coffee, and hugs, and how big their boobs were."

"I remember that," Katrina laughs.

Terry's face lights up with amusement.

Uncle Floyd giggles.

Suddenly there is a loud crashing ruckus upstairs. Very loud like the boys are throwing toys all around the room and down the stairs. Like they are smashing things against the walls.

"God damn it," Terry's big eyes widen in anger and the nostrils of his long nose flare as he stands from his chair.

"They're throwing my cars! My farm equipment?" Floyd stumbles from his green stool in the corner.

All four adults rush forth from the dining room through the kitchen and up the stairs.

Upstairs Katrina stands with her hand covering her mouth, frightened and at a loss for words.

Everything is in order. The room is neat and clean. All the toys, everything is right where it should be as if nothing has been touched. Terry and Katrina peek in at Karl and Kurtis and both are sound asleep as if nothing happened.

"That's strange," Terry whispers.

"How did that noise not wake them up?" Katrina is astounded.

Terry raises a black eye brow. He wants to be mad at the boys but can see it's obvious they're asleep. He doesn't know what to believe.

"You leave those boys alone," Candace scolds the unseen spirits she assumes are in the room. "Let's go back downstairs," she suggests. "Everything is fine up here. It's only restless spirits pouting for attention. Spirits can't hurt you, Terry. They're around us every day, everywhere. All around us.

Overpopulating the universe."

"So why is this spirit raising hell?" Terry asks, smug and unconvinced.

"Who knows," Candace answers, "A temper tantrum. They're just like people. They just don't have bodies. Sometimes you just have to tell them to shut the hell up."

Karl stands in the living room with his nose in the corner. Terry's orders. Karl was running through the house. Terry stopped him and pointed out that running through the house is against the rules.

Terry is watching a Clint Eastwood western on the television with a 2 liter bottle of cola at one side and a package of Oreo cookies at his other side. The credits at the beginning of the movie were just ending as Karl first put his nose in the corner as his punishment for running in the house.

Karl doesn't know how long he's been standing in the corner but it seems like eternity. Karl peeks over his shoulder at Terry who is lounging, relaxed, with his legs luxuriously propped up on the coffee table. Karl's mouth salivates for the cookies and cola. He struggles not to watch the cowboy movie too.

"Keep your nose in the corner," Terry growls, "Or you'll earn a spanking."

"Sorry," Karl meekly and obediently returns his nose to the corner.

"Don't you think it's been long enough?" Katrina pops her head in from the doorway of her mother's bedroom. The movie is half over, it's been around 45 minutes.

"Absolutely not," Terry says with authority, "You have to follow through with consequences and they need to be severe enough to leave a lasting impression to prevent the boys from repeating their negative behavior. He's staying right there at least until the movie is over. Maybe another hour."

Karl hears all this without looking away from the corner.

"I see," Katrina reluctantly agrees and disappears back into her mother's bedroom.

"Karl grows more and more restless and bored staring at the angle of the wall and listening to the western movie. Every now and then he sneaks a peek at the movie when he hears a fight or gunfire. At one point when he's peeking he sees Terry picking his nose, pulling out a white booger he rolls between his thumb and index finger a moment before wiping it on his blue jeans.

The long boredom leads to daydreams. He imagines himself walking through the wall and emerging outside in the backyard to play. Then walking further back to hide in the trees with the tree spirits.

Karl imagines his body leaving a smear of red energy behind him wherever he goes. A permanent tracer. He wonders if that really happens. If people leave behind a trace or residue of different colored energy wherever they go. Imagine if he could see that. A different color for every person. Tracers upon tracers since the beginning of time. He'd want to travel as much as he could to leave his energy trail and scent everywhere. To leave his mark in the world. So many people's paths would overlap it that it would look like rainbows of chaos.

Maybe it's true. Maybe it happens and people can't see it. Except for maybe special people with the right eyes. Maybe people are really made of energy.

Karl wishes he could sit in the corner. He's so tired of standing. He can't help peeking at the gunfights, the action scenes, but at the same time he's terrified of being caught by Terry.

Karl's forehead is pressed against the wall, trying not to fall asleep while standing.

The end credit's roll on the Clint Eastwood movie.

"Karl," Terry barks, "Come over here."

Karl starts, straightens, and obeys. He is standing at his stepfather's side in a second like an attentive soldier obeying a drill instructor.

"You did a good job," Terry smiles and ruffles Karl's hair affectionately. "I'm impressed."

Karl beams with pride, "I tried real hard."

"Here, you earned them," Terry hands Karl a pair of Oreo cookies.

"Thank you," Karl smiles, shoving a cookie in his mouth, feeling like he is finally bonding with his stepfather. "Well," Karl confesses, "I did peek once during the last gunfight because you were watching such a good movie. But I only peeked once."

Terry smirks and leans back in his chair, shaking his head in disappointment, "Karl, Karl, you have to learn. You can keep the cookie, but I told you there would be a spanking if you peeked again. What would it teach you if I didn't follow through with consequences."

Karl's eyes widened in disbelief.

"Pull your pants down and lean over my lap," Terry instructs, taking the leather belt off.

Big tears well up in Karl's eyes as he swallows the last of the cookie in his mouth and unbuttons his pants. He leans bare bottom over his stepfather's lap.

The belt makes a loud swish and slapping sound as it whips Karl's buttocks leaving red thick welts. Karl tries uselessly not to sob. The pain is too much to bear. Sharp, stinging, burning, rapid. Karl's tears plop against the living room carpet. Karl involuntarily screams in pain.

Katrina looks in from her mother's bedroom door, frightened and silent.

Karl, Kurtis, and Uncle Floyd crawl around Floyd's bedroom floor on all fours pushing toy cars around and making motor sounds with their mouths.

"Deputy Sheriff Barney is pulling you over for speeding, Karl," Floyd pushes a toy police car behind a little red corvette over the wood floor. Downstairs on the main floor the floors are carpeted but upstairs they're all wood floors.

"No way," Karl smiles, "You can't catch me!" He keeps pushing the little red corvette around making motor revving sounds pretending to outrun the police car.

"Pull over!" Uncle Floyd hollers.

"Okay, okay," Karl giggles. "I'll pull over."

"Get out of the car," Uncle Floyd says in a drawn out, humorous voice.

"Fine, I'm out," Karl says.

"Lie down," Uncle Floyd holds back giggles.

"What? No?" Karl responds.

"Lay down," Uncle Floyd says again.

"Okay," Karl does.

Uncle Floyd puts his butt near Karl's face and let's a loud, sour fart rip.

"Oh, god," Karl rolls away, plugging his nose, "That is so stinky!"

Kurtis covers his nose and mouth, "Yuck!"

After they catch their breath from laughing they sit for a moment in silence.

"Do you think this house is haunted?" Karl asks his Uncle Floyd.

"Haunted?" Kurtis echoes.

"I mean do you think a ghost lives here?" Karl asks.

"Yes, yes, yes," Uncle Floyd rocks his head back and forth as he answers.

"How do you know?" Kurtis asks.

"She drinks coffee with me. She likes to sit and talk with me over a cup of coffee," Uncle Floyd explains.

"You talk to the ghost? And it's a girl?" Karl asks, astonished.

"Yes, yes," Floyd says with a hint of pride, "Her name is Mrs. Sisten."

Karl and Kurtis are enthralled with Uncle Floyd's ghostly tale.

"Who is she?" Karl asks.

"She used to live here," Uncle Floyd explains with a sudden lucidity, "Her husband built this house. They both died here in the house. A long time ago. She doesn't want other people in the house she doesn't approve of. She says it's still her house. She doesn't really want anyone here."

"Why doesn't she want us here?" Karl asks.

"It's her home, not ours," Floyd simply says.

"She's nice to you?" Karl asks.

"She's my friend," Uncle Floyd smiles.

"Oh," Uncle Floyd searches his memory. "Lots of things. We talk about the Cheryl Gang and the weather. She likes to talk about the stars but I don't like outer space stuff. Mrs. Sisten said when they first built the house the road out front was dirt instead of pavement. She doesn't like cars. She likes coffee."

"Did she have kids?" Karl asks.

"No," Floyd says.

"Do you see her when you talk to her?" Karl asks, enticed.

"Sometimes," Floyd answers.

"What's she look like," Kurtis pipes in.

"Old," Floyd explains, "Very old. Long white hair. Hair that hangs to her feet. She's very skinny. Kind of looks like a skeleton with skin and eyes."

"Can we talk to her?" Karl asks, feeling hair raise on his arms.

"No," Floyd answers.

"Why not?" Karl asks, disappointed.

"She doesn't like people to see her," Floyd explains.

Karl is stunned.

"Why not?" Kurtis asks.

"I don't think she likes people seeing her now. She says she used to be pretty," Floyd says. "Now she looks dead. And I don't think she really likes anyone."

"She likes you," Karl says.

"I share my coffee with her," Floyd says as if that should explain everything.

"Tell Mrs. Sisten to come out and talk with us," Karl says, "Or Kurtis, Casey, and I will have a seance to talk with her."

"She's listening to us from the hallway attic right now," Uncle Floyd says.

"The walk space?" Karl asks.

"Yes," Floyd answers. "She spends most of her time there."

Karl feels gooseflesh rise all over his arms again.

"Tell her to come out," Karl says, "I want to meet her."

Kurtis looks unsure of himself and the conversation.

"She's getting mad," Uncle Floyd says.

"She's not real!" Karl yells, upset, disturbed, "You're making it up! Trying to scare us!"

For a moment Karl and Floyd only stare at each other, a brief battle of wills as Kurtis looks back and forth between them, baffled.

The attic door in the short hallway opens of its own accord, revealing only the thick darkness beyond the entrance.

Karl and Kurtis both squeak in fright, dashing down the stairs and outside to the safety of the backyard.

Uncle Floyd smiles warmly at the darkness beyond the attic door. "Would you like a cup of coffee?"

Karl and Kurtis lay on the living room carpet watching cartoons. A strange cartoon called *the Danse Macabre*, with music playing and dancing skeletons in a cemetery on the television screen. Both boys are fascinated by the program with elbows on the carpet, chins propped up on their palms.

The front door slams open. Their mother, Katrina, rushes in with Terry at her heels. Terry is barking behind her, "Why do you think he was talking to you, Kat? You think he wants to be friends? Are you that naive? I saw him looking down your shirt!"

"Enough, Terry!" Katrina shouts at him, "I won't fucking talk to anyone! Is that what you want? I just won't talk to any men again. Now mellow out!"

Karl and Kurtis jump, pale faced, mouths open at the sound of Terry slapping their mother across the face. Terry continues slapping at Katrina as she tries to block, backing into Candace's bedroom. The boys run into the bedroom where the altercation is occurring, but it happens too fast for them to see it all.

It's only the loud muffled noises, grunts, shouts, and screams of Terry and their mother backed into their grandmother's bedroom closet fighting. They stumble and fumble deep back into the closet disappearing into the hanging clothes and shadows. They hear the sounds of slapping, punching, the fury of their stepfather, the heart wrenching shrieks of their mother sobbing in pain and fear, bodies bouncing off the walls, a ruckus. Followed by a sudden silence. Only the heavy breathing of Terry and Katrina. Then the awful sound of their mother crying.

"Mom?" Karl asks in a mouse-like voice.

"It's alright, boys," she says from the closet. "Go play. Everything is fine."

Terry stomps out of the dark closet and yells at the boys, "Get upstairs to your room!"

The brothers sprint from their grandmother's bedroom all the way upstairs to their bedroom in the upper front end of the house.

Karl is outside by himself in the backyard near the garage. There are wasps flying about near the top of the garage. Karl strolls over and looks up at the under edge of the garage, just where the roof ends and hangs over a bit. On the underside Karl sees wasp hives.

Curious grey sponge things with a multitude of black holes in them. Wasps buzz around and climb in and around the papery hives. Karl finds something about the sight repulsive. Frightening. The wasps' appearance, behavior, and hives seem so alien. There seems to be nothing remotely human about them. Tiny black bubble eyes. Black legs. Pincer mouths. The strange buzzing. Worse of all they can sting you and it hurts. Karl was stung by a wasp a few summers ago and he'll never forget it. It sting his finger and hurt so much he cried. His finger turned pink around the sting and swelled. His only consolation was that someone told him wasps die after they sting you.

What do they do in those ugly grey, pocked, spongy hives? Karl shivers at the thought of touching a hive.

He stays alert, making sure none of the wasps get close enough to sting him.

This cannot stand. The backyard is his world. His safe zone. Wasps are not welcome.

Karl makes his way over to the side of the house and turns on a water spicket with a long, bright green hose attached to it. He is not supposed to play with the water without permission. This is not play. It's war.

Returning to stand beneath the wasp hives, Karl feels a hint of guilt as he sprays the water up at the garage knocking all circular sponge hives loose and they fall to the ground. He can feel the violence the wasps direct at him. They are aliens. They can't be from the planet Earth.

Katrina and her mother Candace are washing dishes together in the kitchen. Candace is washing, Katrina is drying and putting dishes away. Sunlight shines in from a kitchen window on the northside of the kitchen. The floor is off white with a crackling design of light blue.

Karl, Kurtis, and Uncle Floyd are in the backyard.

Terry is at work.

"You should leave him," Candace tells her daughter.

Without thinking about it, Katrina's hand goes to the bruise on her cheekbone, "I can't. I love him."

"He's not going to change," Candace shakes her head, "No matter how much you love him. What are you going to do when he hits the kids instead of you?"

Katrina says nothing, focusing on drying dishes and putting them away.

"I see," Candace nods with a disappointed grimace, "It's already happened."

"He doesn't mean to do it," Katrina defends, "We're early in recovery. He doesn't know how to live sober yet. How to cope with his emotions without drinking. He's working on it with his sponsor, Bob, to get better. He's agreed to go to anger management classes. I'm working on my recovery too. It's an everyday process. I'm not ready to give up. We will get through this."

Candace looks at her daughter with an expression of tough love, "I think it would be a good idea if you leave the boys here with Floyd and me when you and Terry move out. That way you and Terry can keep working on yourselves instead of letting him beat the boys. If you're going to let him hurt you, that's one thing. You're a grown woman. You make your own decisions. But the boys need to be protected from him."

Tears sparkle in Katrina's eyes as she looks at her mom, still drying dishes, "I think that may be a good idea for now."

"How long until you and Terry can get your own place?"

"Another month I think."

Candace nods, "One month."

Terry stands in the doorway of Kurtis and Karl's bedroom. Tall. Lanky. Intimidating, Angry. There always seems to be anger fuming just below the surface of the skinny, black bearded Terry. His face always turns a dark shade of red when he's enraged. Something both Karl and Kurtis are always fearful of seeing.

Karl and Kurtis are cleaning their bedroom while Terry stands on watching, making sure it is done right. Kurtis is putting toy action figures into a football shaped toy chest on the southside of the room. Karl is dusting the headboard of the bed.

Terry spots a baby blue plastic basket underneath the bed. He points to it and barks at Karl, "What's that?"

Karl shrugs, crouches, and pulls it out, immediately recognizing it as his Easter basket from earlier this year. "It's my Easter basket," Karl peeps. Inside he sees it is filled with thick spider webs and dozens of little baby spiders. Karl lets out a squeal and jumps away from the basket, leaving it to bounce on the bed.

Kurtis stops putting his toys away to watch the interaction between his stepfather and his older brother.

"What? What's wrong?" Terry frowns, stepping fully into the bedroom.

"There are spiders inside of it," Karl explains.

Terry gives a devilish smile, "You're afraid of a few bugs?" He picks up the basket from the bed and inspects the contents, "Yep. Quite a few little spiders in there. A mother must have laid eggs there. Don't be afraid, Karl. Clean them out."

"It's okay," Karl stands with his back to the wall, "I don't want it anymore. We can throw it away."

"Come here, Karl," Terry orders, placing the spider and web filled basket back on the bed.

Karl hesitates, forcing himself to step closer, one foot at a time.

Terry grabs Karl with both of his large hands. One hand pins Karl's arm behind his back, the other grips the back of Karl's hair. Terry's grips hurt. Karl feels his eyes go hot with tears.

"The only way to overcome fear is to face it," Terry explains, as he proceeds to shove Karl's face fully into the spider infested Easter basket.

"No, please!" Karl begs,

Kurtis stares in horror.

"Don't fight it," Terry hisses, putting painful pressure on the arm behind Karl's back.

Karl can feel the webs sticking to his face. His eyes are squeezed shut. He feels little spiders crawling over his cheeks, nose, and forehead.

Karl only cries and Terry holds his face inside the basket. His nose is pressed against the bottom of the basket now.

It seems like forever that Terry holds Karl's face in that basket.

With no warning Terry releases Karl and says in a quiet tone, "Finish cleaning this room. It's a mess." And he walks out, back down stairs.

Karl wipes webs, spiders, snot, and tears from his face as he hiccups on the floor trying to calm down.

Karl is in the backyard, the furthest section from the house. He doesn't want to be caught, having stolen matches from his grandmother. Grandma Candace has a chest of drawers against one wall in the dining room, on that is a brass colored decorative tea pot filled with books of matches for lighting candles. She loves to light candles, they're all over the house. Some nights she will turn out all the lights and the family will sit in the dining room or living room talking by candle light. Karl loves the smell of the burning candles.

Karl sits cross legged in grass that needs to be mowed, holding out a plastic green army man with one hand, and a lit match in the other, watching the plastic burn and melt. It doesn't smell good. He watches the army man's head, arms, legs, and gun curl and liquify. Thin lines of black smudges wave through the melting plastic. The hot plastic drips to the ground.

Karl drops the remains of the melted soldier to the grass and lights another match, burning another toy soldier. He doesn't know why he's burning the soldiers. He knows he'll get in trouble if he gets caught. There is something forbidden and fun about it. The fire is fascinating, beautiful, and dangerous. And Karl is in control.

A drop of scorching melted plastic drops down onto Karl's leg, his bare calve, he's wearing shorts. He howls and yips, dropping the matches and the soldier. Karl hops and rolls around clutching his burnt leg. The plastic dries quickly and sticks to his skin. When he picks it off it will leave a scar.

Karl sits back in the grass, squeezing his leg with both hands around the sharp, hot stinging sensation. It really hurts, throbs. The skin is raw and red in a small oval shape.

Karl feels like he deserves it for stealing the matches. Like it's nature's way of making him pay for playing with fire.

Fire. Fire. Fire.

He plays with fire.

He dances with fire.

It's a dark and windy night, wet outside, chilly for summer. It's been raining and storming on and off all day. Now the storms seem to be over but the heavy wind is a reminder that it has only just passed.

The grownups are all awake downstairs playing cards at the dining room table. Karl and Kurtis are in bed in their room. They share a bed. It's dark in the room except for a deep luminous blue glowing in through the windows from the moon and the street lights. Black clouds move fast across the sky tonight.

Kurtis refused to go to bed tonight because he's afraid of the dark. Terry ended up giving him a bare butt, bare hand spanking to make Kurtis obey. Karl is afraid of the dark too, but he's more afraid of Terry. He understands why Kurtis is afraid to sleep in the bedroom, but tonight he was more afraid than usual. Enough to defy Terry.

He was crying that he didn't want to sleep in this room tonight before the spanking and now he's whimpering hidden under the blanket next to Karl. The sound of his younger brother crying upsets Karl. He whispers to Kurtis, "Kurtis, it's okay. It's just dark. If we stay together nothing will happen."

Karl looks in the directions of the shadowy closest and the hallway where the attic crawlspace is. Seeing only blackness but always sensing something watching. Something uncaring and malevolent. Harmful and ugly.

Karl closes his eyes, trying to ignore his brother's sniffling and the ghosts he knows are in the blackness. Just sleep. He tries not to think of anything at all. He tries to count sheep, but the haunter in the darkness keeps returning to his thoughts. Invading his attempts to sleep and escape fear into pleasant dreams.

Kurtis suddenly cries louder than whimpering.

"What's wrong?" Karl asks in the shadows.

"Listen," Kurtis whispers.

Karl listens. It takes a moment for him to realize what his little brother is referring to. At first he thinks the noise is the tree branches outside the window rattling in the wind against the roof outside.

Outside their bedroom window on the west and front side of the house there is a roof level with the window which lids the porch beneath.

Karl listens to the rhythm of the tapping outside the window. It might not be branches. The tapping doesn't seem random. It's like a song being tapped out. Like quiet tap dancing. It sounds like someone is tap dancing on the roof outside the window in the wind and the drizzle.

"He's out there," Kurtis whispers ever so softly.

"Who's out there?" Karl whispers back.

"The goat man," Kurtis whispers, now beginning to cry quietly again, "The Devil is dancing on the roof."

"No he's not," Karl whispers, "The Devil isn't real." As he says this he feels as though a silent watcher hidden in the darkness of the closet is grinning at him.

"Just go to sleep," Karl tells his brother, even though he's afraid to look out the window himself. "The sooner you fall asleep, the sooner it will be morning."

Kurtis nods and goes back to hiding beneath the blankets, trying not to make a sound.

Karl rests next to his brother waiting for him to fall asleep. It seems like hours pass as he listens to his brother's breathing and the pattering on the roof outside.

Finally Karl can tell Kurtis has fallen asleep by the slow, deepness of his breathing, but outside the window the tapping has not stopped. Karl tells himself it's just the branches blowing back and forth over the shingles. That's what he imagines in his mind's eye.

The rattling, tapping changes its tempo. Karl can't stand not knowing any longer. Forcing himself to look over the lump of his sleeping brother and out the raindrop covered window.

Karl wants to shriek when he sees it, but his vocal cords don't respond. Kurtis was telling the truth. There is a goat legged man dancing delicately and gleefully on the roof outside their window. A naked man. A man from the waist up. A fur covered two legged goat from the waist down. Goat legs tapping out the rhythms with its hooves. The goat man has a long phallus dangling with wild hair between his legs. A sick grin on its face with an unsettling glint in its wide goat eyes glaring at Karl as it continues to dance as if mocking Karl.

It's a dark hairy thing with two small horns protruding from its forehead and a goat's tail wagging behind him. Karl realizes it's him, not just an it.

The goat man stops dancing and approaches the window so it is just on the other side of the screen from Karl, only a foot between them. "Rex," it says in a deep, melodic voice.

Karl retreats under the blankets next to his brother, hiding, trembling, cuddling next to his sleeping little brother. He is too afraid to look again. Too afraid to move or make a sound. Too afraid of Terry to get out of bed.

Karl doesn't remember falling asleep but some of his last thoughts were that he is more afraid of his stepfather than the Devil if that is who is on the roof.

The morning sun is shining in from the hall to Uncle Floyd's room. Karl looks outside the window and there is no sign the Devil was on the roof last night and no sign there was a storm other than a few broken branches on the ground. Karl wonders if the goat man was only a dream. He and Kurtis do not discuss it.

Karl and Kurtis are on the living room carpet building small space ships with LEGOs. Little plastic bricks of red, blue, white, green, and yellow that latch together. Toy building blocks that click together. The brothers are arguing as they play.

"I want to be Han," Kurtis argues.

"I'm Han Solo," Karl disagrees, "You should be Luke Skywalker. He's the hero."

"Nope," Kurtis shakes his head, "I'm Han Solo. You are Luke."

"I'm Han," Karl gets mad and tries to convince Kurtis to give in, "Luke is a Jedi and he has a lightsaber. Lightsabers are cool. And he has an X-wing fighter and R2-D2."

Kurtis comes back, "I'll be Han with a lightsaber and the Millennium Falcon.

"No," Karl gets more irritated, "Han's not a Jedi. He's a smuggler. He can't have a lightsaber. I'm Han and you're Luke flying his X-wing."

Kurtis shakes his head, flying his LEGO spaceship around the living room, "I'm Han! I'm flying the Falcon! I have a lightsaber and a blaster and Leia is my girlfriend. You can be Chewbacca, my co-pilot."

"No," Karl snaps, "I'm Han. You can be Lando or Yoda."

"I'm Han Solo," Kurtis taunts.

"No," Karl pouts.

"Settle down boys," Grandma Candace pops her head out of the kitchen door and then back inside.

The front door opens abruptly and Terry storms inside the living room, having just gotten home from work. He looks tired and angry with sleepy bags under his eyes. Terry takes in the scene before him. LEGOs and other toys scattered all across the living room. Karl and Kurtis are running in circles pretending to fly their LEGO spaceships.

"God damn it," Terry hollers, kicking the LEGOs across the room. He snaps into a rage and begins to stomp on all the toys, effectively breaking them. "I work all fricking day! Is it too much to ask to come home to a little peace and quiet?!

Both boys freeze in place and stare at Terry with fear and anticipation. Terry's face is turning red and his eyes are bugging out. Both boys know that look means trouble.

Kurtis happens to be the closest one to Terry and pays for it. Terry kicks out full strength, his foot connecting with the stomach of Kurtis. The single blow is so forceful it sends Kurtis reeling back through the air and he smacks into the wall by the television. The little boy falls to the floor gasping, trying to breath, in shock and pain.

Grandma Candace charges out of the kitchen with a flour covered rolling pin in her grip. She cocks it back ready to swing at Terry, "Don't touch my grandchildren, you son of a bitch! If you want peace and quiet, find your own place to live. Or better yet find a woman without kids. This kind of behavior is not happening in my home."

Terry looks at the older woman, deflated, head down in shame.

"Get out of my house," Candace orders.

Terry gives a single nod and wordlessly walks back out the front door.

Candace takes Kurtis in her arms to make sure the boy is alright. He cries and clings to his grandmother.

Later that night Candace and Katrina have a heated discussion before it's agreed that Terry can come back inside the house.

Karl races inside the house through the backdoor and directly into the bathroom. He's pinching his crotch and prancing. He has to use the bathroom so badly. When he lifts the toilet lid Karl freezes in fear.

There is a fat, long bright green caterpillar crawling inside the toilet bowl. It's not in the toilet water, but creeping up the white porcelain.

How did it get in there? This makes no sense to Karl. How could it crawl all the way inside from outside and then into the toilet bowl? It couldn't have. The toilet lid was down when Karl came inside. Who put it in there? Maybe it was on someone's clothes when they came in to use the bathroom. It would be easy for Uncle Floyd to not notice the bugger riding on his shoulder.

Karl wonders what that green crawler would do if he sat down to poop. What if he had sat on the toilet without noticing it? Would it have crawled up his buty like Casey's little brother? Would it have bit him?

Karl is clenching his cheeks. He has to poop so bad it hurts, but he's afraid of the caterpillar. Taking a deep breath for courage Karl flushes the toilet and watches intently as the water swirls around like a whirlpool and sucks the green critter down to wherever poop and toilet paper go when you flush the toilet.

He sits on the toilet in glorious defecation and a long sigh of release. So paranoid something will crawl back up out of the toilet Karl has to keep inspecting the toilet bowl until he's finished his business.

After he's finished pooping Karl decides to play mad scientist in the bathroom sink. He gathers bottles of everything he can find in the bathroom and mixes it all together in the sink. Shampoo. Conditioner. Vaseline. Mouthwash. Toothpaste. Hair gel. Comet. Toilet bowl cleaner. Makeup.

Peroxide. And other things he's not quite sure what they are.

    After about fifteen minutes of playing mad scientist Karl decides to wash all the evidence out of the sink and then down the drain. He knows he could get into a lot of trouble for the mad scientist game, but it's too fun to resist and he really feels like he's doing something important when he's doing it.

    Karl has a fresh idea. The other day he was in the basement with Grandma Candace while she was doing laundry. He enjoys snooping around the basement, but never goes down there alone. There are so many old things in the basement it looks like a dusty museum.

    There is a work bench filled with strange, greasy, and rusty tools and metal things. Worn leather, wood, and brass chests. Faded magazines. Old black and white photographs. Canned and jarred fruits and vegetables. Racks of vinyl records. Old Army uniforms and helmets. A black priest's robe. Dresses and all sorts of old clothes. Animal bones from his grandfather hunting. A tall standing mirror. Furs and animal skins. All kinds of crates and boxes to rummage through.

    Karl wants to go down there and snoop alone. He saw some old comic books in a chest with magazines he wanted to read. The only problem is the basement is just as scary as the attics upstairs. Maybe it won't be as scary with the light on. He wasn't scared at all when grandma was down there with him. Even though he could still vaguely sense the watchers.

    He makes up his mind to go down into the basement and return with the comic books and whatever other cool supplies he can find. It's a secret mission. He's a secret agent man.

    Karl stands at the top of the basement stairs. The basement door is between the dining room door and the backdoor of the house. He flips the light switch on. The descending stairs are old thick planks. Above the basement stairs you can see the inverted stairs that lead to the bedrooms upstairs. The door to go upstairs is in the kitchen.

    The first part of this daunting challenge is Karl getting down the stairs. What if something reaches up from beneath the stairs and grabs his feet? The hand of one of the unseen watchers. Or a monster or a demon? No. The watchers must be ghosts. He knows the ghost in the basement is a different ghost than in the attics. The upstairs ghost is a woman. In the basement it's a man. Karl's not really sure how many ghosts live in the house. At least two, but maybe more.

    He listens. Everything is very quiet. Forcing himself, he takes the first step down. He'll be like a hero, he tells himself. Uncle Floyd, Kurtis, and Casey will think he's brave. A second hesitant step down. The wood creaks.

    Zoom. Karl dashes down the basement stairs as fast as he can, hoping it's too fast for any ghosts to grab his ankles, leaping the final three steps landing with a cloud of dust, twisting immediately to see there is nothing beneath the stairs. He wonders why the floor is dirt beneath the stairs and a small section next to them. The rest of the basement is cement floor.

    Along the back wall next to the stairs the shelves of canned and jarred goods. Behind that wall is a small room with a closed door partially broken from its hinges. Karl doesn't know what that room is for. He peeked in there once when he was down here with Grandma Candace and she told him to stay out of that room. It was an empty room with a loose dirt floor, broken boards, and thick cobwebs hanging from the rafters. Karl is afraid of that mysterious room. He's pretty sure that's where the basement ghost usually stays.

Making his way through the maze of artifacts and junk, Karl opens the chest he found the comic books in. Casper the Friendly Ghost and several other old comics from the 1950s mixed in with a variety of magazines.

Turning to run back upstairs with arms full of a stack of comic books he stops dead in his tracks. He sensed the watcher before he came down, just standing at the top of the stairs. The watchers are always there. Now it feels stronger than ever before. They are bolder when he is alone. Karl can feel someone standing in the basement watching him. It wants him. He doesn't know why, but he knows that is not a good thing.

He feels like the watchers want to eat him or suffocate him, but not normal eating or suffocating, the kind of eating and suffocating that never ends. The watchers want to hold him close and never let him go. To violate him eternally. Bad people who die and suffer on and on, continuing to be bad. They are trapped in a prison between lines of reality watching and reaching out for life and freedom, hungry, desperate. They want something terribly, but Karl doesn't know what it is.

Karl senses the watchers strongly. It feels like there are several of them in the basement with him now. The most magnetic feeling comes from that closed room with the broken door hinges. A most blaring and glaring sensation. He doesn't know why he can sense these things, he does question it, it seems natural, like breathing and seeing.

That thing in the room. He has to look in there. He doesn't want to, but he has to know what's going on. Something in his center is urging him. What are these ghostly watchers? What do they want? What do they look like? Why are they in Grandma Candace's house? Are they all evil? He's almost certain they are the lost souls of dead people.

Karl walks ever so slowly toward the closed door of the little room in the corner of the basement. With the comic books in one hand, he struggles to shove the broken door open. It doesn't budge easily. The hinges are rusted and the top hinges are broken and the bottom of the door drags against the dirt floor of the interior of the room.

It all happens very fast.

Simultaneously.

Karl screams and screams and screams, drops the comic books to the floor and dashes madly up the stairs and out of the basement as rapidly as his young legs will take him, but the image of the old man in the room is forever burned into his psyche.

A naked old man with grey flesh, a long bushy beard and stringy white hair passed his scrawny shoulders. Naked and sickly thin. Protruding hip bones, ribs clearly visible beneath the saggy, tight skin. Gaunt. A sunken stomach. Knobby, swollen joints. A small shriveled penis between his legs.

What was worse was the look on the old man's face and the uncanny gestures he was making. The ghastly man's expression was perversion, eagerness, and lunatic joy. Eyes wide with starvation. A greedy, drooling grin. Gnarly, dirty fingers and skinny arms reaching out as if to latch on to Karl. The old man laughs hysterically at Karl with wild, untamed hair.

Karl feels weak and insignificant in the eyes of the sick old man. Karl keeps yelling all the way from the ground floor of the house up to Uncle Floyd's bedroom. Floyd and Karl are the only two home this afternoon.

"I saw an old man in the basement!" Nearly out of breath Karl wails to Floyd.

"Who?" Uncle Floyd is startled, sitting on the floor with a green toy tractor in his hands.

"There is some naked, spooky old man in that small room in the basement!"

"Let me see," Uncle Floyd puts down the tractor and struggles to get up off the floor. He sounds angry and grabs his wood cane leaning against his unmade bed. "Get my guns," he instructs his nephew Karl.

Karl takes two toy plastic pistols out of Floyd's top dresser drawer, the sock and underwear drawer.

"Get my rifle too," Uncle Floyd says in all seriousness.

Karl gives a solemn nod and retrieves the toy rifle from under the bed as Floyd buckles a belt with gun holsters on the hips. He slides the pistols in the holsters, "You use the shotgun," Floyd asserts.

"Thanks," Karl utters and follows Uncle Floyd slowly down the stairs to the main floor into the kitchen, then to the top of the basement.

Uncle Floyd always walks slowly.

In the basement Karl stays protected behind Floyd, who has his toy guns out and pointed at the door of the small room where Karl had seen the man of wrongness. "He's in there," Karl whispers.

"Stay back," Uncle Floyd suggests, moving toward the open door of the little dirty room, pointing the toy guns, ready to shoot, "Alright! You're surrounded! Come out of there slowly with your hands up high or we'll shoot you!"

Both Karl and Floyd stand waiting for something to happen. For a bizarre elderly man to come trampling out of the room. The only sound is their own breathing.

"Come out!" Uncle Floyd demands again, a bit of spittle spraying from his mouth.

Floyd whispers to his nephew, "We go in with guns blazing."

Karl nods, pointing the rifle at the door, he fearfully follows Floyd inside.

There is nothing there but heavy layers of cobwebs, the dirt floor, and random broken boards scattered about with a few animal bones. Mostly deer.

They take the time to search the basement to see if the old man is hiding somewhere but they find nothing. They decide not to tell the grownups the house is haunted. The only one that believes it is Grandma Candace but she doesn't care about the ghosts. She just always says to ignore them and don't talk about them.

Karl and Kurtis are under the table together with a cookie jar between them. A ceramic cookie jar made to look like an old moonshine jug. They are both eating Oreo cookies. Their stepfather Terry always has Oreo cookies and a two liter bottle of cola. He does not share these treats with anyone. This afternoon Terry is gone and the brothers decide they could quickly eat a few cookies without Terry noticing.

Karl suddenly has the thought, what if Terry counts his cookies? The thought frightens him as he looks at Kurtis who smiles with brown chocolate cookie covering his teeth. It doesn't matter. Fate plays it's hand and Terry walks in the front door, home early from work.

Katrina comes out of the kitchen, the boys can only see her legs from under the table, "Honey, what are you doing home so early?"

Terry walks to the dining room table, "We ran out of carpet at the apartment complex. Bob ordered the wrong pattern."

Karl and Kurtis sit frozen in fear staring silent at Terry's legs.

"Oh," Katrina says, "It's good to see you home early. Are you hungry? I can warm up what we ate for lunch."

"That would be fine," Terry answers, sitting at the dining room table.

Karl and Kurtis stare at Terry's work boots and jeans, afraid to breathe and be discovered.

Karl sees his little brother's eyes wide and wet with tears of fear. Karl sits perfectly still watching as Terry struggles to pull off a leather work boot. He massages his foot a few minutes before unlacing the other boot.

That's when Terry sees the boys under the dining room table with the cookies in their hands and the cookie jar behind them. Terry flips the dining room table over in a fit of rage.

The boys don't even notice their mother coming into the dining room from the kitchen behind Terry. All they can see is the great monster that is their stepfather Terry standing tall and lanking, larger than life before them. Terry huffs over them, glaring down, nostril's flaring, eyes blazing red with rage, face flushed with anger. A tall monstrous man made of bitterness. The creature called stepfather whips off his leather belt.

The children are like helpless pups trapped under the assault of stinging, welting lashes against their tender flesh. Their shrieks are the high pitched, shrill squeals of the helpless. Their mother is lashed with the belt when she tries to intervene.

This afternoon Karl decides to go visit old Mrs. Falkenrath. She lives two houses south of Grandma Candace's house. The order of the houses along the block is Grandma Candace's house, then Casey's house, and then old Mrs. Falkenrath's house.

    He likes to go over there because she always gives him cookies to eat and juice to drink. All he has to do is listen to her Bible stories. Karl often wonders about her husband. She talks about him all the time but Karl has never seen him. He's never there when Karl's eating cookies and he never sees him coming and going like other neighbors do. Karl feels a sadness like regret in Mrs. Falkenrath's voice when she speaks of her husband.

    She talks about her children often too. A daughter and a son, but Karl has never seen them either. Mrs. Falkenrath says they both live in other cities with children of their own now.

    Mrs. Falkenrath always seems happy when she answers the door to find Karl standing there with a smile for her.

    Today she gives him orange, pink, and chocolate wafers with a small glass of chocolate milk. While he nibbles on his wafers she tells him the story of a man named Lot. Karl doesn't remember much of the story because he is so distracted by one certain part of the story, when Lot's wife looks back and turns to a pillar of salt. This act horrifies Karl. Why would God do that? It's so awful and mean. Karl doesn't question the Bible stories to Mrs. Falkenrath only because he can tell how much they mean to her and she's such a nice lady, he doesn't want to hurt her feelings.

    Karl leaves Mrs. Falkenrath's house and wanders back to his grandmother's backyard in a dazed state of disturbance.

    This God in the Bible is supposed to love everyone. He is everyone's Father, but he's so scary, so uncaring, and so mean. He turned a woman to salt for looking back! He killed her!

    He does so many evil and bad things, like telling Abraham to kill his own son. That story upset Karl more than Lot's wife being murdered by God. Much more.

    Karl thinks about something worse than all of this. God destroyed entire cities with fire and flooded the entire world killing everyone, even little kids and babies and animals.

    Karl is very afraid of God and hopes he never makes Him angry and hopes God can't read his thoughts or at least isn't paying attention to them. He just doesn't know why everyone says God loves everyone when He seems so hateful and warlike.

    Jesus is weird too. Karl doesn't know what to think of Him. They don't seem like the same God. Jesus doesn't quite seem real. Or at least Karl can't sense Him like he can sense God. Jesus seems like a nice guy, a little creepy, and Karl doesn't understand why if God can do anything, he let his Son be tortured and nailed to a cross.

    One thing though is Karl thinks Samson seems cool, even though Delilah cut off his hair.

    Grandma Candace brings Karl and Kurtis to church every Sunday. Karl doesn't mind Sunday school, it's fun to hang out with the other kids, color in biblical coloring books, play with toys, and different group games. The best part of church is when it's over and everyone goes into the basement to drink coffee and juice and eat doughnuts and cookies. The worst part is sitting through the service. It's tortuously boring. Karl can never stop fidgeting and looking around at the stained glass windows and pillars as they stand and kneel and sing and pray. The organ and singing is kind of neat because it sounds spooky.

Grandma Candace gives them little notepads to doodle in some times while the service drags on. Sometimes Karl and Kurtis play tic tac toe on the note pads. Karl especially likes the part where you greet your neighbors, everyone stands up smiling, shaking the hands of everyone around them saying hello and good day. The most relieving part is communion because then Karl know's it's almost over. That and when they pass around the baskets asking for money. Grandma always gives Karl and Kurtis each a quarter to put into the collection basket.

The very last thing that happens is all the people in robes walk down the center aisle holding up crosses and candles and banners as the organ plays. Then the priest stands at the church doors with an overly friendly smile shaking everyone's hands as they either exit the church or head downstairs for snacks.

Karl thinks church isn't so bad. It's just some parts that are dreadfully boring and God is mean. He thinks it would be cool to wear one of those black or red robes some day.

Perry Honeycutt sits in his usual Thursday night 8:00 pm Alcoholics Anonymous meetings on the south side of town. He looks across the table at the man addressing the group. A short, muscular man Perry has known for just over two months now. Fresh out of prison for possession of heroin. Still on parole. Ex-con Darrell.

They all sit around the table waiting for their turns to speak and listen to each other tell their stories or talk about their day or their struggles with sobriety.

Perry's stomach turns as he observes Darrell speaking.

Darrell with his bulldog round face, thick mustache hanging over his lip, and missing tooth talks to the group with mock sincerity. "Hi. My name's Darrell. I'm an alcoholic and an addict. You know when I was in rehab, just out of prison, I thought, what a bunch of wussies when I listened to everyone complain about their problems. My counselor talked to me about this. Not having empathy for other people. That's when I realized you can't measure pain. That was cool. Opened my eyes. Anyways," he points at a thick, worn out blue book on the table before him. "This book is impressive. Full of wisdom. I read it and it blew my mind. I mean how can these guys who lived like a hundred years ago, or however long ago. How can these guys know me? I mean, I'm reading this and it's like they're talking about me. That's pretty cool. That has to mean something."

A few heads around the table nod in profound agreement. Perry is not impressed. He knows Darrell is full of shit, only coming to meetings to get his attendance card signed for his parole officer. He's heard Darrell give the same brief speech three times now, word for word.

Perry tunes out Darrell's horseshit. Perry is annoyed that Darrell is a 13 stepper too. Meaning he comes to 12 step meetings hoping to find women.

Perry's been in recovery for over three and a half years now. When it comes to his turn around the table he simply says, "Hello. My name is Perry and I'm an alcoholic. I think I'm just going to listen tonight."

To close the AA meeting everyone stands together in a circle holding hands and saying the Lord's Prayer, "Our Father, Who art in Heaven..." With hands still joined they bounce their fists together as one chanting one of many mottoes, "It works if you work it, it sucks if you don't!"

The recovering alcoholics and drug addicts graze out into the main lobby of the AA building. Other small meetings are getting over and the participants are filing out. Perry is in an unusually sore mood and avoids talking to anyone.

"Hey, Perry," a familiar voice says and gives him a friendly pat on the shoulder. "How are you doing, buddy?"

Perry smiles at the tall, thin, bearded man, "Hi, Terry. I'm fine." Terry has two women with him. His wife, Katrina, and another Perry doesn't recognize.

"Have you met Stella?" Terry introduces her.

Perry shakes his head slightly and shakes her soft hand, "I haven't had the pleasure," she is pretty he thinks. Tall. Brunette. Sad eyes though. She must be new to the program. Looks like she's been crying very recently. Probably in her meeting.

"Hi," she gives him a delighted smile.

Something stirs pleasantly in Perry's stomach at the nearness of Stella.

"Katrina is Stella's sponsor now," Terry explains, "We're going off for coffee if you care to join us."

Prying his eyes from Stella, Perry answers, "Sounds great. I could use some fellowship."

"We all could," Terry grins, "see you at the diner?"

"Definitely," Perry answers.

A short while later Perry sits at a table in the Karlstein Diner. A milk skinned black haired waitress puts a plate of pancakes, french fries, and an omelet down on the table top before him. He takes his time putting ketchup on the plate. Many people from AA come here for coffee and cigarettes after the meetings to chat.

Sitting around the table this evening are lanky Terry, quiet Katrina, smug Darrell, blue Stella, and level headed, friendly Bob Anderson (Terry's sponsor and boss).

"I'd be happy to be your sponsor," Terry answers Darrell. "I want you to meet my sponsor, Bob. He's got 14 years of sobriety and has helped me through a lot of things. I want you to have more phone numbers than mine to call. Think of Bob as your grandpa sponsor."

"I'm more than happy to give you my phone number," Bob says in a jolly way, "I'm sure Perry will too. You know, Darrell, the real secret is we don't have drinking problems. We have sobriety problems. We don't know how to deal with being with sober. Drives us crazy."

Perry nods, cringing inside as he adds his phone number to a small paper list with Bob and Terry's.

"Call any time, day or night," Bob explains, "call one or all of those phone numbers before you decide to take that first drink or hit."

"Thank you, guys," Darrell shakes Bob's hand firmly, "I will call all of you."

"Picking up the phone is the hardest part," Bob explains.

"I have to let you know, Darrell," Terry advises, "I'm going to work hard for you so I expect you to work just as hard for me. You had to work for your addiction. Work to find the drugs or alcohol or the money to get it. You're going to have to work just as hard to arrest it. I'm sure in the middle of a blizzard you would have no hesitation walking across town for a fix. I expect the same devotion to get to meetings. It's the only way."

"I see what you're getting at," Darrell chuckles, eyeing Stella from the corner of his eye.

The others don't notice, but Perry can tell Darrell has the hots for Stella. It makes a hint of jealousy rise in his heart.

"I want you to read Bill's Story in the big book before next Thursday night's meeting," Terry instructs Darrell, "Underline anything that sticks out to you or catches your attention. We'll meet an hour before the meeting and go over what you've read. How does that sound?"

Darrell grins, "That works for me."

"You have a blue book?" Bob asks.

"Yes, sir, I do," Darrell nods.

Perry notices Katrina and Stella are having their own quiet conversation at the end of the table. It doesn't seem like anything too deep, or like they are discussing the program at all, so Perry joins their talk, "And what are you two beautiful women conspiring?"

Both women giggle.

Stella bats her eyes at Perry, "We're actually talking about ghosts. I told Katrina about a house I grew up in that I think was haunted."

"That's interesting," this genuinely piques Perry's interest. Having been in recovery for what is getting closer to four years now, one of the more attractive things about AA and the 12 step program to him, besides its obvious ability to help cope with sobriety, is the spiritual aspect of the program. In truth, at its essence it is a spiritual program, keeping in mind there is a wide chasm between religion and spirituality. Spirituality is the secret weapon of the 12 step program. A higher power keeps you clean and sober through grace if you follow its road map. What's amazing about this to Perry is that the higher power can be whatever you need it to be. It works if you are Christian, Muslim, Jewish, Buddhist, Hindu, tribal, or whatever religious path you choose. The point is that you can't stop drinking or using drugs very easily on your own will power alone. You have to admit you are powerless over booze and your addiction therefore something stronger than your own will power is required. Something stronger than you. So your God, your higher power, your stronger power, can be anything of your choosing, any god, a tree, nature, the group of AA itself, anything stronger than you alone.

This worked well for Perry because he'd been angry at the Christian God for a very long time. Most of his life. He blamed the omnipotent Christian God for all his suffering as a child. The circumstances were out of his control, but clearly in the control of the omnipotent Christian God.

Since his early days of recovery, Perry has come to terms with this. He is no longer angry at God. How did he do this? He explored dozens and dozens of religions and their higher powers until he found one that felt right for him. The one he felt right about is a god of his own understanding and experience. Gnosticism. The journey has been long, painful, and worthwhile, and is far from over. It's a journey that began the day he was born.

One experience Perry had as a child was seeing the cover of a book called *Communion* by Whitley Striber. At the time he had no idea what the book was about. All he knew was the image of the creature on the cover terrified him beyond words. It was the picture of what today is the standard image of what contemporary culture calls the grey alien. Big head. No hair. Big black slanted eyes. Slit of a mouth. No ears. No emotion. A blank expression.

The picture of that cold, lurking alien set off alarms inside Perry's young mind and heart. It was something straight out of his nightmares. He's spent a lifetime wondering if he dreams of it or if he's truly abducted by aliens some lonely nights. Part of him thinks he is honestly visited by aliens. Another part of him thinks it's a crazy notion, only dreams influenced by the modern myth of the grey alien so embedded in modern culture.

Did he even have the dreams before seeing that book cover or did the dreams start after seeing the book? So many years have passed he can't honestly answer the question. Maybe it's like some kind of unconscious virus, the grey alien virus invading the psyche of humanity.

Perry has always had an interest in religion and spirituality but was not able to become focused and streamlined in his journey until giving up the wild life.

Now Perry believes in a god and has experienced this god. This god only vaguely resembles the Abrahamic theological deities. His god is a god of nature. A goodness and order that sees like chaos from afar and does lead somewhere in the end on a macrocosmic scale.

He doesn't mind being called new age, it explains his philosophies as well as any label. He believes everyone should have their own experience of god and everyone is capable of it. He doesn't necessarily like using the term God, as it is too limiting. Call it godhead. Universal mind. The source. The first point. Whatever. He hasn't found a word sufficient.

So Perry suffered from nightmares of grey aliens coming to him at night. These dreams originated or intensified after seeing Striber's book. The nightmares continue into adolescence. During his teen years when he used drugs along with his drinking problem, he experienced a few psychedelic hallucinations involving grey aliens.

Once he went to rehab and entered recovery, putting himself back together, or together for the first time, Perry decided that besides the AA meetings therapy would be a good idea. Just to make sure he wasn't really crazy. At some point he and his therapist decided to see a hypnotherapist to explore any repressed memories.

The hypnotist was a big, boisterous, balding Puerto Rican psychologist named Dr. Marco. All bluster and confidence. Loud, intelligent, and sure of himself. Perry was fond of Dr. Marco. Envious of his confidence and intellect. He realized he wanted that for himself one day.

Perry was initially excited for the hypnotic sessions but soon became disillusioned with them. He couldn't tell if the repressed memories were real or subconsciously created by himself, Dr. Marco, and his therapist. Was it all just his imagination? The results were entertaining and curious but inconclusive. There was no physical evidence. Nothing that could be measured.

This experience sparked interest in human consciousness for Perry. Shortly after he enrolled in Northington University majoring in Psychology with a minor in Theology with secret ambitions to specialize in parapsychology some day. It's become his passion since entering recovery. His new drug. He is still a student at the university.

Since then Perry has developed the theory that his experiences with the grey aliens are entirely psychological. They have no physical aspect. He is yet to determine what the experiences of the grey aliens are. It is a genuine experience that people have, but what is it? A meaningless delusion? A communication from intelligence outside the human mind? A communication from deep within the unconscious mind? There are many questions to answer.

This led Perry Honeycutt into exploring consciousness in unorthodox ways outside of his university classes. He has pursued all types of supernatural occurrences in hopes of communicating with a ghost or some non-human intelligence.

So when the discussion turns to the subject of ghosts, Perry's fate is sealed. Maybe he should have let his childhood obsessions go after overcoming his childhood fears.

"Tell me more about it," Perry asks.

"There's not much to tell," Stella smiles, almost embarrassed. "We were kids. The babysitter heard something in the basement one night. We all heard it. Like someone walking around and moving things around. The babysitter was too afraid to go down there by herself, so my sibling and I went down with her. We didn't hear any more noise but we all saw it. The shadow of a man moving and hiding behind us. When we saw him we all screamed and ran back up stairs," she chuckles as if not to take it too seriously. "The babysitter called the police. The police looked all over the basement. They searched the whole house and couldn't find anything. There was only one way in and out of the basement. Just one door. No one could have got out without us having seen them. Our parents didn't believe us. Every once in a while we'd hear something down there in the basement or see a spooky shadow, but never like that night. We moved out of the house not long after that."

"Wow," Perry whispers, then says, "That's an interesting story. Truly." He's investigated hauntings before with no success. He's come across nothing to lead him to believe ghosts are real.

Although some of his colleagues at work would dispute that. "Where's the house?"

"I think it was torn down," Stella answers, "Gentrification."

Darrell laughs, "I don't believe in ghosts. That's like the tooth fairy, the Easter Bunny, and Santa Claus shit."

"You don't have to be a jerk about it," Stella says.

"Oh," Darrell realizes his mistake, "Sorry, I didn't mean to."

Terry says, "Katrina's mom thinks her house is haunted."

"Is that true?" Perry asks in all seriousness.

"It's what my mother thinks," Katrina answers timidly.

"Do you think it's haunted?" Perry inquires, noticing a seemingly jealous look from Terry and Darrell continues to ogle Stella like a dog in heat.

Katrina glances at Terry as if she's looking for approval to answer. Terry gives an almost imperceptible nod. Katrina answers, "I think it might be. Weird things have happened there over the years. I grew up there, you know. With my brother Floyd and our parents."

"What kind of weird things?" Perry arches an eyebrow respectfully.

"You can't be serious," Darrell mumbles.

Terry interrupts, "It's nothing. Noises. An old house settling and creaking. Sometimes things fall off the walls. Sometimes it sounds like someone is walking the stairs between the ground floor and the second floor. It's just a very old house."

"My brother Floyd says he talks to a ghost that lives there," Katrina says shyly, without making eye contact with anyone but her coffee cup. "He says she likes to drink coffee with him. Even says her name is Mrs. Sisten."

Perry nods, forehead in a knot of distant thought.

"Nonsense," Terry bellows, "Her brother Floyd is slow witted. He has cerebral palsy. Basically he's mentally handicap."

"You never know," old Bob Anderson sips his coffee with hands leathery from years of hard labor, "The Lord moves in mysterious ways."

"Let's find out," Stella suggests with a smile as bright as sunshine, happy to have found a new group of friends to replace her drug-using companions, "We can hold a seance there. It'll be fun. What's the worst that can happen? A ghost shows up and we know there is in fact an afterlife, or nothing at all happens and we're in the same place we were in before. Sounds like sober fun to me!"

Darrell gives Stella a hungry glance, "I'm down. It's an excuse to get together if nothing else."

Terry looks at Stella with wicked intentions, trying not to let his eyes linger on her cleavage, fighting the naughty thoughts in his mind, "Could be fun for a laugh."

"Okay," Katrina nods nervously.

Perry picks up on the dominance Terry has over Katrina. He also picks up on her reluctance to conduct the seance. He senses that she believes the house is haunted, which makes sense since she's the one who grew up there.

"I don't know," Bob hesitates, "I don't think it's something that should be played with or taken lightly."

"I don't take it lightly," Perry assures Bob, "I'm a God fearing man like yourself, but if there is something wrong going on there we may be able to help rest a lost soul."

Bob seems to chew that over with a non-committal nod.

Candace will be out of town next weekend for some kind of old ladies club," Terry reminds Katrina. "It will be perfect timing. What do you think, honey?"

Perry can tell it's not a question.

"It's fine with me, Terry," Katrina responds. "I don't know anything about a seance. Sounds spooky."

"It is spooky," Bob Anderson mumbles.

"I can run the seance," Perry volunteers.

"You're just creepy enough to believe this shit," Darrell laughs.

Perry looks hurt.

"There's nothing creepy about him," Stella defends.

"It's settled then," Terry likes to take charge of things, "Next weekend. Everyone come over, say 8:00 pm?"

"It's a date," Stella looks pleased with a sparkle in her eye.

"I'll be there," Darrell commits.

With a short exhale Bob says, "I better come and keep all of you youngsters in line."

Karl and Kurtis are supposed to be sleeping in their upstairs room. It's dark and they're whispering a word game they've made up. The game doesn't have a name. They take turns telling each other stories. It's a game that takes place in the imagination. They each pick out two fictional characters to be their partners, one super weapon, and a vehicle to adventure in. Karl picks as his partners *Indiana Jones* and *Batman*, his weapon is *Boba Fett*'s armor and his ship is the *Millennium Falcon*. Kurtis picks *Dr. Doom* and *Dr. Strange* as his partners, his weapon is a *Green Lantern* power ring, and his vehicle is an *Imperial Star Destroyer*, making Karl's storytelling much more difficult.

It's like a choose-your-own adventure story. They present each other with scenarios and make decisions and then the one brother tells the other what happens based on his choices. Tonight Kurtis fell asleep before they were done. Karl lays there in the dark wishing he was asleep too. It's so quiet. Except for a single cricket chirping lonely outside somewhere. It's so dark Karl can hardly see his hand before his face.

He holds his eyes shut against the dark trying to think about things that make him happy. He imagines living on a satellite 22, 300 miles above the Earth with all his favorite superheroes. He's friends with all of them and the superhero girls fight over which one gets to be his girlfriend. Karl loves superheroes and wishes they were real. He wishes he had his own superhero costume to wear. Nothing makes him more happy than getting lost in a comic book.

Just as he is about to drift off into a pleasant superhero inspired dream sleep, he hears something from the closet with the attic walk space door and the attic door in the ceiling.

Karl's eyes open and he stares into the thick, inky black trying to see if there is something there and listening intently, holding his breath.

He can hear a shallow wheezing. Something struggling to breathe hidden in the darkness of the closest.

Karl is afraid to move. Afraid to look away from the black, deep abyss of the closet. Something is there watching him. Tears grow warm in his eyes. His heart pace quickens. Knees begin to tremble with fright.

He sees her. A pale illumination in the dark like something emerging from wind and water. An old, wrinkled, translucent, haggard woman with a pain filled expression in her hollow black eye sockets. Mouth agape, lamenting in agony. She is only half there. Half in this world. Half veiled in an unknown world of blackness.

The old woman floats like a neck broken corpse hanging in the coal black closet reaching feebly out toward him. She speaks to Karl without moving her face from its deathlike posture in a hissing, croaking voice that crawls under his skin, "What are you?"

Karl screams at the sound and sight of the hag, leaping from bed, leaving his little sleeping brother behind. Bolting from the bedroom, through the short hall, passed his slumbering Uncle Floyd. He stomps down the stairs two at a time. Karl doesn't stop running until he reaches the room in which his mother and Terry are sleeping.

Karl blindly shakes his mother awake, crying, "There is an old lady in my closet! She was reaching for me! I don't want to go back upstairs anymore, mom!"

"What?" Katrina rubs sleep from her eyes.

"I'll take care of this," Terry grumbles, rolling out of bed in only his underwear.

"Be nice," Katrina pleads, delicately touching Terry's wrist.

"I will," Terry nods, leaning to give Katrina's forehead a quick kiss.

"I can't sleep up there!" Karl cries, "She'll get me!"

Terry takes Karl roughly by the upper arm, "Come on, bud, let your mother sleep," and Terry tugs Karl out of the bedroom.

"Terry, please," Karl whimpers, "Don't make me go back up there. I saw the old lady in the closet. She talked and she looked dead."

"It was only a nightmare, Karl," Terry grouches as he pulls Karl along by the arm back toward the stairs leading up to the bedrooms.

"No," Karl protests, trying to break free.

"God damn it," without thinking Terry backhands Karl. His knuckles slap across Karl's cheek, dropping the boy flat to the kitchen floor.

Karl lays there in utter shock , clutching his tender cheek, staring up at his stepfather.

"'Let's go," Terry reaches down and lifts him under Karl's armpits. The grip of Terry's fingers pinches Karl and he wants to squeal but he's out of tears, exhausted with fear.

Terry carries Karl up the stairs, scolding him the entire way, "Enough of this nonsense. You're a boy. You're going to be a man. You're too old to be afraid of the dark anymore."

Uncle Floyd's eyes open in the dark, he lay still watching the shadows of Terry carry Karl back into the other room. Floyd pretends to sleep for fear of Terry, but his heart bleeds for his nephew.

Back in the bedroom Kurtis is still sound asleep. Terry puts Karl in the bed and says, "If you get out of bed again I'm going to whip your ass black and blue. You won't be able to sit for a week. Is that understood.?"

Karl nods, wiping snot from his nose with the back of his hand.

"I didn't hear you," Terry commands.

"Y-yes, sir," Karl whispers.

"Good. I'll see you in the morning, Not another word." And with that final statement Terry exits the room.

Karl is trembling, sniffling, wiping his eyes, his cheek still pink and raw, he pulls the blankets close to his chin and snuggles close to his soundly sleeping little brother, all the while staring into the black abyss of the closet.

To Karl's surprise the ghastly woman appears again watching him with empty black eyes. He stifles a scream as the frightening apparition glares at him with a blank expression, but the woman quickly drifts on, following Terry down the stairs. Both Karl and Uncle Floyd witness this and it is apparent to both of them that Terry cannot see the feminine haunt.

Once Karl hears the door close at the bottom of the steps he whispers loudly through the short hallway toward Uncle Floyd's bedroom, "Uncle Floyd?"

"Go to sleep," Uncle Floyd whispers harshly to Karl.

Instead Karl is encouraged knowing Floyd is awake. He knows even if Floyd is slow he wouldn't let anyone hurt him. Karl tiptoes into Uncle Floyd's room. He stands at his bedside, "Floyd?"

"Go back to sleep before Terry comes back," Floyd protectively scolds his nephew.

"He won't come back tonight," Karl sniffs, "Did you see her? Was that Mrs. Sisten?"

Uncle Floyd only looks at Karl with a sober expression that frightens the boy. An expression that reminds Karl that Uncle Floyd isn't quite right in the brain. He feels like Uncle Floyd is in league with Mrs. Sisten or afraid to say anything about her.

"Was it her?" Karl asks more meekly.

"I don't want to talk about that," Floyd hushes.

"Please, tell me. I'm afraid of her. I promise I won't tell anyone. Except maybe Kurtis."

"Don't worry about it," Floyd says with shortening patience. "She followed Terry downstairs."

"Why?"

"I don't know."

"Does she like me?"

"I don't think so. Maybe. Maybe not."

"Why not? What did I do?"

"You were born. And you can see her."

"You can see her. Why does she like you?"

"She likes coffee," Floyd whispers.

"She scares me," Karl admits.

"Just pretend you don't see her when you do. Ignore her. Don't make her mad. Now go to sleep. Everything will be fine tonight."

"Okay," Karl tiptoes back to his room.

Grandma Candace has left town for the weekend to visit a cousin who lives a few counties northwest. A few hours away. Terry and Katrina have invited their AA friends over for their planned seance. Odd Perry. Sexy Stella. Sly Darrell. Carpenter Bob.

The boys, Karl and Kurtis, are fast asleep up in their room. Uncle Floyd sits in the corner of the dining room in his usual green stool, rocking his head in a daydream, and fiddling with his cane as he sips black coffee.

The room is dimly lit by only candlelight. Everyone's face is tinted in flickering yellows and orange for the little wick flames. The room smells of burning candle wax. Terry lit all of Candace's candles and Stella and Perry, who rode together, brought their own which they've lit as well. Perry has also set a clear crystal in the center of the dining room table.

Darrell and Bob drove in separate cars since Darrell recently got his driver's license back. He drives an old dark blue sports car. Bob drives his company truck. Perry drives a compact car that gets good gas mileage. Stella doesn't own a car.

Perry is nervous from the get go. Nervous because Stella rode with him and he has a huge crush on her. She has short blonde hair and bright blue eyes with topaz earrings and blue eyeshadow.

Upon entering the house Perry all but forgets about Stella, caught up in the anticipation of the seance. His gut feeling tells him there may be something to this one. The eeriness in the house is thick for those sensitive enough to feel it. It's more than anything he's felt before. In his few years of exploring paranormal phenomena he's never actually come across any genuine supernatural experience before. This house fills him with a feeling of hope and dread. How can the others not feel it?

A glance at the timid Katrina makes him think she does sense it but has grown desensitized to it over the years.

Perry doesn't fail to notice that Darrell and Terry are both sitting on either side of Stella. The order of everyone around the table starting with Perry is: Perry, Bob, Katrina, Terry, Stella, and Darrell completing the circle.

"I can't believe we're really going to do this," Stella beams.

"I'm still not convinced we should," Bob warns.

"Do you really know what the hell you're doing here, Perry?" Darrell heckles.

"I suppose as well as any of us," he answers.

"That's not very reassuring," Bob says.

"What do we do?" Stella asks with excitement in her bubbly voice.

"We're going to join hands and concentrate on communicating with whatever spirit or spirits are in this house," Perry explains, his smooth crystal ball is in the center of the table, "I want everyone to stare at the glass globe in the center of the table. Hopefully we'll see something in the ball. I'll do the talking. Don't let go of each other's hands until I say it's okay."

Everyone nods in agreement.

In truth Perry is mostly making this up as he goes along. Mostly just doing what feels right. There is a slight tension in the room, as if Perry, Terry, and Darrell are all competing for Stella's attention secretly on an animal level. Like hounds in heat.

"Oh, spooky," Darrell chuckles obnoxiously.

As if in response to his statement a stray screwdriver falls off a shelf above the entryway shelf above the basement doorway. The trajectory is odd. It doesn't fall straight down but at an angle. It hits the floor with a slight vibrating thud, stabbing upright into the carpet. A seeming challenge to all doubters.

Everyone is spooked by the occurrence but no one comments on it.

Everyone is holding hands around the dining room table only looking at the screwdriver standing like a tiny pillar of warning. The room is filled with a sense of unease. "That was odd," Bob Anderson mumbles in a low voice.

None of them notice the sudden perfect stillness of Uncle Floyd in the corner. His eyes glazed and transfixed on something no one else is aware of.

"Alright," Perry takes charge, "Let's begin. It appears the spirits may be eager to speak."

"Yeah, right," Darrell says under his breath.

"Shush," Stella scolds and the bulldog face con nods obedience.

"I want everyone to focus on the crystal ball," Perry orders lightly, "Don't take your eyes off of it. Focus all your energies as if it's a window to the spirit world. Feel the spirits in the house and let them know we mean no harm and only wish to talk with them."

In truth the standing screwdriver sobered everyone enough to begin to take the seance seriously. More than originally intended by most. Especially Terry, Darrell, and Stella. In fact Perry was the only one who originally took it deadly seriously. Katrina did as well but she was more fearful and reluctant to do it at all given her long history with the house.

Everyone stares at the crystal ball centered on the table top, holding hands that are beginning to perspire. Perry occasionally says things like, "Oh, spirits of this house if you are here give us a sign. We beseech you to communicate with us. Join us at the table. Please, respectfully give us a sign of your presence. Let us know your desires. Come to us so that we may aid you."

Perry's passion escalates as he begs the spirits to make their presence known.

"It's getting hot in here," Stella whispers nervously. In fact everyone in the room begins to notice the temperature rise drastically. Everyone is beginning to show beads of sweat on their foreheads. The heat does not seem to affect the paralyzed Floyd watching the events enraptured. The room becomes thick with humidity. Everyone's vision becomes hazy.

Bob is sure he sees something growing in the center of the crystal ball. He doesn't want to believe it. It could be a trick of his eyes brought on by the heat and intense concentration. Bob sees tiny black insects trapped within the clear globe. Flies begin to buzz within. Buzzing around, bouncing off the interior glass sphere, growing in number, becoming frenzied and claustrophobic. Bob's hands feel slick with sweat.

Uncle Floyd moves with a quickness unnatural for his physical prowess. He walks with grace and stealth to stand next to Perry unnoticed. Both hands resting atop his cane as he gazes intently into the crystal ball. A queer look on his face. A look of dreadful desire. He stands perfectly motionless.

Katrina feels a rush of sadness, melancholy. She begins to quietly sob, her head down, hair hiding her face, no longer able to maintain eye contact with the crystal ball.

Darrell feels an irrational fear growing in his stomach. A panic. He wants to flee but is afraid to let go of anyone's hands. He wants to flee but from what he knows not.

Terry grinds his teeth, clenching his jaw. A vein pulsating on his forehead. His eyes wide in jealous rage. He knows he saw Darrell looking at Katrina in the crystal globe. Looking at her in a sexual way. He knows Darrell wants his wife and Terry wants to kill Darrell for it. At least beat the living hell out of him. He begins to squeeze his neighbor's hands too tightly.

Stella sees the room getting foggy, smoky. It's stuffy and hard to breathe. "Is this real?" She whispers to no one.

Bob's pale lips begin to tremble in fear. The crystal ball is so filled with flies it's all black, but no one else seems to see it.

"Show yourself!" Perry shouts, caught up in a mad ecstasy.

Everything happens at once. Everyone sees something different.

In Perry's mind this is it. The moment of truth he has been seeking for his entire life. Finally, clarity. A shift in paradigm. He now knows with certainty there is something more to this world than materialism. A chaotic divinity if nothing else. Or a non-physical aspect of reality. There is something more than man and this life of flesh. The only thoughts Perry can verbalize are a faint whisper of, "Holy, holy, holy."

What Perry sees leaves his head spinning with awe and fear and shock. What he witnesses is a multitude. A spiritual experience of plethora. Hovering and growing above the crystal ball is a sticky, ichorous ectoplasm rising and twisting in the form of a DNA helix grey, white, and sick yellow in color. It dances and swirls upward with an ancient intelligence.

To his left a naked old man emerges from the shadows of the basement doorway, too thin and bony, snow bearded with a crooked yellow toothed grin. Pale moon saggy skin from his arms, stringy, long, unhealthy hair. A deranged madness in his darting, glossy, eyes. He stands snarling and drooling with knobby, skinny fingers holding the edges of the doorway, swaying. Perry feels a vile illness radiating from the dead old man.

In the corner where Uncle Floyd had been standing next to Perry, Perry observes a translucent elderly woman looking more corpse than alive. The woman has hair white as snow flowing like thin wisps to her feet. A look of malevolence in her black empty eye sockets. A look of superiority. A devilish smirk of violation.

On the floors and ceilings and along the walls, Perry sees shadowy skeletal figures crawling in unusual and inhuman methods like bony spiders of dead men. The shadowy skeletal figures surround and close in on the group of seance participants.

"This is killing my heart," Bob Anderson gasps. In Bob's eyes he sees a completely different scene. The table and floors and ceilings have been overrun by creeping, disgusting insects of all shapes and sizes. Flies. Cockroaches. Centipedes. Spiders. Slugs. Alien looking insects. So many bugs it looks like the walls are alive with black chittering movement. They slither and fall over each other. Bob holds back a scream and suddenly clutches his heart, gasping in pain.

Terry stares in the crystal ball seeing nothing but a vision of Darrell having sex with his wife Kartina and Stella at the same time. The rage grows inside him like a disease. He wants to explode and scream at everyone in the room. He wants to murder Darrell. Bash his skull in.

Stella sees what she believes is the Devil in the window looking in at her with a magnificent toothy grin. A man with scarlet glowing eyes and a pair of pointed, stubby horns protruding from his forehead. A sick smile, licking his lips with a forked tongue. The Devil makes obscene gestures, wagging his tongue between two fingers pressed against his mouth. Stella is horror struck by the vision.

Darrell sees nothing but the looks of horror and confusion on the other seance participants' faces. He feels an ever sinking depression, a forlorn worthlessness weighing his soul down like a heavy iron anchor dragging it far below the sea. He knows in truth he is nothing. He is no good. He is a bad man. A criminal. He's done awful things. Selfish things. If Hell is a real place it's where he deserves to go. No one truly likes him. Anyone who truly got to know the real Darrell would be revolted and hate him. He's a broken man. Broken as a child. No one loved him. He's never been loved. His father deserted him as a child and his alcoholic mother beat him and called him awful names growing up. He is nothing. He doesn't deserve anything. He doesn't deserve friends. He doesn't deserve to live. Tears pool in his eyes.

Katrina looks at Terry and realizes she hates him. Hates him more than anything in this world. She thinks about everything he's done to her since they started dating. And the things he's done to her boys, Karl and Kurtis. Terry started out so sweet and tender. He had a real way with words. Then once they were married the anger came out of hiding. His abuse. She remembers every fight. Every time he yells at them. Every time he's threatened or hit her or her sons. Every name he's called them. Every scratch, bruising pinch, and hair pulling. Every broken promise to never do it again. Katrina hates him. Hates him with all her heart and she's his prisoner. She hates everything about him. She hates his face and the way he carries himself. She hates his voice. She hates him for making her afraid. She wants a divorce but is afraid of what he'll do if she says it. Katrina wishes Terry was dead.

Upstairs Karl and Kurtis are sound asleep. Floating in midair above their bed, simply hovering there as if held up by some invisible force. The goat man is tap dancing on the roof with a delightful glimmer in his crimson eyes. The attic door creaks open and multiple eyes of twinkling diamonds peer out.

Back downstairs around the dining room table, Bob sees black and grey insects begin to crawl, creep, and swarm up his legs and arms, covering his body in a coat of bugs, climbing inside his mouth, nose, and ears, underneath his clothes, burrowing into his skin.

"The dead?" Perry asks with an unhinged smile, sweat dripping over his face.

"Sisten!" Uncle Floyd shouts above all the mental ruckus with a disposition and authority, not his own, swinging his cane overhead, bringing it down on the crystal ball centered on the table shattering it into a million pieces. The globe shatters outward in an explosion of glass shrapnel covering all the seance participants in silvery, sharp splinters.

At the same moment they all involuntarily release each other's clammy hands and upstairs the boys instantly fall back to the bed, the attic eyes vanishing in the dark. The boys wake startled, but only look at each other confused before rolling over to go back to sleep.

All the myriad visions everyone had been experiencing are relinquished. The room temperature drops so suddenly as to give everyone a sudden chill.

Uncle Floyd looks at himself again yet confused as to why he is standing by the dining room table.

The seance participants exchange looks of horror and wonderment, clothes and faces dripping with sweat and fear, wide eyed, and taken back.

Bob Anderson is gasping at his chest, struggling for air, before falling back to the floor chair and all.

Katrina only stares in dazed confusion.

"Bob!" Terry shouts, running to his sponsor and boss's side, kneeling down to aid the ailing elder man. Darrell joins Terry's rescue effort.

Stella sits in shock with her hands over her mouth, tears making lines of black mascara stream down her cheeks.

Perry stands, stunned, horrified, and overjoyed at the same time. A dizzying mix of emotions.

"Call 911!" Terry shouts to everyone in the dining room.

The fire department arrives first followed by the police and an ambulance. It's too late. Bob Anderson has died of heart failure on the dining room floor.

Perry vaguely tries to talk about the things they've seen tonight, but none of the others are willing to discuss it.

Perry and Stella leave the house together once the emergency services have left. They say little on the ride home. Everyone is still shaken up by the incident.

Perry and Stella drive in silence for the first few minutes. Both distraught over the sudden death of Bob Anderson.

"He's the only one who didn't want to do it," Stella laments.

Perry nods, "I know. It's a tragedy."

After several more moments of silence Perry says, "I must be crazy. No one else saw anything. I saw ghosts. Several of them. All over the room. I know I did."

"I believe you," Stella answers softly gazing out the window at the passing traffic and street lights.

Perry notices the guilt in her tone and expressions, "You saw something too?"

Stella lights a cigarette and cracks the window, looking at him for a moment trying to decide if she should trust him or not. "Promise you won't tell anyone. I'll deny it."

"I won't tell anyone," Perry reassures, "I promise."

Stella shakes her head in disbelief as if trying to shake the images from her mind before saying them out loud, "I think I saw the Devil."

Perry nods with empathy, hiding his shock and excitement, "Bob must have seen something too. Something so frightening it killed him."

"My God, Perry," Stella says in a reserved tone, "Why didn't the others see anything? What the hell did we do?"

"I suspect the others did see things. Things awful enough they don't want to acknowledge them."

"I'm never going back to that house," Stella makes clear.

"Something terrible must have happened in that house," Perry guesses.

"I don't want to know what it was," Stella responds.

They don't say much more for the rest of the ride home. Perry wishes her well as she gets out at her apartment complex.

Darrell sits in his motel room staring at a syringe on the nightstand next to a half bottle of whiskey. The muted television is the only light flickering in the small room. A digital clock alarm clock plays sad music quietly so as not to arouse the attention of the other motel tenants.

He hasn't been himself since the night of the seance. Darrell just can't seem to shake this feeling of hopelessness that entered his soul that night. A feeling that's always been there just under the surface, but that fateful night brought it glaringly to the forefront of his thoughts and feelings. He can't kick this depression and the booze is not helping. He stopped going to meetings weeks ago. The depression is eating through his insides like a corrosive disease. A black depression weighing his every thought and movement down. All his smiles are fake.

What's the point of staying clean and sober if it's just as miserable as when he's using?

Darrell can't shake the memory of Bob dying either. It bothers him. If they had only taken the seance more seriously or not done it at all. Seeing good, old red nosed Bob on the floor drooling and pissing his pants. Darrell just can't shake it.

The funeral wasn't much better. Bob's corpse looked so stiff and deflated in the casket with too much makeup on his face. It hardly looked like Bob at all.

"Jesus Henry Christ on a Crutch," Darrell mutters, wondering what the point of life is. To be born, suffer, suffer the rigors of nature and age, of hardship, and heartbreak, all to croak in the end with no meaning behind it.

The most spiritual Darrell's ever felt has been when he's fucked up chemically. When he's high or drunk. That's all we need. Escape from the world of shit. Escape from the slavery of the rich.

The funeral. That was the last time he'd seen anyone from that blasted seance. Terry, Katrina, Perry, and Stella were all there along with all the other AA chumps. None of them mentioned what happened that night around the dining room table. That was the last time Darrell has seen anyone from Alcoholics Anonymous. He's been holed up in this dingy, flea infested motel room ever since. Drinking everyday. Hiding from his parole officer. He quit his job the day after the funeral. It's pointless. Life is a preparation for death and nothing more.

The alcohol is not enough.

Darrell lights up a joint before picking up the needle on the nightstand. The rig is already to go. He wraps a shoe strip around his arm and feels that old, familiar snake bite sink into his vein. The blood rushes. A welcome home of blissful oblivion.

Yes.

To go nowhere.

Perry stands outside an AA meeting after it's over waiting for Stella to come out. He'd seen her go into a different meeting room than he had. Perry hasn't spoken to anyone from the seance since Bob's sad funeral. It's obvious the participants have all been avoiding each other. Word is that Terry and

Katrina have started attending meetings at another clubhouse on the west side of town.

Perry stands by a lone tree outside the AA hall waiting to catch Stella. The sun is setting as the first of the AA members begin to trickle out the front door of the clubhouse.

"Hey, Perry," a tall, thin man with long grey hair tied back in a ponytail with a pair of sunglasses propped up on his forehead and wearing a colorful Hawaiian shirt approaches Perry with a friendly smirk as he lights a cigarette, offering to shake Perry's hand.

"Hey, Toomes," Perry takes his hand with a nod, "How are you?"

"Another day sober," Toomes smiles with his cool cat voice. "How about yourself? Haven't seen you around the meetings lately."

"I'm good," Perry answers, "Been busy with school and some side projects."

"Don't get too busy with the program, man," Toomes recommends.

"You're right," Perry agrees, "I have been slacking on my meetings lately. I will be changing that."

"Good to hear. Listen, my man, anytime you wanna ride to a meeting together just give me a call," Toomes offers, "You've got my number."

"I do," Perry says, "I'll likely take you up on that offer soon."

"Good to hear," Toomes says, waving at another couple of AA members exiting the building, "That's my newest sponsee over there. I better go catch up with him. Don't be a stranger, Perry."

"I won't," Perry answers as Toomes walks away only half listening to what Perry just said.

Just then Stella steps out the door and her face lights up with recognition and hesitation at the sight of Perry standing alone by the old tree.

He waves at her with a welcoming smile.

Stella stands for a moment as if deciding what to do, then gives into fate and approaches Perry.

"How are you?" She asks him in a reserved tone.

"I'm okay. You?"

She sighs and lights a cigarette, "I've been better."

"Sorry to hear that, Stella," Perry responds with sincerity. "I need to talk with you Stella. Do you have the time?"

She exhales a short series of smoke rings, about to say no, but something in her changes her mind, "Alright. You can give me a lift home."

"I'd be happy too," Perry can't hide his little smile and they walk together to his car which is parked on the street. A few familiar AA's wave and nod hello as they make their way to Perry's car.

Perry thinks AA is like the perfect example of a well functioning secret society. Not as secret as it's meant to be, but the network created by the members of AA creates a natural situation in which members help each other out with jobs, finances, connections, things like that. It's not intentional, it just happens when a group of people ban together to become involved in each other's lives helping each other stay sober, sane, and spiritual. Thankfully there are no nefarious agendas of the 12 step programs.

In his research Perry has come to believe in some sort of occult connection involved in the founding of Alcoholics Anonymous. Exactly what, he doesn't know for sure but he has found suggestive evidence that the original founder of AA had some type of connections with angels, Ouija boards, and some types of Christian Masonic Lodges.

Perry's search for God has led him down some admittedly strange avenues. The AA/occult connection doesn't alarm him much, only because AA seems to be a force for good. Unless of course it's a conspiracy to dumb the masses, but he hasn't given it much thought,

Once Stella and Perry are driving they share a few moments of silence. This will be the first time they've spoken since Bob's funeral. After a few minutes Stella asks, "Did you hear about Darrell?"

"No, I haven't seen nor heard from him in quite awhile."

"He's dead."

"My god, how?"

Stella wipes a single tear away that was forming in her eye and lights another cigarette. "He relapsed. Went on the run. He overdosed in a motel room."

Perry's heart sinks. He didn't care much for the guy but he didn't wish him death. "This is a fucking heartbreaking disease."

"It is," Stella agrees, "So what is it you wanted to talk to me about?"

Perry feels hurt and alone, rejected by her reluctance to talk with him. Then he reminds himself, she is here, in his car, and has agreed to hear him out.

"Terry and Katrina don't return my calls," Perry starts.

"No surprise there."

"Have you talked to them?"

"Not really," Stella answers, "I saw them at a meeting once since the funeral. Talked with Katrina for a few minutes but Terry cut it short."

"Why would they be avoiding us?" Perry is perplexed.

"I'd say it's pretty obvious after what happened. I don't like to think about it. I'm sure they want to forget it as well. Hell, I'd prefer it if I could completely forget it ever happened. I'm not even sure what happened anymore."

"I need you," Perry says, "You saw something. I saw something. I think it's safe to assume Bob saw something too. He had to. It must have caused his heart failure whatever it was. I'm suspecting

Darrell saw something too."

"Why do you need my help?" Stella asks, curious.

"To convince Terry and Katrina they need to get out of that house. I need you to help get them to listen to me. They're in danger. That house is evil. Maybe even the entire plot of land. It's cursed. It they don't get out of there that house may kill them or worse. Maybe possess them or drive them insane. We have to bless the house or smudge it. Cleanse it in prayers. Maybe burn the unholy place to the ground."

"Katrina and her family grew up there," Stella wonders, "Why hasn't anything happened to the family in the past?"

Perry gives her a quizzical look, "We don't know that it hasn't."

"Burning the place to the ground sounds a little extreme," Stella points out.

"A last resort," Perry says, "Hopefully it doesn't come to that."

"That's crazy talk," Stella says.

"You told me you saw the Devil in the window. I saw much more than that. Please, just hear me out, Stella," he takes his hand in hers and kisses the back of it as he drives. Her hair is in bright blonde curls with big earrings and gaudy sparkly sunglasses shaped like stars tucked up under her hair. "Stella, you know me. I'm asking you to trust me."

Stella looks at him with doubt spread across her face. She does believe Perry is a good hearted man. He seems to take his recovery as a serious priority. He is intelligent, if a bit eccentric. She knows he is working on a graduate degree at Northington University.

Perry pulls his car up to Stella's house. She lives in an apartment building designed for people in the early stages of recovery. It's not a bad place. There is a groundskeeper to check in on the tenants sobriety with breathalyzers. She has to meet with a case manager once a week and a group therapy session with the other residents, besides being required to attend four AA meetings a week.

Besides the focus on chemical dependency the facility also teaches basic living skills such as how to budget money and social skills. Stella is making friends there and is hopeful about the future. She is genuine about putting her all into her recovery.

"Alright," Stella nods, "You can come in for a cup of coffee and tell me more about this haunted house."

"Thanks," Perry answers with relief.

Stella's apartment is a very small place. A small bedroom with a living room/kitchenette that are only separated by a division in carpet designs.

They sit on a sofa in the half living room, cups of coffee on an ebony coffee table. Stella is forever smoking a cigarette, a habit she hopes to break once she's got some solid sobriety under her belt. "Hungry?" She asks, "I have some leftover spaghetti I can heat up."

"Actually, now that I think about it I haven't eaten all day," Perry rubs his belly.

"Sure, It'll just take a few minutes in the microwave."

Several minutes later Stella is sprinkling fresh Parmesan cheese on the heated plates of spaghetti. "So," she says between mouthfuls, "What more do you have to tell me about this haunted house of Terry and Katrina's?"

"It's a long story. Hard to believe. That house on the hill on top of Maine Street has quite a colorful history. Please give me the benefit of the doubt with what I am going to share with you. You know I'm a student at Northington University. My extracurricular studies have a somewhat esoteric bend to them. There is a small group of like minded individuals who have been taken under the wing of a very eccentric Professor Somers. She has access to non-public publications. I mean a virtual library of old, dusty books ranging from old Masonic texts, to old Applegate city records, local church records, old newspapers, unique historical texts, and rare arcane tomes. I've had a fellow student friend of mine named Bon Denbraven helping me research the history of that house."

"You've got my attention," Stella tilts her head, arching a brow. "You have my full attention even if I'm not entirely sure what you've just told me. If I'm getting this right, you have access to a private library at the university."

"Right on," Perry gives a nerdy grin, "So this is going to take a bit of a history lesson."

"My favorite subject," Stella says with sarcasm.

"Okay," Perry begins, "Here it goes. In 1871 there was a secret group called the Vril Society founded by a small group of people who believed in a race of super beings that lived deep inside the hollow of the Earth. They believed the center of the Earth was hollow, something like Jules Verne's *Journey to the Center of the Earth*, except this super race lived underground. They were descendents of the survivors of Atlantis."

Stella, always chain smoking, lights another cigarette, giving Perry a look of absurdity.

"Keep in mind," Perry goes on, "In the eighteenth and nineteenth centuries it was very much in vogue to belong to secret organizations like the Masons and the Illuminati and such."

"Okay," Stella shrugs, "Go on."

"Some time in the 1800s another secret group was started called the Order of the Black Sun. It is believed this clandestine organization had historical ties to pagan Rome and the black nobility of the survivors of the Merovingian royal bloodline."

Perry clears his throat before continuing, "The third secret society connected to this house on North Maine Street was called the Thule Society. They believed the Aryans came from a lost land called

Hyperborean. It's capital was Thule Ultima. This group was also founded sometime in the 1800s. The exact dates of the foundation of both these groups are uncertain."

He continues his narrative, "The memberships of these groups mostly came from Germany, Austria, Prussia. The Aryans we're discussing here have nothing to do with the modern conception of the white, blue eyed, blond human that came about as disinformation and propaganda of Nazi agenda."

"Okay," Stella nods, "what do these three secret societies have to do with the house on North Maine?"

"Bare with me," Perry tells on, "These particular three societies worked closely together, among others, at a time aiding in the rise of Hitler and the Nazis coming to power. They were magicians, hypnotists, mesmerists, esotericists, theosophists, spiritualists, mad scientists, and the like. Men and women who experimented with minds, bodies, and spirits. Magi that were learning to make things happen with will power alone. Or some said with the power of vril. They learned to communicate with non-human intelligence. In 1933 a prophet of the Vril Society named Dagobert selected members from each of these three groups to move to America with the supposed intention of founding new chapters of all three orders. When they left Germany Dagobert chose thirteen apostles who believed in his words and felt the call to spread his gospel."

Perry takes a breath before continuing his brief historic discourse, "Some of the names of the apostles are known: Dagobert's wife, Uschi Rothenberg and the Norwegians Astrid and Jarle Sisten, originally of the Black Sun; Gottlieb and Gisela Ebner of Thule; and Reinholdt and Svenja Rothenberg of the Vril. Dagobert himself was a high ranking member of the Vril Society. The other seven apostles are unknown."

"I have faith this history lesson is leading somewhere," Stella says as she brings the empty spaghetti plates to her small kitchenette. "More coffee?"

"Yes, please," Perry answers politely, thrilled she's been listening so intently.

"Before we go on, Perry," she sets a fresh coffee in front of him, ""How the hell do you know all this crazy shit? This is a little hard to swallow."

"A valid question," Perry agrees. "Like I mentioned, a colleague, Bon Denbraven, helped me with research and I already told you about Professor Somers private library at Northington. Somers comes from a wealthy family. Old money. Academics. World travelers."

"How long is this story?" Stella slides closer to Perry on the sofa.

"Just a bit more. And it gets more bizarre. In fact I think the entire history of our little city of Applegate here weird and queer, but that's for a different time."

Stella nods, with a smirk.

Perry leads on, "The prophet Dagobert foresaw the defeat of Adolf Hitler in 1945. He couldn't let this be known among any but his most trusted disciples, who became his 13 apostles. Dagobert secretly brought his apostles to the middle of nowhere." Perry gives a climatic grin, "Applegate, South Dakota. The New Atlantis. The apostles built homes here. Jarle and Astrid Sisten built the house on the top of the hill on North Maine Street in 1934."

Stella's face brightens like a light bulb has just lit up, "The Sisten's are haunting the house!"

"Absolutely," Perry says, "I think there may be more to it but I don't know. I know when Dagobert and his followers arrived they infiltrated the local Masonic Lodges. The mad prophet Dagobert founded his own new secret society based on a conglomeration of all three previous groups' belief systems fused into one solid religious belief system with Dagobert as the prophet of the coming of the return of the Merovingians. Dagobert claimed to be a demigod, a direct descendent of Yeshua ben Yosef. This new cult was called *the Antiqua Clericis de in Noctus Sol*."

"I'm impressed Perry," Stella admits, "and I think you're little cabal of Northington cohorts may be more than they seem."

"Not really, just a small group of academics interested in unusual things. I guess you could call us *the X-Files* of Northington University. Nothing mysterious, just pursues curiosities."

"So what happened to the Sistens?" Stella asks.

"Black magic rituals gone array is my best guess," Perry answers. "Dagobert wanted to create a new race of supermen based on the idea of the Vril-ya. The next dominant race of Earth. The next step in evolution. There were all kinds of perverted black masses and if it's to be believed, human sacrifices in that house."

"Mother Mary," Stella's lips tremble.

"The things I'm telling you, Stella, we have to keep them to ourselves. If *the Antiqua Clericis de in Noctus Sol* still exists we could be in danger. There is no accounting for seven of the apostles of Dagobert. We'll have to make it clear Terry and Katrina understand this."

"I don't think I can handle this," Stella crushes out a cigarette in an ashtray. "What happened to the Sistens? How did Candace and her husband end up owning the house?"

"It's murky," Perry answers, "The Sistens were found dead in the house under unsolved circumstances in 1947. Astrid was found dead in the attic. Jarle in the basement. Candace and her husband, Volker Barnes, purchased the house in 1949."

"How were the Sisten's killed?"

"Jarle hung himself in the basement with the bodies of several dead and decomposed children found along with him. Astrid was suffocated in the attic by unknown means."

"Jesus," Stella gasps, "What the fuck is this nightmare?"

"The house itself has seemed to become a conduit of evil," Perry deduces, "Such awful things have happened there it's weakened the fabric of reality between our world and who knows where. Before the house was even built on that spot there was an American Indian medicine man named Painted Bear that was slaughtered there with his small band of followers. Including women, children, and the elderly. It was said Painted Bear cursed the land with his dying breath."

Stella's face is an expression of disbelief, "You think the Sistens and their followers and maybe even these Native Americans are haunting the place?"

"Maybe," Perry goes on, "Maybe something more or less than that. I don't know for sure. I'm only guessing, trying to connect the dots. These followers of Dagobert were ceremonial magicians to say the least."

"You believe in magic?" Stella asks in all seriousness.

"I'm beginning to," Perry continues, "Through Dagobert they supposedly spoke with non-humans. I don't know what. Aliens. Ghosts. Demons. Angels. Gods. Something. Dagobert and *Noctus Sol* made a pact with some entities. If it's to be believed we are talking about the fallen archangel Samael and the first woman God created, Lilith. In exchange for Dagobert becoming lord of the world, Samael and Lilith would be incarnated in human flesh. Dagobert would also be gifted with immortality. To be the king of men again. The return of his bloodline as the rulers of humanity, all things great and small."

"Obviously this didn't happen," Stella observes. "What happened? How do you know all of this if no one else does?"

Perry nods at the wisdom of her questions, "Something obviously went awry. Once again it's speculation. As I told you before, Applegate was a hot spot for the weird and abnormal. Applegate and the surrounding areas were crawling with other secret societies, most of which had been here longer than *Noctus Sol*. I don't know which groups were here but I know for certain there were lodges of the Masons, the Rosicrucians, and the Hellfire Club. One of these groups must have intervened and they were only able to do it with the help of one man. Gottlieb Ebner. I know everything I've told you because Professor Somers has the diaries of Ebner in her private library. Ebner was a true traditionalist. He wanted nothing to do with Samael and Lilith. Bon found the legal documents in old city records concerning the sale of the house to the Barnes family."

"It's too much to take in," Stella lights another cigarette, "It's like a god damned episode of *the Twilight Zone* or something."

Perry nods, "After the deaths of the Sistens, Dagobert and the others disappeared. There are no records. As if they just fell off the face of the Earth."

Stella only shakes her head, "This is pretty heavy, Perry. I mean what are we supposed to do with this information? It's an unbelievable story."

"We have to convince Katrina's family to get out of that house immediately," Perry answers.

"That's not going to be easy," Stella says, "Where the hell are they going to go? Katrina and her mom pretty much have spent their whole lives in that place."

"I don't know," Perry admits, "I know Toomes has plenty of space in his house since his wife passed away years ago. You know he's always willing to help people in the program out. Besides that I think it'd be good for him to have some company for a while."

"A whole family?" Stella sounds doubtful.

"Toomes is very committed to AA. He might do it."

"Okay," Stella says, "Let's assume I believe half of what you're telling me. What was that thing I saw in the window that night?"

"Samael, I think."

"And remind me again. Who are Samael and Lilith? Samael is a fallen archangel. The angel of death. Patron of ancient Rome. The seducer, accuser, and destroyer. Samael's consort is Lilith and she was the first woman God created before Eve, but she rebelled against Adam and God becoming the goddess of the night, slayer of children, the mother of lamia and abominations."

"This is beyond us, Perry," Stella sounds apprehensive.

"It's not," Perry assures her, "I think Astrid and Jarle Sisten are still bound to their oaths. If we can lay them to rest this could be over. It could be the end of it."

"I don't know why," Stella exasperates, "I must be crazy, but I believe you. What are we going to do?"

"I have a plan, Stella," Perry grins, "I just want you to know something before you agree to help me with this. Once you step out of the ordinary world into this darker place, nothing will be the same. You will see glimpses of what reality truly is. The spooks and astral zombies will sense you and take notice. Once you've crossed the line into the world of the supernatural there is no turning back."

Stella sits a moment contemplating everything Perry has just said before answering, "Terry will be a problem. He's an overbearing ass hole."

Perry laughs, "Terry is a prick."

"So what's the plan," Stella asks.

Perry smiles again, "A twelve step intervention."

The twelfth step is passing the message of hope for recovery and a better way of life to actively struggling alcoholics and addicts. A group of AA members usually one or more visit a person struggling with addiction they want to show a way out of their addiction or a fellow member of the program they fear is in danger of relapsing.

"Oh, god," Stella chuckles.

"I told you about a fellow student at Northington named Bon Denbraven. He's a good man who's had some experience with the supernatural. I thought we could bring him and Toomes."

Stella nods, "What kind of experience has your friend had with the supernatural?"

"His fiance was killed by a South American witch doctor," Perry answers grimly.

Stella just looks at Perry unsure how to react to that statement.

"I think Toomes will go for it," Perry changes the subject, "He has twenty years sober and he's a retired psychologist. He still does volunteer work as a shrink. He may even be open minded enough to buy into all of this."

"What do you want me to do?" Stella asks.

"Katrina was your former sponsor. I think she still would be if it weren't for Terry. Besides that I think Terry has a crush or something on you. I just want you to come along for support. I think they both may be more open to listening with you there. I'll speak with Toomes and set it up as soon as I can."

Spur of the moment Stella leans over and kisses Perry on the lips. Perry welcomes the kiss and pulls her down to the sofa with him.

Since the seance things have gone from bad to worse between Katrina and Terry. Terry hasn't found a replacement sponsor for Bob Anderson and he's been out of work since Bob passed on. Terry has been picking up as many odd jobs as he can lay his hands on, but it's been tough. The economy is not good and unemployment is at a high. Terry and Katrina have frequent fights about finances. Candace has taken more and more to herself ignoring Terry and Katrina and spending as little time as she can with them. They are not even eating meals together anymore.

Terry would never admit the insecurity he's feeling about struggling to provide for his family. Candace is less happy because she wants Terry and Katrina to move out. Terry at the very least. She can't stand the man. They've overstayed their welcome and summer is almost over.

Terry and Katrina have started attending AA meetings on the west side of town instead of the south side of town which makes Katrina even more miserable. She's naturally shy and has a hard time meeting new people. She was comfortable at their southside AA meetings and finally felt like she was making some friends. The change in meeting locations has more to do with Terry's irrational jealousy more than the death of Bob Anderson. Katrina has become afraid to talk to any men at all let alone look at them. Which is not fair because Katrina is not the kind of woman to take her wedding vows lightly. She is committed to Terry for better or worse.

Ever since they were married Katrina realized Terry has a temper. A frightening, unpredictable temper, but ever since the death of Bob Anderson, Terry always seems angry now or on the verge of losing it. He is just not his old self. Katrina wonders if Terry needs to see a therapist or at least talk to someone about Bob's death.

Every night they have sex but Katrina derives no pleasure from it. Terry is too rough and acts like it's her wifely duty to give him sex every night.

Katrina doesn't talk back to Terry anymore. It's an easy way for her to end up with two black eyes, then be stuck at home hiding them until they heal. She's come to the point where she doesn't speak to Terry unless she is spoken to.

Upstairs in Uncle Floyd's room Grandma Candace has grounded him from all his toys. She's packed then away in boxes in the hallway crawl space attic between the two bedrooms. He's grounded for trying to touch one of Candace's church ladies friends' boobs when she gave him a hug after dinner the other night.

"That stinks," Kurtis complains.

"Yes, it does," Floyd says angrily while sitting on his bed rocking vigorously and chewing on his tongue.

"Maybe we should sneak a few out and put them back before she notices," Karl suggests.

The sandy haired neighbor girl, Casey, is up in the bedroom with them, "It's kind of boring without the toys."

"I don't want to get in any more trouble," Uncle Floyd grumbles.

"Yeah," Kurtis sits on the wood floor in need of a good sweeping with his head hanging low in boredom.

"Maybe we can play school," Casey suggests, "I'll be the teacher."

"No," Kurtis laments, "School is starting for real soon. I don't want to think about summer being over."

"I hate it when summer ends too," Casey agrees.

"I hate it when we're grounded from Uncle Floyd's toys," Kurtis complains. "He's the one that's grounded. Why shouldn't we still get to play with them?"

"Because they're my toys!" Uncle Floyd is insulted.

"Let's just get in the attic and take a few out," Casey gets excited. "We'll put them back before your grandma ever knows."

"Floyd's right," Karl looks defeated, "It's probably not a good idea."

"We won't get caught," Casey smiles and winks at Uncle Floyd.

"Are you sure?" Floyd hesitates.

"I'm sure," Casey gives a more cheerful smile.

"I wanna do it, I wanna do it," Kurtis agrees.

"I'm not doing it," Karl crosses his arms and sits next to Floyd on the bed. "If you get caught it was you and Kurtis, not me and Uncle Floyd."

Casey and Kurtis ignore Karl, which irritates Karl because Casey is older than Kurtis and should know better.

When Casey and Kurtis open the short attic wall door it sends a shiver through Karl. It doesn't seem right. He doesn't think they should go in there.

Inside the attic crawl space the north wall is slanted to align with the roof outside. There are several cardboard boxes filled with Floyd's toys. Casey and Kurtis tear into the boxes like it's Christmas morning.

"It's pretty dark in here," Kurtis points out with slight trepidation in his voice. He tries to stay as close to Casey as he can to hide his fear of the dark.

"Don't worry about it," Casey gives a carefree smile, "We'll be out of here in a couple of minutes. Don't be a scared-y cat."

"I'm not scared of anything," Kurtis puffs up his chest like a rooster.

Outside the attic, sitting side by side on the bed, Karl asks his uncle, "What was the seance like?"

"I'm not supposed to talk about it," Uncle Floyd answers tight lipped.

"Oh, come on," Karl begs, "I won't tell anyone. I promise. Besides, we don't keep secrets from each other."

"I guess we don't," Floyd responds in a low voice.

"Remember at the beginning of the summer when you, me, Kurtis, and Casey became blood brothers in the backyard?" Karl reminds his uncle.

"I remember," Floyd tries not to smile at the memory.

"That was a blood pact between us. For life. No secrets. We're blood brothers and blood brothers die for each other. And they always help each other."

Floyd nods sadly, "I guess you're right."

"I'll tell you what happened to Kurtis and me," Karl offers. "We had the same dream and saw the goat man dancing on the roof again."

"Well," Uncle Floyd hesitates, "I don't remember much. Mrs. Sisten and I were drinking coffee together. She got real mad when she saw them doing the seance. But she said it was alright because this house is almost in the spirit world and now she and Mr. Sisten can finish what they started a long time ago. After that I lost my memory. I don't know what happened."

"Sounds kind of scary," Karl says.

Inside the attic, Casey says with a handful of toys, "It's really dusty in here." She coughs, "It seems bigger on the inside than on the outside."

"Yeah," Kurtis makes sure to stay close to her. "I think we should get out of here. I am getting scared. It feels like the walls are moving. Like they're breathing."

"Oh, come on, Kurtis," she takes his hand, "Just a little further. It's like an adventure. We might find something cool, like a treasure or something."

"Okay," Kurtis whispers, feeling reassured by his hand in hers. They have crawled far enough into the attic that Kurtis is only staying with Casey because he's too afraid to go back on his own.

Abruptly the attic door shuts on its own accord leaving the two children in utter darkness. Both Casey and Kurtis gasp with little squeals. Kurtis begins to cry. Both clutch each others' hands tightly.

Outside the door Casey and Kurtis can hear Karl trying to open the door and his muffled questioning, "Are you guys alright? Why did you shut the door?"

At the far west side of the long, narrow attic walkway the thin, ghastly Mrs. Sisten, face eager with hunger and violation in her dead, hollow eyes, appears as a phantom from nowhere. Kurtis and Casey's mouths both open as if to scream, but instead Mrs. Sisten's arms elongate unnaturally, her fists impaling so deep in the children's mouths the bulk of them can be seen convulsing under the skin of their throats. The hags arms move about making their necks' skin look like the scales of a python having just swallowed a large animal.

Tears gush from both children's eyes and down their cheeks as the ghost of Sisten utters arcane words as she suffocates both of the youths. Sisten's words are in a language entirely alien to the kids. In her rasping, vile voice, Mrs. Sisten says in a thick Norwegian accent, "Let it be done."

When Casey and Kurtis stop moving, stop breathing, the rotting hag removes her arms covered in slick liquid from their throats and mouths. The children lay dead on the attic floor, with Karl still knocking at the attic door, "Karl? Casey?"

Mrs. Sisten reaches out a bony finger anointing the foreheads with a black soot. A pair of short parallel lines crossed with a pair of angled lines. Like a double cross with the central cross of the "T" slanted to one side.

"Heil Dagobert," lifeless Astrid Sisten breathes with a guttural whisper, "The Oath and Pact of Noctus Sol. We are so close," dry tears of joy drag down her flesh barren cheeks. "Arise angel of death! Arise mother of abominations!"

Both dead children, Kurtis and Casey, gasp and gag in the first breaths of renewed, stolen life.

The children stand, perfectly capable of seeing in the darkness. For several moments they study their little hands and limbs, their childlike bodies. They practice moving and testing their joints, opening and closing their mouths.

"You must still pretend to be children until our lord's second coming," the hag whispers, fading from sight.

Kurtis and Casey exit the attic with innocent grins, carrying toys, and looking at Karl. "What's wrong, big brother? Scared of the dark," Kurtis chortles.

"Scared-y brat," Casey snickers.

Karl is confused, "No, I was just worried when the door shut. I wanted to make sure you were okay."

"We're fine," Kurtis smirks, "Let's play."

Stella is taken back by the sight of Perry Honeycutt's college mate, Bon Denbraven. Not at all what she expected. She expected a bookworm with a pocket protector. A total gamer nerd without tact or class. Not this humorless, handsome man, covered from what seems to be head to toe in scars. Slashes all up and down his skin and body. Healed not more than a year or two ago. Some cut deeper than others. Some simple lines and some crisscrosses. The linear scars of differing lengths and gouges cover his arms, hands, and face. Stella suspects his legs and the rest of his body appears the same. She's uncomfortable as to how to react to his deformities. It's obvious someone or other took their time torturing this man. She feels empathy for him. She sees a pain in Bon's eyes she knows will never leave.

"So," Stella tries to break the awkward silence, "Did you both read Ebner's diaries?"

"Yes," Perry answers.

Bon nods. He has a sheathed sword resting across his thighs as they pull up to Toomes house.

"Um," Stella asks Bon, "Do we really need the sword?"

"I'd rather have it and not need it than need it and not have it," Bon grumbles.

"Don't mind Bon," Perry smiles, "He's not always all doom and gloom."

Bon looks annoyed at Perry and Perry smiles, "I've also been told I have a big mouth in the past. More than once."

"It's true," Bon agrees.

Perry sighs, "We're leaving the sword in the car, Bon. If we need it you can come back out for it. If we try to go into the Barnes' place with the sword they won't even let us in the front door."

A tall, skinny man in his mid-sixties with bumbling strides and his hair back in a ponytail wagging like a tail behind him opens the passenger side of the car door, sitting next to Perry. Toomes gives them all a toothy grin, with a modest air of arrogance, "A twelve stepping we a go!"

Bon and Stella are in the back seat and Bon slides the sheathed sword to the side to hide it from Toomes.

As the quartet drives away, Stella accuses, "You didn't tell Toomes the truth about this twelve step call, did you, Perry."

"The truth?" Toomes appears alarmed.

After several long, question filled minutes later, Perry and Stella have filled Dr. Toomes in on the supernatural aspect of their supposed twelve step call with Bon listening smug and amused in the backseat of the car.

Toomes shakes his head looking out the window at the absence of traffic along this residential lane, "So to make a long story short, you've all gone fucking insane."

"Uh," Perry appears genuinely hurt, "I hope that's not the case."

"How come you didn't tell me the truth from the beginning?" Toomes asks.

"I didn't think you would come," Perry admits, still looking sad.

Toomes nods, clears his throat, "You're right. I wouldn't have."

"Everyone respects you and the things you have to say in the program," Stella jumps to Perry's defense. I wouldn't believe this crap either if I didn't see it with my own two eyes." She reaches forward from the backseat and gently squeezes Toomes shoulder, "Bob and Darrell are dead because of this house. More people are going to die if we don't do something. I know it's unbelievable, Toomes. I'm only asking you to trust Perry and I. Give us the benefit of the doubt this one time. We really need you. We need your help. Please."

Toomes rides along next to them in silence for several minutes contemplating all the outlandish things he's just heard before he finally speaks, "Alright. I've known you for a long time, Perry. Since you first started showing up in rehab when you were just a punk kid. I believe Stella is honest and working on what seems to be a solid program." He glances back at Bon, "I don't know a thing about you, wild card."

Bon gives Toomes a respectful nod.

"I love you like a son, Perry," Toomes admits, "I'll come along to at least make sure things don't get out of hand. I'll try to mediate things."

"Thank you, Gene," Perry smiles at Dr. Toomes' narrow face as they share a smile revealing a long, and caring history.

Perry pulls his car up to the cursed house at the top of the hill on North Maine Avenue. The children Kurtis and Casey are sitting on the front steps stoically observing the new arrivals.

"Do you see that?" Bon asks from the backseat of the car.

"What?" Stella asks, at a complete loss as to what the mystery man is referring to.

"What are we looking for?" Toomes backs her up.

"The basement window," Bon answers softly.

All four of them see what he is talking about. Staring out from the short, front basement window just at ground level is the image of a shirtless haggard, old, long haired man staring angrily out at them. The same man Perry remembers coming up from the basement the night of the seance.

"He's the fucking ghost I saw before," Perry whispers almost too quiet for anyone else to hear him.

"And upstairs," Bon mumbles.

In the upstairs window they can vaguely make out the sick decaying image of Mrs. Sisten glaring out at them just as angry as her deceased husband in the basement window, Mr. Sisten.

"So there are people in the windows," Toomes sounds nervous, "What does that matter?"

"I can tell you're an intelligent man, Dr. Toomes," Bon says, "The brain doesn't want to accept what disturbs the physical senses. Those are the restless spirits Perry and Stella told you about. I know rationality is fighting it off in your mind. I've been there before. But you are a spiritual man from what I understand and you know those are spirits. We don't have time to debate it. The time to act is now."

Toomes gives Bon a look of shocked appreciation as the four of them get out of the car together.

"The sword stays," Perry reminds Bon.

"The sword?" Toomes exclaims.

"Don't worry about it," Stella puts her arm under Toomes' as the four approach the front door. All four notice the old man and woman from the windows have vanished.

Stella throws Kurtis a sweet smile, "How are you, Kurtis?"

"I'm fine," Kurtis answers with a touch of annoyance in his voice. "My mom and dad don't want any visitors right now."

"Oh," Stella looks concerned, "Are they alright?"

"They said they don't feel well today," Kurtis answers, then rudely walks away with Casey at his side.

Bon muses as the pair of kids walk abruptly away.

Stella leads the way, knocking at the door.

After enough time passes that the group begins to think their friends aren't going to answer the door at all, Katrina opens the door a crack with a nervous, forced smile, "Stella. Perry. Toomes. What a pleasant surprise. What brings you here?"

"We were hoping we could come in and have a little impromptu AA meeting with you and Terry," Toomes answers her in a voice as cool as a cucumber.

"How thoughtful," Katrina's voice sounds weak, defeated, as she opens the door to invite them in. Bon notices the yellow brown of a bruise almost healed near her eye.

In still silence, everyone is gathered around the same dining room table where the seance took place. This is a different gathering. A displeased Terry. A timid Katrina. A caring Stella. A nervous Toomes. An excited, curious Perry. An alert Bon. Uncle Floyd sits on his usual green faded stool fiddling with his cane, grumbling about how he wished he had some coffee.

Terry pipes up, "This is utter bull shit and you know it. To come in and pretend you're here because you're concerned about our recovery? That's pretty fricking low. You can't be serious. Are you children believing in ghosts in the closets and under the bed?" He glares at Toomes, "I can expect such garbage from this space cadet, Perry, and this whore Stella, but I'm shockingly disappointed in you, Toomes."

Toomes face turns red with rage rather than embarrassment, "I admit I thought it sounded outrageous, but to tell you the truth your behavior has me more worried than anything else that has been said today."

Terry shakes his head, eyes red with frustration, "Let me guess, Perry, we can come stay at your place to hide from the ghosts so you can try to bed my wife?"

"Terry," Stella has tears in her eyes, "We're only trying to help."

Katrina looks meek and embarrassed.

"And who's this freak of nature you brought with you?" Terry yells, "If you're looking for monsters it looks like you already brought your own."

Bon stands up in a threatening manner, the entire dining room table jerks.

Uncle Floyd looks on, transfixed by the drama unfolding.

"I want all of you out of my house," Terry screams, "Now! None of you are welcome here. I don't want to see any of you around me or my family ever again!"

"It's alright," Toomes holds out his hands in a peaceful gesture, "We're leaving. I'm sorry we bothered you. We only had the best intentions in mind."

They all get up to leave.

Bon is the last one out the door. He turns to face Terry. Terry's rage subsides into a moment of fear when he sees the look on Bon's face and Bon tells Terry in a rasping, low voice, "You've made a mistake today. You've insulted my friends. Left your family at risk. Why don't you hit me once, tough guy, and see if I hit back harder than a woman."

Bon makes both his hands into white knuckled fists.

Terry takes two steps back in fright.

Perry takes Bon by the arm, "My noble friend, this is not the way or the time."

Terry appears relieved it's not the way or the time and hopes that time never comes. Something about this stranger called Bon makes him nervous, but then again it's natural for men who beat women to be afraid to fight men.

Both men leave with Terry not only shutting the door behind them but locking the deadbolt and chain as well.

Grandmother Candace saunters out of her bedroom. She gives Terry a look of disgust and disrespect, "You handled that well Mr. Langley. Like a real courageous man."

"Watch your mouth, old lady," Terry snarls, gritting his teeth.

"Or what?" Candace sneers with no fear.

"Or maybe I'll snap you're fucking neck, you old dusty bitch!" Terry roars at his mother-in-law.

Katrina's face visibly trembles with panic.

"Maybe you will someday," Candace says with utter calm. "But not today. It sounds like you have more important things to worry about, like ghosts."

Terry catches himself internally, embarrassed he just threatened Candace's life. He feels his anger is getting out of control. He just keeps getting more and more hateful and furious every day he feels like he's losing his mind. He doesn't trust himself. He feels like he's going to snap and do something he'll regret and can't take back.

"I didn't see any damn ghosts," Terry huffs. He looks at Katrina, "Did you see any fucking spooks?"

Katrina makes brief eye contact with Terry before lowering her eyes and shaking her head no.

Candace gives her daughter a stern knowing look, Katrina looks away from her mother too and Candace says, "If there are any lingering spirits in this house Katrina would have seen them. It's the way of our family. It's in our blood." Candace shrugs, "If my daughter hasn't seen anything there mustn't be any of the dead here." Candace walks toward the back door, "I have my sun tea to attend to."

"Ghosts," Terry rattles his head, "Bunch of grown folks acting like scared little kids."

Katrina nods and wanders into the kitchen to start making dinner.

"Ooga booga," Uncle Floyd giggles at Terry, twiddling his cane.

"Exactly," Terry says, sitting down on a recliner, picking up a remote control, clicking the television on to an old John Wayne western movie, taking a chug of his 2 liter bottle of cola, and digging into a fresh package of Oreo cookies.

Karl, Kurtis, Casey, and Uncle Floyd are in the backyard playing freeze tag. When someone is "it" they chase the others and if they tag a person, that person has to stand perfectly still as if frozen, until another person who hasn't been frozen crawls quickly between the frozen person's legs, effectively unfreezing them and putting them back into the game. When everyone is frozen, the first person who is frozen is the next person who is "it".

Kurtis is it and he tags his older brother Karl next to the garage with a sprinting speed that surprises Karl. He didn't realize his little brother could run so fast. He must be growing. Karl used to be able to outrun Kurtis without breaking a sweat. Kurtis giggles devilishly and commences to chasing Casey.

Standing next to the garage, pretending to be frozen, Kurtis hears a familiar buzzing and looks up to see dozens of wasps crawling and flying around fresh grey papery hives. Kurtis wonders if the wasps are angry at him for destroying their old hives earlier this summer.

The long, thin wasps seem to buzz and fly closer and closer to him, making Karl skittish. Karl is afraid of the oblong insects and their potential stingers. Black, blank eyes, long yellow and black striped fuzzy bodies with dangling angled legs. Getting closer and closer. Like their hive mind remembers what Karl did.

Karl stumbles away as the insects get closer to him. Uncle Floyd is frozen on the swing set. He can't run very fast and doesn't like to try.

"Cheater!" Kurtis hollers, dashing toward his old brother.

Casey joins in the singing, taunting of Karl, "Cheater! Cheater! Cheater!"

Both Kurtis and Casey dance circles around Karl teasing him.

"No fair!" Karl argues, "The wasps are coming at me! I don't want to get stung again!"

"Who's afraid of wasps? Who's afraid of a little sting?" Kurtis laughs like a little king holding his arms out in the shape of a V up toward the wasp hives.

Karl takes a step back astounded and baffled by what he sees as the first wasp lands on his little brother's extended index finger and crawls harmlessly around his little hand.

Karl is shocked. Casey looks on, grinning. Uncle Floyd watches from the swing set, staring hard with curiosity, head tilted to one side.

Karl's mouth opens in warning as a second wasp lands on his little brother's other hand. Followed by another. And another. And another. Soon what appears to be all of the yellow and black striped wasps are covering Kurtis from head to toe. They buzz, fly, and crawl all over Kurt's body. Karl can make out the maniacal smile of Kurtis beneath the layers of insects and the proud lust in his young eyes. His little brother Kurtis has become what looks like the king of wasps.

Casey jumps up and down, clapping her hands in glee.

"Kurtis!" Karl almost cries.

"They are only bugs, big brother," Kurtis laughs.

Then as if nothing at all happened the wasps all fly away at once leaving the children in peace.

Kurtis sighs, "I'm tired of freeze tag. Let's play something else."

"I don't feel like playing anymore," Karl responds, walking back into the house as both Kurtis and Casey watch him go with entertained expressions.

The next afternoon Karl sits on the swing set in the backyard with his Uncle Floyd. He is sitting in a swing, looking glumly down at his feet dangling on the grass.

"Where's your brother?" Floyd asks, sensing his nephew is blue.

Karl shrugs apathetically, "Back in the trees playing with Casey somewhere. They don't like to play with me anymore."

"Oh, I'm sure they do," Uncle Floyd climbs off his own swing with a goofy grin, "Come on. Let's go fart on them and make them eat shit sandwiches."

Karl laughs hard, holding his belly, then follows his uncle further back into the long backyard.

As Uncle Floyd walks into the third section of the backyard almost to the point where the real little forest begins they see Kurtis and Casey come marching out of the trees like soldiers returning victorious.

Karl and Floyd both stop in place with looks of horror and disgust at the gruesome image before them. Kurtis and Casey both proudly hold up long forked branches they've made into some kind of impromptu spears. At the end of each spear is a freshly killed rabbit. Dead. Lifeless. Dripping with blood and open blank staring little eyes.

"You killed bunnies!" Karl's voice cracks when he says it, almost retching.

"We're just play hunting," Kurtis says, annoyed by his older brother's reaction.

"Maybe we should eat them?" Casey suggests.

"No!" Karl protests.

"Why not, big brother," Kurtis taunts, "I know you like to play with fire."

"No, I don't," Karl defends, wondering how Kurtis could possibly know that.

"Calm down, you sally," Kurtis says to his brother, "We're just playing."

"I'm telling mom," Karl turns to walk away.

"Oh, come on," Kurtis calls after him, "Don't be such a baby."

Karl ignores him and keeps walking back toward the house.

Casey drops her bloody spear and jogs after Karl, pushing her way past a distraught Uncle Floyd. She grabs Karl with both hands and pushes him between two trees. "I'll kiss you if you don't tell," she says faintly.

"Gross!" Karl almost gags, "Why would I want to kiss a girl?"

Casey leans in to kiss Karl even as he evades her lips, she still manages a kiss on the cheek.

"Yuck," Karl wipes his cheek off, "I won't tell if you don't try to kiss me again."

Casey smiles, "Someday you'll want me to."

Katrina is tucking Karl and Kurtis into bed. She just finished saying goodnight prayers with them. They always start out with a list of, "God please watch over so and so," followed by the Lord's Prayer. Uncle Floyd is already snoring in his bedroom across the hall. As she is getting up to turn out the light, Kurtis says with all innocence, "Mom, do you know what my favorite part of that prayer is?"

"What's that, honey?" She asks in a soft, loving voice that only mother's have.

"Deliver us from evil," Kurtis answers.

"You just like the word evil," Karl rolls over, annoyed by his brother for talking so silly.

"Karl," Katrina explains, "He can like any part of the prayer he likes. Deliver us from evil is asking God to protect us all from bad things." She asks Karl, "What's your favorite part of the prayer?"

"Amen," Karl answers.

Katrina smiles and kisses both her sons on the forehead before flicking the bedroom light off and exiting the room.

Kurtis sticks his tongue out at Karl as soon as their mom is out of sight.

Karl punches Kurtis in the shoulder leaving a Charlie horse.

"Mom!" Kurtis yells loudly.

Karl thinks his brother is about to tattle.

Katrina bolts back in the bedroom and switches the light back on, "What's wrong?"

"You have to leave the lights on tonight!" Kurtis cries.

Katrina sits on the bed next to Kurtis and gently runs her hand through his hair, "It's okay. There is no reason to be afraid of the dark. Karl is right here next to you and Uncle Floyd is just in the next room. Neither of them would let anything happen to you. And Terry and I are just downstairs. And Grandma Candace will be back from Bingo soon."

"No! No! No!" Kurtis screams as loud as his little lungs will let him and begins jumping frantically up and down on the bed.

Karl looks worried and baffled by his brother's unusual behavior.

Katrina tries to calm Kurtis down with no success.

Karl feels his stomach upset with fear of what's coming. He doesn't understand what Kurtis is doing. He's never done this before. The only thing Karl knows for certain is that Kurtis is about to bring the wrath of Terry upon them all.

The temper tantrum of Kurtis is escalating out of control. He is still jumping on the bed, screaming, and now throwing things around the room. He's even managed to rip one of the pillows open making the room snow feathers.

Karl's stomach churns. Grandma Candace is gone. There is nothing to hold Terry back.

"Hush, now, Kurtis, please," Katrina's eyes fill with tears as she begs her youngest son to behave.

Uncle Floyd is awake now, but pretending he's still asleep with his eyes half open.

They all hear the heavy footsteps of Terry's work boots ascending the creaking, old, wood staircase.

"Kurtis," Karl whispers with despair, "It's okay. Just go lay down. I'll tell you a story or we can play the imagination game."

"I want the lights on!" Kurtis shrieks.

Tall Terry appears in the bedroom doorway. Karl wants to hide beneath the blankets. With a long, drawn out deep breath Terry asks, "What the hell is going on here?"

"It's nothing," Katrina attempts to placate her husband, "I can handle this."

"It doesn't sound that way from downstairs," Terry takes a foreboding step into the boy's bedroom.

"Please," Katrina tries to hold back tears of fear for her son, "Let me handle this."

Kurtis stops jumping on the bed and stares at his stepfather as the last of the feathers from the busted pillow drift down around him, "What the hell?" Kurtis growls with more defiance than Karl or Katrina have ever heard before, "What the hell is going on? I want the lights on!"

Karl feels his body go stiff as a board, terrified. You do not raise your voice to Terry. Ever.

In an eerily calm voice, Terry orders, "Katrina. Go downstairs . Now."

"Terry, please," the tears are now steaming over her cheeks.

"Deliver us from evil!" Kurtis screams and begins jumping up and down on the bed like a boy who has lost his mind, "Fuck you, Terry! Go fuck yourself! Fuck you! Fuck you! Fuck you!"

Karl and Katrina both gasp.

Katrina tries to grab Terry's arm before he punches Kurtis, but instead she is knocked back against the wall and falls to the floor. Terry's fist connects with Kurtis's face with a loud crack. Blood spurts from the little boys mouth and nose at the same time. It's obvious the nose is broken at the very least.

Karl slides out of bed and bounces onto the wood floor. He climbs under the bed to hide from Terry.

Katrina screams from the floor at the sight of her bloody faced son, Kurtis, laying dead or unconscious on the pillow. Blood trickles from his nose like a faucet. Katrina leaps from the floor having found somewhere deep inside the motherly instincts of a grizzly bear. She launches into Terry slapping, scratching, pulling hair, and biting at her maniacal husband.

Terry fights back with no hesitation. The two adults disappear into the short dark hallway and tumble into Uncle Floyd's bedroom.

Karl climbs out from underneath the bed, looking at his younger brother, tears welling in his eyes because he thinks Kurtis is dead.

Karl can hear the screaming and clobbering going on between Terry and Katrina in his uncle's bedroom. The sounds hurt Karl like nothing he's heard before.

Karl walks into Floyd's bedroom, hearing his mother scream, "Deliver us from evil!" Uncle

Floyd's bedroom is partially illuminated by the light bleeding in from the boys bedroom.

Uncle Floyd is sitting up in bed, a twisted look of loss and helplessness on his face.

What Karl sees next seems to happen in slow motion. His mother, Katrina, pulling away from Terry with such force Terry is left standing with a handful of her hair in his closed fist. Katrina is unable to catch her balance from the momentum and tumbles down the old wood stairs end over end. Terry stands panting, sweating, looking at the handful of hair in his grip with a look of utter confusion as to what has just happened.

"Mom!" Karl screams out.

Terry's head jerks to the side, face red and huffing in the shadows, giving Karl an unreadable expression. Then the expression of a mad dog. A rabid animal.

Terry dashes down to the bottom of the staircase. Seeing the angle of Katrina's neck and the unnatural bend of her knee he immediately knows she is dead before checking her pulse.

Karl and Uncle Floyd look at each other completely lost and dazed like they've just crossed over into a parallel universe as they listen to Terry's howl of abandon at the bottom of the stairs. Terry's wailing barely sounds human. Floyd shivers.

Next comes the steady sound of Terry's heavy footsteps coming back up the stairs.

Karl quickly crawls in bed next to Floyd, afraid to do anything else. The boy is hiccuping uncontrollably, his cherub face glossy with tears. Uncle Floyd protectively puts an arm around Karl's shoulders, like bringing him under his wing.

Terry stands at the top of the stairs with Katrina's limp body in his arms. Her head, arms, and legs dangle. Her long lustrous hair almost reaches the wood floor.

Tall Terry's face seems longer than normal, slack with remorse, "It was an accident," he chokes, with a tearless gaze at the two on the bed. "You saw it Floyd. It was an accident. You both saw her fall!" His voice rises, "I didn't do it! I didn't push her! She fell! It was her fault! Not mine!"

Uncle Floyd nods, eyes wide with worry, nodding agreement, "I saw. I saw."

Karl says nothing at all, only hides beneath his uncle's arm.

Lanky Terry looks through the hallway into the other bedroom, the open, lit doorway directly in front of him and the small body of Kurtis deathly still on the bed, face red with blood. Terry can feel his heart in his gut. He feels like vomiting. "I didn't mean to do anything. I didn't mean to hurt anyone." Inside one thought begins to dominate his mind. He doesn't want to go to prison. He will not go to prison.

With a demented look in his eyes, mouth agape, Terry looks at Floyd and Karl with one burning thought. One word burning in his brain like a worm eating his soul. Witnesses.

"Floyd," Terry commands, the tone of his voice deepening, "Go downstairs and wash the dishes."

Floyd looks annoyed, "Mom said I can wait to wash them in the morning."

"Things have changed," Terry feels his fingers gripping Katrina's dead body so tight they are digging into her flesh. "Now go!" He growls like a feral devil, "Do what I tell you. Don't mouth back.!"

"Okay," Uncle Floyd pouts, still worried but now seeming more disturbed by having to wash the dirty dishes. He hates washing dishes and it's one of his only chores. Karl doesn't want to let go of Floyd's arm. "Sorry," Floyd says with sincerity, "I have to wash the dishes, nephew."

"It's alright," Karl sniffles, trying to hold back tears and be brave.

Uncle Floyd hobbles down the stairs into the kitchen below.

Karl wraps himself in one of Uncle Floyd's blankets. It's still warm from body heat. Karl tries to hold back a whimper viewing the shadowy figure of his stepfather holding his dead mother in his arms. Karl can feel her death in his heart.

Terry stands there, breathing deeply, face exaggerated by the shadows from the light shining in from the other bedroom.

Karl quivers uncontrollably for a brief moment.

"Karl," Terry asserts in an uncannily calm voice, "Go to the hallway. I want you to open the attic door."

Karl's eyes expand. He feels like he has to pee his pants. Trying so hard not to pee his pants. Karl's body moves of it's own accord. He feels disassociated. His mind is blank except for pee. His mother is dead. Maybe Kurtis too. The wood floor is cold on his bare feet. In a daze into the hallway. In a daze as he opens the attic door to pitch black. The door stands half the size of a regular sized door.

A little light falls in from the boys' bedroom.

Karl stands motionless at the door awaiting further instructions. Terry is going to kill him and he has to pee. If he pees his pants Terry will kill him for sure. Maybe if he doesn't pee his pants Terry will let him live.

"Go inside," Terry remains calm.

Karl does as he's told, moving to the far east side of the narrow attic.

Terry has to crouch to get into the attic, grunting, carrying Katrina's corpse inside. He lies her down gently, arranging her body flat on it's back with arms resting at her sides. Carefully he brushes the hair out of her face with his long fingers.

Karl stands with his back pressed against the east wall, watching, wordless.

Terry doesn't bother to acknowledge Karl's presence. As if he's forgotten he's there. Or that Karl is insignificant. Terry kisses both Katrina's closed eyelids before crawling out of the attic.

It feels like eternity as Karl stands with his back against the wall waiting for something to happen next. Feeling sweat on his face, chest, and back. He has to pee so much it hurts.

Terry crawls back into the attic dragging little Kurtis. Without looking at Karl, Terry props the small boy next to his mother in an unceremonious manner.

At that moment both Terry and Karl hear a faint hissing sound coming from the darkness of the west end of the attic crawl space.

Both look in that direction to see the pale face of the decaying hag appearing in the darkness. An angry, witchy face floating in nowhere. The same spirit Karl has seen before. Mrs. Sisten. Her black eyes accusing pinpoints. Hair growing and floating wildly slow around her.

Karl only looks at her, too numb to feel emotion. Broken. Maybe he is now broken.

Terry stares at the ghastly apparition in shock momentarily then a chuckle crescendos into full belly laughter.

The ghost vanishes.

Terry's laughter is the laughter of madness. The laughter of a mind that has crossed a point it will never return from.

Abruptly his laughter ceases, his dagger-like eyes focus on Karl, "If you ever make a noise I will kill you. If you ever try to leave the attic I will kill you. Do you understand and obey?"

"Yes," Karl responds blankly.

"Good boy," Terry tussles Karl's hair in a friendly manner then leaves the attic, closing the door behind him. In utter darkness Karl can hear Terry locking the attic door.

Karl turns to a west end corner of the attic, pulls his pajamas down and pisses on the wall and floor. He feels some of the pee sprinkle his feet.

Outside the attic, besides locking the door, Terry struggles to slide a heavy dresser from the boys' bedroom into the hall and shoves it snug against the attic door. Then he shuts off the bedroom light and goes down stairs.

The kitchen light is on and Uncle Floyd is mumbling to himself as he scrubs dishes at the sink. His hands are wet with suds and water, pajama sleeves rolled up to his elbows.

"Go back up the stairs and go to bed," Terry grumbles.

"I'm not done?" Floyd is perplexed.

"There is only one rule in this house from now on, Floyd. Do what I say. You can finish the dishes in the morning like Candace said. Now go to bed."

"O-okay," Floyd dries his hands on a dish towel. His fingernails are in need of trimming.

"Hurry up," Terry starts a pot of coffee brewing.

Floyd creeps upstairs and slides silently into bed.

Terry sits at the dining room table and lights a cigarette. He takes a cell phone out of his pocket, scrolls through a list of contacts, then dials. After three rings she answers.

"Terry?"

"Hey, Stella. How are you this evening?"

"I'm well," she answers. "Is everything alright?"

"No. Not really."

"What's wrong?" She sounds concerned.

"You were right. You were all right. I saw the ghost."

"Oh, God, Terry. Are you okay?"

"I feel like drinking."

"That's not the answer. You know that."

"Will you come over and talk with me? I could truly use some company."

"Of course, I can do that, Terry. Where is Katrina?"

"She left me tonight," he lies, "she took the kids with her."

"What? I'm sorry. Terry. What happened?"

"I found out she was drinking again. And having an affair." He intentionally sounds pathetic.

"Oh, Terry. You just hang on. Don't do anything stupid like drink. I'll be there soon."

"Thank you, Stella," he tries to make it sound like he's about to cry when in reality he doesn't feel that at all.

Terry hangs up the phone and goes into the kitchen to pour himself a cup of coffee.

Stella stands in her bedroom, slipping on a pair of blue jeans, her cell phone propped in place between her ear and shoulder. A twelve step call for real, but something doesn't feel right. Perry answers on the other end of her cell phone.

"Hey, babe," Stella states, "I just got a twelve step call from Terry, if you can believe it. He doesn't sound good. He said he saw a ghost and that Katrina started drinking and left him."

"Wow," Perry responds, "I'll meet you there as soon as I can."

"Sounds good."

"I love you."

"I love you too."

Stella and Perry started dating over the past few weeks but have not shared this information at AA meetings because it's looked down upon to get in a relationship before being clean and sober for at least a year. They both know their sponsors wouldn't approve. Not long after the seance Stella found a new sponsor to replace Katrina.

Terry answers the door with a broad smile, "Stella! Thanks for coming." He gives her a tight hug before she can react. "God, I'm glad you're here. I truly need someone tonight. Come on in. I have a fresh pot of coffee on."

Stella forces a smile, feeling spooked by Terry's mannerisms and the odd tone in his voice. A bizarre strain in his buggy eyes. "Of course, Terry," she says, thankful he released her from the hug, "That's what the fellowship is for. We keep each other sober. Drunks keeping drunks sober."

"And sane," Terry grins as he brings her a cup of coffee to the dining room table.

"Thank you," Stella sips the coffee and then lights a cigarette. Alarms are going off inside of her. Something is odd, creepy somehow.

They sit across from each other looking for a moment. Terry has a strange smile. Like a fake smile, his mouth partially open as if he's going to speak but doesn't. An unhinged smile.

"So," Stella clears her throat and adjusts in her chair, crossing her arms and legs, "Tell me what's happened."

Terry grins at Stella as if they are sharing a secret and playfully shakes his head, "Katrina left because of you. Because of us."

Stella's eyebrows scrunch together, "Excuse me? What are you talking about?"

"Stella," Terry says amorously, "There's no reason to hide it any more. Katrina's gone. She got jealous and left. She said it is obvious that you and I have feelings for each other. You know what I'm talking about. We don't have to keep it a secret anymore." Terry lightly places his hand upon hers. The hand in which she is holding her coffee cup.

Immediately she moves her hand away from his, trying to sound calm and friendly, "I don't know what you're talking about, Terry. I'm sorry if that's what either you or Katrina thought, but you've both got the wrong idea. I'm your friend. Just your friend. I have a boyfriend."

Terry boils, "Who?"

"That doesn't matter," Stella replies, trying to hide her fright. "I'm flattered that you would think of me that way. That you have a crush. I really am, but I'm sorry I just don't have the same feelings for you. I think of you as a great friend and would love it if we continue doing just that. Being good friends."

"Friends," Terry mocks.

Stella senses Terry's anger rising, his face is becoming flushed. She wishes Perry would hurry up.

"I'm not a fucking idiot," Terry growls, "I'm no one's fool. I saw what you were doing. I picked up on everything. Every look and flirt."

"Terry, calm down," Stella almost whispers, bracing herself.

"Are you telling me you're just a tease? Huh? Are you a cock tease? Taunting your tits and ass around married men? You fucking Jezebel! You fucking harlot!"

"Whoa," Stella raises her hands in a gesture of peace, "Cool out. I think you're crossing a line here, Terry. Let's just calm down and talk. Boundaries. Let's both take a deep breath and talk. Sort this mess out. What do you say?" She forces a smile again, trying not to let on that she is scared out of her wits.

Terry stands, slapping his hands on the table top, nostrils flaring.

Stella takes her cell phone out from her back pocket with the intention of texting Perry.

"Who are you texting?" Terry roars, "The boyfriend?" Like a snake's strike he snaps the phone from her grip and looks at the screen.

"Perry!" Terry booms.

"I was texting him for you!" Stella feels her eyes getting warm. She will not cry. "He's on his way to help you! A twelve step call! Please, give my phone back."

Terry's eyes scroll quickly through recent text messages, "This phone?" With a raving grin he smashes the phone against the dining room table. His coffee cup topples, sending a puddle of black liquid across the table.

Terry's breathing seems frantic and uncontrolled.

Stella backs away from the dining room table, "I'm leaving, Terry. Don't try to stop me. Maybe when Perry and Toomes get here they can help you. I'm not comfortable with what's happening. You're scaring me."

Like a serpent's strike Terry's arm whips out again, grabbing Stella's bicep. "You're not going anywhere," he informs her.

"You're hurting me, Terry," Stella pleads.

With an unforeseen surge of fury and force, Terry picks Stella up and slams her hard on top of the table. She lands flat on her back. Her head impacts the hard wood table causing a swelling lump. She feels scratches on her arms where Terry has grabbed her.

Stella attempts to roll away to fall to the floor and escape, but Terry is quicker. He grabs her by the hair and punches her in the stomach knocking the wind from her. Once. Twice. Thrice.

"You're a fucking teasing whore!" Terry rants, "Jezebel!" He grins diabolically climbing onto the table top and straddling her. She tries to push him away but he slaps her across the face several times.

"A fucking slut," he pulls her hair and bounces her head against the table a couple of times, "Once a bar slut, always a bar slut. I bet you were fucking Bob and Darrell too!" Terry uses both hands to rip her shirt open.

"Please," Stella weeps.

"I'm going to fuck the Jesus Henry Christ right out of you, bitch." He begins to fumble taking her blue jeans off, "You'll be screaming hallelujah before we're done."

Stella wipes snot, blood, and tears away from her face, "Oh, God, Terry, please don't do this."

"Welcome to the city of God," Terry's face trembles with demonic rage as he rips her bra off. She sobs as he begins licking and fondling her roughly.

Karl stands in the darkness in the corner of the closed attic. He hasn't moved since being locked in. His eyes have begun to adjust to the dark. He can feel the presence of Mrs. Sisten at the other end of the attic. She is an old female ghost making unnatural breathing noises occasionally. Sometimes wheezing. She seems excited by Karl's presence. He can hear Terry and Stella struggling downstairs. He can hear his younger brother's shallow breathing. His senses seem to have become more acute. His feet stand in a puddle of cooling urine.

He's been standing there this entire time only looking at the east wall inches before his nose. Feeling nothing. Feeling numb and dead inside.

Thought returns to his mind. Not thought like the child Karl. Thought like something has died and been reborn. Thought like memories returning. He can stand here. Do nothing. Die. Again.

No.

He is not afraid.

He turns with slow grace and the confidence of divinity to face everything in the attic. His dead mother's body. His unconscious brother. The hag across the attic crawl space from him.

"What are you?" Mrs. Sisten asks in a broken rasp and croak.

He can feel the chill of her presence.

"What are you?" The spirit asks in a deathly, dry voice.

"I am a boy." He answers her. "I am Karl. Karl Roth Barnes."

The wicked crone looks through him with empty black eyes, "What are you?"

Karl's voice deepens as much as a boy can, "I am the blood. I am Dagobert."

"YES!" The ghastly, ghostly Mrs. Sisten explodes in dull, dark fireworks of joy.

Perry keeps texting Stella getting no responses. He's worried. It's not like her to not answer. Who knows what it could be. Maybe her battery died. He's being ridiculous. Maybe she's just busy with helping Terry.

Perry would have been there sooner but after picking up Toomes he thought maybe he should bring Bon along just in case. Stella did mention the ghost.

AA is all about helping other people. Helping people. Serving other people keeps you sane and sober. It's about being honest, about service work, about turning your life over to a higher power. Being selfless. Doing God's will. Doing what God wants you to do instead of doing what you want to do. Help others. Admit mistakes and make amends. No one is perfect but genuine effort is what matters. Like the vikings of old fighting evil even when they believed they would lose during Ragnarok in the end. The vikings believed evil wins in the end, but the valiant, nobleman fought for good against all odds, to do what's right even in the face of Armageddon. Who said that, Perry tries to remember.

Toomes has a reputation for having his shit together and being a somewhat expert when it comes to interpreting the twelve steps and helping people in recovery. Once Dr. Toomes got sober he gave up lots of money to go work in the field of recovery instead of what he did before. Toomes is the real McCoy.

Toomes is in the passenger seat and notices that Perry keeps texting Stella while he's driving and it's making him nervous. "I'm sure everything is fine. Focus on the road," Toomes assures him.

Bon sits silent in the back seat watching houses pass by out the window.

"I know," Perry agrees, "You're right." Why is he worried? He's working hard to maintain the speed limit.

Finally they pull up in front of the house on North Maine Avenue.

In the neighbor's house Casey casually goes into the kitchen and withdraws a thick butcher knife from a utensil drawer.

Casey wanders into the bathroom. Her younger brother floats in pink water with open eyes reminding her of dead fish eyes. His mouth and nose are beneath the water with most of his body. The bathtub water swirls with hundreds of pale, some yellow, some white, long stringy worms like the one he pooped out earlier in the summer. The myriad of slithering eyeless worms nibble at the dead boy's flesh leaving tiny bite marks everywhere. Some of the worms slide in and out of his mouth, ears, and anus. Her new children.

Casey thinks her brother would be happy to know that he doesn't have to go to school now that summer is almost over. She smiles at her little brother one last time before making her way to her parents bedroom. Her bare feet are silent against the carpet.

She stands over her parents watching them sleep for a while. She is disgusted by how fat her mother is and how weak her father is. She remembers when she was just Casey Falkenrath and loved them. Loved all of her family. But now she is Casey and Lilith. And sacrifices must be made to move forward. It's all about service to a higher cause. It has been decades in the making but the time has finally come. It has been generations of blood magic.

With the effective precision of experience Casey deeply slices her mother and father's throats while they sleep. Her mother wakes up giving Casey a nightmarish look before quickly dying. Her father is too passed out drunk to even notice he died.

A few minutes later Casey has killed her older sisters as well. She is eager to be remarried to Kurtis and for the two of them to serve under the throne of the enlightened throne of Dagobert.

Perry, Toomes, and Bon climb out of the car together. Bon is wearing a long, black trench coat with his Samurai sword hidden beneath it.

Perry and Toomes make straight for the front door, hearing a woman's scream.

Bon notices a very old woman come out of her house in a nightgown. From the house right next to Candace's house a young girl steps out bare foot in her pajamas, a bloody butcher knife in her hand. Both females just watch the trio of men.

Bon stands unsure of what to do.

Perry bolts to the front door of the house. It's locked and he begins trying to kick it open with no such look. Toomes is too old to be much help.

Bon shakes his head, makes his choice. Perry is not an athlete. He runs to Perry's side and with a single blow, throwing his body against the door it crashes and splinters open.

The trio barge into the house, Bon leading the way. They are all horrified to see Terry in the act of beating and attempting to rape Stella. Her short blond hair is strawberry with blood.

Perry charges, screaming and crying at once, "Stella!" He cold cocks Terry before Terry can evade the attack. The punch splits Terry's lip open.

"Oh, dear god," Toomes runs to Stella's aid.

Terry falls off the dining room table and Perry begins to kick him while he's down. One of the kicks blackens Terry's eye.

Terry is swelling with inhuman rage and demonic fury. He is able to get a grip on Perry's foot and knock him off his feet.

Terry and Perry are wrestling on the floor. Terry is more physically fit than Perry. In a moment Terry breaks Perry's nose.

Toomes has Stella off the table covering her in Bon's trench coat.

Bon licks his lips as he removes the black sheath from his sword, watching Perry and Terry fight.

At that moment Candace walks in the front door, returning from bingo, "I made big money tonight," she smiles, looking over the chaotic scene, oddly serene, "Grandma won big tonight." She looks at Toomes, "Mind telling me what the hell's going on in my house?"

Perry spits out a tooth, trying to crawl away from Terry who is now on his feet again, pant's still around his ankles. Terry clubs Perry in the side of the head with a coffee mug, spilling more blood on the floor.

With very few quick steps Bon steps forward, sword point extended out before him. The katana impales Terry's chest, directly through his heart, and the red blade sticks half a foot out of Terry's back. Terry looks down at his chest in shock, mouth gasping like a fish out of water. Bon lifts a booted foot and pushes Terry's body off of his sword.

Terry falls to the floor dead.

Perry, Toomes, and Stella all look stunned.

With a second fluid movement Bon spins around, his sword decapitates Grandma Candace.

Stella cries.

Perry is speechless.

"What the fuck!" Toomes shouts as Candace drops to the floor as dead as Terry.

"She was one of them," Bon explains. "I'm going to look for the kids." Perry and Bon share a look and Perry nods.

"What?" Toomes can't fathom what is happening.

"Trust me," Perry says to Toomes, "Help me get Stella in the car."

Giving Toomes something to do seems to calm him momentarily.

Minutes later Bon joins them in the car. Perry is in the backseat holding Stella. Toomes is standing next to the car.

"Get them out of here," scar faced Bon orders Dr. Toomes. "Perry knows where to go."

"We have to call the police," Toomes protests.

"You leave with them now or I'm sticking a sword in your ass," Bon threatens, "There is more happening here than you comprehend. Now go. Save Perry and Stella. Drive away."

Toomes stands there with a look of terror on his face.

Perry leans forward, his face blooded, and says in a nasally voice due to his broken nose, "Please, Toomes. Just do what he says. It's true. I know where to go."

Toomes looks back and forth between Bon and Perry. Up and down Maine Avenue all is quiet. "Alright," Toomes nods quietly and gets in the car. Perry hands Toomes the keys and Bon watches them drive away.

A day or two later Bon Denbraven, Dr. Gene Toomes, Perry Honeycutt, and Stella Williams sit in the private library of one Professor Farah Somers (who is not present). They sit together around a round table.

"Well," Perry addresses them all, still sounding nasally with a white piece of tape over his broken nose. "We have some decisions to make. There is a war that has been waged since before time. Bon and I are soldiers in this war, so to speak. The two of you need to decide what you're going to do with the knowledge of what's happened. I understand if you end up going to the police Gene."

"We've been locked up here for days now," Toomes complains, sounding cranky, "I'm ready to know what the hell is going on. Then I'll make my decision."

Stella says nothing. Her face is swollen. But she does hold Perry's hand.

"Here is what happened," Bon stands to speak. "A long time ago, 1933 to be specific, a cult of fanatics was founded. They are called *the Antiqua Clericis de in Noctus Sol*. Most of them were from Germany and Austria. They moved to the United States in 1934. They set up shop here in Applegate, South Dakota. To remain hidden in the middle of nowhere. There were fourteen in all. One leader and 13 apostles."

"What does this have to do with anything?" Toomes asks.

Bon gives Toomes a bored look, "We know eight of the cultists came here to Applegate, including their leader, Dagobert Rothenberg. We don't know where the other six set up shop. Somers has had the diaries of Gottlieb Ebner for years. Nothing much was thought of it. She inherited them from her father like she did most of his legacy. Gottlieb betrayed the cult, deciding to stay loyal to his original beliefs as a member of another cult called *the Thule Society*. It's always been thought that schism was the end of *the Antiqua Clericis de in Noctus Sol*. It was only this summer that we learned the cult is still very much alive and active. They believe Dagobert is a Christ. They will do anything it takes to ensure Dagobert becomes ruler of the world."

"This is fanciful nonsense," Toomes crosses his arms.

"Yes," Bon admits, "You have to be open to the belief in the possibility of the supernatural to believe this. I searched for the kids. Karl and Kurtis Barnes were both gone. After you left I did my best to banish the Sisten ghosts. I don't know if I was successful or not, but I did burn the house to the ground. I found Katrina dead in the attic, I'm pretty confident Terry killed her."

"You burned the house down?" Toomes puts his hands on his head, "I'm a prisoner of psychotic lunatics."

"Floyd Barnes was gone too. That little girl we saw with the bloody knife. She killed her entire family that night. Her name is Casey Falkenrath. Granddaughter of Reinhold and Svenja Falkenrath, both members of *the Antiqua Clericis de in Noctus Sol*. The old woman in the night gown we saw come out of her house. She disappeared that night too. Her name is Gisela Ebner. Also a member of *the Antiqua Clericis de in Noctus Sol*. Gisela was born in 1904. It's 2014. She's 110 years old and looks like she's 60. Her husband was the traitor."

Toomes sighs, shaking his head.

"Regardless of what we think, these cultists believe Karl Barnes is the reincarnation of Dagobert. Katrina Barnes was the daughter of Dagobert Rothenberg and Candace Barnes. This cult works in black blood magic that covers generations. We may be the only ones who know they exist. We may be the only ones that can save the world from them. The only ones to oppose them."

"And who are you or we to stop them if I play the devil's advocate and say this is true?" Dr. Toomes asks.

"A fair question," Bon smiles, stretching scars on his face, "Once there were groups like the Rosicrucians, the Masons, the Illuminati, and the Knights Templar to name a few. The world is controlled by powers unknown to most people. These groups have died out or become worthless imitations of what they once were. Hamilton Somers founded a group to take the place of the fallen orders. Perry and I are initiates of that order."

Dr. Gene Toomes sits silent for several minutes.

"You know I'm with you," Stella says to both Perry and Bon.

Toomes sniffs twice and looks around the room at the other three. His expression somber, "I knew Professor Hamilton Somers. I didn't realize Farah was his daughter until I saw that photograph on the wall over there."

They all look at an old framed black and white photograph of Hamilton with his pencil thin mustache smiling at the camera.

"You know my beliefs about a higher power. About doing God's will rather than my will." Toomes says.

Perry and Stella nod. Bon says nothing.

"I think God wants me here," Toomes says.

"There was never anything to fear. Not spiders. Not worms. Not wasps. Or any bugs. There was no reason to fear the dark. No reason to fear ghosts. No reason to fear our stepfather. No reason to fear death." Karl stands at a river's edge watching the water current rush along. It's a warm autumn afternoon. Kurtis and Casey stand on either side of him.

Karl looks back at a small gathering of people behind him including Uncle Floyd and Gisela Ebner among others and continues speaking. "Childhood fears are gone. All fear is gone. We have come to shape the world."

"Lord Dagobert!" The small gathering of followers cheers together.

Made in the USA
Columbia, SC
11 May 2022